AEE-1536

McCLAIREN'S ISLE

The Passionate One
&
The Reckless One

McCLAIREN'S ISLE

The Passionate One

&

The Reckless One

CONNIE BROCKWAY

A Dell Book

Published by Dell Publishing, a division of Random
House, Inc., 1540 Broadway, New York,
New York 10036

ISBN 0-7394-0833-X

Printed in the United States of America

F
BRO

CONTENTS

McCLAIREN'S ISLE

The
Passionate
One

*For the nameless young dog killed in
Minneapolis, and for all nameless neglected,
mistreated, or abused animals everywhere.
God grant them safe haven.*

ACKNOWLEDGMENTS

Thank you, David, for listening way beyond midnight on so many nights, and thank you, darling Rachel, for never complaining about the thrice-weekly pizzas. Many thanks to my agent, Damaris Rowland, for her belief in me and to my editor, Maggie Crawford, for her talent and support. Thank you, Mrs. H. (AKA Christina Dodd), for always finding the weak spots and more important, always pointing them out. And finally, thank you, Anne Horde, a great sister-in-law, and a better friend.

PROLOGUE

In 1523 the McClairen chieftain, Dougal of Donne, stood on northern Scotland's high headlands, looked out at a rocky island rising from the churning sea, and ordered a fortress built there. He had carefully picked this particular ground, it being an isolated, pine-strewn island connected to the headland by a single ramp of flinty rock more oft submerged than dry. No man would step foot on that isle without being seen and no army would cross that narrow land bridge if Dougal deemed differently.

Dougal designed the castle in the shape of a U, the short central façade facing squarely north against the sea while its two wings swept back, forming an open courtyard on the south. Below the courtyard he had a terraced garden cut into the rock where, protected from north gales by the castle's bulk, orchards and kitchen gardens could flourish, making the fortress proof against any siege.

For four years the proud castle gradually took form under Dougal's careful, albeit impatient, eye. Yet, for all its foreboding strength, Dougal did not stint on supplying his castle with creature comforts, blanketing the chill walls with thick tapestries, and carpeting the flagstoned rooms with Oriental rugs.

When it was done, Dougal set off to bring back the inspiration for his work, Gordon McIntere's black-haired daughter.

He'd seen Lizabet only once before, on her thirteenth birthday. Dougal knew that McIntere had planned to align his child with a richer clan than the McClairens. It mattered not to Dougal; he swore to have her whatever the price. He persuaded the old McIntere chief of the fervor of his suit with gifts and coins—and the sight of Dougal's seventy well-armed high-landers. Happily the wench had not yet married, though Dougal swore to his deathbed it wouldn't have mattered if she had. And so they wed and he carried her back to his island.

Legend says that on their arrival Dougal stopped some distance from the isle rising from a sea of mist, and pointed at the great castle, and vowed that once in those walls Lizabet would remain innocent of any man's touch save his own. The lassie's cheeks grew red on hearing her new husband's ardent oath, thus christening the great, gray fortress with the unlikely name of Maiden's Blush.

Maiden's Blush she had remained throughout all Dougal's long life and that of his sons. Throughout the bloody sixteenth century not once did she fall to enemy hands—not even when Scotland's Queen Mary was be-headed.

The castle remained a loyal Stuart keep through the Hanovers' rule and civil war, and into the seventeenth century. When James II was exiled to France and the German George took the throne, her thick stone walls listened to a gathering of Highland chiefs swearing allegiance to the "king across the water."

Maiden's Blush herself kept George from seeking redress against the McClairens. The castle was impregnable. Any army attempting to take it by force was doomed to failure. It could only prove an embarrassment when it stood against the might of George's army—and held. Thus the crown never ventured and Maiden's Blush never fell, nor was she ever threatened.

Until, that is, one rare summer in the third decade of the eighteenth century when heather grew so thickly it hid the island's sharp old bones beneath a mantle of lavender flowers, and a gentle trade wind charmed a riot of brambled roses into bloom. That year Maiden's Blush housed a score of McClairens from diverse branches of that clan, all living under the care of Ian McClairen, Marquis of Donne.

Ian had come unexpectedly into his rank of chief. His three older brothers had died as a result of their part in the uprising of 1719. Colin, his younger brother, had gone to make his fortune in the East Indies, leaving Ian laird.

Ian never married. Instead, over the years, he gathered his clan in the castle. All of them were black-haired and fervent, with the McClairen knack for loyalty and the McClairen curse of bullheadedness. The youngest and prettiest of these was Ian's distant cousin, Janet, whom Ian doted on as the child he'd never had. He would have given her anything in his power to give, anything she'd wanted.

She wanted an Englishman named Ronald Merrick.

Merrick was the eldest son of the Earl of Carr, the half-mad scion of an ancient Sussex family. He'd befriended one of the McClairen men in Edinburgh and come up to McClairen's Isle on the young man's invitation.

Ian had heard the rumors about his cousin's new English friend, that Merrick was profligate and ruinously extravagant, that he'd been in Edinburgh fleeing a huge pack of London creditors. But Ian, having more heart than insight, paid little heed to the tales. All young men, Ian reasoned, were wont to such excess if they lacked purpose, and everything Merrick said gave Ian reason to believe that the Englishman had found his purpose, the same one Ian owned, returning James III to the English throne.

Ian little suspected that Merrick had long been in the throes of quite a different driving passion, one far more compelling than any political loyalties.

Gorgeous, charming, and urbane, well-read and inbred, Ronald Merrick was a penultimate example of amorality. Yet Merrick was by no means the black sheep of his family. He was representative of that breed, being no better or worse, simply blessed—or cursed—with a spectacular combination of good looks and an agility of mind that allowed him to better serve his master—his own desire.

Merrick's desire was simple: He wanted society to bend its collective knee before him.

His self-absorption was unparalleled, his sense of duty nonexistent. He served what best served his purposes and those purposes were whatever best served himself.

Of course his companions knew naught of this. To them he was simply a charming guest who had the devil's own luck with cards and a right handsome way with women.

But Fate has a fine sense of the absurd, she does. For though Merrick *wooed* the McClairens, thinking to cheat from them and their friends what Highland riches he could, he *won* Janet. Before he quite understood what had happened, he found himself wed to a rich, highland heiress. She was bonny and generous of heart and body and she adored Merrick. And if Merrick considered the world a penal colony and himself a prisoner barred from the center of his universe, that being London, at least he'd found himself a comfortable cell with a comely cell-mate.

The years passed and Merrick got two sons on his beauteous highland bride, so pleased with her that he almost forgot his purpose, his desire. Almost.

But one day as he rode into the courtyard, he thought how he would have liked to replace the central stone well with a marble fountain . . . if Maiden's Blush were his. A seemingly harmless, idle thought, but a seed of evil planted in a fertile bed swiftly bears poisonous fruit.

Thenceforth, each time Merrick entered the courtyard he would see some other item that he would replace or embellish or alter if it were only his to do so. Quickly other irritations chafed his never easy peace. Soon he could not dine without being acutely aware that the food he ate had been prepared to please another's palate, or that the dogs lounging in the hall were suffered there because another man willed it, or that the flowers spilling from the silver urns had been placed because of another's preference.

Envy grew in him like a canker, insidious and deep. It became so entwined in his every thought, so directed his every decision, that soon his hunger defined him. Not even his bonny bride could ease it.

He grew to hate the McClairens and all things Scottish, seeing them as manacles keeping him from his true desire. His eyes began to turn ever southward toward London, like those of a deserted lover pining for a former mistress. The newly rekindled desire burned in his imagination until it became an all-consuming conflagration. He needed to return to society. To London.

He kept the canker well hidden. Only Janet knew of it—and that only because she'd seen the cold distance in his eyes when he looked on their sons.

About this time, Colin McClairen, Ian's long absent brother, sent his wife and children to McClairen's Isle while he remained abroad. Ian offered them rooms at the castle but Colin's bride chose instead to live on the mainland.

Then, two years later in 1745, Bonny Prince Charlie landed in the north of Scotland. The McClairens rallied to him and were instrumental in his triumphant march to Edinburgh. They would have been instrumental in his even more triumphant march to London—but someone had betrayed their plans.

Prince Charlie was routed at Culloden and fled to France. Ian and his comrades were captured, taken to Newcastle, tried, and executed. Even Colin's sons were imprisoned while the Duke of Cumberland, who'd led the king's troops, swept through the Highlands like a burning scythe in a monstrous demonstration of merciless reprisal.

At first, Janet did not suspect Merrick of her clan's betrayal. But when he accepted Maiden's Blush from King George she grew uneasy. She fought to believe him when he told her that he'd accepted the castle because, as an Englishman, he could better hold it until, Colin, the new laird, returned.

Treachery had achieved what no amount of force could; for the first time in two centuries no male McClairen lived on McClairen's Isle. The new laird had not returned, and with no voice raised in their defense, his sons rotted in London's Tower.

Merrick commenced renovations on the castle.

Janet knew then, though she did not ask. She'd dared not. It was too late for Ian and his men, Colin's sons, but it was not too late for *her* children.

Or so she'd told herself.

For a time she grew more ill with her suspicions. Now, as twilight rolled across the North Sea, she turned from where she sat at the far end of the terraced gardens and gazed at the castle.

A wit had renamed it Wanton's Blush because of the embarrassment of ornamentation with which the old fortress had so lately been bedizened. It was an apt enough appellation. For centuries she'd worn the battered armor of a guardian; now she resembled nothing so much as a self-conscious and elderly bride. Decked out in fresh plaster, her dark bones covered in the tuck-pointed brick, her mossy roof replaced by gleaming slate, she'd been remade.

Even her ancient setting had been reappointed. The gorse and windstunted pine that had tangled like squabbling retainers at her feet had been replaced by curtseying ranks of tame gardens. Only the old kitchen gardens where Janet and her children rested remained intact. The stone walls still held the manacled limbs of ancient espaliered pear and apple trees, while thin onion stalks glowed fluorescent in the half-light, and marjoram and mint scented the air.

"Is it ours?" her eldest son, Ash, asked.

Lady Carr brushed the silky black curls from his forehead, a tender expression on her face. He was a beautiful boy and just coming into manhood, slender and elegantly fashioned.

"No," she answered. "We're just minding her a spell until Colin McClairen is free to claim her."

"Father says Wanton's Blush is his," Ash insisted in a troubled voice.

She must be careful of how she dealt with this. Of her three children, Ash was the most passionate one. He felt things too strongly; he saw things too clearly. No wonder his father avoided him. Ash had always been able to see beneath his father's thin veneer of charm to the emptiness within.

"She belongs to the McClairen, laird of the clan."

"Then where is he?" Raine appeared suddenly beside her, taking a combative stance.

Two years younger than his brother, Raine was already nearly as tall, answering Ash's fine-boned beauty with his own rough, elemental grace. He was her reckless one, impulsive and impetuous, capable of generosity as well as ruthlessness.

"Where is who?" At the sound of the smooth English voice, Ash stumbled to his feet.

A man moved down the marble steps toward them, sparkling like one of the marzipan fantasies the new French chef created. His coat was encrusted with gems, stitched with metal threads. Glittering gold lace cascaded from beneath his square jaw, and the white wig he wore shimmered with diadem dust.

Lord Ronald Merrick, now Earl of Carr. Until his father's recent death Janet hadn't even known Merrick's father had lived, let alone that he'd been an earl.

Carr arrived at her side, his expression becoming annoyed when he saw Fia asleep in her arms. "Where is the nurse?"

"I wanted to rock her to sleep myself, Carr. She's my own bairn. I don't need strangers to raise her."

"If you want to flaunt your coarse ancestors, so be it." Carr's voice was uncharacteristically indulgent. "But at another time. Our guests will be coming down soon and you need to get dressed."

"I am dressed."

Carr ignored her, peering instead at the little black-haired toddler she held. "You did well with this one."

Janet gazed down at Fia's creamy cheeks and pink rosebud mouth. Though just a child, even now one could see the beauty promised by the fine, regular features and dramatic coloring. Fia would be the ravishing one.

"Very well," Carr murmured. He glanced at Ash and Raine, a glance that did more to dismiss than acknowledge. "She'll have a thousand hearts laid at her feet—and her pick of a thousand titles," Carr predicted. "But not for a few years, eh?"

He flicked the edge of Lady Carr's plaid scarf with his fingertip. "Despite your mumbled bravado, my dear, you are not yet dressed. Did you honestly think I'd let you wear that McClairen rag to my ball?"

"I thought it was *our* ball," Janet said quietly.

"Why would you think that?" Carr's forehead lined with puzzlement. "I am the one who was lost to society, my dear. I am the prodigal whose return they've awaited, and you will not exhibit your political sympathies by wearing the McClairen plaid at my ball."

The wind ruffled the gold lace at his throat. "Such an act would not only be stupid, but dangerous. 'Tisn't that many years since the McClairen were ruled traitors. Or have you forgotten their fate?"

Beheading. No, she hadn't forgotten.

"Mother says Wanton's Blush doesn't belong to us," Raine interrupted suddenly, thirsty for his father's attention. "That it belongs to a laird."

"Does she now?" Carr queried, directing his sardonic smile toward his youngest son. "And were you so stupid as to believe her?"

Even in the faded light she could see Raine's skin darken.

"And what of you, boy?" Carr's probing gaze swung toward Ash. "Did your mother's prattle scare you? Did it offend you to think some unknown hairy-legged brute might someday stomp in and declare your inheritance for his own?"

"No, sir," Ash said.

"No?" Carr's brows rose. "Then you are a fool or a weakling." His smile never wavered; the gleam of amusement did not die in the brilliant eyes. "I despise both."

She did not know why he loathed his sons so. But he did. Each year more so than the previous one. Perhaps he hated them for their Scottish blood, or for having a stronger claim to Wanton's Blush than he, or simply for their youth and promise, promise he'd turned his back on years before. Only Fia seemed to have escaped his animosity.

"Sir, I only meant—"

"There will *be* no inheritance," Janet interrupted, unable to watch him toy with the boy any longer. "You've spent all my dower on tricking out Maiden's Blush like a cheap Vauxhall whore. And she *isn't* yours." The words came from her in a rush, long held, now finally spoken. "She belongs to the McClairens. You swore you'd plead Colin's case, explain that he wasn't even in the country when Ian plotted against the crown. But Colin is living like a pauper in a tumbled tower and you've done nothing to aid him."

"I've done what I could to deal with Colin McClairen." Carr's perfectly smooth face frightened her.

He'd done something to the new laird. She could see it in his eyes. A trembling began within her. She would have done anything for her children, anything. She'd held her tongue for their sake, but now, for the first time, she wondered if she'd done them a disservice. The truth might arm them better for the life they were destined to live than could her silence.

"Since the crown gave me Wanton's Blush—I do so enjoy that name—

until its future is decided," Carr continued, "I shall make it tolerable. I daresay I shan't be here long. This evening's affair is important, a first step in my return to London. Know this, dear wife, I will use, I *have* used, whatever means necessary to see that I am restored to my rightful place in society."

Once she'd loved him and it was more toward that memory than the living man that she stretched out her hand. "You used to care for me, Carr," she murmured. "You had so much promise, such intellect and address, but it's been wasted!"

Carr's face rippled with violent anger. He grabbed her arm and dragged her upright. "It's late. You'll not wear that plaid."

She twisted. The sudden motion jerked awake the little one. Her plaid scarf ripped with a sharp sound. Fia cried out.

"I am the Earl of Carr. I have waited ten years for this night, ten years to begin my return to that strata to which I was born, which is my right. You will not do anything, *anything,* to jeopardize that."

He was flushed, furious. So, too, was she. She'd buried the truth from herself for nearly two years but she could do so no longer. The McClairen plaid hung in pieces from his fist, a fitting emblem of her clan's fate— shredded by Carr's implacable greed and ambition.

"Carr," her voice vibrated with her demand, "the truth. Did you sell my family to the English? Did you? Tell me!"

"Tell you what?" he hissed. "That superior men oft reach their goals by climbing atop the corpses of their enemies? Of course. Don't be naive."

"*Men?* Or you?" Lady Carr asked, in a low harsh voice though she knew the answer. She'd always known. "Did you betray them?"

"Get you to your rooms and get dressed, madame!"

"I won't," she said. "I loved you once, but no more. I won't betray my clan by living with their deceiver. If pride is the only legacy I leave my children, so be it."

"You may regret your words, madame." Carr flung down the scarf and snatched Fia from her, thrusting the little squirming girl at Ash. "Take her away. Take the other boy with you!"

"But—"

"By God, you will do as I say!" Carr's face grew mottled beneath the rice powder.

Janet's heart pounded with her body's intuitive terror. But her mind could not feel the fear, *would* not feel it. For too long she'd buried what she'd known, held her loyalty to her husband above the loyalty she owed her clan. No more. She would leave, take the children, go to her laird—

Raine had begun to cry silently. The tears on his cheeks caught the glint from the torches on the terrace high above.

"Please!" Ash pleaded. "Mother—"

She bent quickly, retrieved the scarf, and wrapped it about Fia's shoulders. "It's all right, Ash. Take Fia up." Her gaze found Raine, his fists balled, his chin thrust out. "Take your brother, too. Promise me you'll keep Raine safe, Ash. Please."

"I will," Ash's tears were flowing now. "I promise—"

Carr's palm jolted into the boy's back, sending him stumbling up the shell path. Ash caught Raine's hand and dragged him forward.

Carr turned toward Janet.

The cream of London's society had traveled Scotland's newly laid roads to see what the Earl of Carr had made of his unlikely acquisition. Now, as the party began, they descended from their rooms shedding powder and bon mots as they observed and judged the magnificence designed solely to impress them.

Within an hour the party was acknowledged to be a smashing success. Carr's guests were impressed, they were titillated, but best, they were amused. And Carr, even more gorgeous than he'd been a decade ago, held court.

Several there had known him in his last days as fashion's most disreputable and prideful leader. They'd whispered as his assets had been sold off and they'd stared at the packs of creditors waiting daily at the door of his town house. They'd nodded sagely when he'd finally fled the city rather than risk debtor's prison. They'd never expected to hear from him again.

But here he was, glowing with pleasure. He traded sallies, lavished compliments, and directed a league of servants to see that every desire was met, every courtesy extended, every convenience offered. He did so fine a job of hosting, in fact, that it was some time before anyone noted his wife's absence.

Finally an elderly roué mentioned this to Carr. Carr dispatched a servant to fetch his wife. The footman returned a short time later with the information that Lady Carr was nowhere to be found.

Carr went in search of her, his handsome face wearing the smallest degree of irritation. She was not in the gaming room. She was not in the ballroom. Neither was she in the Great Hall nor in any of the small antechambers.

The house was warm, Carr explained offhandedly. The crush, the excitement, the noise—she was, after all, unused to society. She might have gone to take some night air in the garden overlooking the sea. His companions volunteered to accompany him on his search.

The gardens were lovely. Paper lanterns had been strung along the perimeters and little candles flickered in the colored glass balls lining the footpaths. At the far end they found a gossamer scarf by an open gate.

Carr retrieved it with a dutiful husbandly cluck. His wife, it seemed, had an affinity for the sea. With a rueful shrug he turned back toward the castle saying that whatever his personal inclination, etiquette made clear that a party cannot have two absentee hosts.

Tipsy and amused and not at all averse to having a role in the little domestic drama, his companions pledged to find the errant lady. They lurched through the gate, laughing and calling her name, leaving Carr behind.

An hour later they burst through the terrace doors. Wigs askew, clothing in disrepair, they trembled on the edge of the dance floor, flushed and sobered and appalled.

The din of conversation faded. Slowly, every head turned toward them and then, instinctively, toward their host. Those closest to Carr stepped away, leaving him alone within a circle. Handsome head high, face taut with ill-suppressed emotion, he demanded an explanation.

"There's been an accident," one of the disheveled band exclaimed. "Lady Carr. She's fallen from the cliffs."

"Where is she?" Carr's body trembled. "Is she . . . alive? God, man, answer me!"

The man sobbed, shaking his head. "We saw her body on the rocks below. We tried to get down to her but it was no use. The sea took her."

CHAPTER 1

Lord Tunbridge was cheating.

In the dank, smoky back regions of Rose Tavern, the young bucks' festive mood had long dissipated. First their purses, then their jewelry, and finally their inheritances had bled into Tunbridge's hands. They sprawled in the malodorous abandonment only four days of fevered carousal can imbue, staring at visions of paternal rage, or worse, debtor's prison. There was nothing left for them to do now but wait for an end to their purgatory.

Because, though they knew Tunbridge was cheating—no one had so devilish luck—no one could say how. Certainly no one would dare make complaint to Tunbridge, an acknowledged duelist with an accredited five deaths to his record.

Only two men remained playing, Lord Tunbridge and Ash Merrick. A slack-mouthed wench snuggled on Tunbridge's lap, her soft pink flesh glistening with the oppressive heat in the room, while outside a blustery, cold day reminded those abroad that winter had only recently ended.

Tunbridge ignored the doxie, his slim fingers straying like albino snakes amidst the piles of guineas and stacks of silver. It was not so great a heap as those that had already been won at that table, but it was a substantial sum, enough to recoup a decent portion of even the worst losses.

Tunbridge's cold gaze fixed on his opponent. Thus far Merrick had fared better than his companions. It was rumored he had arrived in London months ago, after a two-year stay as a guest in Louis XV's prisons, and had since seemingly fixed on making up for lost time.

London's rakehell cubs had taken him up immediately, as one would a new toy. And a prime entertaining toy he was. No man was wittier, no company more obliging, no guide in the ways of dissolution more knowledgeable. And no one was less bound by society's rules and had less care for society's opinions than Ash Merrick. But that was only to be expected.

Lord Carr was his father, after all, a man who'd been exiled to the Highlands rather than face his creditors and then been forced to stay in exile losing three rich Highland wives in short succession.

If Merrick was notorious, his father was infamous and the titillation of following so nefarious a leader had proven irresistible to the bored elite.

But if they adulated Merrick, it was a tainted adulation, well tempered with contempt. He was a no one. Prison fodder. His own sire would not underwrite him, and his mother had been a known Jacobite bitch. He lived by his wits on the fringes of society, and therefore, while being amongst them, he was patently not one *of* them.

More provoking, he did not want to be. And he did not care to hide that from them.

He allowed them to follow him; indeed, he encouraged them, holding wide the doors to a nether world of pleasure. Then he stood aside. Often he profited from a night spent gaming but they did not take exception, as his profit was never great enough to cause speculation. Besides, he earned their money in other ways, they reasoned, by showing them a London they'd never known existed.

Even now, even against Tunbridge, he'd only lost a few hundred pounds. Merrick rarely lost, so those capable of wakefulness, and thus malice, watched his imminent downfall with petty satisfaction. Except that is, for Thomas Donne, an obscenely wealthy, mysterious, and cursedly suave Scotsman—and some said Merrick's friend. Donne's lean countenance conveyed a wicked, subtle amusement.

Merrick, his lawn shirt open at his throat, his dark hair falling loose from its queue, sans wig, sans jacket, sans reputation, smiled obliquely and fingered the pearl-handled stiletto with which he'd been prying open nuts. His dark eyes, raised to catch Tunbridge's considering gaze, were vague and unfocused. Drunk. Tunbridge began shuffling the cards.

"Merrick," Tunbridge drawled, "I'm afraid there's no catching me this day. Another night is come and my taste for this sport wanes as my taste for another grows." The maid on his lap giggled. "What say we call quit?"

"Surely not yet," Merrick answered in wounded surprise. "You would not deny me the chance to retake what you've won?" The slight pause before he uttered the last word was less than a hesitation of breath. No one could say more and yet Tunbridge's face reddened beneath its sweat-streaked powder.

"Well, then, since there's just us two, what say to a game of piquet?" Tunbridge asked.

"Delightful," Merrick murmured, his attention fixed on raising the tankard of ale to his lips. Tunbridge cut the cards and Merrick did likewise, sighing resignedly when Tunbridge's king trumped his knave.

"Poor luck," Tunbridge said. "Doubtless you'll fare—"

The door leading to the public rooms swung open and a youth, dressed in the fashion of a courier, entered. He stood blinking in the smoky room, vapor rising from his wet cape. Spying Merrick, he picked a path over the outstretched legs of slumped bodies to Merrick's side and bent low to whisper his message.

For an instant Merrick's indolent gaze sharpened and the flesh seemed to cleave tighter to the well-shaped bones of his face. He held out his hand. With a furtive glance in either direction, the courier laid an envelope in it.

"I've your leave to interrupt play?" Merrick asked.

Tunbridge dealt the last of the five cards and shrugged. "By all means."

"My thanks." Merrick slid the stiletto's tip beneath the seal and flicked off the embossed wax. He opened the note and scanned the contents before crumpling it. With a peculiar violence at odds with his gentle expression, he tossed it unerringly into the open fire. "It seems my services are needed. I must away."

"Ah well." Tunbridge commiserated with a small smile.

"But nothing is so pressing I need leave before the end of this game," Merrick added courteously.

Tunbridge's hands, hovering over the pile of coins, froze and for a second something in the atmosphere alerted even the least sentient to something potentially dangerous occurring in the room. Then Tunbridge's teeth flashed white in the dim light and he gathered his hand. "But of course."

He studied it awhile, allowing a small expression of satisfaction to play upon his lips before calmly discarding. Merrick shouted for the innkeeper to bring more drink and then, with only a glance at his hand, flung down eight cards.

So it went.

Each hand played slowly. Whatever Merrick had read in that letter seemed to combine with four days of relative abstinence to give him a powerful thirst. Aided by his fellows, encouraged by the constant refilling of his cup, he drank steadily and deeply. Between hands he peeled roasted chestnuts with his knife, muttering disconsolately as Tunbridge's point total grew steadily toward the hundred needed to end the game and take the ante.

With each hand, with each drink Merrick downed, Tunbridge grew more expansive and more contemptuous. His barbed goads grew sharper and his predatory smile flickered like guttering candlelight over his sallow countenance.

Finally, Tunbridge stood only eleven points from the win. He dealt. Merrick did not pay any great attention, being too busy draining the dregs of his ale into his mouth. Tunbridge's mouth pleated with satisfaction. He reached out to gather his cards.

And Merrick, with a speed belied by his clouded eyes, struck savagely, instantly, skewering Tunbridge's hand flat against the tabletop with the pearl-handled stiletto.

Tunbridge howled. The sound exploded in the thick, closed room, startling the sotted company to wakefulness. He clutched at the handle that stood quivering in the meat of his hand, swearing viciously.

Merrick rose, no hint of drunkenness in the graceful movement and swept the coins from the tabletop into his purse. Only then did he take hold the handle of the stiletto. For a moment his gaze locked with Tunbridge's.

"If there is no card beneath your palm, Lord Tunbridge, I must most sincerely apologize." With a savage jerk he freed the sharp knife from its fleshy bed. Instinctively, irresistibly, Tunbridge snatched his bleeding hand to his chest.

With a low laugh, Merrick swung around, pushed his way through the men lurching to their feet, and strode from the room. On the table behind him lay the bloodied ace of hearts.

CHAPTER 2

The day was glorious, spiced with the distant hint of sea marsh, the sky scoured clear blue and the forest minty green with new leaves. From beneath its canopy rode a group of young hunters and huntresses, brilliant in their velvet habits and flush with exertion.

At their lead rode a young woman with tanned, rosy cheeks and dark mahogany red hair lying damp upon her brow. A feather coiling jauntily from her hat teased the corner of her smile. Others were more seasoned riders than she, but few could match the pace Rhiannon Russell set.

Mounted at midmorning and having ridden without bothering to break for nourishment, they'd been unsuccessful this day, thwarted by the dry, crisp air and an old March hare who'd first led the hounds then lost them, streaking from a bramble thicket while the dogs milled wild-eyed in the overscented underbrush.

At the stables, the party dismounted as the kennel master collected the pack of lean-flanked quivering hounds. Yelping plaintively, Rhiannon's yellow gazehound, Stella, limped from the edge of the wood. With a laugh Rhiannon turned her horse and went to accompany the hound's limping progress. Stella was the last gift she was to have from her stepfather, and therefore doubly treasured.

"It's a worthless bitch," the kennel master said coming up the drive to meet her. "My granny has better eyesight." Her companions had by this time dismounted and were heading toward the manor where Edith Fraiser had promised their repast would be waiting.

"Aye," Rhiannon agreed, because she was a most agreeable girl. "Mayhap. But she's young yet and may prove herself worthy. Please? Take care of her?"

With a heavy sigh the kennel master agreed, for who could resist hazel eyes and the sweet request of one of Fair Badden's prettiest lassies? Rhiannon grinned her gratitude and dismounted, hurrying up the front steps after her friends.

At the door a young maid met her. "An English gentleman—a *London* English gentleman—" the girl said, "come to see you, miss." Her face was bright with awe, her voice hushed with the same.

Seldom did English gentlemen come to their small hamlet. More seldom still did *London* gentlemen make the trip to this rural outpost, for pretty though it undoubtedly was, it had nothing more to recommend itself than the prospect of its ownership, a prospect that never transpired as the land had been long held by others.

"I doubt he's come to see me, Marthe. I'm sure it's Mistress Fraiser he wants," Rhiannon said, unimpressed and uninterested, looking about expectantly for one tall, robust figure—Phillip, Squire Watt's youngest son.

"No, miss," Marthe insisted, recalling Rhiannon's wandering attention. "He come to see you. Not Mrs. . . . . Ain't that right, Mrs. Fraiser?"

A stout, apple-cheeked woman with iron gray hair bustled down the hall toward them, adjusting the lace handkerchief tucked into her square décolletage.

" 'Tis true, Rhiannon." Edith's round face was fashioned for complacence, not surprise. The line lifting her brow betrayed her amazement.

"But why?" Rhiannon asked.

"I do not know," Edith muttered and held out her hands.

Obediently, Rhiannon peeled off her yellow leather gloves, tucked them into her belt, and laid her hands in the older woman's. Mistress Fraiser turned them over and *tch*ed gently. "Dirty nails." She looked Rhiannon over with ill-concealed resignation. "Unkempt hair. Dusty habit. Well, it can't be helped. He's been waiting three hours already and it would be rude to have him wait longer."

Though she wanted to protest that her dishabille made her unfit to receive strange gentlemen, Rhiannon did not. She owed too much to Edith Fraiser to ever willfully contradict her, let alone refuse her directions. She'd come from the Highlands to Fair Badden a decade ago, a scrawny lassie fleeing the aftermath of Culloden, looking for some kinsman to shelter her.

Though Edith Fraiser was only a second cousin of Rhiannon's mother, the Fraisers had taken her in. A successful and well-respected squire,

Richard Fraiser ranked high in Fair Badden's countrified society. From the offset he'd treated Rhiannon like a daughter of the house, lavishing upon her every benefit of his wealth and prestige.

Their unstinting affection had harried Rhiannon's blood-soaked memories into hiding. Only at night, and then rarely, did phantoms stagger bleeding through a blasted, burning landscape, did uncles and cousins roar in torturous din as they sought to escape Butcher Cumberland's retribution against those who'd supported Bonny Prince Charlie. During the day, Rhiannon scarcely remembered her life before Fair Badden.

She lived in Fair Badden as though it had always been her home and she had always been accepted, at peace, content. Even her Highland brogue had disappeared over time. Then, ten months ago, Richard had died. Rhiannon and Edith clung together, finding in each other the slow healing only shared grief can offer.

Now Edith fussed over Rhiannon's hair, untangling knots and rubbing a smudge of dirt from her brow. That done she bussed Rhiannon warmly on the cheek, accepted a hug in return, and turned her by the shoulders. She gave her a little push.

"Along with you," she said, shepherding Rhiannon down the hallway. "Your friends will wait as long as there's ale to drink and cakes to eat." Her smile grew sly. "And your beau would wait without the lure of sweets, kisses being a sweet enough lure, I'll wager." She chuckled at Rhiannon's shy expression and stopped before the library door. "Go on."

"You're not coming in with me?" Rhiannon asked in surprise.

"No." A troubled thought shadowed Edith's soft features. "The gentleman asked to see you alone for a few minutes. He said he had news regarding your future.

"I'm thinking—that is, I'm hoping—he might be a lawyer sent from London with word of a lost entailment. Perhaps a little forgotten keepsake from your dear mother to act as a dowry. I only wish I had something more to give you myself, but it's all long since bespoke."

Rhiannon took Edith's hands. "You've already given me more than I can ever repay."

Flustered, Edith twitched Rhiannon's jacket shoulders into alignment. "Go on, now! I'll be here waiting when you come out." She opened the door and pushed Rhiannon inside.

A man sprawled in Squire Fraiser's favorite chair, one foot stretched out before him, the other bent at the knee, his fingers laced over his flat stomach. He gazed out the window, his face averted. All she could see of his head was a carelessly pulled back tail of coal black hair tied with a limp ribbon.

He wore a coat of deep burgundy velvet, a white linen shirt beneath it. Brussels lace fell gracefully over the first knuckles of his long, lean fingers, and more lace cascaded beneath his chin. His breeches were tight and made of tawny doeskin. His dark leather boots climbed past his knees and were folded in cuffs over his muscular thighs. The tip of his sword, sheathed in a leather scabbard and hanging from his belt, touched the floor beside him.

He would have been exquisite had he not been so disheveled. The burgundy coat was dusty and the faded linen shirt went wide of being pristine. The lace of one sleeve, delicate as gossamer, was ripped and soiled. His boots were stained and scarred and the scabbard containing his sword was likewise ill-used.

He did not look like any lawyer Rhiannon's imagination would have conjured.

A bit of pique flavored Rhiannon's curiosity. A gentleman—particularly a *London* gentleman—visiting the Fraiser's home should have stopped at The Ploughman's Inn to repair the damage travel had caused. But then, honesty goaded her generous mouth into a smile; a lady receiving a gentleman should have paused to repair the damage a hunt had caused.

He turned his head carefully, as if he were concerned to startle her and she thus knew that he'd been allowing her time to assess him. He looked tired, worn too thin and used too roughly. His eyes were jetty dark, the brows above slanting like black wings, but the skin beneath them looked bruised. He sported an old-fashioned clipped beard amidst the shadows of lean, unshaven cheeks, and his skin was very pale and very fine and somehow fragile.

Fleeting emotion, subtle and reserved, flickered over his aquiline features.

"Rhiannon Russell, I presume?" His voice was baritone and suave. He didn't bother to rise and his pose remained preternaturally still, like a cat at a mouse hole, watchful but not hungry—not yet.

"Yes." She became unaccountably aware of the hair streaming down her back, the sweat and grime from her leather gloves embedded beneath her short nails, and the mud splattering her bottle green skirt.

He rose. He was tallish and slender and his shoulders were very straight and broad. His mouth was kind but his eyes were not. His throat looked strong. The torn lace ending his shirtsleeves tangled in the carved gold setting of a great blue stone ring on his little finger. He flicked it away.

Even without the cachet of being a Londoner, the ladies of Fair Badden would have found him attractive, Rhiannon thought. Since he was from that great fabled city, they'd find him irresistible. Indeed, she herself could have found much to recommend in his black and white good looks . . . if she hadn't already succumbed to a golden-haired youth.

"You're not English."

"I am. A quarter," she said. "On my father's side."

"I wouldn't have guessed." Having spoken, he fell silent, studying her further.

She struggled to remember the lessons in courtesy Edith had instilled but none of them applied to meeting strange, elegantly shabby young men alone in her foster father's library.

"I'm afraid you have the advantage of me, sir," she finally ventured.

"Could I only be so fortunate as to claim as much with all my acquaintances," he said and then, "but didn't Mrs. Fraiser inform you of my name?"

"No," Rhiannon said. "Mrs. Fraiser has no head for names, unless they're the names of unscrupulous tradesmen. She only said that you'd come from London to see me and that you had news regarding my future."

"I am Ash Merrick." He sketched an elegant bow, his watchfulness becoming pronounced now, as if his name should mean something to her, and when he saw that it did not, he went on. "The name Merrick is not familiar to you?"

She cast about cautiously in her mind and found nothing there to trigger a memory. "No," she said. "Should it?"

His mouth stretched into a wide grin. It was a beautiful smile, easy and charming, but it never quite reached his eyes. "Perhaps," he said, "since it's the name of your guardian."

CHAPTER 3

"I don't have a guardian," Rhiannon said and then, with her usual candor, amended, "I mean, not an official one. At least, none that I know of . . ."

She trailed off, visited by an imprecise memory. She was maybe eight years old, standing on the street of a strange city, squinting up at a door frame filled with beckoning light. The old woman who'd brought her had cold, gnarled fingers. They twisted round Rhiannon's wrist like ropy grape vines. A strangely accented voice spoke from within the warm, yellow light. "You want another Merrick, witch. Not Lord Carr."

She was to have lived with an Englishman. He was supposed to have been her guardian. She remembered the old lady saying so. She'd forgotten. But there'd been so much about those days and all the days preceding them that she'd forgotten. Flight and cold, fear and confusion, the days—weeks?—had bled into one long, seemingly endless nightmare from which she'd only awakened upon arrival in Fair Badden. Even when she tried to recall, it was insubstantial, flickers of sensation and images, more emotions than actual memories.

Rhiannon stared at the man arrayed in damaged elegance. Surely he was too young—"Are you Lord Carr?"

Once more the gorgeous smile lit his dark visage. "No. Lord Carr is my father. And you're perfectly correct if you're thinking him a negligent sort of guardian. He is."

She was unable to read the flavor of that amused estimation. His manner, his address, were nothing like those of Fair Badden's young men. "I don't understand."

"Neither do I, and I thought I had," he murmured, one brow climbing. And then, "I think Carr would like you to believe that he has simply misplaced you these past years."

"Did he?"

Ash Merrick's enigmatic smile spread. "I doubt my father has ever misplaced so much as a toothpick."

Each of his answers only provoked more questions, and each statement this Ash Merrick made only increased her discomfort. She once more felt she was standing at the door leading into that forbidden, enticing house. She was afraid to step over the threshold. It would cost her a price she could not name and was uncertain she could afford. And yet it beckoned.

"What is it you want, sir?"

"I? Nothing. I'm merely here to escort you to Wanton's Blush because *he* wants you, Rhiannon Russell."

"Why?" The sleek cat had tired of watching, he was playing with the mouse now.

"Your aunt was cousin to his wife," he said.

"*We're* cousins?" she asked. Impossible to believe that this black glossy creature and she were related.

"Oh, no. No. My mother had the distinction of being the *first* Lady Carr. Your mother was related to his second wife . . . or was it the third? Carr has an unhappy habit of losing wives to early graves."

"I see." But she didn't. With his explanation the exhaustion had returned to his dark, mobile face, touching her tender heart. "You've traveled a great distance, sir. Would you like something to drink? To eat?"

He looked up abruptly at the offer, his brows knit with surprise. "No," he said. "Thank you. We've business to conduct, you and I. Perhaps later."

"I don't understand," Rhiannon said. "Why now, after all these years has your father sent you to find me?"

"Unreasonable chit," Ash Merrick chided comfortably. "You are not supposed to ask questions. You are to fall into paroxysms of joy that Carr has deigned to offer you his protection . . . such as it is."

She studied him in consternation but forbore comment.

"What?" he queried when she did not reply. "No paroxysms? He'll be disappointed. But to answer your question, Miss Russell, Carr sends you the message that now that he has found you, he is willing—nota bene, my dear, he did not go so far as to declare his *eagerness,* merely his *willingness* —to accept his responsibility for you."

Her frown was severe, her concentration fierce. He spoke obliquely and his manner was mocking but impersonal, as though the jest he saw was more at his expense than hers.

"And what do you say, Mr. Merrick?" she asked carefully.

"Miss Russell, a lady never puts a gentleman in the onerous position of making a judgment," he said. There was kindness—or perhaps pity—underscoring the ironical tone. "Particularly about his sire's motives. I never make judgments, Miss Russell, ergo I never misjudge. If I were following my own inclination, I would never have come here. I am only my father's agent. I do not question his edicts. I follow them."

His voice had grown terse. It was as if he'd decided to dislike her before they'd ever met. She could think of no reason he should do so—unless he resented his father's interest in her. Perhaps he was profligate and his purse light, she thought, eyeing his shabby raiment, and feared his father would be overly generous with his newly discovered ward.

The idea explained Ash Merrick's subtle antagonism and melted her earlier resentment. She could put him at ease. She didn't want his father's protection or his guardianship or his generosity. Nor did she need them.

"What did you do to your face?"

His question caught her off guard. He'd come closer while she'd been lost in thought. He grasped her chin, tilting her face into the shafts of late afternoon sunlight.

"My face?" Was he, too, going to scrub her cheek clean? She went still, embarrassed and unnerved and not at all certain it wouldn't be a touch thrilling to have this exotic, masculine creature offer so intimate a ministration.

At the wayward thought, heat climbed to her cheeks. "Forgive me, sir. We just finished hunting and I didn't have an oppor—"

"You received this wound hunting?" he asked incredulously, lifting his other hand and lightly tracing her cheek.

Warm little tendrils of sensation danced beneath his touch. His fingertips were rough, the knuckles large, and his wrists braceleted with old scars. No gentleman had hands like that. Not even a London gentleman. Particularly a London gentleman. Who *was* Ash Merrick?

Her gaze roved over his face as he frowned at the mark on her cheek. The lashes framing his dark eyes were as black as his hair, thick and spiky and long as a lassie's, and that was the only soft or feminine thing about him. This close, even his fashionably pale London skin seemed nothing more than a comely happenstance. The single purpose of that fine flesh was to shed water, avert wind, not to attract. Though it did that, too.

"Did you?" He released his clasp of her chin.

Ah, yes. He'd asked about her wound.

"No," she answered, no longer concerned with the words they spoke but rather with some other interplay occurring between them, some communication happening just beyond the scope of her mind to facilitate.

"Then how did this happen? One would imagine such a prize would awake the instinct to protect."

She did not understand. Her skin was unmarked by pox and not too browned by the sun, but no one had ever deemed it a prize. He looked into her eyes and his facile smile wavered and disappeared.

For the first time since she'd entered the library, Ash Merrick did not seem completely master of the situation. He drew away from her, looking puzzled, like the lad who has unlocked a secret drawer and found something he'd not anticipated and wasn't sure he liked.

"You were about to say?" His voice was smooth enough.

"Footpad," she answered faintly. "We were coming home from the neighbor's when we were accosted by a villain. He shot his pistols at our carriage as our driver whipped up the team. One of his bullets grazed me. As you can see, we escaped."

"Highwaymen? Here?" His tone was incredulous.

"Rare enough," she admitted. "But it happens."

He'd turned away from her and was rubbing his thumb along his dark, stubbled jawline.

"It looks worse than it ever felt," she offered, obliged by his obvious concern. His eyes slew back toward her, a flicker of astonishment in their dark depths.

"Ah . . . good."

"I'm afraid it will leave a scar, however," she added apologetically.

His expression grew bewildered. "Scar?"

"Yes."

"Nonsense. One won't even notice it," he dismissed the mark roughly.

It was gracious of him to reassure her—if that's what those grudging words had been an attempt at—but she really wasn't sensitive about her looks.

She knew her assets well enough and a two-inch line traversing her cheek hadn't devalued their worth. Phillip certainly didn't seem to find her any less attractive . . . Phillip.

With a start she realized they had not yet finished discussing the reason for Ash Merrick's presence here.

"I appreciate your kindness, Mr. Merrick," she said, moving away from the magnetism surrounding him and taking a chair, "but you needn't worry about me. I am perfectly fine. I've been fine for over ten years and while I am . . ." she searched for some gentle way to reveal to him that his long journey had been unnecessary ". . . I am very warmed by your father's offer, I must refuse it. And your escort to his home."

"Offer?"

"Yes," she nodded, "of his guardianship. You see, I already have a wonderful family who have seen that all my needs have not only been met but are surpassed."

"I don't think you should view this as an offer, Miss Russell."

"No?"

"My father is determined you'll come live with him."

He simply didn't understand. His expression was cold, aloof, giving her a glimpse of the hard implacable will driving him. With a frisson of trepidation, she tried another smile. He couldn't very well kidnap her from her home.

"I hate to disappoint the gentleman," she said, "but as I've tried to explain, there's no need for him to assume his guardianship of me. Indeed, I would much oppose it. Mistress Fraiser, with whom I've lived these many years, is but recently a widow and I could not repay her loving care by abandoning her now."

"I assure you, my father will provide any accoutrements of wealth and privilege you should require," Ash Merrick said, his gaze on the ring adorning her hand.

"My affection for Mistress Fraiser is honest, sir," she snapped with uncharacteristic ire, stung by his inference that she wanted to stay here simply to keep herself well clothed. "My support of her is heartfelt. And I would not have you suggest otherwise!"

She took a deep breath, unnerved as much because he'd provoked her so easily as by his offensive suggestion.

"Perhaps Mistress Fraiser can ill afford the luxury of your heartfelt support," he suggested, looking pointedly at her pearl ring.

The notion of Edith Fraiser selling off the family silver to buy her a second-rate piece of frippery restored Rhiannon's usual good humor. This time her laugh was warm and spontaneous. "This ring and a piece of amber are all I have from my mother, sir, and its value is almost solely sentimental. I pray you only look about you. I assure you I am not causing Mistress Fraiser any financial hardship."

He made a cursory inspection of the room, tallying the fine furnishings, the ornate plaster mantel—Mistress Fraiser's pride and joy—the satin covered settees and silver mirror.

Then his gaze returned, once more, to her.

It flowed down her body and slowly, incrementally, roved back up her person, settling on the brocaded lapels of her hunting jacket. Her pulse quickened beneath that lazy regard, and her hand instinctively fluttered to her throat.

His gaze drifted up to meet hers, the dark centers of his eyes glowing like a hot cauldron of pitch.

"As good as anything you'll see in London, I'll wager," she said inanely, fingering the silk embroidered plaquets.

"Indeed." His voice was deep, heavy and smooth.

"It's French."

His mouth quirked. "I thought Scottish."

Her laughter was nervous. "Oh, no. You'll not find many Scottish fingers working over a piece like this."

"It *would* seem to require a more sophisticated hand," he agreed suavely.

"Yes." She nodded, knowing full well he was twitting her but unsure how. She smiled uncertainly. His lids narrowed, the thicket of lash hiding the brilliance of his eyes.

He hadn't looked the least reproachful when she'd snapped at him a moment before. There was not one person in Fair Badden who would not have looked shocked at having heard the sharp edge of Rhiannon Russell's tongue. There was not one person in Fair Badden who had ever heard it. She'd always been mindful of her debt of gratitude, careful never to give offense.

"I agree, Miss Russell, you've been well tended."

"Yes," she said. In a few minutes he would walk out of this room and ride away back to London. She didn't want him to go. Not yet.

"But being well tended isn't the only issue," he went on. "However tardy in his assumption of the role, my father *is* your legal guardian. He wants you at Wanton's Blush."

Wanton's Blush? She remembered that name. Her aunt had lived there. She froze. "In the Highlands?"

"Yes. Last time I was there, I believe it was in the Highlands. On McClairen's Isle."

The place name ambushed her from out of the past. Her heart leapt to her throat. Fear confounded her ability to breathe and she stared at him, stricken. He didn't even realize he was uttering what to her was a threat.

"And that," he stated, "is where you'll go and where you'll stay, until you marry or die or my father tires of this unprecedented whim to foster you."

"Marry?" Relief rushed over her. She would be able to thwart Lord Carr's demand. And if the smallest bit of regret tempered her relief, well, she'd already admitted to herself that Ash Merrick was fascinating. "Then we've no problem."

"Did we have a problem? I hadn't realized." He held out his hand, inviting her solution to the problem they didn't have.

"Yes, sir," she said. "I mean no, sir. We don't. Because, you see, in three weeks I'm to wed Phillip Watt."

Ash Merrick's hand froze in the act of reaching for her. Seconds clicked by as unreadable emotions flickered in rapid succession over his handsome, weary face. Then he threw back his head and laughed.

CHAPTER 4

The gentleman from London was laughing.

Edith Fraiser straightened from where she'd had her ear pressed fast against the door. She hadn't been able to discern much of what they'd been speaking about, but she could all too easily discern the timbre of that laughter. It wasn't *nice* laughter.

She pushed the door open and waded into the room amidst the rustle of her heavily draped skirts.

"My felicitations, Miss Russell," the dark young man was saying.

"Thank you." Rhiannon replied. Her glance at Edith was grateful and slightly bemused but free from any alarm.

Edith bustled forward. "Ah, Mr. . . . Mr.—"

"Merrick, ma'am. Ash Merrick." He executed a very nice bow. Edith beamed.

She was an uncomplicated and amicable soul, reluctant to judge others unkindly, staunchly believing the best of her fellow man. If Rhiannon hadn't taken umbrage at the man's laughter, then as far as she was concerned, no umbrage need be taken.

"Of course you are. And whom was it you said you represent, Mr. Merrick?"

"He isn't a lawyer, ma'am." Rhiannon came to Edith's side, hooking her arm companionably in hers.

"No?" Edith asked, unable to keep the disappointment from her voice. She'd had such hopes. "Then there is no diamond brooch? Not even a wee entitlement?"

Color flooded Rhiannon's tanned cheeks. "No, ma'am."

"Brooch?" Ash Merrick questioned.

Edith turned to Rhiannon for an explanation. "Well, if he hasn't brought you a brooch and he's no lawyer, who is he?"

"*He* is Lord Carr's son, ma'am," Ash Merrick said.

Edith swung around at the silky pronouncement, abashed by her momentary lapse of manners. She could easily enough identify the source of steel in his tone; it came from being spoken of as if he weren't present. But where the amusement came from, she could not guess.

"And who is Lord Carr?" Edith asked. London gentleman or no, this young man had something about him that made her uneasy, something more than sophistication.

"Lord Carr is Miss Russell's legal guardian," he replied. "I've come at his request to fetch her."

"What?" Edith gasped. Recollection brought with it a surge of passionate outrage. "*Merrick,* you say?"

Rhiannon took her hand. "Ma'am, don't overset yourself—"

"Merrick!" Edith squawked, stomping forward and brought up short by Rhiannon's hold on her. "*Now* I remember where I know that name. 'Tis the name of that fellow who wouldn't take Rhiannon in when she fled Cumberland's men. Legal guardian, indeed. A coldhearted villain, sir!"

"Please, ma'am," Rhiannon pleaded. "Everything will be all—"

Edith spun around and hauled Rhiannon into a tight embrace, pulling the girl's face down against her soft plump neck, glaring at Ash Merrick above her hair. Poor, sweet motherless lass.

"A scoundrel, the man is!"

Rhiannon mumbled unintelligibly against her neck.

"An unfeeling knave, a—"

"I quite agree," Ash Merrick interrupted calmly.

Edith gaped at him, her arms loosening just enough so that Rhiannon's head popped up. She gasped for breath.

"Unfortunately his suitability as a guardian is not at issue," Merrick said. "Miss Russell's future is. Though, I must admit, it appears she's rather circumvented my father's intentions."

Edith eyed him warily. "Come again, sir?"

"Miss Russell tells me she's to be wed."

"Aye, she is." Edith's strong jaw thrust out combatively. If this fellow tried to stand in the way of true love's sweet course, he'd have to go through her to do it. "In three weeks time, right after May Day. She and Phillip Watt but I don't . . ." Realization dawned on her like a lightning strike. "Oh . . ." she crooned on a low exhalation. "I see. Aye."

"Yes," Rhiannon soothed. "It's all right, ma'am."

"That does put the mud in Carr's barrels, don't it?" Edith said to the gentleman. His expression had more than a touch of the complacent conspirator in it. "I mean, you can't drag a girl out of her marriage bed, can you?"

His answering smile was ambiguous. "Don't be too fond of that thought."

"Sir?"

"Of course he won't," he said pleasantly. "It would attract too much attention. No, my pater will just have to abandon his plans—whatever they might have been."

Edith released Rhiannon. The threat to her foster daughter having appeared and been vanquished all in the space of a few minutes, she allowed herself to feel magnanimous toward Carr's son. "You'd honor us, sir, if you'd stay for the nuptials. You bein' Rhiannon's *legal* guardian's spokesman and all, it would be fitting you be here in his stead to witness her marriage."

"Witness?" Ash queried. "Now there's one role I've yet to try."

"Oh do, sir."

Edith looked around at Rhiannon's unexpected support. The sunlight streaking in through the west windows set the lassie's mane aglow with highlights. Her cheeks were flushed with pleasure and the green in her hazel eyes sparkled like emeralds.

Looking at her, Edith thought she spied the vestiges of her bold Highland blood. She ignored the perception as unfair. Rhiannon had always been a dear, unassuming girl. The gleam in her eye didn't mean a thing except that she was courteous as well.

But what did the gleam in Ash Merrick's dark eyes mean?

Enough, thought Edith. She'd never been a fanciful sort and she wasn't about to become one now. What would a cosmopolitan gentleman find interesting in a simple country lass—even one as pretty as Rhiannon Russell? To hear their neighbor Lady Harquist tell it, pretty women stood ten deep in London's fashionable salons.

"We've room aplenty, Mr. Merrick," Edith said, determined to be hospitable. "Please stay."

Ash Merrick's smile caught her unawares. Lord, a man with a smile like that was a danger pure and simple, but the offer had already been made and she couldn't go back on it now.

"You are too good, madame. I accept your kind invitation. I'd be honored to join your prenuptial celebrations and stay to see Miss Russell safely wed."

An odd choice of words but Edith attributed it to London fashion. "Good!" She clasped Rhiannon's shoulder and spun her about. "You go have the maids fix up the master's chamber, Rhiannon."

"But Master Merrick will be hungry and our friends are—"

What had gotten into the girl to question her? thought Edith. Rhiannon always did what she was told. " 'Our friends' will wait. The good Lord knows they always do. Spend more time loitering in my halls than their own! Be off with you. I'll see Master Merrick properly fed and introduced to your sweetheart, never fear. You join us after you've cleaned the stables from your hands and hair."

Without further protest, Rhiannon left, sending one last lingering look over her shoulder at the dark young man watching her so casually. Too casually. Once more a premonition threatened Edith Fraiser's complacence.

Edith Fraiser had been a beauty in her day, a country beauty but a beauty nonetheless. As much as she wanted to, she doubted that men from London were cut from so different a cloth as men from the country. Such determined nonchalance meant the same world round.

Happily, whatever this Ash Merrick's interest, Rhiannon's was fixed on Phillip Watt. Rhiannon was a loyal creature. There was no cause for alarm here and it might just benefit Rhiannon if Edith could enlist the goodwill of Lord Carr's heir. Perhaps a bit of a dowry . . .

With that thought Edith closed the door on Rhiannon's departure and turned. Ash Merrick eyed her with that touch of unsettling amusement, as if he knew full well what she'd been thinking.

"Mistress Fraiser," he said.

She made her way to the settee and dropped heavily into it. "She's a sweet-tempered girl, is my Rhiannon."

"Yes."

"And as biddable as a lamb despite her blood. Highland blood, you know."

"So I've been told."

"And a loyal girl, too. Faithful one would say."

"A veritable saint."

"No," Edith said consideringly. "Not *quite* a saint. You should see her on horseback, riding like a fury. I think she ran wild in those mountains of hers," she added thoughtfully. "And I know she's seen things no gel ought to see. Murderous things. It made her . . . I don't know."

She pulled at her hands, at a loss to describe the element of Rhiannon's character that had always eluded her. Not that it mattered. She loved

Rhiannon without needing to fathom every aspect of her. And because she loved Rhiannon she would do her best for her.

Edith slapped her broad palms on her knees, her momentary and uncommon sojourn into introspection ending with a return to practicality.

"Will the Lord Carr be making some settlement on her, do you think?"

Ash Merrick's mouth curled in gentle derisiveness. "I very much doubt it."

"No?" Edith frowned.

"Not a farthing."

"Well, a fine guardian he's turned out to be. It's a blessing he didn't have her care earlier. She'd be dressed in rags if she'd been left on her own."

Ash cocked his head, studying her closely. "Would she now?"

"Ach, yes." Edith's head bobbed. "Poor lassie arrived here half-starved and white as a gull's breast, wrapped in her dead father's plaid."

"She has *no* property?" Ash pressed.

"Property?" Edith snorted. "A poor bit of amber and that wee pearl ring."

"Who brought her to you?"

"Some old hag." Edith dismissed the memory of the wizened, dirt-encrusted old lady with the fierce blue eyes. "Brought her to my doorstep but never set a foot inside herself. Delivered the goods, you might say, and went on her way."

"And she didn't leave any trunks or luggage with the girl?"

"Luggage?" Edith gave a bark of laughter. "My good sir, they *walked* here. Walked all the way from your father's house in London if I've the memory right. No, sir, they hadn't any luggage."

Ash's brows dipped in concentration. "What about family?"

Edith shook her head. "No, sir. Cumberland's men killed her only brother. Burnt in a croft with his uncle and all his cousins, so they say. Weren't even a body to bury."

No need to tell him that Rhiannon's brother may, just may, have escaped. The fellow was an Englishman, after all, and an earl's son, and there was still a price on the head of any clansman who had stood with the Pretender. Besides, they hadn't heard a whisper of the lad in all the years since Culloden.

She lowered her face and dabbed piously at her eyes before lifting the clear orbs once more to Ash's. "So you see, sir, the lass hasn't a thing to call her own. Nor any family to tend her. I'm only distantly related to her myself, you know. Not that I don't love Rhiannon like she were my own. I do. But love doesn't provide food or shelter, does it?"

When he didn't reply she pushed on, determined to make him, as his father's agent, see his duty.

"Master Merrick, let me be clear. I've no property of my own to settle on Rhiannon. I have the manor and the income from the land until I die because that's the way Squire Fraiser wanted it, bless his soul. But upon my death everything goes to my son what lives in the heathen orient and works for the East India Company." She included this last with undeniable pride.

"Really?"

"Yes. I was hoping what with Rhiannon being set to wed and all, perhaps you might enjoin your father to dower her a wee bit. Nuthin' grand, mind you. Just something to make the dear couple comfortable. Phillip, he's a third son and lucky enough that his father is willing to settle a sum on him at his marriage."

"Unusual. Most younger sons don't fare so well." His eyes were shuttered behind the thicket of dark lashes. His voice was as still as ice.

"Aye. But Watt dotes on Phillip. He's the child of his old age and he would not deny him whatever is in his power to give."

"But who would want an impoverished orphan for a bride?" he quizzed, his dark brows dipping.

"Any man what knows her worth," Edith said staunchly.

"But how is a man to discover that?" he murmured.

CHAPTER 5

"—if both men died, who paid the wager?" Rhiannon heard Margaret Atherton ask as, combed, clad, and freshly doused in rose water, she slipped unseen into the drawing room.

"The earl's widow paid," Ash Merrick said, "claiming it was worth the price just to see her husband finally complete a ride."

Scandalized laughter broke out amongst the group of Rhiannon's friends clustered at the far end of the room. Phillip; pretty, silly Susan Chapham; ripe Margaret Atherton; and steady, sensitive John Fortnum . . . every head was turned toward Ash like seedlings toward light. Even Edward St. John, the Marquis of Snowden's grandnephew—whose already generous conceit had been further puffed up by several seasons in London—hovered near.

"Ah! Here she is. Our Diana," John Fortnum cried upon spying her.

"*My* Diana." Phillip Watt broke from the group and came toward her, his face alight with possessive pride. Taller than any man in the room by half a head, brawny and robust and golden-haired, he was extraordinarily handsome. He caught her around the waist and lifted her above his shoulders, spinning until she gasped with laughter.

"Phillip!" she begged. "What will Mr. Merrick think of us? I doubt London ladies let their beaus toss them about like this."

"But I'm more than a beau, I'm a fiancé," Phillip said, smiling triumphantly. His blue eyes sparkled with proprietorship. "Mr. Merrick knows this is not London and if he thinks less of us for our country ways, then he's the worse for it, ain't he?"

"But Mr. Merrick does not think the worse of you," Ash said. "I think Mr. Watt is an exceptionally lucky young man."

"Well, whatever Mr. Watt and Mr. Merrick think," Edith Fraiser said, glowering from the doorway, "Mrs. Fraiser thinks it a right improper way to act and reminds Mr. Watt that she can still wield a switch with the best of them. If a man acts the bumptious lout, 'tis a lout's penalty he'll suffer!"

"Say not so!" Phillip enjoined, setting Rhiannon on her feet and striding through the room toward the door. There he gripped Edith about her ample waist and hefted her up and over his head. " 'Tis jealousy that speaks, ma'am, and with no cause. Only your refusal to accept my hand forces me to make do with this chit."

The belligerent expression evaporated from Edith's square face and her cheeks grew scarlet as she batted at Phillip's head, huffing insincere castigation. "Let me down, you young rogue! Let me down, I say. You best save these demonstrations of your manly vigor for your wedding night!"

The others broke into cheers and Phillip, grinning hugely, lowered Edith to the ground and swept a low bow before her. "I heed your sage advice, ma'am. Pray consider my . . . vigor duly hoarded," he said, his gaze fast on Rhiannon.

It was too warm a jest. Rhiannon's skin heated as knowing winks turned in her direction.

"What say you to that, Rhiannon?" Edward, ever the instigator, demanded.

"I? I know nothing of men."

Hoots met this demure evasion and Rhiannon, smiling with an uncharacteristic impishness, stilled her audience with a wave of her hand, aware of Ash Merrick's gaze resting on her with dutiful patience. She suddenly wanted to prick that indolent lack of expectation from his face, prove her wit was as sharp as any London lady's.

"But of beasts I know much," she continued, "and it is my observation that what a squirrel so dutifully hoards in anticipation of his winter bed, ends all too often nothing but . . . rotten nuts."

Laughter erupted in the room. Even Edith, after a gasped "Rhiannon!" broke into loud guffaws. And Ash Merrick's eyes, which Rhiannon had been watching, widened with gratifying surprise before he, too, joined in the laughter.

Only Phillip did not fully appreciate her wit. She was seldom forward, never ribald, and the look in Phillip's eye suggested he'd fostered a kitten and just discovered it was a fox. For an instant his handsome face soured before his innate good nature reasserted itself.

"Mr. Merrick!" Phillip called to their guest. "In London what would a man do with so saucy and bold a wench?"

"It depends—" Ash answered consideringly, coming toward Rhiannon. Once at her side he put his hand on his hip in the attitude of a connoisseur looking over offered goods. Her friends, alert to the fun, moved in, encircling them.

Slowly, he began walking around Rhiannon. She notched her chin up at an angle, her pert attitude delivering him a challenge she found herself incapable of explaining.

"Depends on what?" She refused to turn like some cornered hind. She did not need to. She could feel the heat of his regard as intensely as if he touched her.

"On many things." His voice was as smooth as French brandy warmed over a candle, intimate and close. His breath—surely it was stirring the hairs on the nape of her neck? Surely his lips hovered inches from her skin? He couldn't under Phillip's eye— He shouldn't—

She spun around. He raised his brows questioningly . . . from a good five feet away. Their gazes met and locked. Gray. Clear. Soft as an April fog, cool as a November sea. Impossible to look at anything besides those dark-thicketed eyes, to look deeper into their depths and find . . . Weariness. Such awful weariness behind the calm, pleasant façade—

"For instance?" Phillip prompted.

Ash's gaze broke from hers, severed like a spider's strand by a razor's blade. "For instance," he said, "where in London 'the wench' is. There are different customs for different countries," he said.

"Countries?" Susan Chapham asked.

"Yes," Ash answered. "London isn't simply one great heap. It's an entire world with a myriad of tiny countries existing side by side, each barely aware of the other. Covent Garden and Seven Dials, Spitalfields and Whitechapel. In London's vast acres these are principalities ruled by kings and princes without so much as a last name."

"And would Rhiannon be a princess there?" Susan Chapham asked, and dissolved into giggles.

"I'd think she'd be a princess anywhere," Ash said with calculated charm.

"Well, then she best not go to London since it would mean a coming down in the world," John Fortnum stated.

"How'd you figure that?" Phillip asked.

"In three weeks' time, she'll be queen of Fair Badden," John offered.

"Queen?" Ash Merrick asked as the others laughed.

"Queen of the May," Susan explained, her tone resigned. "Three years running now. 'Tisn't fair."

"True enough," Edith cut in. "I don't see an end to it until the girl is wed and ineligible. Only virgins can rule on May Day, you know."

"No," Ash said. "I didn't."

"Never fear, Miss Chapham," Phillip said. "I can promise you Rhiannon won't be eligible next year. Or next month, for that matter."

The way he looked not at her, but at the group of their friends, as though he spoke for their benefit more than hers, made Rhiannon uncomfortable.

"What say we get married earlier, Rhiannon, and give these other beauties a chance at the crown?" he asked, smiling.

The chattered gaiety faded in awed interest. The proposed marriage of Phillip Watt to Rhiannon Russell was the most extraordinary—and in some people's eyes the most foolhardy—piece of romance within Fair Badden's memory. Phillip's father, because he was enormously rich—and some said enormously dotty—had not only agreed to the wedding, but had settled enough money on his son so that Phillip could take the bride he desired and not the one he needed. And that woman was Rhiannon who, though pretty and darling, had no name, no family, and no dowry.

She could not help but leap at the chance to legalize her union early, before Phillip or his father came to their senses. They all looked at her, awaiting her flattered and hasty acceptance.

"No," Rhiannon said.

"No?" Phillip echoed.

Several jaws grew slack. Few people had ever heard Rhiannon utter that syllable, and never so flatly.

She fidgeted, her twisting fingers betraying an unease her cheerful voice did not. "I . . . I willingly if shamefully concede my greed. If there's any chance I should be fortunate enough to be May Queen again, I'll snatch it."

"But you'd be queen of my heart," Phillip said. "Is that not kingdom enough?"

Pretty words. A lovely sentiment. But Phillip's back was still to her and he had opened his arms in the direction of their friends, appealing to them, not her. Several nodded in agreement. If he had just looked at *her* when he said it . . .

Ash Merrick was looking at her.

Of all those present, he was the only one. He watched her intently.

Her heartbeat hastened. His regard was more than a summation of her physical self. He gauged her, weighing her reaction, studying her as if all his conscious thought were centered on her. She had never been the focus of such acute concentration. Not even Phillip's.

Phillip glanced over his shoulder at her, awaiting her reply. She should say yes. She should be grateful. She *was* grateful. Phillip could have chosen a gentlewoman, an heiress, perhaps even better, but he had chosen her. He represented everything she had ever needed. She would wed Phillip and be safe and happy in Fair Badden for the rest of her life.

But not yet. Not so soon.

"I have admitted my greed," she said, forcing a bright smile to her lips. "I cannot help it that I want both crowns."

Phillip blinked. Indeed, the entire party seemed nonplussed.

"If that can please you, Phillip?" she added faintly, suddenly despairingly aware of what she'd risked with her ill-advised teasing. For that was all it was . . . teasing. Of course she would marry Phillip. Tomorrow if he insisted. But deep within, a half-drowned Scottish-tinged voice begged different.

Phillip's face grew ruddy.

"Ach, you great oaf!" Edith suddenly barked into the quiet room, stomping forward to cuff Phillip smartly on the ear. He yelped and jumped back from her onslaught.

"Have you no finer feelings? No dab of sentimentality?" Edith demanded. "Can you no see the gel wants her wee bit of courting and the trimmings of a fine and well-planned ceremony to mark the occasion of her wedding? None of your harum-scarum elopements for my Rhiannon. You'll wed her fit and proper. Not hieing off like some stable hand with his milkmaid, you great . . . *man!*"

The storm clouds lifted from Phillip's handsome face as comprehension took its place. "Is that it, Rhiannon?" he asked, his fond gaze just the smallest bit patronizing.

Edith caught Rhiannon's eye, clearly warning her.

"Aye," Rhiannon said. "That's it."

"Well, then, you'll have the grandest wedding Fair Badden has ever seen!" With the pronouncement the men and women surrounded Phillip, clapping him on the back and calling loudly for drink to toast his magnanimity.

And Rhiannon smiled, and demurred, and accepted the ladies congratulations on wresting a feast from her bridegroom and the gentleman's appreciative sallies about knowing her own worth, and she lowered her eyes in embarrassment and did not look at Ash Merrick again. Because she knew he'd sensed her lie.

CHAPTER 6

Ash lay on his stomach beneath the bud-spangled limbs of an ancient elm. A fair breeze flirted with his cheek. Bees, woken to industry by spring's beckoning warmth, murmured in the clover. Beneath him a bed of fresh-sprung grass cushioned his abused body.

The months of drunkenness and debauchery had taken their toll. That atop two years chained to a French ship's galley as a "political prisoner."

The thought still provoked his bitter amusement. He'd never had the least interest in politics and neither had Raine.

He and his brother had stumbled into the trap the McClairens had set for his father in retaliation for his betrayal of them. The clansmen hadn't quite known what to do with Carr's evil progeny. Being McClairens and thus relentlessly faithful they couldn't quite bring themselves to murder Janet McClairen's sons. Though, Ash thought with a twist of his lips, they'd come damn near three years before when they'd beaten Raine to a bloody pulp for supposedly raping a nun.

Ash's eyes narrowed. It still made no sense that they'd spared Raine after they'd captured him the second time. Though right at this minute Ash wasn't sure Raine would be grateful, because the McClairens, thinking to break Carr's back financially if not literally, had sold his sons to the French. They, in turn, had demanded a ransom from Carr.

A ransom that hadn't been forthcoming. Until Carr had capriciously decided to pay for Ash's release—but not Raine's. Carr's decision to leave Raine to rot still bit into Ash's heart like saltpeter in an ever-gaping wound. It, as much as anything else, compelled him beyond endurance and exhaustion to find the means to secure his brother's freedom.

Little wonder his health was depleted and near breaking. But though he was exhausted unto death, sleep was hard coming.

Even though he'd been in Fair Badden a week, he still felt as alien as if he'd been shipwrecked on Africa's dark coast . . . and just as wary. Fair Badden was simply too good to be real, particularly with what he knew of the world.

Yet at night he slept on a feather mattress with the sound of crickets clicking beneath his open window like the nervous worrying of papal beads in a novitiate's hand. Each morning he was greeted with smiles and pleasantries. Each day he drank sweet water from a deep, clear well and ate fresh bread, smoked meats, and farmhouse cheeses.

Each day Rhiannon Russell and Edith Fraiser divided homely duties between them: preparing confits and honey; distilling clover into a fresh, pungent wine; stitching sun-bleached clothing; and tending the rows of herbs outside the kitchen door.

He watched all this domestic harmony skeptically, looking for some sign of dissent. He did not find any. Though sometimes Rhiannon Russell would catch his eye and the tranquil submissiveness that seemed the hallmark of her character would be betrayed by a roguish gleam or a conspiratorial flash of a smile when one of his more subtle sallies blew far over the head of the worthy Mrs. Fraiser.

He wished Rhiannon didn't smile like that and that her eyes didn't gleam like that because, against all likelihood, Ash Merrick was charmed. And that surprised and alarmed him.

She was interesting. Lovely. And natural. And he'd had a surfeit of artifice.

More, she accepted *him*. As decent. As a gentleman. And no one here was wise enough or discerning enough to warn her differently.

Why should they? They were of the same opinion: the ambitious and self-satisfied Edward St. John; homely and sincere John Fortnum; all the eager lads who clamored for a story that they might taste secondhand London's dangerous habits. Even that great gold monolith Phillip Watt.

Restlessly, Ash rolled his tense neck, the movement releasing the grass's fresh perfume, a scent at variance with the darkening of his thoughts. Watt was heavy-handed and complacent and his status as fiancé had fired his ardor. Several times Ash saw the boy attempt to sweep the unwitting Rhiannon to some secluded enclave for a spot of slap and tickle. Or perhaps not so unwitting, Ash thought with a small smile.

That was part of her charm, after all, the flash of amused knowledge that leapt to her greening eyes when she blithely upset one of Phillip's amorous plans. She might be innocent but she was not gullible.

Neither was Edith Fraiser, the canny old cat. She'd certainly manipulated him adroitly enough.

She'd spent the week watching Ash. Every time he looked at Rhiannon, the old dame was looking at him. A few days ago, after sending Rhiannon on some errand, Edith had cornered him. Smiling and bobbing her head she explained that she was old and stiff and not nearly the duenna she need be. Therefore, she declared with impeccable reason, in Carr's stead Ash must be Rhiannon's chaperon.

The notion was so bizarre that he'd been blindsided into acquiescing. Since then he'd spent hours padding after the courting couple to see that Rhiannon's chastity remained intact.

In fact, that was what he was ostensibly doing now—chaperoning the happy couple. His orders were clear: Under no circumstances were Rhiannon and her swain to enter the yew maze, where "untoward" things might occur. He'd accepted with outward amiability but had taken himself off as soon as Phillip had steered Rhiannon through the maze's entrance.

For while he might enjoy letting down his guard and having these people assume him noble and gentlemanly, he wasn't quite ready to rap Watt's knuckles if they chanced too close to Rhiannon's breast. Because if he witnessed that, he would imagine his own hands brushing her velvety skin.

He imagined far too much regarding Rhiannon Russell.

He imagined her as he'd first seen her, flushed and pretty and awash with pleasure. Only in his mind her pleasure was sexual and the heat rising from her throat brought there by his touch. *His* hands had loosened her hair and *his* mouth had brought the full color to her lips. And *his* palm had molded to the sweet swells and lush line . . .

God, what was he thinking? He frowned, casting about for an explanation for this . . . fancy. He would not give it any weightier title.

The answer was simple: He hadn't had a woman in years. Upon his return to England he hadn't dared offend his newfound London "friends" by lifting their sisters' or wives' skirts. He wouldn't spend any of his hardearned money on an expensive whore, or his health on a cheap one.

Of course he wanted the girl. He wasn't so used up, he thought angrily, that he wouldn't appreciate swiving a fresh, vivacious chit. He stirred uneasily.

Damn her for thinking him a tame and friendly sort. It irritated and fascinated him. How dare she think him better than he was? The only thing he'd ever been loyal to was his brother, and even that loyalty was blemished, for he could *not* quite bring himself to wrest Rhiannon from Fair Badden and deliver her to Carr and accept the money Carr offered for the job. Not even for Raine. Not knowing that once at Wanton's Blush she would in all likelihood die. All Carr's brides died.

Even closed, Ash's eyes narrowed in concentration. He'd assumed his father had sent him here to fetch another rich bride but Rhiannon had nothing. Less than nothing. Yet why would his father have sent him here otherwise?

Carr only concerned himself with that which brought him money or influence. He'd even let his youngest son rot in a French prison rather than pay his ransom.

Raine's ransom.

Ash's mouth flattened. It was the carrot Carr always dangled before him. How many times had his father cajoled and manipulated him with the promise of Raine's ransom? How many times had that promise been "postponed"?

If only Ash could earn enough money on his own. But each pigeon Ash plucked at the gaming table, each program he undertook to earn the fantastic sum the French demanded for Raine's life, brought him only marginally nearer that goal. As much as Ash hated his father, Carr alone had the wherewithal to purchase Raine's freedom.

But then, Ash thought bitterly, why should he? Carr had found a faithful puppet in Ash, one he could make dance with the tiniest jiggle of the strings. But when Ash had arrived here and discovered that his father's plans had been trumped by a country boy and his doting father . . . When he'd seen Rhiannon . . .

It was rare that Carr was thwarted. Ash would enjoy each moment to its fullest. And finally, with the familiar and poisoning vitriol singing in his blood, Ash fell asleep.

The black stone walls oozed cold, inky sweat. Chill seeped into the murky corridors. Ash slumped in the middle of the slanted stone floor beneath his prized rag of a blanket, capturing what warmth he could from his own breath, past shivering, merely enduring.

Behind him the cries and mutterings of the other prisoners faded. He tensed, waiting for the inevitable attack, the latest test of his waning strength, the newest contender for the stinking rag he himself had fought over. Animal and base, he strained to hear the muted approach.

There. A touch. Experimental and wary.

With a thick oath, Ash grabbed his assailant's shoulders and pitched

him to his back. He threw himself on the prone figure. Snarling, he throttled him, meeting—

—Rhiannon Russell's panicked eyes.

With a gasp, he jerked his hands from her throat.

"My God." He'd nearly killed her. What had he become that even in his
sleep he could kill? He struggled to clear his thoughts. He needed to say
something, do something. He closed his eyes, dazed and sickened.

Cool fingers touched his cheek. Shocked, his eyelids flew open. She
raised her other hand and with her fingertips brushed his mouth. Then
gently, soothingly, she bracketed his face between her palms.

"It's all right," she whispered.

No fear. No indignation. No reproach.

Astounded, he realized she was *comforting* him. Comforting him with
the marks of his hands still red around her throat. With his body heavy
and penalizing on hers.

"It's all right, Merrick," she whispered.

She could not have done more or worse to him. With those simple
words she robbed him of his half-formed apology, the explanation and
excuse. She cut his soul from him, leaving him mute and exposed beneath
her tender, pitying gaze.

She'd recognized him. Not his ruthlessness or the debauchery he'd so
willingly embraced—those were still hidden from her. No. She knew
something more profound: his vulnerability. His fear. Because she shared
it.

She, too, had walked through nightmares. There was no other explanation for her immediate recognition, her spontaneous understanding . . .
the succor she offered. She had mapped that same terror-filled geography.

He swallowed, breathing too hard, pressing his eyes closed against her
pity. He didn't want this. He didn't want the connection. He wanted her
body. Nothing more. And Lord, was it not enough?

Robbed of sight, he could only feel. She lay beneath him, supple and
light-boned, locked into a parody of mating, her hips nested into his own.
The image tormented him with its immediacy and impossibility. Blood
surged through him, hardening him.

"It's all right," she repeated softly. "I have nightmares, too."

He opened his eyes and stared unseeing at her. She didn't understand.
He didn't give a damn about nightmares. He wanted to press his bare
flesh against hers, to feel her moving beneath him.

"Merrick!" Fear now. Clear, cold, recalling him. He couldn't have her
afraid. It wasn't part of his plan.

"Merrick?"

"Aye." He rose unsteadily to his feet, attempting a smile, failing. "Aye. A dream."

He offered his hand and trustingly—damn her—she took it. He helped her up. She should have leapt back, but she didn't. She studied him worriedly while he averted his eyes from her loosened neckline. It dipped too low over her breasts, her nipples inches from being exposed. Would they be pink and rosy or tawny and dark? Large or small? Would they pucker against his tongue—?

"I didn't mean to disturb you," she said. "I only . . . I saw you sleeping and"—her gaze fell to a hitherto unnoticed buttercup wilting in the grass at their feet—"Mrs. Fraiser used to wake me by brushing a flower across my face. She said the scent promised a pleasant waking."

"A pretty conceit," he said, finally producing an inane smile. She had no idea what he'd wanted. He fought to find the mild persona he'd adopted in this little rural community. He found it. "But I assure you, 'tis I who must humbly beg your pardon. Believe it or not, I'm not in the habit of throttling lovely young women who wake me."

"You were having—"

"There's no excuse for my behavior. Even in one's sleep manners are important and I believe strangling a woman would definitely be considered a breach of such. Don't you agree?"

A small frown puckered her brow. "Yes," she said, "I suppose."

"Where's your fiancé?" He looked away from the trap of her green eyes.

"He left." She began brushing the grass and twigs from her skirts as blithely as if nothing had happened.

"Without seeing you back to Mrs. Fraiser?"

"Phillip knew you were here," she said. "And some of his friends were to meet at The Ploughman. He didn't want to keep them waiting."

Only a fool, he thought, would leave such as her for the company of fatuous, overindulged young men.

"Oh?" The sight of her long tanned finger combing bits of leaf from her hair captivated him. It had come free of its coil and fell in waves about her shoulders. Had his hands undone it? Had Phillip's?

"They were going to play cards," she said. "Oh, yes. He related an invitation to you to join them."

Cards? Fiercely, Ash forced his thoughts to the matter at hand. Rich, bored young men were meeting to game away their allowances. They wanted his company. Isn't that what he'd been maneuvering for? They could easily be induced to play for higher stakes and he could gain something from this trip . . . besides an unwanted passion.

CHAPTER 7

"I miss London terribly," drawled Edward St. John. "I don't doubt I shall go back for the season. A year seems a long time in the country. You've had a season, Phillip. Cut quite a swathe, I believe." His manner, though mild, hid a barb.

Phillip flushed slightly and quaffed the rest of his ale. He wiped his mouth with the back of his sleeve and motioned the innkeeper's son, Andrew, over to refill his cup. "Yes."

Edward turned to Ash. "I've met your father, you know," he said. "In fact, I spent two weeks at Wanton's Blush a few years back. Quite a fascinating man, your father."

They were ensconced in the only private room The Ploughman boasted. The others of their party had left. Only Phillip Watt, John Fortnum, St. John, and Ash remained.

"Isn't he," Ash murmured noncommittally. He was not surprised that St. John had found his way to Wanton's Blush. He wagered incautiously and ostentatiously. A plump little pigeon like St. John would certainly have attracted Carr's far-ranging notice.

"It made quite an end to what was a grand season." St. John looked around to make certain that his audience was suitably impressed. When no one responded, he finished scooping the small ante from the center of the table into his pocket.

Ash stretched out his leg, mentally tallying the wealth of jewels bedecking St. John's exquisite persimmon-colored silk jacket. It was amazing St. John had escaped Wanton's Blush apparently unscathed. Few did.

"You were regrettably absent, however." The little spark of malice in his eyes told Ash that St. John was well aware Ash had spent that season in a French gaol.

"I had prior commitments. Or rather, I was committed previously."

St. John burst out laughing and Phillip frowned, disliking being excluded from the joke. Men like St. John always enjoyed excluding others. Wearily, Ash waited for St. John to relate the amusing story of his incarceration.

How would Rhiannon react when the tale reached her? Would she find it vastly diverting to know she'd nearly been throttled by a gaol rat? Or horrifying? He was curious, he told himself, no more.

He glanced up to find St. John regarding him with a bland smile. Apparently he'd decided to keep the matter their little secret. Doubtless because as men of the world they understood the humor in his having been a prisoner while these country louts could never appreciate the jest.

Not that Ash appreciated it himself. But he appreciated men like St. John. They were so easy to anticipate. Ash nodded at him, promising himself that St. John would pay for his sport . . . and for reminding Ash of Rhiannon when he'd almost excised her from his thoughts.

"Your father, now there's a gaming man," St. John went on. "Unhappily for you, you don't seem to have inherited his luck with the cards. Happily for me, however."

"Yes," said Ash, "he's a rare devil all right." He plucked a wrinkled brown apple from the bowl at his side and began paring the soft skin with his stiletto. He was in no hurry; he had nowhere to go.

Today he'd primed the pump for his future gambling by establishing himself in the others' eyes as a fellow with questionable skill and no great luck. When he eventually left Fair Badden, his newfound companions would shake their heads over his belated good fortune, never bothering to tally the slow but steady stream of money that had made its way into his purse. No one would be the wiser. No one would be hurt.

He had to stay focused on that, on his hidden talents, on maintaining his persona as an entertaining companion, a bon vivant who tarried amongst them for a few short weeks.

"Exactly, sir," St. John said, "devilish."

"How did you meet Carr?" Fortnum asked.

"I was in Scotland staying at the home of some mutual acquaintances. He was there and invited me to stay at Wanton's Blush. How could I resist?" St. John held up his hands. "It's magnificent. A miniature London with all its varied pleasures."

"I didn't like London," Phillip Watt suddenly put in.

"Oh?" St. John asked, openly amused. "Pray tell, why?"

"Why should I go elsewhere for what I already have here?" Phillip leaned his great blond head back and beamed like some Adonis. "Fair Badden has everything I want."

Ash glanced at him. Doubtless within five years Watt and Rhiannon would have littered the rural landscape with little golden godlings and goddesses. Ash looked away. He'd always hated mythology.

"I have fine wine to drink," Phillip went on, winking at Ash in a friendly manner, "when the tide is right. Prime horseflesh to ride as well. Fine fellows to be my companions. And damn pretty girls."

"To ride?" St. John snickered.

"Aye!" Watt laughed, a shade too loudly.

Ash's wandering attention abruptly sharpened on Watt. The bloody fool would probably give Rhiannon a case of the pox on their wedding night.

"I agree with Phillip," John Fortnum put in. "Not about the ladies." His ears turned pink. "About the other thingies. I hear London is a dangerous place these days. Packs of young aristos roving the streets like mad dogs, assaulting good people. Damned impertinent."

St. John shrugged. "It's not as though violence hasn't found its way here. Watt's own bride-to-be was nearly killed not long ago."

Ah, yes, Ash remembered. The shallow furrow across her cheek. Another inch and the eye socket would have shattered, the clear hazel green eye rendered sightless.

"They never apprehended the man who did it?" he asked.

"No. He hasn't been caught," Phillip answered tersely.

"Shouldn't wonder that he will be soon," Fortnum said. "Stupid bugger."

"How so?" Ash asked.

"Well, look at who he picked to rob." Fortnum's face was alive with disgust. "An open carriage carrying two ladies on a fine afternoon. What did he hope to get? Tiaras?"

"I thought Mrs. Fraiser was well-to-do," Ash said.

"Aye," Fortnum answered, "she is. But she wouldn't be sporting what finery she owns in the afternoon. Maybe they do so in London, but in Fair Badden we keep out glitter for candlelight."

St. John, openly bored with the turn of conversation, picked at a hangnail.

"Perhaps he thought they carried deep purses," Ash suggested, his thoughts whirring.

"Why would he think that?" Fortnum asked. "Simple carriage. Unescorted ladies. What raises my hackles is that even after the driver whipped up the horses, the bastard shot at the ladies. He needn't have done that."

Ash allowed that he had a point.

"The blackguard had a mask on," Fortnum continued. "He wasn't going to be identified. If me and my dad hadn't been on the road and heard the pistol shot . . ." He trailed off, shaking his head.

Incredibly it sounded as if the carriage carrying Rhiannon and Mrs. Fraiser had been specifically targeted. Ash frowned.

He sighed gustily, as though the ways of evil men were beyond the ken of his civilized understanding, and rose from the table. Casually he collected his jacket and depleted purse. But as he took his leave of the others, he was already composing a letter to Thomas Donne.

Scottish expatriate, enormously wealthy, suave and perennially bored, Donne had little allegiance to anyone or anything. But he did have a supreme desire to find ways to fritter away the hours. He just might consider the challenge of finding out what he could about a Highland orphan interesting enough to accept.

The afternoon sun glanced off the whitewashed wall of the Fraiser's manor, warming the garden. On the grassy path separating vegetables from herbs, Rhiannon sat rolling Stella's silky ear between her fingers.

The young bitch yawned hugely, displaying large white fangs and a long, curling pink tongue. Then, grumbling, she stretched her great gangly body across Rhiannon's lap, moaned in contentment, and fell asleep once more. Rhiannon smiled. So fierce a bloodline this hound had, yet so tamed by simple kindness.

Like Ash Merrick.

For a moment, earlier that day, when she'd struggled beneath him, she'd been truly afraid. Yet when she'd called to him and touched his face he'd shivered, *shivered*. She wondered when last he'd been touched without violence or threat of pain.

Which was absurd. He was a London gentleman and a very handsome one at that. Many women must have explored the texture of his glossy black hair and caressed his lean, beard-shadowed cheeks. Yet, where had those scars on his wrists come from? How to account for them?

Disconcerted by her thoughts, Rhiannon fondled Stella's other ear. The truth was she was drawn to Ash Merrick. She should be ashamed. It smacked of disloyalty. Yet . . . well, what if she was?

What harm could it do? She was not so stupid as to confuse fascination for some more permanent emotion. She was simply intrigued by the discrepancies she saw in him: the glib tongue and watchful eyes; the shabby raiment and aristocratic manner; the fine-boned hands with the battered wrists and callused palms. What woman wouldn't be interested? That didn't mean she would be anything less than a faithful and attentive wife. When the time came.

As Phillip would be a husband. When the time came.

She knew Phillip had occasional assignations with some of the village women. That they might not have ended wasn't surprising. Phillip was gloriously handsome and genial and generous and—

"Rhiannon! Ah, there you are. Good." Edith Fraiser came bustling around the corner of the house, her cap fluttering in the breeze. She stopped by Rhiannon and glanced around.

"He's not here," Rhiannon said.

"Good," Edith replied, nodding. And then, eyeing Rhiannon suspiciously, "*Who's* not here?"

Rhiannon blinked in feigned innocence. "Who do you *think* is not here?"

Edith blustered. "Phillip Watt, of course. Who did you think I meant?"

"Phillip, of course," Rhiannon replied and then ruined the virtuous response by laughing at Edith's doubtful expression. "Dear, dear, Mrs. Fraiser, your concerns are groundless—whatever they may be."

"You know me too well, Rhiannon Russell," Edith declared, spreading her skirts and dropping down beside Rhiannon like a roosting hen. She looked at Stella still snoozing contentedly. "Spoil that hound, you do. 'Tisn't natural. It's a beast, not a baby." A sly smile overtook the disgruntled expression on her face. "Soon enough you'll have your own babes and yon hound will be back in the kennels where she belongs."

"Never," declared Rhiannon. "I'm faithful, I am. Something you might recall," she added gently, "when misgivings send you flying from the house without your shawl."

"Humph," Edith said. "I see the way you circle Mr. Merrick. Like a shy colt spying an offered apple, wary but sure that the extended hand holds something sweet. Take a lesson from that colt, Rhiannon. More often than not the hand that holds out the apple is hiding the one what holds the noose."

Rhiannon laughed. "You are wise and knowing, but your imagination is running wild. I assure you Mr. Merrick has no desire to trap me with a noose or anything else."

Edith shook her head. "Can a girl raised in my house be so green? Must be so, for from the look in your eye I see you believe your own words. It's not that I don't understand the temptation of him. He's a fair way with him and he's rare pretty, too—when he's dusted off." She smoothed her

skirts and released a gusty sigh. "I know you think I'm only a simple country woman and so I am—"

"No!" Rhiannon burst out. "I trust your judgment above all others. I look to you for guidance."

Edith straightened, smiling smugly. "Then be guided here, Rhiannon. Stay away from Mr. Merrick. He's dangerous."

"Dangerous? Isn't that perhaps a bit strong? He's affable and gentle and courteous and perhaps a bit more polished than we are accustomed—"

"Are you *arguing* with me?" Edith stared at Rhiannon openmouthed. She could not have been more surprised if the dog had spoken. Rhiannon never contradicted her. It was not like her to dig in her heels—except in matters of hunting and Stella.

Rhiannon's smooth brow puckered and her gaze fell in equal parts abashment and militancy. "Mayhap," she murmured, fiercely concentrating on plucking a burr from Stella's coat. "Forgive me."

Edith scowled. She knew what she saw and she saw a man whose gaze went dark and hot whenever it encountered the form of her darlin' Rhiannon. More worrisome still, whenever that same man was about, she saw a young woman not given to blushing turn the color of a red sunset.

But after hearing that tone from sweet, biddable Rhiannon, she knew that to pursue the conversation further was folly. She might be used to Rhiannon's amenable ways, but she'd also raised a strong-willed son. She recognized the obstinate set to Rhiannon's lips. It was only surprising that the willfulness most youngsters experienced in adolescence had in Rhiannon's case been so long delayed.

"I have a list here of the things that need doing," she said in a neutral voice. "It's going to be rare busy here about. There's the young people coming here tomorrow afternoon, and Lady Harquist insists we attend her annual ball." Edith sighed in exasperation.

Lady Harquist's husband had been made a baronet for his patriotism during the last Jacobite uprising. He'd never actually fought in any battle, but he'd supplied the local weavers with the free wool that was necessary to make uniforms for His Majesty's men.

Lady Harquist—nee Betty Lund—took her new position seriously. Thus each spring Fair Badden society enjoyed its one and only ball. It was no accident that Lady Harquist had set the date for her gala just before May Day.

She wished to contrast the rough-and-rowdy country entertainment with her own sophisticated party. Fortunately, Lady Harquist never real-

ized she alone thought that in a contest between May Day and her ball, her ball prevailed.

"Who'll all be there?"

Edith glanced up at the innocent tones. "Everyone. Including Mr. Merrick, if that's what you're asking."

"Not at all!" Rhiannon's eyes widened. "You must try to overcome these prejudices."

"Hm." Edith studied the girl before turning her attention back to her list. "Then there's all the arrangements to be made for the wedding itself. Your dress isn't even half done and—"

"Oh!"

At the sound of dismay Edith's head shot up. Rhiannon scooted back and Stella's head landed on the ground with an audible thump. The dog cast an aggrieved look around and promptly went back to sleep.

"Hadn't we best make plans for the May Day first?" Rhiannon asked anxiously. "I mean, the wedding isn't until after—"

"The day after May Day."

"Yes. Well. Still *after*. There's still much to do for Beltaine night. You promised we'd bring clover wine and we haven't even bottled it yet."

"There's enough to drink on Beltaine night without our adding to the general insobriety," Edith said virtuously.

"Mayhaps, madame." Rhiannon smiled and Edith felt her virtuous mien slip in answer to the girl's wheedling ways. "But would you condemn our neighbors to the aching heads and roiling bellies you know they'll suffer if they've only The Ploughman's vile bran ale with which to celebrate the eve of May Day?"

"Maybe they shouldn't drink so much." Edith sniffed and colored, conscious that she might have on one or two Beltaine nights imbibed a bit more than was seemly herself, but unwilling to admit it to Rhiannon.

"Ach, now, dear." Rhiannon reached over and tickled Edith under the chin, her smile conspiratorial. " 'Tis once a year we in Fair Badden have an excuse to play at being varlets and laggards and buffoons. The rest of the year we're too sober by half. What's a celebration without your good clover wine?"

The girl was right. Edith herself didn't want to get, er, *festive* on The Ploughman's rotgut ale, and intend to get festive she did.

"All right, Rhiannon," she capitulated with a grumble. "We'll bring the clover wine but if there were less celebrating on Beltaine night mayhap we mightn't have so many baptisms nine months hence."

It was true, particularly amongst Fair Badden's younger, farming population. The old custom of young people pairing up and going off into the

dark woods on Beltaine night to collect hawthorn blossoms often ended with the courting couple having an incentive to move past courting to the altar. Often that incentive was a babe.

"I wouldn't know about that," Rhiannon said. "I've been Virgin Queen of the Virgin May three years running now."

"You just make sure you *keep* running this Beltaine night, girl," Edith said severely. "At least until after your wedding."

CHAPTER 8

"Hide and seek?" Susan Chapham echoed Margaret Atherton's suggestion. "In the yew maze?"

She glanced around as she said it, an unnecessary precaution as Edith Fraiser had shepherded their parents into the drawing room where innumerable games of whist, coupled with matching glasses of port, would keep them busy all afternoon. "Dare we?"

The young men, reluctant to be caught instigating such naughty sport, remained mum but their smiles related their accord with the proposed entertainment. Only Ash Merrick remained uninvolved, his gaze distracted, his expression polite but bored. More than anyone Rhiannon had ever met, he provoked the mischievousness in her. She simply could not let him dismiss her and her friends.

"Why not?" Rhiannon therefore asked. " 'Twill be good practice for Beltaine. Mayhap we ladies will discover some hidey hole to keep ourselves safe from roaming males that night."

"And how do you propose to conduct the game?" Ash Merrick asked. He unfolded his whipcord length from where he'd been idly leaning against the maypole the villagers had erected that morning.

His time in Fair Badden had bestowed a tawny hue to his pale skin and since he so adamantly denounced wearing any wig, his hair, freshly washed, glistened like polished ebony.

"Everyone hides and one person tries to find them all?" Susan suggested.

"Sounds confounded tiring to me," St. John said, yawning behind his gloved hand.

"Have you a better suggestion?" one of the other young ladies asked.

"I do," Phillip declared. "The ladies hide and the last one to be found wins."

"But that isn't fair," Margaret said plaintively. "Rhiannon will be the last woman found. It's her yew maze, after all."

"Besides," John Fortnum said in his gruff, forthright way, "seems to me that since the men do all the work, the men ought to reap some sort of reward."

An inspired smile appeared on Phillip's face. "How about this? The gentleman who finds the last lady hidden in the maze shall be rewarded with"—he looked around—"a kiss."

The ladies tittered. The men grinned knowingly. And Ash Merrick leaned toward Margaret Atherton, saying something in a voice that did not carry. Something for her ears alone.

"Aye. A kiss it shall be!" Rhiannon declared.

"But Phillip knows this maze nearly as well as Rhiannon," Susan complained. "He'll be sure to win. . . ." And then, as realization struck her, "Ohh!"

Phillip's golden brows rose in feigned innocence. "I am sure Rhiannon knows hiding places I've yet to discover."

He was so sure of himself, thought Rhiannon, and the same quality that had driven her to support the game, the same thing that spurred her to race breakneck speeds when putting her horse to a hurdle, was pricked awake by his certainty.

She did indeed know a place or two Phillip had never discovered. Besides, Margaret knew the maze nearly as well as she, and from the manner in which she cast sidelong glances at Ash Merrick, she might well prove to be the last lady discovered . . . if Ash was the seeker.

Sure enough, Margaret lent her support to the proposal. "All right. I'm game."

"Indeed?" One of Ash's black brows climbed consideringly, a lazy sexual quality in his regard.

Margaret tittered unconscionably and Rhiannon felt her cheeks grow warm. She chided herself viciously. Why shouldn't he flirt with Margaret? He was unattached—as was Margaret.

She moved away from them, her feet carrying her swiftly as, with heated faces, the other young women in the party added their approval. As soon as it was decided that the women should have the count of two hundred before the men came to find them, they disbanded, multicolored skirts belling out as they fled amidst laughter into the maze's evergreen corridors.

As soon as she passed beneath the rose arbor that led into the maze, Rhiannon broke to the left. Experienced hunters like her friends would drive to the back of the maze and scout for a hiding place there, amidst thick hedges in the densest part of the garden. But not her.

She would stay on a side path. After the men had passed, she would sneak back toward the front and the rose arbor she'd ducked under. There, the rose vine entangled with an ancient yew, hiding a little nook she had discovered years ago. Outside the maze she would be barely visible, but from within the maze no one would be able to see her.

She waited for the men to enter, her heart racing. She heard a muted hunting-horn sound and then the men crashing through the entry, calling out. Before long Susan Chapham's squeal of outrage proclaimed her the first woman to be found. Had it been Ash? Or was he seeking other quarry?

Cautiously Rhiannon peered around the corner. The only sound she heard was that of St. John's perennial complaints. She sped swiftly back toward the entrance. Crouching low, she angled her body sideways and pushed her way through the thick growth.

And then she was in.

She looked around. The very center of the huge yew had rotted away, making a small empty room with living walls. Slender needles of sunlight pierced the higher boughs, stabbing the earth with brilliant pinpricks. The tight, unfurled buds of the red rose adorned the dark green walls like rubies. Beneath, her feet crushed fifty years of accumulated yew needles. Their fragrance rose, sharp and pungent.

She hadn't been here for years. Not since she was a little girl, driven from her bed to hide from the red-coated devils who rode thundering through her dreams. Or had they been dreams? Memories most like, taking advantage of sleep's vulnerability to attack once again.

Thank God, she'd found haven. She'd found Fair Badden. She'd never have to face the landscape of her nightmares again. Ever.

She vanquished the memories, as she always vanquished the memories of her life before her arrival here. She would think of nothing unpleasant. She was playing a game on a lovely spring day and she was going to win. She could imagine Phillip's surprise when he strode confidently toward the bower he expected she'd be occupying only to find it empty.

She grinned. She would wait until he'd given up and then she'd walk serenely from the gate, stringing a chain of daisies as she came.

Ash Merrick might even smile.

Within a few minutes a triumphant call signaled the discovery of another lady and then another. Two more ladies had been flushed. Another cry and more laughter. That left only Rhiannon.

"She's here somewhere," she heard Phillip say from nearby.

"Aha, Watt! She's outmaneuvered you! Best think twice before marrying a wench what's smarter than you." It was John Fortnum.

"I'll find her."

But he didn't. A few minutes later Phillip called out, "There's nothing else for it, lads. We'll just drive her like a partridge. She'll be far back where the trees overhang the maze. Likely she's clambered up one and is swinging her legs overhead, laughing as we stumble about nose to the ground."

"Well, even if I don't win the kiss, you've just offered me reward enough to gain my aid," another man laughed. "Rhiannon Russell must have pretty legs."

Rhiannon's face grew hot.

"I'm for it, too!" John Fortnum answered, his voice moving off. "Lead on, Watt."

Rhiannon settled down to wait, leaning her head against the yew's shaggy trunk. It could take a goodly while before Phillip called quits. He was tenacious and he disliked being bested.

Perhaps it was the cool dimness chased with golden lights, or perhaps the hushed stillness, the rich damp scent of a hiding place, but soon her eyes drifted shut and she fell into a light, easy sleep.

"Tha thu agam." I have you.

Her eyes opened slowly, uncertain of what she'd heard. Gaelic. She hadn't heard the Gaelic tongue in ten years. She raised her head, her vision slow in adjusting to the sharp contrasting light.

Ash Merrick stood over her.

Sunlight dappled his broad shoulders, sparkled in his black hair. His head was cocked to one side and in the odd light she could not make out the expression in his dark eyes, though she could see clearly enough the dark lashes surrounding them, the shadow beneath the high cheekbone, the shape of his mouth.

"You spoke to me in Gaelic."

"Did I?" His voice was quiet. "I was raised in the Highlands, for all my English blood, you know."

"Aye. English . . . How would you . . . ?" She stuttered, stopped herself, went on. "I didn't hear you enter," she said, self-conscious beneath his mute appraisal. "How can that be? I should have heard the sound of yew boughs breaking and—"

"Easy, Miss Russell," he said. "I came in by the roses." He gestured toward a low opening leading to the grassy gardens outside. "I walked the outer periphery of the maze. Sometimes a man needs to stand back to see what's before him."

"Oh." She swallowed, brushing the hair back from her face. It didn't seem fair that he'd left the maze. It set unexpected anxiety shivering through her and she didn't understand why.

She tilted her head back. He bent down, startling her. She jumped a little. He went motionless for a heartbeat and then with a slow, wry smile, reached down and gently removed a sprig of yew from her skirts. Flustered, she brushed the needles from the folds.

"I've won," he said.

"Aye." She did not meet his eye.

"You didn't expect anyone to find you."

"Nay."

"You dislike it that I did."

"Aye," she replied sullenly.

"Why is that?"

"I don't know," she muttered. "I'd hidden where no one would find me. I thought I was safe."

" 'Safe.' An interesting choice of words considering we were playing a game."

"It's a feeling, is all," she explained grudgingly. "I used to come here when I was just a lassie newly arrived from . . . newly arrived at Fair Badden."

"From the Highlands."

"Yes."

"You were what? Nine years old? Eight? Your family had fought for the Pretender, hadn't they?"

She nodded.

"Did you hide? When Cumberland's men came? Why? The troops didn't seek children."

"They sought anyone that wore a plaid," she replied in a hushed voice.

"And you hid in the woods." The words seemed to come from him without volition.

"Yes."

"And no one found you."

"Me or the old lady my mother sent with me." She hadn't ever told anyone of those days. Not even Edith Fraiser. She'd tried once, but Edith had tucked her shivering body onto her lap and told her to forget everything that had happened to her before she came to them.

Rhiannon had tried to do what Edith said. Like she had tried to do everything else the Fraisers had asked, to be good and dutiful and never give a moment's distress. Mostly she had succeeded. She could barely recall her own parents' faces. "We watched the croft burn."

He did not ask her to elaborate and for this she was grateful. But he understood. She could see it. Sense it. Following Cumberland's defeat of Prince Charlie's Highlanders at Culloden she'd lost everyone: father, brothers, uncles, cousins.

"Do you have family . . . besides your father?" she asked.

"A sister. A brother."

She nodded. "Where are—"

"Then you found your way here," he cut in. "But you still felt hunted."

"No." She shook her head. "Only sometimes at night. When the thunder came. I didn't want to be a coward and I didn't want to hurt Mrs. Fraiser's feelings—and they would have been sorely hurt had she thought I didn't feel safe in her own good home—so I'd steal outside and come here.

"No one ever found me. No one knew about it. I thought no one ever would—lest I told them. So it was safe, you understand. And now it isn't anymore, because you found me and I don't know that I'll ever feel safe here again." Or anywhere, she thought.

He studied her for a long moment before extending his hand as he had yesterday after wrestling her beneath him and making her aware of his strength, his tensile length, and his weight. He'd made her feel weak, vulnerable. Yet it was not a conscious aim of his. She could not fault him for making her feel that way, or in some odd way liking it. Because if she'd felt weak, he'd felt strong and she knew he would use that strength to protect her.

She placed her hand in his. Effortlessly, he assisted her to her feet. He stepped away.

"You should be safe. You should *feel* safe," he murmured, an edge of anger sharpening his tone.

"No matter now."

"I won't tell anyone about this place," he said. "In a few weeks I'll be gone and it will be your sanctuary once again." His words came rapidly, as though he must say them.

He didn't understand. Whether he went or stayed, wherever he was, she would always be cognizant of the fact he knew about this place. She would never be alone here again. *He* would be with her. But his impulse was kind and she could not rob him of that.

"Thank you."

"But"—he stepped nearer and she could see his chest rising and falling as though he'd been running—"I still would have my reward."

He stepped forward and she moved back until her shoulders pressed against the yew's green branches.

"An toir thu dhomh mo pog?" he whispered. *Will you give me my kiss?*

She lifted her gaze; it became entangled with his as surely as the rose vine entangled with the yew at her back. As steadfast and ineluctably. "Aye."

Slowly, carefully, Ash drew near her. His hands hung loose at his side, his eyes held hers. He angled his head and lowered his mouth until she felt his breath on her lips. Her eyelids fluttered closed. Their lips met.

As soft as summer mist. Delicately as dawn's first colors. Tenderly his mouth molded over hers, moved with breath-stealing sweetness and her own lips, readied for an overpowering assault, were conquered instead by exquisite gentleness.

He raised his arms and she, prepared to lean into his embrace, found that he did not embrace her at all and that instead his strong arms reached past her, bracketing her head, and finding purchase against the living walls behind her. He leaned forward, deepening the kiss.

She sighed, her head falling back, overwhelmed and shaken. She felt weak, her body drugged, her pulse erratic. Unsteadily she laid her hand against his chest for support. His heart beat thickly beneath her palm.

His mouth opened over hers, his breath stole between her lips. She could feel him, taste him, complex and exotic, spicy wine and fresh mint. The tip of his tongue gently lined her lips, coaxing them farther apart.

Her legs trembled. Her thoughts grew faint. All she was aware of was his mouth, his tongue gently playing, seeking the sleek lining of her inner lip, the tip of her own tongue. His heart thundered beneath her hand in an acute counterpoint to the leisurely intoxication of his kiss.

A sound rose in her throat. Her mouth opened wider. Her hands stole around his shoulders, pulling her body tight against his hard chest— He let her go.

Dazed, disoriented, lips sensitive and lush feeling, she stared at him. He stepped away from her, clasping his hands behind his back. His face was still. His dark eyes shuttered. Then he smiled and bent forward in a deep, courtly bow.

"I am well rewarded," he said. "I heard the others coming back. You'd best go. Now. Meet them outside the entrance. I'll follow later."

"But—" she stared at him without understanding, naive and stupid and ill, for he'd awoken with his kiss such feeling as she'd never experienced for Phillip Watt. Never.

Mrs. Fraiser had been wrong. Ash Merrick wasn't dangerous. He was courtly and genteel and his kisses were soft and stirring. Her feelings, *they* were dangerous.

"Go." He was still smiling. "You see, you've won."

She turned away, gathering her skirts and bolting into the too bright light. And so she did not see Ash Merrick's gaze follow her, or see him take his hands from behind his back and turn them over. And she did not see the bloody hands that had been torn strangling the thorny vines behind her so he could keep from crushing her to him.

CHAPTER 9

During the next week, Rhiannon saw little of Ash Merrick. Edith Fraiser needed her services in a myriad number of ways. Her foster mother sent her on lengthy errands to neighboring estates, occupied her mornings with overseeing the processing of spring honey, and decided now, of all times, to teach her the secrets of brewing a potent clover wine.

When Rhiannon did see Ash Merrick, perpetually on his way out to join the young men—of which Phillip was one—at some masculine entertainment, he was invariably polite and courteous but nothing more. He evinced none of the stunned bewilderment she herself so acutely felt, none of the sensual attraction she fought so hard to hide.

Their kiss meant nothing more to him than the meaningless prize it had been proclaimed. It was a simple meeting of lips, a casual misbehavior.

She only wished she could be so worldly and unaffected. But there had been nothing simple about her response to his kiss.

It had incited a maelstrom of emotions and sensations. The memory of it heated her blood, pooling a restless longing in her lips, her fingertips, her breasts. . . .

It frightened her. It haunted her. When she closed her eyes at night, Merrick's lean, hard form and dark-lashed eyes appeared with startling and all too revealing clarity. She'd been careful since to avoid his company.

Tonight, however, there was slim chance she would be able to avoid his company—or he, hers. Tonight was Lady Harquist's ball. She would have considered it the usual overpopulated, uncomfortable, and crushing affair it generally was, if not for the anxiety of wondering whether Ash Merrick would be there.

She assumed Ash had been included on the guest list but then, doubtless, even if invited he would decline. He had a more than adequate excuse; he'd brought no clothes fitting for a ball.

The thought brought relief at the same time as an acute, guilty regret. Edith Fraiser had been right after all; Ash Merrick was dangerous.

"Begad, that creature you're riding is unfit to feed my dogs, Merrick!" Phillip avowed blearily.

Ash, jouncing along on a squat pony some distance ahead, clad in black silk, three quarters of his face covered by a mask, did not appear to have heard. The others in their party did. They raised drunken voices in boisterous concurrence. Even the gypsy rogues they traveled with had fallen prey to Ash Merrick's bonhomie. Teeth flashed beneath the fantastical papier-mâché masks as shouts in the Romany tongue filled the night air.

Phillip, in no mood to be ignored, spurred his pony forward. Far ahead of them, the Harquist manor blazed with light, a beacon in the dark.

"You're a right Mogul," Phillip proclaimed on reaching Ash's side.

Ash's dark gaze flashed sidelong but he simply smiled in that lazy way of his and took another swig from the leather skein bouncing on his hip.

When he didn't respond, Phillip went on. "Bedamned if this isn't a grand notion. Don't know why one of us didn't think of it years ago."

It was indeed a splendid notion, spectacular and hilarious. Earlier that day they'd been disconsolately draining tankards of ale at The Ploughman, complaining loudly about the deadly dullness of the fete they were obliged to endure that evening—Lady Harquist's spring ball.

Ash had been taciturn—an increasing tendency in the last few days. Even though Phillip had put himself out to entertain, Merrick was not to be cajoled. His obvious boredom had infected the others' moods, blighting their usual gaiety until a band of filthy, beggarly looking rascals had entered the inn.

Merrick's elegant head had lifted and he had watched them with more interest than he'd evinced all afternoon. A light of inspiration had slowly ignited in his silver eyes. He'd clapped his hand on the table.

"If the evening's entertainment promises tedium, my dear sirs, you've but two course open to you," he'd declared. "You can forego it—"

"Not bloody likely," John Fortnum interjected disconsolately. "Me old pater would disinherit me if I gave the snub to Lady H."

"Me, too," Phillip confessed.

"Then you have only *one* option," Ash said impatiently. "*You* become the entertainment." He cast a knowing look in the direction of the foreigners. "Lest I be mistaken—and I am rarely mistaken in these matters—yonder sits An Opportunity."

Before anyone could protest, he had hailed the band's leader, Raoul, a gray-headed fellow as wiry as a river alder, to join them. Over the next two hours—and a keg of strong cider—Merrick had ascertained that the gypsies were in fact a troupe of acrobats and tumblers "what been hired to entertain at the big house."

Forthwith Ash had bribed Raoul with sweet words and sweeter coin into allowing them to join their company for the night, masquerading as fellow tumblers. So it was that St. John, Fortnum, and Phillip himself—as well as a half-dozen nameless rascals—were trotting down the road leading to Lady Harquist's, dressed in black leggings and shirts, faces concealed behind whimsical masks, drunk as lords, happy as angels, and as set on mischief as Satan's imps. All thanks to that infernally amusing and fascinating fellow at Phillip's side, Ash Merrick.

Phillip was dully aware he had a case of hero worship. Usually 'twas he, because of his height, his breadth, his looks, or his father's wealth, who attracted admiration. But Ash Merrick was utterly unimpressed by any of Phillip's attributes, having looks and address enough without seeking its reflection in others.

He was simply the damnedest, most dauntless, and most interesting man Phillip had ever met.

Phillip gazed blearily at his idol. Merrick was slender and hard as an épée. Even half-sotted, he fair stank of élan.

The thing of it was, thought Phillip, Merrick had the trick of making everything into a game. Take, for example, a few days ago when Merrick had suddenly announced that the local magistrates were old and blind and thus incapable of tracking down the rogue who had assaulted Rhiannon and Mrs. Fraiser. The task, he'd explained, belonged to young, sharp-eyed gentlemen.

Thus for the rest of that day and the next, Merrick had led his merry, confused companions over the countryside, interviewing hostelry workers, waylaying farmhands, searching for any clue as to the whereabouts of the highwayman.

They didn't find anything—of course not—but that wasn't the point, was it? The point was it had been fun. Exciting. Like this.

"I don't know that this is such a good idea after all," Fortnum called out from his position at the rear. The curling horns of his ram's mask bobbed in agitation. "There'll be the devil to pay when we're caught!"

"What are we to do with them, Watt?" Ash sighed. A feeling of pleasure suffused Phillip.

"I don't know," he said, trying to discern Merrick's desire.

"I suspect we'll just have to sweeten the game." Merrick placed a fist on his hip and eyed St. John and Fortnum severely. The wind ruffled his black locks and plastered his loose linen shirt to his chest. He looked every inch a black-hearted devil. There was about him a fateful ferocity that Phillip admired greatly.

"Let's see. How can we make this a worthy game for our friends here? You are betting men, are you not?" he asked.

Both men agreed.

"Ha! I knew I'd taken your measure right. Here it is, then. I wager that I can dupe everyone attending Lady Harquist's party for a full hour.

"And furthermore, I bet you that when my identity *is* finally divulged, not one word of censure greets that revelation no matter how crudely I misbehave, no matter how lecherous my leers, no matter how deeply I drink—and make no mistake, my dears, I intend to be very, very drunk." His smile was fierce and challenging.

"Oh, come now, Merrick," Fortnum sputtered.

"Ha!" St. John burst out. "I'll take that bet."

"Will you?" Ash tipped his head. "But I haven't said what the stakes are."

"What?" St. John asked.

Ash smiled. "Two hundred pounds."

Phillip caught back his surprise. Two hundred pounds was more than he'd ever wagered on a single bet before.

Ash's cool, mocking gaze scanned their faces. "I thought not," he murmured pleasantly. He took another deep draught from the wineskin.

"I say you can do it!" Phillip declared staunchly. Ash passed him the flask. Phillip slurped it greedily, eyeing his lily-livered companions scornfully.

"I'll take that bet," St. John finally said.

"Excellent, St. John," Merrick declared. "I knew *you* were a game one. First, the rules. None of you, by action or word, must betray your acquaintance with any of Lady Harquist's guests. You must, on your honor, keep strictly away from those you call intimates, be they friend, father, or lover." His glance found Phillip. Heat rose to Phillip's cheeks. "Agreed?"

They all nodded.

"Good. Now, I'll want a sharp blade and a steady hand to hold a mirror."

"But why?" Fortnum asked.

Merrick laughed. "I fear overcoming the clue my beard provides would strain even my thespian skills," Merrick said. "Who can help me?"

It was one of the gypsies who found amongst his travel kit the means to rid Merrick of beard and moustache. Ten minutes later, the razor's sharp blade had revealed a square and manly jaw, a pair of deeply bowed and sensual lips. Merrick held the mirror up and gave a mocking laugh to his own reflection before pulling the black silk domino back down over his blacker hair and upper face. "Now, away my lads."

A short time later they were following Merrick down the cobbled drive that led up to the Harquists' manor. The weak moonlight washed over the contours of Merrick's thighs and shoulders. His hands were pale against the black silk cuff. Phillip quaffed more from the flask.

Who could possibly take exception to a man like Merrick? Yet, Rhiannon appeared to have developed an aversion to him. Odd. Especially since she had seemed to like Merrick well enough at first. But in the past few days Rhiannon had grown uneasy in Merrick's company, skittish. Through no fault of Merrick's.

Merrick was all that was pleasant and respectful to Rhiannon, even courtly. Perhaps he drank a bit much, and each day seemed to increase his thirst, but what of it? Phillip was perhaps imbibing more than usual, too. Especially now, with his impending nuptials closing in.

He twitched away the unpleasant sensation the thought awoke. Being a touch goosey about being leg-shackled was surely normal.

Rhiannon had best learn right now that Phillip was loyal to his friends and that his companions ranked high in his esteem. *Nothing* was more sacred to a man than his friends. They sustained and encouraged and understood him in a way a woman never could.

Phillip took another swig, arguing away his sense of unease. Rhiannon wouldn't interfere with him, he reasoned. It was why he'd settled on her for his wife. That and his father's prodding.

The old man had specifically chosen Rhiannon Russell as his youngest son's mate, explaining that Rhiannon was kind and loyal and grateful. She would quietly accept whatever Phillip did. She would not demand things a man could—*would* not give.

The old man was right. Rhiannon was the perfect choice for a wife. Besides he was fond of her.

Yes, it was time he wed. Though still young, he felt this subtle resistance to the idea of marrying grow each year. If he waited too long he might not be able to bring himself to do the deed at all—there was so much about living a bachelor's life that appealed to him. Freedom. Not being accountable to a woman for his whereabouts or his actions. Friends. And of course, he added as an afterthought, other ladies.

But he did want a family. He quite looked forward to having a couple brats, and the old man wanted grandsons, something his older brothers had yet to provide. Rhiannon would make a good mother.

As if he had read his mind, Merrick suddenly spoke to him. "Your darlin' bride-to-be is at tonight's festivities, is she not?"

"Yes."

"And any number of other rich young wenches," John Fortnum added. "Now that Phillip here is going all connubial, me dad's all in a lather for me to marry. Perhaps I should take advantage of this evening's sport to look over the prospects, unbeknownst to the prospects, of course. Just because Watt can sustain a penniless bride does not mean I can."

Merrick slew about in his saddle, peering at Phillip. "Just how is that, Watt? How came you to offer for the penniless, if lovely, Miss Russell?"

"Phillip here is proof of an old man's passion," Fortnum supplied before Phillip could speak. "And his father does therefore love him dearly. If it would keep Phillip in Fair Badden, his father would let him marry a tavern wench.

"A rich wife might want a London house. A well-connected wife might have family to visit on long extended trips away. Miss Russell has no reason to leave Fair Badden, nor any desire to do so."

Sober Phillip might have taken exception to such revelations, but he wasn't sober. He was deliciously drunk and surrounded by his bosom friends and on his way to a fine piece of sport. What and why would he keep anything private from these men?

"True," Phillip confessed. "But that's not the only reason. Rhiannon's clever enough to spend the rest of her life being grateful to me for making her my wife." He grinned. "What other woman would have that sense?"

CHAPTER 10

They were rough, uncouth fellows. And they were exquisitely, hilariously, vibrantly alive. Fair Badden had never seen their like.

Other traveling performers measured Fair Badden's high society as the self-conscious, priggish band of yawners it was and suited their talents accordingly, somberly enacting philosophical vignettes or singing plodding chorales. Not these fellows. Rude and boisterous and bawdy, they had about them a joie de vivre that was infectious. True, the big silent fellow had no more important a role than letting his smaller fellows clamber over him, but he played the part of mountain well. Another masked man circulated through the room, snatching goblets of wine from Lady Harquist's guests' well-manicured hands and giving back salacious ditties in a high, inane falsetto.

They were unpredictable, thrilling, and novel. Even the most consummate snob in Lady Harquist's company could not restrain an occasional smile at their antics. They sang ribald songs with leering enthusiasm, mocked their betters with uncanny insight, and quaffed expensive wine as though it were cider dregs. They tumbled and juggled, danced and somersaulted one over the other. Their short morality plays dissolved into delicious double entendres.

Rhiannon welcomed their vibrant company with relief, taking the opportunity to escape her unwelcome preoccupation with Ash Merrick by entering wholeheartedly into their heated word games. It was early yet. Not everyone had arrived. Cornered by a lean fellow in a black silk domino, she giggled, intoxicated by this unexpected freedom from her troubled thoughts.

"Ah, pretty ladybirds!" His voice was slurred and husky, and his thick French accent was so authentic one could not help but wonder if it were real. He peered owlishly at the young ladies tittering behind Rhiannon. "A full gaggle of them and all squawking love songs!"

He swept a crumpled tricorn from his head. A tight-fitting scarf of silk covered his hair. He bent over in so low a bow that his forehead nearly brushed the floor. Just as he was about to overset himself and crash face first into the ground, he snapped upright, blinking woozily.

Part of his act, no doubt, Rhiannon thought. Because though his voice was slurred, he moved with the grace of God's own fool, dodging the vases his fellow acrobats hurled at him, catching them midair, and sending them back. Through it all the inane smile remained plastered on his lower face. But behind the mask his dark eyes gleamed with feverish light.

"Here now, miss," he said snatching at Rhiannon and missing her by inches. Merrily, she danced out from his reach, twirling away in a cloud of jonquil-colored brocade. A tendril of hair escaped its knot and tumbled down her neck.

"Come, dearest. My haughty, devilish, quick-footed Mab," he crooned, reaching for her again. "You look an adventuresome wench, a curious kitten. I've heard it said that all 'ladies crave to be encountered with.' Admit it, sweetling, 'tis a fact that virgins dream of what a gypsy's embrace might be like."

A French gypsy who knew Shakespeare? Not likely.

Rhiannon snorted. "If I allowed your arms about me, sir," she said through her laughter, "I'd be wondering still."

His head swung up. A flicker of surprise appeared in his shadowed eyes.

"Oh ho! What are you saying, *mon amie*? That I'm not what I appear to be"—his voice lowered, became silky with innuendo—"or that *you're* not?"

Why, the audacious cur! The knave! Rhiannon thought in bemusement and could not help grinning at his audacity.

"Tinsel gypsy!" she declared.

"Downy child!" he returned in his low, rough voice, grinning drunkenly.

"I'm not so easily gulled." Rhiannon denied the charge of naïveté, placing her hands on her hips. She cocked a brow at him. "For have I not discovered *you*?"

She leaned forward, studying him closely, the marble smoothness of his blue-cast chin, the full sensual lips. They were unfamiliar yet . . .

"I know you," she murmured, mystified.

"No, Mademoiselle." He shook his head sadly. His dark eyes caught and held her own. "For how can you know me when I do not know myself?"

Around them the noise from the tumblers and jugglers dimmed to a hum. She was scarcely aware of her friends, moving closer.

Faithless flirt, she chastised herself hopelessly. Was it not enough that in her heart she'd betrayed Phillip with a black-haired Londoner, but now she betrayed both men to this . . . *actor* who had honed each slippery, honeyed word on a continent of twittering, blushing girls.

"Who *are* you?" she asked.

He shrugged. Stepped back. "Who do you want me to be? Tumbler?"

He folded at the waist and snapped suddenly backward, head over heels, landing lightly. Around them the ladies clapped. He did not acknowledge their applause; his eyes remained riveted on her.

"Minstrel?"

He withdrew a slender flute dangling from his belt and placed it to his lips. A frolicsome tune flushed from beneath his fingers. Once more the applause broke from the little group of watchers.

"Buffoon?"

He laughed, an unpleasant, helpless sound that caught at Rhiannon's heart, propelling her forward a step. He held out his hand, backing away as if her spontaneous movement somehow threatened him.

"No! Not yet the fool. Though there's always hope you'll witness it yet this night. You wouldn't want to miss it. I play that role best of all."

"Yes!" A young lady in an elaborate wig and diamond ear bobs cried. "Play the fool for us now!"

The tumbler's head turned toward the speaker. "Forgive me, *ma chérie*, but I must decline. That particular mask is threadbare, a shoddy, shopworn piece of work. Unfit for such exalted company. I'll retire and late this evening when you lay sighing upon some worthy"—he paused and the ladies gasped—"pillow, I'll mend it. When next we meet, I swear, I'll be a knave."

He stood rigidly a few seconds and then abruptly grinned. "But tonight I've a grander notion."

"What's that?" the girl asked, but he was not looking at her anymore.

His attention had returned to Rhiannon. Fascinated and charmed, she stayed though her conscience urged her to leave.

"Perhaps tonight I am . . . a hero? No?" He dropped to his knee and stretched a beseeching hand in Rhiannon's direction. "Chevalier? Knight gallant?"

She smiled and would have taken his hand but he snatched it away. He plucked a silver stiletto from where it was hidden in his boot and uncoiled with lethal grace. The knife flashed deadly in his hand.

"Or perhaps mercenary? Villain? Only tell me what you'll pay . . . and I'll tell you my price." His voice had gone flat, emptied. The tip of the blade moved in a threatening arc before the company of giggling women. It stopped at Rhiannon, held, wavered, and was abruptly snatched back.

"A rogue? Or a friend?" He flipped the stiletto into the air and caught it on its descent. Once, twice more.

He was breathing quickly now, each breath exposed by the clinging shirt, the rise and fall of his muscular chest. "A fribble? A blackguard?"

No drunkenness now marred his speech or clouded his bright eyes. He slunk closer to her, his feet sliding ahead of his taut body, his head angled away from her, approaching her like a feral dog.

"Only tell me what *you* desire, *mon coeur*," he said. "What do you want? I'll become it. Anything. It's what I am. What I do. My stock-in-trade."

His voice was hypnotic, base insinuation and bitter mockery underscoring a vast bleakness. The audience around them grew hushed. Margaret shuffled on her feet, her eyes darting nervously. The smile of another bewigged young lady remained fixed on her face like a beauty mark she'd forgotten to take off.

And then the moment was gone. The dark tumbler flung himself back and away.

"No suggestions?" he complained. "You'd leave me to my own devices? My own imaginings? Not a safe place to leave a man such as me."

He sighed heavily. "Then I'll be a juggler. *Here*, my friends, to me!"

At his call several of his fellow acrobats abandoned their pursuits. He called out again, raised his stiletto, and flung it over the heads of Lady Harquist's guests. As one, the guests ducked and shouted in alarm. The blade whistled high above their elegant coiffures, their feathered, puffed, and swollen wigs.

A short, bandy-legged fellow perched atop the giant's shoulders cackled gleefully and caught the dark tumbler's missile. Magically, its twin appeared in his other hand. With a hoot, he hurled first one then the other back at Rhiannon's would-be hero.

He caught them both and sent them chasing one another in an arc above his head. A third knife joined them, and then a fourth, as the other members of the troupe sent their blades spinning and flashing toward the black-clad figure.

Effortlessly he caught and added each to the sparkling, glittering circle of death that flew above his head, occasionally plucking one from the circle and sending it out amidst the party, only to have it returned seconds later chased by a new one. The company held their breath, clasping their gloved hands to their mouths in fascinated terror.

He made it look so easy, so effortless. But Rhiannon, standing closest to him, saw the sheen break out on his closely shaven chin and exposed throat, witnessed the intensity with which he watched the tumbling blades fall toward him, an intensity at odds with his easy banter and fluid movements.

Now, released from his attentions, the niggling impression of familiarity returned to tease her. The lean, hard acrobat's body hidden under dusty, ill-fitting finery, the supple grace, even the choice of words, though spoken in an accent . . .

Her gaze flew toward the young giant standing currently unemployed and idle against the wall. His mask had gone askew. One bushy golden brow appeared in the jagged eyehole.

Phillip?

Her head snapped around. The juggler had reached above his head to catch a knife thrown a shade too high. The cuff slipped up his arm.

A thick, pale rope of scarred flesh decorated his wrist.

"Merrick?" she whispered, jerking forward.

From the corner of her eye she saw a silver gleam, then heard a thunk. She wheeled about. Behind her a stiletto vibrated in the paneled wall.

Exactly where she'd been standing.

CHAPTER 11

Rhiannon stared at the still quivering blade. Some hand had grown sloppy with drink, she thought breathlessly. Had she not moved . . .

Ash tore off his silk mask, looking beyond her, his gaze hunting through the assembled crowd. A gasp followed his revelation and was pursued by the rumbling of a hundred voices.

"It's that Merrick fellow!"

"Merrick? The fellow staying at the Fraisers'?"

"Merrick. Ash Merrick. Carr's son—"

A flicker ignited in the cool depths of Ash's dark eyes as he searched the faces turned toward him. He was not drunk, he was pretending, Rhiannon thought. And all those things he'd said, all those words he'd played upon . . .

"What sort of a game is this?" she heard Edith Fraiser exclaim. The company parted and she sailed forth, her skirts bunched in fists on either hip, her face rouged with concern. Purposefully, she stomped toward Merrick, bypassing the knife without a glance.

With a start, Rhiannon realized that her foster mother, as well as the vast majority of those present, was unaware of how close that blade had come to separating Rhiannon's spirit from her flesh.

"Is that really Mr. Merrick, then?" Edith demanded.

"Aye, madame," Merrick murmured in a low, distracted tone. "And I, too, would like to know what game this is."

He turned and suddenly his face wore a lopsided smile. "Ala*th* . . . I mean alas . . . I am revealed!" he called, bowing inelegantly. "And since *I* am revealed, I insist my cohorts suffer likewise. Unmask! Unmask!"

With a drunken shout, Phillip tugged until his mask came off. "Me, too!" he cried jubilantly. "Revealed, that is!'

The others followed his example. Around them, Lady Harquist's astounded guests stared, snickered, smiled, and finally laughed. Even Lady Harquist, seeing how well the fake acrobats were received, allowed herself a moue of self-congratulation.

True, a few ladies sniffed—these, confirmed sticklers—but overwhelmingly the crowd approved. A spattering of applause even broke out and Phillip's father, hunched and crippled with gout though he was, banged his cane upon the floor in approval.

"This your doing, Mr. Merrick?" the old man demanded. "Good for you, sir. Our society is grown stale of late. We're wanting a bit of piss to shine the pewter!"

With a debonair swoop of his hand, Ash saluted the crowd and then ruined the gesture by staggering sideways and tipping into the wall. His shoulder hit the paneling with an audible thud. He stayed there, canted against the paneling, his face six inches from where the knife protruded. He cocked his head and studied it.

"What's this? What's this?" he muttered.

He was drunk after all, Rhiannon thought and then castigated herself for being disillusioned.

So? She'd mistook a spark of reflected light in his pupil for keenness and the candle-made shadows beneath his cheeks for taut alertness. She'd supposed his words filled with meaning when they were filled only with mead. She averted her eyes from him. They felt hot and she would not cry. She had no reason to cry.

Ash craned his head around and, seeing her, smiled stupidly. She winced and then, realizing how unfair she was, forced a smile. It was no part of his fault that she'd dressed him as her knight and that the shining armor did not fit.

His expression betrayed a momentary puzzlement and then he pointed at the knife. "You were standing here, weren't you, Miss Russell?"

"Yes," she answered. "What of it?"

Curious partygoers, finally alerted to the presence of a knife in their hostess's linen-paneled wall, had gathered in a loose semicircle around them.

"He thinks someone hurled a knife at Miss Russell," a lady said.

A snort of masculine contempt. "Some bungler missent it. Accident."

"Probably one of Watt's fool friends," an older man declared. "Not a grain of sense amongst the lot."

A low murmur rippled through the assembly.

"What's that Merrick fellow doing now?" a lady near Rhiannon asked.

"Who cares? Just let him stretch the cloth tight across those shoulders once more and I'll be counted content," a low feminine voice whispered in approval.

"Handsome creature, is he not? Dark as a storm-tossed night," another lady concurred.

"Aye and I'd be tossed right enough . . . if I could arrange to meet him of a night," came the throaty rejoinder.

Rhiannon bit back a reply. It was no concern of hers what these trollops thought. Ash finished his scrutiny of the stiletto and turned. His gaze lit on her.

"Begad! I have it!" he declared with an air of sudden inspiration. "Someone here has mistook this tasty morsel for his dinner!" He pointed at her. Dozens of eyes followed his gesture with amused interest.

He clucked his tongue. "Now what knave would seek to use a knife on what is so clearly . . . finger food?"

Heat raced up Rhiannon's throat and burned in her cheeks. Several of the men caught back their laughter, and smiles were traded behind the shield of lace handkerchiefs and widespread fans. He was easing the tensions that had grown in the overheated room, Rhiannon realized. Relaxing them. Why?

"Come now," Ash said, "someone must claim this knife. Where did it come from, friend rogue?" He hailed the wiry acrobat who'd clambered on Phillip's shoulders.

She'd forgotten Phillip. She looked around. Her fiancé was no longer sitting on the floor. He'd disappeared.

"I do not know where that comes from," the gypsy answered. "I was concentrating on the knives. *My* knives. That sticker isn't a Romany blade."

Ash jerked the blade from the wall. "True," he said. "No gypsy threw this pretty steel."

He ran his fingertip along the blade, testing the edge. He withdrew a finger marked with a thin red line.

"And as we all can attest, the only reason a blade leaving a Romany hand would hit this wall is because that is where the gypsy wanted it. Why would one of them do that, do you suppose? It's a far bit too early for them to be expressing disappointment in the tips."

Laughter met this unassailable observation. Merrick sighed gustily, squinting at the knife. "Whose then?"

He lurched toward Rhiannon and without warning grasped her upper arm, pulling her near. His grip was strong; his body exuded the remnant heat and scent of his exertions. Earthy. Masculine.

His dark face moved close. His rum-soaked breath sluiced over her face. She should have been disgusted and part of her was, but another was not. Another part of her wanted to discover if his mouth tasted of the drink, if drunk he could still make her knees grow weak with his kiss, if his body was as hot as it seemed.

"Who do you think flung that knife, miss? And why? Did someone think to make symmetry on that lovely face of yours with a twin scar?"

"I'm sure it was an accident." She pulled back; it would be too easy to lean forward.

"Aye. Accidents."

"Here now, Merrick!" Phillip's loud salutation broke over their heads like a thunderclap. He appeared behind them, towering over them like a convivial giant.

He swung one of his huge arms around Rhiannon's shoulders and another around Ash drawing them both together in an embrace that brought them within inches of each other. "It won't do any good, Merrick!" he said, fondly ruffling Ash's black hair.

"What won't do any good?"

"Fussing over that damned sticker won't divert anyone's attention from the fact that you owe St. John two hundred pounds!" At this, Phillip crowed with laughter.

"That's right, Merrick," St. John said, making his way toward them. "Your disguise didn't last the hour you promised."

"What's this about a bet?" one of the gentlemen asked.

"True, sir," Phillip said. "Mr. Merrick here bet St. John that he could cozen you all into thinking him one of these gypsy knaves for just as long as he wanted. Well, he lost and now he can stay and take his comeuppance."

Phillip exerted another powerful squeeze on his hapless prisoners. Ash was no proof against Phillip's strength. He stumbled toward Rhiannon who, manhandled in a like manner on Phillip's other side, toppled forward. Ash's hands flew out, catching her around the waist and steadying her.

His touch set her afire. She swallowed, willing herself not to react, not to flush, not to melt.

Even through the thick satin material, his touch burned her. So little a thing, so harmless, and yet, it stirred her blood, incited riotous visions. Visions she had no right entertaining.

She was worse than any flirt; she was a right molly, a slut, but that knowledge did not stop her from hating it when he took his hand away. She looked around in a panic, anywhere so she wouldn't have to encounter his eyes, and found Phillip watching her.

"*Th*ass right." His handsome golden head bobbed with soggy approval. "Make up. Be friends."

"Why should they?" St. John's humorous voice intoned. "She's the author of his loss. 'Twas she who called out Merrick's name. She revealed him."

"Did she, now?" Phillip asked, eyeing Rhiannon proudly. "What do you think of that, Ash Merrick? I think I ought to collect half the winnings."

"Not bloody likely," St. John said before Ash could answer. He leaned in close, his mouth inches from Rhiannon's ear, but though he whispered close to Rhiannon 'twas Ash his gaze fixed on.

"Best watch that girl, Merrick," St. John advised. "She'll be the ruin of you."

Ash blinked at St. John, a vague smile on his handsome face. "Unless I'm wrong, I believe she already has been."

He smiled throughout the rest of party. He smiled as he drank his way through an additional two bottles of port and he smiled as he traded suggestive sallies with Margaret Atherton. He smiled as he danced and he smiled as he counted out two hundred pounds into St. John's plump, gloved hand. And he smiled, by God, as he saw Rhiannon's confusion become disappointment then hurt.

When dawn stained the sky with her orchid-colored blood, he smiled and accepted Lady Harquist's offer of a bed. He was smiling as he staggered from the salon, and when he turned the door handle to the bedchamber, he was smiling still.

Because while tomorrow his obligation to his brother might make him a cheat or a thief or even a murderer, here, tonight, in this place, he was a congenial rascal, a bon vivant. A smiler.

But when the door shut behind him and he leaned his head against its panels, his smile died. He'd lost two hundred pounds because of her. Raine rotted in a French prison and he played fast and loose with money that could buy his freedom. And why? Because someone had thrown a knife too near her and he'd immediately concluded that her life was in mortal danger and he must save her, revealing himself—and losing his bet

—in the process. At least he'd had enough presence of mind to mask his concern beneath a façade of drunkenness.

He should be strung up and gutted. One minute of lucid thinking would have shown that it *had* been an accident just like the highwayman having targeted Rhiannon's carriage had been simple ill luck.

Ash had searched the countryside without finding a trace of the robber. And the reason for that was simple: He'd found none because the bounder had fled. There was no malevolent assassin lurking about waiting for the opportunity to kill a penniless girl.

Ash sneered. Either the two accidents had been just that, unconnected misfortunes, or someone in Fair Badden wanted Rhiannon dead. And who would that be, and why?

He was the worst kind of fool, one who needed to romanticize simple lust. He'd spent most of the week trying to get drunk enough to lose his erection. It hadn't worked.

He closed his eyes, willing the liquor in his blood to erase the taste of her soft mouth, the fragrance of her dark hair. . . . Six more days. Then she'd belong to that big, congenial boy.

Ash's hands clenched at his side, as he forced one last smile around his teeth. He had to get out of here. He had to get out of this damnable place, these terrifyingly defenseless lambs. The wolf should slink back to the black forests and leave the sheep wholly innocent of what had, for some short weeks, moved undiscovered amongst them.

He could leave now. There was no real reason for him to stay. He pushed himself away from the door. He *would* leave now.

Except that someone *had* thrown that knife. At her heart. He knew it.

He twisted, pounding his fist against the door. The stiletto had impaled the paneling at chest level. It stood at right angles to the wall. Someone had hurled it with deadly speed and precision.

He cursed roundly and viciously, but in the end it didn't affect his decision. He'd stay until she was another man's concern, another man's responsibility.

Another man's.

CHAPTER 12

Edith Fraiser sat on the bench outside the kitchen door, the gay ribbons that would adorn Rhiannon's May Day dress spilling over her skirts. She peered at the horizon. Dark weather was coming. Not today or this night, thank the Lord, which was Beltaine Night. No one enjoyed a soggy Beltaine. But perhaps tomorrow—which would be a shame as a soggy May Day was almost as sad.

She wiped her damp forehead, wondering if it really was as unseasonably warm as she thought or if her own frets and stews only made it seem so. She glanced at Rhiannon who, with Stella in attendance, was busily plaiting wild anemones into a maypole garland.

Two more days, Edith thought, returning to her task. It would be all right, after all. Two more days and the wench would be safely wed.

For a bitter moment there at Lady Harquist's ball Edith had thought for sure that the dark Londoner was simply going to pick Rhiannon up and carry her off like some rogue medieval knight come looting. The man certainly looked the part with his black good looks and the tension vibrating in his lean figure.

But nothing like that had happened. Not only hadn't he carried Rhiannon off, he'd paid scant attention to her for the rest of the night, and the days and nights that followed.

Perhaps she was simply getting fanciful in her old age. What with the strain of praying Squire Watts didn't change his mind and withdraw his consent to the marriage and hoping Phillip remained resolved to wed, was it any wonder if she was a wee bit overprotective?

But now she could relax. Tonight all Fair Badden would turn out for the Beltaine Eve festivities and Rhiannon would be under the watchful eye of not only herself but the entire community. Then tomorrow was May Day with its innocent—and blessedly sunlit—pleasures and the afternoon hunt Squire Watt had arranged as a special wedding present to the bride, the last hunt of the season. Rhiannon would never miss a hunt.

And then . . . Edith clipped off a length of bright red ribbon and pleated it into a fat rosette to affix to Rhiannon's skirts. The next day Phillip and Rhiannon would wed.

She sighed gustily, drawing a glance from Rhiannon. She smiled fondly at the girl. True to her sweet nature Rhiannon returned the smile twofold. Edith bent her head over her sewing, nodding happily.

Aye, she could relax.

It was Beltaine Eve, and Fair Badden's marketplace overflowed with revelry. Stalls and carts, piled with toys, confections, and trinkets lit by rush torches and lanterns, cluttered the cobbled square. In the center of the square the traditional Beltaine fire was being erected. Flowing around the unlit fire and hapless staggering of goods, all manner of people milled and jostled, trading smiles with egalitarian abandon.

True to its ancient traditions, the May Day celebrations stripped each resident of Fair Badden of office and status. Manor-bred mingled freely with baseborn. Peasant and aristocrat alike had dressed in simple country garb sewn over with bright ribbons. Bells tinkled, dogs yapped, and the pennants snapped from atop the four corners of the open-sided pavilion set at the square's far end.

Under this tent's billowing canopy stood a huge plank table, its surface sticky with spilled ale, honey cake crumbs, and cheese rinds. Beneath the table a young gazehound bitch scavenged tidbits.

Rhiannon Russell, Queen of the May, drunk as a lord and teetering like an unfledged owlet, dug her bare and dirty toes into Stella's silky fur. Beside her was her lady-in-waiting who—for reasons Rhiannon could no longer fathom but which she distinctly remembered having been hysterical about some hours earlier—was a brown cow named Molly. The lady-in-waiting stretched out her neck and tried to snatch the royal tiara off the royal brow. With a frown, Rhiannon rapped the cheeky wench across her broad brown nose, the movement upsetting the balance of her clover blossom crown.

"King" Phillip, slumped on the oak keg throne next to hers, roused himself enough to grab hold of Rhiannon's crown and jerk it from Molly's mouth. Having successfully attended to his consortly duties, he lapsed once again into his former vapid, grinning state.

Rhiannon studied him with soggy affection. Good ole King Phil. Steady, handsome, dependable, undemanding, sweet King Phil. She smiled at him. He didn't notice.

She slouched back, feeling magnanimous and sentimental and over-heated. Around her the "court" buzzed and murmured, drank and sang. She knew them all. Every one. This was her home. These people were her family. No matter what ghosts called to her spirit from their graves—and what man called to her other far more earthy parts—here she was loved and respected and safe.

An unsteady hand reached over Rhiannon's shoulder and slopped May wine into her goblet. Her *royal* goblet.

"To the good people of Good Badden. Fair Badden. Not so Badden," she declared. Gripping the cheap pewter cup with both hands, she tossed the contents down her throat in one long, noisy gulp.

"Long live Queen Rhiannon!" the crowd yelled.

"And her king. Don't forget the king." Phillip announced, a spark of consciousness brightening his eyes.

Not that they needed brightening. Phillip had truly bright blue eyes. Very beautiful. Really nice. And she was lucky—no, Rhiannon thought earnestly, she was *privileged* to be the woman who got to marry them . . . him. She reached over to refill her goblet.

Phillip smiled vaguely at her, as if he couldn't quite place her in his memory but knew she had some status nonetheless. "Pretty Rhiannon. Pretty Queen," he muttered fondly. "Favorite of everyone. Fellows all envy me."

Abruptly, he linked a giant paw around the back of her neck. Toppled from her throne by Phillip's enthusiasm, she flung her arms around his neck to keep from landing on her bum. The room exploded with hoots of approval as his mouth came down on hers in a loud, wet smack.

He kept kissing her. Demandingly, forcefully, and oddly passionlessly, and Rhiannon, woozy and complacent, allowed it. Finally he released her.

"You'll make a good Queen won't you, m'dear?" he asked.

He patted her cheek awkwardly, his expression begging for reassurance. His sudden insecurity caused acute and lethal guilt to eat its way through Rhiannon's agreeable alcoholic haze. Unable to meet his anxious gaze, she glanced away and so caught sight of a dark, masculine figure disappearing abruptly into the darkness beyond the pavilion's lights.

It wasn't him. It wasn't Ash.

"We'll live here and be hap—content. I'll be a good husband," Phillip was saying. "You couldn't do better."

He was right. She was marrying far above her station, better than anyone could ever have expected. And she *would* be . . . content. Then why was she still staring at the place where the dark figure had disappeared?

She glanced at Phillip but he had already slouched back on his throne, his eyelids falling over his gorgeous blue eyes. A second later he was snoring. She slipped from his lap, regarding him ashamedly. Every time Ash Merrick was near, she forgot her soon-to-be groom.

Drat Ash Merrick and his flashing smile and his cautious eyes. Drat his hard body and his soft mouth. Drat a man who made the very word "content" seem a laughable, pallid notion. Drat him for taking that wagered kiss. Drat him for stopping at that.

Where the devil was the man? Rhiannon glared at the crowd about her. He was a guest in her foster mother's home. He'd been invited to take part in the festivities. He should be here.

"I'm Queen, aren't I?" she demanded of her heifer-in-waiting. In answer, Molly once more plucked the crown from her head. Rhiannon let her have it. "What good's a crown if the wearer doesn't rule?" she asked loudly.

The crowd looked up at her outburst, primed for play. If their queen had a game in mind, they were all for it.

"If I'm Queen, I should be able to make laws, shouldn't I?"

"Aye!" A chorus of voices agreed. "Aye, you're Queen! What law is it you're wanting to make?"

"I want . . . I want every one of my loyal subjects to bend his knee before me, er, us, and swear his fealty."

The crowd, amused and rowdy, traded glances and shrugged. "We already done that."

"No, you haven't," Rhiannon corrected them. "Not *all* of you."

"Who ain't performed the proper respects?"

"The Londoner. Ash Merrick," she announced darkly.

"Why, that's right," John Fortnum said in the amazed tones of discovery. "He hasn't been round most of the day. The maggoty knave didn't even attend the coronation!"

"Well, we'll set that to rights," announced a burly "knight," "won't we, lads?"

At this, those still capable of action streamed from the pavilion, dispersing into the crowds outside. Fired by alcohol, they swept through the market, calling and clamoring for "the foreigner, Merrick."

As the hunt progressed, those who had no part in it began shouting for the King and Queen of the May to come to the Beltaine fire and leap across it. It was a custom as old as Beltaine itself, a pledge sealing a couple's matrimonial fate. The call gathered force until it could no longer be gainsaid. The revelers entered the pavilion, snatched Rhiannon and Phillip from their thrones, and carried them out into the night to the fire's side.

At the same time, the hunters finally met with success. They found Merrick at The Ploughman, wiping the froth of ale from his upper lip.

"Merrick!"

Gleefully they encircled him. He turned tiredly.

"St. John," he said. "I'm not in the mood, boy."

St. John's eyes widened in mock despair. "He says he's not in the mood," he told his fellows. He looked back into Merrick's eyes. "Too bad, old fellow."

"What's this all about?"

"You're wanted at court, Merrick. A royal decree."

"Oh?" Merrick turned his back on them, motioning the ale seller to draw him another tankard. "What for? Does His Majesty need instruction in seduction? I'm afraid I have no advice to offer."

He took a deep draught of ale before placing the tankard with telling precision back on the counter. "From what I saw, he looked like he was doing fine. The royal wench was warming his lap and her royal mouth was encouraging his ardor. It all looked most promising. But then, I've never enjoyed spectator sports. Mind you, don't let that stop you, lads."

They jeered and winked at his insolence. Then, before he could resist, they'd surrounded him and tied his arms behind his back. With much laughter they shoved and cajoled and half-carried him back to the May Queen.

They found her standing before the bonfire, weaving slightly. At her feet sat Phillip, sunk in drunken fascination with the recently ignited fire.

"Queen Rhiannon!" they called out and, wresting Merrick from their midst, shoved him before her and stood back, well-pleased with themselves.

She stared at him in surprise, having forgotten she'd sent these men to return with him. His hair tumbled over his brow; his expression was unreadable.

"Here he is," St. John declared.

Ash tilted his head to the side, regarding her intently. Dear Lord, why had she drunk so much of that clover wine?

She steeled herself. It was too late to fret over how much she'd imbibed. Besides, she felt daring, and why shouldn't she? He'd befriended her and then abandoned her. He had dallied with her and then ignored her. Why, he had caused her to betray a husband she did not yet have!

And the memory of his kiss played havoc with her body.

"Well, Your Majesty?" St. John said, his brows climbing. "You wanted him. Here he is. Now what?"

She swayed slightly, the taste of wine thick on her tongue, the crackle and pop of the green-wood fire masking the buzz in her ears.

"Your Majesty?" John Fortnum's voice. Reminding her of her role. She was Queen.

"Be you Merrick of London?" she asked.

Ash eyed her guardedly.

"Answer her and it'll go well with you," John Fortnum promised kindly. "She's a most munificent ruler. Perhaps she'll knight you."

Merrick smiled, his face turned away from her and toward the crowd. "Fortnum, if your tender treatment of me is a sample of her munificence I'll have to refuse any further samples. I may not survive a knighthood."

The men and women laughed in appreciation. Rhiannon scowled.

She did not want him charming them; he charmed too easily by half. She would not allow him to turn this into a marketplace for his charisma.

"You'll have no offers from me gracious or otherwise," she declared loudly. She held out her hand and motioned for the wine bottle a lass near her held. With a grin the girl handed it to her.

Eyes locked on Merrick, she moved toward him, her hips swaying slowly, provocatively, her lids heavy with wine and the yearning he'd incited and would never satisfy.

She halted within arm's reach, close enough that he could not help but see her. Only his eyes moved, rising slowly to meet hers from under dense, black lashes.

"Lord, but you are exquisite." The words seemed torn from his lips, a spoken thought not flattery.

She tipped her head back and drank deeply from the bottle. False courage, she knew, but any courage was welcome when a woman was faced with Ash Merrick's dark and passionate eyes.

"What do you want of me? Whatever I own is at your disposal." One side of his mouth lifted in a crooked grin. His gaze held hers. "Whatever skills I possess are yours to command."

"Not enough," she breathed, stepping closer, vaguely conscious that she skirted too near the fire, both figuratively and literally.

"Really?" His tone was mead infused, intoxicating and low and sweet, pitched for her ears alone. "What queen could ask more of her subject? And what would that be?"

She hesitated, craven and coward that she was, afraid to tell him the truth.

"Only say it and I will give it to you."

She tore her gaze away from his, raised the bottle to her lips, and took another draught of bravado, an increment away from declaring what she did indeed want of this man. But then she would lose all that she'd spent years in attaining. She took another drink. It burned going down.

"Yes?" he prompted, a tense note hidden in his gentle cajolery.

"Your regard," she burst out and then, "your note. Your attention." Fearful of how revealing her words were, she straightened, forced a laugh between her stiff lips. She lifted her goblet to those watching. "A Queen's due from her vassals."

"Here! Here!" the crowd responded.

"But I'm not your subject, madame," Merrick reminded her gently. "I'm a foreigner, a sojourner, an alien. I'm not one of them." His eyes flickered over the crowd. "But then, neither are you, are you . . . Your Majesty?"

She froze. With so few words he named her an outsider, an imposter, an orphan. Abruptly the focus of her concern shifted. A trembling of fear began in her heart and lungs, filling her chest.

She fought the sensation. She *did* belong here. She'd done everything, become everything anyone could want. She'd lost her accent, even her memories. All of it done so that she could stay. She had purchased her right to be here and she had paid for it with the coin of her heritage.

Beneath her feet the earth seemed to rise like the arching back of a cat. Ash was watching her.

"Sir." Her voice sounded faint, distant. "You are in my kingdom. You will demonstrate your fealty."

"I've had enough games, Rhiannon."

His voice was pitched so only she could hear him, and yet she lost the meaning of his words, it so unnerved her to hear her Christian name for the first time from his lips.

She tried to focus but the earth was dipping dangerously and the fire was stretching toward her. He was too close. He was always too close—or too far. Out of the corner of her eye she saw Phillip stirring.

"Rhiannon? Why's Merrick got his hands tied up?" Phillip lumbered to his feet. Oh, God. She'd forgotten him again. She closed her eyes and immediately felt the effects of Edith's clover wine. "Rhiannon? Merrick?"

Her husband. Her lover. Safety. Danger. Home. Refuge. Outsider. Her eyelids fluttered. She swayed.

"What are you doing to Merrick?" Phillip shouted in a bewildered voice.

She heard a crash behind her, from Phillip's direction. The crowd erupted in a cacophony of alarm. She started to wheel around but the movement sent her spinning madly, the world darkening.

"Catch her, you fools!" she heard Ash shout and then the ground rose up like a blow.

CHAPTER 13

Watt had either sprained his ankle or broken it.

He'd launched himself through the boughs waiting to be fed into the fire and caught a foot. He landed in a heap of wide-eyed disbelief. With the simple conciseness of the very drunk he'd then announced that he was hurt and proceeded to apologize to Rhiannon explaining that he would not be able to jump over the bonfire and seal their betrothal. Since Rhiannon was sagging unconscious in John Fortnum's arms, she did not respond.

Phillip's friends turned their attention to consoling their King. With a huzzah, they hefted Phillip above their heads and took him back to the pavilion where he was duly splinted, saturated with drink, and finally propped on a chair.

Ash witnessed it all with a mixture of anger and helplessness. He had no right to hold, administer to, or even touch Rhiannon. He hovered until Margaret Atherton took charge of Rhiannon, then he found his way back to the tavern where he spent the next several hours. But the thought of Rhiannon being untended and vulnerable during the rest of this night of free-for-all carousing prevented him from drinking and preyed on his imagination until it became an obsession. Someone *had* shot at her. A knife *had* nearly pierced her chest. A night like this would present the perfect cover for an attempted murder. . . .

The blasted witch had coiled herself into the tangled mess of his life, and like a knot, she would not come free. Not unless she was cut out, which marriage to that golden-haired oaf would certainly accomplish.

But for tonight . . . Ash slammed the half-full tankard down on the counter. Damn it to bleeding hell! She was likely sitting on Watt's good leg, purring in his arms, as he stood here poleaxed by misguided fear.

But what if she wasn't?

He pushed the tankard away and stepped over several bodies sprawled senseless on the floor, heading through the door. Outside, a few knots of women and men still clustered about the grounds. Few young people were present, however, and Ash remarked it uncomfortably. Where had Fair Badden's youth gone? He scanned the area for Rhiannon and spied Edith Fraiser sitting with her eyes closed, the hound Stella resting her heavy head on Edith's lap. The marketplace was much quieter than it had been a few hours earlier and it wasn't even midnight.

At the end of the square Ash found an old man gazing at the moon and smiling, a look of fond remembrance on his seamed, leathery face. Ash asked him where everyone had gone and why they'd abandoned their revelries so early.

The old man snorted and after shaking his head in a profoundly pitying fashion, explained to Ash that the revelries hadn't ended, they'd simply been transferred to a more private setting.

Over the course of the last few hours, it would seem, the younger girls had gone into the woods to gather hawthorn blooms to ensure good luck for the coming year. But the shawls they carried on their arms and the back-long glances they'd sent the young men who watched them go were invitation to another sort of hunt, the old man explained with a chuckle and a wink.

The young men hadn't needed any prodding to follow after, stepping into the forest's dark embrace to seek another embrace entirely. Not that all the young women were so inclined, the old man hastened to point out, but if a lad were lucky . . .

Ash left him, his thoughts haunted by images he could barely tolerate.

Were Watt and Rhiannon among their numbers? Ash wondered. Was she straining beneath him right now?

His hands flexed at his sides and his eyes glittered like flawed diamonds, a black carbon core corrupting their brilliance. A peel of raucous male laughter coming from the pavilion drew his attention and he turned in its direction.

Inside, Watt sat on his throne, his lower leg padded thick and stiffly bound to a board. Immediately the tension drained from Ash. Of course Watt wouldn't be with Rhiannon. He couldn't even follow her on that leg. Watt's ever-present coterie of friends was with him. They were arguing over something. When the company saw Ash, several flushed guiltily, except for St. John who grinned like an evil gargoyle, winked at his fellows, and clapped Ash on the back.

Ash was in no mood to play St. John's cat's-paw. Or to entertain and charm. He looked around for Rhiannon. She was not there. She must have gone home, though it was odd she'd left without Edith.

"Gads, I'm glad you're here, Merrick! *You* of all people must know the song." St. John laid his arm over Ash's shoulders. "Popular a few years back. I heard it in the Highlands, matter of fact."

Phillip looked away, his face turning dusky red.

"We know the front part but can't figure out quite how the bloody thing ends," St. John went on. "Here. Tell us."

Ash narrowed his eyes on the group. One of them tittered and hid his lips behind his palm. Another's eyes went wide as he struggled to contain his amusement, and suddenly Ash knew the song they'd been singing. It had been popular some years back, soon after the incident that had inspired it. Ash's mouth went dry.

"It's a thing called 'The Ride of the Demon Brood.' " St. John smiled.

Ash struggled for composure. He'd disparaged these men for being naive and unaware. God, how the fates must be laughing at him. He'd assumed that here, in this tiny outpost in nowhere, here at least he would escape his notoriety. With empty eyes he gazed at St. John's puckish countenance. He wouldn't give him the pleasure of seeing how well he'd scored, how sharp the knife, how raw the wound. He was far better at hiding pain than this man could imagine.

And as far as the embarrassment St. John obviously hoped to provoke in Ash if St. John thought some antique ballad could bring shame to a name that had no understanding of the concept . . . the idea wrung a laugh from Ash's throat, startling St. John.

"Why, certainly," he declared hoarsely. "What lines were you having trouble with?"

The other men had sobered and were regarding Ash warily.

"No one recalls?" Ash asked lightly. How to tell them. Part of him wanted to explain, to insist they believe him if he claimed the ballad a lie, a piece of propaganda, a hideous hyperbole of the truth. But what difference? His past had taught him that people wanted to believe the worst. So be it.

"Then let us recap. The story goes like this: In order to save her brothers' lives, a Scottish lassie must prevent the ragged remnants of her clan from hanging the worthless youngest son of the Demon Earl.

"The lad is accused of raping a novitiate and the clan's call for his blood is well justified. But the poor girl's brothers languish in London awaiting trial for their part in the uprising of forty-five." Ash grinned savagely.

Raine hadn't raped that girl. Ash had never asked but he didn't need to, he knew his brother. He looked around at the rapacious faces. They hung on every word, unhappily transfixed by the sad, sordid tale.

"I swear I have told this story so often I have managed to encapsulate the entire tale in a fifth the time it takes to sing the damned thing!"

His sweeping gaze caught and held each man present. They squirmed uncomfortably.

"Let's see, where was I? Oh, yes. Our pitiful heroine. Eight? Ten years old? And all this drama to contend with. The thing of it is, the thing that breaks the heart, is this: That very night while her father is away pleading for his sons' lives the girl's mother has died in childbirth.

"Now, if her clansmen kill the English Demon Earl's cub she can kiss adieu to any hope that King George will be merciful and free her brothers. Is it any wonder she makes such an effort to halt the boy's lynching even though he is her enemy?"

In his mind's eye he could still see that raggedy girl-child, her thin white arms wrapped tightly about Raine's throat, her gold hair streaming down her nightgown, her bare feet sunk in the ice- and mud-rutted road. He wanted to tell them that she'd been the only spot of mercy in a night black with vengeance and retribution. That he'd ached even then for that child. That he'd regretted what had happened.

But they wouldn't understand the choices he'd made, they'd all made, all the actors on that cold, winter stage. They wouldn't believe him and he wouldn't allow anyone to dine on his grief.

He continued. "Well, the lass prevents the bloody deed by flinging her arms around the bound boy, shielding him with her own wee body—and I say the tale would have been a sight more interesting if the girl had been sixteen rather than ten but then Highlanders are an odd breed. Anyway, while thus, the Demon Earl himself rides up, a hundred redcoats with him. At his side are his devilish eldest son and, behind, watching, the little black-haired witch who is his daughter."

"Aye, that's the spot we'd gotten to," a slurred voice called from the shadows.

"Is it?" Ash queried, fighting the revulsion threatening to overwhelm him. He would not succumb. Not in front of St. John and some of these others.

A few of them shuffled, miserably wishing to be elsewhere but held captive by his recital of the old tragedy.

"Go on," St. John urged and then added, "if you've the guts."

"Allow me to satisfy your . . . thirst for knowledge. I will recite," Ash said, shifting a leg forward, placing one hand on his hip, and spreading the other across his chest. His heart pumped dully beneath his palm.

The theatrical stance, the melodramatic timbre of Ash's voice mocked the listeners, openly chastising their prurient fascination; and they resented it. They'd counted him a friend and none looked more aggrieved at his defection than Phillip. Ash began to recite:

> With rapier drawn, the eldest son
> Dragged his brother up before him.
> And brandishing his blade, death he gave
> To the men who barred his way.
>
> Blood bloomed thick on the hoary ground
> As Scotsmen were mowed down.
> Like a sickle cuts through wheat,
> They died as one, the clan complete.
>
> When all about had silent grown
> The laird's young orphaned daughter moaned.
> And the Demon Earl kneed his stallion near
> And bending low, lent his ear.
>
> "Why saved you my worthless son from death?"
> He queried low, beneath his breath.
> "To save my brothers," she replied.
> "Whom George would kill if your son were to die."
>
> The Demon Earl then laughed,
> A sound so wicked, the redcoats gasped.
> "John of McClairen's head now sits on a pike,
> Set above Temple Bar last night."

The words clogged his throat, damning and true yet a truth without honesty. The ballad did not tell how sickened he'd been by his act, how savagely the clan had beaten Raine, the number of soldiers who died in the confrontation.

"Do you want the rest?" he asked, praying they would say no. "Some versions tag on a rather tiresome denouement."

"Is the song about you?" Phillip whispered. "Is it true?"

"True?" Ash asked. Would they believe him if he said no? He wouldn't risk being doubly hurt by his recitation. "Dear me, no. I can attest to the fact that my father is no demon. All too human, just lately evincing signs of gout—"

"Did it happen that way?" John Fortnum's honest, homely face was etched with sadness.

"Yes." His anger died on seeing the shocked misery of the listeners, leaving behind only self-disgust. They'd not known what they were doing. He had. He'd punished them for his own past.

"Rhiannon will be so hurt," John murmured. "She thinks you're such a nice gentleman."

She was worth any ten of them. And they didn't know it. They had no idea they harbored a refugee. Good, obedient Rhiannon Russell. Willing to trade her freedom for sanctuary. Yet beneath that dutiful exterior lay a core of tempered metal, forged by war and its aftermath. But never tested. Hidden here, instead. Like a Spanish blade that is packed in wool and tucked away in an attic chest. He turned, suddenly exhausted, and started to leave.

"Best she didn't stay to hear this," Phillip said mournfully. "Best thing she went off to collect flowers."

Rhiannon was *alone* in the woods? Ash wheeled around. He strode back to Phillip's chair, grabbing him by his shirt and hefting him half out of his seat. "What did you say?"

"Lemme go," Phillip cried. "Don't mind tellin' you you're disappointin' to me. First I find out you're some sort of a demon-spawned murderer and now you're being flat-out offensive." He batted ineffectually at Ash's hands.

Ash shook him. "Didn't she go home?"

"Course, not! She's Queen of the May. Went to pluck posies in the forest—"

With an inarticulate sound, Ash dropped Phillip back in his seat. Rhiannon was alone in the woods after someone had flung a knife at her but a few days earlier. Without another word, he left.

CHAPTER 14

It was too nice a night to go home, and there was no one to go home with, but most important Rhiannon didn't know which way home was. The basket hanging from her arm banged against her hip as she walked. Only weak moonlight illuminated the forest floor, and a rising, drifting mist obscured any familiar landmarks.

Rhiannon hesitated and drew to a halt. Perhaps she should have stayed in the square and found someone to help her take Edith home. But she was Queen of the May, Virgin Queen of the May, and the Virgin Queen of the May always, *always,* spent Beltaine night gathering hawthorn flowers for her May Day coronet.

Of course, the Queen of the May also always went into the woods knowing that the King of the May would be in hot pursuit. Traditionally the Queen then spent the night fending off the King's advances so that the next day when she was crowned with those pure, white hawthorn blooms the knowledge that she was just as pure kept her from blushing. And that was important.

Wasn't it?

Not that Phillip had ever pursued too hotly or pushed too heavily. He was a gentleman, after all.

But then again, in past years when they had been king and queen, they had not been betrothed. Tonight Phillip might have pressed his suit and she, bedeviled by unfamiliar urges, might have been receptive. But then he'd gone and broken his ankle.

She gazed glumly down. Unfortunately, just because the King could not fulfill his role, did not mean she was exonerated of *her* obligations. And, by the Virgin, hadn't she done a ripping good job of it? Over a hundred damn flowers filled her basket.

Realizing her profanity, Rhiannon frowned. She was a good, decent young lady. She had been ever since she'd come to Fair Badden. But lately she didn't feel very "good."

She didn't understand what was happening to her. She seemed to always be edgy and irritable. The constant need to be "good" had begun to chaff—even with Edith Fraiser. Only with Ash Merrick did she feel truly at ease.

Perhaps it was because she owed him nothing, no debt of gratitude, no unspoken vow of obedience. Not that she didn't *love* her life here, and Edith Fraiser, and all her friends, but sometimes it was hard to discern between love and obligation. She was more . . . natural in Ash's company.

And more likely to do abominably stupid things.

With a groan, Rhiannon closed her eyes. She would never have believed herself capable of such outrageous behavior. Ash Merrick had always treated her with gentlemanly courtesy—even in his kiss. In return she'd had him hunted, tied, and brought before her like some criminal. Then she'd proceeded to fall over in a drunken stupor. How he must loathe her.

She hastened forward as though she could outdistance her memory, humiliation burning her cheeks. She'd gone some distance when off to her side came the muted sounds of dalliance, pleading and private as a novena.

The sound stopped her as effectively as a stone wall. She strained her ears, listening, swaying slightly on her feet, as the effects of Edith's clover wine had not yet fully left her. She couldn't see a thing. Darkness and mist combined to hide the figures making those earnest sounds.

She didn't dare venture farther and risk stumbling onto a tryst. What if it were Margaret Atherton and—

She wheeled around, her head spinning, and began retracing her steps. She'd almost reached an ancient, spreading hawthorn when a muted giggle reached her ears. Once more, she stumbled to a stop.

More lovers? she wondered in despair. The soft provocative laughter moved off but because of the fog, she was unable to tell in what direction. With a sound of frustration she sank to the ground beside the tree's great trunk.

Stupid Beltaine customs.

She would just have to stay here, until the mist lifted or the moon grew stronger or some friendly woodland sprite took pity on her and led her out of this fantastical world of blue shadows and earthbound clouds, ghostly luminescence and heady night-born fragrances.

She leaned her head back against the tree trunk and closed her eyes, letting the magic of the place bewitch her, creating fantasies she had no right entertaining, things she'd fought against but now, here, she found impossible to resist. She forgave herself.

It was Beltaine night, after all, and she was alone and she did not want to be the Virgin Queen of the Virgin May. She wanted Ash Merrick.

The moments grew one into another. The moon rose with benign leisure as images of a dark, angular face and a hard lean body filled Rhiannon's thoughts. He was like Oberon, she thought, king of the sylvan spirits. Aye, Ash Merrick would make a fit sovereign of dark enchantment. He'd come silently, materializing from the shadows, a spirit of pure desire conjured into flesh—

"Rhiannon."

She opened her eyes, gazing at him without surprise. *"Oberon,"* she whispered. Dark forest prince, black light-devouring hair, and eyes gilded like steel.

He'd been on one knee beside her but now he slowly straightened. The mist swirled in agitation as he rose, slipping from his shoulders like a fairy's cloak and leaving a dusting of moon-silvered moisture on his pale skin.

"Ash."

She sighed, entranced and warmly intoxicated—by wine and want and by the beauty of him. She smiled and he stepped forward as though drawn. A light laugh escaped her with the thought that she might draw him with her smile. But she did not believe it and her smile turned sad.

"You're safe," he said.

"I'd thought so," she answered, not yet willing to cede her dreams to reality. As long as they stayed here in this little island surrounded by mist and magic he was hers. And wasn't that what Beltaine was at its core? A night of abandonment . . . to dreams and wishes, wants and hopes? And she had never before taken advantage of its magic. She deserved one Beltaine night.

"I'd thought I was safe," she murmured again. "But now, I'm not so sure."

He tilted his head and the movement placed his face in shadows so that when he spoke his voice seemed disembodied, carrying through the moisture-laden air with startling intimacy. "Why is that?"

"You're here and so too am I and I doubt much whether that is a safe thing," she answered simply.

She heard him catch his breath. "Do you fear I would hurt you?"

"Never."

A short telling pause. "Unwise, little Titania."

Titania. Oberon's queen. He might have read her thoughts.

"Unwise for whom?" she asked gazing into the dark shadows that hid his expression.

"Exactly."

His shirt rose and fell in deep, increasing measure but in no other way did he move. Intuitively she knew he would not make a gesture nor say a word, that he was forcing her to decide what next happened.

Two days hence and she would be married and belong to another. Two nights hence and he would leave.

It was Beltaine, she told herself with frantic insistence. Beltaine existed apart from the rest of the year. Its revelries were above the laws governing the rest of the days and weeks. No one was held accountable for what they did on Beltaine night.

The rest of her life she would be another's but not tonight.

She wet her lips with the tip of tongue, her fear of his rejection nearly paralyzing her, her mouth dry. She didn't know what to say, how to win him and he stood so silently, an attitude of fearful expectancy about him.

Instinctively and utterly without design she leaned forward, her head lifted, and she raised one hand, palm up, in supplication. "Please."

She saw a light shudder pass through his body.

"Please, Ash."

Abruptly, as though some cord binding him had suddenly been severed, he surged forward and dropped heavily to his knees beside her. Roughly, he pulled her up and into his arms. His mouth fell on hers with undisguised urgency. He bent her over his arm, holding her there.

With a sob she wrapped her arms around his broad shoulders, holding fiercely to him. He rained kisses on her mouth and cheeks, hungry kisses, desperate kisses, kisses long denied and passionate. His free hand moved, roving over her body in trembling haste, as though collecting the measure of her, the feel and form of her—a blind man learning to see.

She cupped his jaw between her hands, hoarding each sensation—the rasp of his beard against her palms, the silky coolness of his hair between her fingers, the hard angle of his jaw.

His tongue moved insistently against the seam of her lips. She opened her mouth and the warm tip delved deep within. Her head spun.

Her hands skated down his strong throat to his collarbone and beneath the loose shirt to his heated flesh. Sinful, satiny skin. She wanted more, she wanted to arch her body against his naked flesh like a cat.

She pulled at his shirt until he became aware of what she wanted. He broke off the kiss. Her head fell back into the lee of his arm. He stared down at her.

"We're near a place where there is no return," he said, his breathing ragged. "I am not a nice man, Rhiannon. I've little honor and less restraint. This is the extent of both noble traits. From here out I will take whatever I can, whatever portion you'll allow even knowing it was never meant to be mine."

His face was set, and his words were brutal and honest but she didn't want to listen, hear, or heed them. She touched his cheek. He turned his head and pressed a hot kiss against her palm.

"It's Beltaine night," she whispered hoarsely. "Nothing we do tonight counts against the dawn."

For one long second he looked down at her and she thought she saw a wound within their silvered depths. He smiled with terrible resignation. She opened her lips to ask him why, but he set his finger against her mouth and hushed her, easing her down onto her back and straightening up on his knees. With one smooth, economical movement he grasped the edge of his shirt and peeled it from his body. She stared in awe at the masculine beauty he revealed.

The moonlight outlined the hard ladder of his ribs and played with intimate sensuality over the muscles of his chest. Dark hair covered his breastbone in a triangle and more dark hair grew low on his ridged and taut stomach, disappearing beneath the waistband of his breeches.

His arms were long, the biceps well developed, his wrists supple and powerful beneath their scars.

Slowly, his eyes never leaving hers, he put one hand then the other alongside her hips, tipping over the basket of hawthorn blooms as he did so and scattering the shadowed ground with white petals. He lowered himself until his chest just brushed against her.

"Nothing counts," he whispered hoarsely and then his mouth claimed hers.

He hadn't lied to her. There was nothing of restraint or composure in his actions, nothing courtly or obsequious in his manner. He quite simply, quite ruthlessly lay siege to her senses.

One arm snaked beneath her, hauling her up against him as the other hand reached between them and jerked her bodice down, exposing her breasts. He lifted his head, something feral and possessive in the gaze that met hers. She should have been afraid of his ill-contained violence, but she wasn't. She drew a deep shuddering breath and her breasts grazed his chest.

He looked down at the dark puckered tips, smiled, lowered his head, and licked a nipple.

She gasped, embarrassed and panicked by the unfamiliar sensations that shot through her. She grabbed handfuls of his long dark hair in her hands, trying to pull him back. He ignored her, taking the hard nub deep into his mouth, until it grazed the back of his tongue. He drew hard on it, suckling her with devastating deliberation.

Her gasp turned into a moan. Sensation after sensation assaulted her untried body, pulled chords of response from her nipple to a point between her legs. Her fingers loosened in his hair. Her back arched. With a sob, she silently offered more of what he'd so roughly taken.

The sound seemed to set a spur of need through him. His hands traveled down over her quivering belly to the waistband of her skirts. He grasped bunches of the cheap material, rucked it high above her thighs, all the while plying her breasts with his attentions, dazing her with physical sensations she'd never imagined existed.

Dimly she became aware of cool night air tickling her thighs and whispering gently over the down-covered vee at their apex. Reality spun into focus with a shattering jolt. She snatched her hand down to cover herself.

He grabbed her wrist, easily pulling it up and away and pinning it beside her face.

"Ash—"

His lips found hers. His tongue plied the interior of her mouth with deep, rich strokes. He nudged his knee between her legs. Reflexively, she clamped them together.

He would have none of it. He forced his knee between her legs, spreading them apart, and at the same time she felt his fingers there, at the very entrance of her body. Mortification brought a strangled sound to her throat.

"It doesn't count," he muttered against her lips. His tone was dazed and dark and bitter and lost, but his mouth was sweet and pleading and tender.

Gently he caressed her mound until he found the sleekness beneath. She jerked, but the movement only moved his fingers deeper into that nether cleft. The trembling that had begun deep within her spread and centered there. She moaned as he rubbed and fondled her.

Her legs went lax with the exquisite sensations he roused. He cupped her mound, his callused palm pressing tight against her as his fingers gently eased into her very body, stretching, testing—driving her mad. She had no idea her body could be played like an instrument, that so much pleasure could center in as small a nubbin as the one that Ash caressed with such mind-wrecking genius.

And it wasn't enough. She shuddered with the unsatisfied craving he'd inspired. Her hips lifted, instinctively trying to force a deeper contact.

He stopped. She sobbed and he covered her mouth with his own, drinking her need as though it was an opiate. Then the heel of his hand moved against her, building the sensations all over again, carrying her toward the brink of that unnamable place. Dimly, she heard her own ragged breathing. Her eyelids fluttered, shutting out the night sky above—

He stopped again. She sobbed in frustration, clutching at him.

"Aye, *daor*. Want and want more and then maybe you'll begin to know my own desire." His fingers moved deep within, his palm rubbing quicker and quicker. There. Nearly . . . almost . . . !

Gratification exploded within her, bringing with it crescendo after crescendo of pure, physical pleasure. Her back arched, pulled taut by her crisis, her limbs went rigid, her hands clutched into fists. And then it was over, the tension seeping from her, leaving her sated and spent.

She felt him ease his fingers from her. Weak and shaken, she opened her eyes. A crooked smile twisted his sensual mouth. A mouth she could not for the life of her look at without wanting to kiss.

"It's all right, Rhiannon." His voice was soft, gentle. "It truly didn't count. You're a virgin still."

She barely heard him. Dear God, she must truly be depraved. Because simply looking at him, the darkness and light molding to his hard body, the moonlight trapped in his dark-lashed eyes, caused desire to pool anew in her breasts and lips and between her legs. She struggled up, heedless of the cool air on her naked breasts or her hair tumbling down her back. Her eyes riveted on the bemused expression that was slowly replacing the gentle mocking one he'd worn.

She stretched out her hand and touched his throat. The skin was hot and damp beneath her fingertips—as though he'd exerted himself in some arduous test. Her touch moved slowly downward. His muscles tightened reflexively beneath it. She covered his heart with her palm, her hand riding the heavy rise and fall of his chest.

She *needed* him. A piece of the heart he held so carefully apart. Once again she had no words for what she wanted or why, having never allowed sentient thought to frame the words.

"Please, Ash."

A hoarse sound, brief and heartbreaking. Anger or regret? She could not say. But then, without a word, he swept her into his arms and snatched his cape from the ground. He rose and carried her out from under the dark moon shadows cast by the hawthorn's boughs. She wrapped her arms around his throat and rested her cheek against his chest and listened to the deep, even beat of his pulse.

He carried her out into a grassy clearing bathed wholly in soft light. He spread his cloak and laid her gently down. With unconscious grace, he lowered himself beside her.

"Can something that does not exist be killed?" he asked her, gently stroking the tangled hair from her brow.

"I don't understand," she murmured. His fingers moved lower, brushing over her breasts. The tips budded beneath his teasing. She could not think when he touched her like this. But hadn't that been her goal this night? Not to think? Hadn't she told him that?

"Look there," he said in a low ragged voice, sweeping his arm out over the moon-bathed field. "If I am Oberon, then this is my dawn. This is my moontide noon, and here . . . it counts." He said the last savagely, intently.

Something elemental and vital seized at her emotions, demanded recognition, but then he rolled his hips into hers, driving all thought from her mind.

His member bulged against her mound, provocative and erotic. He rocked his hips against her, and desire, so lately sated, bloomed again, this time ripe and mature. She gasped in startled pleasure. He met her gaze as he bunched her skirts about her waist and gripped her thighs, moving them apart. Something hard and masculine touched her center.

His gaze did not release hers. His mouth was tense and hard, his eyes gleaming as he held himself still, letting her accustom herself to that part of him. She moved and the thick knob rubbed deliciously against her, dragging little moans from her.

Helplessly, she pulled his head down to hers and opened her mouth, hungry for his kiss. Wine. Cinnamon. Heat. Her head spun and whirled, her senses flashed and floated. She wanted to be absorbed into his hard body, to meld herself with his strength, burn with the passion she sensed he trembled on the brink of unleashing.

He slid his hands behind her knees and lifted them over his hips, poised in the very entrance to her. Then he slipped his palms beneath her buttocks, effortlessly lifting her. His erection rubbed wet and silky between the soft folds. She squirmed, her breath hitching in her throat at the promised pleasure.

He closed his eyes. His lips curled back from his teeth, clenched tightly together. She watched him, wanting more, wanting all of him.

"Please, Ash."

Moisture beaded his brow. His skin was dusky, his eyes savage.

"Moonlight doesn't make this any more real, make it count for anything more," he said. "It's madness to want things you can't afford, and I can't afford you." His words tumbled out in a rush, violent and inarticulate. He dropped his head and kissed her again, deeply, passionately before lifting his head. She returned it desperately, uncertain why he'd stopped, what she'd done.

"I want you, Ash. I *need* you. *Please* want me."

"Need." His eyes were dazed. He shook his head.

He gripped her hips and pushed into her, stretching her. Impossibly big, impossibly hard. His expression was taut, his eyes lost in the shadows created by thick lashes. His hair fell in a black unkempt mane about his throat. Sweat gleamed on his bunched shoulder muscles and straining biceps. Her fingers dug deeply into his trembling arms, trying to find purchase against the torrent of sensation buffeting her.

"No going back," he whispered hoarsely. "No second thoughts. Open your legs wider. Yes. There."

A sharp, brief pain. She gasped. He grated out a sound against the back of his teeth, a curse or a prayer.

He filled her, deeply and utterly, and held still, his arms faintly trembling, sweat coating his chest. Slowly, pleasure returned, then more spiraling waves of pleasure. Nothing had ever felt so good. He moved. A rich, thick slide of silken steel. He retreated. Again. A hard, slow thrust.

Her world spun with heady gratification. Instinctively she met the next thrust. And the next.

"Yes," he breathed. "Yes."

He rocked into her and she clung to him, riding the increasing tempo of his thrusts.

"Slowly, *eun*. Easy."

But it wasn't easy! It was hard, passionate work. Her heartbeat thundered. She panted. Struggling to reach that point again, she whimpered as it danced just beyond her reach. He grasped her buttocks, driving deeper.

"Thoir dhomh," he demanded. *Give to me. "Gabh, me eun."*

There. There. And there. Light and dark careened and splintered as pulse after pulse of exquisite, wrenching pleasure beat through her, in her, to her very core. She sobbed with the exquisite release of it.

Then his arms clamped tighter about her. Again he drove into her body. His head snapped back and he lifted himself up on his arms. His hips ground against her own. A deep, body-wrenching shudder racked through him.

And when it was over, his head fell against her damp throat, his breathing harsh in her ear.

"Damn the dawn," he ground out in a thick, dazed voice. "Damn the bloody dawn."

CHAPTER 15

Beltaine night slipped away, its shadows replaced by the bright raucous colors of sunrise. The freshening wind whipped color in the wan cheeks of maids and boys for whom a night of revelry was no excuse for sloth. By noon even the privileged had awoke, emerging to resume the business of celebration. By midday most of Fair Badden had once again congregated in the town square around the gaily decorated maypole, waiting for the next round of activities.

Not all, however. At the Fraiser's house, Ash Merrick sat at the long, scarred kitchen table, a mug of milk cupped between hands that unaccountably trembled. He grimaced at the white liquid.

Milk, for God's sake. He really had forgotten who he was. Last night he'd carried Rhiannon's slumbering form back to her room and left before Edith Fraiser scurried back to find Rhiannon's bed empty. It was a small enough act of kindness and one he owed her after having taken her maidenhead on the day before the eve of her wedding.

He drew his hand across his face. He hadn't intended to take her.

Or had he? He still couldn't believe he'd succumbed to the misguided impulse to find her and keep her safe from predators—two-footed as well as four. He'd found her all right. Half lying against a tree, her head thrown back, and her long, delicious throat arched as if for a lover's kiss.

But it hadn't been the sweet abandonment of her pose, or the swell of unbound breasts, or even the length of exposed thigh that he had been incapable of resisting. No, 'twas her feet that had overset every last shred of decency in him.

Bare and elegant, long and slender, they'd emerged from beneath the garishly decorated milkmaid's skirt. Though the pink soles of her feet were stained with grass and dirt, the nails of each small toe were nonetheless clean, glinting in the moonlight like abalone shells.

He would have bet his last penny that not one other of Fair Badden's young ladies pretending to be simple country lassies had gone unshod. Only Rhiannon Russell had kicked off her shoes and felt the grass springing wet and fresh between her toes. The hint of wildness, the suggestion of a sybarite waiting to explore a sensual world, had filled him with lust.

He'd wanted her more in that moment than he'd ever wanted anything before. He wanted to be the lover she arched her neck for. Every other consideration had evaporated before that sudden, single-minded intent.

So he'd set his mouth to the base of her throat and felt the pulse quiver like a wild bird in a trapper's palm, sealing their fate. Because once he'd touched her, there had been no turning back. Whatever brief prick of conscience had begged him not to deflower a virgin before her marriage had been devastated by the answering ardor of her mouth. Her strong young body had surged upward to meet him with beautiful abandon, wrecking his tepid scruples, a battering ram destroying a straw hut.

His futile attempt to demonstrate his self-control had never been more than a bluff. She'd only to whisper "please" for every other consideration to burn to cinders before their cumulative need.

She'd been more honest than he, he thought with a wry smile. For at least she'd known that their pleasuring of each other had been a night-bred thing. Not real. He closed his eyes. She'd said it wasn't real. He must remember that.

Indeed, morning would doubtless erase the easy truce she'd made with her conscience. Now it was time to pay. One always paid.

She would be filled with condemnation, as well she should be, for on her wedding night there would be questions, and Rhiannon, honest, damnable Rhiannon, would answer them and ruin herself in the process.

He scraped his hair back from his eyes and stared out of the kitchen window. Rhiannon's big bitch, Stella, lay idly regarding a rabbit munching Edith Fraiser's comfrey plants. Ash watched her, remembering Rhiannon tenderly stroking the useless monster's ears. Smiling. Relaxed and happy. She should always be thus. His hands tightened around the mug.

He would have to stay until after Watt had married her. Because though Ash could offer Rhiannon nothing of himself—having nothing worth offering, not even the decency to resist the bride of a man who considered him a hero—at least he could offer her the protection that fear inspired. That, at least, was one thing he owned: the ability to instill fear. Today he would find opportunity to explain to Phillip in very clear, very explicit terms just how dangerous renouncing Rhiannon Russell would prove—

"Ash."

He closed his eyes a second. He should have known she wouldn't avoid him, that she would confront her seducer rather than avoid him. These people didn't understand her at all. They did not understand that though she had been subdued by wounds garnered at Culloden, it was not in her nature to be subdued. He plastered a suitable smile on his face—nothing too intimate, nothing too cavalier. The smile of a lover who didn't count. He looked around.

Her satiny skin appeared more delicate than he remembered, and the sunlight revealed violet-tinted stains beneath her eyes. They looked greener today, her hair darker.

"Rhiannon. Miss Russell." He held up his hand, offering her the choice of what she would have him call her.

She frowned and skirted the room, moving to the window and a ceramic vase filled with wild anemones. She touched the rosy petal delicately—like she'd touched him last night.

"This is so hard," she murmured.

In profile her hazel eyes looked glassine and brilliant. Tears? Yes. Of course there'd be tears. He steeled himself because there was nothing else he could do.

"It was wrong."

"Yes." Wrong, right—when had either made any difference to him? He gazed at her, tired beyond endurance. "It was wrong."

"I'll make him a good wife, you know." She glanced sideways, to see whether she'd convinced him. "I will. I know what we did last night was a sin and I know that you are Phillip's friend—" God help him before he laughed or sobbed, the pretty naive wench. Did she not understand even yet? "But I must ask you . . . no, I must beg you, please do not tell him."

He exhaled in relief, tension draining from his body. Good. She'd resolved to hold her tongue, the only thing she could do if there were any chance at all she would escape last night without consequence. She was still intent on marrying Phillip and that was just as it should be—and this odd sense of betrayal? Nothing.

Phillip could give her so many things and he could only give her— *passion*. Why, in some twisted greedy corner of his heart, did that seem to him enough when he knew, rationally, logically, it was not? "Yes. I mean, no. I won't."

"Swear it." A pleading note softened the demand.

"I swear."

She turned toward him, the movement swinging the soft waves of her unbound hair to settle over her shoulder. It was like a cloud of silk, he remembered. But why unbound? Ah yes, she was Queen of the May.

"You don't know Phillip as I do and I . . . it's not that I think you would purposefully hurt him but if you felt bound by honor to tell him he would feel obligated to call you out. He mustn't be hurt." She held out a hand in an impulsive gesture of appeal.

"Of course."

"You must understand, it's best if I—"

"You don't need to say another word," he broke in softly, unable to listen to more.

"Thank you." Her smile was sad and grateful. After what he'd done to her, she gifted him with that wholly beautiful smile because—his eyes widened in shocked recognition—because she believed that he felt the same. That he *cared* about Phillip Watt! *Because he was a gentleman.*

The enormous irony of it, her horrendous mistake, hit him like a blow. He looked away.

Enough of this, he thought, suddenly savage. *I'm sick to death of carrying the weight of her good opinion.*

He would tell her he didn't give a damn about cuckolding her betrothed. He'd tried to tell her of his true nature last night. Perhaps he should try again, disabuse her of her provincial notions regarding his gentlemanliness, show her just whom she'd lain beneath last night.

He'd only cared about one thing: spending himself between her thighs. He still only cared about one thing, as evidenced by the hardening of his loins as he looked at her.

Yet, somehow, this little thing—her wrong-headed belief that he would act chivalrously, that he was, in fact, better than he was—kept him from speaking.

"You are hurting," she said. She moved from the window, slowly diminishing the space between them. He held his breath, willing her to stay put. She didn't. "I can see it in your eyes. I am so sorry."

Why was she saying this? What was she doing to him?

"It was . . ." Whatever she'd been about to say died on her lips. A sad, lost smile gently turned the corners of her mouth, like an echo of innocence. "Oh, Ash. I know it is wrong, more wrong than anything I have ever done, but I cannot regret last night."

Utterly destroying him.

"I will keep the memory of it," she went on inexorably, softly singing her way to the very core of him with her lethal words. "It may seem to me now a meager sort of thing, a memory, but in years to come I am sure it will— Please," she moved a step closer. Uncertainty clouded her expression, a quavering note of abashment colored her voice. "Please, won't you kiss me good-bye?"

He stared at her, unable to speak.

She must have taken his silence for acquiescence. Hesitantly she rose on her tiptoes and brushed her mouth over his. But in forming the word "good-bye" her lips lingered an instant too long. Long enough for the stunned paralysis to leave his limbs, long enough for him to snake his arm around her supple waist and pull her closer, deepening the kiss into something darker, stirring . . . infinitely more satisfying.

She kissed so sweetly. So tantalizingly. Her mouth was fruit, delicious and succulent, and he was starving. Had been starving for years. Hungrily he traced her lips with the tip of his tongue, slipping into the sleek, moist interior. Her tongue fluttered against his and he stroked it lavishly, deeply.

With a sigh of defeat, she wrapped her arms around his shoulders, tipped back her head, and surrendered. She kissed him—Lord, how she kissed him—with all the longing of a tragic, final leave-taking: yearningly, tenderly, despairingly. He cupped her delicately molded skull between his palms, combing back her silky, dense hair, mouthing soft, incoherent words of ravishment and seduction. Desire coiled and sprang, confounding him with its power.

She withdrew from the kiss and he followed her retreat. He lifted his free hand and rubbed the pad of his thumb back and forth against her lower lip. His body shuddered with the restraint he exercised. "Rhiannon . . ."

With a sudden, hopeless sound she dropped her hands and pushed against his chest. She broke free of his embrace and twirled. He heard the swish of her hem, the rapid tattoo of her fleeing shoes, and the breathy echo of her sobbed "Good-bye." By the time he looked she'd disappeared through the kitchen door.

He slumped against the table, groping for support, realizing what she thought. She thought him her lover, her tender, considerate companion in guilt and that kiss had been his severance pay, a memento. His lips curled back.

Absurd. Horrifyingly naive. Unendurably so.

He'd bedded the wench. He'd had what he'd wanted. It was past time he remembered why he was here and where he was going. He should be in London, at the gaming tables, working for Raine's release, not here, lusting after some wench who had a wrongheaded notion regarding his nobility.

His fists clenched at his side, the thick scar tissue glistened like white. He stared about the kitchen as if looking for a means of escape.

He must think of Raine. He'd promised his mother he would keep him safe, and right now he didn't even know whether Raine was alive. Abruptly, Ash swept the mug of milk from the table, shattering it. Like the reproachful stain of a maiden's lost virtue, the sweet milk spread across the tiles and seeped into the earth between. Tainted. Lost. Gone.

He strode from the kitchen, out into the backyard, and to the stable, calling for the boy to saddle his horse.

The town square hummed with drowsy activity, the bright streamers bedecking several pink-cheeked lads and lassies attesting to the fact that the maypole dance had recently ended. Watt and his cronies had gathered around a square table in front of The Ploughman.

Good, Ash thought. With very little effort he should be able to repair the damage done by his ill-advised recitation and St. John's gossip. They were a provincial, gullible lot.

A vague sense of self-disgust crawled up Ash's throat. He swallowed it down, like he had every bit of vileness in his life, accepting it whole. Watt wanted to like him.

Deliberately he forced his gaze past Rhiannon, sitting on the ground beside Watt, fussing over his splintered leg. Watt covered her hand with his great tanned paw, leaning over to speak earnestly. They were absorbed in each other, deaf to all others, but Ash's ears were damnably acute.

". . . of course you must ride this afternoon, Rhiannon," Phillip was saying. "I refuse to allow you to stay back because of my injury. Besides, Father arranged this hunt particularly for you. Really, Rhiannon, you must go. I insist on it!"

She dashed the back of her free hand across her cheeks, ridding herself of tears. Ash clamped down on his insane impulse to snatch her up into his arms and kiss the tears from her face.

"—really are too kind, Phillip," she answered. "I don't deserve you."

Phillip awkwardly patted her cheek. "It's all right. Nerves. A day before our wedding and all."

She colored violently, and pulled her hand from under his. Ash saw the moment in which her honor extinguished her common sense. "Phillip, I have to tell—"

She mustn't do it.

"Watt!" Ash hailed.

Rhiannon glanced up. Her mouth looked bruised.

"Miss Russell." Ash nodded his greeting. "Are you not going to join the delightful game Miss Chapham has arranged?"

He smiled brilliantly. She needed a few lessons in deception. She'd best learn them soon. *Before* she entered Phillip's bed. He swung his glance back to Phillip. The blond giant regarded him sullenly.

"Watt," Ash said, "if you don't take a care to warn visitors of the potency of your village scrumpy, you'll end up with a great line of dunderheaded knaves queuing up before your magistrate trying to account for their idiocy."

The hurt somewhat evaporated from Watt's expression, but the wariness remained.

"I barely recall what type of an ass I made of myself last night," Ash said with winning candor, "but I'm sure it was a large one. I'm liable to lay claim to all sorts of crimes when I'm in that state. And make promises I can't keep and swear allegiance I have no intention of remaining loyal to. Forgive me?"

He ignored the hurt in Rhiannon's eyes. Of course she would think he was addressing her.

"Pay it no mind, Merrick," Phillip said, clapping Ash on the shoulder. "And never mind what was said or sung or . . ." he blundered on, "whatever. Fair Badden's scrumpy has caused the best of us to make ridiculous claims. And," he shot a dark look at St. John, "there are those who will always derive pleasure from carrying tales. Whether true or no."

"You are too kind," Ash murmured.

"Here. Sit by me." Phillip waved Andrew, the innkeeper's boy, to bring another chair. Ash sank into it. Rhiannon scuttled away from him.

"I say, what's that they're playing, Miss Russell?" Ash asked pleasantly, needing an excuse to look at her, to examine just how deep he'd driven the spike.

"Blindman's Bluff," she said, eyes lowered. "Would you care to play?"

He stretched his long legs out in front of him. "Dear me, no. Wouldn't know how."

"But everyone knows Blindman's Bluff," she said.

"Not me," he said. "There was no nursery where I grew up. No playroom. No classroom. Not a nanny or a governess. Only a twisted, misshapen old nurse that worked cheap and was for whatever reason loyal to my mother's family name."

As soon as the words had crossed his lips, he regretted them. Rhiannon had gone still, her face numb.

He glared at her. She'd bewitched him, forced confidences from him that he had not intended to give, brought a ripple of unease to the smooth tableau he'd been working to create. He sought to regain lost ground.

He shook his head. "By Jingo, one must tread carefully about you and your softhearted bride, Watt. I can understand her frailty, being country bred and lacking wisdom in the ways of the world and worldly men." *He must not look at her.* "I didn't mean to suggest I did not play games as a child. We played aplenty."

Desperate games. Feral games. His father had been a master at teaching them.

"Mostly games of chance. Inveterate gamblers, we Merricks. Same with your people I imagine, eh, Watt?"

"Yes. Indeed," Phillip blustered.

"Now, tell me about this Blindman's Bluff. Can one bet on the outcome?"

"I suppose," Phillip said consideringly.

"I'll wager you a shilling to a crown that Margaret Atherton is the first to be caught," he said to Watt, avoiding Rhiannon's eye. There was still something to be taken from Fair Badden. Even if it wasn't the thing he wanted.

Rhiannon rose to her feet. She hesitated, uncertain of whether she ought to stay, but Phillip had forgotten her and Ash would not look at her. She walked away, silently praying her trembling legs would hold her until she'd rounded The Ploughman's corner and found the bench set against its sunny outer wall. Her knees did not betray her but the moment she stepped in front of the homely bench they gave out and she sank down, finally finding a moment of privacy in which to try and sort her wild thoughts and indiscreet heart.

She couldn't stop shivering, a deep shudder that began inside and worked its way out. She knew its source. She'd betrayed Phillip and the guilt of it was eating her from the inside out.

She buried her face in her hands. Tears sprang to her eyes and washed down her hot cheeks and she cursed herself roundly for it. Tears did no good; guilt did less, for neither could call back last night and let her replay those fateful hours. Even if they could, she was not sure she wanted those hours altered.

Except he did.

She saw it in his cool dark eyes this morning in the kitchen and heard it in the veiled warning he'd issued her with his words about "worldly men and naive country lasses." She scrubbed at her eyes and pressed the heels of her hands against her temples trying to think, to make some decision.

Clearly she had to tell Phillip what she'd done or she'd become so shaken by the keeping of this secret that she'd fly apart. Twice now she'd tried and twice Phillip had managed to stymie her. It was almost as if he already knew what she would say and feared it and sought to keep her from telling him. She twisted her fingers in her lap.

Nonsense. It was only her own wishful thinking. How much easier this would be if she could convince herself that Phillip was best off not knowing. And she could, with very little difficulty, convince herself of just that. She knew Phillip had no great love for her, that he'd chosen her as his bride because she was biddable and undemanding. He'd even told her once that his father had quite succinctly pointed out her suitability to be Phillip's wife because she had no aspirations to live anywhere but Fair Badden, no inclinations to travel, and no social ambitions regarding the London season.

And the old man had been right. She and Phillip were perfectly suited. She did not want to leave Fair Badden. It was lovely, quiet, and safe. Just the thought of venturing elsewhere added ripples of panic to her shivers of misery. Out there—bad things happened.

She should have thought of that before she'd risked her future—the lovely, genteel future that even now was still within her grasp—on a night of surrender to her long-buried passionate nature.

Time to bury that nature again. Deeper this time. So deeply that it would finally die, never again to be resurrected.

An involuntary sound of anguish escaped her lips. Unsteadily, she stood up. She couldn't think anymore, each thought circled back onto itself, a snake eating its tail. She felt dazed and frightened. The light glancing off The Ploughman's whitewashed wall dazzled her eyes and she looked away. She mustn't think anymore.

She saw Edith Fraiser moving gingerly across the town square, a thin envelope in her hand. Behind her one of the men held a brace of hounds straining at the leash.

The sight instantly calmed Rhiannon, releasing the poisonous tension coiling within her. *The hunt.* The hunt would clear her thoughts and sweep the confusion from her heart. A race with the wind that would leave behind every vestige of her life, every concern, obligation—and betrayal. Aye. She'd follow the hunt.

Ash flicked the envelope Edith Fraiser had given him beneath his chin as he watched Susan Chapham being blindfolded.

He should be quite pleased. His purse was nearly fifty pounds heavier; he'd reestablished himself amongst these well-fleeced sheep as a harmless lambikins; and he'd kept Rhiannon from running to Phillip in full mea culpa cry before her wedding.

He *was* quite pleased. This feeling of heartsickness was simply the result of too much country. A surfeit of vegetables. Too much sun.

He opened the envelope, and glanced at the signature. It was from Thomas Donne. Ash's interest sharpened as he read. The letter suggested a reason for the attacks on Rhiannon—an improbable conjecture, but a reason nonetheless. He frowned.

It had been his plan to leave soon but because he owed the lass some small part of his consideration he would wait around and play watchdog. All would come right, for then she would once and for all be Phillip Watt's concern.

And if he could not account for the hurtful rhythm of his heartbeat, he did not try.

CHAPTER 16

"Go on without me. I'll just stay back and enjoy the day," said Ash Merrick from atop the back of his steed.

The two young men he addressed, the last members of the hunting party to mount up, regarded him dubiously. Ash waved them off and watched them go, his smile dissolving. He wasn't about to inform them that for him those years a young man dedicates to refining his hunting skills had been spent in a dungeon.

His gaze picked out Rhiannon Russell's figure. Clad in midnight blue velvet that turned her roan tresses incandescent, she lagged near the rear of the group rather than the front where he would have expected her.

Behind her, Stella darted into a patch of bushes. Rhiannon called out to her. With a crash the hound burst from the tangle of brush, tongue lolling, tail wagging.

Would that all curs be so well favored, Ash thought. The other hounds barked and danced at the end of leashes, waiting for the Master of the Hunt to loose them to the trail, but Rhiannon's dog enjoyed its freedom. And Rhiannon's love.

He frowned and pulled Donne's letter from his waistcoat pocket, scanning the missive for the portion that had made him reconsider leaving:

—if this man in the French islands is, indeed, Miss Russell's long-lost brother, should he die without wife or brat his plantation would revert to his next of kin. Since she is Scottish, Miss Russell would be next in line, even though she is female. We Scots are so barbarously nonpartisan with regard to women, aren't we?

However, should Miss Russell wed one of your Englishmen, her property becomes his. Someone might take exception to this. I think I would make some inquiries about Miss Russell's extended family.

But all this presupposes a brother precipitously restored from the grave and just as precipitously returned, as well as a secret family member plotting from the shadows.

Instead I would look for a potential murderer in Miss Russell's jealous rival or some person harboring a grudge. If Miss Russell has trapped herself a groom by becoming enceinte, I would say look there. Or perhaps the elder Watt cannot abide the thought of a Jacobite daughter yet dares not risk alienating his son by refusing to countenance the marriage?

Now, enlighten me as to whether those rural strumpets know any interesting tricks that have eluded their urban cousins—

Ash refolded the vellum and pocketed it. Interesting. He hadn't realized that the Scots laws governing inheritance were so different from the English. Certainly a molasses-producing plantation would be prize enough to commit murder for.

No wonder Carr wanted to marry Rhiannon.

But as Donne suggested, the tale of the long-lost brother did seem unlikely. Perhaps Rhiannon had beaten out other favorites for the Watt name but he'd seen no show of animosity amongst her friends. He, above all others, knew that Rhiannon had not trapped Watt into marriage by conceiving, and Watt's father had apparently handpicked Rhiannon to be Phillip's wife—

A thought niggled at Ash, impressions, chance phrases. He sifted through them, scowling in concentration. Phillip. Handsome, athletic Phillip. Always surrounded by his boon companions. Gruffly boastful of his romantic conquests. Yet in the month since his arrival not once had they sought out women of easy virtue. No one had even suggested it.

If Phillip had not wanted a bride . . . if there was in him something that resisted yet could not be voiced . . . if he feared a wife might expose something he wanted left alone—

Ash shook his head. He was being overly imaginative. These incidents were just what they seemed. Still, the hunt setting with everyone tearing off would present a prime opportunity to manufacture yet another "accident."

He touched his heels to the gelding's side and loped off in the direction of the disappearing hunters.

Rhiannon's heart was not in the hunt. Always before when she'd needed to escape, the hunt offered her the opportunity.

Not today. She reined her horse at the edge of a thick copse of hemlock and watched the others hurdle down the steep embankment after the pack of trumpeting hounds. Absently, she looked for Stella's rangy form and when she could not find her, she smiled wanly.

The dog was a disaster. She'd rather chase squirrels then add her voice to those of her littermates. Three times already today Rhiannon had had to call her from her own doggy pursuits and lead her back to the pack. It was becoming increasingly obvious that no amount of cajoling or scolding was going to turn Stella into a decent gazehound.

Rhiannon nudged her mount forward, riding along the fringe of the woods, listening for the telltale sounds of a dog playing.

The minutes ticked by, becoming half an hour and then an hour. Rhiannon began to grow concerned. The other hunters had long since disappeared from view and the sun's rays slanted across the long forms of oak and larch. Soon it would be dark and Stella would be lost.

Rhiannon lifted herself in the saddle, calling out and listening. Nothing. She turned the horse back and retraced her route, certain now that Stella had gone east rather than west as she'd assumed. Her raised voice sharpened with fear when she heard a sudden high-pitched howl.

She moved toward the sound, into a dense tangle of overgrown shrubbery that formed a wall along the forest's edge. She dug her heels into her mare's flanks, but the horse shied from entering.

Another yip dissolved her caution. She set her whip against her mount's rump and the skittish horse gathered its haunches beneath it and plunged into the thicket. Immediately vines and brambles caught and tore at Rhiannon's hair and face. The mare neighed in distress, jumping and lurching in fitful forward motion through the net of bindweed clutching at her legs.

Rhiannon held her arm up, warding off the worst of the nettles and barbs. Fifty yards, and then seventy. Several slashes sliced through her skirts and sleeves. A new fear took hold. Her horse could be blinded by such savage growth.

She reined in. The mare thrashed her head back and forth, fighting the bit in her mouth, frightened by the unseen enemies pulling at her legs. Rhiannon could no longer hear Stella. She searched the area for easier egress. To her left and farther in she made out a patch of light through a low, thin corridor: a deer trail. She pulled her mount's head around, crooning encouragement.

The horse blundered onto the trail, her flanks twitching with excitement, her ears flat against her head. Rhiannon raised herself in the stirrups to see where the trail led. A rabbit darted from beneath the ferns, shooting across her horse's path.

It was too much for Rhiannon's frenzied mount.

The mare bolted, catching Rhiannon unawares and snatching the reins from her hands. Free, the horse raced like a devil fleeing hell. Rhiannon threw herself flat along its outstretched neck, snatching unsuccessfully for the reins streaming along its withers.

Clots of black earth spun from beneath the mare's hooves. Green and gold, light and dark passed by Rhiannon's face in a stampeding blur. Without foothold or handhold, her velvet habit became a slide. She skittered in the polished leather saddle. One sharp turn, a sudden stop, and she would lose her grip. She buried her fingers in the mane, crouched over the mare's withers, and prayed.

A shout ahead. A crash. The thunder of pursuing hooves. Her horse veered, hurtling her forward—

A strong arm snatched her from the saddle. Her back slammed into a hard body, her hips banged into a thigh. She twisted, clutching wildly. The arm around her yanked her up and settled her between hard legs.

Ahead, her horse's low bunched hindquarters disappeared. The black-gloved hand before her drew back on the reins of the horse. She slewed around to face her rescuer knowing, certain, yes . . . Ash.

"I thought you were supposed to be some sort of bleeding Diana!" he shouted angrily.

"What—"

"You! Everyone says you ride like a centaur. I've seen better riders on a costermonger's cart!"

"I lost my reins," she whispered, stunned by his anger.

"Lost your *reins*? Damnation!" His arms tightened around her. "The middle of a poacher's trap is not the place to lose one's reins. Or didn't your equestrian instructor teach you that?"

"Poacher's trap?"

She blinked up at him, confused and disoriented. Heat and power radiated from him, soaked through his shirt, warming her, bracing her.

"Yes. Poacher's trap. The bloody deer run is ringed with razored barbs. If you had made it down the chute—"

His eyes glittered as he stared over her head. His voice was a dangerous thing. Beneath the blue-black shadow of beard his jaw hardened.

"What the hell are you doing out here, anyway?"

"Stella." She remembered suddenly. She pushed at his chest, scrambled to free herself of his implacable grip. "Stella!"

A thready howl answered her call.

"Please!" She grasped his arms. Muscles bunched beneath her fingers. "Please. She's hurt. Can't you hear?"

His gaze locked with hers. Abruptly, he swung her to the ground, one hand still imprisoning her wrists as he followed her.

"I'll go. Wait here. Hold the reins. *Keep* holding the reins."

"Yes. Please. Thank you—"

He'd already gone, moving with catlike grace down the leaf-canopied trail and disappearing into the flat disc of sunlight ahead.

The moments extended in thick, heartbeat-accented measures, one after the other. A branch snapped nearby and a covey of partridge flushed, air trembling beneath their wings as they broke skyward. Rhiannon waited. A high-pitched yelp jerked her to the end of the reins tethering her to Ash's sweat-foamed horse.

"Ash!" His horse snorted at the sharp tone and danced backward. "Ash!"

"Yes."

She peered down the trail and saw a dark masculine figure break from the light and stride forth, carrying a huge animal in his arms. She knotted the reins to a sapling and flew down the trail heedless of Ash's barked order to stay.

She had almost reached them when she saw the blood. It ringed the dog's neck with a crimson collar and streaked her hindquarters. One hind leg dangled awkwardly from Ash's clasp.

"Stella," she whispered.

The dog lifted pain-filled amber eyes and whined. Gingerly Rhiannon stroked the silky head and worked cautious fingers through the sleek coat. Her fingers grew wet with blood.

"What happened?"

"She was in the middle of the trap. Couldn't get out."

"Will she be all right?"

He didn't meet her eye. His own face was flushed, his eyes hot. "Her leg is broken."

She spun around and returned to the tied horse, calling over her shoulder. "We have to get her back. Mrs. Fraiser can set the bone of any man or beast."

Ash followed her. "Mount up, Rhiannon. I'll hand her up to you. Keep her still as possible."

Rhiannon clambered astride. The horse shifted but did not shy when Ash lifted Stella up onto Rhiannon's lap. The dog whimpered and Rhiannon whispered soft comforting words, painfully aware of the dangling leg.

Without a word, Ash took the reins and led the way back up the narrow path. They emerged at the far end of the thicket, a good distance from where Rhiannon had entered. She looked down at Stella. The dog panted shallowly, her eyes half-closed against the pain. Blood stained Rhiannon's skirts.

"How long will it take to bring her to the Fraisers'?" she asked Ash.

"Two hours. Maybe less. I don't want to—"

"Hallo!"

At the sound both Rhiannon and Ash looked up. A pony cart was jostling its way along the forest track toward them. Phillip drove it, his splinted leg resting on the front axle. "Hallo!"

"Thank God. We can rest Stella on the seat beside him." Rhiannon lifted her arm, waving wildly. "Here! Phillip! Here!"

Ash remained watchfully silent as Phillip pulled up beside them, his grin fading to an expression of concern. "What is this?"

"Stella has broken her leg and lost a great deal of blood. Oh, Phillip. You must drive her back to Mrs. Fraiser's."

"Of course," Phillip said, shifting to the side of the cart. Wordlessly, Ash took Stella from Rhiannon and placed her alongside Phillip.

"I'll see her forthwith to the manor," Phillip promised, his big hand on the dog's head. In that moment Rhiannon felt sick with gratitude and affection and guilt. He was such a good man. A decent, kindhearted man. "Rhiannon, you ride along behind me. If Stella grows restive she'll need your voice to calm her."

"Stella won't grow restive. She's lost too much blood," Ash said, breaking his silence. "Don't get down, Rhiannon. You're staying with me."

Rhiannon, in the process of alighting, froze. "Phillip is right. I can help Mrs. Fraiser—"

"No," Ash said, approaching his horse. Before she realized what was happening, he'd grasped the back of the saddle and swung up behind her. One strong arm wrapped around her waist, pulling her tight against him, imprisoning her there. "You won't be going back to Mrs. Fraiser's. Now or in the foreseeable future."

"What the hell is this?" Phillip demanded. Pain and betrayal filled his handsome countenance. "Rhiannon? Is this—is he what you've been trying to tell me? That you and he—? You bastard!" Phillip erupted. "You bloody bastard! I thought you were my friend!"

A cold, acid bath of fear gripped Rhiannon. Stunned beyond coherent thought she twisted in Ash's grip. "Ash, you can't. You can't do this." She tore at the arm imprisoning her. She might as well have been clawing at iron manacles.

"Why are you here, Watt?" Ash's voice, so close to her ear, came deadly and soft. "This isn't the course the hunters followed. The only thing here is a poacher's trap, set to catch a young girl and baited with a tortured dog."

"What?" Rhiannon gasped.

"There's nothing in that trap that would break a dog's leg," Ash went on. "Someone broke her leg on purpose and then twisted it to set the hound howling so that its fond mistress would follow the sound."

"No one would do something so vile!" Phillip declared. "You're mad to suggest it."

"Am I? Why all these accidents? How many times in the past month has Rhiannon nearly been killed? How many times were you there?"

"Rhiannon! You don't believe this madman, do you?"

"No!" she shouted. "Ash, I don't know what you're about, why you're saying these things. You can't mean them. Phillip couldn't have done this. His leg is broken. Only think!"

A low, nasty laugh tickled the hairs by her ear. "So innocent. It has its appeal, I'll admit, but *you* think, Rhiannon. The trap could have been laid a long time ago. A contingency plan, eh, Watt?"

Phillip rose awkwardly. His face suffused with color. "Let her down! You have no right—"

"I have every right and you might be so good as to inform Mrs. Fraiser of such so that she does not set any of your local magistrates after us."

Phillip sank down on the seat. "What do you mean?"

"I have letters naming me Lord Carr's agent, with the legal right to act in his behalf. And as Rhiannon Russell's surrogate and oh-so-legal guardian, I'm exercising those rights. There are new laws, Watt, making it illegal for a woman to wed without her guardian's consent before she reaches the age of twenty-one. I believe Rhiannon is younger."

"No!" Each calm, cold word sounded a death knell to her future, her life. Ash Merrick was snatching it from her. All of her life she had been ripped from those she loved, fled or chased or taken away. It was beginning again. No choices. Simply robbing her of her right to make her own decisions.

Wildly, she twisted in Ash's hold, fighting him. "No!"

"For the love of God, man," Phillip pleaded. "Can't you see she's frantic? Let us go back to Fraiser's. Discuss this. Whatever you and Rhiannon have done—"

"What we have done?" Ash laughed harshly. "I have *had* her, Watt! I've taken her maidenhead. Don't you understand? She's no longer a virgin bride. You won't marry her now. No one would expect you to."

Rhiannon hissed with fury at Ash's betrayal. He'd promised! And he'd not only lied, but was deliberately provoking Phillip, taunting him.

Savagely she wrenched around in Ash's arms, scoring his wrists with her nails. He did not even counter her frantic clawing. There was nothing malleable or soft in him.

"If you are trying to assuage your guilt over abducting her, it's not that easy, Merrick." Phillip's face was pale, white lines bracketing his nostrils, his jaw trembling. "We can still marry. Other brides have not been virgins. Leave her here, Merrick. I assure you, no one will call off the wedding."

"You leave me no choice but to take her," Rhiannon thought she heard Ash say under his breath. His horse danced sideways.

"You cannot simply steal her like this," Phillip said.

She felt more than saw the curl of Ash's lip as he turned his horse away and set his heels to its sides.

"Oh, but I can."

CHAPTER 17

Late that afternoon in an unnamed hamlet thirty miles west of Fair Badden, a single horse rode into the yard of the local blacksmith. It carried a dark man riding behind a tousled young woman. The smithy abandoned his bellows, wiping his own hands on his leather apron. He did not like the looks of this pair.

First off, they were quality. Dusty quality, sweat-stained and travel-worn quality, but quality nonetheless. But, it weren't that they were quality alone that set a nerve twitching beneath the smithy's eye. It were that they were quality on the run, and running hard from the looks of them and their barrel-chested, lathered horse.

The girl looked exhausted. The man, a hard and tensile-looking creature, took no note of his companion's condition. He dismounted, leaving the girl sagging in the saddle.

The smithy, a fond father with daughters of his own, moved forward until he saw the sparkle of fury in the girl's bright eyes. A lovers' spat, perhaps, thought the smithy. Perhaps his interference would not be appreciated. Though if his lover had looked at him like the girl glared at the man's back, he'd have looked elsewhere for his sport no matter what the lure of reddish hair and a full bosom.

A glance at the watchful way the dark man waited—limbs balanced just so—added its counsel urging the smithy to mind his own business. A nasty-looking customer, the stranger.

"I need a horse." The man pointed at the roan mare fenced in the yard beside the smithy.

His speech marked him a city man, as did his tight breeches and the pearl blade handle protruding from the folded edge of his boots.

"And a saddle, too. Not a lady's saddle. I'll pay in coin," he said and named a sum far exceeding the worth of either horse or leather, and the smithy, what with all those beloved daughters, abandoned chivalry in the interest of practicality. Daughters liked dresses.

The smithy caught the mare and tied her at the fence before fetching an old saddle from its peg.

"May I get down?" he heard the lass ask. From the stilted sound of her voice and the blood rising in her cheeks, the smithy guessed she disliked making the request.

The man studied her a minute. She lifted her chin defiantly. Proud lass. Foolish lass. The man's mouth tightened but he went to her and without word or warning plucked her from her perch.

"No." Her single word was denial—repudiation and calm, frigid command. "Don't touch me."

The man's narrow face dulled with color but he did not set her down. He swung about, the lass in his arms as stiff as a paste doll.

"You'll go round back there," he said to her. "And you'll come back before the mare's done being saddled."

He set her down, stepping back before she could push him away. She yanked up her heavy skirts and paced off behind the smithy, her hem swishing angrily.

"Yore wife?" the smithy asked, pricked again by the unwelcome call of gallantry.

"Don't think of interfering, friend," the man advised. "It will only get you hurt."

The smithy could fair believe that but still if the lass needed him . . .

The young woman reappeared a minute later and watched while the smithy finished cinching the girth strap. Nothing was revealed on that pretty face. It was as blank as a churchyard angel's. As soon as the saddle was on, the man tied a lead rope to the mare's bridle and called to the young beauty.

For the first time, something other than anger showed on her face. Her eyes shimmered with telling moisture. The man called out again. She bit down on her lip, approaching the mare at a foot-dragging pace.

Once more he swept her up into his arms. Once more she went rigid, a shudder passing through her slight frame. And then, as if against her will, she flung her arms full around the man's neck. With a soft whimper, she pushed her face against his throat. Tears ran down her smooth cheeks. She clung to him like moss to a rock, her body—before so rigid and denying—now malleable and entreating.

The man froze, a slight check no longer than a heartbeat, before disentangling the girl's arms from his throat and lifting her into the saddle. He turned his back on her at once.

All the fight seeped from her posture; a lost and bewildered expression appeared on her face. And when she looked at the man, something bled from her eyes that the smithy recognized from long ago and that mostly from dreams, and troubled dreams at that.

How could the man rebuff this woman?

Then the dark stranger strode past the smithy to mount his own steed. His face was averted from the lady and the smithy saw him close his eyes, clenching them tight, and the smithy knew that the cost of his seeming callousness was immense.

They traveled north throughout the evening. Ash stopped once at a farm and bought some bread and cheese from the timid woman who answered the door.

Rhiannon did not speak. After forging that outrageous tale about someone deliberately maiming Stella and trying to kill her, Ash had made no attempt to speak, either.

For her part, she had no words to say to this . . . devil. He'd taken them in with his polished manners and ready laughter, his easy smile and amiable charm. They'd fed him, and sheltered him, allowing him time to regain his strength, unaware they'd harbored a predator in their midst.

Bitterly, she wondered what he wanted now. She'd already given him what men value most. Perhaps, the acrid thought occurred to her, he'd never considered allowing her to marry Phillip. Perhaps he'd merely taken the opportunity for a profitable holiday, all along planning on taking her to this Lord Carr. Perhaps her infatuation had merely been an agreeable happenstance.

Clearly, he no longer wanted her as his lover. He touched her, yes, but only to assert his strength and her comparative weakness, to show her, she was sure, how easily he could have of her whatever he wished. To frighten her.

He succeeded.

With no reins to clutch, her fingers had grown numb from gripping the rolled edge of the saddle. Her back ached with each step the mare took but she would not ask for mercy. Her thoughts swirled between a dream and waking state.

She had no idea how long he intended to ride. The moon had long since

risen above the rutted country road. Its pale light smothered the landscape in a ghostly cowl. Crickets chimed from the grass, and an occasional
night-dwelling predator rustled in the ditches, yellow eyes glowing flat and
incurious. She'd seen their like before.

Images and sensations flicked through her mind. Memories were like
wolves waiting for the door to open to come ravening in, and each mile
forced the door open, inch by painful inch.

The sharp line of moonlight cresting the mountain. Muted voices whispering from the hiding hole in the clansman's croft. The staccato of hoofbeats. Scarlet coats made black by the night, suddenly illumined by torch
fire. Discovery. Panic. Shouts . . .

No!

Her head snapped upright, her stomach roiling, the taste of bile thick
on her tongue. Dizzy and disoriented she stared about her.

They were rounding a curve. Ahead, an inn squatted beside a cross-
roads. Bright light poured from small windows, and a curl of smoke stood
pale against the indigo sky. Ash halted, waiting until she was alongside
him to speak.

"We'll stop there for the night," he said. "You won't say anything or do
anything to cause a . . . situation."

"Why won't I?" she muttered, head aching dully.

"Because it wouldn't do you any good," he replied. "I have papers
naming me your guardian in my father's stead. No commoner is going to
challenge the Earl of Carr's will or, by extension, mine. And if you should
bedevil some half-drunk farmer into thinking himself Galahad to your
damsel in distress, remember, his wounds would be your doing."

"No. Please."

No, please! Come out! The smoke . . .

"You wouldn't want more guilt on your tender conscience, would you,
Rhiannon?"

She shivered.

"I would think that particular cup is full."

"Bastard."

"Unfortunately quite legitimate." He yanked on the lead rope.

At the inn, he dismounted and came to her side, lifting his arms.
Weakly, she slapped his hands away. He stepped back and watched her
pull her feet free of the stirrups and slide to the ground. Her legs, numbed
from so long in the saddle, buckled.

He reached her as she collapsed, lifting her. "Don't be a fool. Hurting
yourself isn't going to make me return you to Fair Badden."

"What will?" she asked weakly.

"Nothing." He clipped out a command to care for their horses to the tired boy who materialized beside them. Then he kicked open the inn's door and ducked beneath the low lintel.

A gristle-cheeked innkeeper blinked at their sudden appearance.

"I need a room," Ash said. "And the lady needs a basin of fresh water, towels. We'll eat now, while you prepare it."

Rhiannon squinted around the room, praying she would recognize someone of authority, someone who could stop this madman. There was no one. A pair of rough-looking travelers eyed her interestedly until their gazes fell on Ash.

"See them scars on his wrists? Manacles," she heard one mutter to the other. "Seen 'em before. Tattoo of the prisons."

Manacles? Prison?

"Now," Ash barked at the innkeeper.

"Yes, sir!" The man pattered off behind a door.

With a predatory smile at the two travelers, Ash moved to the fire. He set her down on a stool and dragged a small table in front of her, settling himself on a chair across from her, effectively penning her into the corner.

Heedless of him, she leaned her head against the wall. Her eyelids drifted shut until a rich, earthy aroma filled her nostrils. She opened her eyes. Two steaming bowls sat on the table beside a half loaf of dark bread and a bottle of wine. Her stomach rumbled loudly as she tried to focus her vision. A sickeningly familiar sensation of near-starvation swept over her with all its eviscerating power. Saliva drenched the interior of her mouth.

"For God's sake," she heard Ash say, "eat."

Shamelessly she lifted the wooden bowl and slurped down the thick, viscous liquid in great gulps. She *was* starving. Ravenous. Her hands shook as she tore into the stale bread and rammed a piece atop the mouthful of mutton stew.

She was breathing too fast, eating too fast, and the wine she sloshed into her mouth to chase down each mouthful of bread stifled the air from her throat.

Memory became present.

Time turned inside out.

Hunger. Excruciating hunger. She hadn't eaten in days. Nothing but berries and water. They hadn't dared poach a rabbit or build a fire. The redcoats would see.

Fear and flight. Hounded and hunted on roads, on foot, at night. The mocking moon made crossing the fields near suicidal. They skulked in the ditches, as the soldiers drove the roads, hunting down clansmen, all those men who'd answered the McClairen's call. The smell of gunpowder. The smell of blood. Men screaming. The mountains looming. *The Highlands.* She stared wild-eyed at the cold-eyed stranger sitting opposite her. He was taking her back there.

Her head pounded. A rushing noise began in her ears, dimming the sound of the others' voices. Her vision swam and she stared into his eyes. Pale like the betraying moon, cold, like a Highland night, beautiful and uncompromising. She rose shakily to her feet, clutching for the edge of the table, spinning, out of breath—

Ash snuffed the guttering candle flame between his thumb and index finger, steeping the room in darkness except for the thin moonlight that trickled from the window and blanketed the slumbering woman on the mattress.

She'd fainted hours ago and had yet to come fully conscious. He'd seen the like in prisoners who'd gone too long without food and were finally fed.

He'd experienced it himself, his first night of freedom from the French gaol. A crease furrowed Ash's brow. Amongst prisoners such an occurrence might be commonplace but not in gently reared young ladies. Not that his experience with that breed was extensive.

Rhiannon had downed that vile broth as though it had been her only meal in a month. And when she'd risen to her feet, horror had clouded her eyes, a deeper, older horror than that which had blazed from her eyes since he'd taken her from Watt.

He pulled a chair near the narrow cot, cocking his head and studying her. Her lips parted on soft susurration. Not only was she exhausted, she was frightened.

It was his doing, of course. He'd pushed her too far. He should have recognized that earlier, but she wore bravery so well and he'd not much experience with fear, having become inured to it long, long ago. Yet he'd felt a lick of it earlier that day, when he'd recognized what had been done to the dog and realized a trap had been set for Rhiannon. And later, when they'd come out of the forest and seen Watt's cheerful approach, that lick had become a flail.

He reached over and tucked his jacket up around her throat, taking care to wipe her square little chin. So elegant a jaw, so proudly fashioned . . .

Abruptly he straightened, raking the black hair back from his face. What the bloody hell was he going to do?

He couldn't let her return to Fair Badden to be murdered, and murder was exactly what he feared had he left her in Watt's suspect care. Granted, Watt's reason for wanting to kill Rhiannon eluded him. He was not satisfied that Watt's motives could be wholly ascribed to his aversion to marriage—yet the attempts on her life seemed to have begun with their proposed marriage. Nothing else had changed, or threatened to change, the status she'd held in Fair Badden for ten years.

But Watt had refused the excuse to withdraw his suit that Ash had offered him. Yet his vow that he would still marry Rhiannon hadn't been made by a besotted man, nor even one too proud to acknowledge himself cuckolded. A desperate man had made it. Which made no sense.

And if Ash wouldn't allow Rhiannon to marry Watt, he would not allow her to become one of his father's short-lived brides, either. He couldn't marry her himself. Even if he could find some place to hide her until she came of age and no longer needed Carr's permission to wed. Or if he could persuade her to marry him in Scotland where Carr's permission wasn't needed.

He had nothing in this world: no friends, no holdings, and no future. What money he had was promised to his brother.

Abruptly he stood up, the chair scraping loudly in the hushed room. The only thing in this world that he owned was a promise he'd made to his mother on the day of her death: to watch out for Raine.

All his life it had seemed enough, been his lodestar. When Raine had been taken by that tattered McClairen mob, he'd fought and killed without remorse to free him.

He would not forsake his promise. He could not. It was the only thing he'd *not* forsaken, having abandoned faith, and hope, and lo—and everything else that romantics wept over and pious madmen preached. Nothing he'd done or become had diminished that obligation.

Nothing until Rhiannon Russell.

He stared down at her, and as he watched, she twisted her cheek into the deep velvet pile of his jacket collar, murmuring in distressed tones. Unable to help himself, he loosed a coil of hair that had caught against her lip and tucked it behind her ear.

She opened her eyes. For an instant they lightened with recognition but then the light died, killed by fear. She scooted up, heels drumming the mattress in her climb to the headboard.

"If you touch me, I'll kill you."

Well, yes. The thought was distant, like an echo in a cave, hollow and detached and having nothing to do with a body that seemed incapable of motion, a mouth that refused to speak the denial that clamored for expression.

Why, yes. If she refused to believe she'd been in danger, she could only think that that was why he'd taken her. It hurt. God help him, it hurt, and he nearly laughed at how ridiculous it was that such a little matter as a girl's misplaced fear could cause such immeasurable pain.

And was it so misplaced? Would she be wrong at that? All day he'd taken any excuse, however feeble, to hold her, embrace her, touch her; he wanted her so damned much.

And if something in him shriveled before the fearful suspicion in her eyes, well, it was a weak, trifling part of himself that succumbed, a part that he'd never even realized he'd owned, now happily dead.

He reached down, grabbed her arm, and yanked her to her knees.

He was better off without it.

CHAPTER 18

What little light came through the window did not reach Ash's face. He didn't say a word. He just stood over her, like a child's golem, a construct of darkness and earth, holding her like a child's cloth doll. Only the violence of his grip bespoke the deep well of anger his silence could not quite contain.

Well, Rhiannon, too, was angry. Years of obeisance fell from her like rusty shackles. Fair Badden had been an opiate, a sweet illusion of kindness and gentleness. But she'd only needed to pass beyond its borders to be wakened to the world she'd left behind, one of treachery, desperation, and deceit.

She pitched herself against his hold and he released her. She fell back on the bed on stiff arms.

"Is that what you think?" he whispered.

"What else?" she spat up at him. She was not half dead with fatigue now, not lost in a labyrinth of hellish, living memories. She knew where she was, what she was doing . . . what was being done to her. She'd fought once and survived. She would fight again.

"I'm taking you to my father's to keep you from being killed."

"You are too good." Even as she jeered, some misbegotten part of her wanted him to convince her that he believed what he said. Even if it was madness, madness she could forgive. But he was not mad, nor misguided. He was simply a devil.

He didn't expend the paltry effort of a reply.

"I don't know what you hope to accomplish by telling me this," she said, in spite of herself. "Why would someone want to hurt me or kill me? Why would *Phillip* want to kill me?"

His gaze slipped away from hers and she noted the involuntary act with bitter conviction. He would lie now. "Watt did not want this marriage. He may not even know why himself. Perhaps his father was forcing him to it and he saw no other way to escape."

She laughed. "Not want this marriage? I went to him yesterday, to tell him what I had done. He wouldn't let me, even though it was clear from what he said in the forest that he suspected. Is that the act of a man looking for a way out of a marriage?"

"You were going to tell Watt? Why?" He sounded shocked. "You asked me not to tell him."

"Of course." She bit off the words. "Because I feared you would say it in such a way that he had no recourse but to call you out—just as you *did*. You told him in the cruelest manner possible. I could not have gone to my marriage bed with that lie waiting to be discovered and I would not have deceived him. But you would have no understanding of that, would you, Lord Janus?"

A flinch? More likely contained laughter.

"None at all," he said. "I was going to advise you to prick your thumb as he slept and smear your thighs."

She felt the blood flee from her face, her skin grow cold, but she was stronger now. She ignored his crudeness.

"What I would like to know is why you have even bothered weaving this pitiful story," she said. "I would think a man of your talents would have at least come up with some better tale." Her lip curled back in as much contempt for herself as for him. "In fact, why fabricate this Banbury tale about assassins at all? I mean, you *have* the bloody letter naming you my surrogate guardian, don't you?"

She peered through the darkness, trying to find some sign she'd struck a human chord in that inhumanely still countenance. All she could see was moonlight shimmering over his black hair.

"You didn't really need an excuse to take me, did you?" she insisted.

"No," he finally answered in that cool, dead voice.

She could hear his breathing, the slight draw and exhalation, light, measured, as if he were consciously regulating it.

"So if you don't mean to rape me—and make no mistake, that is the only way you will ever again take your pleasure between my legs—what *do* you want?" With bitter satisfaction she heard the small, sharp inhalation of his breath. Pain or anger, it made no difference to her, as long as it discomforted him.

She waited for his answer, head up. A long moment passed.

"Don't you know?" he finally ground out.

"Money," she said flatly. It made sense. In hindsight his entire stay in Fair Badden had been one, long, well-orchestrated bit of dodgery: the charming, unsuccessful fumbler slowly transformed into a peerlessly lucky gamester.

"There'll be no money from Mrs. Fraiser," she promised. "The lands and everything on it are entailed to her son and he's far beyond the reach of your stratagems."

No reply.

She bent forward into the light from the window so that he could see her contempt, read her disdain.

"You've no chance of blackmailing *anyone* into paying for my return." A small satisfaction, but she would take what she could. "Whatever Phillip might want, Squire Watt will never accept me as his daughter-in-law now."

"So sure? I'm not."

She shook her head, and the long, tangled skeins of her hair settled around her cheeks and throat like a widow's webbed veil. "He might overlook the lack of a dowry but not the lack of a maidenhead."

"Oh, Rhiannon, I assure you, you've more to recommend to that particular marriage than a simple intact piece of skin."

"I loathe you."

"I know."

He would not be baited, nor pricked with the contempt she was wielding like a blade. His heart and soul were immutable if, indeed, he owned them at all. How could she have been so deceived?

"How lucrative was your stay in Fair Badden?"

The shadow shape shrugged, drifting back a pace, dissolving further into the gloom. "Four hundred pounds. More or less."

"You admit it?" she asked.

"Why not?" he countered. "You've already discovered me. I see no advantage in promoting your naïveté. If you could not stand to—how did you phrase it?—'go to your marriage bed with that lie waiting to be discovered,' how can I be any less noble? Only honesty between us now, eh, Rhiannon? Unless," his voice dropped, became low and mocking, "you'd rather we dispensed with even that inconvenience . . . ?"

She shrank back from its ugliness.

"No? Ah, well."

He was every bit as terrible as she conjectured. How much worse could he be? She had to know the extent of her gullibility.

"The song?" she asked. "Is that true, too?"

"Which song?" he asked.

" 'The Ride of the Demon Earl's Brood.' "

"St. John must have tripped in his haste to tell you that little tale."

"Is it true? Did you?"

"Why?" he countered. "Are you wondering just what sort of evil seed you received?"

She gasped at his crudity, at the calm passionless manner in which he delivered it.

"All right. Here it is. I slashed through a line of men armed with pikes and staves. I made my sword bright with their blood. I trampled them under my horse's hooves."

She wrapped her arms around herself.

"I aided redcoated Brits in killing Scottish peasants." And then, so quietly she barely heard him. *"I saved my brother from being killed."*

She raised her eyes, speared the darkness that hid him with her gaze. "Those peasants were my clan. McClairen was my laird."

He stood as still and motionless as the night.

He'd seduced her on the eve of her wedding, killed her kinsmen, and stolen her from the home she'd so carefully fashioned, from the life she'd so carefully cultivated.

Well, she thought, she needn't be careful anymore. There was no one here whom she wished to please.

"You can't stay awake all the time," she whispered. "But you'd best try, Ash Merrick. For as soon as you're asleep, I'll be gone and you'll be lucky if I don't leave that silver blade of yours sheathed between your ribs."

"Trading threats, are we?" he mused softly. "Well, it's my turn now. Listen carefully. You're right. I can't stay awake until we reach Wanton's Blush. But if I catch you trying to run away, or trying to induce some poor fool into interfering with us, I'll not hesitate to punish you. Severely." Not a chord of warmth was revealed in his voice.

She huddled back on the mattress, glaring at him. She heard him take a deep breath.

"And as for your 'killing me' if I touch you—" His head shifted in the gloom and she caught the glint of his dark eyes. "Any time I want, anywhere I want."

For three days a tempestuous sky dogged their travel. It hounded them along faint, ancient drovers' paths up to high pastures and secret paddocks, the traditional hideouts of the raiders and thieves.

Ash did not try to break Rhiannon's silence. With her savage denunciation, she'd finally made him confront his own motives. His notion that

Watt would want to kill her because he preferred the company of men was feeble and ridiculous. Her best interest hadn't been at the heart of his decision, his loins had been. He'd deluded himself, and that tortured him most of all. He'd always been honest with himself if with no one else.

With no reason to enjoin Rhiannon's good opinion, having repudiated it, he punished himself by seeking its opposite, her contempt—something she was more than obliged to give. It was a painful scourge. It was damn near killing him.

As for Rhiannon, she watched the rod-straight back before her with sullen hostility. She had little doubt Ash meant his threat to hurt her if she tried to flee. But it wasn't that or the bruising pace he set—or even the fact that in spite of his claim she'd yet to see him asleep—that kept her from trying to escape. She had no place to go.

Each night she met his mocking smile with a tilt of her chin but held her breath until he'd wound a blanket about his shoulders and settled with his back against the door of the inns where they'd overnighted. He ignored her then, his gaze fixed on the floorboards, leaving her to wonder what drove him now to complete whatever plot he'd devised.

She little cared. And if the haunted expression she sometimes glimpsed upon his fierce, exhausted countenance might have once confounded her, bitterness left no room for such speculation. She simply welcomed whatever pain he felt. He'd destroyed her life.

During their travel her gaze slew cautiously about. It was all so intimately recognizable: the feel of the wet, cool air; the dark, drenched colors; the scent of flinty rock and gin-spiced conifers. It had been waiting for her return for a decade, like a witch's unwanted familiar.

The winnowing wind whispered a spurious greeting and the chill mist stretched milky fingers up to brush her legs in mock obeisance. Here the McClairens and all those sworn to support them—including the Russells —had returned from Culloden's bloody battlefield seeking sanctuary. Here Lord Cumberland's dragoons had found them. Here they'd been hunted down. Here massacred.

Even in moonlight the mountains seemed stained with blood, the ground, salted with her clansmen's deaths, forever inhospitable and barren. A thousand high, craggy acres of graveyard.

She shuddered and closed her eyes against it. They'd made her home a potter's field.

In such a manner they traveled for four more days and nights. On the fifth night they crested a high, tree-bereaved hill overlooking the sea. Below them and some miles off, a thin bridge of land connected the headland to a big, crescent-shaped island. It surged out of the sea, blocky and jagged with rock. At its inner curve it rose to a high shelf of land overlooking the sheer, dramatic cliffs facing east. On this apex perched a mansion, or castle, or fortress.

It was impossible to tell what exactly the place was, or had started out as, or looked to become, it was so rife with turrets and buttresses, cupolas and columns, friezes and pediments. A mad architect's maddest creation.

Lines of windows cast beacons across terraced lawns and pockmarked sweeping staircases. All about, pinpricks of light—lanterns?—swung and swayed about the massive fortress's base, like fairies dancing maniacally about the skirts of some mammoth, beleaguered matron.

Flitting in and out of the open doorways, through beams of light and patches of shadow, darting and settling in clusters and singly amidst the blackening lawn, were people, ladies and gentlemen, dozens and dozens of them.

Bemused and disconcerted by the spectacle, Rhiannon looked to Ash. His gaze was already on her, thoughtful and remote, his face stained with fatigue. He smiled tightly, and flung out his hand in a cavalier's overmannered gesture.

"Welcome to McClairen's Isle," he said, "and Wanton's Blush."

CHAPTER 19

They left the horses with a liveried servant and climbed the front stairs through the carved panels into a great hall ablaze with light and mirrors and gilt.

Beneath the beatific gaze of the plaster angels high overhead mingled dozens of people. They nibbled cakes and licked gloved fingers, spilt iced punch on Persian carpets, and laughed and posed and sweated in their rich gowns and piled wigs.

Ash led Rhiannon through the little queues of revelers and knots of gamers. Few noted their progress. Most had gone days without sleep, sun, or fresh food. They were swollen on wine and excitement, dull and fog-witted, groping through the mire of senseless spectacles and animal plea-sures his father designed to keep them entertained . . . to keep them careless with their money. For, when all was said and done, Wanton's Blush was simply the most dissolute, the most licentious, the most sump-tuous gaming hell in all the British Isles.

In a few minutes they had broken free of the crush in the main hall and stood in a narrow corridor behind the curved staircase. A laughing woman burst out of a nearby door, her gown slipping from one shoulder, a trio of flushed and hound-eyed men tumbling in pursuit. Ash snatched Rhiannon up and out of their way.

His arms tightened convulsively. The salty, musty scent of travel filled his nostrils. The feel of her body stoked the appetite he'd held in check into a veritable blaze. He looked down. She'd averted her face.

Temper surged through him. What did he care? He thought fiercely. He did not need her scorn to tell him who he was.

"Fa! Carr never said we were to have a masque tonight!"

Ash looked up. A pink-ribboned, satin-clad creature in a lavender wig leaned against the door frame.

"But 'struth, must be so for here's Little Red Ridy Hood herself!" The man's plucked and pencilled brows rose in twin semicircles above shallow, lashless eyes.

Smoothly, Ash lowered Rhiannon to the ground. She did not step back. Of course not. She'd never give him the satisfaction of showing fear. Neither did she say a word or rebuke him in any way. She did not need to. Her silence was eloquent enough. She expected he'd stolen her from Watt to satisfy his carnal appetite.

The lavender-headed fop's gaze drifted from his interested inspection of Rhiannon to Ash, sizing up the filth of travel, the five-day growth of beard, and the tangled tail of black hair.

"And this is either the woodsman or the wolf. I say, fellow, which are you supposed to be?"

"Pray commence trembling, Hurley, that's Merrick you're twitting." A gorgeous young girl appeared beside the plump, pink Hurley. Her young, pure face was absolutely smooth and her poise was unassailable. The gray of her elaborately powdered wig contrasted jarringly with her obvious youth, somehow making a mockery of both.

"Merrick?" the perplexed Hurley asked.

"My brother," the girl replied.

"Fia," Ash said, inclining his head. She was fifteen—or was it sixteen? —and having known so little of her mother, was utterly her father's creature. Ash trusted her less than anyone else, perhaps because in spite of himself he felt the bonds of blood between them, urging something different.

"Merrick? Carr's son?" Hurley stuttered.

"One of them," Ash allowed coolly.

"The ruthless one," Fia said with a small, practiced smile. She moved her salved lips close to one of Hurley's pink ears. Ash could practically see it quiver. "The dangerous one," she whispered loudly. "The passionate one."

Hurley's expression of perplexity gave way to a licentiousness. He reached out to tickle Fia beneath her chin. Calmly Fia slashed her fan across his knuckles. He snatched back his hand, staring at her in wounded wonder.

"Be gone, Lord Hurley. Before Merrick decides to misinterpret your attentions to his little sister." Her face was as smooth as a porcelain doll's and yet a little sneer curled around her words.

The white powder covering Hurley's face could not hide his flush, and with a mumbled adieu, he escaped. Fia ignored his departure.

Beside Ash Rhiannon stirred.

"What is this you've brought, brother?" Fia murmured. "Something for Carr? A new toy?"

"His ward," Ash returned shortly. Rhiannon's head remained bowed, her eyes downcast, her shoulders slumped. She looked as if she'd been beaten which, Ash decided, was probably just what she wanted to look like.

Fia, a little smile chasing cross her features, dipped her head and peeked up.

"He has a ward now, does he?" she said in a voice as gentle and dangerous as the sound of a snake slithering over a dry lawn. Calmly Ash stepped between them. Fia glanced at him in surprise. "Who'd have thought?"

"I would," a deep masculine voice with a distinct Scottish burr announced.

At the sound, Ash turned. Approaching him was a tall, broad-shouldered man. The chandelier light polished his dark mahogany head to a metallic sheen.

"Donne," Ash greeted him. He was surprised to see him here, at Wanton's Blush. Carr usually picked his guests carefully and while Donne was certainly rich enough to be admitted, he did not display the proper susceptibility to drinking, gambling, or wenching.

A smile carved deep dimples in each of Donne's lean cheeks, mirroring the cleft in his chin. There was a watchfulness about the long, narrow eyes currently fixed on Fia. She'd straightened abruptly at his appearance but now stood regarding the Scot with the calm imperturbability she'd owned since childhood.

Rhiannon, like some damn silent statue, remained motionless at Ash's side. He needed to get her upstairs before Carr discovered them. He was tired and edgy, in no condition to deal with his father. Still, if Donne was here, perhaps he'd come with some interesting information.

"What the devil are you doing here, Donne?"

Donne shrugged. "I came along as part of a set. Hurley's house party, you know. I simply could not refuse the opportunity to game a bit and, of course, such charming company."

At his last words he bowed in Fia's direction, and though the movement was easy and elegant, a quality of practiced boredom robbed it of politeness and made it instead an actor's gesture, cruelly meaningless.

If possible, Fia's young, unnaturally beautiful face grew smoother; her large eyes went dark as obsidian in a black rill's bed.

Donne turned to Rhiannon, bowing again, and this time the movement was respectful, the gesture an acknowledgement rather than a caricature.

"Since Ash refuses to be civil, pray allow me to satisfy the amenities myself. Thomas Donne at your service, miss."

She lifted her face, her gaze latching on to Donne's handsome, lean visage, drawing Ash's cold consideration. She was pitifully easy to read.

In Thomas Donne's braw Scottish face she looked for a champion.

A sliver of pity touched Ash. Donne was the last man who would come to her aid. He knew little about Donne; he'd never asked, but what he did know was simple. Donne had been abroad and, in some mysterious place, had won, earned, or stolen a monstrously big fortune which he kept monstrously big by the simple expedience of not giving it away to any fool that came begging.

This apparently hadn't set well with his Highland cousins for, according to Donne, they'd long since blotted his name from the family Bible, an act that had in no way discomforted Donne. Instead, self-avowed coward and sybarite that he was, Donne simply eschewed the clan that had exiled him.

It would be a waste of time to seek an ally in Donne. Ash forced his gaze from Rhiannon. She would be living at Wanton's Blush. She'd learn soon enough that there would be no champions. Every person here had been handpicked because they possessed just exactly those characteristics that champions lacked: greed, self-interest, cowardice, insolence, and vanity.

His own sister was a prime example.

"I think Merrick has brought us a mute," Fia said. "Did you have to take her tongue to keep her from denouncing you, brother?"

This brought a swift glare from Rhiannon.

"I assure you, she is quite capable of denouncing me. Make your curtsey, Miss Russell," Ash said. "One of your Scottish baronets has introduced himself to you."

He may as well have spoken to stone, her disdain and self-containment were so complete and so completely excluded him. Excluded them all. But then, he'd stolen her from her home and family under the most feeble of pretexts. He'd taken from her her good name and her maidenhead.

And if he'd twice now sought to convince her of his honest concern, twice now she'd refused to believe him. So how could he, he asked himself as he gazed at her averted profile, who had so little experience with honesty, fail to accept the verdict of one who understood it so well?

He was done with trying to realign his nature. He *was* as corrupt as she imagined.

"She won't speak to you, Donne."

"Not yet, perhaps," Donne said thoughtfully. "But, surely, as two Scots in a house full of Englishmen, we'll find in each other's company a wee bit of comfort, eh, Miss Russell?" His offer surprised Ash.

Donne's accent, a thing he slipped on and off as comfortably as a pair of slippers, had grown pronounced. Its music drew another of those grudging glances from Rhiannon and this time the light revealed her complete exhaustion, the pale mouth and ringed eyes. She wove where she stood.

She must be near to collapsing. He needed to get her out of here. Somewhere where she could wash and sleep.

"Not yet?" Donne said and Ash could not remember ever hearing such gentle tones from his mouth. "I can wait."

"I fear you wait in vain, Lord Donne," said Fia. "Perhaps the lady is discerning in her choice of companions and simply exhibits her good taste. Would that it extended to the matter of her attire."

The chance reference to her apparel caused Rhiannon's hands to flutter hesitantly about her heavy, muddied skirts.

"It looks as though Ash dragged you from a particularly feverish hunt."

"He did." These were the first words Rhiannon had spoken. Her glance slew up and speared Fia so that the younger girl, in spite of an upbringing that should have inured her to even the most violent of glares, stepped back.

Fia looked around, disconcerted by such honest animosity. "Let me send one of the servants for your trunks."

"There are no trunks," Ash said. "She has nothing."

"Odder and odder," said Fia. "Whatever is she here for?"

"That's easy," Donne said, without looking at Fia but instead studying Rhiannon. "Carr dotes on you so, Miss Fia, that he's imported a sister with whom you might trade girlish confidences."

The thought of Fia, even though still chronologically a girl, as anything in the least childish, was absurd, and well Donne knew it. But Fia refused to be baited. Her cool, silky gaze fastened on the tall baronet. "It's only fair," she said, "seeing how he's misplaced one sibling, that he replace it with another."

The reminder of Raine's whereabouts struck Ash painfully. With an effort, he kept his expression neutral, wondering whether Fia had chosen her words to hurt him, or rebuke Donne. It was impossible to tell with Fia. She kept her own counsel so completely.

"Still, new sister or not, Carr dislikes ugliness. He'll be horrified if he sees her like this," Fia said. "She looks to be near enough my size that she might borrow a dress. If she's to meet Carr, she'll need all the confidence she can find—or borrow."

Ash hadn't thought of that. Fia was right. Appearances were of the utmost importance to Carr. Gaining his approbation might prove prudent. The question was what Fia hoped to achieve by offering her aid.

Her face was as serene as a Madonna's, her eyes wells of unfathomable darkness. After an instant consideration Ash decided it didn't matter what she wanted.

This was Wanton's Blush. Subterfuge and treachery were the games of *his* childhood, and they were compulsory. There were only two rules here: Play at one level deeper than your opponent and never forget that everyone is your opponent.

He nodded. "Give her over to Gunna," he said, naming the white-haired woman who had been Fia's nanny since toddlerhood and the only bit of warmth any of them had encountered at Wanton's Blush since their mother's death.

"Yes."

"There's no need to rush an audience," he added casually. "She can see Carr tomorrow."

"Yes," Fia agreed once more. She moved to Rhiannon's side and linked her arm through hers, calmly ignoring Rhiannon's attempt to pull free. "Please come with me. I'll order a bath and we'll find you some clothes. Something to make you feel invincible," she said, drawing Rhiannon away.

"You won't run away will you?" Ash heard Fia ask as they left.

"No," Rhiannon replied without a single backward glance. "I've nowhere to go."

CHAPTER 20

The sun was full up when Fia slipped inside of the sumptuously appointed bedchamber where Rhiannon had slept. Though the girl entered on a light, furtive step Rhiannon came fully awake at once. She kept her breathing even and opened her eyelids to mere slits, studying the girl.

Today, Fia had eschewed last night's dramatic midnight hues in favor of an exquisitely worked butter yellow dress of astounding indecency. The tight, square bodice pushed her young breasts high above the décolletage, barely maintaining modesty. Pearls draped her slender throat and dangled from her earlobes. A tiny black patch flirted with one smooth white cheek and rosy salve coated her lips.

She looked like a dressmaker's mannequin, thought Rhiannon dispassionately, a dressmaker with a demimonde clientele.

A week ago a creature as exotic as Fia would have rendered Rhiannon tongue-tied. But when one was a prisoner such matters as another's demeanor ceased to be important. Or even very interesting.

Besides, Rhiannon thought with a brittle inner smile, it was so patently apparent that Fia expected to unnerve her—and everyone else. Last night Fia had perched herself on the foot of the bed and watched as a maid stripped the filthy riding habit from Rhiannon's back. In a tender, composed voice she had recited salacious stories about Carr and Ash and another brother named Raine. When her tales failed to invoke so much as a gasp, she'd become openly disconcerted. Her smooth white brow had knit with perplexity and she'd finally left Rhiannon alone.

It was a telling point and Rhiannon re-estimated Fia's age to be much younger than she'd originally surmised. A faint memory came back to her, her uncle advising her to "know well one's enemy."

Enemy, lover. Sanctuary, prison. Home and exile.

Now that exhaustion no longer kept such notions at bay, they prowled through Rhiannon's waking thoughts, mocking her with her own culpability. She'd succumbed to Ash's potent magnetism. She'd sought his company and flirted with him, burning with curiosity over what his kiss would be like. And after discovering that, she'd still not been content. Knowledge had only fed the craving, consumed her until she'd felt she'd *needed* to know passion—*his* passion. Well, she thought, biting hard upon her inner cheeks, she now had that knowledge, too.

If only it had been a shabby, tawdry thing, an act that *felt* as sordid as she knew it to be. But it *hadn't*. It hadn't felt like lust or rank sexual appetite. It had seemed her soul's imperative. It had been . . . wondrous.

If it hadn't, she wouldn't have hated him so much now.

It wasn't only that he'd deceived her but that she'd deceived Phillip, that he'd robbed her of the opportunity to confess what she couldn't explain. And though she knew that laying such blame on Ash's door was unfair, she no longer cared.

It was unfair that Ash had ridden into her life a scant three weeks before her wedding. It was unfair that his eyes were dark, his wrists scarred, and his soul as tattered and patched as a gypsy's cape—and that she recognized the cut.

A ruthless man, Fia had said. A dangerous one. Well, the Highlands had bred a rare, pure line of that sort. Hadn't she been ruthless in getting what she wanted, never thinking past the morrow, or of where her headlong dash into pleasure would lead her? Or anyone else. She turned her cheek into her pillow, sickened with guilt. She could see again the knowledge of her betrayal in Phillip's beautiful eyes, the disappointment, the hurt— She jerked upright in bed.

Startled by the sudden movement, Fia spun around. "You're awake."

Rhiannon seized on the distraction. "Yes. I'm sure you knew that, though. Otherwise you wouldn't have come in, would you have?"

The girl tipped her head in calm agreement. "Of course."

"You wished to see me?" Rhiannon settled back against the thick bolster of pillows. *Calm. Breathe.* Yesterday she'd been a victim but today she needn't be.

"Gunna is outside. She wishes to see you."

"Gunna?" Rhiannon asked. "The nanny? Why would your nanny wish to see me and why would she need you to act as a vanguard to that fact, Miss Merrick?"

"She's brought some gowns for you to try on and I— Well, Gunna is most . . . unprepossessing. Actually quite hideous. But—" Fia hesitated. Whatever she'd been about to confide she decided against it. "She's served me faithfully. I would not want her hurt."

Fia smiled wryly at Rhiannon's obvious skepticism. "She still has her uses," she explained coldly.

"Bring her."

The young woman's eyes narrowed fractionally at the commanding tone and Rhiannon smiled. She was Rhiannon Russell and her distant cousin had been laird of McClairen. Ash had dragged her back to this place, rousing that long dormant knowledge. Let him see what he'd awakened. Whatever airs this hybrid English girl owned, she'd adopted. In Rhiannon's warrior heart five hundred years of pride and audacity churned for expression. "Now, Fia. Before I fall asleep again."

The girl smiled once more, this time an honest, rueful smile of such poignant charm and humor that in spite of every instinct that told her to beware of her, Rhiannon found herself warming toward the young girl.

Without a word, Fia drifted—there was simply no other term that adequately described Fia's modus of locomotion—toward the doorway and opened it. "Gunna!"

A moment later a bent and twisted figure in black wool crept in, a half-dozen gowns filling her arms. A mantillalike veil of black lace covered her head, pinned so that one side draped over the left portion of her face, concealing it. The open side exposed a deformed jaw, a large drooping eye, and a twisted caricature of a nose.

If poor Gunna had chosen this side of her face to present to the world, Rhiannon could only be moved to pity imagining what the rest of the veil concealed. The woman turned to Fia who hovered by her elbow in an oddly protective manner. "Jamie says yer father is looking fer you." Gunna's deep voice was thick with a Scottish accent. "Best be to him. Go on. Sooner gone; sooner back."

With a disgruntled sniff, Fia twirled and departed. The old nurse chuckled at her ward's flouncing departure before looking back at Rhiannon.

"Highlander, they said ye were, in the kitchens. What clan?" she asked, hobbling closer. Her tone was slightly brusque, the manner in which she regarded Rhiannon touched with enmity.

Rhiannon swung her feet over the sides of the bed and dropped lightly to the cold floor. "McClairen."

A flicker of surprise passed over the exposed side of Gunna's face.

"McClairen? Ye don't have the look of the McClairen. They're a black-haired breed with white skin."

Rhiannon tugged the blanket from the bed and wrapped it around her shoulders. She didn't want to be reminded of those old clan affiliations. She'd left them behind a decade ago.

Wordlessly, she moved past the old woman and went to the window. Below, a gunmetal gray sea battered the island's base.

"Forgive me, miss," she heard Gunna say. "I don't know my place and that's a fact."

Pride and coldness had replaced the woman's former grudging interest. Rhiannon felt ashamed. It wasn't Gunna's fault that she'd been brought here.

"I'm not a McClairen," she said. "My father was a chieftain in his own right but when McClairen called for men to fight in forty-five, my father answered." She closed her eyes. "And my brothers. And my uncles."

"Yer an orphan then," Gunna murmured, her manner thawing slightly. "No one left?"

"No," Rhiannon said. "They were all hunted down and murdered. Out there." She pointed at the bleak landscape outside the window. She stared at it unseeing. "Dear God, how I hate being here."

A light touch on her sleeve begged Rhiannon's attention. Gunna had moved to her side. Her hand was rough-skinned, the nails bitten down to the quick, but the long fingers were surprisingly elegant.

"Aye?"

"Of course," Rhiannon said impatiently. "Who wouldn't? This place is filled with ghosts and a bloodied lot they are."

Gunna sighed, her one eye following Rhiannon's gaze out over the sea. "I find," she said carefully, "that the ghosts that follow closest are those we've fled."

Rhiannon glanced at her and frowned. "There were no ghosts where I came from."

It wasn't strictly true, but those phantoms faded with the light. Not these. In one day she'd remembered more of her life in the Highlands than she'd thought about—or allowed herself to think about—in over ten years in Fair Badden.

The exposed corner of Gunna's mouth tucked into a smile. "Not all hauntings are hurtful."

She only meant to be kind and though Rhiannon doubted her wisdom, she appreciated her concern. "I hope so."

Gunna tugged on her arm, leading her back to the bed where she'd spread out the gowns she'd carried in. She scooped up one shimmering leaf-green damask and held it to Rhiannon's face.

"Ye'll be a beauty in this and that's a fact. Carr will be pleased." She watched Rhiannon carefully. It mattered little to Rhiannon what Carr thought of her appearance. Apparently Gunna read her lack of concern in her expression for she shook her head. "You seem a fair bit unconcerned what yer groom thinks of yer appearance."

"Groom?" she echoed dumbly, staring as the implications of that single word took hold. The woman's former disapproving attitude suddenly made sense, wringing a harsh laugh from Rhiannon. "I'm not going to marry Lord Carr."

"Truly?" Gunna asked.

"Truly," Rhiannon returned, regarding the old woman dryly.

"They say Mr. Ash brought you," Gunna said after a second's hesitation.

His name brought a flood of warmth sweeping up Rhiannon throat and face. "Yes."

"Carr's beast of burden." Both women spun around at the sound of Fia's voice. She was standing inside the door, leaning back against the panel. "Poor Ash."

Gunna ignored her charge's smooth, false tone, replying to the words rather than the timbre—a course of action that Rhiannon thought she might do well to emulate.

"Carr best have a care," Gunna said, returning the dress she held to the bed. "Methinks Lord Carr will get no more service out of that particular beastie until he gives up one of the carrots he's been danglin' in front of Mr. Ash's proud nose. Here, miss, let me take that blanket from you. We best get you dressed."

"Ash will do whatever he has to do," Fia replied, coming forward as Rhiannon complied and Gunna scuttled across the room to fetch a water pitcher and basin. "Ash would never do anything that might harm Raine."

"Raine? Carr's younger son?" Rhiannon could not help but ask. The one that was supposed to have raped the nun?

"Ye donna ken, do you, Miss Russell?" Gunna said. She dipped a soft towel into the water and rubbed it with soap and handed it to Rhiannon. "About Ash and Raine."

"No," Rhiannon said tersely, her voice muffled by the towel as she scrubbed at her face.

"It's an interestin' tale," Gunna went on. She took the dirtied towel and splashed more cold water in the basin in preparation for a cold, but much needed hip bath. Even with just her face clean Rhiannon felt better.

"And one we don't have time for right now," Fia interjected. "Carr wants her in the gallery before the hour."

"What?" Rhiannon asked, her gaze flying to the mantel clock. It was barely fifteen minutes before the hour.

Fia shrugged. "I told him I thought that would be fine."

Rhiannon looked down. She still wore the same soiled chemise she'd had on for five days. She had no time to bathe now and Fia knew it. So much for last night's concern about Rhiannon making a good impression.

But then, Fia was a Merrick. Doubtless she had her own agenda. Well, let her.

Rhiannon may have been over ten years from this land, but being reared on a Highlands battlefield produces a pupil well versed in combat —of all kinds.

At the end of another long corridor the footman finally opened a door. Rhiannon swept back the green skirts of her borrowed dress and entered.

Ash Merrick stood in the center of the room, his hands clasped behind his back, his black hair tied negligently at the nape of his neck. He regarded her watchfully. His stance was broad and challenging.

At the sight of him her breath caught. She hadn't expected him and he was so damnably beautiful. "Your father sent for me. Where is he?" She sounded angry. Better than dazzled.

"Fia said you would have an audience with Carr. And so you shall."

"I have nothing to say to you." She forced the rising note of panic from her voice. "We have nothing to say to each other."

"I miss you." His words came out low, nearly inaudible, more whispered admission than declaration.

Her head snapped up in astonishment. Whatever she'd expected it had never been that.

Admission? Lie. He was a consummate opportunist. He simply wanted an accommodating prisoner, not a difficult one. Hadn't she proven already how susceptible she was to him?

No more.

She lifted hot, angry eyes to his light, unrevealing eyes. "How unpleasant for you."

"Tit for tat, eh?" His mouth tilted mockingly. "Standard practice in my family. I should tell you, in the interest of fair play, I've vast experience with payback." The smile dissolved, replaced by an intent, hungry look. "I never meant to hurt you, Rhiannon. Use you? Yes, I admit to that. Have you? Definitely. But I never wanted you hurt."

His eyes stayed locked on hers as he strove to convince her that he told bedded me in the first place. Did the thought of a nameless orphan marrying into your English aristocracy so offend you?"

Amazingly, he laughed. "Now there's as fascinating a motive for deflowering a girl as ever I've heard."

She'd sought to shame him and instead he mocked her. Humor glinted in his dark eyes though his mouth remained hard. A mouth that had moved with exquisite tenderness over her skin, burnishing her nerves with pleasure.

"At least I've given you some plausible explanation for your actions. I have no excuse for willfully betraying my betrothed."

His nostrils flared slightly. "You don't consider lust motive enough? I assure you"—his gaze unraveled over her face, her mouth, her throat and bodice—"it's a most potent imperative."

He didn't move but she suddenly felt as though he'd surrounded her. She drew back a step. Her pulse tripped thickly in her veins. "But why bring me here then? Not for lust's sake. If forcing a woman could pleasure you, you would have forced me by now and you haven't."

Strangely, her words seemed to anger him. "I would not rely too much on such an assumption."

Once more she backed away from whatever emotion he strove so hard to suppress. His hands shivered at his sides.

"Let us say for the sake of argument that you are right," he grated out, "that I would find no ease in forcing myself on you. Now for one minute, just one, allow that I am astute enough to realize that in taking you from Fair Badden I could only secure your contempt." The very rigidity of his posture bespoke his fervor, forcing her to listen.

"Suspend your disbelief just a bit longer." He held out a supplicating hand—this man she doubted had ever been a supplicant—and confusion rippled through her resolve, shaking it.

"Say that I took you here for no other reason than the one I gave you. That I believed your life was in danger and that I suspected Watt of being responsible. If you can find no other reason for my act, could not that one, as fantastic as it might seem, be the truth?"

His voice remained firm, insistent. His eyes pleaded with her. But the notion of Phillip intentionally setting out to harm her, or that anyone could conceive him capable of such, was absurd.

"Please, Rhiannon." She'd never heard so raw a tone before. "Please."

But then, Ash did not know Phillip as well as she. He *might* mistake Phillip's nature. . . .

Her gaze raked his face, trying to see what his expression might betray.

the truth. She even half believed him. It didn't matter. In Fair Badden, soft heart would have turned to warm wax with his confession. But Highlands bred no soft hearts or weak resolves. Only those who wo fight for their survival rather than allow themselves to be used and aside had survived.

"Too late." She watched for a telltale sign that she'd pricked his h heart. "You should have gone away. I could have made some sor recompense to Phillip."

"I told you. Someone tortured that damn dog of yours on purpose She felt the color bleed from her face.

"The same someone who scarred your face with a bullet and hurled that knife at you at the Harquists' party," he went on in a biting voice.

She glared at him. "You misread Stella's accident," she insisted. " as for the other incidents? Nonsense. And well you know it."

His gaze flickered away from hers, the tiny involuntary gesture ju ing her suspicions. But instead of the vindication she might have expe she only felt hollow, emptied, and lost.

He *had* manufactured the whole story for whatever covert purpos his own. Purposes he had no intention of revealing to her.

"It's not too late," she heard herself saying in a dull voice. "You send me back to Fair Badden."

His expression tightened. He sneered.

"No matter what Watt claimed, you would have ended an outcast were lovers and Phillip knows that. He'd never accept you now."

How could he speak of it so unemotionally? But then, she remi herself, he'd only been involved in the physical act. He'd given her no of himself that he hadn't reclaimed the minute he'd left her.

"You didn't offer me any choice, did you? Or Phillip," she accused "You bludgeoned him with the knowledge of my betrayal. You lied in that, too."

His eyes clouded. "I thought I was keeping you safe. I thought to it impossible for—"

"Phillip to marry me?" Rhiannon finished coldly. "Well, as y kindly have explained, you did that."

"I thought to give him an *excuse* not to marry you."

"I still want to go back," she said, ignoring his fantastic rubbish. needn't do anything but get me to a coaching inn."

He shook his head. "There's nothing for you at Fair Badden. It's d

Her breath felt hot in her nostrils but she made herself speak in tone of coldness. "I do not know why you forced me here or why you

She moved closer, close enough to hear the ragged draw of his breath, so intent she was barely aware of a movement behind her.

A voice—cultivated, bored, and imperious—spoke. "Well, Ash, now that you've fetched her I suppose you'll want the money I promised you for your trouble."

CHAPTER 21

Ash saw the spark of uncertainty in her eyes die, snuffed out with Carr's words. She'd been searching for a reason for his actions; Carr had supplied one. Hatred of his father seethed in him. Carr's words left him nothing. Nothing but the rattail shreds of pride and Ash refused to lose those here, in front of him.

Rhiannon was lost to him. Her cold, appreciative smile flailed him with its lack of accusation. That was the worst of it. He'd done no less than what she'd expected. He'd almost duped her again.

He looked away. There was still Raine to consider. He would always have Raine.

Carr had sauntered into the room and begun a slow circle around Rhiannon, one perfectly manicured finger raised to his lips in concentration.

"Two thousand pounds, I believe," Ash said dully.

Carr ignored him, continuing his study of Rhiannon in her borrowed finery.

Fia's gown, like all the ladies' gowns at Wanton's Blush, was designed to titillate and impress, provoke and advertise. Rhiannon wore the borrowed finery with regal disdain for its provocative qualities. Layered over some sort of hoop contraption, the heavy leaf-green silk de Chine shimmered with little gold glass beads. Treble ruffles of lace were gathered at the elbows and cascaded over her forearms.

Under Carr's dispassionate stare, the faintest blush stained her slender throat and marked the upper curves of breasts uncovered by the low, square décolletage. She'd refused a wig. Her hair was coiled in a thick knot at the crown of her head.

The sight of her and of Carr studying her made Ash's mouth dry.

"What shall I do with you?" Carr murmured.

In spite of his calm tone, it struck Ash that Carr was upset. The lines fanning the corners of his eyes were pronounced as were the twin grooves bracketing his aquiline nose. His lips had thinned with discontent. Carr, whose life revolved around beauty and appearance, class and status, would never have willingly shown his ire.

He obviously regretted whatever impulse had led him to offer Ash money for his services. He must suspect how close Ash was to realizing Raine's ransom. Once Raine was out of prison Carr would be deprived of one of his more effective agents. He would hate that.

"Send me back, sir." Rhiannon's voice broke Carr's contemplation and caught him off guard.

Ash smiled. Carr was unused to young women speaking in that tone to him. It was bound to exacerbate an already foul mood, and, indeed, the lines at the corners of his mouth deepened with displeasure but then smoothed.

"My dear," he said, "you have only just arrived."

"I have no desire to be here, Lord Carr." She did not look at Ash and her voice rose as she spoke. "Indeed, I am here much against my will."

"How is that?" Carr's brows rose.

"Your son *stole* me on the eve of my wedding!"

A heartbeat's pause while Carr absorbed this, then he gasped a melodramatic, "No!"

"Yes, sir!" Rhiannon said, nodding vigorously.

A wave of pity washed over Ash and he met her triumphant gaze wearily. She thought Carr had taken her part. She thought she'd horrified him with this tale of her son's ruthless perfidy.

"The blackguard!" Carr's tone rang with indignation and he spun on his boot heels to face Ash. Immediately the horrified indignation on his face was supplanted by indifference. He saw no reason to mask his real reaction from Ash. He looked up and saw Ash regarding him.

"What do you have to say for yourself?" Carr asked in a voice rife with displeasure, but his expression was incurious.

Ash refused to defend himself. It would only amuse Carr, and Rhiannon already thought the very worst of him. "You sent me for her. Here she is. You owe me two thousand pounds."

Carr composed his face to the proper aggrieved lines and turned back to face Rhiannon. "My dear, please forgive me. Had I known you were about to wed I would, of course, never have dreamt of tearing you from your foster home. I am amazed Ash was so fervent to do my bidding. Believe me, it is most uncharacteristic."

Ash watched Rhiannon eagerly examine Carr's benign countenance; saw the instant she perceived the tiny, false note of sympathy; saw her earnestness die and distrust replace it. Carr saw it, too, and for a second his eyes narrowed as he realized she did not wholly buy his act of sorrow, that she would not be, in fact, so easily gulled.

In spite of himself Ash felt proud of her.

"Why did you send your son for me after all these years?" she asked suddenly.

"I did not know where you were until most recently and then only by chance. A man who had come to Wanton's Blush with a party of my friends, some native son of your little hamlet, mentioned your surname and I recognized it as the same as my own dear wife's cousin."

"Which wife was that?" Ash asked sardonically and was rewarded by a lethal glance from his sire.

"My second wife."

"Why would anyone mention my name?" Rhiannon asked doubtfully.

Carr held up his hands before his eyes as though framing her. "My dear . . . such modesty is most becoming if a trifle, just the merest bit, *jeune fille*."

Rhiannon colored and her gaze fell. Point for Carr. His smile was not without malice but Rhiannon, eyes still averted, did not see this.

" 'Struth," Carr said, "You are a most beauti—"

"Why did you turn me away all those years ago?" Her gaze flew up, discounting his flattery. He hadn't won her. Not at all. "We came to your front door," she went on. "My mother's old nurse and I. She had a letter, she gave it to the man there and he took it away. When he returned he refused to let us in—"

"He did?"

Ash had to credit Carr, his expression of amazement was superb, especially followed as it was by that convincing blend of indignation and sorrow.

"I . . . I had no idea! I swear on all that is sacred, until this moment I did not know you had ever come to my home." Carr moved closer to her and drew one of her hands up and between both of his, chafing it lightly. "I heard of what Cumberland was doing, of course. I knew your family would likely be punished for being dragged into taking a stance on the part of The Pretender—"

"My family *gave* their lives for him. Willingly!" Rhiannon burst out.

"They were not coerced. They committed themselves with valor and honor and pride. And James Stuart is no 'pretender'!"

Her outburst seemed to startle Rhiannon as much as Carr for as soon as the words had escaped her, she bit hard on her lips and scowled. Carr looked briefly taken aback but then, seeing Rhiannon's discomfiture and confusion, he smiled sympathetically.

"Of course, my dear. Of course," he crooned. "And after I heard that Cumberland had satisfied his depraved need for vengeance, I sent men to search for my dear wife's relatives, most especially you, my wife's ward and thus mine. Alas, they returned empty-handed." He lifted one hand and with his fingertips tilted her chin up, so that she would be forced to meet his eyes.

It took all of Ash's self-control to stand still then, but if he were to indicate by word or deed that Rhiannon meant anything more to him than the two thousand pounds Carr had promised for her, Carr would use that to his advantage. And without a doubt Carr's advantage would be Rhiannon's disadvantage. So Ash stayed where he was even though the blood thickened in his veins and pounded in his temples and his hand shivered above where the stiletto hid in the top of his boot.

"What is this?" Carr suddenly said. "What is this scar on your face?"

"Nothing." Rhiannon said, jerking her head back. "A highwayman shot at a carriage in which I rode. The bullet grazed my cheek."

"Damn the bastard!" Carr's low words vibrated with anger.

Ash stared, confounded. He knew every gesture and expression in Carr's repertoire and the darkening of his sire's throat and cheeks was beyond even Carr's thespian talents. He was truly furious.

"I escaped, my lord," Rhiannon said evenly.

"And did *he*?" Carr spat. "This . . . this *highwayman*?"

"Yes."

"Damn!" Carr bit out. "Damn him to a painful death!"

"Really, sir. I suffered no great harm." Her tone was amazed.

Carr took a deep breath, releasing it slowly. "Yes. Yes. We must accept what we cannot change. You are here now. You are safe."

"I was safe in Fair Badden." Rhiannon kept her gaze locked on Carr, as though by ignoring Ash, she could somehow make him cease to exist. "I wish to return there."

Carr scowled, released her chin, and folded his hands behind his back. "Return there? But how would that look? I mean by dusk everyone at Wanton's Blush will know you are here, that you are my ward. How would it appear if I were to shun my obligations and ship you back?"

"Returning me to Fair Badden won't be a detriment to your good name, sir."

Poor Rhiannon, Ash thought, too honest by half. She hadn't been able to keep the sneer from her voice and Carr noted it. His eyes shot to her face, glittering. Gamely she continued. "You'll be returning a bride to her fiancé."

Carr pulled thoughtfully at his lip.

"Please," she urged him.

"Well, perhaps," Carr allowed.

Ash froze. Whoever endangered Rhiannon, it was someone in Fair Badden. She couldn't go back there. She mustn't be allowed.

"Put in such a manner, one could understand."

"Exactly! You'd be righting a wrong done to an innocent girl—"

"Not so innocent," Ash drawled, careful not to make any impression of urgency. "No, I don't think that will do. You see, Miss Russell's rather precipitate exit on the eve of her wedding will doubtless give rise to all sorts of sordid speculation. I fear her reputation is quite in tatters. As for her erstwhile bridegroom"—Ash paused and shook his head sadly—"I doubt he'll have her now."

"Bastard!" Rhiannon hissed.

Carr's pale gaze flickered back and forth between Rhiannon and Ash. He moved across the room to Ash's side and leaned forward. In a voice gauged so that Rhiannon could not overhear, he whispered, "Is that the way of it? I must say, she doesn't look so very fond of you. Perhaps you lacked finesse? What say, Ash? Wasn't she very good? Or weren't you?"

It was a ploy, Ash knew, a simple gambit to discover what Rhiannon meant to him. Still, he nearly betrayed himself. He wanted to choke Carr to silence so very, very much. Instead he kept his expression blank.

"What the people of Fair Badden speculate on and what is truth—" Ash shrugged eloquently. "Surely you know how interchangeable such notions are. Ruining Miss Russell's reputation was simply a matter of expedience. You wanted her. She wouldn't go and I doubted whether her bridegroom would release her without a reason. I provided a reason. But remember, one can ruin a reputation without troubling to ruin anything else."

Rhiannon, on the other side of the room, had lifted her chin proudly.

"Ruin?" Carr, his back still to Rhiannon, snickered. "Such vanity. I'll tell you a secret: Ladies love to be *ruined* and in truth are quite peevish if you stop at their reputations. Witness Miss Russell's ire."

"What of it?" Ash asked in bored tones. "I'm more interested in my fee."

Carr's humor evaporated. He stepped back. "I'll see you're paid by day's end," he said, "then you can go wherever it is you go."

"No hurry," Ash replied, fervently pleading with a deity he no longer believed in that Carr would not send him away from Wanton's Blush—and Rhiannon. He would do whatever necessary to stay here and watch Rhiannon until he knew what Carr planned for her.

"I've seen your guests, Carr," Ash said. "Fat purse, rabid appetites. High stakes tables, I should imagine."

"You're a vile drunk, Ash. And a violent one. You could embarrass me or my guests."

Ash laughed humorlessly. "*Your* guests, Carr? Your guests would pay in gold for the titillation of my company. Their sort is so often drawn to the sordid for their entertainment."

Rhiannon flinched as though his words hurt her. Impossible. He was imagining things.

Carr considered him through narrowed eyes. "True," he finally murmured. "All right. You may stay. But for God's sake, find something decent to wear. I won't have you offending my eyes looking like that."

"Of course," Ash said.

"Now leave us," Carr said. "Miss Russell and I have much to discuss."

To hesitate now would be disastrous.

Ash walked out of the room smoothly and easily, without looking at Rhiannon.

"My dear Miss Russell," Carr said, "please be seated. Where are my manners?"

The young woman hesitated a second before taking the seat Carr had indicated and settling her dress about her. She was clearly unused to such extravagant skirts. But having no experience in society did not mean she should be underestimated. Indeed, the sharp glances he'd already received from her were indicative of a keen perception.

"Sherry, m'dear?"

She nodded, watching him doubtfully. "Please."

In his youth such suspiciousness would have presented an irresistible challenge. To succeed in seducing a woman already on her guard would have been high entertainment. He busied himself pouring two glasses of sherry.

Unfortunately he was no longer so easily diverted. Even the piquant pleasure of bedding a girl his son wanted wasn't incentive enough to woo this girl. Not that he wouldn't do it at some future point if it profited him.

He'd seen the glimmer of possessiveness in Ash's eyes. The girl might be useful in manipulating his recalcitrant eldest son. But for right now, seducing the chit wasn't necessary, and he allowed finally, his mouth flattening, he was no longer so young that the idea roused him.

Only one thing still had the same power over him that it had always had: his ambition to return in full glory to his former position in society— a position from which he'd been exiled over twenty-five years ago. But if he didn't return soon he'd be too old to enjoy his triumph.

He handed the girl her glass. She accepted it with a mumbled thanks and took a delicate sip of the sherry; a flicker of appreciation appeared in her hazel eyes. Thank God they were not sherry-colored.

As *hers* had been.

Knowing Rhiannon shared McClairen blood, even diluted by half a dozen generations, Carr had been . . . anxious that she might have the McClairen eyes. Like Janet.

Thank God, Fia did not have her mother's eyes. He didn't think he could stand it. And Ash, too, cold as his eyes were, had little of Janet in him. Only the other boy, Raine, carried his mother's stamp in feature and character.

The thought brought with it a ripple of sentimentality, and for a brief moment Carr indulged it. Some, he knew, said he had no heart. If they only knew how still, to this day, he grieved for his first wife. If they only knew the truth about Raine's incarceration, they would not slander him so.

It was his younger son's resemblance to his mother and not his father's greed, as was widely reported, that kept Carr from ransoming Raine. Well, honesty forced him to admit, perhaps Raine's usefulness in bringing Ash to heel also contributed to his continued incarceration—but *mostly* it was his resemblance to Janet.

Was not that romantic? Was that not indicative of the power of his passion, that he let his son rot in jail because the look of him was too painful to bear?

Janet would think so. She was the only one who'd ever truly understood him. He gazed out the window at the lawns spread below. All the rooms he occupied and entertained in faced front. He disliked looking out over the cliffs where Janet had fallen. Indeed, he could barely bring himself to venture into those sea-facing rooms. Once, just before the break of dawn, when all his guests slept, he'd found himself in the back library overlooking the terraced gardens. He'd thought he'd heard Janet singing, her voice soft and light—

"Sir?"

He looked around. The girl—Rhiannon—was regarding him as though she'd spoken several times.

He pulled his thoughts together. He had other matters to consider. Like this girl. This Rhiannon who might, if things did not go as they needed to go, prove troublesome.

"Your son is wrong in his estimate of my situation," she said. "I am sure Mrs. Fraiser will not deny me the home I have known for over ten years."

She waited, her body angled forward in entreaty. He steepled his fingertips before his lips, regarding her intently, thinking.

He wanted to believe her. But if Ash had destroyed the girl's reputation to return her to Fair Badden and the stigma of being used and abandoned could only be seen as an act of cruelty. The Prime Minister's letter, ostensibly written to express his condolences on the death of his third wife, had made it clear that Carr dare not be delinquent toward this or any woman.

He remembered the pertinent parts by heart:

> *His Majesty has watched in amazement and deep grief as three of his subjects, all well endowed in feature, form, and fact, have died whilst in your care, Lord Carr. There are some who have suggested to His Majesty that your series of sorrows have benefited you materially. His Majesty is wroth with such slanderous talk. He is certain that no woman shall ever again come to grief or be caused sorrow while under your care. Indeed, he is most adamant.*

He glanced at Rhiannon, doing little to disguise the dislike in his eyes. Not only could he not return her to Fair Badden, he must make certain that while she was here she enjoyed only the best of health. That meant keeping her from his guests who were apt to see her fresh innocence as part of the entertainment.

As for the other matter—that would have to wait. He had some time yet. Something would occur to him. It always did.

He slapped his hands down on the arms of the chair and pushed himself to his feet.

Rhiannon blinked at his sudden movement. "Lord Carr?"

"No, Miss Russell. I must, for your own sake, refuse you. You will stay here."

"But—"

"Perhaps later you can return to this place. I will think carefully on it, consider the ramifications of your return and the alternatives."

"Alternatives? Please!" She threw out a hand. "I don't want to stay here. I don't *belong* here!"

"Miss Russell," Carr took her hand and patted it, a gesture that seemed both awkward and unnatural, "the best I can do is to assure you, you will not be here too long."

CHAPTER 22

"**A**sh must look quite like one of the Russian *vampirs*," Fia said. As had become her custom in the nine days since Rhiannon had arrived at Wanton's Blush, Fia had arrived in Rhiannon's room just before dawn and perched herself on the edge of the bed. Rhiannon had recently vacated.

Rhiannon faced the young girl with a carefully bland expression. Fia's beautiful, still face was as cream in the half-light, her immodest, sumptuous gowns wilted by a night of carousal. Yet, fatigued though she must be, each day before retiring she appeared in Rhiannon's room to relate the evening's exploits and debauches. Too often they involved Ash.

"I have never heard the term," Rhiannon said now.

Fia's rare smile flashed and disappeared. "It's a folk legend of the Russian people. A count came to Wanton's Blush last year. He grew . . . fond of me and being uncertain whether I would be more beguiled by fairy tales or salacious palace intrigue, he amused me by alternating the two." She leaned over, a spark of mischief in her dark eyes. "I preferred the fables. The Russians are quite savages, you know."

"Yes?" Rhiannon asked. "What exactly is this *vampir* you compare your brother to?"

"A *vampir*, my dear Miss Russell," Fia instructed, sitting back, "is a dead creature that rises at night to dine on the blood of the living."

"Disgusting," Rhiannon said coldly. She shed her nightgown and drew on a chemise and petticoats. It would do no good to order Fia from the room while she dressed. She would simply ignore the order and none of the servants would dare put hand to her. Besides, Fia was the only person with whom Rhiannon spoke, Carr having abandoned her whilst he "pondered" what to do with her, and Ash, besides stalking her with his gaze, having kept his distance.

Fia shrugged. "I simply report what is told me and make the observation that Ash could be a model for these creatures."

Rhiannon hesitated. She didn't want to ask. "Why do you say that?"

"Because," Fia raised her eyes to the ornate plaster ceiling for inspiration, "because he looks like such a predator. And seeing him night after night hunt through Carr's guests, I must own he *is* a predator. Not that the ladies mind. I think any number of them would like to be mauled by my brother."

Rhiannon ignored this statement, though she had no doubt it was true. She'd seen the type of woman who visited Wanton's Blush. Rapacious, hungry. Eyeing Ash with the same expression she'd once seen in him regarding her a lifetime ago. It had thrilled her then. God help her, it still might.

"He looks . . . I don't know," Fia continued thoughtfully. "His eyes . . ." she made a circular motion in front of her own face. "They're barren, empty, as though he simply moves by instinct rather than sentient purpose. He drinks too much. He rarely eats."

Rhiannon inhaled sharply. It wasn't that she cared for him; it was just that she so hated a waste.

"He'll be a corpse in truth if he continues on his current path," Fia said glibly. "He burns from within. 'Tis quite a spectacle. You ought to come down from this tower of yours, Miss Russell, if only to witness Ash's last bright hours."

"Don't say that!" Rhiannon snapped, startling the young girl. "What sort of unnatural creature are you that you can speak so of your own brother?"

"Ach, Miss Fia, Miss Russell be right!" The reproach came from the doorway where Gunna stood. Fia turned to face her onetime nanny "Ye shouldna speak so. Miss Russell does not understand the ways of yer family."

"How could she?" Fia asked calmly, but the color was high in her smooth cheeks. "I don't understand them myself. You should have seen her, Gunna. She all but bit my head off simply because I told her what Ash was getting up to—"

"I don't wish to speak about him," Rhiannon said, trying to drive the image of Ash, burning and spent, from her mind.

"Then we won't," Gunna declared, crossing the room to the tall chest on which lay a comb and brush. "Ye'll be going for yer morning walk as usual, Miss Russell?"

"Yes," Rhiannon answered gratefully.

"Then best let me comb out that tangle. And best ye be in bed, Miss Fia," she said pointedly. "Yer lookin' none too well yerself."

This news did not hasten Fia on her way. If nothing else, the girl was wholly lacking in vanity. She cared less for her looks than anyone Rhiannon knew, and in many ways even abused her beauty.

"Go on, Fia," Gunna urged more gently. "Ye can come back and talk to Miss Russell this evening, before ye go down."

"Oh, all right," Fia agreed, dropping lightly to her feet and sliding gracefully across the room. She did not turn at the door, nor did she give any gesture of farewell when she left.

Gunna watched her go and Rhiannon studied the old woman curiously. Gunna was genuinely fond of the unnatural witchling.

"She hasn't had yer advantages, miss," Gunna murmured, her eyes still on the door through which Fia had departed. "She canna be anythin' other than what she is and that's better than anyone has the right to expect, or anyone has the imagination to see."

Immediately Rhiannon felt ashamed of her lack of charity. Who knew what she would have become had she been raised in this odd, displaced pleasure palace?

"You shame me, Gunna. It is only that Fia seems not to feel any pain for . . . another and I find that unnatural."

"She feels pain, mark me she does," Gunna muttered and then turned her one good eye on Rhiannon. "As do you, miss. Fer *his* sake."

Rhiannon shook her head in violent denial. "I would have as much care for a mad dog."

"Tenderhearted are ye?" Gunna asked and cackled. "Then ye must have learned that trick in that wee small hamlet of yours fer no Russell I knew of was ever accused of being softhearted."

"You knew the Russells well enough to have marked their character?" Rhiannon seized on the change of topic, glad of the diversion.

"A bit," Gunna replied.

Several times now Gunna had made a casual mention of Rhiannon's family, and with each remark Rhiannon found her interest sharpening. A surname would sometimes bring with it an image from her childhood: Ross of Tilbridge with his great shelf of eyebrows; Jamie Culhane, an old man with impossibly red hair; and Lady Urquardt, a thin lady whom everyone knew by her retinue of wee spaniels.

Piece by piece, Rhiannon fit together a past she'd denied and a history she'd never been told.

"My father." The words slipped unthinkingly from Rhiannon's mouth.

"What of him?" Gunna asked combing out her hair.

"Did you . . . did you know him?" She heard the caution in her own voice.

"I knew *of* him."

"What was he like?"

"A fine, decent man," Gunna said shortly, frustrating Rhiannon.

The old woman shuffled over to the chest of drawers at the foot of the bed and opened the lid. She rummaged inside a second before withdrawing a pale blue wool gown. "This may keep ye warm on yer walk, miss. Though it be cold this morning. Ye should ask Miss Fia fer a cloak to wear if ye must go traipsin' out by the sea." She gave a little shiver. "Canna see what draws ye there."

Rhiannon stood up and let Gunna slip the bodice about her and fasten the ties. "What was he like? I don't remember much of him."

"Yer father?" Gunna asked. "I thought ye dinna *want* to remember. *Any* of it. That's what ye told me the morning after ye come here and that's more than a week gone by."

"I won't be remembering," Rhiannon whispered. "I dinna . . . I mean I do not think I ever knew him enough to remember him."

Faintly now, every now and again, she could hear a trace of her mother's soft rolling burr in her own voice. It disconcerted her. She belonged in Fair Badden, not here. Yet slowly, day by day, she felt her former self slipping away and a new creature emerging to take her place, a bold creature with a Highland accent and, if Fia Merrick were to be trusted—which she was not—a direct, impervious expression.

"Oh, then that's different," Gunna said mockingly, holding out her hand to support Rhiannon as she stepped into the pooled circle of wool on the floor.

"Gunna, please," Rhiannon said as the old woman drew the skirts up and over stiff petticoats, since Rhiannon eschewed hoops.

The old woman sighed heavily. "He was an honorable man and a loyal one, Miss Russell. When the McClairen called, yer dad came forthwith and brought with him such men as he could muster."

"But what was he like?" Rhiannon urged.

"I dinna know him." Gunna shook her head.

It was no more than she'd expected. Where would an old serving woman become intimate with a minor Highland chieftain?

"Is there anyone here, anyone at Wanton's Blush who might remember him or my mother or brother? Anyone who could tell me some stories?"

Gunna shook her head. "This wasn't Russell land, dear. 'Twas Mc-Clairen."

Rhiannon caught Gunna's hand. "But my family was loyal to the Mc-Clairen. Perhaps there is a McClairen hereabouts who might have known my family?"

Gunna hesitated.

"Gunna? Please. I thought when I came here that I would be haunted by the souls of those murdered in the reprisals. But if there are ghosts here, they're a timid lot and must be lured from hiding to tell their tales."

"The McClairens are an outlawed breed, miss," Gunna said, gently pulling her hand free of Rhiannon's light clasp.

"I just want to hear the stories, Gunna." When had this become so important to her? "The stories my mother never had the chance to tell me."

Gunna stared at her a second then cleared her throat. "Will ye be walking with Mr. Donne this morning?"

Rhiannon's gaze fell in disappointment. Apparently Gunna had decided she was not to be trusted. She would have sworn that the old woman knew a McClairen or two. Well, the only way to win her trust was not to force her confidences.

"No," she said. "Not today."

Thomas Donne had made it his habit to meet her after an early breakfast and escort her on her turn about the back garden. He was handsome, urbane, and his attentions were warm with consideration. But today she wouldn't be satisfied with a walk in the seaside gardens. Today she wanted to follow the path she'd spied from the far gate, a thin line that skirted the cliff tops.

Gunna said nothing more, simply finished fastening the waistband and then pinning the embroidered stomacher in place. Finished, she stepped back and eyed Rhiannon critically. "Be careful, miss," she said. "I dislike the thought of ye bein' out there alone."

"But I won't be," Rhiannon replied, her thoughts returning to Ash in his window, vigilantly watching over her.

Rhiannon swung open the old gate and picked her way cautiously along the narrow path that followed the cliffs. She'd gone some distance before she came upon a rocky outcrop jutting over the sea. Heedless of Fia's borrowed dress and her thin shoes she scrambled atop and stood up.

The wind blew heavily here, lashing her loosened hair across her cheeks and throat and whipping the heavy skirts back up and over her petticoats. Far below, the sea crashed against the jagged teeth edging the island's shore, the subsequent fine mist shimmering in the air below. Above this, a phalanx of pure white gulls had caught the updraft from the sea and hovered, suspended just beyond her reach.

Rhiannon closed her eyes and lifted her arms, letting the gusty wind buffet her body, pretending she too might fly. A sense of homecoming enveloped her. She'd done this before! She'd stood on some high point overlooking this same sea, spread her arms, and imagined she was flying.

She shivered, but not with the near panic with which she'd looked out at the sea on her arrival here. She shivered with emotion. She'd once loved the sea. She'd forgotten—

"Step back."

Her eyes flew open at the sound of his voice and she started to spin about but her shoe heel caught in the shale and she began to slip— Strong hands snatched her up, pulled her back tightly against a hard chest.

"Dear God, what were you thinking?" Ash's voice, warm and low, swept over her ear, his lips tangling in the loose hair at her temple.

The hands gripping her upper arms did not release her. Between her shoulder blades she could feel his heart pound against her back, the muscle of his thighs press against her rump.

And, God help her, God forgive her, that's all that was needed to bring a wave of longing rushing over her with such devastating power that she nearly turned in his embrace and wrapped her arms about him.

What was she that she longed to lay beneath this man? Mad or craven or as dissolute as the women whom Fia watched pant after him?

"You mustn't!" he grated out. His voice vibrated with anger. "You can't. God, *not here*. Not anywhere!"

She started at his unexpected words, tried to break free but his grip held fast, bruising her upper arms. Abruptly she realized what he was saying. Dear Lord, he thought she'd been about to fling herself into the sea when in fact she'd been lusting after him!

A burble of hilarity escaped her and he shook her violently.

"Damn you! *Damn you,* if you think to escape me by such foul means."

She twisted but still he would not let her go, instead wheeling her violently and catching hold of her again. He grasped her chin, forcing her head up, forcing her to meet his eyes. His lips curled back over his teeth in a feral expression. "I will tie you to my bed and force food and drink down your throat and keep you there for all eternity before I will let you harm yourself."

He meant it. The violence he held in check scared her, and he'd never scared her before. Every vestige of the man who'd arrived in Fair Badden was gone, leaving this stranger with his burning eyes and punishing grip.

"I was not going to throw myself off," she said, and swallowed. "I swear it."

The fury stayed in his eyes a full minute as his gaze raked her face, searching her countenance. Slowly the fingers digging into her skin relaxed, the tautness about his mouth eased and with it her fear.

Anger took its place. He thought her so pitiful that she would kill herself rather than live here? That she was so undone by his betrayal that life no longer held any meaning for her?

God help her, she might be unable to banish the memory of his haunted, passion-filled eyes from her thoughts, or forget the soft touch of his hand caressing her, but she still owned her pride. She was still Rhiannon Russell.

"Nothing, *nothing,* you or your family could ever do to me could make me take my own life," she said in a voice quivering with ill-suppressed emotion.

He watched her intently.

"I watched my father bayoneted to death rather than give away the whereabouts of his men. I saw my uncle shot in the head still defiant even though he lay helpless on a frost-covered moor. I share their blood. How dare you think I'd kill myself over the likes of you?" she spat out.

"I beg your forgiveness," he said through stiff lips. "I should have known better."

"Yes." She raked him with her scorn. "Take your hands from me! They're filthy. I'm not one of your fascinated jades panting to discover if your embrace is as feral as your looks!"

His chin drew back sharply. He dropped his hands as if she'd scalded him and he tore his gaze from her, as though he found the sight of her painful. He looked down at the crashing sea, breathing heavily through his nostrils.

She regarded him angrily. The unkempt tangle of the black hair falling down his lean cheeks and beard-darkened jaw was dull and lank. Mauve stains marked his eyes, and an old bruise colored one brow.

She was about to look away when she discerned the faintest tremor in his hands hanging loose at his sides. She looked back up at his averted profile, studying it closer.

She saw now that his pallor hadn't been unhealthily white, the blood had literally drained from his face. She knew this because the hue was slowly returning. His lips were still chalky and the manner in which he held himself suggested a sudden overpowering enervation, not anger. My

God, she realized with a sense of discovery, of wonder—he'd been afraid. Not merely afraid. Terrified. For her sake.

Confusion churned her emotions into an unrecognizable brew. She wanted to touch him, to smooth the fine lines from his forehead and the corners of his eyes. She wanted to shout at him and rail against what he'd done to her—to them.

She did neither. She drew back and had begun to move past him when she saw the long length of material on the rock behind him, a plaid woven in rich heather, gold, and emerald greens. She frowned and picked it up, turning to regard him askance, and found he was already watching her.

"What is this?" she asked.

A corner of his mouth turned up in mockery. "Gunna said you'd come out without a cloak. I'll not have you dead by any means, Rhiannon. Not by your hand or nature's ministrations. That's the McClairen plaid."

She stared down at it. He confounded her. She did not know what to expect from him next.

"Why?" she breathed.

"Gunna said as you'd been asking after your family. Your family's history and my mother's were interwoven." His voice was flat. "Take it. But don't let Carr see it. Any token of the McClairens enrages him."

With so few words he gave her a piece of her history, a piece of her past. Emotion clotted her throat. He could not know how important this was to her, how much it meant, and yet she could not rid herself of the notion that he *did* know. She carefully draped the tartan around her like a precious relic.

"Thank you." She touched his arm in a spontaneous gesture of gratitude. His lips curled derisively.

"Don't thank me. It's not but an old rag. And don't come out here again." His gaze shifted down toward the boulders at the cliff's base. A little tick jumped in his cheek. "It isn't safe."

Before she could reply, he brushed passed her and strode away. He did not look back.

Ash heard Carr speaking in the hall just outside the door. Quickly he shrugged out of his jacket and pulled his shirt free of his breeches. He flung himself into one of the gothic chairs that stood beside Carr's desk.

He would never have dared entered his father's office at all had he not noticed Carr leaving the gaming table in the adjoining room via the hall. The office door had remained unlocked.

Rifling through Carr's desk had been a risky venture, but since Ash's arrival it had been his first opportunity to discover the reason behind Carr's interest in Rhiannon Russell.

Now, when Carr opened the door, he would find Ash sprawled in one of his prize imports, his leg draped over the arm, his head lolling forward on his chest, his arm hanging bonelessly by his side, and his hand brushing the neck of a half-emptied wine bottle. The cool draft of an opening door filtered over Ash's hands. He strained his ears and heard the candles lighting the orderly surface of Carr's desk sputter irritably.

Ash opened his eyes to slits, taking the chance that it would be a few seconds before Carr's eyes could adjust to the dim light. Carr's gaze darted about the room, falling on the position of the few papers on his desk, the surface of the drawers, and flicking, for just one telling instant, over the mantelpiece.

So, that was where Carr kept his treasures. The rigidity in his father's body eased, he turned his attention to Ash.

"What are you doing in here, Merrick?" Carr asked, his voice pitched low, testing.

Ash sighed deeply.

"Merrick!"

"Humph?" Ash grunted. "Say, what? Did I win then?"

"What are you doing in here?" Carr again demanded.

Ash peered woozily up at his sire as if he could not quite remember the name that went with the face. He pushed himself up a ways in the chair, grimacing, and looked around the room. "Ain't this the privy?"

"What?" Carr thundered.

Ash let an expression of confusion become dawning comprehension and finally drunken hilarity.

"Damme, sir," he sobbed through his laughter, "I *am* sorry. Bit foxed, you know. Had to leave the fellows midgame. Methinks I thought this chair was the privy! Sat on a few in London, don't you know." He leaned over and examined the baroque carved legs of the chair. "I swear I've never seen a more likely candidate."

Carr's face turned ruddy with rage. "You swine! I had that chair shipped here from a Moroccan seraglio! If you've soiled it I'll—"

He grabbed Ash's arm, hauling him to his feet. Ash made himself hang loose in his father's vicious grip. He grinned foolishly. "Nah. Think I fell asleep first."

With a sound of disgust Carr shoved Ash away. Ash fell back heavily in the chair. The suspicion evaporated from Carr's face, leaving it blank as a reptile's.

And why should he be suspicious? Ash asked himself. He'd spent nearly two weeks convincing Carr he'd plumbed new depths of depravity—would take any bet, do anything to earn the sum needed for Raine's release. A glimpse in any mirror revealed a gray complexion and eyes red-rimmed with lack of sleep. Where other men scented their bodies with perfumes and powders, Ash anointed himself with stale beer and sweat.

"You're filthy with drink again, Merrick," Carr said. "Though I appreciate your efforts. I've acquired quite a tidy sum betting on just how many bottles you'll upend before passing out each evening."

"Care to split the winnings?" Ash asked cheekily. "No? Didn't think so." He fidgeted in his seat. "For a chair that ain't a privy chair, this is deuced uncomfortable."

"It's invaluable."

"Doubt that," Ash replied flatly. "I'd wager you can set a very exact price on it." He wrapped his arm over the back of the chair and hung his weight from it. "New, isn't it? Lots of new geegaws in the family manse—not our family manse, I realize, but who's to know?"

"I'm remodeling," Carr said coolly. "You never did understand what I was trying to do here. How could you?"

He wandered behind Ash's seat, his fingers caressing the back of the chair. "I need beauty like you need drink, Merrick. Life is a simple process of animal adaptation but Art is a controlled mutation that only a connoisseur is qualified to direct. . . ."

Ash had heard the speech before. Once launched into his discourse, little would stem Carr's flow of words. Ash kept his gaze fixed on Carr's face but allowed his thoughts to uncoil along their own path.

He'd had little time to rifle through Carr's desk. He'd scanned through his ledger discovering in the neatly penned columns two things: First, the refurbishment of Wanton's Blush was costing Carr far more money than he owned. Second, a large sum of unidentified origins was deposited quarterly in Carr's accounts.

As for the letters, Carr's communiqués had proven uninteresting if often sordid. Pleas for extension on debts outnumbered anglings for invitations to Wanton's Blush. Interspersed amongst these were detailed plans for plaster ceilings and marble friezes; bids and specifications from architects, artisans, and garden designers; payment demands from marble cutters and weavers.

Only one note had caught Ash's attention, a terse missive from one of his father's many victim-cum-debtors, none other than Lord Tunbridge. Of the pierced hand. After begging for a few more months in which to make good his debt, Tunbridge had closed his note: "I shall do all that I can to convince His Majesty that you are indeed reformed. This may take time and whilst I am engaged on your behalf, I adjure you to be in all matters circumspect."

Unfortunately, before Ash had had time to look for other letters carrying Tunbridge's seal, he'd heard Carr.

"—Donne might take her off my hands."

Ash's head snapped up before he could control the movement. His father's gaze was waiting. Carr smiled obliquely.

Ash swiped up the bottle of wine and took a long draught to mask his reaction. "Take who? Fia?"

He knew Carr was not speaking of Fia but of Rhiannon. She plagued his dreams and subverted his reason. Even whilst sunk in the deepest of carouses, he found himself reliving the moment when Carr had told her that Ash had been paid to bring her to Wanton's Blush. He saw again the frail promise of her trust shatter and become bitter cynicism; and when he was not drunk, he could not escape the contempt in her voice, telling him he was filthy and feral.

But most haunting of all was that moment on the cliffs when pitiful gratitude for his mother's torn tartan had overcome her natural, her so well-justified, revulsion and she'd whispered thank you and touched his arm. He still felt that touch as distinctly as if his flesh had been branded.

Like a fever that would not break, she lived in him, destroying his resolve and making mock of his intentions. He should be focused on winning enough money to ransom his brother. But he was in here, looking for clues as to why Carr had sent him to fetch her.

"Not Fia. My new ward."

"Donne has offered for Rhiannon Russell?" Ash mumbled, holding his wine bottle up and eyeing the three fingers of liquor disconsolately.

"Not yet," Carr answered. "But he dogs the girl's footsteps, or so I'm told. Weren't you?"

No, he wasn't and he should have been told. He'd paid well for information about Rhiannon Russell and he'd received detailed reports for his coin: what hour she woke, what gown she wore, what book she read. But not that Donne courted her. Ash shrugged noncommittally.

"Why do you want to get rid of Rhiannon Russell?" Ash asked as if just struck by the thought. "You just gave me a fat purse for bringing her here. Don't make sense."

"One can't be too forward-looking," Carr pronounced silkily. "I'm simply ascertaining my options."

"You've never so much as written the first word in a letter without already having planned the last line," Ash said. "So what I'm asking myself, is what you planned when you sent me for Rhiannon Russell?"

Carr's gaze met his. "Busy thinking, Merrick? Why is that?"

But Ash had found a dint in Carr's skin. He knew Carr's tactics; he would not be diverted by his questions. "What do you want with Rhiannon Russell?" He pressed the slight advantage.

Carr casually took a seat, settling and smoothing the satin cloth of his breeches before answering. "I really didn't know where she was until now," he explained in bored tones. "A man mentioned her name and said she lived in his village. I recognized it and asked him about her. It became clear she was the girl my valet had turned away from my London town house years ago."

Ash laughed nastily. "Don't try to tell me your conscience had been pricking you over her loss."

"Of course not," Carr said with a flash of annoyance. "I was *told* she was comely. I *knew* she was the last of a once wealthy family. I *assumed* that as such she would be heir to whatever trinkets and coin they had managed to hold. I gambled 'twas so."

"So simple?" Ash took another swig of wine. "Fascinating. Pray continue."

"The rest is, in hindsight, sloppy. But in my own defense remember I felt compelled by some urgency. Hoping to prevent some provincial boy from securing her inheritance by marrying the chit, I sent you for her. And, Merrick"—he looked up from the rings bedecking his pale hands— "had circumstances been different and Miss Russell an heiress, in fact, I would have been extremely upset had you returned with the news that she'd wed."

But Ash was more interested in how much Carr had divulged. Too much. Carr never explained anything to anyone. How much was lies and how much simple misdirection?"

"Alas," said Carr, "the girl doesn't own a thing. She's utterly a pauper. As I'm sure you know."

"Yes." Ash wiped the wine from his mouth with his sleeve. "Who did you say told you she was in Fair Badden?"

"I didn't. But since you ask, it was some blond Goliath named Watt. He came here with his fellow rurals in order to taste society." Carr smiled serenely. "They were quite surprised at the cost."

Watt? Ash remembered St. John saying he'd met Carr but no one had ever mentioned Watt being here. Certainly not Watt. Why the oversight?

"My turn," Carr said. "I find your interest in this girl inexplicable."

Ash was ready. "Not so inexplicable," he said. "I need money. I thought she had some. Put some effort into makin' meself pleasant, you know. Hate to see it go to waste."

"You *did* seduce her."

Ash waved his hand. "No. Though she might well think she's been seduced. You know how these sheltered little virgins are. You fumble 'neath their skirts a minute and they think they've been done."

"Indeed. Well, if Thomas Donne is overcome with patriotic fervor and decides to offer for the wench, I'm sure he'll appreciate your restraint." Carr's gaze lay carefully on Ash's face.

Donne's hand moving over Rhiannon's silken flesh. Her mouth opening beneath his. Her long, smooth thighs wrapped tight—

"That would be bloody convenient, wouldn't it?" Somehow Ash managed to smile disinterestedly.

"How long is it you're planning on staying at Wanton's Blush, Merrick?"

A vise tightened about Ash's throat. Carr *couldn't* send him away. He shrugged. "Don't know. Why? You can't spare the room?"

"The room yes but you've been winning more than losing and at *my* guests expense."

Ash snorted. "Didn't mean to encroach on your feeding grounds."

"But you have," Carr said. "I'm afraid I don't see any real advantage in having you here after all."

"I don't have anywhere to go," Ash said sullenly.

"If you'd like to remain here you'd best make yourself not only useful but lucrative," Carr said. "To me."

For a second, Ash held his father's gaze, clear gemlike blue eyes meeting cool, unfathomable dark ones. The orders were clear.

"Oh, I think I might be able to amuse you—*and* enrich you." With that Ash let his head fall back against the chair and his eyes drift shut.

"Make sure you do," Carr said.

Ash did not respond, playing the sulky mute. Five minutes passed before he heard Carr's footsteps retreating across the room. The door opened and shut.

He opened his eyes and pushed himself wearily to his feet. His head felt thick, his tongue dry, and his belly rebelled against too many days with too much wine and too little food. The sticky sheen of sleeplessness coated his skin, and he stank. He was burning himself out.

He should walk away. But he wouldn't. God help him, he couldn't leave her here. And the great jest of it was that staying would earn him nothing. Not even her smile. To her he was less than human. A rutting, sotted animal. Carr would never allow him to stay at Wanton's Blush if he weren't thus. As long as Ash appeared bestial and seemingly drunk, he was tolerated. Carr would never feel safe otherwise.

He longed to tell Rhiannon this but he dared not. She was too ingenuous, too candid. She didn't yet understand the layers upon layers of deception that were part of life at Wanton's Blush. Besides, she would never believe him. Carr was handsome, charming, and attentive.

Ash . . . Ash was the monster.

It was the price he paid to stay here with her. And as long as he did not have to witness her abhorrence, it was a price he was willing to pay. With that comfortless thought, Ash staggered to the door leading to the foyer and wrenched it open, blinking like some subterranean creature into the brilliant sunlight. He stretched out his hand, groping for the support of the wall.

It was then he saw her. The sunlight affixed itself to her smooth skin, shimmered in her hair, molded a warm shadow beneath the fullness of her lip, and picked out with exquisite detail the contents of her expression. Disgust. Pity. Revulsion.

It was too much.

"You," he rasped out. "Get out of here. Now!"

CHAPTER 23

"Up with you, you great stanking hound!"

Ash rolled over on the mattress, groped for some missile to hurl, and finding none, snarled, "Get out, Gunna! Your tender ministrations are not needed!"

The door slammed shut. Ash winced at the reverberating echo in his head. Good. He only wanted to be left alone. He'd stood just about all he was willing to stand—

A surprisingly strong hand grabbed a hank of his hair and jerked his head back. "Damme, witch! Are you seeking to tear my head off?" he gasped.

"I dunna want it," Gunna spat in disgust. "Many more days on yore present course and yer head will be so far pickled it'll be useful only as garnish. Ha!" She cackled.

"You're a witch, Gunna."

"Aye, and you're a knave. What are ye thinkin', Mr. Ash? Destroyin' yerself like this isn't going to win the lassie's good opinion."

Ash went still. Gunna had always had uncanny insight into his mind and motives.

"I don't want her good opinion."

He heard Gunna click her tongue. "Her heart then, lad. And dunna bother to contest that, 'cause I'll not believe a word of any denial."

"You're getting cursed mawkish in your old age, Gunna." His ire had spent itself, leaving only overwhelming weariness. He smiled slightly.

"Though you always did insist on finding the good in a thing. Surprising since you've spent so many years in his employ."

"He's not all bad," Gunna said and then added with the flat practicality that Ash had so needed during his early years, "though I'll allow he's *mostly* bad."

He laughed weakly. Gunna regarded him with something like fondness. "You'll do, Mr. Ash, if you'll just give yerself a fair chance. You're strong and hard, hot-forged and bright shining like that dirk ye carry. A passionate man. But there's no shame in that."

Her words eviscerated his laughter. "God! Look at me; think back on what you know me to have done. I am *not* 'bright shining'!"

"Aye, ye are, Ash," Gunna said softly, and touched her hand to the back of his head.

In reply he moaned.

"You probably think Raine a saint, too."

"*Too?*" Gunna echoed. "I dunna recall naming you 'saint,' Ash Merrick. Far from it. And no I dunna think Mr. Raine a saint. He's just reckless is all, as willing to let his emotions sweep him away as you are to keep yours hidden."

"Raine is a devil." He craned his head around and peered up at Gunna. She stood primly at the foot of his bed, her hands folded neatly at her waist, the ravaged side of her face composed. "If one pledges one's life to protecting a devil," he queried interestedly, "what does that make one? A demon?"

Gunna ignored him. "It's Miss Fia I fret most about. She's so vulnerable."

Ash rolled fully over. "Don't waste your time worrying about Fia. She's as self-possessed a little mannequin as ever I've seen. In a contest pitting my little sister against the world, I'd wager on Fia and give the world a ten-point lead. Carr dotes on her."

"Aye," Gunna murmured. "She's yet to see him for what he is. When she does, I fear what it will do to her."

"Give her a newfound appreciation of sin, I suspect."

Gunna's lopsided mouth creased in lines of disapproval. Though it was hard to gauge expression on that ruined mien, he'd long ago learned to read it in her eyes. He'd hurt her. She cared for Fia, honestly and deeply. Sometimes, however, a kind heart saw only what it expected to see.

"You might ask Rhiannon Russell about perception and reality," he muttered, flinging his arm over his eyes.

"Might I?" Gunna padded closer to the bed. "What did you do to her, Mr. Ash, that has you in such pain?"

Why bother to deny it? Gunna would only ignore any protestations to the contrary.

"Oh, destroyed a few of her illusions," he said. "You know, seduced her then trumped up some fantasy about her groom trying to kill her. Abducted her on the eve of her wedding. Dragged her here." He shrugged. "That sort of thing."

"Mr. Ash."

"Quite the bright-shining blade, aren't I, Gunna?" he asked calmly. He was not surprised when he heard her shuffling step carry her from the room.

"Come, lass. There's naught for it but to obey. Carr's made an edict and you'd best not cross him," Gunna said.

"I don't want to meet his guests," Rhiannon said, shaking her head.

It was late afternoon and Rhiannon had spent the day wandering through the seaward-facing bedchambers on the third floor. Most of them were unoccupied, draped in cobwebs and sheets.

Gunna had found her there, in the oldest part of the castle, a turreted tower that had been untouched during Carr's renovations. The walls were bare and the floor uncovered, but the cushioned window seat was soft and dry and the sunlight warmed Rhiannon's skin.

"Ye canna to hide up here forever, lassie," Gunna said gently.

"I'm not hiding," Rhiannon protested, knowing full well that she was. She could not see Ash again. Not as she'd last seen him. "Why should I hide?" she added weakly.

"There's been some idle gossip about the servants' hall."

"Really? And what do these gossips say?"

"You don't want to know it." Gunna took her hand and tried to pull her up. "Idle blather. I should know better than to open me mouth and spout such."

Rhiannon remained seated. Outside the sun sparkled on the sea. "I should like to know."

The sunken, drooping eye exposed by the draping of her veil regarded her cautiously. Rhiannon had the distinct impression the old Scotswoman was deferring judgment.

"They says in the servants' hall," the old woman finally began, "that Mr. Ash did ruin you and that's why ye'll have naught to do with him and that's why ye keep here by yerself. For fear of him."

Rhiannon drew back from Gunna's hold. They all knew. They all knew so much and so little.

"Others, however," Gunna continued carefully, "says yore breaking yer heart over him. I don't mean to be forward, miss, but I know how it can be. My sainted sister loved a man who broke her heart. He took from her everything a woman can offer and then he cast her aside. Is that what Ash Merrick has done to you?"

Rhiannon stared at her. Gunna's sister and she shared similar histories, but the man who'd used Rhiannon had not abandoned her. He'd done worse; he'd stolen her—and her heart.

With a start Rhiannon realized how much she wanted to confide in Gunna. She missed Edith so very much. Even though she'd never fretted Edith with her problems, her beloved foster mother had comforted Rhiannon just with her presence. Rhiannon glanced at Gunna. It had been long years since she'd confided in anyone. Ash alone had been the closest to breaching the high walls she'd built to keep others out and herself safe from her past.

"Did he, dearie?" Gunna repeated softly.

Perhaps it was time.

"If by 'ruin' you mean physically force me," Rhiannon said slowly, "no. He disguised his true nature, though, and I would not see past his beauty to his treachery. I betrayed myself."

Gunna's deeply lined forehead furrowed. "You could not . . . forgive him, of course."

"He doesn't *ask* for my forgiveness," she replied. "He'd do the same again. He told me so."

"Would *you*?" Gunna asked. "Would you be deceived a second time?"

Rhiannon stared at her hands, fingers lacing and unlacing, unable to answer. Would she? She'd like to have said "no, of course not," but her tenacious core of honesty did not allow equivocation.

The truth was she was deceived every time she looked at him. She still felt the pull of his attraction, the overwhelming lure of his masculinity.

"Do you love him?" A query so hushed it might have been Rhiannon's own heart asking the question.

"I don't *know* him. He fascinated me. But he was not what I thought." Was she telling Gunna or reminding herself? Gunna tugged on her hand and she stood up.

Leaning on Rhiannon's arm, Gunna began tottering toward the steep tower steps. "How's that?"

"He's cruel. And ruthless. He obtains what he wants and he wanted me. For one night."

Gunna began a cautious decent, leading Rhiannon. Her eyes stayed fixed on the stairs but after a moment she said, "I been here many years, lassie, and I dunna claim to know Ash Merrick well. He was more man than boy when I came to take care of Lady Fia, but while I might allow that he's ruthless, it's in my mind that that's what he's had to be. If he's ever wanted something, I have never seen him admit to it. He'd never give Lord Carr that sort of advantage. Carr already has too many ways to bend Mr. Ash to his will."

"Why?" she asked, trying hard to understand this man who'd so much power over her.

Gunna paused at the landing. "Carr's guests talk. They say that Ash Merrick is the best gambler in Scotland, England, or anywhere in between. And you must ken that Mr. Ash knows how to use that blade he carries. People are afraid of Mr. Ash.

"Now, lassie, wouldna such a man be useful to whisper a threat into an enemy's ear? Or issue a challenge? Or do any bit of a deed in London that Carr cannot because he's been made to live here?"

Despite the heat in the narrow spiraling stairwell, Rhiannon shivered. "I knew Ash was ruthless. I did not name him evil."

"Evil?" Gunna's lopsided mouth twined. "Mr. Ash isn't evil. Think on him as a fine Spanish blade and having about as much choice in where its owner plunges it."

"Carr."

"Aye," Gunna agreed. "And Carr would not like to lose that particular weapon."

Yes. She could see Ash as a weapon. Yesterday, storms blowing in from the ocean had kept her indoors. She'd been coming down the stairs to the main level searching for some way to occupy her time when a door had swung open.

Ash had reeled through it. He wore neither waistcoat nor jacket. His shirt was open halfway down his chest. A soiled stock fell like a noose about his neck.

He'd lifted his head, squinting against the weak light. His black hair fell across his soot-fringed eyes. He stumbled forward and only saved himself from falling by bracing his hand against the wall.

Then he'd seen her. His eyes had narrowed as though he had trouble focusing them and she realized he was drunk, debilitatingly drunk. "You," he'd said hoarsely. "Get out of here. Now!"

She'd needed no further encouragement. She'd fled like a hind from the hounds but she hadn't been able to flee the image of him. Yet she found herself deliberately thinking back over those few moments, just so she could evoke them.

"Best hurry, lass," Gunna said.

They'd come to the landing on the floor where her rooms were located. Impulsively, Gunna smoothed her hand down Rhiannon's cheek. Rhiannon flushed, deeply moved. "You're too good a listener, Gunna," she said.

"And you're too good a mute," Gunna murmured. "Now, Carr wants you and that's nothing to take lightly. Especially as his valet says he's been in a vexatious mood these past few days."

Rhiannon smiled ruefully. "I doubt Carr has even noted my absence."

"I would not count on that," Gunna said, opening the door to the stairwell and leading Rhiannon out into the wide, sunlit corridor. "Carr must fair dote on a beauty like you. What is it he plans for you, do you think, lassie?"

"I don't know," Rhiannon replied honestly. "I haven't spoken with him since my arrival."

"Ha!" Gunna straightened, her one exposed brow lifting in surprise. "Carr's not bothered with you at all?"

"Not a word."

"There's a wonder," Gunna murmured. "Why is Carr wanting you to be present today of all days?" She worried the slack portion of her lip with her teeth as she shuffled quickly toward Rhiannon's room. "Why would he want you to see Ash Merrick in such a state? Or maybe it's Mr. Ash he's wanting to do the seeing—"

"What are you talking about?" Rhiannon asked, scurrying to keep up with her.

The single eye gleamed with inspiration. "Carr might be using you to regain the use of his . . . Spanish blade. He knows Mr. Ash is taken with ye."

Rhiannon's curiosity faded. The old woman was a romantic after all, building fairy tales. Rhiannon would not make that same mistake. "Ash doesn't love me."

Gunna spared her a brusque glance. "Fa! He would'na lay with you lest he had feelings for ye, lassie."

An image of Ash's face stark with longing filled Rhiannon's mind's eye. Beltaine night. What she remembered may not have existed at all. She shook her head, willing it away. "He takes whatever appeals to him."

Gunna pulled her along. "He doesn't bed any of the ladies here. Last night Mrs. Quinton give me the key to her chambers to slip in Mr. Ash's hand, and he slipped it right back," she said impatiently. "There's somethin' in ye calls to him and I'm thinkin' he may not like it any more than ye."

Rhiannon *would not* let it happen again. And yet . . . God help her. "Why are you so sure he wasn't simply dallying with me?"

Gunna looked at her in patent disgust. "That's easy enough," she said. "Ash Merrick hates his father. He would never use a woman for mere sport if for no other reason than that his father would."

CHAPTER 24

The crowd gathering in the great hall for the midday entertainment vibrated with excitement. Titters of excited laughter rose from behind the agitated flutter of fans. The novelty of rising early these past few days still fascinated this jaded group. Besides, when the spectacle ended, nothing prevented them from returning to their beds, which they often did.

Thomas Donne stood near the bottom of the marble staircase and glanced up to where a flash of bronze satin on the landing high above had caught his eye.

So the Scottish fledgling had escaped her gilt cage, he thought. Perhaps when Carr's guests moved to the stable yard, she would descend, but not until then. She was as leery of human contact as a kestrel. Donne could not fault her. She was out of place in this cesspool.

After a second's hesitation, Donne stationed himself at the foot of the stairs and waited, vexed by his unlikely concern.

Rhiannon Russell touched his heart, and Thomas Donne thought he'd long since mastered every bit of that organ. But her wild, fragile beauty and that loose, easy stride of hers recalled other girls with auburn hair and free-moving grace. Even all those English manners some matron had imposed on her could not mask her direct gaze or canny nature.

He'd forgotten how differently the Scottish raise their lassies. There was no falseness in Rhiannon. One got the notion that she saw every deceit a man perpetuated on others . . . and on himself. It was a compelling sensation and an unsettling one. He knew better than to rhapsodize over the past.

But in Rhiannon Russell he saw the best of Scotland. He looked at her and recalled brae heirs and valiant sons, killed or imprisoned or sent off to rot in England's penal colonies. Aye, looking at Rhiannon Russell was a bittersweet endeavor but one he could not deny himself.

A week ago he'd discovered that she woke early and moved about the castle freely while the rest of Carr's guests slept. Since he seldom found peace in slumber and even less here at Wanton's Blush, he'd made it a habit to seek her company.

She didn't seem to mind. Over the course of those short hours he'd discovered Rhiannon had other traits besides beauty and honesty. Each day she seemed to gain more of a singular strength, the sort of strength that comes from abandoning oneself to fate, of moving past fear. It was a characteristic with which he was well acquainted. He and Rhiannon Russell had much in common.

He leaned back against the newel and scanned the thinning company. Beneath their piled wigs, their faces were slack with witless hunger and numb desire. If he had a jot of red blood in his veins, he would take Rhiannon out of here this very night. No one would miss her until dawn. During the evenings she kept to herself and Carr never asked after her . . . Carr. Aye. That was the danger and the enigma.

Donne was not the only one who thought so. Several times, when the revelries had wound to a temporary end, Ash Merrick had sobered up and sought Donne out. Ash belabored Donne on every point he'd discovered about the Russell family and Rhiannon's hypothetical brother. Despite his penchant for debauchery—and just lately his wholehearted pursuit of it—Merrick still owned a subtle intelligence.

The reminder killed Donne's urge to chivalry. No one would notice if he took Rhiannon Russell—no one except Ash Merrick. A ruthless sort of gentleman, one a wise man would not lightly cross.

And Thomas Donne was a most wise man.

"Do you still pine for your bucolic home?" Fia looked over Rhiannon's shoulder and met her reflected gaze in the mirror.

"Yes," Rhiannon replied. "I miss Fair Badden very much."

Fia's heavy eyelids sank over her dark eyes. "Well, darling, you don't seem to be wasting away from the effects. You're in blooming good looks."

Rhiannon finished twisting her hair into a knot atop her head and pushed herself away from the dressing table. "Thank you. I think."

"Why is that, do you suppose?" Fia asked silkily. "Do you suppose you were not as happy at Fair Badden as you claim? Or perhaps your heart was never as fully engaged as you thought?"

The little witch, Rhiannon thought with a sharp glance at the girl. Her expression softened when she saw that her glare had disconcerted the girl. That was the trouble with Fia; innocence and jaded knowledge inexorably twined together to form her character.

Most of the time Rhiannon couldn't decide whether Fia's questions were deliberately provocative and biting or astoundingly innocent and honest. And perhaps she was angered with Fia because Fia was in some small way right.

"I do not doubt, Miss Fia, that I loved well Mrs. Fraiser. Every day I think of her and miss her very much and hope that she does not grieve for me or worry." Fia was watching her fiercely, her brows puckered uncharacteristically in concentration.

"But, perhaps," Rhiannon went on, "Fair Badden does not hold the place in my heart I thought it did. Perhaps no place is anything more than what memory and experience make it."

The girl held Rhiannon's gaze for one long moment before Fia nodded shortly. "You should write a letter to your Mrs. Fraiser."

"I can do that?" Rhiannon asked in surprise.

"Of course," Fia said coolly. "This isn't Bedlam, Miss Russell, it's a castle. We do have servants for that sort of thing. Write her a letter—she can read? Good, and I'll have it delivered."

Nonplussed by Fia's detached magnanimity, Rhiannon rose to her feet and smiled tentatively. "Thank you . . . I will. Your kindness—"

"You really should let Gunna fit you with a wig. With your eye color a pale silver would be astonishing." Rhiannon quelled the impulse to smile. Fia was as disconcerted by having made the offer as Rhiannon had been on hearing it and she was seeking to cover her awkwardness. The least Rhiannon could do was to help her out.

"I dislike wigs," Rhiannon said. "Nits."

"I don't have lice!" Fia cried.

Rhiannon raised her brows. "Of course not."

Fia frowned. "We'd best be going. Have you finished? No powder, either? No beauty mark?"

"No." Rhiannon swept past the girl and through the door, smiling when she heard the trip of Fia's feet hastening to catch up. She was a tiny thing.

"Carr won't like your dress," Fia warned breathlessly on making Rhiannon's side. She eyed Rhiannon's gown as they began descending the stairs. "Too *jeune fille.*"

Rhiannon was unconcerned with Carr's sartorial approval. Ash Merrick and Fia's curiosity about her family in Fair Badden occupied her thoughts. "You have another brother, do you not?"

"Yes. Raine. He's a few years younger than Ash. Big, rough-looking fellow."

"I don't believe I've met him."

"Well, darling, you wouldn't lest you'd been loitering about French prison yards," Fia said complacently.

Rhiannon halted. "Prison?"

Fia sighed and stopped also. "Yes. I thought you knew. I thought everyone knew. Ash was imprisoned, too. Until Carr ransomed him almost a year ago."

Prison bracelets. The scars he wore were from manacles. "What— But why—"

Fia *tch*ed gently. "Carr does not tolerate stuttering."

"Why were your brothers imprisoned in France?"

Fia shrugged with elegant unconcern. "My mother was Scottish, you know. She was quite the little Jacobite loyalist, I'm told. She sought to involve Carr in her dramas. Carr played along with her."

Did it not occur to the girl that she was Scottish, too? Rhiannon wondered.

"Her relatives eventually proved valuable during the rebellion of forty-five. Carr furnished the Duke of Cumberland with information he'd acquired through them. In return, Wanton's Blush was given to Carr."

Rhiannon barely heard the last part. *Cumberland*. The Butcher of Culloden. The floor dipped beneath her feet. She looked up, light-headed, and found Fia's lovely gaze fastened on her in puzzlement.

"Go on," Rhiannon said faintly.

"After Culloden, those of my mother's relatives still living discovered Carr's true allegiance."

His treachery, thought Rhiannon.

"They plotted to ambush and kill him. Only they caught my brothers instead." Fia's slight, childish shoulders lifted in a dismissive shrug. "Their captors didn't know what to do with them. For probably the only time in their lives my brothers had cause to bless their Scottish blood.

"For valueless as my mother had been to her relatives, they were a loyal lot. They disliked the thought of killing her sons. So, they handed them over to their French allies to be used as hostages, thinking they would break Carr's back financially. Within days of their capture Ash and Raine were in a French gaol. The conspirators were, by the way, soon after rounded up and dispatched."

"Why is Raine still in prison?" Rhiannon asked in bewilderment. "Your clothes, the jewels, the food, this place . . . surely Carr can afford to ransom him?"

"He didn't try." Fia's elegant chin rose. "To give in to such demands would only encourage further tactics of that sort. He explained it to me."

Dear God, Rhiannon thought numbly, what manner of wasps' nest was this? A father who would not ransom his own sons long after the hostilities that had resulted in their captivity had ended? A cold, emotionless girl who supported such monstrous disloyalty?

"But Ash is free," Rhiannon said.

"Yes . . ." Fia's brow lined in perplexity. "Carr ransomed Ash. I must own, he never explained that to me. . . ." She glanced at Rhiannon and her brow once more smoothed. "Not that it matters. I'm sure Carr had excellent reasons. It's imperative that one see each situation for what it is without allowing sentiment to cloud one's judgment."

"Is that what paternal affection is, a clouding sentiment?"

"You don't understand."

"Don't you miss your brother?"

Color simmered beneath the smooth powdered surface covering Fia's face. "I don't know him. I don't know either of them. Carr said they had been too much under the influence of my mother as children and it has irrevocably marked them. He says they are unfit companions for me. Besides, Ash and Raine have never demonstrated any concern for me." A sliver of bitterness disturbed her usually suave voice.

"But still, they are your brothers," Rhiannon insisted. "Don't you wonder how Raine is? If he suffers? If he hopes for release and is doubly tormented in captivity by knowing his father refuses to pay for his freedom . . . perhaps even his life?"

"I don't wonder at all. What could such conjecture possibly accomplish?" Fia slowed her steps, as though she wished to draw away. "*You* are too emotional. An unfortunate characteristic Carr says is endemic in the Highland Scot.

"Besides, Ash will see that Raine is eventually freed. He's obsessed with the idea. Why do you think he agreed to waste all that time fetching you?"

Rhiannon could not answer. Her thoughts spun in a chaotic whirl.

"Money. To be used for Raine's ransom," Fia said in disgust.

Rhiannon stared at her unseeingly. "Are you sure?"

Fia lifted her shoulders indifferently. "I conjecture. What else is he spending his money on? Certainly not clothes!" She sniffed.

"Miss Russell!" A deep, masculine burr drew Rhiannon's stricken gaze from Fia's inimical one.

Thomas Donne strode up the stairs two at a time, his hard face softening at the sight of Rhiannon. Beside her Fia's expression grew guarded.

The girl drew back on Donne's approach, as though she could not bear for him to see her with her eyes bright and her skin flushed. Donne did not spare her a glance.

"You're not going to the fight, are you, Miss Russell?" he said to Rhiannon.

"I'm afraid I don't know what you mean," Rhiannon mumbled, the implications of what Fia had told her wheeling through her mind. "Lord Carr insisted that I attend some sort of entertainment. He said nothing about a fight. Not a cockfight? Or bear baiting. I can't abide either."

Donne glanced sharply at Fia. "No, Miss Russell. This is men fighting, bare-knuckled street savagery. Nothing a lady should witness."

"Carr specifically asked for her," Fia said calmly. "And many other ladies will be present, *have* been present all this week. It's not as abhorrent as you make out, Lord Donne. I doubt Miss Russell is so much more sensitive than the rest of us."

"Other ladies will be present?" Rhiannon asked doubtfully. She had no desire to see two men beat each other but if it provided the chance to press Carr about leaving here and, perhaps, discovering more about Ash and Raine, she would take that opportunity.

"Other *women* will be there," Donne allowed flatly. "But I would not place Miss Russell amongst their ilk. Refuse, Miss Russell," Donne urged. "Your attendance can only cause you distress. It's scandalous even for Carr. Even for this crowd."

"You've become a prude, Lord Donne," Fia said haughtily. " 'Tis nothing more than an interesting demonstration. Personally, I agree with you that the thing should be called off, but only because it makes him so unprepossessing to face over the dining table. But why should Miss Russell care? If she really was kidnapped, as 'tis rumored, she might even enjoy seeing him receive a good thrashing."

Donne swung on Fia, his mouth smiling politely but his eyes flat with scorn. "Don't measure another's capacity for decency by what little you . . . see in others. Whatever Miss Russell has suffered at your family's hands, I cannot think she wishes to witness Merrick's crippling."

"Merrick?" Rhiannon echoed in unwilling alarm. "How is that?"

Donne stared at her. "But . . . didn't Fia or Carr tell you?"

"What?" Rhiannon asked.

"Ash Merrick is one of the combatants."

CHAPTER 25

Ladies and gentlemen clad in last night's stained, rumpled silks, whey-faced and flabby-skinned in the unforgiving morning light, hung from the windows overlooking the stable courtyard and milled four deep around its border. A carnival mood infected them. By pitting an aristocrat against a commoner in a bare-knuckle fight, Carr had orchestrated a delicious scandal. And not just any aristocrat but Carr's own son, Merrick, and not a single fight but fisticuffs for three days running now.

They wouldn't have missed being part of this no matter how much it cost—and it had cost them plenty. London hadn't offered anything so infamous in a decade. And though they panted to be away to London to spread the tattle, they dare not leave lest something even more outrageous occur.

Their murmurs quieted as Baron Paughville's groom entered the stable yard. He was stripped to the waist and oiled, his shorn head likewise greased to frustrate an opponent's handhold. Rumor had it he'd wrestled on the Continent. More telling, he was Scottish. The chance to break English bone and pound English flesh would have been enticement enough without the fat purse Carr offered for winning.

Ash Merrick stood chatting with the crowd at the rail with all the appearance of amiability. Surreptitiously, he noted the groom's long, thick arms and short, bowed legs and the forward tilt of his crouching gait. The Scot would be hard to get off his feet and onto the ground, where street brawls—and prison brawls—were won or lost.

Three days ago Ash would have been certain of his victory. If nothing else, he'd had the element of surprise to aid him. His opponents, all culled from the stables and fields hereabouts, were laborers. They did not imagine an aristocrat would deal violence so brutally or so expeditiously. Three days had taught them differently.

But it wasn't surprise alone that gave him an advantage. He'd learned to fight not only unscrupulously but also fearlessly. He could block out every external distraction including pain, narrowing his focus down until only he and his adversary existed.

What set today apart was simply his body. He was no longer physically up to the task. Though his spirit had risen to do battle through sheer instinct, spirit alone could no longer compensate for three days of brutal pummeling. The preceding victories had come at a price.

He suspected one rib was cracked. For a certainty two fingers of his left hand had been broken. His left eye was swollen as a result of having become intimately acquainted yesterday with a combatant's boot heel, and purple welts tattooed his torso. Today would be his last fight, no matter what his father "urged."

The thought of Carr made Ash smile.

His father had lost a great deal of money betting against his son, while Ash had made a nice profit. His smile faded. Today, though . . . today Ash simply wanted to survive and have an end to it.

"What do we do now?" The Scots groom demanded of the crowd in general. He approached the cleared center of the stable yard and eyed Ash expectantly. "Is there anyone to make a beginning or end to it?"

Ash glanced about, looking for Donne. The elegant Scotsman had held Ash's bets for the past days. Not finding him, Ash tapped a nearby exquisite on the arm. The startled young man backed up. Ash grinned.

"Don't worry— Begad if it ain't Hurley!" Ash exclaimed. "Hurley, m'dear, be a fellow and make me a small wager, will you? Fifty pounds says I win." He seized Hurley's gloved hand and pried open the stiff lavender-sheathed fingers, slapping a fat purse into his palm and curling the fingers back over it. "There's a lad. And since you've been such an accommodating fellow, let me give you a tip. I wouldn't follow suit. My bet is only by way of incentive, don'tcha know."

"N-n-no," Hurley stammered. "I mean . . . y-y-y-yes. I mean, I am sure you'll win, Mr. Merrick."

"I did warn you." The small diversion palled and Ash dismissed Hurley without another thought. Best get on with it.

In a single motion he stripped off his jacket and then pulled the cambric shirt over his head. Whispers of female gratification sizzled beneath roars of masculine approval. Ash faced the Scotsman still standing awkward and self-conscious in the center of a ring of beautifully clad ladies and gentleman.

"No one starts and no one finishes it," Ash explained, approaching the other man, "save we two. There are no rules. There is only one manner in which to win and that is to leave here upright." He stopped just out of arm's reach of the other man. "Exquisitely simple, *n'est-ce pas?*"

"I gets it," the groom growled and launched himself forward.

Ash had been right; the man had experience. He came in low and aimed for the knees, seeking to take Ash to the ground rather than battering haphazardly—and ineffectually—at the head. Ash locked his fists together and swung down, chopping across the back of the groom's oncoming neck.

Pain jolted through the broken fingers and thundered through his hand. The Scot tumbled and sprawled flat under the blow. Ash wheeled back, cursing and shaking his injured hand even as he felt arms grapple him about his calves. Damn the man, he was still conscious.

Ash kicked out and twisted sideways but the arms about his legs tightened relentlessly. With a thick grunt, the Scot heaved upward, pitching Ash into the air.

The ground slammed into Ash's back like a smithy's hammer. Pain drilled through his side with red-hot intensity, driving the air from his lungs, blackening the edges of his vision. He gasped, rolling to his side and curling up, protecting the injured ribs. The Scotsman recognized his agony and paused, his eye glinting with anticipation. It was only a second's gloating, but it was a second too much.

Savagely, Ash kicked out, his heel smashing into the groom's kneecap. A loud, sickening pop sounded above the shouts of bloodthirsty approval from the crowd. The Scot howled in agony, clasping his broken knee and stumbling backward.

Ash heaved himself to his hands and knees, shaking his head to clear the threatening mist from his vision, his ears roaring with the din of the crowd and the sobbed curses of his injured foe.

Stay focused. Stay with it. Two hundred pounds. Four-to-one odds. He needed to render the groom unconscious before the bastard did as much to him.

Ash found his feet and wheeled around, surprised to find the Scot, too, standing. The groom favored his injured leg, swaying from side to side. His mouth moved with a string of silent invective, flecks of red foam spraying from the corners of his broken lip.

The battered Scot charged again, coming at Ash with animallike tenacity, seemingly impervious to the blows Ash rained on his battered face.

Time and again the Scotsman came at him, what he lacked in skill more than made up for by his sheer ability to endure. Time and again, Ash managed to dance out of reach of the huge swinging paws and deliver a series of unanswered punches.

By now both men were gasping for breath, filthy with grease and sweat and stable dirt. The crowd roared with approval as Ash staggered back once more from a glancing blow to his jaw, each minute using up precious breath, expending energy he did not own. He jabbed out over and over again but try as he might he could not deliver enough power to end the fight. His blows only seemed to enrage the man.

He was going to lose.

The Scot fought from passion and Ash had thought he was fighting for money but now he suspected he fought for something marginally more interesting . . . his life. Without a doubt the Scot would kill him if he could.

"Shall we finish, *mon ami*?" Ash panted. "I have a lady waiting and I would like to—"

With a strangled sound of fury, the Scotsman launched himself once more at Ash. This time Ash was ready. He met the onrushing figure with knees bent, arms flexed. When the groom's bull-like figure collided with him he did not try to stand up to the charge. He folded, letting his opponent propel him backward and adding his own weight to the impetus by digging in his heels and grasping the Scot's thick arms. With a huge grunt, Ash jerked the Scot into him rather than thrusting him away.

Ash's shoulders hit the ground and he heaved back, pulling the groom down as hard as he could. The groom's face crashed into the unyielding ground. His thick body cartwheeled heel-over-head. The arms around Ash went slack and the heavy body completed its loose-limbed tumble, dropping into the dust with a powdery thud.

Clenching his teeth against the pain, Ash lay flat, waiting for the Scot to rise again like some bloody phoenix and kill him. He couldn't have stopped him. Not an ounce of energy remained in his body. It was all he could do to breathe, his chest heaving up and down, his eyes staring in bewildered appreciation at the obscenely clear blue sky overhead, the dust settling like Pentecostal ash on his trembling limbs.

The Scot did not move.

For a long second there was absolute silence. The crowd began to murmur with delighted scorn. He heard a plunk beside his head and glanced over. A bitter smile curved his lips. They were tossing coins at him. Gold coins. God bless them.

The he heard the familiar voice.

"For God's sake, get up, Merrick, or we shall be forced to declare a miscontest," his father said, "and from the look of her, I doubt my dear ward would be able to stomach another bout."

The pain in his side and hands and lungs evaporated before the wretchedness welling through him. He'd thought he understood his father's game. He hadn't even begun to understand.

Unable to help himself, he turned his head. His gaze found her figure with unerring accuracy. She stood between Carr and Thomas Donne. Carr held her arm, his long fingers stroking her hand comfortingly as he whispered in her ear.

She was not listening. Her head was erect, her posture poised for flight. Dark red-gold coils of hair gleamed in contrast to a face as pale as bleached linen. Absolute horror suffused every feature.

Ash's lids drifted shut. Against the black tapestry of his lids he saw himself through her eyes, bloody and broken, covered with stinking dirt and rancid grease, a body he'd rendered unconscious—or worse—laying half across his legs along with that for which he'd beaten him. A few gold coins.

"Well, to give the lad his due, he fought ingeniously," Carr said.

Rhiannon had been so transfixed by the hideous spectacle that she'd failed to note when Carr had taken her hand. She pulled it back.

No matter what depths she imagined Ash to have reached, he always managed to find a more profound debasement. The crowd was flinging coins at the two inert bodies. A redheaded wench dashed into the makeshift arena and knelt by the Scot. She grasped his upper body and tried to heave him upright, at the same time scraping the guineas and shillings into her skirts. The crowd roared with laughter.

"I have never seen anything so degrading," Rhiannon said.

"I daresay Ash would agree," Carr replied. "But everyone at Wanton's Blush must pay for the privilege of being here, by whatever means they can."

"You mean that you asked him to fight? You risked your own son's life against that mountain of flesh?"

"*Asked?* I don't *ask,* Miss Russell." Carr said. He was not trying to charm her today. In fact, it seemed as though he was deliberately provocative, trying to alienate her. "I command. King George may rule in London, but I rule here. I may be exiled, but I still have my court." He made a sweeping gesture around the crowd. "I don't suppose I can let Merrick fight again tomorrow. Who would bet on him?" He scowled, displeased, but then his expression cleared. "But if he were by some miracle to win, think of the odds he'd have overcome! At least twenty to one—"

"You're hateful." As she spoke she saw Ash turn his head toward her and open his eyes. Something so raw passed between them that she had to look away. When she looked back, he'd lurched to his hands and knees, his head hanging low.

"Isn't someone going to go to him?" Rhiannon swung on Carr.

He met her gaze disinterestedly. "Such concern. You have a soft heart, m'dear. But to answer your question, no. There are very few rules in this sort of thing but one of them does require the victor to leave the arena under his own power."

"He needs attention," she insisted.

"Does he? Well, I don't know where he'll find it. As far as I know there are no quacks in my castle."

Rhiannon looked at her companions. Beside her Thomas Donne maintained his enigmatic composure. She glanced at Fia, expecting nothing from that quarter, and was surprised to find the girl looking greenish, her gaze flickering unwillingly toward the dirt in which her brother lay.

"I'll go to him," Fia murmured.

Carr's head snapped around. "What?"

"I can clean him up. If you will just have some of the servants—"

"You will not!" Carr hissed before recovering his poise. "Absolutely not. Don't forget, you are my hostess. Can't have you coming to the table smelling of vomit and"—he glanced once more at Ash—"whatever other excrement Merrick has rolled in."

He was all the monster Gunna had suggested and Fia had unintentionally substantiated. The charm Carr had exercised on their first meeting hid a soulless fiend. Even Fia looked startled by Carr's venomous tone. And though Rhiannon was suspicious of why he would suddenly reveal himself to her, she was too concerned about Ash to pursue such thoughts.

A small cheer from the crowd drew Rhiannon's attention. Ash had made it upright. He lurched toward the ring of spectators. They opened before him and swallowed his figure, closing behind. Now that a victor had been established, voices rose as wagers were claimed and satisfied.

"I'm going to him," Rhiannon said. "You can't stop me. You may rule here, Lord Carr, but you do not rule me."

"Just as I feared." Carr sighed. "As you will, Miss Russell. Come along, Lord Donne."

He secured Donne's arm and led him off through the crowd. "I believe you actually bet on my son? How perceptive of you—"

Rhiannon looked toward Fia. "Where can I find Gunna?" she asked.

"She'll be in my rooms," the girl murmured distractedly. "How odd—" But Rhiannon did not stay to hear what Fia found odd.

Carr looked too well satisfied. Few others besides Fia would have realized it. Rhiannon had just challenged his edict. Her disobedience should have been like a spark to tinder but Carr had left calmly, a buoyancy to his stride that bespoke complacency.

It made no sense. For days now Carr's temper had been building. She'd heard him pacing in his office several times. Once, when she'd cracked the door thinking to offer him her company, she'd discovered him scribbling on a piece of paper, stabbing it with his pen. He'd been so involved that he hadn't even realized she'd entered—in itself a telling sign. Carr noted everything.

Finally he'd thrown the writing instrument down and balled the paper up in his hand, hurling it to the floor. "How? Under what excuse? Simply have a change of heart and send her back? No. Someone must take her back, or forward. Or any bloody where but here."

Fia had been too long under Carr's tutelage to ignore the import of such a rare outburst just as she was too wise to let Carr know she'd heard it. She'd closed the door as quietly as possible and run to her room.

Now, watching Rhiannon stride off in the opposite direction from Carr, for the first time in her life Fia felt the pull of divided loyalties.

The problem was Fia liked Rhiannon. Of all her acquaintances the Scotswoman alone—with the exception of Gunna—treated her in the manner Fia imagined other fifteen-year-old girls were treated. At least, Fia amended, Rhiannon didn't treat her like the polished and precocious woman everyone else assumed Lord Carr's daughter must be.

Since her twelfth year Fia had been presented not as a child but as an unnatural hybrid—part woman, part doll. She'd been bribed with toys she was too old for and offered experiences she was too young for.

Rhiannon Russell did not flatter or patronize her. True, Rhiannon also neither trusted nor particularly liked her, but even this Fia found refreshingly candid. She was as close to a friend as Fia had ever known.

She didn't want Rhiannon hurt.

She was being silly she supposed. She knew Carr had a reputation as a diabolical fiend. It had always amused her. Carr was no monster. He was a genius who chose not to be governed by the irrational emotions or the asinine laws made by lesser men for lesser people. It made perfect sense.

Or, Fia thought, her young face troubled, it always had before.

CHAPTER 26

Ash couldn't make it up the servants' stairs and he refused to ask the snickering footmen to carry him. By gritting his teeth and concentrating very hard, he managed to stumble into one of the small antechambers behind the great hall—a mean, dark room, presently unused and therefore as devoid of furnishings as it was of light.

Gratefully, Ash sank to the floor, his back against the wall. His ribs throbbed dully. He forced himself to twist and was pleased when it hurt no great deal worse than before, indicating that just perhaps his ribs weren't broken. Scant comfort but all he was likely to get. His hand felt as though it were being crushed in a vise. His skin stung where the sweat and grease ground into innumerable abrasions.

He would have lain on the floor and allowed sweet oblivion to overcome his senses but each time he closed his eyes he saw her face and read again her horror. The pain in his body faded, becoming faint compared to the pain of that recollection.

From his earliest years he'd understood what he was. He'd never wasted a moment regretting it. A wise father may well know his child, but it was more important that the child recognize not only his sire but those parts of himself his sire had bequeathed.

Somehow he'd forgotten that. Indeed, it seemed lately that he'd lost the part of himself he knew best. Well, he'd bloody well remember, because this pain—this pain was unendurable. It had to end. It *would* end.

He'd finally accrued enough money to ransom Raine. He'd even written to the French demanding particulars of how and where the trade would occur.

The door opened and a bar of light fell across his injured eye. He winced, flinging up one hand against the intrusion and placing the other palm flat against the floor. He heaved himself to a crouching position, facing whoever entered.

He squinted against the bright rectangle of the door frame. "Another challenger?" he asked with a bitter laugh. "Why not? It might not be a very interesting confrontation but it might prove satisfying—for you. Hell, for both of us. Though being a gentleman I should ask you to take your place at the end of the queue."

"Ash."

It was *her* voice. Ragged and low and it nearly undid him.

He swallowed hard. Had his father sent her as a special reminder of the many ways in which he could bring his eldest son to heel or had she sought him for her own purposes?

"What, Rhiannon?" A small pleasure to speak her Christian name, but one he wouldn't cede. "Have you come to condemn me for my chosen path, my ill-gotten gains, the depth to which I have sunk? Don't waste your breath or my time. I don't give a damn what you think."

Liar.

"No." She turned and spoke to someone in the hall. He climbed to his feet, weaving slightly. His little speech had cost him dearly.

"I'll need more water than this and hot," she was saying to whomever waited without. "Very hot. And bandages and he'll need a shirt."

"You're not going to clean me up," he ground out, sickened by the thought of her hands sloughing the filth from his limbs.

She ignored him, hefting a pail from the floor outside and setting it inside the room. She closed the door behind her, sinking the room into twilight.

"Where are you hurt worst?"

"What the hell are you doing here?"

"You already know that. I've come to patch up your wounds."

"The hell you say." He made himself stand away from the wall. Sweating with concentration, he moved toward her. She did not back away and as he drew near and his eyes adjusted to the murky lighting he saw that she wore one of those new gowns Carr had insisted she don, a shimmering bronze striped through with rich green.

She looked elegant and regal, no longer the modest little beauty. No, quite evolved now. Quite different from that pretty wench.

This gown dipped low, far lower than anything she'd ever worn in Fair

Badden. Her bound breasts, pushed up by the constricting bodice, trembled in an agitation delicious to behold. He'd never had the time nor inclination to lechery, owning a full complement of sins that already commanded his attention. But even battered and broken, just the sight of Rhiannon made him grow hard.

Yet it was not *his* hand that reached out and hovered inches above naked flesh. It was hers. Incredulously, Ash realized she meant to touch his naked chest. Like a wild thing unused to human contact, his stared at her in startled wariness.

Rhiannon shivered before the threat she read in his hot, smoke-dark eyes. He looked cornered, dangerous, and unpredictable. If she had sense she would leave. Whatever he was to his brother, he was her enemy, a scoundrel who'd used her, lied to her, and stolen her from her home for money. She began to move back toward the door and safety but her gaze, released from his, fell on the purpled skin sheathing his ribs.

He hadn't wanted to fight the Scotsman. Carr had forced him to it.

Her hand rose, closed the distance, and gently, carefully, traced a deep gash across his breast. His eyelids fluttered shut. She sidled closer, her touch feather light, warily watching his face for signs of—

He grabbed her wrist, spinning her round and catching her by the throat with his free hand, shoving her violently against the wall, hissing as his swollen hand, cushioning her wrist, slammed into the wall. His eyes opened on a blaze.

"You've changed, little Rhiannon," he muttered thickly. He angled his head sideways. Around her throat his fingers tightened. "You've grown bold and headstrong. What happened to the sweet, obedient young woman I met? Don't you remember, Rhiannon *alainn*? Or is that it? You want a reminder of her fate?"

There was nothing of kindness in him. She'd been wrong. Wrong to stay. Wrong to be moved by his pride and his plight—

"Remember now?" he whispered, the soft rough music of his voice mocking his violent actions. He pushed his body flat against hers, dominating her slighter frame. Even through the layers of thin silk petticoats and draped satin skirts she could feel the swollen part of him brand the outside of her thigh.

"Or now?" He thrust his hips graphically against hers. Her courage wavered. Eyes wide with stricken, mute appeal she stared at him. A muffled word—a curse? an endearment?—escaped him and then his mouth closed on hers, punishing and brutal.

His tongue dove between her lips, thrust deeply within her mouth, and stroked her tongue, seeking the warm sleek side of interior cheeks. Passion exploded within him.

Rhiannon.

He felt the weight of her breasts flattened against his chest. Her throat was a silky column in his palm. Her wrist was as delicate as a bird wing.

He could have her. Here. Now. Pain speared his side and throbbed in his hand. Pain sat like a vise in his chest and burned like acid in his thoughts. He knew only one way to make it stop—

He fumbled low at her knees, bunching the heavy satin up, savoring the long, smooth slide of his knuckles up her thighs. He dragged the skirt higher, and cupped the softly rounded swell of her buttocks, lifting her, pressing her even more tightly to the wall, vaguely aware that she was clutching his shoulders.

His gaze devoured the sight of all the ivory skin he uncovered, remarked the dark stain left by his dirty hands as they traveled up the long lines of her lovely milk white thighs. She'd been clean.

He laughed softly and laughed again when he saw her face go still with apprehension.

Cleanliness. He'd never been clean. He'd no experience with anything unpolluted. Until her. She was fresh and sweet and innocent. In spite of her nightmares. In spite of being stained by the blood of battle. *In spite of him.*

The scent of her filled his nostrils. The cool polished feel of her hair slipped in silky waves over his forearm. Why should he not have her when she'd wrung from him the one thing he'd always had—the knowledge of who he was.

He dipped, bending at the knees. She could not resist. Her body was imprisoned between his and the wall. He rocked forward against the hidden delta he'd exposed. Erotic pleasure surged through his limbs, pooling in his groin. He couldn't stop, would not stop, he would take her, use her, pitch and flux and drown in the sin of ravishing her. He *wanted* to overpower her, force her to pliancy, punish her for making him—

Through the thundering of his heartbeat he felt a faint vibration, a shiver no stronger than the pulse racing in her throat. She was sobbing.

Not the sweet sob of abandonment he'd heard on that warm, cursed Beltaine Eve. Not the sound of newly discovered passion, of pure desire. It was not a pleasured sob like the one she'd offered to the night sky when she'd so artlessly, so ravishingly given herself to him. It was a pitiful gasp for a breath he would not allow.

Dear God, let me rape her, he prayed. Let me be done with her. With a thick sound, he wrenched his mouth from hers.

Rhiannon breathed.

She opened her eyes and found Ash's thick-lashed eyes inches away, fierce and alien. Had she once thought them cold? Impossible. Molten lead and green wood smoke, heat and ash, nothing cold here. Nothing recognizable.

His hand about her throat tightened fractionally as if he read in her pleading expression something he would not endure. Anchored only by her hands braced on his shoulders, her hips jammed to the wall by his, she stared at him. For a long second their gazes locked. Fury roiled just beyond expression in Ash's battered face. She took a deep, shuddering breath.

"Let me go," she commanded him.

The edges of his nails dug deeper into her throat.

"Why should I?" he sneered.

She wanted to whimper, to claw at the hand on her throat. It would be futile. She'd seen Ash's expression on the faces of the soldiers who'd bayoneted her cousins. The redcoats had been ordered to commit acts that none of them would have willingly done in the normal course of their lives. But because it was war, because Cumberland said to, they'd obeyed, burned crofts, shot men like wild dogs, bayoneted boys.

They couldn't stop. Their brutalized minds wouldn't let them. They wouldn't stop for even an instant and consider that the Highlanders were people. And *nothing* must remind them elsewise. When her youngest cousin had shed a tear, a soldier shot him, furious that the boy had reminded the redcoat that he was murdering a child.

She saw in Ash's embattled countenance that same frantic need to kill an overburdened conscience with one heinous, unforgivable act. To finally take that last step over the line and free-fall into an abyss of moral blackness, a place where choices and options no longer tortured him.

And yet, in spite of all she knew of him, she did not think he had been brought to that place. She locked her hand about his strong supple wrist, praying she was right.

"Because," she said very clearly, very firmly, "you are hurting me. You are frightening me."

He stared at her a second as if he could not comprehend her words. Slowly the fingers around her throat loosened. He released the skirts he held crumpled at her hip. He did not say a word, only stepped back, a single step, just enough for her to move away.

Swallowing, keeping her gaze fixed on his, she slipped sideways, skirting the room's edge. He watched her stonily, mutely, his hands loose at his sides, his eyes bleak and exhausted and terrifying. Fumbling behind her she found the door latch and twisted it, pushing the door open. Only then did she dare turn her back and leave.

Fia found Gunna lugging a heavy-looking pail down a corridor. The old woman puffed as she staggered under the weight. With a quick glance around, Fia hastened forward. The startled old woman dropped the bucket the few inches she held it above the floor and snatched her veil before her face. Seeing it was Fia, she relaxed.

"What are you doing?" Fia hissed. "If Carr sees you downstairs, you know he'll dismiss you."

"Ach! He'd naught do so," Gunna snickered. "He couldna replace me and well he knows it. Dinna worry, darlin', I'm just heading in there." She jerked her head toward a half-ajar door. "I must bandage up the lad is all."

Fia glanced at the door. "Ash is in there?"

"Aye, most likely unconscious. But, hold lassie. If he ain't, I'd no be entering that particular lion's den just now. He's like in as black a mood as Lucifer in sunlight."

"Why?"

Gunna shrugged as Fia latched her fingers around the bucket's handle and lifted it. "I dunno. Perhaps he's in no mood to have his lover become his stepmother."

Fia stopped. The water in the bucket sloshed, soaking the bottom of her skirts. She barely noticed. "His lover?"

"Aye," Gunna said, *tch*ing gently and bending down to dab at Fia's jonquil-colored skirts.

Fia watched her in surprise. Gunna seldom gossiped and did not encourage it in Fia.

She shouldn't ask Gunna more. But Carr had taught her the import of knowing about everything that affected one's life.

"What?" Gunna said, reading Fia's wide eyes. "Did you think that all Mr. Ash's drinking and carousing was for the hilarity of it? I had it from the lassie herself that Mr. Ash and she were lovers. Only once, 'tis true, but I'm thinkin' Mr. Ash would like to make it twice. Mayhaps even more." She winked at Fia.

"But," Gunna went on, "Carr must have other ideas. Why else would he send Mr. Ash to bring the lassie here if not to marry her himself? No matter *what* the lassie herself believes." Gunna chortled and picked up the bucket. "It's no wonder Mr. Ash is in so foul a temper, is it?"

"But Carr *didn't* bring her here to marry her," Fia murmured, following Gunna's bent form down the hall. "He can't."

Rhiannon and Ash were lovers? Yet Carr had commanded Ash to bring her here and Ash had done so. Why? And if Carr had wanted Rhiannon here badly enough to send Ash for her, why was he now pacing the floor and muttering about finding someone to take Rhiannon Russell away?

"Why can't he marry Miss Rhiannon?" Gunna asked casually, stopping outside the door.

"Because," Fia answered distractedly, still trying to sort through what she'd learned, "the Prime Minister gave an edict to Carr years ago, after the death of Lady Beatrice. He said that if one more of Carr's wives died, no matter what the cause, Carr would answer to the king and he would answer with his life. Upon hearing this, Carr swore he would never marry again—no matter what the inducement."

The old woman frowned and pushed the door to the darkened room open farther. A hiss of pain from the darkness just inside greeted them.

Gunna turned to Fia. "Best you be gone now, dear. Afore yore father comes seeking you and finds you here, with him."

Before she could reply Gunna slipped into the room leaving Fia to hasten back the way she'd come, her thoughts in a whirl.

CHAPTER 27

His arms were strong and sheltering, his body a rock-hard instrument of pleasure. Rhiannon moaned softly and Ash lifted her with big, warm hands on either hip, sliding deep within—

A sudden wild clattering brought Rhiannon upright in her bed. She looked wildly about but there was no lover, phantom or otherwise, beside her. With a little moan of distress, she sank forward, bracing her forehead against her upraised knees and rocking back and forth.

Two days now since Ash had so nearly raped her and yet it was not her escape from so heinous an act that occupied her thoughts. No. She remembered instead the blue-black welts marring his beautiful body, and his pain-filled eyes. Even when she managed to push him from her waking thoughts, he found other ways to come to her, at night, in her dreams, as the lover with whom she'd shared such passion on Beltaine night.

A light tapping on her door brought her head up. The sun had just crested the sea, unraveling strands of rosy light across her bedroom carpet. It was early, far too early for even the servants to be about. Another soft rap preceded a sound of wild scrabbling.

"Miss Russell?" A young male voice queried desperately. It was vaguely familiar. "Please, Miss Russell! Answer soon! I can't keep her still!"

Rhiannon swung her legs off the bed and slipped to the floor. Donning a dressing gown, she crossed the room and opened the door.

A huge yellow monster erupted from the floor, launching itself directly at Rhiannon, dragging the thick linked chains that leashed it clean out of its handler's hands. The creature hit Rhiannon square in the chest, knocking her flat to her back.

Like a lion over its prey, the huge animal stood over her, curled lips exposing huge ivory canines.

"Stella!" Rhiannon cried.

The grinning gazehound dropped its enormous head and swiped Rhiannon's entire face with a tongue the size of a small hand cloth.

"Oh, Stella!" Rhiannon wrapped her arms around the hound's thick neck and hugged.

In the doorway the young man shuffled uncomfortably, drawing Rhiannon's attention. She recognized him as Andrew Payne from The Ploughman in Fair Badden.

"However did she get here? Did Mrs. Fraiser send her?" Rhiannon asked.

"Nah, Miss Russell," the young man said. "It was Mr. Merrick. Some weeks back Mr. Watt hurtles up to the front of the inn driving a wagon hitched to a wind-broke horse, as furious as ever I've seen a man. He's shouting about how Mr. Merrick has taken off with you and swearing he'll find Merrick and kill him and get you back. He's in such a lather that me father calls some fellows from the public room to see that Watt doesn't hurts himself. Off they hauls him, leaving me to the wagon."

The sound of rattling dishes drew Rhiannon's attention. Still on the floor with her arms linked around Stella's neck, she motioned the boy inside. "Come, Andy. Now tell me the rest."

Andrew entered, snatching his hat from his head, twisting the woven wool between his hands. "Well, I sees Stella here." He nodded at the beast. She wagged her tail in delighted recognition of her name. "She's covered in blood and breathing weak and her hind leg is crooked."

Rhiannon ran her hands over the dog and sure enough, found a thickened lump on her hind leg.

"I always liked her, useless though she be," the boy admitted gruffly, "so I takes her back to Mrs. Fraiser with the rest of the story."

"How did Mrs. Fraiser take it?" Rhiannon asked softly.

The boy shuffled uncomfortably, his gaze skittering away. "She shed some tears, miss, but she sees Stella and she sets right out to patching her up and setting her leg. A few days later, Mr. Merrick's letter arrives and that gave her some comfort."

"What letter?" Rhiannon asked.

"A letter *and* a purse. The letter says how he would not take you without good cause and asks Mrs. Fraiser to fix up Stella."

"What did she do? Was she sad?" Rhiannon asked anxiously.

"Ach," Andy said. "She's a touch melancholy but greatly eased. She says as any man that takes time out of an abduction to write a letter askin' that a no-good bitch be patched and brought across the entire country just to keep a lady company must have a powerful care for the lady.

"And then, well, you know Mrs. Fraiser. She says what's done is done and that ye'll do fine. You're a survivor."

"What do you mean, brought across the country?"

"The money," Andy explained patiently. "Mr. Merrick sent it so someone could bring Stella to McClairen's Isle. I volunteered and glad I am of it. Never seen nuthin' like this place."

He grinned widely, staring around the sumptuous bedchamber and letting out a long, low whistle. Rhiannon stared at him unseeing. *Ash* had caused Stella to be tended and brought here? Ash, the blackhearted deceiver, her would-be rapist? But also, the man who'd brought her an old tartan so she might have something of her family's history. Dear Lord.

"I got in an hour ago," Andy said, his gaze still wandering around the room. "Mr. Merrick saw me straight off, right there in the kitchen while he made sure me and Stella had something in our bellies."

Stella promptly flopped down and rolled to her back, her great dinner plate–sized paws waggling in the air in an attempt to elicit a belly scratch.

"He doesn't look so good, Mr. Merrick don't. And his eyes look a great bit of empty. And— Oh I am thick-headed!"

With a *tch* of self-disgust, Andy fumbled in his pocket and withdrew a folded piece of paper. He handed it to her. "He sent this to you, miss." He grinned at Stella. "And don't you worry, you great sweet-eyed tart, I gots something for you, too."

Once more Andy shoved a hand in his pocket, this time pulling out a beef's knucklebone. He tossed it to Stella and her jaws closed on it in midair. "Got that from one of the scullery maids," he explained. "Nice girl. Accommodating, if you know what I mean."

A considering expression stole over Andy's young face. He slapped his thighs suddenly. "Well then, I . . . I, ah, I best be off. I . . . I left something in the scullery. I'll stop back afore I leave for Fair Badden to see if you've anything you'd like me to take to Mrs. Fraiser."

He plunked his abused cap back on his head and, with a cheeky nod, opened the door. He looked up and down the deserted hall. "Not much for morning activities round here, are they?"

He disappeared, closing the door behind him.

With trembling hands, Rhiannon unfolded the paper. The words were few, the handwriting angular and harsh, without any softening or embellishments—much like Ash himself. She blinked away the sudden moisture in her eyes and read:

Forgive me and accept this dog by way of my apology. Please. I didn't mean to frighten you. Please.

Merrick

But he'd sent for Stella long before the scene in that dimly lit room, before they'd even reached Wanton's Blush. He'd done what he could to see that Stella's wounds were treated and then he'd arranged to have her brought here, so that Rhiannon might not be alone. Because Ash understood what it was to be alone, without allies or confidants.

Or love.

But he'd tasted that emotion in Fair Badden. She was sure of it. He simply hadn't experience enough to recognize it.

He may not be the charming bon vivant who'd first captivated her in Fair Badden. But neither was he an unfeeling monster who'd seduced her only to discard her. He was a hard man in desperate need of tenderness, roughly used by fate and father, seeking a moment's respite from constant strife.

The realization burned through her heart like a dry field afire, illuminating the darkest corners, the cautious frightened places she'd tended and hidden in for over ten years. The safe places.

But Ash Merrick was not safe, and loving Ash Merrick would never be safe— She stopped, her hand stilled in Stella's thick, smooth coat.

Loving Ash Merrick.

She rose smoothly, strongly, sure of herself and her destination. At last.

Ash slouched forward over the writing desk in the corner of his room, staring at a column of numbers he'd written from memory. If he remembered correctly the numbers from Carr's ledger went back seven or eight years. They had no notations associated with them, only dates.

But what, if anything, had they to do with Rhiannon Russell? He sighed heavily, rubbing his palms over his beard-roughened cheeks. By now that lad would have delivered that useless hound to her. They'd be rolling about her bedroom floor in an ecstatic reunion. The thought brought a smile to his harsh countenance and he kept the image there, in his mind's eye, for a minute, savoring the pure sweetness of it before straightening and raking his hair back from his forehead.

He'd more important things to consider. He'd overheard Fia telling Gunna that King George, not content merely to exile Carr to the Highlands for his habit of losing wives, had gone one further, promising to extract retribution if yet another of England's daughters succumbed while in his care.

That must have been what Tunbridge's letter had alluded to—Carr's obsession with his "place" in society. Tunbridge must have been sent to pave the way toward some sort of reconciliation between the king and Carr.

And there was more. Last night Ash had managed to corner Carr's man of business in a bout of intense drinking, a small triumph in itself since Carr had hired for that post a man of nearly pathological discretion.

Ash had spent hours weaving lurid and grossly exaggerated tales about his days in Paris. Under the influence of drink and bonhomie, the wizened little man had finally begun to nod sympathetically. Bit by bit he'd disclosed his secrets. After relating the expense of running the castle, the little fellow had placed his finger alongside his nose and let one rheumy eye close in a careful wink.

"Carr has income near enough to make it all work," he'd whispered. "Information is always worth gold to some. Plus there's the gaming. Certain gentlemen, and I'm sure you can figure out at least one of them, since Lord Carr says you speared his hand, pay His Lordship for the privilege of being invited to his tables. Then there's bonds and banknotes and that property overseas . . ."

Then, as if suddenly aware of just how much he'd divulged, the little man had clapped a hand over his mouth, risen unsteadily to his feet, and fled.

Overseas property? The Americas? Australia?

Ash rose from behind the desk and walked to the window. Ever since Rhiannon's arrival Carr had grown daily more tense. But in the past few days his irritability had given way to a certain expectancy. It boded ill for someone and that person mustn't be Rhiannon.

Lost in contemplation, Ash was only vaguely aware of the door opening behind him. Assuming it was a servant bringing a pot of strong black coffee, Ash gestured toward the desk without turning. "Put it there, please, and don't bother to stay and tidy up. I'll be gone from here soon enough."

He stared out at the sea. The dim, hushed predawn light soothed his burning eyes. It was like Fair Badden's pure sweet dawns. He would have liked to have gone for a walk this morning as he had so many mornings there. He would have liked to have stridden through the dew-shimmered grass with that fool hound Stella gamboling behind him and Rhiannon at his side.

With an exhausted sigh, he rested his forearm on the window above his head and leaned wearily into it. No such pastoral pleasures for him. He had an image to maintain, a reputation at stake.

"No. No sunlit vagaries for me," he murmured to himself. "Not when an entire night beckons me with the promise of untold amusements."

"Ash Merrick, you're a liar."

He wheeled around. She stood in a soft wash of paling light, a cloud of silky lace pooling about her bared feet, her shoulders rising from the froth of her night garment like an alabaster Venus rising from the waves.

He swallowed. It was all he could do. He was too tired and she was too beautiful and he'd tried, God knows he'd tried, to keep her safe from Watt and Carr and most especially himself.

But he hadn't any reserves left; he'd been wrung out of his last drop of self-restraint and he'd never owned any good intentions anyway. He'd wanted her, lusted after her, desired her, and *needed* her and she was here, in his bedchamber with cloudy dawn molding itself to her skin and a haze of soft slumber muzzying her soft, rich mouth.

But he tried. He still tried.

"If you take another step into this room," he advised her, "I will not let you leave until I've had you on your back."

She took a step into the room.

CHAPTER 28

Ash met her before she took another step. He reached her and dipped, sweeping her up in his embrace as easily as if she'd been feather down. Jaw set, he strode across the room and kicked open the door to the adjoining suite, stopping in the door frame.

Little light came through the long, tall windows facing out over the sea. A storm rushed down from the north, steeping dawn in a clotted blue-gray, making the room twilight. A great canopied bed, counterpane pristine as a sacrificial altar, stood in the center.

The windows rattled with a sudden gust of wind, breaking Ash's stillness. He carried Rhiannon to the bed, laid her in its center, and followed her down, imprisoning her between his arms. Trepidation clouded her exquisite gold-green eyes. Too late. He braced himself above her on shuddering arms.

His gaze devoured her, roving greedily over her shadowed eyes, touching on the mane spread across the counterpane, and moving lower to the deep, lace-edged vee of her sheer nightgown. It exposed the creamy column of her throat, the delicate collarbones spread like wings beneath fragile flesh, and the velvety shadowed valley between her breasts. She'd grown thinner in the last month.

"Oh, Ash," she said, reaching up and delicately touching the bruised flesh beneath his injured eye.

She ruined him. She saved him. He turned his face into her palm, branding it with a hot, fervid kiss.

He didn't want to rape her or rut with her . . . he wanted to make love with her.

He lowered himself, pressing her body into the thick feather mattress, intent on simply kissing her. He bent forward; his lips touched hers.

His head spun with light-headed pleasure. Her lips were as cushioned and warm as he remembered, but softer now, slightly, shyly, breathlessly opening for him. He sipped in her breath, tasting the corners of her mouth with his tongue with feigned languor.

"Kiss me, Rhiannon," he whispered, hopelessly vulnerable now, wretchedly aware that petitioning her favors guaranteed his rejection. How could she do anything else? She'd been someone else's bride-to-be and he'd seduced her.

"A kiss." He brushed his lips over the velvety shell of her ear, hoarding sensations, pleading with gentleness, begging with restraint. Her fragrance intoxicated him: warm and clouded floral, the sharp tang of sea and pine, the musk of arousal . . . *arousal.*

He angled his head, licking the base of her throat. Her pulse fluttered beneath his tongue.

Carefully, he slipped one hand beneath her waist, crept his arm up her back between her shoulder blades, and cradled the back of her head in his palm, lifting her body up. The thick satin mass of hair fell down over his arm.

"Rhiannon."

She kissed him. She lifted her head and molded her lips to his. He shivered with the unexpected voluptuousness of it, his body growing hard with burgeoning desire. The tip of her tongue teased just within his mouth, both bold and hesitant, untutored and wise.

His mind teemed with gratification, overwhelmed by every exquisite detail: her softness, her graceful curves, the beat of her heart. A beautiful female body lay beneath him, vibrant and glowing with slowly awakening appetite. But all this could not explain his total absorption, because he was involved with so much more than the body that yearned beneath his hands and lips.

Rhiannon. Rhiannon's heart, flesh, and bone. Rhiannon revealed to him, beneath him, surging up to cling to him. It had been Rhiannon since Beltaine night. He could no longer fight that knowledge.

She undid him.

He settled his hips against hers, rocking into her with little irrepressible jerks. Her thighs relaxed, she tilted her hips. He shivered, fighting for control, fearful of crushing her. Mouths still melded, hand still cupping her delicate skull, he shifted away and swept his hand between them, encountering fragile silk and gossamer lace. He no longer thought, he reacted instinctively. The material that kept her from him hissed as it tore.

Startled, her eyes flew wide. Her hands instinctively flew up to brace against his chest.

He cursed himself. He'd no graces, no art, nothing but this devastating desire growing each moment, and each moment shredding his tenuous mastery of it.

He released her mouth, overwhelmed. His heartbeat raced out of control. He closed his eyes, fighting the imperatives of pure want, forcing his breath to a quieter tempo, chaining desire to his will.

He had not meant to frighten her.

"I won't hurt you," he promised thickly. He bracketed her face between his forearms and, with as much gentleness as he possessed, touched her cheek, her temples, lining one silky-smooth brow and feathering her eyelashes with the back of his forefinger, trying to show her what he could not say.

Beautiful. Lovely and sweet and impossibly desirable. His gaze roved over all the grace notes of her countenance: the slight dilation of her pupils, the thin white scar on her cheek, the delicate blue tracery of veins on the whiteness of her breasts.

Slowly, the taut line of her mouth relaxed as he plied her with soothing caresses. He brushed her shoulder in slow, ever-widening circles, moving gradually to her breast. She sighed, a sweet sound of abandonment. He found the tip of one breast and rolled the nub between his thumb and fingers, watching her face intently.

She inhaled sharply. Her shoulders arched off the bed; her breasts rose in an unvoiced overture. He made no attempt to withstand the offer. His mouth closed on her dark, ripe nipple, sucking gently at first but then more greedily, lifting and kneading the other plump breast.

It was more than Rhiannon could bear. All the words, the terrible names, the warnings and castigations she had been chanting like a charm against his enchantment could not save her. She did not want to be saved.

His mouth pulled forbidden sensations from her while his hand fondled her other breast into peaked and ready arousal. The hardness pressed against the vee at the top of her thighs rubbed with intimate promise, swirling into a rush of titillation.

Unable to resist, she combed her fingers through his long, tangled black hair, stroked his face, and felt the rasp of his unshaven cheeks. He drew harder, deeper. A throaty purr vibrated from deep in her throat.

The sound caused him to release her. His eyes flashed up to meet hers, black and unreadable. For a timeless moment she stared into their depths and then he lowered her shoulders to the bed. Slowly, like a prowling beast, he moved up over her, his legs on either side of her hips. He braced himself on his arms, suspended above her, his hair falling forward, masking his features. The only sounds she could hear were the pelted spatter of rain on glass and her own harsh breath.

He suddenly pushed back, knees spread wide, and rested on his heels. His gaze locked on her mouth. He grasped his shirt bottom and pulled it from his breeches and over his head.

It had been dark on Beltaine night and thus she'd never fully seen what she'd clutched and stroked and petted and strained to join. And when he'd fought he'd been filthy and battered. Now, finally, she did.

For the first time she saw how beautiful he was, more beautiful than her imagination had allowed. His hips were narrow and his shoulders broad, his body taut and lean. His clear skin sheathed hard muscle and long, clean bone. Her gaze dropped and fled. The evidence of his arousal strained the fabric of his breeches.

His gaze followed her own. "Yes, *boidheach*, readied, hard and urgent, for pleasuring you, for pleasuring myself. For passion's sake."

"No other reason?" she whispered, trying to ignore the sliver of uneasiness his words had caused.

If he heard he gave no indication. His eyes were nearly black with arousal, focused and intense. He stretched out his hand. Purposefully, he ran his knuckles in a long, drawn out caress starting from the base of her throat, moving slowly between her breasts down over her belly to the thicket of soft curls between her thighs. She writhed beneath the gentle contact, trying to remember what she'd asked and why.

"Need there be another?" he whispered hoarsely.

She did not answer, for his fingers had found her nether lips and were gently stroking the silky interiors. Moments and hours, he played upon her body, stroking and urging, nibbling and licking, tender kiss and sharp nips ending just the pleasure side of pain. She lost herself in the vortex of sensation, liquid with want, the agitated sounds of constricted pleasure humming from her throat, foretelling her crisis.

Finally she could take no more, she held up her arms, her eyes wide and unseeing. He fell upon her like a sea eagle on a dove, jerking his strained breeches away, unerringly finding the moist cove he'd so thoroughly prepared. He entered in one long, sense-shattering slide.

She caught her breath, instinct and need supplying what befuddled memory withheld, and shifted her hips to accommodate the length of him. She would surely die. It felt that good; it promised that much.

"Rhiannon," he gasped, grasping her hips in his big callused hands, the scarred wrists shining like a strand of milky pearls in the dim light. "This time it counts." His gaze held hers until finally she surrendered.

"Aye. It does."

He began moving, his teeth grinding together and his eyes clenched in extremity. Unbearable stimulation, too rich a broth, too heady a brew, her body riding waves of increasing desire, pulling her muscles tight with anticipation, forcing her hips to rise, to accommodate more, to welcome the increasing power of his thrusts. Her back arched, her hips bucked, and her mouth opened on soundless supplication as her hands flew up to seek purchase against the storm of sensation buffeting her from within.

They found Ash's rock-hard body. A sound like a growl vibrated from his throat. The muscles of his arms and chest and throat stood out, straining and corded-over with dark veins. He thrust forcefully, caught up in the intensifying rhythm, aggressive, masculine, moving in her, taking her.

There. And there. All the swirling sensations condensed and telescoped with dizzying speed to a single center.

Then it exploded.

Every inch of her skin, every fiber, every bone flooded with rich, boundless pleasure.

There. There. She panted, riding the tidal wave of feeling, absorbing it, shivering with its aftermath. She clung to him, dimly becoming aware of the runaway thunder of his heartbeat beneath her ear. He flung his head back, lifting her and clamping her to him.

"Rhiannon. *Chan urrainn dhomh ruith tuilleadh.*" *I cannot run anymore.* "For my heart's sake. It always has been."

Words had no meaning here, the only truths were his arms and body, his kisses and his strength. His words barely penetrated her thoughts, sweet verbal caresses when her whole body was being stroked.

"Rhiannon!" He thrust into her one last time.

His whole body shuddered. A low cry of triumph surged from his throat. He froze, holding himself deep within her, straining and raw and beautiful in the act of completion.

Gradually the rigidity melted from his body. His face fell forward into the lee of her throat. His breath sounded harsh in her ear. With a small groan, he set his shoulder to the mattress and rolled, pulling her over onto him. His forearm looped about her waist, keeping her there.

He was hot and damp and solid and she'd never felt anything so good, so perfect. Lush with completion, she drifted, disjointed and detached from time and memory, his chest her pillow, his body her bed.

"Sleep, Rhiannon," he murmured, stroking her hair from her temples. His breath was warm. "The day will wait."

She sighed, utterly content, and nuzzled her cheek against the rising plane of his chest and, beyond all expectation, fell asleep.

Rhiannon woke slowly. The warm skin beneath her cheek rose and fell in measured cadence. *Ash.* She opened her eyes. It was still early, the room was still dark. A glance at the boiling gray sky outside the window told her why. A storm had taken hold of the coast. It might be days before it blew over.

She lifted her gaze to Ash, studying him as he slept. She was startled by what she saw.

She'd always thought of Ash as a man, fully mature and well into his prime years. But now, with slumber erasing the jaded sophistication from his face, and his eyelids hiding his bleak, world-weary soul, she realized that Ash Merrick was a young man, a *very* young man. Perhaps no more than a few years her senior. Tenderness filled her.

Being careful not to disturb him, she swung her legs over the edge of the bed and sat up. He sighed in his sleep and flung one long, tapering arm out across the bed, as though even in his sleep he searched for something. She leaned forward, intent on bestowing a kiss on his bluish-cast cheek, but thought better of it.

She had to leave him, before someone discovered her in his bed and told Lord Carr. She'd no doubt that Ash's father would use the information in some hurtful way. She did not want to be another flail Carr wielded over his son. She wanted only to love Ash.

She smiled sadly. She'd been correct in Fair Badden to think she'd been prey to a girlish infatuation. She'd been besotted by Ash's black and white good looks, by the forbidden danger suggested by his scarred wrists, and by a susceptibility to his glib tongue and urbane manners. She'd been enamored of a mask, a character Ash had created to hide the real man, a man so much more complex, so much more vulnerable, and yet so much stronger than that play actor. A man in need of love.

Well, Rhiannon thought, he had her love if he wished it and even if he didn't. She loved Ash Merrick.

How sad, she thought, that she'd spent so many years amongst loving, gentle people and never learned the simplest truth of that emotion—that the heart does not need reasons to love, only the opportunity.

She'd never had to earn Richard or Edith Fraiser's love. She'd never had to be careful in securing Phillip's affection.

The thought of Phillip ambushed her. How ill she'd used him! How grievously she'd wronged him! She could never begin to make up to him what she owed—but she must. She would never know peace until she tried.

She stood and gathered her ruined nightgown about her as best she could. With one last, lingering glance at Ash, she slipped from his room and down the dark corridor.

CHAPTER 29

The stable was warm, the dawn was cooled by sheets of rain, and young Andy Payne was as hot and cocky as only a sixteen-year-old male newly initiated into the world of carnal pleasure can be. His darlin', Cathy? Carly? had left earlier and he'd dozed a bit—this tupping business was most strenuous play—but now he felt quite up to a cup of milk and a bit of beef.

Whistling happily, Andy clambered down the ladder from the hayloft, leaving the stables and heading for the kitchen building. The smell of baking bread was just beginning to ride the gusting east wind. He followed it down the path between the alehouse and the icehouse, and in doing so ran smack dab into a human mountain.

Andy staggered back, staring up into a once handsome visage now ravaged by sleeplessness and pain.

"Mr. Watt!" Andy cried.

Phillip clamped his hand over the boy's mouth, hushing him in a low urgent voice before half dragging him into some scrub larch fifty feet away. A half-dozen men materialized from the brush and encircled Andy. Their faces were grim, their clothes hard worn, their boots scuffed with travel.

Andy counted three he knew besides Phillip Watt: John Fortnum, Ben Hobson, and Edward St. John. The other two men were vaguely familiar but the glint of excitement in their eyes he knew all too well from his years working his Dad's tavern. Troublemakers, this lot. Up to no good. He'd stake the guinea in his pocket on it.

"What are you doing here, Mr. Watt?" Andy asked, though he suspected he already knew, and that knowledge lodged in the pit of his stomach and made it ache. "Where'd you come from?"

"We've been here three days, boy," Phillip said tightly, "waiting for the chance to get word to Rhiannon. Thank God you've come along."

"But all you'd have had to do is write her a letter and send it by courier. Or give it to her yourself," Andy said in bafflement. "She walks out on the cliffs each morning. They aren't keeping her prisoner, you know."

"Ha!" Phillip's laughter was bitter, and bitterness from this man, whom Andy had always known as a jovial, fine chap, was as odd as summer snow. "She's watched day and night. I've seen her guards. We all have." He looked around at the others; they nodded in curt concurrence.

"Is . . . is she all right?" Phillip asked gruffly.

"Miss Russell?" Andy asked. "Aye. She maybe lost some weight but she's not being mistreated. I think she's mayhap lonely."

Phillip's lip curled back in a sneer. "What? Even with Merrick—"

He bit off whatever he'd been about to say and grabbed Andy's hand. He thrust a single folded and sealed piece of paper into it. "Take this to her. Give it into her hand and hers alone."

The look on Phillip's face sent Andy stumbling back. The others watched approvingly.

"Aye, sir." Andy gulped audibly. "Aye. Right away, sir."

He knuckled his forehead and backed away, scooting clear of the larch, apprehension chasing him. Apprehension not only for himself, but for Phillip Watt, who looked as changed as a man can be, and even more apprehension for Rhiannon Russell. Andy hadn't liked the look in Phillip's eye when he'd asked after her.

Andy peered back over his shoulders. The men from Fair Badden had vanished and— For the second time that morning Andy ran directly into the tall broad figure of a man. Strong hands steadied him and a smooth Scottish voice spoke from the darkness, "Now, then, lad. Why don't you be tellin' me about your friends out yonder?"

Donne saw Rhiannon walking swiftly toward the conservatory, a cape over her arm and a huge, lanky yellow hound pacing beside her.

"You're not thinkin' of going out today, Miss Russell?" Donne called after her.

She looked round in surprise and smiled doubtfully as he approached. This morning she wore her beauty full open, a lush highland rose radiant with youth and promise. He only wished his heart allowed room for something so fresh and honest. Alas, it was too full with the need for revenge.

"Well, yes . . . I was," Rhiannon said.

"You'll be blown from the cliffs, Miss Russell. But if go you must, allow me to accompany you."

"That is most kind of you, Lord Donne," Rhiannon said, "but I confess today I would most enjoy my own company."

"But I insist," Donne said. He moved close to her and looked down at her shining cap of unpowdered hair. "I have a note for you from a friend of yours."

"A friend?" she repeated.

"Aye. A friend from Fair Badden." He offered her his arm, and after that first startled hesitation, she placed her hand upon his forearm. "Not another word, Miss Russell. Carr was quite right to term Wanton's Blush his kingdom and he the king. A despotic king. He rules through many means, intimidation and blackmail being but two. Whenever you speak, whatever you say, I advise you to be oblique."

"Lord Donne, pray remember that Lord Carr is my guardian," she said uncomfortably, her eyes searching his face.

Yes, he thought, during her short stay at Wanton's Blush she'd learned to be wary, to trust no one. Pray God she wouldn't have to stay and learn harder lessons still.

"So he is," Donne said smoothly. They'd reached the conservatory doors. He took her cape from her arm, spread it wide, and settled it gently on her shoulders. Once more he offered her his arm. "Shall we walk?"

She nodded and he drew her outside. The rain fell in fits and starts, stripping the petals from the flowers. The small ornamental trees in the formal gardens danced with each gust, the creak of their branches underscoring the rushing sound of wind.

He drew her close to him, angling himself to protect her as best he could. He led her out onto the terrace and from there down the stairs, ducking beneath the arch that gave entry to the kitchen gardens and from there the sea.

At the seagate he finally stopped and positioned himself so that he acted as a barrier. He handed her the letter. She stepped back, half turning for privacy, and broke the seal. She read and as she read her fine, gold-buffed skin paled, the color bled from her lips, and her hands shook.

"I would go to him, Miss Russell," he said.

Her eyes snapped up.

"I intercepted the messenger your fiancé sent, a boy named Payne. I convinced him I had only your best interest at heart. He was scared. The young should never be burdened with such responsibility," he murmured, his gaze distant. He gave himself a little shake and looked toward her. She was watching him closely. "He told me about it. About Phillip Watt, and Merrick kidnapping you."

"You don't understand."

He shook his head gravely. "I do. Ash Merrick is a ruthless man. I know him. I understand him and in some ways," he admitted with a wry smile, "I even admire him. And because I understand him, because we are in some ways but different sides of the same coin, I tell you this, Miss Russell. There's no room in his heart for anything so fragile as affection or so nebulous as honor.

"There is nothing for you on McClairen's Isle but pain, Miss Russell. If you stay you will end up being a pawn. Carr already has an interest in you, which is frightening enough. Add to that Merrick's interest and you have a very unprepossessing future. Did you know that Merrick specifically asked me to discover how your death could benefit someone?"

Her head snapped up at this, her gaze unreadable but intent.

"Yes," Donne said gravely, unwilling to hurt her but knowing he could not spare her, "Merrick, too, is trying to determine your worth in this mad chess game being played."

"Thank you for your concern, Lord Donne." She sounded breathless. "It is much appreciated."

The fear he'd hoped to engender was nowhere to be seen in her lovely, composed face. Only a deep sorrow and, oddly, something like peace. Frustrated Donne tried again. "You don't understand. This isn't simply a rather nasty family. It's evil.

"Carr *killed* his first wife and then killed the next two. No one says it, especially those dependent on him for their gambling. Who would dare? But in London everyone knows it, accepts it as fact—including the king.

"Carr is not living here because the air suits him, Rhiannon. He's here because he's been *exiled* here. The king will not have him in London and what's more, the king has promised to separate his head from his shoulders should any other heiresses die under his care.

"That's what your guardian is, Miss Russell! He left his sons to rot in God knows what form of hell rather than spend his precious money to ransom them.

"*And Merrick is his son.* The same blood runs thick in his veins, believe me. I've seen him skewer a man's hand for cheating and you saw him fighting—"

"He had to," Rhiannon broke in. Her eyes had grown cold and her face frozen. "He has to do what he does in order to free his brother."

"His *brother* raped a nun! He is as bad as his sire. They all are." Donne shouted, infuriated by her inconceivable faith in Merrick, her abysmal naïveté. "Fia is nothing but Carr's whore, groomed to fetch the largest marriage settlement possible!"

"Lord Donne," Rhiannon said, the mist beading on her lashes and coating her lips in salty spray, "I . . . I am so sorry."

"I don't want your condolences. I want your promise that you will go to Watt. That you will leave this cursed place." He grabbed her upper arms, unable to keep himself from shaking her. "I am *trying* to *help* you, Miss Russell!"

She lifted her chin, her gaze scouring his face, a slow dawning inspiration turning her expression first to amazement and then to consternation. "Yes," she swallowed. "I promise. I will go to him."

He released her and she turned, the wind catching her cape and sending it billowing out behind her as she retraced her path, leaving him behind in the heightening wind.

Fia heard the receding crunch of Donne's boots on the gravel path. He was leaving.

Her knees buckled and she slid down the outside of the garden wall, her sodden cloak pooling around her on the muddy grass. She closed her eyes. *Murder. Whore. Mad.*

That small child who still dwelt, hidden and secret beneath Fia's sumptuous, worldly exterior whimpered. She wished she'd not come here. She wished she could forget what she'd heard.

She'd come down the stairs and seen Donne approach Rhiannon and speak. Whatever he'd said had arrested Rhiannon and with every appearance of consternation, she'd allowed him to lead her off.

Mindful of Carr's instruction to gather whatever information one could, she'd slipped along the outside of the kitchen garden wall until she'd heard them speaking.

It had not been hard. Donne's voice had risen above the rush of heightening wind. She'd heard every word.

She wished she had a knife like Ash's. When Rhiannon had left Donne she would have met him at the terrace bottom and pierced his black, lying heart. But she didn't have a knife and Donne was large and strong and harder than any man she knew, harder even than Ash.

She had thought Thomas Donne was perfect: polished, hard, yet with a core of something immutably . . . compassionate. She rolled her head against the hard, gray stone, sobbing on laughter. Compassionate.

She'd fallen in love with him two years ago, the first day she'd seen him, when he'd come to Wanton's Blush with friends and stayed a weekend. Since then she had loved him with all the intensity of her passionate young heart, doing whatever she could think of to attract his notice, to secure his regard.

It had been hard. Every day she'd had to fight to overcome the shyness that drowned her whenever she was in his presence. Too often she'd succumbed to the insecurities that made her flee a room he'd entered rather than risk making a fool of herself in his presence.

She'd adopted every artifice and embellishment that instructors and governesses, artists and dressmakers, perfumers and wig makers could provide. For him. And he hated her. Hated them all.

Because—she bit her lip until it bled—because, or so he said, her father had murdered her mother. And Ash was evil and manipulative, and Raine had raped a nun, and she? A little keening sound rose from deep in her chest. She was a whore. Carr was her procurer.

For the first time in years, tears sprang to her eyes. They spilled from her lids and streamed down her face mingling with the pouring rain. More and more of them, a torrent of them, all the tears she'd never shed and all the ones she would never allow again. And when she had spent them all, when she was exhausted and soaked with rain and shivering with nausea and cold, she planted her fists wrist-deep in the muddy ground and pushed herself upright and made herself walk through the storm back to Wanton's Blush.

To her father's office.

CHAPTER 30

"**W**hat do you mean you're not coming with me?" Phillip's voice rose. Rhiannon met his gaze sadly. The rain had faded to a soft misting drizzle. Her eyes were as calm and impenetrable as an autumn pool. She did not look like Rhiannon. She looked like a stranger, a sad, pitying stranger both older and wiser than the Rhiannon of Fair Badden. Too wise. He wanted to erase that wisdom from her eyes.

"I can't go back, Phillip," she said. "I came because I owed you more than a note, not because I intended to leave with you. I'm so sorry, Phillip. I appreciate it so much that you came here. I only wish I could have spared you the journey."

"Appreciate?" He shoved his hand through his wet hair. "You *appreciate* my coming here? That's all?"

She didn't reply and he felt the fury that now always seemed to be simmering just beneath the surface of his thoughts boiling forth. "What will you do? Go back to that," he flung his hand in the direction of the castle, "*brothel*, and whore for Merrick? Is that what you choose over me?"

If his words hurt her he could find no evidence of it. Her lovely face only grew sadder; her pity became more pronounced.

"It's no use, Phillip," she whispered. "Even if I agreed—which I never would—your father would never let us marry and you'd be thankful. Because in your heart, you do not want to marry me."

"Don't say that!" His glance slewed back to where his companions waited beneath the dripping trees. Even from a distance, he caught St.

John's disgusted expression and Fortnum's miserable one. "We can find a way round my father. He'll come round. As long as we live in Fair Badden, he'll come to accept it. Why, for God's sake, he all but chose you to be my bride in the first place!" He tried to deliver a laugh and failed.

She shook her head.

He ignored her rejection, anger overwhelming cautionary reason. The moment Ash Merrick had entered his life, he'd begun destroying it.

God, how he hated the man! thought Phillip. Merrick had turned his world upside down, charmed and mesmerized him, and then betrayed him in the most basic sense. Betrayed them all, Phillip thought, looking back at the others who'd lost money and peace of mind to that dark prince.

Merrick would demonize them no longer.

Phillip grabbed Rhiannon's arms, hauling her close, vaguely aware that she winced, but too overwrought to care.

"We don't need to get married in a church," he said. "We're in Scotland, dammit. We have only to say the words before a proper witness. We can return to Fair Badden with the deed already done."

"But I won't say the words," Rhiannon answered softly.

He shook her hard, a terrier with a rag, unable to stop himself. "What is it, Rhiannon? Do you think to become mistress of that castle? Don't you know what Wanton's Blush is? It's a byword for perversion."

She squirmed in his hands. "Phillip, please. You're hurting me."

"I don't care!" he thundered, his roar rising above the gusting wind. "I don't care. I have been hurt, too!"

She stilled. Her head dipped, but with sadness not shame.

"I know," she said. "I know. But this isn't the way, Phillip. This isn't going to make it stop hurting."

"Maybe not," he ground out, "but I won't let you throw yourself away on him. I couldn't live with myself if I allowed you to become his creature."

"Oh, Phillip—"

"He won't marry you, Rhiannon." Phillip shook her again, trying to reason with her, well acquainted with the strength of the spell she was under. "He'll just play with you for as long as you amuse him and then he'll betray you."

Her eyes lifted to his, no longer a girl's unlearned gaze, but one filled with compassionate understanding. He could not look at them. He drew a deep breath through his nostrils.

"I won't let him have you."

He dipped and caught her under her hips, tossing her over his shoulder. "Phillip! No!"

Jaw bulging with determination, he strode back to the others, ignoring her pleas and her vindictives, her flaying arms and thrashing legs. He was a decent man, a good man, and he'd offered her his name. She'd been promised to him. He'd only to get her away from that devil's influence and everything would return to the way it had been before Merrick. The way it should be.

In front of him, his companions broke from their awed observation and scurried for their mounts, trading roguish smiles and excited murmurs.

And if Phillip felt more ill than victorious, they needn't know and would never suspect. They'd only know that Rhiannon was his and he would not let her go.

It was late afternoon when Thomas Donne found Ash Merrick and his father outside Carr's office. Ash's voice was low, Carr's expression flat with animosity. No other guests were present. They were readying themselves for the nightly bacchanal.

Donne's smile thinned with satisfaction. He could not have asked better. He wanted to see Carr's face when the bastard realized that whatever plan he'd had for Rhiannon had been thwarted. And, Donne admitted, he would not be averse to witnessing some small pain on Ash's proud, dark countenance when he discovered she'd rejected him in favor of another.

It was little enough revenge against the family that had decimated his own, but small satisfactions were all he would allow himself until he found the means to bring this house down in its entirety. Watt had been a gift, a bit of unanticipated pleasure. How piquant that the situation allowed Donne to maintain his role of pretended friendship even as he delivered the blow.

"Merrick! Lord Carr!" he hailed.

Ash looked up. Carr's brows rose questioningly.

Donne hastened to their sides, taking care to compose his features into lines of concern. He pulled Watt's note from his hand pocket. "I just returned from Miss Russell's suite. I had gone there to ask her if she would care to walk in the conservatory. Her door was ajar. I entered and found this on the floor. I know it does not speak well of me, but I read it. I think you had best read it, too, sir, seeing as how you're her guardian."

He held the missive out. With a frown, Carr took it. As he read it, his frown disappeared and was replaced by an expression of surprise. Donne waited, his heartbeat thickening with anticipation, careful to reveal none of it. And then—and then—Carr's face bloomed with pure, unfettered exultation.

Carr looked up, his eyes shimmering with satisfaction. And relief. Stupefied, Donne stared at him, aware that Ash, too, was regarding his father with consternation. Ash snagged the letter from his father's hands.

"Bloody well good for her." Carr had managed to rid his expression of pleasure, but he could not erase the gloating quality in his voice. "This is what comes of offering foundling brats a home. Ungrateful baggage." His gaze settled on Donne. "You saw, didn't you, Donne? I offered her a home, dressed her like a princess, introduced her to my friends, and she turned her back on it. There was nothing more I could do, was there?"

Donne was so completely offset by Carr's reaction, he could not think of a reply.

"I couldn't stop her, could I?" Carr insisted.

"No," Donne answered.

Carr's head bobbed up and down. "Well, that's that then. She's gone and I still have guests who require my attention." Carr clapped his hands together, only just refraining from rubbing them together. He strode away on a buoyant step.

Donne watched him go, trying to account for Carr's reaction. He would have staked his life on the fact that Carr had plotted some ill use for Rhiannon Russell.

He glanced at Ash. His glance stayed and became a stare, riveted by what he saw.

Some small pain. That's what he had told himself when he'd devised this scene. If Carr's reaction had lacked evidence of his being injured, Donne's wishes in regard to Ash had been answered tenfold, a hundred, no, a thousand.

Donne had never before witnessed such raw anguish on a man's face, a pain so extreme that no mask, no experience with torture, no instruction in endurance, *nothing* could hide its eviscerating power. It turned Merrick's eyes to arctic ice and then ashes and then emptiness. Merrick's hands hung loose at his sides as though he had no power to lift them, as if just the act of standing tested him beyond his measure.

"She's gone, you say?" Ash's voice was quiet, empty.

"Yes. Gunna says she walked out early this morning. Hours ago. I found the boy who delivered this message to her."

"Boy?"

"Andy. Yes."

He glanced up as though he was having trouble forming cohesive thought. "But you just came from her room," Ash murmured. "You didn't mention questioning the boy."

Donne cursed himself for a fool. "I did not think it advisable to let your father know any more than necessary about her whereabouts. And that's not the point. Listen, Ash. The lad says Watt was with a great number of men. That they'd camped on the far side of the island. There's no good going after her. And no point."

"Yes. I know."

God help him, he had no stomach for this sport. Ash had been gutted, sure and proper, and Donne saw no sense in playing with the entrails. "She's out of Carr's grasp, Ash. That was all you *really* wanted, wasn't it?"

Ash turned his head slowly, seeking Donne's gaze and pithing him with such sudden searing understanding that Donne knew he'd given himself away and revealed himself as an enemy. And he also knew it made no difference to Ash, that nothing made any difference anymore.

Ash turned without a word and walked away, leaving Donne standing alone. He decided then to leave this place and to stay away until his resolve returned, because the long-lost hereditary laird of the McClairen's did not feel any of his anticipated pleasure in revenge.

Dressed in sumptuous, scandalous scarlet and gold, face painted in a mask of unrivaled beauty, Fia threw herself into that night's festivities. Abandoned and scintillating, she danced with countless nameless men and flirted with as many more. Throughout Wanton's Blush, at gaming tables and in back corridors, masculine and feminine voices alike re-marked her extreme behavior. She shone with a fascinating sharpness, a diamond newly cut.

When the meat of the night was being served, when strong heads and weak had been plied with their nightly opiate of wine and titillation, Fia heard dimly, like a cricket's song beneath the squall of a storm, the great clock in the center hall chime the eleventh hour. Calmly, disinterestedly, she removed Lord Hurley's hand from her naked shoulder and without bothering to explain herself, left him panting and red-faced in a shadowed corner of the conservatory. She walked to her father's office.

Once there, she looked around to make sure she was alone and then unlocked the door with the key she had stolen earlier that day. She en-tered. It was dark but she knew this room well. She struck the tinderbox beside the door and lit a lamp on a nearby table.

She did not waste time going over the items lying on Carr's desk. Instead she moved to the ornate marble mantel and pried her nails into a seam on its top. A thin square of marble came up in her hands, revealing the deep niche where Carr kept his most valued papers.

She did not know what she looked for. Proof, she supposed. One way or another an answer to Donne's accusation.

Carr had once told Fia that her mother, Janet McClairen, for all her insane loyalties, had been the one woman he'd loved. Fia had believed him for the simple fact that he obviously hadn't *liked* loving the woman.

Love, he'd said, clouded the judgment, absconded with reason, and diminished a man's effectiveness. This was so in keeping with everything she knew about Carr that she'd believed him. But perhaps he'd been a better play-actor than she'd imagined.

She'd always adored her father, even as she feared him, because cold and analytical as he'd been, he'd always been direct with her. Honest. He'd made it their especial bond. Others could be lied to, manipulated, occasionally—and necessarily—hurt through deceit, but he would *never* use her in such a way. Certainly he would never barter her to the highest bidder like . . . *like a whore.*

But perhaps Carr *had* lied. Perhaps everything he'd told her had been deceits, equivocations, and sophistry told to keep her malleable, to distance her from her brothers because they knew the truth, to keep her shut away from the world while he groomed her for her future . . . sale.

Perhaps Carr had killed Janet McClairen.

Her mother.

Carefully Fia removed a thick packet of letters and papers and returned to the desk. Carr would be occupied for hours with "subjects."

She had time to discover the truth. God help her . . . and perhaps Carr.

CHAPTER 31

Rhiannon sat huddled against one of the boulders ringing the small clearing. She drew her knees up, folded her arms, and waited. The men from Fair Badden were sleeping.

As she watched, a curl of smoke floated up from the smoldering campfire like a phantom fleur de lis and dissolved into the black night. No moon or stars shown in the ebony sky. It was a good night for prey animals to be afoot. A good night to walk away.

Phillip had not bothered to set a guard. He'd assumed that a woman alone would never dare flee into this desolate wilderness. He'd been mistaken. She was a daughter of these unforgiving mountains. Whatever they threatened her with could be no more painful than that which Phillip had already done to her: taken her from Ash.

Rhiannon waited another fifteen minutes before gathering her damp skirts and creeping forward. Nearby—too near to chance saddling—the tethered horses nickered softly. Silently, she rifled through the belongings scattered about and found a skein of water. She slipped its leather thong across her shoulders, anger thrumming through her.

Her entire life had been a series of fear-inspired flights: the escape from the Highlands, her abduction from Fair Badden, and now Phillip's "rescue." She'd been taken from her home and then from her adopted home and now from Ash, always for the same reason: so she would be *safe*. And in the process she'd left behind those people and things she loved.

No more.

She would stay in the Highlands and if by staying she was destroyed, then she would be destroyed fighting for what she wanted, not fleeing what she feared. True, Ash Merrick was dangerous and passionate and complicated. Perhaps he would even be the death of her. But she loved him, with all her heart she loved him, and she would fight to stay at his side.

At the edge of the campsite, she lifted her hem and sprinted into the woods, her eyes riveted on the east. And Ash.

There was not much to pack, but then there never had been. A shirt, an extra pair of breeches, woolen socks. Ash thrust them into a leather satchel atop the belt stuffed with the money for Raine's ransom.

He still had his promise. He must hold on to that. It was all he had now. All he'd ever had, really, except for those brief incandescent hours before she'd left.

He understood. He did not fault her choice. Whatever magic they'd wrought as lovers had dissolved with Watt's note and sanity's return. She'd weighed Ash's poverty—not merely a paucity of coin—against all Watt had and represented. Watt had won. How could it be different? What could Ash offer her that could compare with friends, family, security, and home?

He'd thought of going after her—but it was a brief madness, the desperate last measures of an injured heart. He wanted her happiness too much to delude himself any longer. He couldn't pretend Phillip wanted her dead. That wretched giant would never harm Rhiannon.

Ash's gaze strayed to the adjoining room and the bed that still held their fragrance, the unique perfume of their lovemaking.

He'd made love with Rhiannon. He allowed the words to sweep over him with all their sweet, shattering power. He'd loved Rhiannon.

He braced his arms atop the satchel, his head falling forward. He'd loved Rhiannon and he'd never told her. In a life rife with misadventure and iniquity he knew that was the one act for which he would never forgive himself.

He threw his head up, inhaling through clenched teeth. It was as well for her that he'd never told her. It would have only added to her confusion. She loved Fair Badden. She cared for Phillip. If she would never again know such passion—he stopped, forcing himself to bitter honesty—if *he* never again knew that passion, many lived without it.

If this emptiness held at its core a hurt that threatened any second to erupt and consume him, he would survive that, too. It need only take time to heal. Say, a few eternities.

Yet, he thought, he would not have traded a second in her arms, a single word, not one of her smiles in order to extinguish all his anguish. Whatever pain it cost him was well worth the remembrance of her.

He released a long, shuddering breath and forced himself to buckle the satchel's straps. France waited.

He threw the pack over his shoulder and without looking back, walked away from the room, along the empty corridors, past the silent servants' furtive glances, down the filth-littered staircase, and out into the bleak morning light. He headed across the moss-slick cobbles toward the stables.

A dog's plaintive yip echoed through the yard. Dully, he looked about. A big yellow hound had been tied to the rail. Though the rope bit into her muscular throat she strained against her bounds. A prime case of Wanton's Blush tenderness, he thought bitterly, and went to the beast, bending down and unknotting the choking noose.

"Best leave," he muttered. "Take your chances in the mountains. Wanton's Blush is no place for man or beast."

The dog tucked tail and loped off, it's stiff hind leg in no manner impeding its speed. Ash stared after it. "Stella?"

The hound stopped at the stable yard entrance and looked back.

"Stella," Ash spoke quietly. "Come."

The hound turned its great head in the direction of the mountains, black nostrils quivering.

"Come."

Reluctantly, the dog returned to him. It was Stella. A tiny fire seeped through Ash's numb heart. Rhiannon would never have left Stella at Wanton's Blush. Whatever she'd intended when she'd gone to meet Phillip, she'd planned on returning. She had not willingly left here. Joy mingled inexorably with anxiety. He needed to find her. He started for the stables at a trot.

"Ash!"

He looked back. Fia was hastening across the courtyard, her cape whipping in the swirling wind. "Wait!" she called again.

He paused, anxious to be off, but he waited until she'd reached his side. "You're leaving," she said.

"Yes." He was eager to go, but Fia obviously wanted a few words, and he knew that even if Rhiannon was an unwilling companion, she was in no danger from Watt.

"You were not going to bid father a fond adieu?" Her smile was bright and mocking. "Or your little sister?"

His own raw vulnerability identified the subtle disappointment in Fia's young voice. He regarded her sadly. Whatever Fia was, she had been made that way through no offices of her own. "Fia, do you want to leave here?"

His words took her aback. Her smooth face softened with astonishment. She searched his face warily, as if suspecting a trick. "No, no . . . I can't." The words tumbled out. "Where would I go? What would I do?" She lifted her chin. "Why would I want to leave, anyway?"

"I can't take you with me now," Ash said, reading the distrust in her gaze. "Not now. But if you wish, I will come back for you, Fia."

She opened her lips to frame some stinging reply but her mouth snapped shut without uttering it.

"Think on it, Fia. I'll write. I promise."

He called the dog to his side and had started past Fia, when she caught at his sleeve. "Where are you going?"

"Rhiannon," he said shortly.

Her brow puckered. "She's gone?"

"Yes."

"But she can't. She mustn't." Fia's silky voice had roughened with such fear that Ash halted in the act of uncurling her fingers from his sleeve.

"What is it you know, Fia?" Ash asked. She hesitated. "Fia!"

"I think Rhiannon is in danger from Carr. I read his letters last night, all of—"

"What did you find, Fia?" Ash cut in.

"Her brother, Ian Russell, he's alive. He lives on one of the French-owned islands by the Americas."

"Still alive?" Ash's tension eased. "Then Rhiannon is not an heiress. She should be safe. Unless Carr has hired someone to kill her brother."

He threw the consideration out without thought and was shocked when he saw Fia blanch. Dear God, he thought in astonishment, she had not known what Carr was capable of and was only now discovering it.

"Yes," she said in a distant, hushed voice. "I don't think . . . Russell has been sending Carr money for Rhiannon's support and a substantial dower. Over the last ten years Russell has sent Carr thousands of pounds. Money Rhiannon never saw."

The quarterly entry in Carr's ledger. The overseas property Carr's little man of business had mentioned. Of course.

"There's more," Fia went on, lifting her face and speaking calmly now, too calmly. "I found a letter from this Ian Russell. Though he's a Jacobite fugitive, he grows homesick. Ash, he's coming here for one day, to see Rhiannon and then return to his island. I think Carr plans to have him arrested or . . . or killed."

One day. Realization swept over Ash in a cold, tidal wave of fear.

"No, Fia," he said. "Carr would never allow his association with a known Jacobite to become public or Russell to testify; it would end any hope Carr has of returning to society, if not forfeit his own life. And Carr can't take the chance that a hired assassin might fail. Russell is an unknown quantity, an adult, a battle-tested man who may well arrive with his own complement of companions."

He turned from Fia and began moving away, but Fia caught his arm again. "Why do you look like that?" she demanded. "What does he plan?"

He jerked his arm from her hold. "He plans to kill Rhiannon." He threw the words over his shoulder as he broke into a trot, his thoughts racing. That is why Carr had sent him to Fair Badden. Ash had been sent not to retrieve Rhiannon, but Rhiannon's corpse.

Ash ran faster, the king's edict ringing in his head: "No flower of England must die while under Carr's care." Carr had made sure that Rhiannon wasn't under his care, that she was miles away, that she had, in fact, never even met Lord Carr. Why, Ash himself would provide witness to that fact.

He burst through the stable doors and raced to his horse's stall, snatching it open and entering. Carr had planned it so perfectly. Ash would return with the body. Carr would strip the rings from Rhiannon's cold fingers and give them to Ian Russell, who would be too overwhelmed by grief to ask questions, and soon after gone forever, never realizing that not a penny of his money had reached Rhiannon. Should Russell find out otherwise, there was no telling what retribution he would seek, what he would do.

Hands flying Ash bridled and saddled his horse and leapt into the saddle, grabbing for the reins. No wonder Carr had been so stricken when he'd arrived at Wanton's Blush with Rhiannon. It was the one place on earth Carr could not allow her to die.

But now she'd left, and Carr's agent, whoever he'd hired or blackmailed into killing her, could finish the job.

Ash dug his heels into his horse's sides, flaying it with his hand and calling out loudly as the steed launched itself from the stable doors.

He had to get to Rhiannon before the assassin did.

"Where the bloody hell has she gone?" Phillip roared. His voice sent the starlings shrieking from the pine branches.

"Back to her lover," St. John sneered, crawling to his feet.

"I'll get her back," Phillip declared. His fury was a living thing. Merrick had taken her not once, but twice now. This last time Merrick might not have dragged her off, but she hadn't left here of her own volition. She'd become Merrick's doxy, chained to him by carnal desire.

"Nay, Phillip," John Fortnum said gravely. "Nay. The lass doesn't want to be rescued. It's clear to see."

Phillip swung on him, his hands balling into fists at his side. "She doesn't know what's good for her. She's fascinated, under his spell. I'll break the hold he has on her when I break his filthy neck."

The others gained their feet and traded cautious glances.

"I didn't come here to commit murder," Ben Hobson finally said.

"Is it murder to rid the world of a devil?" Phillip demanded. "He taints whatever he touches and destroys what he seduces. He deserves nothing less than death!"

"No, Phillip," Fortnum pleaded. "Think what you're saying. He's a man, Phillip, like any other man. No demon."

Phillip ignored him, ignored them all, stalking past the shuffling, muttering men and slinging his saddle over his mount. He laced the cinch straps and tightened the girth, the air hot in his lungs as he put on the bridle. Finished, he swung into the saddle, yanking back on the reins and spinning the horse around.

The men had not moved and Phillip scoured them with his glare. "Go then! Tuck tails and run! I'll find him without you!"

CHAPTER 32

"**H**ie on!" Ash shouted.

The great, yellow bitch darted about the cold campfire with increasing agitation, her hackles rising and foam spattering the huge muzzle sweeping the ground. At the edge of the clearing she suddenly lifted her head and shot into the brush, angling back the way they'd come. Ash hesitated. There would be no reason for Watt to take Rhiannon back toward Wanton's Blush. Nothing lay between here and there but rough wilderness.

He bent over in his saddle, studying the ground. The majority of hoof prints clearly led south and to the west, yet Stella's attitude had been nearly frantic, as though the scent had been thick in her nose. She'd not led him wrong yet.

Ash spurred his horse, plunging down the rocky slide of land after the hound.

The beast had been misplayed, he thought watching her. She was no gazehound, but a scent hound. She'd taken the lead from the beginning, quartering in sharp angles ahead of him, her nose to the earth, following a trail only she could discern. It was almost enough to make Ash believe in a benevolent deity, one who'd sent Stella to him as guide, for without her he would never have been able to pick up Rhiannon's trail in this unmarked wasteland.

But the hound had been crippled and the day had worn perilously hard on her injured leg. Except for sporadic bursts of speed, she lagged now, loping on three legs.

With increasing regularity Ash had circled the failing dog in ever widening rings, stopping often to rise in the stirrups and call Rhiannon's name. Each minute now portended a coming crisis, a fatal meeting between Rhiannon and Carr's assassin.

Around noon Rhiannon reached a high pasture. She sat down and pulled off her half boot. She tore another strip of silk from her underskirt and replaced the bandage covering the open blister on her ankle. A shiver racked her body and she shrugged out of her damp jacket, hoping that the weak sun would warm her.

She shouldn't be stopping at all, but she was beyond tired—wet and still cold from her night out on the mountain. Twice now she'd thought she'd heard the sound of pursuit. Once she'd glimpsed a lone rider on the lower slopes of the mountain. But that had been early and she'd kept to the steep upper slopes since then, eschewing the easier footing below.

All of her years as mistress of the hunt stood her in good stead. She knew the tricks of backtracking, the importance of moving with the wind through the densest brush and of staying away from the open places. Each time she utilized these lessons, she swore she would never again chase down an animal for sport. She understood too well now what it was to be the prey.

She forced her swollen foot back into the half boot and stood, looking cautiously down the long, empty pasture. The storm had blown over at dawn, leaving only a thin fog that the sun had quickly burned away. Before her the field grasses bowed low, fanned by a chastising breeze.

It would be criminally easy to spot a dark-clad figure moving across that flat green expanse but the alternative of climbing through the steep banks flanking the narrow valley would cost her hours. Hours Phillip would put to good use. He had the advantage. He knew where she was going and he must know she dared not spend another night exposed to the elements on the open mountains. Her only hope lay in reaching McClairen's Isle before he found her.

Once more she looked around, peering intently at the edges of the pasture, straining her ears to hear any sound of pursuit. She crouched down and hobbled into the sea of grass.

Stella's heart was more able than her body. She limped now with painful determination, no longer capable of loping. She held her head up, nostrils quivering but moving on a direct if painfully slow course, as if pulled by an invisible string. Driven by a sense of foreboding, Ash left her behind. He cantered in the direction she traveled, soon far outdistancing her.

Whatever path Rhiannon had taken had obviously been the most torturous route possible. Several times Ash had to dismount and lead his horse up a shale-slick incline or around a series of jagged outcrops.

The sun was high overhead when he entered a narrow valley a half-mile long. He pulled his mount to halt, scanning the rocky walls embracing the glen. He saw nothing. He carefully surveyed the swaying grasses before him. Again, nothing. His heart thudded dully.

Stella could easily have switched directions and even now closed in on Rhiannon while he floundered about in an ocean of grass. He'd lost not only Rhiannon but also the hound that had been leading him to her.

He stood in his stirrups and cupped his hands and called out, "Rhiannon!"

He would not give up. She was somewhere. Perhaps not here, but near. He could bloody *feel* her.

"Rhiannon!"

He waited, his body stiff with tension, every nerve stretched. He would find her. He would search the entire damn country if need be, but he would find her. His voice rose, filled the valley, echoed off the stony mountain walls. "Rhiannon!"

Far away, near the end of the glen a slender figure rose from the spring green grasses, a wood sylph called by a mortal's implacable summons. The sun blazed off her rich, dark mane.

"Rhiannon!" He spurred his horse forward and galloped like a madman across the field. He'd almost reached her. Joy animated her wholly beautiful face—vanished, became terror.

She stared past him, shouted words made unintelligible by the rushing wind. He leaned forward, only one thought driving him now; he had to reach—

A blow like thunder caught his side, throwing him from the saddle. He hit the ground hard, his momentum catapulting him sideways and tumbling him yards before he settled. Blackness swam in manic circles around the edges of his vision. A woman was shouting. *Rhiannon.*

He slew about and caught back an agonized cry as a sharp, lacerating pain drove through him. He peered down, trying desperately to focus. His right arm was trapped at an awkward angle beneath his body, and a dark, warm stain was seeping through his shirt. He didn't have time for this.

He shoved his good arm into the ground, pushing up on his knees. The world spun madly. Arms swept around him, the scent of pine tar and sweat and *her.* He clenched his teeth, fighting the enveloping void.

"My God!" he heard her say. "Dear God, Phillip, what have you done? Help me!"

Watt. Of course. How well he'd courted that man's hatred. . . .

Rhiannon eased Ash down to her lap, cradling his head, sheltering him as well as she could. He gritted his teeth at the movement. Tears sprang to her eyes that she was hurting him more than he'd already been hurt.

A shadow fell over his face and she looked around, crouching lower over Ash's body. Phillip Watt stood above them, the pistol still smoking in his hand. His face was white, his eyes startled and empty, like a dreamer who'd been awakened too abruptly from a nightmare.

"Is he dead?" His voice was numb with disbelief.

"Dead?" She spat the word. "If he were dead, Phillip, then either you or I would be, too, for surely I would lose my life in trying to see that you lost yours!"

The low, intense venom in her voice took him aback. The hand holding the pistol dropped to his side. He lurched forward a single step. "I didn't know. I didn't realize. God help me, there's so much blood—"

"Get your horse," she commanded. "We need to find help for him."

"Yes," Phillip mumbled.

Ash stirred in Rhiannon's arms. She returned her attention to him, hovering over him in a protective attitude, her eyes searching his white countenance. With shaking hands, she brushed the long black hair from his temples. "Quiet, my own, my heart. Easy. Be still, my love."

"Well, what are you waiting for Phillip? Kill the bastard."

At the sound of that smooth voice, Rhiannon's head snapped up. Edward St. John sat his horse a few yards behind Phillip. One fist rested on his hip; the other held a primed pistol.

Phillip spun around, like a child being called by too many voices, his expression confused and miserable.

"Kill him," St. John urged calmly. Rhiannon tensed, her arms tightening around Ash.

"I . . . I can't!" Phillip burst out.

"Of course you can," St. John said. "He really is a devil, you know. Or if not the devil, the son of one. At least a devil with cards. I can testify to that with some authority. Carr quite, quite has me in his debt. Indeed, in my short two weeks at that hellish Eden called Wanton's Blush I lost every bit of money I owned. Plus quite a bit I did not own. In fact, I lost my entire inheritance."

A flash of deep, burning hatred revealed itself in the trembling of St. John's smiling lips. "You aren't going to shoot the bastard, are you, Phillip?"

Dully, Phillip shook his head. With a disappointed sigh, St. John reached down with his free hand and withdrew another pistol from his belt. "I thought not. You really are Milquetoast under all that manly bluster, aren't you, Phillip? No matter. I would have had to kill you anyway. I was simply hoping you might accomplish at least one decisive act before your death. It was to be my gift to you. For old time's sake, don't you know."

"But why?" Phillip asked.

"Because you're a witness," Ash said. Rhiannon looked down at him. His gaze went past her, fixing on St. John with cold enmity. "A witness to Rhiannon's murder."

"True." St. John laughed and Phillip lurched forward a step. St. John jerked the pistol barrel around, aiming it directly at Phillip's chest. Phillip checked.

"Now, now, Phillip." St. John suddenly grinned. "Really, this has worked out so much better than I'd hoped. I shall kill the girl and then you, Phillip. When I send Fortnum and the others—oh, yes, our companions are still staggering about these godforsaken mountains somewhere— they shall find this little tragedy. Merrick, you *will* do me the favor of dying shortly? That's an awful lot of blood you're spilling."

Ash's hands groped feebly down his side and over his hip. His fingers grew red with his blood.

"Yes," Ash murmured. "I think I can promise you my cooperation."

Ash's gaze met Rhiannon's and she realized what he was seeking. She sobbed, doubling forward over him, her hands aiding his search. "Leave him alone!"

"Good!" St. John said, ignoring Rhiannon's rocking figure. "Because you simply must die. I'd shoot you myself but I haven't got an extra bullet. But perhaps I should keep you company whilst you expire."

"You're too kind," Ash said weakly.

"Not at all. Of course, I could just—move things along a bit." His eyes were flat and cold.

"I don't understand," Phillip said.

"The cornerstone of your character, Phillip." St. John shook his head, his gun still trained on Phillip. "Allow me to explain. With my help our sad friends shall piece together an entire unsavory tableau: A rapist—Merrick —shoots his rival—you. When his slut, having finally come to her senses, objects, he shoots her, too. Phillip, you get to be a hero. Because before you die you manage to get off the shot that ultimately kills Merrick. All very tragic, what?"

"But why?" Phillip asked again.

St. John's smile disappeared. "Carr promised to forgive my debt if I did this thing for him."

"Carr will never forgive your debt," Ash laughed weakly.

"We shall see—or rather, *I* shall see." St. John aimed the pistol at Rhiannon's back.

"Nothing personal, my dear," St. John muttered, "but as I said, Carr is a devil and the devil must have his due—"

The stiletto flashed from behind Rhiannon's concealing skirts. Hurled by a master hand, it flew straight, but the eyes guiding it were clouded and so rather than St. John's heart it pierced his shoulder, shattering the bone. One pistol dropped from his nerveless fingers; the other discharged into the ground and fell from his hand as he clutched for the knife buried in his shoulder.

"Bedamn!" St. John gasped.

Phillip leapt forward but St. John was too quick. He groped for his reins with his good hand and caught them up. Digging his spurs into the mare's flanks, he sawed back on the bit. The horse reared, her hooves flailing out, striking at Phillip. Then she shot forward and tore across the field.

Phillip watched St. John flee, torn by the need to pursue him and his debt to the man who was attempting to rise from Rhiannon's arms.

"No." She wrapped her arms around Ash and held on grimly. He closed his eyes and sank once more in her embrace, finally allowing the beckoning darkness to take him. "Go, Phillip," Rhiannon said to him. "Find the others. Now!"

There was nothing for it. Catching his horse's reins Phillip swung into the saddle. He knew what honor demanded. He rode for help.

At the far end of the glen, a scent filled Stella's nostrils. Not *her* scent. That was nearer now, but still some distance. Her scent was a promise.

This scent was a threat.

She knew it well. Her hackles rose in response, and a growl rumbled from deep in her powerful chest. It was the one who'd tied her so she could not move and twisted her leg until it hadn't worked and then twisted it more until she'd howled.

His odor rushed toward her on a warm, driving wind. She lifted her head and saw a man on the horse coming toward her, oblique and at an angle. Her stamina had failed her hours ago and she had no vigor left on which to draw. She was a kennel dog, a lady's coddled companion. But hatred is a power in itself and of that she had plenty.

Deep within Stella's heart a feral beast still reigned, its ferocity held hostage by kindness, its savageness imprisoned by love.

The scent that filled her nostrils set it free.

If anyone had been watching, they would have seen the mounted man reach the glen's far end and look back over his shoulder. They would have witnessed his relief as he realized he was not being pursued and so stemmed his mount's headlong dash to a slower gait. They would have seen him smile with malicious triumph as he entered the forest.

And if they had watched a bit longer they would have seen a long, muscular form racing with all the speed of vengeance through the winnowing grass and vanishing in the same spot.

Ash felt tears falling on his cheeks and lips. Woozily, he opened his eyes. The afternoon sun swam in golden pools above him, blinding him, and he turned his head away. Stella's huge head swam into focus, her tongue lolling clownishly. Good beast, Ash thought vaguely, she'd found them.

"Ash?" He peered up at the shadowed face above him. Worry and grief marked her voice. She turned her head slightly. The sun caught and caressed her features, limning her cheek and throat with light and tipping her eyelashes in gold. Her hazel eyes glinted with green fire. She was beautiful and courageous and everything to him. Everything.

He'd almost lost her and he hadn't told her he loved her and he had to correct that. She had to know.

"Rhiannon."

"Hush," she murmured. "The others will be here soon. You'll be fine. I've washed the wound and stopped the bleeding. It really—you *have* to be fine."

"So pretty. I never . . . said." He raised his hand and brushed the tears from her cheeks. She *would* weep silently, he thought. She'd done so as a child when she'd first come to Fair Badden. He remembered, a story told mostly by her omissions. "I need . . . to tell you."

She smiled down at him, her trembling lips soft and musing. "I know," she whispered, her fingers caressing his jaw.

He rested quietly a minute, savoring her soft caresses, the fragrance of spring grass and sun-heated skin, his gaze roving her features with calm deliberation until a thought occurred to him. "Where were you going?" he asked. "Where were you heading when I found you?"

A look of exquisite tenderness came over her face. "To you, Ash."

Once more he nodded, commanding himself to be content with that answer. But he was a passionate man and he was starved for an answering passion, *her* passion, her heart, her love, starved for words he could not ever remember hearing, and so, though he knew he was being greedy and taking shameless advantage of her tender heart, he did not hesitate before asking, "Why?"

This time her smile was fuller, richer, more certain, hearing in his commanding tone a promise of a future that had only hours ago seemed an uncertain thing.

She thought of all the years ahead in which she would tell him she loved him and all the ways in which she would demonstrate it. And because for the first time in her life she felt sure of another's love, of owning it purely and wholly, she could afford to be the slightest bit roguish. And so she gave him back his answer with the same words he'd used when he'd first told her he loved her.

"For my heart's sake, beloved. For my heart's sake."

EPILOGUE

Carr watched his daughter. She stood at the end of the servants' hall facing a small group of men—dirty, mud-coated peasants. He'd come upon them quite by accident. Usually he gave up the redoubtable pleasures of the servants' quarters altogether but this afternoon he'd needed to talk to his wine steward.

The men fidgeted, eyes downcast, faces sullen with the universal expression of the yeoman. Fia's face, as always, remained composed, as unrevealing as a sphinx. She said something and with much bobbing of heads the men disappeared, shuffling backward through the servants' door.

Fia turned and saw him, hesitated a second. Something bright flickered in her black eyes and then she sailed gracefully toward him. For a second she looked just like Janet. He shivered.

"What did those men want?" Carr asked her when she'd reached his side.

"They've found a body about fifteen miles west," she said calmly, "on the mainland."

"In the mountains?"

"Yes."

"So?" Carr asked. "What of it?"

"It's apparently a nobleman. The clothes, or what are left of them, are fine and there was an expensive wig."

There must be more to the story. "Yes?"

"He looks to have been savaged by a wolf."

"Impossible." Carr snorted, his interest in the tale fast fading. "There haven't been any wolves in Scotland for over a hundred years."

"As you say."

He began to turn, intent on finding the wine steward, but something about her complacence made him uncomfortable. She'd ever been cool, like a beautiful ice princess. Now she was hard as ice as well. And no longer cool, but cold. That type of coldness that burns. "Who was the man, did they say?"

"Edward St. John." Her eyes stayed on his face, soft and intent as a cat's mesmerizing gaze. "You look upset. Did you know him? Ah, yes. I recall. He was here last year, was he not? He lost a great deal of money to you. Losing money to you must surely be the way to your heart, for upon my faith, Father, you are pale with the news."

"Was he alone?" Carr demanded.

"Quite alone."

The bloody, bloody bungler. Carr had all but handed the Russell bitch to him. He deserved to die. Now he would have to make another plan before Russell arrived, find some other puppet whose strings he could pull. . . .

"I wonder why he was traveling alone in those mountains?" Fia smiled.

She was toying with him! The realization struck him like a slap across the face. The audacious chit! How dare she? Anger clotted his cheeks with high color. His mouth compressed. He wheeled and began stalking away from her.

"Oh, Father?"

He looked around. She stood exactly where he'd left her. Her hands were clasped lightly before her.

"What?"

"I forgot to mention earlier but a messenger came for you last night."

He scowled. "What is it, Fia?"

" 'Twas a message from a Mr. Ian Russell." She tilted her head. "I don't recall knowing anyone named Ian Russell. And I have quite a memory for names."

Russell. No! He wasn't suppose to arrive until late summer!

Carr's heart leapt to his throat. A thick, dull pain lanced through his side. His throat constricted and his fingertips tingled. The blood surged and boiled to his face.

"What?" he demanded in a choked voice. It was hard to breathe. His hands felt dulled, numbed. "What about Ian Russell?"

"Odd message," Fia said slowly.

"Damn it, Fia," he gasped, "what . . . did . . . it . . . say?"

"Oh, only something about the political climate not being favorable for sailing and that he must delay his trip indefinitely. Isn't that odd?"

Carr closed his eyes. Relief washed through him, but the cost of his momentary panic was high. The vise around his chest eased only slowly, the feeling returning to his fingertips in increments. When he finally opened his eyes, Fia was gone.

Le Havre France
July 1760

It was a nice inn, relatively new, and very nearly clean, particularly the private room in which the dark young man had carefully ensconced the pretty young woman. The innkeeper's wife, an earthy practical woman had winked at the handsome fellow when he'd demanded the room have a lock and he the only key, and remarked that a fine stud had no need of a tethered mare.

He'd laughed, returning a sally in coarse Parisian patois. Surprising because the gentleman looked a good measure better than his gutter speech declared him. And certainly the little mademoiselle looked patrician with her red glinting hair and wide hazel eyes and her blushes. . . .

Ah well, he was certainly handsome enough to lure a decent girl of good family and she was certainly beautiful enough for him to risk that patrician family's wrath. And the way they watched each other . . . ! The innkeeper's wife smiled and shook her head. It had been many a year since something so small as a look passing between a man and a woman had had the power to awaken her imagination. But these two!

Still smiling, she banged on the door to the private room, balancing a tray in the other hand. It contained the meal the man had ordered. The door opened and the beautiful woman stepped back, motioning toward the table. She did not speak. In fact, the innkeeper's wife had yet to hear the girl utter a word. She shrugged. Perhaps she was a mute and perhaps that was why she settled for a coarse-spoken beau. No matter how powerfully built or how passionately he watched her, a girl like this . . . she should be in a castle. Unless something was wrong with her.

Ah, well. It was no concern of hers. They'd paid in coin. She set the tray down and, after bobbing a little curtsey, left.

Rhiannon glanced at the steaming plate of stewed chicken and returned to the chair she'd pulled up beside the window. She knew the innkeeper's wife wondered at her lack of speech but she hadn't the "advantage" of Ash's years in a French gaol to teach her the nuances of an accent. She smiled tenderly, as always impressed that Ash could recall any part of his years in prison and find value in it.

Outside in the little seaport town the late summer sun was finally giving up the sky and sinking into the horizon. Ash should be back by now. He'd left yesterday at daybreak, making her promise not to open the door to anyone save the innkeeper and swearing he would return with Raine by nightfall the following day.

She'd begged to go with him but he'd refused. Rightfully so, she suspected. She could only be a burden to him on his covert mission to ransom his brother. England and France were at war and her speech marked her nationality quite clearly. If she was caught, well, even though born Scot, Rhiannon now owned an English surname—Merrick.

Rhiannon Merrick. Nearly a month had passed since they'd stood with Edith Fraiser and John Fortnum just north of the Scottish border and declared themselves husband and wife. Edith had cried. Rhiannon had never been so happy. She was still happy, deliciously so. Each day revealed more of the depth of honor and integrity the man she'd wed owned; each day proved the depth of his love for her. It was there in the care he took with her, in the passion and tenderness with which they made love, and in the worry that he could not quite hide. They had nothing. Except Raine's ransom.

Then, a week ago, he'd offered even that to her. It was, he said gravely, a fair princely sum. With it they could live wherever they wanted, anywhere in the world. His eyes had been still, his face composed, the offer utterly sincere—but she knew him now. She saw the haunted shadow behind the tender smile.

She knew then that he'd do anything for her, be anything she asked him to be—but all she wanted him to be was Ash Merrick. And Ash Merrick had vowed to ransom his brother. So here they were.

The sound of a carriage clattering on the cobblestones outside the window drew Rhiannon's attention. She pushed open the window and hung her head out. The carriage pulled to a halt before the inn's front entrance and the driver clambered from his seat. Before he could descend and pop open the door, it swung open and a lean dark figure leapt unaided to the ground. Rhiannon held her breath waiting for a second figure to emerge.

The driver went to the solitary man's side and held up his lantern; the swinging garish light swept over Ash's face as he counted out coin into the driver's outstretched palm. His expression was bemused, taut, his brows dipping low over his eyes. He glanced up and saw her. A wave of pure pleasure lit his whole dark countenance. He swung away from the driver, heading for the entrance, and Rhiannon slammed the window, hastening into the hall.

A moment later he strode down the narrow corridor toward her. She stretched out her arms and flew to meet him. His strong arms caught her up in his embrace, his head bent, and his mouth closed greedily on hers. She scraped her fingers through his hair, held his beloved face between her palms, and returned his kiss.

He pushed the door behind her open, still kissing her, and carried her into the room, kicking the door shut behind him. Finally he raised his head.

"Raine?" she said, unable to keep from lifting her hand and stroking his cheek.

Slowly he set her down. He shook his head. "I don't know, Rhiannon. I don't know."

She gazed at him questioningly.

"I went first to the prison to speak to the head gaoler. I wanted to make specific arrangements as to the time of Raine's release before I *visited*"— his lips curled back in a sneer—"the politician who was to accept Raine's ransom."

"Yes?"

"I went to the prison. I spoke to the head gaoler. Rhiannon, Raine is not there."

"What do you mean, not there?" Rhiannon asked, a dull sense of horror growing within. "Dead? Oh, Ash, did he die?"

"No!" Ash shook his head violently. "Not dead. Of that I am certain. I even 'interviewed' a few of the guards late last night at a local tavern they frequent in order to make certain."

"Then where is he?"

"I don't know. No one seems to know. He simply seems to have disappeared. If there were someone else who might have ransomed him I would suspect the French already released him."

"Your father?"

"Carr?" Ash's glance was incredulous but then, seeing her anxiety, his gaze softened. "No, Rhiannon. I forget your soft heart. But no. Not Carr. There is no one."

"Then he escaped," Rhiannon said.

"To where?" Ash asked.

Rhiannon touched his cheek gently. "He wouldn't go to Wanton's Blush, would he?"

"Not unless he'd a very good reason."

"Then perhaps he's just . . . looking for his life," she suggested softly.

He scowled and then sighed and finally moved his hand over her temples, brushing back the soft tendrils with infinite tenderness. "What a wise creature you are, Rhiannon Merrick. How much I love you."

She turned her face into his open palm and pressed a kiss against its center. "What are we to do now?"

He stared at her and then suddenly smiled, his expression far lighter than she'd ever seen it, free of shadows, obligation, or the past, filled only with love and anticipation.

He reached beneath his cloak and withdrew a long, heavy belt of double stitched leather. He held it up. "My dear, it seems we're suddenly quite rich—indeed, heirs to a fair princely sum."

She stared at the money belt in bemusement. Though all that money meant little to her, she knew his inability to assure she would have a comfortable future had troubled Ash greatly, so she smiled, too. "But what do we do with it?" she asked.

"Why, my beloved, we find our happy ending."

McCLAIREN'S ISLE

The
Reckless
One

CHAPTER 1

A fine drizzle seeped from the low, gunmetal-colored sky above the prison yard. The head jailer, Armand, bounced his cudgel in his palm, his already bad mood exacerbated by having to stand outside in this weather. Well, he promised himself, he wouldn't stand in it any longer than necessary.

"Hold his cursed head down in the water till he passes out if you must," he barked at the two beefy warders straining to force the half-naked man to his knees before a water trough.

They were having little success. The man fought like the devil. He'd always fought like the devil. Ever since he'd been sent here from the prison at Le Havre, after his short-lived escape.

Armand pulled his timepiece from his pocket and angled the face into the rush light. Five o'clock and it was already dark. Cold too, he thought, noting the vapor lifting from the prisoner's bare skin. *Damn* cold.

"Curse your misbegotten birth, hurry!" he shouted.

Madame would be arriving soon, heralded by a note received less than an hour before telling him to have ready an assortment of "exotic specimens." Spontaneous visits were unlike Madame Noir. Usually she gave Armand ample warning of her intentions—and her needs—so that he could make certain that her arrival did not coincide with that of his superiors. They would not look kindly on Armand and Madame's little arrangement.

But the perverse itch that tormented Madame this day apparently needed immediate scratching. Aristocrats, Armand thought and spat at the slick black cobbles. Who could account for their whims? If she didn't pay so well for her sport, he would have refused to see her. But she did pay.

A sudden burst of activity at the trough drew his attention. The prisoner had heeled back and rammed his elbow into the older guard's gut. The younger guard retaliated with a vicious blow across the prisoner's temple. A gash appeared above his brow, oozing blood. He dropped to his knees.

"*Non,* Pierre, you imbecile!" Armand sprinted forth, swinging his cudgel. "No marks! Drown him if you must but no marks, do you hear?"

"*Oui,* no marks," Pierre grumbled.

"And you, English *bite,*" Armand said, grasping a handful of the prisoner's hair and dragging his head up. "You had best behave."

The Englishman turned his head. Long, dark hair streamed over his forehead and a rough beard covered the lower half of his face making his features barely discernible. Only his eyes gleamed from the shadowed countenance.

"Or else what?" the prisoner sneered. "You'll kill me?" An evil smile flickered and disappeared in the dark face. "I am afraid, friend Armand, that your threats have quite lost their power to intimidate."

Startled, Armand straightened. The prisoner's gaze followed him, defiant, if edged with bleakness.

"And why is that?" Armand asked.

"You can't threaten a dead man with death," he rasped back in French gutter *patois*—the dialect of the prison. "I saw the clean clothes. Did my father send them for my execution? How sentimental of him.

"No matter. You'll not have them clean off my body, Armand," the Englishman vowed. "You'll not make one penny more off my corpse than I can—"

Pierre's fist plowed into his belly, cutting off his words.

Armand grinned. So that is why the Englishman fought so hard. He thought he was on his way to being hanged. He thought they were bathing him so that after he'd been executed they could strip clean clothes from his body rather than ones stinking of jail. They'd fetch a better price that way. Not a bad notion.

It was amusing and Armand, who rarely had the pleasure of denting this particular prisoner's self-containment, relished the experience. He motioned Pierre to revive the Englishman.

With a grunt, Pierre heaved him over the rim of the trough and dunked his head in the cold water. The Englishman lurched upright, sputtering and coughing—and fighting. Water streamed down his heaving chest, leaving muddy trails on its filthy surface. Muscles and tendons corded and swelled in his lean body. Even in the cold air the sweat beaded on the faces of the two guards straining to subdue him.

Armand watched with concern. The prisoner had come here as a youth, but the years had turned him into a man, a man who, in spite of the deprivations of prison life, still had somehow developed a formidable physique.

This is what came of mollycoddling "political prisoners" and allowing them meat and blankets and a room on the upper levels of the prison rather than in the fetid subterranean chambers where most were held. But Armand's master insisted that political prisoners be kept alive in anticipation of possible ransoms.

Armand thought it a waste—and possibly dangerous. Should the Englishman ever put bulk on that tall, broad frame . . . *Mon Dieu*, even three warders would have a hard time holding him. As it was, soon one of the guards would lose his temper and start using his fists on the prisoner's face. Madame disliked marked faces. Armand waded into the fray, his amusement vanishing.

"Merde!" he shouted. "You guard your virtue like a nun!"

"My virtue?" the Englishman panted, his struggles abating.

"Oui. She probably won't even choose you now," Armand said contemptuously.

"She?"

"Madame Noir."

The man stopped fighting, yet none of the tension left him. He narrowed his eyes on Armand. "She picked *me*? Specifically?"

"Non. She says foreigners. And you, *mon homme,* are one of the only foreigners left. Do not think to make her pass you by again. If you spit at her this time, I swear I will render you useless to any woman ever again."

"He is not useful to women *now,"* Pierre added his voice. "Best take whatever Madame offers, *brut.* It might be your only chance to ever have a woman. Though rumor claims Madame is the one who does the 'having.' " He broke into coarse laughter.

The Englishman ignored the provocation. Armand considered him. *"Should* Madame pick you, do not think to escape," he warned. "No man has ever escaped after one of her nights of pleasure."

A glimpse of teeth flashed in the prisoner's dark face. "Me?" He shook his head. *"Non.* I simply wish to take advantage of the situation, as Pierre suggests."

Armand snorted in disbelief. "You didn't feel that way some months ago when she would have taken you."

The smile disappeared. " 'Some months ago' I still held out the hope that my father would ransom me as he did my brother. I still believed—" He broke off abruptly. After a second's silence he shrugged, a smile flashed once more in his dark face.

"I still believed in something," said Raine Merrick.

"She is unnatural!" hissed the English youth chained beside Raine. "I heard what she is. Depraved! She'll not have me!"

The boy flung himself against the manacles holding his arms spread wide against the rough stone wall next to where Raine was likewise chained. He was seventeen, or so he said. The same age Raine had been when he had been brought to France.

"She'll not use me that way!" The lad's defiance broke in a sob.

Raine ignored him, watching the cell door with cold anticipation as he rubbed his jaw against his shoulder. The pleasure of having his face clean-shaven once again was as heady a sensation as any he'd known in the past five years. Of course they hadn't let him shave himself. They would never have trusted him with a razor. Instead, they'd tied him to a chair for the procedure.

Pierre had taken particular delight in waving the dulled blade above Raine's loins but as Raine refused to react the porcine guard soon grew tired of the sport and contented himself with describing to Raine in graphic detail what "Madame's boys" endured at the hands of the veiled lady.

Raine didn't bother to tell Pierre he already knew all about Madame. She was a legend among the prisoners. It is why, months ago, he'd spat at her feet when she'd arrived to look over her "prospects." He still bore the scars from the beating that little act of rebellion had incurred.

But at that time he'd still been certain that the years he'd already spent in this prison were somehow a mistake and that the two short weeks of freedom he'd had after his escape would soon be returned to him for the rest of his life. Almost a year passed before he'd realized his father would not be sending a ransom and that the prison he'd been sent to was a far harder place to escape than the one from which he'd come.

A desire for revenge had taken hold of Raine. He'd survived in this hellish place driven by a seething need to make his father pay. But this prison had a way of stripping a man of all but his most basic drives. Eventually his pride had withered and died as he focused all his dwindling reserves on the increasingly herculean task of staying alive.

Even the rumor that his father had ransomed Ash could not rouse his sense of injustice. By then he'd seen far worse injustices. No, Raine no longer wanted vengeance; he simply wanted to survive. And that meant escaping or dying in the attempt.

He'd die soon anyway. Few lived as long as he already had, killed by disease or illness, another inmate, or simply the slow inner corrosion that eventually found its physical expression in death.

He had one chance to escape and it depended on Madame Noir's choosing him over the other "candidates" Armand had dredged up. He looked around at the other men. Two were long-time residents: a hatchet-faced middle-aged colonist from the Americas and a slender Prussian dying of consumption. The English youth chained to the wall next to him was new, delicate, and sullen-looking.

Suddenly the door to the cell grated open. Raine peered through the gloom at the dark figure hovering in the outer corridor. His attention sharpened.

Madame Noir.

CHAPTER 2

Madame Noir had arrived to make a selection for her evening's entertainment.

Raine watched the black-clad figure step through the cell door. Hidden beneath a nearly opaque, ebony veil and layers of midnight-hued silk, she moved with an odd hesitant grace. A black velvet cape covered her shoulders and long black gloves encased the slender hands holding her skirts above the stagnant puddles on the floor.

Armand followed her, his face flushed and his ridged brows lowered in displeasure. Beside him shuffled a huge monolith of a man bundled against the cold, a thick cape draped over his massive shoulders and a woolen scarf wrapped about his thick neck. The eyes beneath the brim of his hat were sharp and piercing.

Silently Raine cursed the fates. Why couldn't she be accompanied by someone like Pierre? Big, but dull-witted and slow.

She turned and spoke to her man, stopping in front of the torches. The backlighting revealed her profile through the heavy veil; a slender throat, a sharp-angled jaw, a patrician nose. The men who returned from a night in her "care" swore she never removed that veil. No one had ever seen her face—even Armand—and no one knew her real name. She always registered under the pseudonym "Madame Noir" at the hotel she used for her entertainments.

She finished her whispered conversation and turned toward the prisoners. With what looked like a conscious gathering of purpose, she came toward them, her attendant shadowing her. She paused before the colonist.

"Too old," she murmured in exquisite, aristocratic French and continued circling the room. She stopped in front of the Prussian. He lifted his wet head and gazed at her with dull, hopeless eyes. "This man will die if he is not made warm," she said.

"Yes," Armand agreed uninterestedly. "A Prussian."

She remained studying the shivering man.

"But I might have a desire for a Prussian someday," she said quite calmly, and moved on.

Immediately Armand barked out an order that the Prussian be taken down, dried off, and fed. In another, one might possibly mistake Madame Noir's comments for compassion, Raine thought cynically. She moved toward the English youth.

Armand scuttled to her side. "He's new, Madame. English. Young. Feel." He chattered like an auctioneer. "Go ahead. I have never known you to be shy."

She lifted the boy's chin. His lower lip trembled.

"Very young." She sounded uncertain. "But English, you say—"

"Please! I come from a noble family. I cannot be used so!" The youth sobbed. "I am not the one you want! I am not the one—"

"*I am.*"

Madame spun around at the sound of Raine's calm voice, her veil swirling about her shoulders and settling like the dark wings of a nighthawk. She cocked her head sideways, increasing her resemblance to a small, sleek bird of prey.

"Monsieur is English?" she asked, interest sharpening her inflection.

"Aye." He watched her carefully. "English. You have a taste for Englishmen, Madame?"

Behind the heavy veil he thought he saw the glimmer of her eyes. He forced himself to stand still and turned his palms up, inviting her inspection. "I'm your man."

"Perhaps."

Armand hurried over. He grabbed a handful of Raine's hair and jerked his head back.

"Here, Madame. Come. Examine. Look. I know Madame is most careful in making her selection."

She came within a few feet. Her heated scent filled his nostrils, unexpectedly stirring his senses. A woman's perfume. Without warning, sensual images from his all-but-forgotten past ambushed him, flooding his mind, filling his thoughts.

Musk and flowers, cleanliness, and dark promise. Womanly and virginal all at once. Straining bodies, sweet aftermath. The sudden sensual memory stunned him with its force.

He closed his eyes, breathing in deeply through his mouth, tasting as well as scenting her. He hadn't been in the same room with a woman in five years, having hidden in barns and cave during his short freedom. Yet could that alone account for the thickening in his loins?

This woman was a bawd, a profligate jade, a byword for pollution, and while he'd once been a randy youth eager for most any sexual sport he'd never added perversion to his extensive list of vices.

Yet the mere scent of her stirred him.

"Touch him," Armand urged.

Did she hesitate before reaching out? Did she note the uncontrollable forward cant of his body in anticipation of her hand? Her gloved fingers brushed his naked skin. He forgot everything else.

His breath caught. He backed away. Not because he abhorred her touch. Just the opposite. Because he wanted it. Her fingertips fluttered down his chest to his belly to where his breeches hung low on his hips. He shivered, willing her hand to slip lower still, waiting for that intimate touch, aching with arousal, heedless of the spectators.

Her gaze dropped to the evidence of his arousal. Abruptly, she snatched her hand back, like a maiden.

"Madame wished a challenge?" Armand was asking. "Here is such a one. Arrogant. Young. Healthy."

"I don't think—"

"Forgive me, Madame." Her servant lumbered forward.

"Yes, Jacques?"

"I believe this one would suit very well."

Raine studied the mountainous Jacques. Since when did a servant advise his mistress on her sexual requisites? She did not reprimand him, however, but only hesitated before gesturing toward the English boy.

"Perhaps him," she said, and it sounded to Raine as though she was asking. "He is—"

"Very young," Jacques finished, his tone cautioning.

Raine ground his teeth in frustration. She had to pick him. She *must.*

"I will be whatever Madame wishes me to be." He forced the words out between his lips, surprised at how easily they came, how facilely he abdicated the last shreds of his pride. "I will do whatever Madame wishes me to do."

He held his breath.

"All right," she finally said. "I'll take him."

Jacques nodded approvingly.

"Very good," Armand said. "I'll send two guards with you."

"Not necessary," Jacques said, handing Armand a heavy-looking velvet pouch. Raine blessed the man's self-assurance.

"But it is, Monsieur," Armand argued. "I know this man."

Madame made a dismissive movement with her hands. "Has there ever been a problem before?" she asked coldly. "I do not wish spectators at my sport. I desire . . . privacy with him."

"I understand, but Madame, you must see that if this man should escape—"

"Do you dare to press me?"

"*Non,* Madame!" Armand assured her, hauling a thick set of keys from his belt and opening the lock that held Raine manacled to the wall. "Still, I fear this one." He fastened a length of chain between Raine's manacles. "I have the solution: The guards will ride post, on the back of the carriage. You will have privacy. I will have peace of mind. This is sensible, yes?"

Armand jerked Raine forward and handed the end of the chain to Jacques.

"If you insist," Madame said, irritation vibrating from her slender form.

She stalked from the cell, her skirts rustling. Armand hurried after her, barking for the guards. Raine, who'd kept his head bowed throughout the proceedings, glanced up and found Jacques watching him.

The huge man shrugged off his cape, throwing it over Raine's naked shoulders, robbing the act of charity by saying, "I will chain you in the coach across the seat from her. If you hurt her . . . If you so much as blow your filthy breath in her face, I will rip off your head and piss down your neck. *Comprends?*"

Raine's lips curled back. "I assure you, your mistress is safe with me."

"Good. Be civil, be wise, and all shall go well for you. Better than you imagine."

Raine could not keep the derisive sneer from his face. "Your largesse undoes me. I wonder if hers will."

In answer, Jacques shoved Raine between the shoulder blades. He propelled him through the door and down the low corridor toward a flight of stairs leading up to the prison's receiving yard. There, just outside of the gates, waited a closed carriage. The prison guards were already perched on the footmen's steps at the back. Armand stood beside the open door.

Any attempt to flee now would be futile. Choking down his frustration, Raine shuffled across the yard through the open gates. Outside, he stopped, unable to help himself, and lifted his face to the weeping sky. He drew breath outside the prison walls and closed his eyes.

"Go on, son." Jacques's voice was surprisingly mild. "Get in."

Raine hefted his chains and flung them in onto the floor of the carriage. Jacques reached past him, snapping a padlock through the links and locking them to a bolt on the floor. Damn the man's caution!

Unceremoniously Raine climbed into the carriage. Across the carriage, bootheels scrabbled against the floorboards. *She'd* already entered. He peered through the dim interior.

She was almost indiscernible in her black gown and heavy veils, being tucked as she was as far back into the corner as possible.

As though, he realized, she was scared to death of him.

CHAPTER 3

It was possible Madame Noir regretted her decision to choose him; that titillation had taken a backseat to fear.

But this woman was notorious for her *outré* appetites. The more probable reason for her ostensible fear was that it was all part of some perverse game. A game which, if Raine played it correctly, he might use to his benefit.

If he could convince her to unchain him he would be out of this carriage in seconds, losing himself in Dieppe's twisting alleys. With such thoughts, he crouched low as he entered the carriage, conscious of the part he needed to play.

Mindful of how his shoulders crowded the doorway and blocked the light, Raine slouched down onto the seat opposite her, angling himself in such a way that he did not appear threatening. He could hear her short agitated breaths, feel her tension.

Jacques called out from up top and the horses plunged forward, pitching her across the slick leather seat. Raine flung out a hand to keep her from falling.

"Take your hands off of me," she whispered.

She was not commanding him. She was pleading. As false as he suspected her trepidation to be, her simulated fear worked insidiously on him. His body reacted instinctively to the implicit submissiveness in her appeal. Was she pretending that she was an anxious virgin closeted with a ravening beast? If so, her fantasy marched closer to the truth than she could know.

It had been years since he'd felt such lust.

"Take your hand off me." Her voice quavered. He obliged, releasing her slowly, letting his hands slide down her sleeve. He did nothing to hide the direction of his gaze, allowing it to linger on the agitated rise and fall of her breasts.

Role-playing be damned. He wanted her.

"Madame," he said softly, lifting his arms and spreading open Jacques's cape, displaying his shackled wrists and naked chest, the scars of Pierre's frequent "disciplinary actions" ridging his white prison-hued skin. "As you can see, I am at your disposal, to do with as you please."

She shrank back against the deep, tufted leather seats. "You don't understand," she whispered.

"I do not," he agreed. "You will teach me, though. What *is* your pleasure, *petite* Madame? You touch; I am not allowed to touch? You arouse and then withhold the culmination of the arousal? Is that how you achieve satisfaction? Pray, do your damnedest by me. I am in a lather to be so victimized."

"Quiet!"

"Just tell me the rules of the game, Madame," he said tersely. He was more than willing to pay whatever price freedom demanded. He sank back against the seat, his aroused body flaunted for her perusal. "You have only to look to see how primed I am for whatever sport you chose," he said.

"O Lord." Her whispered epithet embodied the virgin maiden's horror of a lecherous suggestion. 'Sblood, she was a good little actress.

"I am yours." He leaned forward and gently grasped her wrist, drawing her gloved palm forth until it lay flat low on his belly. He drew his breath in on a hiss of undeniable pleasure. "Can you feel my muscles clench with the promise of that which you withhold?"

She tried to snatch her hand back but he kept it there, desperately trying to gauge the nature of his role. How much to ravish; how much to seduce. His very life depended on his ability to judge her reactions. Once, a lifetime ago, he'd been well on his way to being a master of such sensual expertise.

"I was resigned to my celibacy, Madame," he said grimly, "having long since purged myself of the tormenting memories of a woman's soft body, a woman's sweet mouth, a woman's ardent embrace. You've resurrected those, given them substance, teased me with their reality." His voice grew low and fervent. She tried to tug away, but her efforts lacked conviction. She wanted to hear this confession. Bask in it. Damn her.

He grabbed her other wrist and, heedless of her sudden resistance, yanked, tumbling her into his embrace. He hauled her into the lee created by his wide-spread legs. His arm snaked about her waist, the chains locking him to the floor jangling noisily.

She gasped, her hands trapped between them, pushing at his cold chest. The feel of her gloved fingers stroked his nerve endings. His heart thundered in his chest in equal parts fear and arousal.

"Cry out and I'm dead 'ere I've been of any use to you," he grated out. She was svelte and tensile as a young she-cat, her hips narrow. Even through the thick layers of her skirt he could feel the delicate jut of her pelvic bones brand his inner thighs. Her veil settled over his knees in a drift of black silk.

"Let me service you," he whispered, the line between playacting and reality blurring with the heady feel of her. His patience was wearing thin. She would find herself ravished in fact if he played this game much longer. "Let me touch you. Fondle you. Inflame in you a fire to equal my own," he purred. "Enjoy me."

He rocked lightly against her, striving to keep the anger from his voice. Anger as much with himself as with her, at the body that betrayed both his mind and spirit. "Here. Now," he said. "Let me take you. I can-not wait. Only unchain me," he ground out urgently, "and I will swive you as thoroughly as a spring stallion at his first mare."

"Let me go!" The veiled face jerked back. Raine cursed his impetuousness.

He released her arms immediately. He'd read her incorrectly, decided that coarseness would appeal to what he knew of her appetites. Instead, she'd been appalled. He was not mistaken in that reaction; no one could act *that* well.

He forced his features into a submissive expression, dropping his gaze so that she might not see how it burned. Trembling, she scrambled into the seat opposite him.

"Forgive me," he began in a hard, far from humble tone. But he'd been stretched a bit far, worn a bit thin. By this game. By her. "I should not have allowed my desires to make me so bold." His hot eyes lifted contemptuously to her concealed face. "But then, I thought you liked your captives vulgar and base. 'Tis the rumor in the prison where you purchase your toys."

As soon as the words were spoken he cursed himself again. He hadn't planned on speaking thus. The words had simply come. He sneered at his manacled wrists. He'd thought that over four years in prison had culled the impetuousness from his soul.

He waited for the inevitable; a blow across his face, an imperious call to turn the carriage around.

Amazingly, it did not come. She only squeezed herself farther back against the seat. "Sir. Please. Be still. Be quiet. The guards might hear you. Only wait, I pray you," she urged, "wait!"

"I am your creature, Madame. You have only to command me," he replied flatly. "As you well know."

They drove in silence until the carriage lurched to a halt. Raine peered outside. They were in the yard of a hotel. Beyond the three-story building, Raine could see only an occasional light in the distance. They were near the outskirts of the city. Good.

The carriage door swung open. Jacques stuck his massive head in and fitted a key into the padlock securing Raine's chain. He unlocked it, wrapping the links around his fist and jerking Raine across the carriage.

With a snarl, Raine stumbled out. Pierre stood waiting for him. An anxious-looking middle-aged man emerged from the hotel and assisted Madame Noir's descent. Together they hastened into the hotel.

"I will take him up to the room," Pierre said to Jacques. "Once there, he is your responsibility. You best make sure he is returned by first light tomorrow."

Jacques eyed the bloated French jailer with ill-disguised disgust. "Has Madame ever neglected her part of the bargain?"

"No," Pierre said. "Make sure she does not grow lax in her . . . satiation. This one is wily. Reckless. Come."

Without waiting for a reply, Pierre yanked Raine after him, leading the way to the servants' entrance at the back of the hotel. From there they climbed a flight of stairs, stopping before a linen-paneled door at the top. The door swung open and the innkeeper, bowing and smiling, backed out of the room.

Jacques grabbed Raine's arm and thrust him into the ornately shabby room, barking at Pierre to remain outside. Raine stumbled to his knees beside a four-poster hung with dull blue satin drapes. Madame Noir hovered on the other side.

"Madame," Jacques said, eyeing Raine and holding a pistol out to her. "I will pay the jailer and his partner and return."

"Must you leave?" she asked, coming around the corner of the bed.

"I do not trust the guard to give his partner his portion and I would not have you interrupted should the jackal come here looking for his share.

"In the meantime, keep this pistol trained on him." Jacques nodded toward Raine. "If he moves, shoot him."

She took the gun, leveling it at Raine. Slowly, he climbed to his feet.

"*I* will kill him if he tries anything," Jacques promised tersely, and then, with a worried glance at Raine, he stomped from the room, slamming the door shut behind him.

Raine stared at the gun. The pistol bore looked as cavernous as the entrance to hell, which, Raine allowed fleetingly, it just might be.

Without a second's more hesitation he acted.

His hand flew out, snatching the barrel and twisting it viciously. With a cry, she released it. He grabbed her wrist, spinning her around and slamming her back against his chest, pinning her free arm to her side.

His forearm jerked her head back, pressing against her throat. It would be a simple matter to break that slender neck. With one hand he manacled her wrist, with the other he held the gun. Carefully, he released the hammer and shoved the pistol into the waistband at the back of his breeches.

"Scream now, Madame, and die now," he whispered into the veiled ear so close to his lips.

In response she began struggling fiercely, her free hand tearing at his wrist. She kicked, but her movement was hampered by the thick layers of skirt. Still, one booted heel found his instep, crunching down and drawing from him a hiss of pain.

He wrenched her head back against his cheek, bringing the concealed face near his mouth. "Cease!"

She whimpered, her struggles abating but not ending. Immediately he became aware of her buttocks pressed against his loins.

He smiled humorlessly at his body's heated attempt to subordinate reason. Since the moment she'd stepped into that damned cell, she'd bewitched him. Perhaps his years in prison had perverted his sexuality because, 'struth, she aroused him more than a thousand fantasies he'd devised to keep him company over the long years.

"Please," she rasped. "Please. Listen to me!"

"No, Madame," he whispered. "You listen. Heed me well. I will never return to that place. Not alive. And you are the means for me to keep that vow. You are *my* prisoner now."

She moaned, her face twisting away from his, the silky veil slipping against his lips. "Please—"

"Shut up," he growled as a sudden realization overwhelmed him.

He needed to kill her.

Without doing so his chances of this gambit succeeding were well nigh nil. Should he actually make it alive out of the hotel he would not last an hour if he had to drag her along with him. He didn't have time to gag and tie her; Jacques could be back at any moment. And if he left her behind, she'd raise an immediate cry. He should kill her: quickly, silently, *now*.

But he couldn't. As much as every instinct for survival demanded it, he could not kill her. In more frustration than anger, his arm tightened around her throat. She began kicking again and he lifted her, hitching her against his hip, filling his arms with the firm, supple woman.

The old devil-may-care humor that had once been the hallmark of his character awoke in response. The rash, heedless boy who'd died, unredeemed and unransomed in a French prison, was resurrected.

No, he couldn't kill her but at least he could claim something from this night. Damned if he wouldn't see the infamous Madame Noir's face.

He grasped a fistful of dense, gauzy material. "Madame, you are revealed," he said.

He wrenched the veil from her head. Hair pins scattered at their feet, their small, sharp staccato a prelude to the silken whisper of her veil fluttering to the floor. Loosened tresses, soft and heavy as damask silk, cascaded over his bare forearm in shimmering waves.

Red-gold. Antique gold, healthy and luxuriant.

Confounded, Raine seized a handful of the silky stuff and jerked her head back.

Fine skin. Creamy and utterly smooth. Blue eyes, dark blue. Near indigo. Frightened. Young. Very young.

Too young.

"Madame," he said, easing his forearm's pressure from her throat, "who the hell are you?"

CHAPTER 4

The girl—for certainly she was not much more than that—wrenched away, his surprise aiding her escape. She wheeled to face him and her hair came further undone, spilling about her shoulders and tangling with the jet beads decorating her bodice, the black silk a foil for the gleaming gold strands.

Black, too, were her brows. Or so nearly black as to make no difference. The contrast between them and her red-gold hair was startling. Straight, slender and severe, they lowered over the bridge of her nose. Wide, passionately full lips curled back over her pearly teeth, exposing the slight unevenness of the front pair.

"Who are you?" he demanded again.

"I have been trying to tell you!" she said. "But you . . . you idiot! Imbecile! You would not listen. You must grab and hurt and fight before you even know what you are doing. Thrice I asked for your patience!" She pointed a gloved finger at him accusingly. "*Thrice*! Could you not wait? Must you try to kill me?"

"Mademoiselle," he ground out, anger quickly supplanting his astonishment at finding himself harangued by a small, spitting she-cat, "if I'd wanted you dead, you'd *be* dead."

In answer to this, his most threatening voice, she flung up her arms in disgust. "Bah!" she spat. "You English are all alike. Push! Bully! Reckless. Fine, Monsieur. If you must be reckless be reckless with your own life, not mine and not Jacques's."

To claim astonishment would have been understating Raine's reaction.

The girl quivered with indignation. Or, fear. Raine's gaze sharpened. He knew she'd grown pale because of the color slowly returning to her cheeks and the breath, which stirred a few strands of gold, came in pants.

He *had* frightened her. From the very beginning. What he'd read as a jade's deviant role-playing had been real. She probably wasn't even cognizant of the degradation he'd been willing to embrace in order to escape. Hell, he thought, she probably hadn't understood half of what had gone on during that carriage ride.

"Pray, speak, Mademoiselle. I'm a captive audience," he said, mindful of the pistol sticking comfortingly into the small of his back.

He crossed his arms over his chest, noting her gaze drop to his bare skin and skitter away as she blushed. Dear Lord, she looked like a novitiate, Raine thought, and thus was reminded of another novitiate, a lass whose gaze burned with a far more secular fire than this one's. But Merry's dark beauty had been earthy while this girl—well, she was no beauty.

Those brows, for one thing, too boldly, defiantly straight. And her jaw was too square. And her nose too aggressive. Though, 'struth, she'd gorgeous hair. And a lower lip he'd greatly like to sink his teeth into, it was that rich and full. Her eyes—no one would fault them if they could but be appreciated beneath the dark slashes of those condemning brows.

"Stop staring at me!" she said, scowling even more fiercely.

"I'm not to speak, grab, or bully as well as not *look*? Well, now that you've finished looking *your* fill," he said, noting in satisfaction that her cheeks grew rosy once again, "do you think you might enlighten me as to *what in God's blood is going on*?"

She flew the few feet separating them and reached up, smothering his mouth behind her fingertips, hushing him urgently.

"Quiet, you . . . you blasphemer!" she hissed. Dear God, she even spoke like a convent—

The door slammed open with such force that it bounced against the wall and slammed shut again, giving Raine a glimpse of Jacques's beet-red countenance. Raine grabbed the girl and yanked the pistol from his waistband, pointing it at her head just as the door flew open once more and Jacques surged through it.

"Carefully, *mon ami*," Raine advised. Jacques came up short, the sight of the pistol barrel a few inches from the girl's temple stopping him as effectively as a brick wall.

"We should have taken the younger one," the girl said.

"Bah!" Jacques spat contemptuously, his gaze trained on the pistol. "That quaking aspen leaf? No one would mistake him for *La Bête*."

"*La Bête?*" Raine echoed. "Who is The Beast?"

The girl's attention swung to him. "You misheard," she said quickly. "Not *La Bête,* Monsieur. *Lambett.* My husband."

She could not have surprised him more had she announced she had a tail. He could not say why. She simply didn't *look* like a wife.

"Monsieur. Lower the pistol," Jacques urged, making a broad, pacifying Gaelic gesture. The plea in his voice in no manner reached his eyes. "I'll shut this door. You lower the gun. We will explain. Everything."

"And if I choose not to lower the gun?"

Jacques's countenance turned dusky. "Then we sit here until it falls from your numb fingers. Because if you try to leave we will simply call the alarm." Apparently, his conciliatory mood had evaporated.

"I could always kill you," Raine suggested.

"If you shoot, the sound of gunfire is its own alarm," Jacques said with no small satisfaction. "So drop the pistol, eh?"

So Jacques disliked being threatened. So had Raine at one time. It was amazing what one could get used to if the need arose.

"I have a better idea," Raine said. "I keep the gun where it is and you tell me everything anyway."

"You *merde!*" Jacques burst out. "You gallows offal! How dare—"

"Jacques!" the girl broke in. "Please! This is getting us nowhere. Explain to him or I will."

Raine studied her. A sheen of perspiration covered her face, shimmered above her luscious lips. A lie from her would be easy to discern.

"An even better idea," Raine said. "*You* explain, Mademoi—Madame Lambett. And you, Jacques, remain very, very quiet. Or I will shoot you and then I will . . ." He smiled tellingly at the girl. "Well, you won't be around to discover that, will you?"

"You were right," Jacques said to the girl, his eyes on Raine. "We should have taken the aspen leaf."

"Now, one last time, explain."

The girl nodded slowly. "As you will, Monsieur. My husband, Richard Lambett, died a month ago from the fever. He was English."

Raine's interest was piqued yet he remained mute.

"I see you have some appreciation of how unlikely such a marriage is . . . was. But the heart is not always so wise, is it?"

"I wouldn't know, would I? Having spent the years in prison most men are bedding wenches." Raine sneered at her sentiment, causing her indigo gaze to drop.

"Oh! *Pardon,* Monsieur. I have been most callous."

Dear Lord, she was apologizing to him for a breach of etiquette. He could not hold back a snort of laughter and just caught her quick sidelong glance of satisfaction. Damned, if she hadn't fashioned that ingenuous statement to disarm him. She was cannier than he would have suspected —a worthy adversary.

"I now know you own an unwise heart," he said. "Unfortunate for you but having little to do with me. And now pray excuse me, Madame, for *my* callousness."

She delivered him a sharp, assessing gaze. Good.

"Continue," he said.

"My husband, he was a diplomat," she said.

"Apparently not a very good one," Raine said. This time the glance came with a scowl. "Pray, correct me if I err, but England and France are still enemies, are they not?"

Behind her Jacques shifted uncomfortably on his feet.

"*Oui,* Monsieur." Her voice was tight, her eyes bright. Ire or pain? He could not tell. "Still, I would not have you speak unkindly of him. Perhaps if we had not fallen in love, if his attentions had remained on political matters—"

"Dear lady, such catholic willingness to accept blame speaks volumes about the Sisters who had you in their care,"—this won a startled glance from the wench. He'd been right; she *was* convent-raised—"but even nuns might balk at blaming a war on a minor diplomat's amorous daydreams."

The scowl became pronounced and Raine quelled an inappropriate desire to laugh. Regardless of the diversion this wordplay afforded, his life was still held in the balance. And unless Raine's eyesight had suffered during his incarceration, big silent Jacques had edged closer while she'd distracted him. Raine swung the gun toward the giant.

"Come, *mon homme.* Practice the patience your lady upbraids me for lacking. Be still, Jacques, or be dead."

Her lush mouth pursed. Yes, she was definitely piqued.

"Enough background. What do you want of me?"

Jacques nodded unhappily. She took a deep breath.

"A half year ago my husband received word that his uncle in Scotland had died leaving him heir to a great estate. He set about trying to make arrangements for me and little Angus to travel to Scotland."

"Little Angus?"

Her gaze dropped demurely. "Our son."

Son. Raine's gaze traveled down her slender figure to her waist. The necklace she wore could encompass it. Still, a corset could account for its narrow span.

"As you might well imagine, securing passage to Scotland for a French lady and her son is a difficult matter. Particularly for a French lady of some preeminence—albeit diminished. I am an orphan, Monsieur, fostered in my aunt's household, the same household where I have been living since my husband's death.

"Happily, after much searching my husband was able to contact a privateer and make arrangements for our travel. We were—we are—to follow the tide out tonight."

"So why," Raine asked, "are you instead here with me, masquerading as a notorious jade, rather than bustling little Angus through Dieppe's shipyard? Not a word, Jacques," he cautioned the other man.

"Because," the girl said with a sudden flash of ire, "my husband died a few months ago and the man we were to meet on the docks expects to deal with a man, an Englishman. He wrote yesterday. In his note he ranted against having agreed to take a woman onto his ship. He says it is bad luck. That his men will rebel. He even goes so far as to suggest that we find other passage but ends his letter by saying he will grudgingly honor his agreement."

Raine waited. She held out her hand, palm open in a gesture of impatience. "Do you not comprehend? I am alone. The passage has already been paid and I have no more money. There is no reason this smuggler, this . . . *pirate* should honor his obligation. I needed an Englishman and Jacques knew where to find one."

"And how is Jacques so savvy?"

"My aunt . . . *she* is Madame Noir. Jacques is her steward. He always had an affection for me, even as a child and when he discovered my difficulty he . . . he presented a solution." For the first time since he'd dragged the veil from her golden head, she looked self-conscious and abashed.

Raine's gaze swung toward Jacques. He didn't look much like an aristocrat's steward, but admittedly Raine had had little experience with that breed and so withheld judgment. "So 'twas your idea to pluck an Englishman from prison to masquerade as Monsieur Lambett."

"*Oui*," Jacques agreed. "I knew the arrangements Madame Noir made, the pattern, the names of those with whom she dealt. I knew that at so short a notice, the prison was Mademoiselle's only hope of finding an Englishman willing to act as her husband."

Every bit of Raine's instincts for survival urged caution. He didn't like this story. He mistrusted it.

"But"—Raine backed up a few feet, angling toward the door, his pistol still aimed in Jacques's direction— "your plan hinges on finding a *willing* Englishman."

"Monsieur," the girl said, her brows dipping into a V of consternation, "why would you refuse to aid me when you can only benefit from my offer?"

"What exactly is your offer?"

"You go to the docks tonight, pretending to be my husband. You meet with the smuggler captain, then . . ."

"Then?"

"I arrive, we board and sail for Scotland. Once we are on land, we go our separate ways."

"What about little Angus?"

"Angus? He will be with me, of course."

"And once in Scotland you'll walk to this great estate of your husband's?"

"*Non!*" she said impatiently. "Do not be foolish. My husband's people, they await me . . . us." A shadow dimmed the bright night sky of her eyes. She released a barely audible sigh and, catching his eye, smiled wanly. "Little Angus will be the new laird, *n'est-ce pas*? The point upon which all their plans and strategies and hopes hinge."

An odd way of putting it, but Raine supposed that in some families a son might be looked upon with such concentration of pride and hope. Just because it hadn't been so in his family didn't mean it was a lie.

For the first time, Raine found himself believing her. Not all of it to be sure, but that last part perhaps, because of the sadness in her eyes. She looked as he imagined a fond mother might look upon realizing the burden of expectation being placed upon her child: resigned, troubled, a shade resentful.

"Monsieur, will you not help me? What harm have we done you? You have already enjoyed some hours of freedom, clean clothes, and will soon partake of a warm, hearty meal." She sounded tired, as though the strain had finally caught up with her.

As if on cue, there came a thump on the door. Raine's head slew about, looking for some way to escape. They'd only to call out and he'd be dead.

"Monsieur!" the girl pleaded on a soft whisper.

"Come, son," Jacques urged. "What have you to lose and how much to gain?"

He could return to Scotland. How many nights had he lain on his moldy pallet and plotted his movements after his escape? Now he had the chance to fulfill those plans.

First to Scotland and Wanton's Blush, the castle on McClairen's Isle where his thrice-cursed father lived—but not to see his unnatural sire. No, he would go there secretly to retrieve the jewels his mother had hidden shortly before her untimely death. The jewels he'd seen her stow in the false bottom of an oriental tea chest. The jewels he'd never told anyone about. Not even Ash.

And then, with his stolen birthright hard in his pocket, he'd sail for the New World—and freedom. Real freedom. Freedom from Scotland and McClairen's Isle and Carr and, most of all, his past.

The servant outside the door pounded again. The girl watched him anxiously, wetting the full curve of her lower lip.

And, too, there was something to recommend itself in the notion of spending several nights ensconced on a ship—as Mr. and Mrs. Lambett they might even share a cabin—with this black-browed, oddly attractive girl.

He grinned, releasing the hammer on the pistol and shoving it into his waistband. "Open the door, Jacques," he said quite calmly. "I'd as soon eat before we head for the docks."

CHAPTER 5

True to the girl's word, the servant at the door carried a tray loaded with food: crusty loaves of fresh baked bread; meat pies with wisps of fragrant, herb-scented steam rising from the slits in their lard crusts; a cold shoulder of mutton and a mound of hot, syrup-coated apple slices.

Whatever doubts Raine had about the pair's candor, clearly they courted his cooperation. For the first time in years he filled himself to satiation, paying half attention to the girl as she outlined her plan. She gave him the lines he was to say, the manner in which he was to approach the "smuggler captain," the times and place of the meeting. The other half of his attention pursued his alternatives.

But try as he might, he could not come up with any plan that promised as much as the one the girl proposed—*if* it was true. Besides, if he walked out of the room he doubted he would get far. His last experience had taught him the necessity of plans and allies.

He had no allies; he didn't even know what lay beyond the next hill. And even if he did escape, to what? Without papers or money, he would be forced to wander until he was recaptured or had managed to accrue some wealth—if he didn't end his life in some wretched tavern brawl first.

He wanted more than that. His years of incarceration had dared him to consider whether his life could have some value. He'd found he wanted more than that future he'd been pursuing before France: a dingy echo of his sire's brilliant sins.

He glanced at the girl across the table from him. She'd recaptured her golden hair in a knot at the nape of her neck—a pity, as her free-flowing tresses were rare lovely. Tension marked the corners of her mouth as she endeavored to convince him to accede to her plan.

Raine suspected begging did not come easy to her. God would mark a woman with such uncompromising brows only as fair warning to the opposite sex. Raine gave a fleeting thought to her dead husband. She would have any husband on his knees, this one.

Jacques, chewing through a hunk of grizzled meat, remained silent. Wise man to let the girl do his procuring. The light of the tallow candle cupped her cheek in a warm glow. When was the last time Raine had touched anything as soft as her cheek looked to be?

He refilled his cup, trying to vanquish the spell she cast and pick out how much of what she told him was true. Not that it mattered. If all he needed to do was appear on the docks and speak in genteel accents to some English pirate, and by doing so broker a passage to Scotland . . . Well, was it not worth the risk of trusting this pair?

Though Dieppe's docks were crowded, the *Le Rex Rouge Inne* was unusually deserted. But then, Raine thought, peering through the carriage window at the tavern where he was to meet the smuggler, he knew little of life in these dockyards. Dieppe was a fresh-born harbor town.

A gust of wind found its way into the carriage and beneath his newly acquired coat. More from long-forgotten habit than need, he drew the thick wool folds shut. Beside him the girl shivered, her cobalt gaze fixed outside. Since he'd agreed to her scheme she'd been quiet and preoccupied.

On the driver's seat above, Jacques waited for a signal from the smuggler. As soon as he received it he would alert Raine, who would then proceed to the tavern to complete negotiations for their passage. He jingled the three gold Louies in his pocket, money he'd extorted from Jacques by claiming—not without some validity—that he might have to sweeten the pot should the smuggler prove recalcitrant.

If all went accordingly, Madame Lambett would wait within the carriage until an agreement had been made; then she and Jacques would fetch little Angus from wherever she'd secreted him. Fond mother that she was, she hadn't wanted to bring her son to the docks before it was absolutely necessary. The thought of little Angus awoke Raine's curiosity about the young woman's dead husband. "How did he die?"

She turned her head. In the dim light of the carriage her eyes looked nearly black. "Monsieur?"

"Your husband, how did he die?"

"Oh. An infection of the lungs." She averted her face once more.

"You were much attached to him?" he asked.

She remained mute.

She did not want to speak to him. He could not much resent her decision. She knew nothing of him other than that he was English and she'd found him in a prison. She hadn't even asked his name. Of course, she needn't fear for her safety what with Jacques only a heartbeat away.

The thought of the giant servant damped the spark of ardor still plaguing Raine—but did not altogether drown it. He could not forget the feel of her trapped between his thighs, her hands against his naked skin, her body molded to his. Even now, while his mind unraveled the next few minutes into a hundred possible ends, his body was still preoccupied with hers.

The minutes ticked by, the interior of the carriage grew warm with their shared heat. From outside came the clatter of an occasional passing vehicle, the sharp clink of shod hooves on cobbled streets, men's voices, distant and muted.

"Why were you so crude, so rough with me?" The stiff leather seat creaked as the girl shifted.

Her sudden query surprised him. He'd been relaxed, simply enjoying her scent, her warmth, and the sight of her. She repeated her question grudgingly, her gaze anchored firmly outside. "Why were you so crude?"

"The woman you impersonated *is* crude," he said, perplexed. Surely she knew the sort of woman her aunt was, especially since she had used her proclivities so effectively to obtain his release.

"But you touched me even when I made clear that I did not want it."

He was unsure of what she wanted and so remained silent, waiting.

"Yet you speak well, in the accents of the aristocracy. Are you? Are you well-born? Is your crime against the well-born?"

"Madame, is it not a bit late to be asking for a letter of introduction?" Raine asked, amused by her accusing tone.

"Why were you in prison?" she blurted out, this time accompanying the question with an anxious glance. "Did you . . . did you assault some woman? An aristocratic lady?"

She thought him a rapist? Ah well, the mistake had been made before. Still, at one time, he would have been affronted. He would have politely damned her to hell and proceeded to spend the night proving his irresistibility to the opposite sex.

But yes, he supposed she would think that, given how he'd nearly forced himself on her earlier. He rubbed his cheek consideringly and for the first time in years he wondered what a mirror would reveal. He smiled and she misread his reaction, shrinking back against the cushions.

"No," he said to ease her fear, "I have never taken a woman against her will."

"Then"—she hesitated—"then why were you in prison?"

" 'Political reasons,' a phrase I give you leave to interpret into meaning someone hoped to profit by my incarceration."

"I don't understand."

"And you an ambassador's wife?" he taunted lightly; but she'd turned that disconcerting gaze upon him again and he answered with a small sigh, amazed at her seeming youth and perturbed by it.

"What did you do?"

"What didn't I do?" he muttered, and then, "I was imprisoned because I could be and I was *kept* imprisoned because of some French bureaucrat's fantasy that someday someone might ransom me." He leaned closer and was rewarded by her faint, heady fragrance. " 'Twixt we two, however, I can assure you that no one other than yourself would ever have found a reason to set me free. My thanks."

He smiled again, this time without rancor, suddenly heedful that, indeed, were it not for this woman he would not be sitting in a warm carriage, clean and clad, astonished by his unexpected freedom and fearful he might yet lose it.

But instead of reassuring her, his smile seemed to make her even more anxious. The corners of her mouth dipped unhappily and her fingers worried each other in her lap. "You hated being caged."

He laughed this time, in spite of himself, and heard Jacques shift atop the carriage in response.

"Rest easy, friend Jacques," Raine called out in a low voice, "your mistress would play the wit. I simply appreciate her sallies."

He studied the girl. She looked fresh and vulnerable and, he allowed, a bit piqued that he'd laughed at her. Jacques was right to worry about her. Raine had once known a hundred men who would have feasted on such innocence as hers. They'd once been his boon companions.

"Aye, Madame. I hated it. But never so much as now."

"Why is that?" She moved forward, her curiosity momentarily making her forget her fear. The carriage window framed her head and shoulders, the light outside glinting off her hair and spinning a bright nimbus about her silhouette. She would, indeed, be unsafe traveling unescorted. She was, he thought distantly, unsafe with him.

"Because I'd forgotten what freedom was like," he said, "and now I remember and the comparison is . . . keen."

Backlit as she was, it was impossible to read her expression.

"Why did your family not—"

"My turn," he cut across her query. Ash was gone, Fia probably bartered off to the wealthiest suitor by now, and he did not want to think of Carr. He had no interest in his sire, nor any desire to ever again behold him. Though he supposed it might prove inevitable once he'd reached Wanton's Blush.

Wanton's Blush.

Once again his future held choices, options, and prospects beyond the simple ambition not to be killed in the next prison brawl. The realization rushed in on him with heady force.

"Monsieur?"

He blinked like a man coming into the sun after too long in the dark, overwhelmingly aware of the debt he owed this young woman. Even if, as he suspected, there was more to this girl's scheme than she was letting on, at least tonight possibility existed where yesterday there had been none.

"I owe you a debt," he said.

"Please, Monsieur. You owe me nothing. You are aiding me." She dipped her head, studying her gloved hands. A long tendril slipped over her shoulder. She looked fresh, soft, and tantalizingly vernal with a youth he'd never experienced himself. "I am in *your* debt," she murmured.

Now, to ask the heavens for *that* boon would take even more audacity than even he had ever owned. But she'd made the declaration and he had never denied being an opportunist. "It would seem we are mutually indebted, eh *ma petite* Madame?" He paused. "Can I . . . May I touch your hair?"

It hadn't been what he'd meant to say and he heard in the stumbling hesitation of his voice a yearning controlled only by some remnant of pride. *Oafish bore,* he berated himself, *blathering fool. How polished, how urbane. 'May I touch your hair. . . .'*

Yet he awaited her answer.

He saw the slight dip of her chin, the barest of assents. Slowly he reached out, as careful of alarming her as if she'd been a Highland colt seeing a man for the first time. She held herself just as still, just as cautiously. His fingers hovered above the gleaming tresses, moved. Felt.

Silk. Cold silk. So polished as to seem crisp, so slickery cold. He rubbed the lock between thumb and forefinger, closing his eyes, intently cataloguing its texture and richness. His fingers worked higher, moving up, identifying the point where the strands lost their metallic coolness and grew warm with proximity to her skin. He opened his hand wide, letting the strands flow between his fingers, crushing the silky mass in his fist and releasing it and the faint fragrance of soap. He sighed.

"How old are you, Monsieur?" he heard her ask wonderingly. He opened his eyes.

"I am a few years into my third decade, Madame."

"So young? *Mon Dieu*," she breathed. "How many years were you in prison?"

"What matter—"

"How many?" she insisted.

"Four."

"You were just a youth . . ." He barely heard her and the horror in her voice made him uncomfortable. Disconcerted he looked away and then immediately back again because he'd not feasted his eyes on a woman like her in years.

"It is unfair," she murmured. "This is not right."

Once more her naivete goaded awake the long-dormant devil within, a misplaced part of himself that could still be amused by such things as a girl's innocence. " 'Right,' *ma petite*? What has *right* to do with my fate . . . or yours?"

His hand was still in her hair. Slowly, his eyes never leaving hers, he wound a handful about his fist. She resisted, but not adamantly. With each light tug, the stiffness of her body melted like warm wax before a brassier. Her lips—as full of voluptuous promise as her brows were of stern disapproval—parted slightly in astonishment. He saw the glint of her white teeth, a flicker of surprise in her eyes. Sweet clove-scented breath fanned his—

"There he is!" The small, driver's hatch flew open and Jacques looked down at them.

The girl jerked back, wincing as she came to the end of her tethered tresses. Raine freed her. Damn Jacques.

"Remember, speak only English," Jacques hissed. "Wait until he is very near. He won't want you to draw attention to him and I daresay his French is abominable."

He snapped the trapdoor shut. Raine looked at the girl. The odd light had leached the color from her skin.

"A kiss for luck, *ma petite*?"

Her eyes grew round. "*Non*, Monsieur! I am but recently a—"

"—and I am but recently free." He clasped the back of her head and pulled her forward, crushing her petal-soft mouth beneath his. For just one heady instant her mouth was pliant and then she fought, pushing him away.

"Get on with it," Jacques called down.

Raine angled his head in a courtly bow, reached past her, and opened the carriage door. "Madame, your debt is paid." He jumped down to the street and without bothering to look back crossed toward *Le Rex Rouge.*

A tall man stood under a lantern hanging beside the door. He held his voluminous cape close to his body, warding off the stiffening wind. His expression was eager, his body tense.

Raine slowed his pace, glancing about. Three men stood huddled together at the corner the building, rubbing their hands together above the sullen glow of a small brassier. At the end of the street, a driver slumped atop a closed landau, his ill-matched pair shifting in their traces. It was too quiet.

The tall man stepped beneath the lantern. He'd a pale, cruel face.

"Lambett?" he called out.

"Yes," Raine answered. He halted. Jacques had warned him to be discreet, yet the smuggler called his name loudly across a nearly deserted cul-de-sac.

At the corner, one of the men lifted his head. Down the road the chaise door opened. The tall man nodded with evident pleasure, extending his hand, moving rapidly forward, his pale face—

Pale.

No seafarer had a face so pale.

He'd been set up. He heard the woman's voice call out behind him. "It's a trap! Run!"

The advice was unnecessary. He was already running.

The girl watched the tall figure of the nameless young man sprint past the soldiers tumbling from the carriage and be swallowed by the night. From his position atop the carriage "Jacques," also known as Jamie Craigg and more currently "La Bête," cursed roundly, whipping up the horses and heading for the docks.

Once he got over his anger, Jacques would see she'd not only done the right thing, but the best thing. Soon the soldiers from the docks would join their fellows in chasing down the man they thought was *La Bête,* the most notorious smuggler to ever make mock of the French authorities. For the first time in a fortnight the docks would be relatively free of troops. The real *La Bête* could thus, in relative safety, load important cargo before heading back to his native Scotland.

The "cargo" touched her fingertips to her bruised lips. She had never been kissed before. Never known an unrelated man's touch. His had been the first. A tall, hard Englishman with sherry-colored eyes, sprung from a fetid jail. He would not have liked his fate had she really been Madame Noir, of that she was certain. Then why did she feel so guilty?

The honesty the Sisters at Sacré Coeur had demanded of her provided a quick answer. She was no better than Madame Noir. She'd simply put the young man to a different use.

She bowed her head and offered a short prayer that he find his way to freedom. Yet, even as she finished her prayer and crossed herself, guilty at having used another being so wretchedly, she knew she would not have done one thing differently. She did not act on her own behalf now.

She drew back from the window, snapping the curtain shut as though by doing so she could shut out the Englishman's image. What she did, she did for her clan, to rectify the decade-old wrong she'd caused them.

She was the only who *could* rectify it.

She'd been reared on that knowledge, molded and shaped by it. Even in the French convent where she'd been sent so many years earlier, the letters from Muira Dougal had kept her obligation ever before her. Now, finally, the time had come for her to act.

Favor McClairen was going home.

CHAPTER 6

It took an hour to row out to the ship. The half dozen men in the long boat strained silently against the oars. At the helm, Jamie guided their way, threading the heavily laden boat through black water like Charon bringing the newly departed across the river Styx.

Except she wasn't dying, Favor reminded herself. She was going home. She should be ecstatic. They'd made it when all odds were against them.

For days the entire north coast had been covered with not only soldiers but guards and laborers, merchants and seamen, all seeking the notorious smuggler, *La Bête*—or more to the point seeking the unheard-of sum being offered for his capture. Apparently Jamie had made fools of the French authorities once too often.

After a few days in his company she understood how he'd managed that not inconsiderable deed. 'Twas Jamie who'd determined that their best odds in evading capture lay in hiding in plain sight. He'd anchored his ship in a port, not in one of the tiny inlets smugglers generally favored.

Still, while most of the authorities' efforts had been concentrated on coastal areas, they hadn't altogether neglected the harbor towns. It had been necessary to arrange a diversion that would give them time to load their contraband—as well as Favor. Again, Jamie came up with a plan. But for it to work they'd needed an Englishman—an Englishman they could leave behind. But where and how to find a willing dupe?

Amazingly, it was Sacré Coeur's Most Reverend Mother who provided the answer.

Now, perhaps the Abbess had information from other sources, but it was certainly interesting that her brother, Father Dominic, was also Madame Noir's confessor. For whatever reasons the Abbess was uncommonly well versed in that notorious lady's habits and for this Favor was grateful.

The plan had been simple. One of the convent's milkmaids dropped a word into a French lieutenant's ear regarding the Abbess's anticipated windfall of fine Scottish wool blankets on a certain night at a certain locale. In the meantime Favor went to the local prison disguised as Madame Noir to select an Englishman who might readily be mistaken for the infamous English smuggler.

Everything had gone as arranged.

Except for the Englishman's eyes. And that he'd sworn he would never return to prison again. And that in asking her permission to touch her hair he'd looked quite as naked as Favor had ever felt.

The rowboat bumped lightly against the side of the ship's barnacle-covered side. Favor frowned. She had nothing to feel so guilty about. Once the guards realized they didn't have *La Bête*, the Englishman would simply be sent back to prison where he'd have ended up if she had been Madame Noir.

Hushed voices called out from above and Jamie answered in kind. A second later a rope ladder dropped down and two men leaned over the side of the ship. She took hold of their hands and they hauled her onboard. A second later Jamie, panting and swearing, hoisted his girth up and over the gunnel, followed shortly by his men.

"Get her to the cabin," he ordered in a heavy Scottish accent, jerking his head in Favor's direction. "Hoist anchor and put yer backs to settin' sail. We're fer home, laddies."

A rumble of approval met this announcement. Curious glances followed her as a balding man took her elbow and steered her through a doorway into a small cabin. Before she could turn, the door closed behind her.

She looked around. A narrow cot was nailed to one wall, likewise a table on the opposite wall. On this stood a chipped washbasin. Gratefully, she dipped the end of her kerchief into the frigid water and dabbed at her face.

Outside the door she heard a woman's voice. Apprehension followed her surprise. It could only be Muira Dougal, the woman whose iron will and driving determination had shaped Favor's last nine years. No one had told Favor Muira would be onboard. She hadn't prepared herself to meet the woman who'd . . . Favor floundered for a word that could adequately describe the degree to which this woman had influenced her life. All of it done from hundreds of miles away, mostly through letters.

In some very real ways, Muira Dougal had invented Favor McClairen. Certainly the child who'd arrived on this foreign soil no longer existed.

"How did it go?" Favor heard her asking Jamie.

"Well enough, Mistress," Jamie Craigg answered deferentially. "The guard at the prison didn't blink twice when the girl said she was Madame Noir."

"Is she any good then? Will she succeed in what she must do?"

Jamie paused before continuing. "Aye. She'll do. Though I'll say this"—a deep chuckle rumbled out—"if a man was in on the joke, so to speak, he would see right enough that the lass dinna understand the woman she played."

"Well, Jamie Craigg"—Muira's voice dropped in pitch, became biting and hard—"I'm glad you're so amused. But this isn't a joke. It's our last chance to regain what was stolen from us and if you no longer hold that a sacred endeavor, there are those of us that still do."

"Forgive me, Mistress," Jamie said gruffly. "I just found the lass—enchanting is all."

"Enchanting?" the woman echoed thoughtfully. "Good. She'll need to be enchanting, and more, for her purpose. What happened next?"

Favor pressed her ear to the door, straining to hear Jamie's reply. ". . . wary and hard, as hard a man as I'd not like to cross. But she had him eating out of her hand soon enough and sending him into the arms of the French as docile as a lambkins."

Favor's throat knotted with guilt.

"But then, just as he's about made it to the lieutenant's side, the lass calls out a warning. The Englishman dashes one way and we dash the other."

The door to the cabin suddenly swung open and Favor scuttled back. An elderly woman stood before her, her lantern raised. Favor squinted at the bright light, trying to see past its glare.

"Listening at doors, Miss?" the woman asked.

"If it aids my cause," Favor answered calmly.

"Ach!" A wide grin split the face of the thin woman. She turned her head toward Jamie, who filled the door frame behind her. "Bold!"

The bright light dangled a moment longer in front of Favor's face. Finally, irritated by it, she forced herself to face it squarely. "Would you kindly take that thing out of my face, Madame?"

A low chuckle greeted her imperious tone. The old woman lowered the lantern to her side. "Speaks like a McClairen wench. Uncrowned royalty is what the McClairens always thought themselves."

Muira's smile faded. "That's good, lass. You'll need all that queenly bearing and more. But tell me, come nightfall does a haughty manner keep the vision of Merrick murdering your kin at bay? No." She answered her own question fiercely. "Only an act of recompense will do that."

Favor backed away, caught off guard by the old woman's bald-faced reference to the night Favor had all but destroyed her own clan. She chided herself for her naivete. She'd thought Muira might offer her a word of welcome. She should have known better. She'd had a decade's worth of letters to instruct her differently.

The old woman studied her impassively and Favor returned the examination. Muira Dougal, *née* McClairen, had the sort of face seen on ancient Greek coins, genderless and refined, arrogant and haunted. Her eyes were heavily hooded, the narrow face hung with crepelike flesh. Her thin mouth was uncompromising. Only the bright blue eyes blazed as though lit by a fire from within.

For a full five minutes the two women faced each other, neither willing to break the silence. Even Jamie seemed loath to interfere in their silent discourse. He shuffled uneasily on his feet, glancing anxiously from one to the other. On the one side stood the woman who had for nearly a decade, single-handedly bound the far-flung McClairen clan together. On the other side stood the girl whose brother was that same clan's long-missing laird, in essence an uncrowned king, the girl that Muira Dougal intended to sacrifice in order to return the McClairens to their full glory.

"Yer nineteen years old." Muira finally said, her tone giving nothing away.

"*Oui*, Madame," Favor answered.

"Jamie says you improvised your escape here. Called out a warning to the English bastard you'd duped. Is this so?"

"*Oui.*"

"From here on there'll be no more improvising. None at all. Is that understood?" The woman's hand darted out like a striking snake and grasped Favor's chin.

"*Oui*, Madame. *D'accord.*"

"Agree? I did not ask you to agree. I asked if you understood."

Favor felt herself flush. "*Oui.*"

"And there will be no more French," Muira muttered distractedly. "*She* had only a smattering of French. Remember that." She looked over to Jamie. "You knew her. What do you think?"

The big man cocked his head. "I don't see much of the McClairen in her, that's a fact. They be a black-headed breed, like yerself. All of them taller than she by some measure. Regal, yes, but gay. This one is handsome enough but fierce-looking."

"Hair can be dyed, brows can be plucked," Muira murmured. "A resemblance can be created out of gestures and habits, a way of standing, a turn of speech."

She twisted Favor's chin, pulling her face this way and that in the light. "There's not much here to work with, I grant you, but it's there in the angle of her jaw and the purity of her skin. Her nose is all McClairen. And when I add the rest . . ."

Resentment made Favor pull away from the cold, dry fingers. She disliked being spoken of as though she were unformed clay waiting the potter's hand. She already had a set of features, individual and her own. 'Twasn't much, true, but when one could not call her future her own, even so little was precious. Though she did have Thomas. The thought of her long-unseen brother brought an attendant wave of worry.

"Thomas is gone?" she asked.

"Aye, lass," Jamie answered.

"Good," she said, but she could not keep the wistful note from her voice. She hadn't even been aware her brother was alive until a few years before when his letters had begun arriving at the convent. Thomas McClairen, bondage servant, sea captain, Marquis of Donne and laird of the McClairen.

She hadn't seen him since he and their older brother John had been taken to London to await trial for treason. He'd been sentenced, deported, and sold into bondage for his part in the uprising of '45. Their older, thus more "dangerous," brother, John, had been hanged, drawn, and quartered. John had been sixteen.

"He'll be gone a fair length?" she finally asked.

"Long enough for us to accomplish what we must," Muira answered.

Favor nodded. Thomas would be a dangerous man to defy and impossible to deceive. He'd spent his years of servitude on the deck of a ship, his master being the captain-owner of a small shipping business. He'd won his master's respect and later his trust. After his bond had been satisfied, Thomas had bought a share in his former master's shipping business and become captain of his own vessel.

He'd prospered and looked to prosper even more but his sight was set on a different goal. He'd returned to Scotland seeking the downfall of the man who'd betrayed the McClairens and stolen their birthright: Lord Carr.

To accomplish this he'd taken "Donne" as his surname, it being one of the McClairen lairds' old, long-forgotten French titles. In London he'd established himself as a disreputable ne'er-do-well and attached himself to a group of young devils who habitually made a pilgrimage to Wanton's Blush, once the McClairens' castle, now a hellhole of gaming and debauchery. There he'd befriended—to whatever degree such a creature as Carr was capable of friendship—Carr himself, all the while looking for the perfect manner in which to, in one fell stroke, destroy Carr and all he owned or held dear.

All this Thomas wrote to Favor in letters, in dribs and drabs. Favor pieced the hints together, discerning Thomas's goals in what he said and what he omitted. But something had gone wrong with Thomas's plan. His last letter to Favor had said only that his resolve had been shaken and he needed to regain it somewhere far from Scotland. Which was good for Favor's purposes.

Thomas knew naught of Muira's plan. If he caught wind of it he would do everything in his power to keep Favor from becoming involved. But she was involved. Muira had written hundreds of pages to her elucidating just how very involved she was.

Because Favor was responsible for her clan's near extermination.

And if the good Abbess at Sacré Coeur had eventually convinced Favor that God had forgiven her, she knew very well that the same could not be said of her clan.

Favor pulled her thoughts away from her dark musings. She looked up, finding Muira's cool, appraising gaze fastened on her. How could she have thought that woman would have a kind word for her? Muira held her responsible for the death of every person she'd ever loved and more, of the death of her heritage.

Favor's return to Scotland was no prodigal's homecoming, no happy end to a decade-long exile.

It was penance.

CHAPTER 7

Lord Carr looked down from the tower window at the bleak courtyard of Wanton's Blush. A storm was coming in. A stiff wind smote the rocky island with backhanded fury, ripping what leaves were left from the branches of oak and rowan and hurling them across the square. Overhead, dark mauve-veined clouds rolled ominously westward. If one turned around and looked out the east windows, one would see huge waves shattering themselves on the jagged rocks surrounding the island.

If one were to look out the east windows. Which Carr would not. Had not, in fact, in years if at all avoidable. Not that his present view pleased him any too much.

Like a cheap whore too long in the trade, Wanton's Blush was showing her coarse antecedents. All the accoutrements Carr had so painstakingly plied upon her homely surface could no longer hide what she was: a Scottish drab.

The redbrick he'd ordered to cover her façade had crumbled in places, the gaping pox marks exposing the gray hand-hewn rock beneath. The courtyard he'd had paved with shimmering pink granite had heaved, pushed from below by tough Scottish turf that sprouted like hairs on a hag's chin.

The corrosion had seeped inside, too. Oh, not drastically—and not yet too apparently—but the signs were there. The expensive plaster moldings had cracked in several rooms. Chipped marble mantelpieces went unrepaired. Water stains darkened the walls of the south wing. Nothing too remarkable but telling.

Carr had acquired Wanton's Blush for the price of some information. In his youth he'd come to Scotland for an extended vacation, thinking to stay until his creditors in London forgot the immense sums he owed them. He'd accepted that he was bound for a lengthy visit. There he'd met Janet McClairen, the doted-upon cousin of this very castle's one-time owner, Ian.

She, being rich and smitten with him, and he, having nothing much else to do, married. They'd lived here, under Ian's benign auspices until Carr had decided he was tired of the *décor*. So, when the opportunity had arisen with the ill-fated Jacobite rebellion of '45, he'd relayed pertinent information about its leaders to Lord Cumberland. After the rebellion had been squelched and Ian and his kin either executed or deported, the grateful Cumberland had seen that Wanton's Blush and its lands went to Carr. Then, Carr had changed the *décor*.

He'd made Wanton's Blush over, sparing no expense in converting her into a showpiece. A U-shaped fortress built on the highest outer curve of the island, the main body stood perpendicular to the sea. Two wings sprouted from towers at the north and south corners, protecting the wide interior courtyard from the constant winds. Italianate gardens had once bedecked the terraces Carr had cut beneath the courtyard but the years had watched the slow encroachment of the native weeds. And since none of Carr's guests were wont to spend their waking hours idling there—their waking hours being primarily nocturnal—he did not fight too hard for those Italianate conceits.

The problem was, Carr admitted without regret, Wanton's Blush no longer interested him. It had served its purpose—indeed, *still* served its purpose: enticing from afar the wealthiest and most notorious gamblers of England's most distinguished families.

Carr was no fool. He still poured enough money into the cursed place to tempt jaded palates. Wanton's Blush still boasted the best wine cellar in Scotland, the best chef in England, and still contained a premier collection of artwork and artifacts, treasures he would take with him when he left here and returned triumphant to the scene of his former humiliation. The old venom seeped to the surface.

After Janet had died, Carr had set about accumulating enough wealth to pay off his dunners and set himself up as befitted his station. It had been slow going. Too slow. So he'd married another heiress whose wealth hadn't been nearly as grand as she'd intimated to him, the bitch. She'd met with an accident, as had his third wife.

By then he'd had the wealth he needed, but King George, grown sancti-monious in his dotage, had long since taken umbrage with Carr's unfortu-nate habit of losing wives. He'd not only made it clear that Carr would not be welcomed back in London, nor in any society that the king—damn him —controlled, but he'd written him an edict: If any female ever again died while under Carr's care, Carr would pay for it with his own head.

And so, Carr had sat up here in this northern nowhere for twenty-five years. Twenty-five years in unofficial exile—first self-imposed, later im-posed by a king's will.

But soon all that would be over, Carr thought, drumming his fingers. Wheels were turning. The wooing of some, the blackmailing of others, flattery, coaxing, threatening . . . all his exertions were on the cusp of bearing fruit. Soon. A few months and he would once more reign in London's exalted society.

But first, he thought, turning from the window, he needed to attend to a few immediate matters, a bit of housekeeping before he quit Wanton's Blush once and for all.

He crossed the room, approaching a shriven, unkempt figure hunched over a littered table. He wondered if the old witch knew the reason the sea-facing windows were draped. Probably. She seemed to know every-thing. Not that he cared overly much. What could one old Gypsy do to such as him? Except be of use.

"Well, what do you see, Pala?" Carr asked, examining the nails of his hand.

The woman shifted, her layers of discolored shawls and patched skirts swirling out and settling over her feet. A seamed and leathery face peered up at him from between a curtain of lank gray hair.

"Well?" he prompted.

She stabbed one filthy finger at the little pile of ivory knobs scattered across the table's mahogany surface. "She loved you. No man owned so much love as you had from her."

A little thrill, all the more exotic for being so very rare, ran up Carr's spine. Pala was referring to Janet, his first wife, the only woman he'd ever truly loved. For a second, Janet's face danced before him: a black silken fall of hair, pale skin, dark amber-colored eyes. She smiled, an off-balance smile, utterly charming. Her eyes glowed with unhappy affection, unhappy because loving him had never made Janet happy.

"Yes," he said to himself. "She did."

"She loves you still."

The Gypsy's voice abruptly dispelled his sentimental mood.

"She loves you even from the grave." The Gypsy's sly accents curled through the air, wheedling and testing.

Calmly Carr sauntered over and looked down at the table where Pala had spread her divining tools.

"Oh, yes. I'm certain she does." His lips curled into a semblance of a smile. "Is *that* why she's haunting me? Her and her thrice-cursed clan? Because she *loves* me so much!"

He slammed his fist down on the table and the intricate configuration of bones burst apart, skittering across the surface and falling to the floor.

Pala speared him with a venomous glare and dropped to her knees. She scooped up the knucklebones and cradled them against her sunken chest, crooning indecipherable gibberish under her breath. "You have broken one!" she said accusingly.

"Yes?" His brows lifted with mild annoyance. His composure had returned. "What of it? You could buy the hands from a dozen corpses with the money I've given you."

"Pala never asks for money."

Carr smiled. At times the old Gipsy could be amusing. "Of course not. I forget your exact words but the gist of it was that such an act might sully the purity of your discourse with the spirits. Yet you've never refused my 'gifts.' Correct me if I'm wrong."

Pala crouched lower. Her mouth was sulky.

"How much do you imagine my 'gifts' have amounted to since I found you lurking in my stables two years ago?"

"I am not lurking," she protested feebly. "I . . . I follow the spirits. They tell me you are in danger. I come to warn you. Did I not warn you of the mad dog?"

Carr regarded her through hooded eyes.

"You know this true!" Pala insisted, jerking her head up and down. "For you, I read the portents, I listen to the spirits whisper, I see what has gone before and I see what will come. Has Pala not been of use to Your Grace many, many times?"

"A few," Carr allowed, pulling a chair out from beneath the table and dropping down into it. Pala *had* warned him about the rabid dog. Just as she'd seen the foundering of a smuggler's ship and the rich trove that washed ashore from it. And certainly she knew more about him than any other living person, far more than anyone could without supernatural aid.

He stretched out his legs and laced his fingers across his flat belly. The feel of the silk-embroidered waistcoat soothed him.

"Please, most gracious sir." Pala's voice dropped to an unctuous mewl. "I read the bones for your guests, too. They like."

"You've been an effective little diversion, I'll grant you that," Carr murmured. "It is hard enough to lure Lord Sandwich away from his cursed Hellfire Club and harder still to keep him here with his rich and largely insensate companions. You sometimes manage to do that, what with your augury and omens. How much real, I wonder? How much fraud?"

He leaned forward, fixing Pala with a meaningful stare. "Don't ever take me for a fool, Pala. Don't ever be so unwise. Or greedy."

The Gypsy's gaze slipped away from his. She dropped her bones into a leather pouch, drawing the thong about her neck and tucking it into her bodice. "I don't lie to you. I tell you only what the spirits tell me. What the bones say. If they lie . . ."

She shrugged and Carr smiled at her sophistry. The old witch was a woman after his own heart. If the bones lied, how could it be her fault? She was simply a messenger.

"You know why I trust you, Pala?" he asked. "Aside from the fact that if you were to ever prove untrustworthy you know I would kill you, that is?"

The cheap necklaces about her thin throat rattled as she cautiously shook her head.

"It is precisely because your messages from the spirit world reek more often of gin than brimstone. An infallible witch? An honest one?" He laughed. "Those qualities don't exist among noblemen so how could they exist in the likes of you?

"No, Pala, it is precisely because you fail and cheat and whine that I listen. You are treacherous and cowardly. Only the dead could prompt someone like you into risking her neck by claiming she hears them." He settled back once more. "It isn't so long ago that witches were burned. But you know that, don't you?"

Pala hunkered in the center of the room, like a rabbit baited for a fox.

"Now then, I know you heard something, saw something, or even smelled something among those bones of yours. Something to do with Janet. What was it? And no more drivel about her undying love." A little prick of something like regret rose within him. He ignored it. The dead returned for one reason only: to annoy the living. "In point of fact she did die. Now what . . . did . . . you . . . see?"

A sudden blast of wind rattled the glass in the windows as a low moan issued from the chimney.

"I cannot help what I hear," Pala finally whispered. "You ask and ask, you know when I lie. I *not* lie. She loves you. Even now, even after what you did. She forgives."

"Oh." He stood up and was about to walk away when he heard her speak, her voice flat and soft, marked by the lack of inflection in which she issued all her most accurate portents.

"She desires . . ."

"Yes?"

"To be reunited with you."

Carr snorted, disappointed. More maudlin sentiment. He'd over seventy guests in residence this day. Since Pala did not appear to have any suggestion on how to rid the castle of the haunts, he'd best go attend the living.

"She wants to be with you."

"Well, I'm afraid the dear girl will have to wait a bit, won't she?"

His smile faded as he saw the intensity with which Pala stared at him. He was not mistaken. He'd engendered it in enough men to be wholly familiar with its every aspect. Pala was afraid.

"There is more," he prompted. "What do you know!"

"She is *not* waiting. She comes back. To forgive. To protect from them. As she always did."

Them. The McClairens. Alive, Janet had shielded him from their unproven certainty that he'd betrayed them, refusing to believe he would do such a thing. At least, at first. By the time she'd died, so too had most of her clan. Later, thanks to the fortuitous whoring of his son Raine, he'd had the excuse he needed to kill off any remnant of that cursed clan.

In truth it had been no great surprise when the McClairens had begun creeping from their graves, seeking in death the retribution they'd been denied in life—though they'd certainly bided their time in coming back.

Janet . . . now Janet was a different story. Yet here was Pala claiming Janet was only now returning. It made no sense; Janet had been haunting him for years.

"In what form will she haunt me? When will she come back?"

"Now."

"I don't understand."

"She is no spirit no more. She has found a vessel. Here. At Wanton's Blush."

"What do you mean?"

"She is reborn in another. One who is not aware she shares her body with another soul. But you will know. You will recognize her."

His heart hammered painfully in his chest as he moved forward, grabbing the old woman's arm and hauling her to her feet. "If you are lying I will tear your heart from your chest myself and force it down your throat."

"I not lie!" Pala cried. "She loves you. She wants to be once more with you!"

Carr flung the old woman away, running a trembling hand through his peruke, shoving the wig back on his head.

Janet returned, he thought numbly.

He had to find her.

The door to the tower room slammed open. Pala, her skirts bunched high, scuttled out and disappeared down the steep tower staircase. Carr followed a moment later, his expression distracted. Blindly he followed the winding stairs downward and through a low arched door. He turned sharply and collided with a stooped female figure.

A thick black veil concealed the left side of her face leaving the right side uncovered, exposing a twisted mouth, deformed jaw, and one sunken eye obscured by a drooping, nerveless lid. Carr recoiled. It was hideous.

The creature shrank against the wall, her twisted body trembling.

"Who in God's name are you?" Carr demanded.

"Gunna, Yer Grace," the old woman mumbled in thick Highland accents, lifting the corner of her veil across her mouth.

"Damn, another witch! Whatever are you doing in my house?"

"I do fer yer daughter, sir. Miss Fia. Have done fer years." The woman shuffled sideways like a land crab. It was repulsive.

" 'Swounds!" Carr swore softly under his breath, looking away. He remembered now. Fia had an inordinate and inexplicable fondness for this creature—Gunna, was it?—and she, in turn, seemed to be the one person who had some influence on his increasingly intractable daughter.

"What the hell are you doing here, hag?" he demanded.

"Followin' yer bidding, Yer Grace," the old woman mumbled.

"How so? By spying on me?" he demanded.

"No! No, Yer Grace! Ye said as how whenever I'm not tending Miss Fia I should keep meself to the east and upper rooms where the sight of me wouldna offend ye or yer guests. So here I be, Yer Grace."

Carr looked about and blanched. Surely enough, the window behind Gunna framed a view of the churning North Sea. Somehow, what with his distraction, he'd taken a wrong turn and ended here, overlooking the very cliffs from which Janet had fallen to her death.

A little thread of apprehension tightened his back muscles and set his scalp tingling. It was as if Janet herself had led him here.

"Yer Grace?" he heard Gunna ask.

He quelled the shudder taking hold of his limbs and fixed his attention on her cowering figure. His pride would never allow him to reveal anything even remotely akin to dread to so wretched a creature.

He brushed past her, sneering as he went, "For a man who loves beauty why do I suddenly find myself surrounded by hags?"

CHAPTER 8

There were close to a hundred guests overflowing the front salon. Carr fixed a well-practiced smile to his face, practicality having reestablished itself. The damned haunts he could deal with. It had been the notion that Janet could actually return. . . . Nonsense! An ignorant woman's ravings.

He waded into the crowd, greeting people as he went. No matter that he did not know a good half of them by either name or face, nor that they appeared at his door as the hangers-on of those who'd received *bona fide* invitations. The more wastrels, the better.

He poured himself a glass of port, downed the contents in one draw and poured another, eschewing the pale tea he drank most evenings. He eyed the crowd with a connoisseur's appreciation. No huge-stakes men here tonight. Mostly middling wagerers. A number of gulls, a cheat or two.

"Your Grace!"

Carr lifted a brow in acknowledgment of the tall, extremely thin man threading his way toward him. It was James Wells, Lord Tunbridge, distant cousin to the future king, George III. Tunbridge was said to be educating the crown prince in royal—and royally carnal—sports. An agreeable situation, seeing how Tunbridge was in his power.

"I would have a word with you, sir," Tunbridge said breathlessly. "I . . . It's important. Very important."

"Really?" Carr asked. "To whom?"

"Why, to me." A light sheen sprouted on Tunbridge's high forehead.

Deuce take it, the man wanted something. Carr was not in the mood. "Later, Tunbridge. My guests—"

"Your guests will wait, Lord Carr," Tunbridge said, his voice hardening. "Please. I have been of great service to you these past few years, as well you know, and now I would ask but a few minutes of your time."

"You're making demands, Tunbridge?" Carr asked mildly. "How very annoying for me and how very dangerous for you."

Tunbridge flushed but raised his chin. He was going to be plaguesomely persistent.

"Very well," Carr capitulated, taking Tunbridge's arm and drawing him through the open doors that led out into the courtyard.

Outside, the sun had relinquished the sky and the wind had died down. A thin fog drifted up the low, flinty apron that sloped away from the castle. The noise from the party within melded with the elemental rumble of the sea.

"Now, what is it, Tunbridge?" Carr faced the tall man.

"Your daughter, sir."

"What of Fia?" Carr asked with awakening interest. Of late his gorgeous young daughter was an unpredictable creature, one minute an unruly jade and hoydenish flirt, the next, a Sphinx, inscrutable and cold.

Her attitude toward him had certainly changed in the last year. Once she'd been his familiar, seeking his company and amusing him with her sardonic wit. But now she'd turned her gifts against him, and honed them, too.

What had Fia done now? Publicly denigrated the fool's manhood?

"Before you choke on whatever it is you have to say, Tunbridge, I feel obliged to tell you that I have no intention of fighting any duels over anything Fia may have said or done," Carr said. He held up his hand, silencing Tunbridge when he would have interrupted.

"No. Listen. If you have a quarrel with the girl that only blood-letting can satisfy, I suggest you find one of her swains to champion her. I shan't."

"No! Of course . . . why . . . I mean . . . no! No!" Tunbridge grew bright red.

For reportedly being one of London's most celebrated duelists, Carr thought impatiently, Tunbridge certainly lacked dash. "Out with it, man! What the devil are you trying to say?"

"I . . . I don't want to *kill* Miss Fia. I wish to *marry* her!"

Carr stared at him a full minute before throwing back his head and laughing. He laughed until his side hurt and tears leaked from the corners of his eyes. He laughed until he could laugh no more and when he'd finally finished, he sniffed and withdrew a lace kerchief from his wrist and dabbed at his eyes and nose, occasionally hiccuping up another little chortle.

"Oh, thank you! I had need of a divertissement. I vow, Tunbridge, I would never have taken you for a wit."

Only then did he see that Tunbridge was not laughing. The color had leached from his face, leaving bloodless lips forming a thin line. Tunbridge had been serious.

When Carr realized this, he also remembered anew that Tunbridge—whose dueling career had been severely curtailed when Carr's son Ash impaled Tunbridge's hand on a stiletto—was still accredited to be more than passing proficient with a rapier. Still, Carr really wasn't in the mood.

"I will give you the benefit of the doubt, sir," Tunbridge ground out, "and assume that you misunderstood my intent, that being to take Miss Fia to wife."

"No, I didn't misunderstand you," Carr said, tucking his kerchief back in his sleeve. "And the answer is no."

"Why not?" Tunbridge demanded. "My lineage is impeccable, I am a baron, but most tellingly I am in the royal family's confidence.

"You, sir, ought to appreciate the extent of my influence on His Majesty as I have used that influence this past year and more in persuading him to revoke his decree that exiled you to Scotland. I have almost convinced His Majesty that your habit of losing rich young wives is, indeed, an unfortunate tragedy and nothing more sinister. I can just as easily convince him otherwise."

For a full minute the two men studied each other in silence, Carr with bored indifference, Tunbridge quivering with outrage. Finally, Carr sighed. "Are you quite through, Tunbridge? Fine. A moment of instruction 'ere we proceed to your suit."

Tunbridge blinked, startled.

"The trick to blackmailing, Tunbridge," Carr lectured calmly, "is that one must be willing—and able—to carry out whatever threats one uses to pressure one's victim into complying with one's purposes.

"Take, for instance, yourself. I know you'll do your best for me because should I fail to return to London—and that very, very soon—you realize that I will have no choice but to console myself with my latest acquisition, that being Campion Castle. How long has it been in your family, Tunbridge? Two? Three hundred years?"

Tunbridge's quivering ceased. His face had fallen into the slack proportions that Carr was beginning to recognize as being as habitual as they were unfortunate.

"Not only that," Carr continued mildly, "but I ashamedly admit that I will then likely enjoy imagining your own situation in a deportation vessel, having finally been brought to justice for the business with that Cheapside whore so many years ago."

"But I was drunk!"

"Ah!" Carr wagged his index finger playfully. "But I was not."

Tunbridge blanched further.

"Now, I have been reasonable this time because finding another toadie with your particular connections so late in the game would prove tiresome. It can be done, of course, and should it prove necessary, will be. Bear that in mind, Tunbridge, the next time you feel the urge to try your hand at extortion." Carr cocked his head. "Do we understand each other?"

Mutely, Tunbridge nodded.

"Good. Now, pray tell me, what is all this about Fia?"

Like a puppet whose strings had been severed, Tunbridge's shoulders slumped. His face betrayed his potent unhappiness. "She is a siren! I swear it. She drives me to distraction."

"Yes." Carr nodded. "I hear she's good at that sort of thing."

"She's bewitched me, I tell you. She's a succubus!" Tunbridge continued, his voice desperate. " 'Tis the only way to account for this obsession she has roused in me."

"Now, wouldn't that be a lovely rumor to start on the eve of her presentation?" Carr muttered irritably. He might have to deal with Tunbridge after all if he continued this sort of gibberish. A "siren" was fascinating; a "succubus" was disturbing.

Tunbridge held out one hand in supplication. "I must have her. I must."

"Don't be ridiculous."

"But why not?" Tunbridge asked pitiably. He looked utterly bewildered and in pain. Carr silently applauded Fia's skill. "I am rich. I am well connected. Whyever not?"

"Because I *already* control you," Carr explained. "Marrying Fia to you would be redundant. No. Fia will marry someone who does not bow beneath any of the other influences I can bring to bear." His smile relayed a certain pride. "Because Fia is the ultimate inducement."

"But . . . but *I want her*!" Tunbridge complained, having abandoned all attempts at manly forbearance.

Carr clapped him companionably on the shoulder. "Come, man. Grow a spine. Besides, Fia would use you up and spit you out within a fortnight. Begads! The chit is but sixteen! Why, she's just using her milk teeth on you. Imagine what she will be at twenty. Thir—"

The faint sound of a Highland pipe drifted out of the fog, cutting Carr's words short. He lifted his head sharply. "Did you hear that?"

"Hear what?" Tunbridge asked indifferently. "What would you say should Fia declare she wished to marry me?"

"She doesn't." Carr squinted into the soft shimmer of the twilight-kissed fog. A dark figure moved therein. He was certain of it. A dark *masculine* figure clad in a belted plaid. "Do you see anything out there?"

"Why won't she?"

Carr spared Tunbridge one dismissive glance before once again scanning the mist. "Why *would* she?"

Apparently, the answer to this pointed query finally convinced Tunbridge of the futility of his petition. With a deep sigh he slunk away. Carr barely noticed. His eyes were turned toward the drifting fog. His ears strained to hear the McClairens' sepulchral pipes. Nothing.

Damned haunts. Had the dead nothing better to occupy their time than with children's games of hide-and-seek? With a curse, Carr quit the terrace and followed the dew-glistened granite steps down into the garden. He strode purposefully along the footpath between the topiaries, bizarre and fantastical shapes clipped from living yew and boxwood. The fog swirled about his legs, the damp seeping through his white silk stockings and staining the pale blue satin covering the heels of his shoes.

At the end of the garden, where yet another set of pink granite steps led to a still lower terrace, Carr paused and peered out. Below him bracken and gorse had infiltrated the once regimented beds of roses and rare botanicals. The shadows had thickened down there. Night had found purchase. The fog was denser, the air colder.

"Come out, you cursed McClairen spirits! I am here! Haunt me!"

No reply met his shouted challenge. No ghostly form materialized. No pipe trilled from the darkness. Nothing.

Every time he'd had an . . . experience it was the same; a furtive movement from the corner of his eye; a gust of chill wind where no wind could be; a drumbeat in the middle of the night that could have been his heartbeat but wasn't.

It was driving him— *No!* It was not driving him anything. It was distracting. An annoyance. That was all.

"What's this?" he shouted to the gloom beneath. "Do the dead still fear the living? Do Scots flee the British even in death? Cowardly phantoms!"

The very silence seemed to mock him. With a hiss of rage he swung around and retraced his route, keenly aware of eyes upon him, of ghostly smiles jeering. He'd begun stalking up the stairs to the terrace when his eye caught a splotch of muted color tangled amid the mist and rose vines beside him. A scarf? Odd he hadn't noted it before, but then, his attention had been on other things.

One of his female guests must have been using the gardens for an assignation. Damned cold weather for an assignation. He leaned over and picked it up. He'd started forth once more when he chanced to glance down. Abruptly he stopped, riveted by the sight.

In his hands he held a frail length of heavy silk, its once bold colors dulled and faded by time or wear or a decade of being drowned beneath the sea. One side was raw and frayed though the other edges were neatly rolled and stitched. Someone had rent it in violence.

He closed his eyes. Opened them. It had not disappeared. Or mutated into some other piece of cloth. He crushed it in his fist. He recognized it.

This was Janet's *arisaid,* a woman's version of a plaid. The McClairen plaid. He could not mistake it. She'd worn it the day she'd died. It had been he who'd ripped it, infuriated that she would dare consider wearing it to his ball. One piece she'd wrapped around Fia. This was the other half.

He'd not seen it since he'd watched it floating beside Janet's body at the base of McClairen's Isle.

Where he'd thrown her.

CHAPTER 9

"**C**arr didn't even look for Jamie and his pipe," Muira cackled. She sat at the dressing table in the bedchamber Carr had reserved for Favor Donne's chaperone.

As Favor watched, Muira dipped a cotton wad into a jar of grease and began rubbing the ochre-tinted paint from her face. "Not that he'd have found him. He may have lived in the castle over twenty years but he doesn't know half her secrets, one being as how a body whispering on the parapet beneath the south tower will sound like he's standing in the gardens below the courtyard."

"You're very sure of what Carr knows and what he doesn't know," Favor said.

"I should be. I've been listening to his raves and curses for two years and I've been watching him for a dozen before that. Aye. I know Carr's black soul as well as my own," Muira said. She tossed the stained cotton into the fire and began rolling the clothes she'd shed into a small bundle that she would later store in the locked chest at the foot of her bed.

Favor looked around the room, wondering what secrets it held. Happily, her own room was unconnected. She disliked the idea of Muira having unimpeded access to her.

"If only I could remember some detail about Janet that only Carr would have noticed," Muira muttered, her eyes narrowed in concentration on her image in the mirror.

"Well, you'd best come up with something soon," Favor said. "We've been guests at the castle two weeks and so far he hasn't taken any more note of me than a scullery cat. Aside from dancing naked in the firelight, I don't know what else I can do to attract his attention."

Muira flashed her an annoyed glance. She finished plumping out her cheeks with a bit of cotton wadding and quickly dusted her face with fine white powder, taking special care with her brows and lashes. That done she twisted her white hair into a bun atop her head.

No one who saw her now, looking so pudding-faced and pale, would recognize her as "Pala," the dark, wiry Gypsy whom Carr had found in his stables nearly two years earlier.

"I've spent two years filling Carr's head with hints and omens about Janet's return," Muira said. "If you fail to make Carr believe you are she, it's because you *want* to fail."

She regarded Favor thoughtfully as she stuffed her bodice with woolen bolsters. "Is that it? Are you wondering what would come of you if you could call your future your own?" Her brogue thickened with her growing contempt. "Yer still thinkin' on that English prison scarecrow, aren't ye?"

"No." Favor denied the charge.

"Aye." Muira nodded. "Jamie says as soon as he returned from France, just before we come here, ye asked him if he'd ever heard what become of the man."

"I know you'll not believe this but I asked because I feel—"

"Guilty." Muira spat out the word. "So you say. So you've said this past half year. Well, it seems to me your fine conscience has developed a large appetite. Now me, I'd think that any lass responsible for the deaths of most all her clansmen wouldna have room for any more guilt."

"You'd be surprised at the things of which I'm capable," Favor stonily returned. The old woman's methods of persuasion were never subtle but certainly one could not gainsay their effectiveness. Since she'd brought Favor from France she had lost no opportunity to remind Favor of what she owed her clan. They'd each learned a great deal about the other.

Favor had learned to hide her vulnerabilities. Muira had learned that the biddable puppet she'd hoped to manipulate was an independent young woman not easily managed. It had been a lesson the old woman disliked and one that had pitted the two women in constant conflict.

"Or," Muira said now, "are you wondering whether or not your blooming sweet youth really does need to be sacrificed after all?"

Favor faced her silently.

"Well, darlin' lassie, all those men that died because of you were blooming with youth, too. And they all deserved bonny brides and plump bairns and warm hearths. My husband, my brother, and my three sons among them."

"I know." Favor did, too. She'd sneaked out to the stables the night they'd arrived at the castle and found Jamie, who was masquerading as Thomas Donne's driver. She asked him to intervene in the battle of wills between her and Muira. Instead Jamie had told Favor about how on the night of the massacre Muira had lost every one of her family yet still found the strength to rescue the wounded and tend them back to health.

But Favor, guided by the Abbess's sweet reasoning, also knew that she was only in part responsible for the tragedy that had occurred that night. It had taken the Abbess years to make Favor believe that. Yet daily, what with Muira carefully tending it, she felt her old guilt growing back.

"We did not hide here, risking the last of our men's lives smuggling French brandy, just to keep you happy in that fine French convent of yours. We did it because we had plans for you, plans you have a blood debt to carry out."

"I have never denied it." Dear God, no. Not she. The weight of the McClairens' expectations had at times near crushed her, but she hadn't bowed before it. She would not break now. No one wanted to pay off that debt more than Favor.

"We did not work and plan and sacrifice for all these years so that you could ruin everything now, at this last stage."

"I won't ruin anything."

"If all goes right—and that's in your hands—the isle and her castle will soon once more belong to the McClairen. Is that not what you want?" Muira demanded.

"Yes."

"Then mind me well, you must not *act* like Janet McClairen, you must *be* Janet McClairen. Do you ken?"

"I've tried," Favor said, unable to hide her frustration. "My face aches with my efforts but Carr doesn't seem to notice."

"Then try harder!" the old woman said grimly.

Favor did not back away. She did what she did for her own reasons, to put her guilt finally and completely behind her. "Time's running short and you've not been able to supply me with the key to Janet McClairen. Perhaps your memories are faulty, your recall not as keen as you think. Perhaps you can't teach what you don't know."

Abruptly, Muira chuckled. "You doubt my thespian skills, child? Don't. Have I not convinced Carr I'm a sweet old lady?"

She blinked myopically, her mouth curving in a benign smile. In a trice she'd become every inch the vague, elderly relative she pretended to be. Favor watched with grudging admiration.

They'd arrived six months ago and taken up residence in Thomas

Donne's empty manor house. Soon after, Muira had forwarded Lord Carr a letter ostensibly written by Thomas Donne, introducing her as Mrs. Douglas, his aunt, and his little sister Favor's chaperone.

As Muira had predicted, Carr couldn't resist adding a wealthy, ill-protected heiress to his guest list. An invitation had been immediately forthcoming and a few days later Muira had trailed Favor up the steps to Wanton's Blush shedding lace kerchiefs and whispered "oh, mys." They'd been at Wanton's Blush on and off as guests ever since.

Muira's smile disappeared. "You're right on one mark, though. Time is running short. You need to find Carr alone tonight. But that'll never happen if he sees me at yer side.

"Damn the man, I think he has yet enough sense to be afraid of your brother. He doesn't want to chance having me report anything amiss in his conduct toward you." The notion tickled her and she chuckled.

"I'll go down soon," Muira said thoughtfully, "I'll drink a wee bit, and a wee bit ostentatiously at that. You come down in an hour. By that time I'll seem to have fallen asleep. You'll be able to catch Carr alone without him worrying on the repercussions."

She stood up, drew on her gloves and picked up a fan. Moving to the door, she paused briefly. "Tonight it must be. 'Pala' promised Carr his dead wife would be returning for him. I saw his expression. He's rabid to see her."

Muira shook her head, fascinated. "Even though he flung her from the cliffs, he still pines for her. He honestly believes he loves her. And that she loves him." She gave a brief, rueful laugh. "Our plan is perfect. Once he finds her again, he'll never let her go."

Her expression hardened. "Only then will you have paid yer debt. After he weds you, and McClairen's Isle belongs to the McClairens once more."

An hour later, Favor McClairen rose from where she'd remained seated since Muira's departure. She carefully arranged the fall of her wine-red taffeta skirts, adjusted the treble ruffles of black lace that fell from her sleeves and exited her room.

Her face betrayed no emotion—and indeed, there was none to betray. She felt like a member of the audience witnessing a play from the balcony seats.

She would convince Carr she was his dead wife come back to life. She would marry Carr. She would then disappear, returning to France where he would never dare seek her. And then she would wait for however long it took for Carr to die and then the castle would be back in McClairen hands. For this was Scotland where a woman inherits her dead husband's estate.

And if between the first and the last something (consummation) occurred (or was forced), which she would personally find unpalatable *(abhorrent)*, she would still, at long last, mark "paid" to the debt she owed—

A black-haired wraith flickered and vanished in the corner of her eye. Startled, Favor spun to face the creature and only then realized that she'd seen her own reflection in a mirror hanging on the wall.

She gazed unblinkingly at the creature—beyond pale, spectral white skin, empty black eyes, soulless as a selkie.

She studied the mirror seeing white flesh, high cheekbones, small bowed lips, a slender throat, and thin arching brows. All of it an illusion, the product of an artist's tricks of embellishment, accentuation, and deemphasis. Powder laced with the finest, iridescent lead created her white skin. Carefully applied salve made her lips look thinner than nature had ordained them, and a bit of rouge accented her cheekbones.

More rouge, beneath the jaw, created the impression of a long neck and Muira's tweezers had produced those thin, arching brows. A drop of belladonna dilated her pupils to such an extent that they nearly eclipsed the blue of her irises, making her eyes appear less blue.

Finally, thrice weekly Muira pulverized bits of roots and berries and dyed Favor's tresses black. A dead color, Favor thought privately, so deep an ebony, lacking any of the sheen of health.

At least in repose, Favor was as close to looking like Janet McClairen as Muira and her paint and potions could make her. For the rest, she needed to rely on the memories of those who'd known that long-dead lady to augment her resemblance. Experimentally, she flicked open her fan. Briskly—because Janet McClairen did nothing languidly—she covered her lips, lowered her eyelids and glanced sidelong. Too coy. She tried again—

"I say, Miss Donne, you won't be so cruel as to use up all those blisteringly come-hither looks on your own reflection, would you? I mean, you will save at least one for me?"

Favor spun around. Lord Orville stood with one shoulder rammed against the wall. His voice was slurred, his mouth puckered scoldingly. Favor backed away.

On her first evening at Wanton's Blush, Lord Orville had cornered her in a vacant room. Without preamble he'd grabbed her and kissed her with lip-splitting brutality. Even now her belly rebelled at the memory of his cool, wet lips. She'd tried to get away but he'd been too strong. She hadn't dared scream. Carr might send her away for being prudish, or worse, form an aversion to her maidenly sensibilities.

Only the timely arrival of Orville's giggling wife being hotly pursued by a disheveled footman had distracted Orville long enough for Favor to break free of his embrace and flee. Since then she'd managed to avoid him.

Her luck apparently had run out.

"Cat got your tongue?" Orville drawled. "Lucky cat."

Sophistication, she adjured herself. It was her only hope. Orville would have no idea how to handle a woman whose worldliness surpassed his own. She forced her breath to an even tempo. Snapped the ivory fan closed.

"Lord Orville"—she rose on her tiptoes and pretended to peer behind him—"is that your wife I see disappearing up the stairs with one of the stable boys?"

He sneered. "What of it? May she have her fill of him—or rather"—he laughed without amusement—"may the lad have his fill of her. Everyone else does."

He pushed himself from the wall, his lip curling back. "I'd much rather have my fill of you, Miss Donne. Bite by bite."

He strolled toward her, tapping his long white chin. "I'd be tasting something rare, something few other men had sampled. Oh, don't look surprised, my dear. I've asked after you, you see. We all have."

"How tedious of you," Favor said, forcing herself to stand still. "I can't imagine why since I've shown not a whit of similar interest in you."

"*Tch. Tch.* Such a rude little Scot. Aren't you curious about what I've discovered?"

"No."

His smile grew. "I know your older brother is some sort of dispossessed Scottish thingie—dispossessed because he chose to go off to the Americas rather than stumble 'round the Highlands with the rest of his Jacobite-loving kin. Seems eminently sensible to me but apparently your clansmen thought it showed a certain lack of fealty."

He was watching her carefully, seeing whether his words caused pain. It flashed through her thoughts that perhaps Orville was one of Lord Cumberland's agents sent to the Highlands to rout further insurrections.

If so, he would get no joy from her. She knew by heart the tale of her brother's supposed cowardliness and dispossession. She should. Thomas had created it. It allowed him to move freely among these English usurpers—despised by them as a traitor to his people at the same time as they embraced him for being a *roué* willing to spend money.

"I'm afraid he's not greatly regarded by his kilt-wearing brethren. But don't look so sad, Miss Donne. I hear his wealth greatly succors him. And you."

Favor continued regarding her reflection, a vain woman bored with the conversation of a tiresome man.

"Do his old clan affiliates threaten him? Is that why he left Scotland so abruptly?"

Favor leaned closer to the mirror and rearranged a black curl on her temple before answering. "Hm? Thomas? Lud, no, nothing like it. As far as I know, my dear brother is in America." She gave him a vacuous smile. "Now, if you'll excuse me—"

She'd almost made it past him before he stepped in front of her. Her smile slipped. "Sir?"

"How is it he left his little sister behind?"

"Perhaps because he's visiting his plantation and his little sister has an aversion to sweat; and sweat, so I'm assured, is abundant on a plantation. Though," she said, her gaze traveling over Orville's damp brow and glistening upper lip, "we don't seem to lack for it here, either."

Orville flushed. "You're a saucy wench, Miss Donne."

"But not nearly spicy enough for a sophisticated palate such as yours." She cursed the pleading note she heard in her voice.

Orville heard it, too. Immediately his confidence returned. "I'll be the judge of that." He leaned forward, his sour breath sluicing over her mouth.

The courage supporting Favor abruptly gave out. She wheeled, grabbing up the hoops beneath her billowing skirts, and ran. For a moment all she heard was the hiss of rustling taffeta, the staccato of her own heels, and the far-off sound of voices growing even more distant as she fled.

Then she heard Orville give chase.

She raced past her own chambers. They could offer no safe haven. She would never be able to fetch the key and lock the door in time. Her only chance lay in evading him.

"How delightful!" he called. "I adore games!"

She made it to the servants' staircase and ducked beneath the low lintel, feet clattering on the worn stone steps, slipping as she went, her skirts choking the narrow, winding passageway. She burst from the door at the bottom and fled on. Through another door, down another set of stairs, always the sound of his footsteps behind. Through more doors, to another dim passage.

She had no idea where she was. She'd been culled like a yearling deer from the herd, driven to the far reaches of the castle, to the dark, uninhabited parts. Her lungs burned, her skirts dragged like dead weights from her hands. She stopped, panting, looking about. She could run no more. Desperately she lunged for the nearest door handle and pushed. Reluctantly the door gave way.

She scrambled into the room, turned and eased the door shut, pressing her back to it. She waited, her heart hammering, searching for another way out.

There was none.

She was in a bedchamber, long unused and neglected. Ghostly sheets draped all the furnishings except the huge bed in the center. Its filmy curtains hung torn and shredded from the canopy like the night rail of an ill-used bride. Boxes and chests lined one wall. A thick stack of paintings leaned against another.

A hushed atmosphere of suspension permeated the room, as though only timid ghosts kept company here, holding their spectral breath, waiting for her to leave. She strained her ears to hear Orville's footsteps. Nothing.

She counted to one hundred before moving cautiously across the room, her wide skirts sweeping a broad swath in the dust. She stopped at the tall bank of windows on the opposite wall and pulled back the gauzy drapery. Her breath caught in her throat.

The evening sky bloomed above a seething cobalt-colored sea. In a gothic excess, day lay bleeding its brilliance on night's black shoulders. She had never seen such a sunset. "My Lord," she gasped.

"Milady."

Her heart checked. Before she'd turned around, Orville was on her. He grabbed her around the waist, hauling her off her feet. He shoved her hard, face first against the window. His mouth fell on the back of her neck, sucking greedily.

She cried out, kicking and sobbing in terror. He laughed. The sound extinguished her fear, cold water on a fire.

She was Favor McClairen. She was not some vile Englishman's doxy. She was not *any* Englishman's victim. Not *anyone's* victim. She reached over her shoulders and clawed at his face, satisfaction flooding through her as she felt his flesh rend beneath her nails.

"Bitch!" He grabbed one wrist and twisted viciously, slamming it against the window frame with numbing force. He grasped her other hand and treated it the same.

"Scottish whore!" he hissed into her ear. "I'll mark you for that and damned be your bastard brother! We'll see—

His words were cut off in a strangled sound of surprise. Abruptly Favor

found herself free. She sank bonelessly to the floor, twisting to see what
had happened.

The room was darker now, nearly black. Two figures struggled in its
center, pitched in an ill-matched contest. One was tall and broad, his fists
spearing through the air with blinding speed and devastating effect. In
seconds, he'd landed a series of brutal blows. He stopped abruptly and
straightened as the slighter figure teetered and crumpled into a heap on
the floor.

The stranger turned his head in her direction. He hesitated but then
came toward her, she thought to offer her his hand.

She lifted her face, shaken and grateful, and gave him a tremulous
smile. "Thank you, sir. I . . . I can't begin to express my gratitude. I . . .
thank you so very much."

He neglected to hold out his hand. She frowned, perplexed by this lack
of manners after he'd just championed her so completely. He took another step, bringing him into the last rays of daylight coming through the
window. She suddenly understood his reluctance to touch her.

She'd last seen him being swarmed by the French soldiers she'd set on
him.

Her Englishman.

CHAPTER 10

The tall man's eyes narrowed on Favor. In a rush of relief she realized that he couldn't possibly recognize her disguised as she—

"Are you thanking me for my current services or the ones you made such good use of in Dieppe?" he asked.

So much for anonymity.

His voice was rough-smooth, his gaze shuttered, the light refracting off the clear, wild honey of his irises. Only the slight curl of his upper lip indicated his current disposition. It was not a pleasant one.

"It *is* you," he said. "What sort of perfidy had you planned for that poor sot?" He jerked his chin in the direction of the motionless Orville. "Damned if I oughtn't dust him off and apologize, for any man entangled with you, Milady Treachery, deserves at the very least his fellow man's pity and most probably his aid."

Favor only half-attended this biting denunciation. She was too busy staring. Lud, he was big. Far taller and wider than she remembered. He wore tight black breeches that had seen better days and the white lawn shirt he wore was untied and loose, revealing his muscular bronzed chest.

He was darker than she recalled, too. The angularly rough features were tanned now, the square jaw blue-black with an incipient beard. His rumpled sable-colored hair fell in loose curls about a strong, broad throat.

But there was some other difference. Something elemental. Something important.

She tilted her head, trying to identify it. She had it. The man who had been shackled spread-eagle to that prison wall had been desperate, pushed to the crisis point. This man owned himself completely.

It put him at a distinct advantage. Now she was the one controlled by fate and others' fortunes. She disliked the reversal in their positions.

He'd moved closer to her, agile and light-footed for so large a man. She shrank against the wall, suddenly realizing that one danger had supplanted another. Her heels beat a tattoo as she struggled to rise. He reached down, grabbed her upper arm, and lifted her to her feet.

She attempted to dart past him but his hand flashed up, circling her throat in a warm, tight grip, keeping her where she stood. She forced herself to meet his gaze. With one large thumb, he tilted her chin back. Her pulse thudded heavily against his palm.

"Well," he murmured, his gaze slipping over her cheeks and mouth and throat like a caress, "what say you, Madame Noir, or Widow Lambett, or whoever the hell you are?"

"Favor," she said. "Favor Mc—Favor Donne."

He went utterly still, his gaze scoured her features.

"Damn you, what trick is this?" He dropped his hand to her upper arm, this time his grip not merely restraining but hurtful. "I don't know what game you're playing now, but I will have the truth."

She winced. His teeth snapped together. "The truth before I . . . the truth!"

" 'Tis the truth, I swear it!" she cried. "My brother is Lord Thomas Donne. He owns the manor house five miles inland on the north highway. You've but to ask anyone here to receive that same answer. I am Favor Donne."

He eyed her derisively. "And what is a nobleman's sister doing in France, masquerading as a licentious bawd?"

She hesitated a heartbeat, searching for a likely explanation. He shook her. "Out with it!"

"My brother . . . He is also *La Bête,* the smuggler," she whispered. " 'Twas he the French sought in Dieppe. 'Twas he I protected by giving you over to the soldiers in his stead."

He thrust his face closer to hers. His eyes no longer looked cool, but torrid. He looked older than he had in France—harder, too. Certainly more dangerous. Silently she prayed that he would believe her.

"I swear it," she rasped.

Slowly, his grip loosened, became less punishing.

"Damn," he finally said but he seemed to be replying to some internal avowal, and not to anything she'd done. "You haven't answered my question yet. What were *you* doing in Dieppe, little falcon? And why the new plummage?"

"What?" she asked in confusion.

"Your fierce brows are gone and you've dyed your hair. Why?"

"Because"—she cast about for a plausible answer—"because the English gentlemen are partial to dark hair."

"I never heard it was so."

"And where would you have heard *anything* about the current modes?" she asked, praying he wouldn't punish her impertinence. "Or did you have the *Gentleman's Quarterly* delivered to your cell?"

Appreciation flickered through his expression. *"Touché."*

"And what are *you* doing here?" she asked haughtily, pressing her momentary advantage. Had he found out her identity and followed her here to extract some sort of revenge? The concept sent a shiver through her. Let that be a lesson to her never to heed the urgings of a guilty conscience. She should have let the French soldiers take him.

"Oh, no, pretty peregrine." He shook his head. "A decent attempt at diversion, but I'm no callow youth to be distracted by a lush mouth uttering haughty demands. We were discussing *you.*

"Why were you in Dieppe? 'Twas it your job to mind the smuggling ship's rudder?" he asked sarcastically.

"Of course not!" she said quickly, examining and discarding evasions with lightning speed. "I was with relatives who'd had the care of me for years. It was safer for me in France than here. Because of Tom." She glanced up, gauging his reaction. Impossible to tell. "You know about Tom, of course."

"Do I?" He abruptly released her, and stood back, crossing his arms over his broad chest. She backed away, rubbing the marks he'd left on her upper arm. His gaze touched dispassionately on the reddened area.

"Tom left the country just after Culloden. Followed by the price the rest of the clan chieftains had put on his head."

"Why?"

She lowered her eyelashes, bit her lip in feigned humiliation. "He was at Culloden but he was just a boy. He saw how outnumbered and outarmed the Highlanders were. Tom"—she paused for effect—"Tom has never been much for a fight. The sight of blood curls his toes. He left the moor when the fighting began."

His sudden laughter made her eyes snap open. She scowled. He was grinning at her hugely, his white teeth flashing in the semidarkness. "God preserve me, you could convince a cat to bark, you little liar."

"Have you no delicacy?" she demanded, brazening it out. "I've just confessed my brother's disgrace."

"That being that he ran away from the battlefield because he's an aversion to blood?" He shook his head. "You'll have to do better than that, love, especially if you're going to chase that fable with one about the same cowardly brother becoming a notorious smuggler. Unless of course, 'La Bête' hides belowdeck whenever there's a spot of bloodshed."

"Don't be ridiculous," she snapped, chagrin supplanting fear.

"No need, as you're being ridiculous enough for both of us."

"I don't care if you do believe me—"

"Oh, you'd better," he broke in quietly, returning her fear to her.

She swallowed. "Thomas orchestrates the smuggling so that there will *be* no blood-letting. Last year the French started closing in on him. They offered a reward for any information leading to his arrest.

"It was only a matter of time before someone told the authorities about me. We would not bring trouble to those who'd fostered me for so long. So, Tom devised a plan whereby I could escape. It needed a decoy."

"Me. And here I'd thought I owed the inestimable Jacques a visit. Where is your gargantuan friend?"

"He's here and his name is Jamie and he's my . . . my brother's driver."

"How delightful to have so multitalented a driver."

"He had nothing to do with your . . . situation. He simply followed orders," she said, envisioning Jamie and this huge, lean man closed in mortal combat.

"Don't worry, sweetling, I won't hurt your tame bull."

She breathed a sigh of relief. His expression flattened. "But tell me, where is your clever brother? I'm all agog to make his acquaintance."

"He's abroad."

"Avoiding more unpleasant things? So why are you here without him?"

If she stuck close to the truth perhaps she could convince him to leave her alone, to go away and do . . . what *was* he doing here? "My brother may appear to be a wealthy man, but he's not. *We're* not. And neither is our clan. In fact, my whole family is quite, quite poor."

"Yes?" he prodded.

"I'm here to . . . to repair the clan's fortune." She skirted closer to the truth than she would have liked.

"Fortune? Do you mean by that you are casting nets in the matrimonial waters, Miss Donne? Here?" His voice revealed his skepticism. "At Wanton's Blush? Well, I give you high marks for originality. Not many a blushing debutante would think to come here to seek a mate."

"Where else would such as I go? A Scottish nobody without lands, family, or connections to recommend myself?" she demanded hotly, for he'd pressed too close to a truth she'd never allowed herself to inspect. Even if she could call her future her own, where would someone like her find a "happily-ever-after"?

"Only at Wanton's Blush could someone like me find a suitor who would not look too closely at my antecedents or, even if he did discover them, care who they were. As long as I am richly gowned, bedecked and bejeweled, here I am accepted as the eligible heiress I appear to be."

"You mean the smuggling business isn't all it's cracked up to be? And here I thought it one of the more profitable occupations open to an ambitious young man."

"Nay," she said harshly. " 'Tisn't. Not nearly profitable enough to repair a fortune stolen by English ba—"

"Be careful, Miss Donne," he interjected dryly. "Your future husband may just be one of those English *ba's*."

"I understand that," she answered tightly. "But you see, I don't have any choice. Your English didn't leave any Scottish men to choose from— rich, poor, or anywhere in between. They killed them all."

She had the impression her words had struck a chord and that he was growing sympathetic to her tale.

"Aye. That has the ring of truth to it," he said after a moment. "But then, I have a certain history with your bell-toned lies."

She'd been wrong. He cared nothing for her people's slaughter. "Ridicule me all you like," she snapped.

"Tuck your lower lip in, sweetling, 'tis too tempting by half pouting thus. But I'm sure you know that full well."

She stamped her foot in annoyance and then stared at the offending limb in consternation. She hadn't stamped her foot since she was a child.

"What a fine tale and what a fine heroine you make, Favor, me love," he said in a light, mocking tone. "So brave and passionate. How noble of you to sacrifice yourself for your clan." His expression flattened. "If only I could believe in that nobility. But you were very willing to exploit me."

"I'd do the same again today. You were already condemned. What did you have to lose? Besides"—she stared defiantly at him—"you escaped, did you not? Well, then you got more than the bargain called for."

"Oh, no," he murmured, "I didn't get *any* of what the bargain called for."

He stepped forward, intent, predatory, his concentration focused to a rapier sharpness. She stepped back. Her shoulders collided with the wall.

He smiled, one side of his mouth turning up and carving a deep line beneath his high, broad cheekbone. A wicked smile, that. A devil's smile.

He lifted his hand toward her face. She flinched but he only reached past her, placed his palm flat against the wall next to her head and leaned in. His stance emphasized his much greater height. He eclipsed her with his breadth. His gaze drifted down her face and throat and lingered where her breasts swelled in agitation above the low, square décolletage.

"I'd been purchased from jail to provide sport for you."

"Not for me!" she denied. "For Madame Noir."

"Who you pretended to be," he reasoned, his voice low and seductive. He angled his head and inhaled, his mouth inches above her flesh. She shrank down; there was nowhere left to retreat. The wall behind her bare shoulders was cool. Every inch of her skin seemed suddenly heated.

"You shouldn't have dyed your hair," he mused. He picked up a lock, his knuckles brushing her collarbone. Sensation danced over her skin in response. He rubbed the tress lightly between thumb and forefinger, testing the texture. "It was prettier before. Plundered gold. Now it's funereal, like a dead raven's eye."

"Flatterer," she whispered.

His gaze shot up to meet hers. His dimple deepened in surprised humor, then dissolved. The wide mouth relaxed, became pensive. His brows dipped, as if in puzzlement.

"Who would have ever thought you . . . of all the women in the world . . . *you*," he whispered in a voice so low she barely heard him.

Watching him studying her body made her feel ripe and lush, liquid and uncomfortable. She couldn't have looked away if she'd tried.

"Please."

"Please what? Please myself? What would that take, do you imagine?" he asked. "I had a kiss from you once and I still remember your taste. Isn't that odd?" He lay the artificially darkened tress on her shoulder, arranging the curl with patient care. "Isn't it?"

"Yes."

"I'd been in jail for four years, you know," he said. "Four years is a long time to remember those carnal pleasures I was just learning to appreciate when I was captured. After I escaped—with your aid—it took me a few days to realize I was safe. But then . . . then I sought out those pleasures —when it didn't mean risking my life."

His face hardened. "And do you know what? Do you want to know something very odd?" His face was very close, his mouth looked very soft, the only soft thing in that hard visage. "Do you?"

She nodded, mesmerized by his low hypnotic voice, the heat of his hand playing just above her collarbone.

"Even in the blistering heat of the most powerful climax, I still tasted *you*."

She tried to hold back her gasp. Failed. Earned another one-sided smile.

"What's this? A blush, little peregrine? Too raw? By God, I believe I've embarrassed the wench." He gave a humorless laugh. "And to think I mistook you for Madame Noir. I really had lost the knack of reading a woman."

"She was my relative," she said.

"Allow a modicum of respect for my intelligence. I doubt you've ever even met the lady—No!" He lay a callused fingertip against her lower lip. "Your mouth begins to form a lie before it's even half thought. Spare us both yet another of your fictions." Hesitantly, as though compelled, he grazed his fingertip back and forth along her lower lip.

"I can't help what you believe or disbelieve," she answered, a sense of panic unlike any she'd ever experienced rising in tandem with the electric feeling suffusing her mouth, her cheeks and throat, her breasts and thighs.

"Damn me, lady hawk, is there any truth in you at all?"

Her voice wouldn't work. She stared in mute appeal.

"Christ's blood," he murmured with that wicked, Satan-inspired darkness flooding his voice, "I can't decide if God is punishing me or you. Let's find out, shall we?"

He closed the short distance between their mouths. His lips touched hers with deliberate delicacy, clung. Her eyelids drifted shut.

Warm breath. Velvet mouth, firm and testing. Just a kiss, just the softest brush of his lips and yet her knees weakened and her head spun. He moved closer. She sensed it, felt his breadth surround her, above her . . . Threatening? Protecting? By the Virgin, she couldn't tell.

Her head fell back against the wall. His fingertips branded one side of her throat with gossamer fire, skated down and across the top of her breasts, found the edge of her décolletage and slipped along it, moving with lingering deftness beneath—

A jolt of molten sensation electrified her. Her eyes flew open, her startled gaze leaping to meet his unreadable one.

"Let me go," she pleaded. "Please. I am not rich and I have no name with which others might seek to align themselves. All I own is my virtue. Please don't take that from me."

Was his breathing staggered? She couldn't say. Her own thoughts were in too great a turmoil to heed another's state, her own breath too ragged.

"Let me go," she repeated. "Please! I don't even know your name."

" 'Tis Ra—Rafe," he said, but his hand dropped to his side and he moved back. "Though I've had far more intimate discourse with women who've had far less knowledge of me than that."

"How dare you speak to me like this?" The words broke from her rising panic. "I'm not one of your women of the streets taking money to lift my skirts."

"Oh, rest assured, I did not find all of them on the streets," he said. "And I had no money to offer."

Fire swept over her chest and throat and burned in her cheeks. "So that's what this is about."

She had known this game she and the rest of the McClairens played would extract an ever-stiffening price. She had not foreseen this, though.

"What's that?" he asked, a smile loitering in his dark gaze.

"You've sought me in order to penalize me for my actions in Dieppe. To take your revenge in . . . in having me against my will," she ended brokenly.

When she finished, he snorted in disgust. "Rest easy. Your virtue is not at risk. Odd as it must seem to you, I would like to hold on to the notion—no doubt a self-deluding one—that I might find pleasure with a woman without resorting to rape."

At her wide-eyed amazement, he broke out laughing, shaking his head. "And as for your idea that after four long years in a hellish hole I had naught better to do with my newfound freedom than hunt you down in order to toss you on your backside . . . By all the saints, Madame, your conceit outstrips even my own!"

Put thus, it did seem improbable. Only someone unhinged would set himself on such a course. She felt another blush rise to her cheeks.

"What are you doing here, then?" she asked.

He regarded her thoughtfully a second before answering. "Have you ever heard of McClairen's Trust?"

"Aye," she answered. Every McClairen knew the legend of the lost jewels. "It's a parure of rubies and diamonds; a necklace, earbobs, brooch, and circlet. 'Twas said to be a gift that Queen Mary gave a McClairen lady in gratitude for her aid in discovering Darnley's treachery."

"Aye," he said. "That's the one."

She frowned. " 'Twas lost. Probably sold to finance yet another glorious return."

"Ah! A cynic and a Scot?" He laughed. "Who'd have thought the two could coexist in one body. As for the Trust, some say that the McClairens hid it at Wanton's Blush and here it remains."

"And *that's* why you're here? I don't believe you."

"Have you a better explanation? Besides the irresistible lure of breaching your own maidenhead, of course. Assuming that you aren't lying and it's unbroken yet."

"Knave!" she said, more from embarrassment at his reminder of her foolishness than at his crudity.

His gaze mocked her. "I've been here a week already. 'Tis been an easy enough venture thus far. Carr keeps most of the east rooms empty, using them as a warehouse. So here is where my search has begun." He swept his arm over the room.

"The McClairen Trust is naught but a child's nighttime story," she said gruffly. "If there were any rubies and diamonds they've long since disappeared. I am surprised you know the tale, though. It's only a local legend. How *do* you know about it?"

"I had a cellmate named Ashton Merrick. He told me."

Her eyes widened. Of course. 'Twas common knowledge that Carr's sons had been captured by some Scots seeking revenge against Carr. They'd sold them to the French as political prisoners and the French kept them for ransom. Just as everyone knew Carr had refused to pay for their return until last year—or so she was told—when Ash Merrick had briefly reappeared.

Mayhap Rafe had met Raine Merrick, the source of all her grief. Mayhap this man even knew something of that thrice-damned rapist's fate. "Ashton Merrick had a brother," she said.

"Aye."

"Did he share your cell, too?"

"No. Raine Merrick was kept in a different city. A different prison. I doubt he even knows if Ashton lives or is dead. I don't."

Favor closed her eyes. "God keep Raine Merrick from that knowledge if it were to provide him a dram of comfort," she muttered.

"You hate this Raine Merrick?" he asked.

She didn't want to discuss that black-souled demon. Not now. Not ever.

Behind them Orville stirred, groaned, and rolled over. She needed to leave. Once more she drew on the Abbess's wisdom: Act a queen and you don't need a crown. She squared her shoulders.

"Orville will shortly awake. Unless you plan to murder him—which," she hastily continued on seeing the thoughtful manner in which Rafe regarded Orville, "will only cause a search of the premises—I suggest you leave here.

"Now, my thanks for your aid. In return, I promise I shall not tell anyone of your presence here." She started past him but he stepped in front of her.

"Oh, no," he said. "I haven't given you leave to go yet. I have been thinking."

Alarm danced up her spine. His expression had grown wolfish. She mustn't let him see her fear. She raised one perfectly arched brow. "Thinking? Ah. I trust this is not a novel experience?"

His mouth quirked appreciatively. "I don't want anyone to know about me. It's been a bit venturesome having to steal food from the kitchen at night. And if I don't find my jewels in this wing, I'll have to search the occupied parts of the castle. I'll need to blend in to do that. That means I'll need clothes. Nice clothes."

"So?"

"So, you will bring me both food and clothes. Unless, that is, you want your host, Lord Carr, to find out that his heiress and her brother are not so flush as he'd assumed."

"You wouldn't dare tell him. You couldn't afford to confront him. He'd have you hanged as a thief."

"I don't need to confront him at all. I have only to write a letter."

"That's blackmail!"

"Yes," he replied easily. "I know. But though it doesn't look to be nearly so interesting a revenge as the one you envisioned, it will have to do."

CHAPTER 11

Raine leaned against the doorjamb, enjoying the sight of the young woman's rigid spine above the tantalizing sway of her hips as she swept down the hall and disappeared into the gloom. He'd seen her crossing the courtyard a few days before. Something had been familiar in her stride, in the set of her shoulders, and the way she held her head. For a moment, in profile, she'd resembled someone from his past but then she'd turned and the sense of long-ago familiarity had been supplanted by a much more recent one. But it wasn't until he'd seen her closely that he'd realized that the black-haired girl fleeing an amorous pursuer was the same golden-tressed widow who'd so thoroughly duped him in Dieppe.

She'd dyed her hair and plucked the fierce slashing brows—which, oddly enough, he rather regretted—and disguised the full sensuous curve of her mouth under a thin painted line. She'd even done something to her eyes, causing the pupils to devour their iridescent blue—a grave error in his estimation should she indeed be seeking a mate.

Had she gone to such lengths to, as she claimed, make herself more appetizing to the English gentleman's palate? Perhaps. She would never be a classic beauty, her sharp-angled face lacking that oval symmetry such demanded. But there was some element that drew the attention, a certain comeliness, some quality that made a man want to watch her mouth move as she spoke, to touch the high outer curve of her cheek.

Raine pushed off the wall, turning and strolling back into the room. Miss Favor should be on her knees right now, thanking God that the past years had taught him restraint. Not a great deal of restraint, but enough that he'd asked her name before tossing her on that rickety bed and finding out just how attentively the holy Sisters had guarded their charge's virtue.

Aye, Favor McClairen was lucky. Her name had stopped him. But in his impetuous youth . . . or should he find out she'd lied again . . .

He sighed. Unfortunately, there was no doubt she was Favor McClairen —whether or not she and her brother chose to call themselves Donne. He'd recognized her. She was no longer a child, but the obstinate set of her chin was the same, as was the fierceness in her eyes.

His smile faded. He glanced down at the unhappy Orville, currently attempting to rise to his hands and knees. Raine dusted off his hands and considered Favor's advice. She was probably right. The last thing he needed was to have Favor's suitor searching for him.

Orville raised his head, peering blearily about. With a grimace—after all Orville hadn't been doing anything Raine himself hadn't considered— Raine rapped him sharply on the jaw. Orville's eyes promptly rolled back and his head hit the floor with a thud.

With a grunt, Raine hefted him over his shoulder and straightened. He headed down the corridor in the opposite direction the wench had gone. He needed to think.

Perhaps Favor really was seeking to repair her clan's fortunes by making a spectacular match. Certainly he, better than most, knew how desperately those fortunes needed repairing. After his father had betrayed the McClairens to the Crown, he'd been rewarded with every bit of property and wealth the clan had once owned. But that hadn't been enough for Carr. He'd made sure no McClairen would reclaim a ha'penny of it by the simple expedience of murdering them all.

Raine dodged the memory of the instrumental part he'd played in his father's plan. He opened a door leading to the occupied section of the castle, poked his head out, and, seeing no one in either direction, dumped Orville. Orville moaned and Raine shut the door.

He followed the tower's narrow winding staircase up to the next level, needing no lantern to illumine his way. He knew Wanton's Blush well, every secret passageway and concealed niche, every hidden room and priest's hole. More times than he could remember he'd hidden here to escape his father, thanking a usually indifferent Creator for the superstition that kept Carr from these rooms.

At the top floor, Raine headed for the small bedchamber he'd been using as his headquarters since his arrival. There he struck a tinderbox and lit the lantern on the table inside the door. Wearily he snagged a bottle of Carr's finest port from a tabletop and kicked a dusty armchair toward the single window overlooking the sea. He sank down on it.

He uncorked the bottle with his teeth, took a deep draught, and wiped the back of his hand across his mouth. He paused at the rough feel of his beard. He needed a shave. His gaze fell to his white shirt, slightly stained in spite of his having washed it thrice since his arrival. He smiled at such delicacy. If nothing else, his years of incarceration in that sty had imbued in him a deep and abiding passion for cleanliness.

He leaned his head back, letting his long legs sprawl out before him. As soon as he found his mother's jewels he'd buy himself a hundred new shirts and as many breeches. He'd never again wear a soiled stockinet cloth or sweat-stained waistcoat again. Mayhap he'd become an eccentric and breathe only through a scented silk kerchief.

When he found his mother's jewels? Today it seemed the more likely question was *if* he found them. As far as he knew he was one of the only people to have ever seen the fabled jewels.

'Twas shortly before her death. He'd been nine years old and on a mission to steal a sugar lump. He'd arrived at the kitchen door to find his mother already there. Knowing her views on small boys who pilfered sweets, he'd ducked into the larder.

As he'd watched, an angry-looking redheaded fellow had entered. Afraid of being caught spying, Raine had hunkered down. Though he hadn't heard much, it was clear the stranger was trying to compel his mother to some act and just as clear she was not to be compelled.

Finally, the stranger left and his mother soon thereafter, her lovely face a mask of worry. Desiring only to comfort her, Raine had slipped out of the kitchen and followed. But rather than head for her private chambers, she'd hastened to the small office she used to receive the local merchants and instruct the household staff. Before Raine could catch up with her, she'd shut the door behind her.

Worried, Raine had peeped through the keyhole. He'd seen her bend over a battered oriental tea chest and begin manipulating the wooden tiles on its surface. Suddenly a shallow drawer had popped up from its center.

Reverently, his mother had withdrawn a heavy gold object from the drawer. It was large, shaped roughly like a dragon, or a lion, and fitted with big, rudely cut stones. She handled it only a second before placing it back in the hidden compartment.

Raine, uncertain of what the object was, nonetheless knew it was something his mother wanted kept concealed. He'd never told anyone about it. Not even Ash. Certainly not his father.

Only later, when he'd begun to hear rumored tales of something called the McClairen Trust, had he realized what he'd seen. By then his mother was dead. Having no great love for her people, and even less for his father, he'd kept mum.

During his years in prison he'd thought often of that homely brooch. It became his lodestar. He'd spent hours plotting exactly how he would liberate it, where he would go with it, how he would sell it and to whom, what price he would ask. He built his entire future around its retrieval, not at all sure he would ever live to experience it.

Now he had the opportunity to realize those dreams.

If he could only find the bloody chest.

Getting into Wanton's Blush without his father's knowledge had been no problem. Raine had simply joined the line of servants awaiting their masters' carriages. He'd grabbed a trunk from the ground, heaved it to his shoulder and followed a footman into the castle and up the servants' staircase. There he'd dropped his burden and taken an abrupt detour to his mother's room, assuming he'd be in and out of Wanton's Blush in less than an hour.

There his plan had gone suddenly awry. Nothing was as he'd remembered it. Worse still, not one item of his mother's remained.

Raine took another swallow of port, recorked the wine bottle, and set it carefully beside his chair. He'd been searching the castle ever since.

The upper stories of the east façade, in general disuse four years before, were now totally abandoned, given completely over to storage. And what storage! If nothing else, the last week had given Raine a newfound appreciation of the demon driving his father. He'd never seen such a testimony to one man's avarice. The place was honeycombed with crates and trunks and furnishings, stuffed with a fantastic mixture of valuables and litter.

Nothing had been thrown. A man could spend half a lifetime sifting through the wreckage and ruin, the treasures and tripe accumulated by a dozen generations, searching for that one small oriental chest.

Not that he had any choice. He had no money, no skills, no past, no future. He couldn't—or rather wouldn't—approach his father. Carr believed his youngest son to be rotting in a French prison and as far as Raine was concerned he could just continue to believe so. He would have been there yet had it not been for her.

Raine laced his fingers across his belly and let his chin rest against his breastbone, pondering. Things had become complicated.

Favor McClairen.

He smiled. He was beginning to think God was not indifferent after all, but simply sat upon His celestial throne patiently awaiting the opportunity to perpetrate pranks upon mankind. Nothing else could account for the

fact that she, of all the women in the world, should have been his unintentional liberator.

Interesting that she was using her real Christian name. He understood
her need to keep the McClairen part mum; Carr would have her flogged
from the place should he know. So obviously she didn't expect the name
"Favor" to be recognized. And truthfully, he allowed, who would remember that the scrawny girl who'd saved his life nine years earlier had been
named "Favor"? Certainly no one in Carr's household would have asked
after that child's name. Except for himself—and that months later, after
his wounds had healed and the girl had disappeared.

He closed his eyes, the taste of the excellent port not quite enough to
purge her own delicate flavor from his lips. Had her name been Sal or Peg
or Anne he might well have done exactly what she'd accused him of
planning and tossed her on the bed.

But she was wrong on one score. It wouldn't have been for revenge.

He'd been deceived and used so many times that her small betrayal
didn't even make an appearance on his most-notable list. Amusing, really,
that she obviously felt the sting of guilt so keenly. His congratulations to
the holy Sisters.

No, he would have taken her because he wanted her.

The lust and longing he'd kept at bay ever since she'd left him abruptly
broke free with devastating results. He inhaled deeply, his muscles tens-
ing. He hadn't meant to tell her how she'd haunted him, how images of
her had primed him for sex more than willing flesh and clever mouths. He
hadn't meant to arm her with that particular knowledge.

But then, she was still babe enough not to even realize the weapon he'd
handed her.

He frowned. How did one account for her implausible mixture of innocence and savvy? That ingenuous, direct gaze and the accomplished lies?
It was a puzzle and, more, it was stimulating. Nearly as arousing as her
sweet little body.

He felt again the texture of her velvety breasts, the supple yield of her
body, and replayed that simple kiss.

He wanted more.

But then, damnation, her name *was* Favor McClairen, a girl who'd every
right to hate him and wish him dead. The one girl in the world whom he
was obligated to aid in every way he could.

The girl whose life he'd ruined.

CHAPTER 12

"**D**rag him up to the gate!"

The ropes binding his wrists snapped taut, jerking him off his feet. He landed face first in the hoarfrost, the shards scraping his chin and forehead. He hadn't the strength to even turn his head.

"Up, ye English bastard! Up, ye puling fucker!" A hard bootheel slammed into his side, breaking what had been cracked. He groaned. It was all he could do. Hands grabbed his arms, jerking him to his feet. He swayed. More hands seized him, half-dragging, half-carrying him to the arching postern before an ancient tower. There they stood him, weaving and half-conscious, beneath the teeth of the raised iron gate. Elbows and fists jostled and shoved; angry voices rang in his ears; the stink of sweating bodies and the reek of green reed torches clogged his nostrils.

A thin, metallic taste drenched his mouth. Blood congealed on his lips and dribbled from his chin. Blood clouded one eye and blood stained his shirt.

"McClairen!" They were shouting now, voices raised in triumph. "McClairen! Come out to us!"

High above him he heard a weak female voice answer, "What is this? Who do you seek?"

A hand in the middle of his back catapulted him forward and he staggered to his knees. Behind him a harsh voice answered, "We come seeking the McClairen!"

He squinted, saw a gaunt middle-aged figure in rags, such fury in that face as to rob it not only of its gender but of all humanity. Hers had been the first staff to break across his shoulders.

"There is no McClairen clan," the voice above answered, fainter this time.

"Nay, lady, you are wrong!" a man's voice answered, "for we be that clan. The English might chase us from our homes and burn us in our crofts. They might harry us like cunny but we've survived. We are McClairen's people, and we've brought the laird an English rapist to teach Scottish justice."

"What? How's this? Who is that boy?" the lady asked, her tremulous voice rising, seeming to mirror Raine's own fear.

"Carr's evil seed who sowed his own germ 'neath the skirts of a nun's habit!" the woman in rags screamed. "A McClairen lass, she were!"

"Dear God, is that Carr's son?"

"Aye. Carr who betrayed and deceived us, who had our pipes and plaids stripped from us, who stole our lands and killed not one but three wives! Well, no more! This we will not suffer! We will have justice!"

The crowd roared in approval.

"Send us our laird so that we might be proud once more!"

"Ye fools!" the woman cried out, despair so ripe in her voice that for an instant it recalled Raine to his senses. "Ye've murdered . . . my sons!"

"McClairen! McClairen!" The chant began behind him, picked up tempo and volume, became a din drowning out even the ringing in his ears.

He tried to lift his head and tell them the truth: He hadn't raped Merry. Aye, they'd found them together, Merry naked and him nearly so, but it wasn't rape. She'd made her accusation because she'd been afraid of them, of what they would do if they discovered she'd willingly given herself to Carr's son.

He would tell them. Tell them, too, that he hadn't been the first to lift her novitiate's robes. He opened his mouth. The words would not come.

He knew too well what would befall Merry at their hands if he spoke. Merry would confess. She would be raped then, by every man there. Raped until she most likely died from the abuse.

A fist came out of nowhere, striking his battered side. The world spun, the angry faces dissolving and expanding in a whirl of flame-stained light and shadow.

Besides, he thought dimly, I'm half dead already. How much more could it hurt?

A noose was thrown over his head, the scratchy hemp quickly greased with his blood. More hands. Another shove. Again he tripped; again he was hauled upright.

"No!"

A new voice. Young. Very young. A child's voice, raised pure and distinct above the guttural roar of the crowd.

"No, ye mustn't!"

A murmur began in the crowd.

" 'Tis the McClairen's daughter."

"The laird's wee lassie."

"McClairen's gel."

He felt a shift of attention thrum through the mob, a ripple of movement as something passed among them. He squinted, peering woozily about. He didn't understand what was happening, half expected to be snatched off his feet at any second and hanged from the gate's tines.

"No, I tell ye! Ye canna kill him. My mother, yer laird's own lady, begs ye to free him."

"The child's daft. Tragedy has chased her reason from her. Go up to her mother, Colin, and find out the truth." A stout young man shoved past Raine, heading into the tower.

"I am not mad! Me mother begs ye to spare this lad. My brothers' lives depend on it."

An unhappy rumble coursed through the crowd.

"Where is yer ma then, bairn?" someone asked.

"Dead!" A voice boomed from the tower window above. "The lady's bled to death!"

The lass burst out a choking sob. And Raine pitied the child, for it was clear she'd made a deathbed promise to her mother and clear she could not keep it. Children take such things hard.

Yet, she tried. " 'Twas more than she could bear, birthing me stillborn brother and then seeing how ye here are sure to cost her the lives of her other sons. She sent me with her dying breath to stop ye. Have ye no honor fer the dead?"

But all the crowd heard was that a McClairen lady had died in this all but tumbled tower where their laird had taken refuge while their enemy prospered in what should have been her home. And their enemy's son was in their power.

"Dead? Ye hear? The McClairen's lady is dead! Haul back on the rope! Draw him high! Make him kick!"

Suddenly Raine felt a small form hurtle into him, thin arms wrap about his torso, a face bury itself in his blood-soaked shirt. Voices broke out around them, shocked and hushed.

"I'll not let ye kill him," she vowed fiercely. "My brothers sit in a London prison and me da rides even now to seek the king's mercy. If ye kill this 'un, ye kill my brothers as surely as if ye wield the ax yerselves!"

He could barely stand with the girl's wee body clinging so desperately to him and his hands tied tight behind his back. The crowd milled uncertainly, their bloodlust temporarily suspended by the sight of the small lass in her *white night rail clinging tenaciously to the tall, bowed form of the battered boy.*

He tried a smile, failed, and whispered into the kitten-soft head beneath his chin, "Stand back, lassie. They'll not let me live this night through and your brothers are dead already. There's no mercy in London for Highlanders."

"The bastard speaks true!" the gaunt Scotswoman proclaimed. "Stand back, girl. Ye don't ken what he is, what is happening. Stand away!"

The child's arms wrapped tighter about his waist, her whole small body cleaving to his like a barnacle on a hull. "Nay! I promised my mother."

"Take her away."

But no one was willing to lay hands on the McClairen's last living child. Thus they stood for what seemed to Raine an interminable time, fixed in place like characters in a tableau vivant, *awaiting death.*

Death did not disappoint.

It rode in with the sound of hoofbeats resonating through the frozen ground, a lurid glow streaming toward them on the black highway.

"Redcoats!"

With something like exultance the crowd turned from Raine, snatching up pike and cudgel, outlawed sword and staff. They erupted into motion, streaming forth to meet the advancing troops. Raine stared, only vaguely conscious of the girl reaching up and pulling the noose from his throat.

And then the soldiers were on them. Horses cleaved the black night with lethal hooves, swords slashed flesh, and cudgels battered bone. Piercing scream, grunted effort, and everywhere grease and sweat-stained faces, taut with strain and rigid with virulence.

He blinked away the blood from his eyes and stared down at the girl. She trembled, shook so violently that he could hear her teeth rattling as she stared in wide-eyed horror at the massacre.

It was over quickly. So damn quickly. One minute the night churned in apocalyptic struggle, the next it was nearly silent. All about them Scotsmen lay dead and dying. A few soldiers strode among them, finishing off the survivors.

"Is he alive?"

Raine lifted his head, trying to find the source of that familiar voice, his father asking his status with immeasurable indifference. But then, who'd have even thought his father would have ridden to his aid?

"Yes." Another familiar voice, rough with concern. Ashton, his brother, ever trying to stand between Raine and his own reckless nature. "He's over there."

"Oh." A moment's silence. "And what is that next to him?"

"McClairen's daughter," Raine heard one of the soldiers answer.

"*Oh?*" Carr asked, his brightening tone evincing the interest he'd lacked on discovering Raine lived. "*How do you know?*"

"*There's a Scotswoman here cursing the little girl. Said if it hadn't been for her they'd have hanged Raine Merrick and been gone by the time we'd arrived.*"

Beside Raine the girl's head snapped up. "*No,*" she whispered.

"*Should I kill her?*"

"*The girl or the Scottish witch?*" his father replied. "*No. Don't bother. The woman looks too old to be breeding any more McClairens. Let her go. As for the girl . . . I suspect that one must consider her a subject of the Crown? And, in a way, now under my care?*"

"*Aye,*" the soldier answered in a confused voice.

"*As I thought.*" Carr sighed. He emerged from the darkness, maneuvering his mount carefully amid the bodies strewn over the frozen ground. He stopped, his attention fully on the child beside Raine, ignoring his son utterly.

"*Don't touch her,*" Raine croaked.

Carr glanced at him. "*I assure you, I have no intention of soiling myself by touching her and as for your tone, my boy . . . well, you have provided me with the excuse I needed to rid my lands of any remaining McClairens. Indeed, thanks to you, Raine, there are no more McClairens left.*" A slight keen issued from the girl and Carr's gaze dropped to the small figure huddled at Raine's feet. "*And thanks to you, too, my dear.*"

He kneed his horse closer, puzzlement drawing his brows together. "*Why did you save my worthless son?*"

The girl's head came up, her eyes shimmering with tears in the torchlight. "*Naught fer love of you, sir, but to save my brothers' lives.*"

Raine's father stared a second and then he threw back his golden head and laughed. All about them the soldiers, who'd been picking through the dead Scots' clothing like jackals among carcasses, lifted their heads and gave Carr their wary attention.

Raine swayed, nausea rising from his belly. He knew why Carr laughed. There could only be one reason. He closed his eyes, for he couldn't bear to see her face when he told her.

"*But my dear, didn't anyone tell you? Didn't you know?*"

"*Know what?*" the child whispered.

"*Why, that at this very moment John McClairen's head decorates a pike above the North Gate.*"

Raine's eyes were closed, but he could not plug his ears. Only a child can voice such anguish, only a child who'd, in one single night, lost mother, brother, and the clan she'd helped destroy.

Because of him.

*   *   *

Raine jerked awake. He was covered in sweat, as though his body, even now, all these years later, must repudiate the events of that night. He eased back against the seat, staring out at the sea.

Whether Favor McClairen was here hunting a husband as she claimed or was here for any other reason, he would aid her and never threaten her again or cause her fear.

He'd never had much experience with honor, nor had he ever cared to become acquainted with such a lofty concept. But for Favor McClairen he was willing to learn.

CHAPTER 13

Carr sat motionless while his new valet finished shaving his hair in preparation for the new wig. The little man—Randall? Rankle?—slid the peruke in place and offered Carr a silver-foil cone. Carr held it to his face as powder descended about him in a fragrant cloud, covering the wig with a fine white coat. Rankle waited a few minutes for the dust to settle and then carefully removed the cape protecting Carr's clothing.

"Your Lordship looks most impressive," he said.

Carr flicked a little clod of powder from his sleeve. "Rankle," he asked curiously, "did you just comment on my appearance? You did, didn't you? Begad, what is this world coming to when servants offer unsolicited opinions on the appearance of their betters? I should thrash you for such impertinence but as that would probably undo the best of your tiresome ministrations, I shall resist the temptation. This time."

Really, first his magnanimity toward Tunbridge, now his valet. He was becoming positively mawkish.

He stood up and held his arms out from his sides waiting patiently while the valet scurried to pull them through the sleeves of his new waistcoat. Violet brocade, an extremely flattering color.

"Henceforth," Carr continued as Rankle adjusted the collar, "Henceforth, bear in mind that I am fully aware that I look impressive. Indeed, I am interested in your sartorial evaluation of my person only should I *fail* to look impressive."

"I'm sorry, sir!" That was the thing about new valets—it took such a deuced long time to break them in, Carr thought with a sigh as he reached down for his gloves and brought them in a blinding stroke across Rankle's face. The crystal beading on the cuff cut the little man's cheek. He raised his hand to the wound, staring at Carr in astonishment. A flicker of what looked like—by God!—anger flashed in his eyes. Impossible. Creatures such as Rankle did not get angry. They fled.

"I didn't ask if you were sorry. I was informing you of my opinion. And you interrupted me. Now, Rankle, should I ever look less than impressive you shall be dismissed. I imagine finding a position in these heathen parts without a letter of recommendation might be a trifle difficult."

The little valet flinched.

"Now, go away," Carr said. "I have decided not to attend this evening's dinner. Have my daughter informed." The valet bowed and hurried off.

Carr approached a wall covered in green velvet and tugged on an embroidered bell pull. The material flew apart, billowing out and settling in banks on either side of an exquisite life-sized portrait. He stepped back, studying it tenderly.

"Janet, my dear, why now?"

He hadn't needed the old Gypsy, Pala, to tell him what he knew in his blood, what he'd sensed every night for a dozen years; that Janet was here, watching him. He was used to it. It neither disturbed nor even greatly interested him. The uses one could find for a ghost, after all, were limited.

But this new notion Pala had voiced, that a spirit could infiltrate another's body and in some sense live again, that Janet had done so, in order to come to him in the flesh once more—If she had found new housing for her spirit, he needed to discover it before he left this cursed castle once and for all.

She'd obviously left her scarf in order to convey some sort of message. But what? Had there been rebuke in that gesture?

Carr opened the lid of a chest that stood beneath the picture. It contained some gold, a few jewels, and remnants of the offending *arisaid*.

The night Janet had died he'd been hosting the first party Wanton's Blush had known since its renovation. The most important people in society had made the treacherous trip from London to attend. Among their number had been the king's personal secretary. The trouble, alas, had begun when he'd gone seeking his beautiful wife shortly before their guests were due to come down to dinner.

He found her—along with their brats—on the cliffs. Apparently she'd finally tumbled on to the fact of his involvement in her clan's . . . difficulties. In a fit of pique, she'd sworn to wear her family plaid to his party as a show of allegiance, knowing full well that the wearing of plaids was strictly prohibited by law. And with the king's secretary there!

She had sealed her own fate.

"In all honesty, Janet," he murmured to her likeness, "wasn't it a shade coincidental that you awoke to my 'duplicity' the day I hosted what could have been the most important party of my life?

"Yes." He nodded. "You might as well have jumped off that damn cliff yourself instead of forcing me to throw you over. You did it to ruin my party, didn't you? But I foiled your little plan, didn't I, my dear?"

Idly, he fingered the silk *arisaid.*

"What did you mean by leaving this for me to find, Janet? For you never were one for subtlety. Tiresomely straightforward, if truth be known. So what's this about?"

Thoughtfully, he dangled the torn half of scarf in front of the portrait. Perhaps, if she hadn't died that night he might not have felt compelled to marry those other heiresses; he might not have facilitated their demises and subsequently been banished.

She really did have a lot to answer for.

Perhaps Janet recognized her culpability. "Did you leave me this by way of an apology? A sort of 'Here, you take the damn thing. It's caused enough grief.' "

The explanation pleased him. "It makes sense. I mean, a scarf isn't exactly the sort of thing one leaves behind as a means of striking terror into a body. I mean, it's a scarf, for God's sake, not a gory eyeball or a pulsing heart, or some such rot."

"Dear me, Father, please advise me should you ever try your hand at striking terror into someone. I shall absent myself immediately," a smooth feminine voice said from behind him. Carr spun about.

Fia stood framed in the doorway, her hands folded primly at the waist of an extraordinarily indecent dress. Another young woman would have looked like an expensive bawd in such a gown. On Fia one barely noted the midnight-blue satin.

Father and daughter regarded each other in silence. Beneath its thin layer of bright makeup Fia's face was perfectly composed. He'd seen an oriental doll once, a porcelain depiction of a theatrical character. It had been fine, detailed craftsmanship, finer than any he'd ever seen. But something about a doll depicting what was in essence a living doll had been unsettling, like seeing a reflection in a reflection. Looking at his daughter gave him exactly the same sensation.

"How long have you been there, spying on me?" he demanded.

She lifted one wing-shaped brow. "I wouldn't spy on you, Carr. Haven't you ever heard the old nursery adage 'He who listens at keyholes hears no good of himself'?"

Her tone was oblique, her brilliantly colored blue eyes, unrevealing. Where once she'd shared every thought with him, now she'd entombed herself in her composure, giving him nothing.

"What do you want?"

"That little man. Rankle. He said you would not be dining. I thought perhaps you'd taken ill. I came to see." Her tone did not imply concern, but impersonal curiosity. "Forgive my inquisitiveness, but does she answer you?" She raised her gaze to Janet's likeness.

Carr snapped the concealing draperies closed. "Speaking in front of a picture is not the same as speaking to a picture, Fia."

"Isn't it? Thank you for explaining the subtlety."

Not a ripple of expression flawed her smooth, ravishing young face. Just as well. His two sons had been hot-headed, emotional children; both had ultimately proven enormous wastes of his time.

Fia was different. Fia was, like himself, a predator.

She would never let maudlin sentimentality cloud her judgment, nor pedestrian principles dull her purpose—that purpose being to see that she made the most brilliant matrimonial match English society—'sblood. *European* society!—had ever seen, thus aligning her father ultimately and irrevocably with power, prestige, and money. So much money he would never again need to waste a moment of his life thinking of it.

"What is that in your hand?" Fia asked.

"A piece of scarf Janet wore the day she died."

"Don't tell me her ghost left it for you?" Fia laughed and then reading his expression with horrifying accuracy, said quietly. "Begad, I do believe I've hit on it." She reached out, brushing her fingertips quickly over the silk and just as quickly withdrawing her hand.

"You know," Fia said coolly, "I should very much like to see my mother's ghost. Should you ever have occasion to chat with the transparent dame, kindly point her tattered parts my way when you're done."

"Are you mocking me?" he asked in his deadliest voice.

She considered him calmly. "Perhaps."

Insufferable, yet he dared not slap her and the reason provoked him far more than any words she could have uttered. He did not strike her because he was no longer precisely sure of what she was capable. Certainly revenge. Possibly more.

"Get downstairs," he commanded her, and waited, hating the uncertainty he felt. She'd never directly disobeyed him before. But someday soon she would. He needed to get her wed before then. "My guests ought not to be left unattended."

"You're right. They'll need a pied piper to lead them in their debauchery."

"I'll be down shortly."

"I hope so." Fia began to turn away. "There's a lady there who feels your absence keenly. She was quite distressed when she heard you were not dining."

Carr's interest quickened. Could it be her? Janet? "Lady?" he asked. "What did this lady look like?"

Fia watched him interestedly. "Elderly. Not yet antique but decidedly venerable."

Horrible apprehension filled him. Janet had died in the full bloom of womanhood. The idea that she might choose to inhabit a body any less lovely than her previous one would never have occurred to him. She couldn't do that to him!

"Who is the lady?"

"Mrs. Diggle? Douglas? A mild-mannered, apologetic old cat. Not your usual guest."

"Douglas," Carr corrected her, his anxiety abating. He knew the lady. Anyone less like Janet would be hard to imagine. "No, she isn't in the mode of my usual guest. But her nephew certainly is and it's for his sake that she and her charge are here."

"Oh?" Fia intoned uninterestedly.

"Yes. He spent the spring here. You remember him," Carr said slyly, seeing an opportunity to reward Fia for her mockery. "Thomas Donne."

Fia had never confessed her infatuation for the tall Scotsman. She hadn't needed to. Every omission, every glance, every stilted conversation Carr overheard her have with Donne told the story of a young girl's first overwhelming passion. Just as her sudden and absolute silence on all matters regarding him told another sort of tale altogether.

Carr was rewarded. Her pupils contracted slightly, her nostrils turned a paler shade about the delicate rims. It was a nearly imperceptible reaction, if one wasn't looking for it.

"Of course," she said briskly. "I remember them now."

"Mrs. Douglas is chaperoning Donne's little sister, a Miss . . . Miss Favor, I believe." He scoured his memory for a face to put to the name and came up with a vague recollection of a comely, well-dressed wench, surprised he remembered that much. He paid little heed to virgins, even wealthy ones. What, after all, was the use? He couldn't marry again and since Favor Donne did not gamble and since he couldn't get at her money any other way, he hadn't bothered with her.

"What is she like?" Carr asked, twisting the knife a little. "Does she look like her brother?"

"I don't recall him that well," Fia said smoothly. "Miss Favor is small. Handsome. Black hair, aggressive eyes, a dark little warrior.

"Now that I think of it, I recall overhearing her asking one of the other guests after you, too."

Handsome? Black hair? And she'd asked after him.

"You know, Fia," he said, "I believe I have changed my mind. I believe I will go down to dine after all."

CHAPTER 14

High above the grand ballroom, hidden in a cleverly disguised gallery cut between the arching buttresses, Raine looked down at the spectacle below. The crowd churned like broken bits of brightly colored glass stirred in a giant bowl. The smell of bodies, ripe with heat and perfume, rose in sultry waves. Their din was as incessant as the surf beating at McClairen's Isle's rocks.

Though his vantage point allowed him only an occasional glimpse of an upturned face, he ultimately discovered the two figures that interested him. He spotted Carr first, resplendent in purple, standing as straight as ever, his gestures elegant and languid.

As a child Raine had despaired of ever achieving even a portion of his father's aplomb. Carr had ridiculed his attempts, advising him not to waste his efforts on so hopeless a cause. And when it had become clear that nothing Raine could ever do would raise him in his father's estimation, he'd sought other ways to win his attention. He could not begin to recall all the damage he'd done in that man's name: harassment of the locals, destruction, drunken fights, and mad carousal. All done to prick, discomfit him, embarrass; to somehow provoke a response—any response —from him.

Raine smiled ruefully. Five years earlier such memories would have awoken bitterness. But then, five years earlier Carr had been important to him. Since then Raine had had his priorities forcibly rearranged. He no longer cared about Carr, not even enough to hate him.

He studied his father with detachment. Still handsome, still rigidly straight and graceful. His gestures were just as smooth as ever, his expression as bland and polished. But even from this distance Raine could make out a slight slackening of the once tautly fitting flesh on his face, a looseness under the square jaw and the beginning of pouches under the fine eyes. Even Carr's will hadn't been able to keep the toll of years at bay.

Raine's gaze traveled through the crowd until he found Favor. Yards of vibrant jonquil yellow swathed her upright figure, the light-killing blackness of her dyed hair as coal dust against her white bosom. She moved unswervingly through the crowd, as though she traveled a narrow corridor without doors or windows but only one egress and that far ahead.

Hardly provocative behavior, yet she didn't lack for attention. A definite pattern was emerging among Carr's male guests. A small train of them had fallen into procession behind Favor. It was subtle, of course; the idiots weren't actually queuing up, but undeniably Favor was gathering a retinue.

He understood the attraction. There was something about her. Something more than a desirable figure—though, by God, she did have that. And, he conceded, a not unhandsome face. Something about her challenged a man or provoked or inspired or—

Inspired?

He'd been imprisoned too long. 'Twas the only way to account for this interest in Favor McClairen. Because she'd saved his life he'd imbued her with qualities she more than likely didn't possess.

If Favor inspired him at all it was with lust, he decided. And it was damned maddening that the woman whose skirt he wanted to toss up was named McClairen. It complicated things. It caused obligation to contend with animal desire.

Obligation would win. After all, for him to owe a debt to another person, particularly one he was in a position to honor, was a unique experience for him. Lust was not.

Once more he focused his attention on Favor. The dowdy female beside her must be her chaperone. At first glance he could not imagine a less effective-looking dragon to defend this particular damsel. But a short observation proved him wrong. Few of the men following Favor made it to her side. Apparently she allowed access only to those who met some standard set by either the old biddy or Favor herself. What would that be?

Whatever the gauge, Raine thought wryly, for a certainty his name would never have made the approved list. But then, he didn't need to chase after Favor McClairen. She was coming to him in—he pulled out his timepiece—about ten hours.

*   *   *

"Here's your food," Favor said sullenly. She flung the tied napkin at Rafe, envisioning the greasy contents making an agreeable splotch on his white shirt.

She hadn't counted on the rogue's having such keen reflexes. He spun away from the window he'd been looking through and snagged the bundle from the air. His shirt was opened, exposing his lean torso. A pistol, tucked beneath the waist of tight black breeches, caused hardly a dent in a flat belly dark with fur. The sleeves of his shirt had been rolled up over broad, tanned forearms.

Her gaze plummeted to the ground, utterly nonplussed by an immediate tactile memory of that warm flesh beneath her hand. This was not Dieppe. He was no longer chained to a wall and she was no longer pretending to be a—whatever Madame Noir was.

More's the pity, an inner voice mocked.

"Why, how civilized!" Rafe said. "With such manners, Miss Donne, I'm certain your brother's doorway must soon be choked with suitors."

"Humph," she said, but could not entirely quell a smile in response to his banter. How odd he was acting, how . . . friendly. She was immediately on her guard.

He clamped a palm theatrically to his chest. "I swear when your mouth twitches like that it sets my heart to racing. Assuredly, whoever instructed you to hoard your smiles knew their power. For should you ever actually grin, I am sure no man could be held accountable for his actions. Certainly I could not testify as to what I would be capable of doing."

She burst out laughing, surprised and amazed. Whatever she'd expected from her blackmailer, it had not been charm or merry foolishness. She'd assumed she would deposit his food in the middle of an empty room and leave. She'd never expected him to be waiting for her.

He smiled back, displaying a full set of even white teeth and surprising her yet again, for his smile filled his eyes with warmth and humor. It was a potently attractive smile, a devastatingly attractive smile, devil-may-care and winning. A man with a smile like that didn't need elegant features and that recognition sobered her.

He sensed her withdrawal, his smile became one-sided and wry. "Ah, forgive me my jest. For a moment I forgot our relative positions and the history that had led us here."

"That being you as blackmailer and me as victim?"

The dimple in his lean cheek cut deeper. "And here I'd cast myself as the injured party. How could I have so misinterpreted our roles? Mayhap it had something to do with you throwing me to the wolves in Dieppe?"

She flushed. Vindicated, he turned his attention to the napkin. He planted a huge boot on the windowsill, using his broad thigh as a table on which he unknotted the linen and spread it open. He bent his head over the package, the movement causing his shirt to gape away from his chest, revealing hard contours she all too clearly remembered. They were even more contoured now. Presumably they would be even harder.

"Beefsteak!"

She jumped. He glanced up, his honey-colored eyes guileless.

"Bless the English for their unholy love of dining on beef. Didn't bring me a set of cutlery, did you, sweetheart?"

"Don't call me 'sweetheart.' And no, I did not. I considered it," she replied dryly, "but rather worried that someone might object to me nipping off with the silver. Believe me, I drew enough odd looks when I dumped my dinner in my lap."

He burst out laughing. "You didn't!"

"I did. How else was I to get your food? I couldn't very well show up at the kitchen door with a sack and a request that it be filled with table scraps. And I most certainly couldn't send a servant. Your presence would be discovered within an hour. Once a servant smells a secret he won't rest until he's ferreted it out."

"Well versed in the ways of servants, are we?" He tore off a piece of meat and popped it in his mouth. His eyes slid half-shut in sybaritic pleasure. He chewed slowly, savoring the process, swallowed and sighed. Deliberately, he licked the burgundy-laced gravy from each finger.

She'd never seen anyone enjoy food so thoroughly. It was fascinating.

He had long fingers, lean and strong-looking. Soft, dark hairs sprinkled lightly across their backs, growing more thickly above his wide, supple-looking wrists. Very masculine, his hands.

He looked up and caught her watching him. He winked. "Four years of moldy cheese and stale bread soaked in water," he explained without the slightest hint of rancor. "I will never again take the joy of eating lightly. Care for a bit?"

"No." She sounded doubtful. She tried again. "No!"

"Please yourself." He shrugged and popped the next bit into his mouth. "Cake!"

His delighted cry broke her reverie. She scuttled back, as though her thoughts were physical things she could retreat from. He didn't notice, being too busy devouring the cake she'd brought—and ruined when she'd hurled it at him. He had beautiful—

Whyever was she thinking these things? She was daft! He was her enemy!

But was he? That sly, internal voice queried. Or wasn't she, if truth be told, his? Or had been.

Since Dieppe, he had done nothing to cause her any harm. He may have frightened her but even that might have been manufactured more from her own guilty conscience than his actions. In fact, he'd rescued her from Orville.

Her eyes narrowed suspiciously. Yet, as he'd already pointed out, he could still denounce her.

She should tell Carr about Rafe. Immediately. And when he, in turn, revealed her she would affect astonishment and pity. Everyone would think he was a ranting madman, especially since by his own words he was hunting for a fairy-tale cache of jewels. It was a good plan. She should implement it.

She *would* have implemented it by now except . . . except he hadn't done her any harm and she'd done him wrong aplenty.

"Should I be expecting a brace of bruising footmen any moment?" Having finished the cake, he dusted the crumbs from his threadbare breeches. "Or have you decided to take pity on me after all?"

His words too closely followed her duplicitous thoughts. She felt contemptible. She disliked feeling contemptible. She reacted badly to it.

"I brought you food, didn't I?" she asked.

"They always fed the prisoners a bit better before taking them out to be drawn and quartered."

He'd startled her yet again. How could he make light of such a thing?

"I haven't told anyone about you."

"Including the old puss?"

"Excuse me?"

"Your chaperone."

Muira. No, she hadn't ever considered telling Muira about Rafe. The old woman would probably have had Jamie hunt him down and slit his throat. Nothing must interfere with Muira's grand scheme. "You mean my aunt. No. She doesn't know about you."

He smiled again. "My thanks."

Her gaze flickered away and back. He grinned more broadly, as though he knew the course of her wayward and wholly unacceptable thoughts and lowered his leg from the sill. "That was good."

He reached his long arms above his head, rotating at the hip as he slowly stretched from one side to the other, his shirt ends swinging like the foundering sails on a tall ship. She felt the warmth stealing up her throat and turned away so he would not be driven to make any ridiculous assumptions about her blush.

"How goes the hunt for McClairen's Trust?" she asked.

"It goes."

She looked about. Most of the boxes and trunks had been opened since yesterday. He'd rifled through the pictures standing against the wall, too. A portrait of a black-haired lady stood at the head of the stack, face out. It hadn't been there before.

She was beautiful, dressed in silvery blue, the frothy gown slipping from her shoulders. She had a tender smile and a stubborn jaw. Her eyes were bold and her expression pleased.

"How goes the husband hunt?"

His words recalled her not only to her immediate surroundings but to her other obligations. How she loathed her part in Muira's plan. For an hour there she'd forgotten. Perhaps that had been the real reason she hadn't informed against Rafe. He'd provided a distraction, made her forget the eerie mixture of cool speculation and feverish intensity in Carr's expression last night.

"Well?" he repeated.

"It goes."

"Any likely candidates?"

"Perhaps."

Carr had brought her punch. She'd thanked him but further words had died in her throat. The man had killed her people, then laughed as he'd told her that her brother's head decorated a London pike. He hadn't seemed to miss her conversation.

He'd stared fixedly at her, a little scowl furrowing that blasphemously noble-looking brow. It had taken all her self-control not to recoil. Which did not, she supposed, bode well for their proposed marriage bed.

She'd seen Muira out of the corner of her eye. Beneath the soft mask of feeble amiability she'd been gloating. Near rapturous. Favor had left the room soon after, Muira bustling after her, commending her on her coquetry in an exultant whisper. On reaching her room, she'd locked the door against Muira.

Perhaps in coming here she was "locking the door" again. Even with the danger and risk Rafe posed, at least it was a danger of her own choosing, a risk only to herself, taken independent of the McClairens and Carr and Muira. Here it was just him. And her.

"You're not considering Orville for a potential mate, are you?"

"Orville?" Favor repeated.

"Your smile was hardly pleasant. I thought perhaps you'd determined Orville had the deepest available pockets and for all his lack of charm would serve your purpose."

She didn't consider telling him the name of her projected spouse. Rafe might be a distraction for her, but she knew next to nothing about him. She would take no risk with Muira's plans. Besides, he'd only laugh at her. Or worse, pity her or even—*damn* that inner voice!—be disgusted with her.

"No. Not Orville. He's married. I haven't really decided on anyone yet."

"Oh?" He moved closer to her. He was very, very tall. She had to lean her head back to meet his eyes. "Then I suppose you'll be in a lather to get back to the mart and queue up the prospects."

She snorted in an utterly unladylike manner. "Hardly." The word came spilling out before she could stop it, giving far too much away.

One heavy brow climbed above a toffee-brown eye. "Good."

"And why is that?" she asked.

"Because," he said, "I've decided that food and clothing—the latter of which, by the way, I don't see—are too little to demand by way of reparation. Especially from someone who was anticipating rape."

Her heartbeat kicked into a gallop. Her mouth went dry.

"What do you want?" she croaked.

"You'll see," he said, his sensual gaze gliding over her face and body. "But first, you'll have to take off those clothes."

CHAPTER 15

Sweat covered Favor's bare arms and neck. The fine hairs at her temple coiled into damp tendrils and clung in little black commas to her throat and collarbone. She licked her lips, sampling the salty mist. Her limbs felt weak and logy. Muscles she hadn't even known she owned ached with overuse.

She looked in the mirror, barely recognizing the well-tumbled-looking, relaxed wench staring back. Her makeup had long since gone. Her skin glowed.

"Oh," she whispered guiltily, "that was grand!"

"What did you say?"

She turned from the mirror, smiling innocently at Rafe. He'd stopped rummaging through the huge crate he'd hefted to the top of a breakfront. "Nothing."

It would never do to admit that helping him search for McClairen's Trust had been more reward than punishment. She'd shed her beautiful gown and donned the old smock he'd unearthed from some box, trying to hide her elation. She'd spent too much time in front of too many mirrors trying to be Janet McClairen. The relief of her release from that role made her giddy.

It had been wonderful. She'd rummaged, poked, and rifled through cabinets and wardrobes, drawers and chests, under beds and through rolls of bunting and stacks of linens. She hadn't found the Trust or the ornamental box he claimed legend said it resided in—though she'd never heard that part of the legend before.

She *had* found little mysteries and precious keepsakes: a child's ebullient account of his life written a hundred years before; a broken scimitar reverently wrapped in a faded Moorish flag; a woman's crystal flacon that still carried the faint scent of roses. They captivated her with their unspoken histories. McClairen histories.

Her history.

She remembered few of her mother's stories and none of her father's. She barely recalled him at all. He'd returned from London soon after the massacre, his plea for mercy refused; her brothers' fates sealed. He'd returned and been met with the news of his wife's death and his people's slaughter. He'd been dead within the year.

Muira had written to her about her ancestors; long lists of names and dry recitations of battles won and lands conquered. But *these* things, Favor gently touched a child's pearl ring, they related intimate stories. For the first time her ancestors had become real.

What fond mother had tucked this leather slingshot into this drawer? Had someone died wielding this scimitar or had it been broken symbolically? This flacon may have been a great aunt's, this diary her grandfather's.

Rafe didn't object to her dawdling—even when she spread a pack of tattered playing cards upon the floor and pored over it until she'd discovered that the knave of hearts was missing. He'd remained silent, systematically going through each piece of furniture and chest along one wall.

Only occasionally she'd crow with delight over some oddity and look up to find him watching her with an unreadable expression. She didn't know what to make of him. These past few hours, he'd seemed nothing more than a young man filled with enthusiasm for their task. It was as if in this room both of them had found some part of the innocent pleasures of a childhood neither had owned.

"Well, this is the last thing large enough to hold a two-foot-square box," she said, tapping on the lid of a traveling trunk. It was just as well. The sun would set in an hour or so. If she wanted to escape an interrogation by Muira, she'd have to be back in her room dressed for evening by the time the old lady knocked on the door.

Rafe didn't answer so she raised the heavy lid. Inside lay carefully folded satin clothing, copper and plum colored, studded with gems and metallic threads, glinting like the scales of an exotic fish beneath long-desiccated lavender sprigs.

"What is it?" Rafe asked, peering over her shoulder.

"I don't know," she replied, keeping her face averted. He smelled of dust and heat and male exertion, a potent scent, distinct and earthy. She dared not turn. He still wore his shirt open.

"Begad, at least one of those Highland heathens was a dandy." His laughter tickled her ear.

"What is it?" she asked, gingerly lifting the gleaming material.

"I believe it's a gentleman's coat in the Persian style. Quite the mode in the last French court."

"It's fantastic!" she exclaimed, shaking lose the folds and holding the garment up by the shoulders. "What is the purpose of these loops of ribbon, do you imagine?" She glanced over her shoulder.

He stood very close behind her. A long streak of grime marked his exposed pectoral like a brand. His labors had sheathed his dark skin in a silky dampness, accentuating each contour and ridge in the slanting light. A white scar on his belly disappeared under the waistband of breeches, which rode low on his hips.

"Decorative." He reached over her shoulder and flicked his finger against a jeweled bauble. "Damn, it's only glass."

"Oh, and you're an expert on gems?" she asked dryly.

He grinned cheekily, his sidelong glance too knowing by half. "You'd be surprised at what areas I excel in."

She rather doubted that.

She looked away, unwilling to be caught and held by his gaze. It had already happened several times too often that afternoon. It was like drowning in a warm pool of honey.

She quashed the errant thought. The longer she spent in his company, the more easily such thoughts came. 'Twould never do. They were . . . well, if not exactly sworn enemies, hardly friends. After all, she was here under duress, not because she wanted to be here. Even if she *did* enjoy being here, he didn't know that.

She was getting damned—she bobbed her head and mumbled a *mea culpa* for her profanity—confused.

"What are you doing?" he asked curiously.

"Thinking."

"About?"

"How . . . how perfect this would be for the masque."

"What masque?"

"Friday evening, a week hence," she answered, glad to escape her uncomfortable thoughts. She peered into the trunk. More garments lay exposed. Buff breeches, garters of pink rosettes and buckles sparkling with crystals. "We're all to dress in costume and conceal our faces."

His expression smoothed to indifference. "Ah. There's good hunting," he said. "Just make sure the bait isn't taken before the trap is sprung."

"Pardon me?"

His smile was suave. "It's a perfect opportunity for a spot of dalliance. How did you so charmingly put it? 'All I own is my virtue'? I'm simply advising you to retain it so that come your wedding night you can . . . deliver the goods. A masque offers a unique opportunity for men—and women—to sample that which they have no intention of purchasing."

She felt as though he'd slapped her. From easy camaraderie, he'd plunged them back into Wanton's Blush's sordid world. She could not think to reply. Her hands fell to her sides, carrying with them the copper-colored coat.

"Here now," he said, "that expression of censure will never do, Miss Donne. As a prime piece in this particular marriage mart you are here to be approved, not to condemn your fellow guests for taking advantage of that which they came expressly to enjoy."

"And what is that?" she asked stiffly.

"An amoral, conscienceless society."

"You overstate the case."

His laughter contained no humor. "Perhaps you choose not to see what is abundantly clear."

"How do you know so much about it?" she challenged him.

"Everyone knows about Wanton's Blush, Miss Donne," he replied. Pity softened his tone. "Didn't you?"

"Of course." Carelessly she tossed the gentleman's coat back into the trunk. "Whatever odd notions you have about me, you exceed yourself. You know nothing about me. Even less than I know about you."

"Which is exactly what?" he asked.

"That you are a thief. You are a blackmailer. You are here to steal jewels and you have forced me to be your accomplice." Her gaze dared him to deny the charge. He didn't.

"I take it our truce is off," he said glibly.

"Yes. I got your food. I helped you search this room. I have done enough for you. I bid you *adieu*, Monsieur." She wheeled about, sailing past him and to the door with stately indifference.

"Brava." *Clap. Clap. Clap.* He was applauding!

The scoundrel! The wretch! She swallowed an angry retort, refusing to acknowledge his audacity. She took hold of the door handle and pulled. It remained stubbornly shut. Damn! She closed her eyes, mumbled a prayerful apology, grasped the handle in both hands and yanked. Nothing.

"Damn! Damn! *Damn!*"

"Miss Donne?"

Frustration vied with mortification. Frustration won. She seized the handle, shaking the brass handle violently.

"Miss Donne?"

"What!" She swung around.

His arms overflowed with emerald velvet, yards and yards of the stuff. "You forgot your dress."

She bit down hard on her lip, refusing to give vent to the string of epithets piling up behind her clenched teeth. She stalked back across the room, snatched her gown from him, turned, marched back to the door, seized the handle in both hands, and, setting her heels for leverage—

"You might want to try pushing the door rather than pulling it."

Striving for some shred of dignity, she pushed. Silently, the door swung open.

"Tomorrow we'll search the room next to this one."

She wouldn't reply.

"Also, though the beef was good, I wouldn't mind some fowl. Try not to mash up the cake next time."

He *couldn't* make her respond.

"And do remember my clothes. I should hate for my aroma to offend you tomorrow and I intend to keep working this evening."

"I'm not coming tomorrow," she bit out.

"Now, that"—his voice, all afternoon so easy and unruffled, now flooded with darkness—"would be a mistake."

"Miss Donne." Carr stood back from the chair he held out, waiting for her to take her seat. For him to have not only taken her in to dinner but then to seat her so high at the table was beyond irregular. Speculative murmurs rippled beneath the squawk of drink-infused conversation. Favor slid into the seat, refusing to acknowledge the glares of those who would point out that by doing so she usurped a marchioness, a pair of baronesses, and at least half a dozen ladies.

"Miss Donne."

Favor looked up and found herself facing Fia Merrick across the table. The girl looked faintly amused. But as far as Favor could tell, Lady Fia always looked faintly amused, her black wing-shaped brows forever canted at an ironic angle, the ice blue of her gaze perpetually glittering with secret wisdom.

"Lady Fia," she returned politely. What could this enigmatic and aloof girl want of her? Though at least three years her junior, in some ways Fia seemed older than any woman in the room.

"Lord Tunbridge begs an introduction." Long, slender fingers moved fractionally, stirring the air in a little ballet of grace, indicating a hitherto unnoticed gentleman. "Miss Favor Donne, may I present Lord Tunbridge. Lord Tunbridge, Miss Donne."

He nodded, his hooded gaze assessing her closely. "Miss Donne, my pleasure."

Tall and cadaverously thin, the unpadded skin of his face cleaved tightly to a well-shaped skull. He looked angry and hungry. His white hands moved restlessly among the silverware, fidgeting and aligning the pieces.

Favor mentally skewered her right cheek with a dimple, emulating Janet McClairen's one-sided smile. "Thank you, sir."

"Tunbridge is a great friend of Carr's," Fia said smoothly. "Aren't you, Lord Tunbridge?"

Beside Favor, Carr remained silent, clearly comfortable in the role of spectator.

"But not so great a friend as he would like to be," Fia said. Briefly, affecting sympathy, she touched Tunbridge's hand, lingering just a shade longer than simple sympathy would merit. Tunbridge speared her with a ravening glance, which she adroitly avoided.

"They appear to have had a falling out, however," Fia continued. "These things sometimes happen among intimates, Miss Donne. Particularly ones with so long a history as Lord Tunbridge and my father. We must apply ourselves to smoothing things o'er between them. It is our duty as women, being the pacific creatures that we are. Don't you agree?"

The girl's lines were designed to give Favor an opportunity to perform her role. Yet she found herself resisting. The afternoon had given her a taste for freedom. How ironic that a thief and a blackmailer should have provided her with a momentary escape from her fate—a fate she herself had chosen, she reminded herself sternly.

Fia was still calmly awaiting her answer.

Favor still had a debt to repay.

"I am sorry to contradict you, Lady Fia, but I have never considered myself particularly pacific. Perhaps it is your nature to forget a wrong. It is not mine."

Beside her she heard Carr's faint but discernable inhalation. The veins on the back of his hands stood out like ropes. *En garde.*

"So you believe in a biblical variety of justice?" Fia asked.

Favor picked up her wineglass, twirling the ruby liquid, studying it. She needed to frame a telling response, something that would draw Carr. But he stank of perfume and the heat from his body clung to him like an oily mist and he'd laughed when he'd told her about her brother John.

"Miss Donne?"

Janet. They were trying to convince Carr that Janet wanted him back. It was their plan—*her* plan. She'd agreed to be Janet and Janet wanted Carr back.

"Forgive me," she said, smiling Janet's smile. "I confess I was fretting over how honest I dare be. I would hate to risk whatever portion of regard"—she divided her gaze flirtatiously between Carr and Tunbridge—"I might have won. The truth is that I am a creature given to my own comfort, both physical and otherwise.

"In addressing a wrong done me I would seek relief—if justice alone would provide that, then justice would serve me. If recompense eased me, then I would seek compensation. If I felt robbed, I would demand back what had been taken from me." She fluttered her lashes coyly. "I suspect you find that quite shallow and self-serving?"

"I find it bracingly honest," Tunbridge declared. "How refreshing to meet a lady who provides so succinct an outline for her behavior. Who informs a gentleman of her character rather than deceiving him."

Favor felt sorry for the man. He so obviously spoke to Fia, whose attention was fixed on the chilled pear a servant had placed before her.

"I think honesty is vastly overrated," Fia murmured, delicately slicing off a thin piece. "I think Miss Donne would agree. Certainly her brother would. I know Carr does."

What did she mean by that? And what had Thomas had to do with her?

"Lady Fia?" She kept her voice calm.

"She insists on being provocative," Carr spoke before Fia could reply, his manner disgusted. "It's a child's trick but then she is a child. You'd be wise to remember that, Tunbridge, next time she involves you in her games."

If Carr thought to vex Fia he was doomed to disappointment. She lowered her head, a little smile playing about her lips.

"A child? Games?" Tunbridge trembled on the verge of saying more. His chair legs scraped the floorboards as he shoved his chair away from the table. He stood up, snapping forward slightly at the waist. "Forgive me, Miss Donne. I fear I am inadequate company tonight."

"Tonight?" Favor barely heard Fia say. Beside her Carr snickered. Favor's head swam, trying to find her way through all the undercurrents she perceived. She dined with jackals. Tunbridge, gutted and hung, could only turn and leave.

But Janet would be used to such behavior. And while Janet had not approved much of what Carr had done and said, she had never publicly chastised him. She had ignored what she did not approve. So said Muira.

"Wherever do you find pears in the Highlands, Lord Carr?" she said, and bit into the succulent fruit. It tasted like clay.

The night would not end. The clock struck the witching hour but the revelry wound tighter, like a watch in the hands of a feckless, spoiled child. Fia disappeared, her inexplicable interest in Favor as quickly gone as it had appeared.

The one-sided smile had petrified like rigor mortis in Favor's cheek. Her spine ached from trying to appear taller than she was and the belladonna Muira had dropped into her eyes to dilate her pupils caused her head to throb and her vision to swim.

Carr, too, had distanced himself. Ordinarily, Favor would have retired but though Carr had left her side, he still watched her. Intently, covertly, hour after hour. So Favor ignored her throbbing head and aching back and listened to Muira who bobbed and grinned and hissed instructions at her.

At two o'clock Carr finally approached her once again and asked her to dance. She obliged. He was a superb dancer, guiding her expertly and wordlessly through the intricate steps. At the end, as he led her back to where Muira sat feigning sleep with her chin sunk upon an ample false bosom, he finally spoke. "I found your scarf."

Favor scoured her memory for some point of reference, some scarf that Muira had told her about that Janet had owned. She could recall none. Perhaps he sought to trick or test her?

"I have lost no scarf, Lord Carr. I fear one of your other lady guests is missing it."

His face stilled. It had been no trick. He had expected some other reply. Damn Muira for this oversight.

Too late to claim the scarf now. At least until she found out from Muira what it meant.

"Ah. My mistake. Thank you for the dance, Miss Donne," he said, and bowed before disappearing into the crowd.

"What was that all about?" Favor looked down. Muira's expression was muddled, like someone coming awake, but her low-pitched tone was hard-edged.

Favor was in no mood to accept Muira's carping criticism. She, too, could hiss through a smile. "The next time you leave one of Janet's scarves laying about for Carr to find, I suggest you inform me first."

Muira's genteel mask evaporated, leaving a hard middle-aged face staring at Favor in angry consternation. "I didn't leave any scarf anywhere."

* * *

Moonlight bathed Favor's sleeping form, embossing her features with blue-white alchemy. Her head burrowed against her pillow, the inky hair spilling across the coverlet and down the side of the bed. Her lips parted slightly and a little frown puckered the skin between her brows.

The tall, dark figure standing at the foot of the bed angled his head, studying her intently. She looked tired, even in sleep, Raine thought.

He'd watched her from above the ballroom most of the night. Her shoulders had drooped with fatigue long before the evening had ended. Even from where he'd been standing the white face powder had not concealed the dark smudges beneath her eyes. And she'd held her head as though it ached.

She shouldn't have come here, he thought. She shouldn't—

She moaned and stirred unhappily. The small sound of distress sent him forward, out of the shadows, his hand poised to bestow a comforting caress. Abruptly he stopped.

No, he realized. It was he who shouldn't have come.

CHAPTER 16

The afternoon sun slanted through the stained-glass oriel, piercing the cool dimness of the Lady's Chapel and casting a mosaic of warm color on the gray stone floor. Overhead, shallow niches flanked the small, grimy rosette window. Within these a pair of dust-mantled saints kept vigil. Though the castle's chapel had long been denuded of bench and altar, it had always had a certain solemn dignity. No longer.

Raine had finally found where his father had banished his mother's possessions. "Damn you, Carr."

He looked about, unprepared for the wash of sadness recognition brought with it. So many memories. Here was a blue dress she'd worn one Michaelmas. He recalled how lovely she'd looked hastening down the stairs, her crisp petticoats rustling. Now it was limp and yellow and housed a family of mice.

Near the bottom of a heap of haphazardly stacked furnishings he spied the bench that had sat before her dressing table, its red petit point tulips dull and moth-eaten. Her favorite fan lay atop it, the painted silk tatters clinging to it, ivory frets like the fragile bones of an ancient corpse.

All jumbled and discarded and abandoned. No careful folding of Janet McClairen's things. No sweet lavender sprigs to retard the inevitable march of decay—The chapel door opened on a loud protest and Favor swept in.

"So, 'twas you! I thought I heard something down here," she announced triumphantly. "This part of the castle echoes strangely, don't you think? I swear I heard you say 'damn' all the way at the other end of the corridor."

Her voice was bright with interest, as alive as these things were dead. She brought with her all the ruthless practicality of her youth. And she swept the sadness from his soul as heedlessly as the riptide scours the shore.

"What are you doing here?" he asked.

She'd angled her head back, looking around. "This is where the Mc-Clairens wed and were christened and from where they were buried," she murmured. "That rosette window was brought from Paris."

"How would you know that?" he asked dryly, curious as to how she would wiggle out of this revealing statement. Clearly she could not afford for anyone to discover she was a McClairen. Carr would have her ousted within an hour.

But Raine had underestimated her. Her wistful expression evaporated. "Oh, it's all in the diaries and journals I've found," she said. "Oh, my! Look. I believe this is Venetian lace. 'Tis criminal someone would leave it to rot like this."

The pleasure she found in the task to which he'd sentenced her was as unaccountable as it was captivating. This was her fourth day helping him search for McClairen's Trust and each day she appeared, she sparkled more. Of course, were he to charge her with such a thing she would deny it. But he doubted she'd deny it to herself. She was a gifted liar, but as with all gifted liars, she would have an uncanny ability to be truthful with herself.

"You're early." He'd told her noon and it was not ten o'clock yet here she was, eager and ravishing and vulnerable. So very, very vulnerable. She had no idea the thoughts taking root in his imagination.

"Sooner begun; sooner done," she quipped, but the sparkle in her eyes belied the indifference in her voice.

Damn his misplaced chivalry. He should seduce her and be done with it. But he wouldn't. For while he was all too certain of his reaction to her, he was uncertain of hers to him.

He assumed she found him somewhat attractive. He'd a wealth of memories that taught him the signs of female interest and Favor, bless her, met the criteria. But he knew nothing of what a convent-raised girl did with such an interest.

And, too, Raine wasn't certain he wished to jeopardize this . . . this whatever this was. In his experience such camaraderie between the genders was unique. He'd never been in a young woman's company without the specter of imminent seduction transforming each word they exchanged into double entendres and each look into mental disrobing.

The young women in his past had been interested in one thing, for one reason, which even then Raine had realized had more to do with his reputation than with any personal recommendation. They'd sought him precisely because of his inability to curb his wild impulses—

"Well?" Favor asked impatiently, her tone suggesting she was repeating herself.

"Pray, pardon me. What was it you asked?"

"Why are you staring at me?" She looked down at her dress in some consternation. "I couldn't very well wear that filthy smock again and it's cold in here."

"I'm not staring. I'm trying to decide how best to put your rather negligible skills to work."

She accepted his excuse, completely unmoved by his criticism. She looked about the room and spied the book he'd placed on a shelf in the huge, teetering armoire near the door.

Like a cat drawn by a piece of yarn, her expression sharpened with interest, she hastened over to it. Gingerly, she opened the first page, catching her lower lip beneath the edge of her slightly crooked front teeth. They added a piquant note to her countenance. A once fierce countenance, he thought, deploring the artificial arc that stood in place of the once proud, slashing brows.

She read avidly and he watched her, feeling ridiculously pleased. He purposely sought such items for her to find, hoping to give her access to the history her clansmen hadn't lived to relate.

If he recalled correctly her father, Colin, had been a second son who'd left the Highlands early in life to seek fame and fortune. Instead, he founded a family—a wife and three children whom he'd sent home to Scotland while he continued seeking that ever-elusive fortune.

He came home in disappointment some years later to find his sons imprisoned for their part in their uncle Ian's Jacobite plottings. Ian had already been executed, and for a short time Colin had been laird.

Favor, Raine recalled, had never even lived at Wanton's Blush, her mother, dispossessed by Carr, awaiting her husband's return in an old deserted tower on the headland. The tower where Raine had been dragged so many years before.

The memory diminished his earlier pleasure. As though she sensed his darkening mood, Favor looked up from the page she'd been perusing. She closed the book, the resultant puff of dust causing her nose to wrinkle.

"It's a sort of account book with personal notations. But it's not by Duart McClairen."

"Pray who might Duart McClairen be?"

"The little boy whose diary I found the other day."

"I see. And why did you think it might be young Duart's?"

"Oh, I don't know." She shrugged. How the holy Sisters must have bemoaned that particular mannerism. "I guess it was wishful thinking. I was rather hoping to discover what happened to Duart after he grew up."

"As I recall you were good for no work that day, your nose being stuck between the pages of the little heathen's memoirs."

"How do you know Duart was a little heathen?"

Because whatever interests you, I find interests me.

"There's not much to do come nightfall. Sometimes I read. Pray, try to compose your expression into bland acceptance, Favor; such ill-mannered surprise speaks poorly of the good Sisters. I can read . . . if I take care to sound out the words. But pray, don't let me interfere with your own reading."

If she noted his sarcasm, she did not reveal it. "No, thank you. I'll read it later. In my room." She tilted her head sideways. "Who exactly are you, Rafe?"

Since that night in the carriage in Dieppe she'd never asked him anything personal. It was as though she feared what she would discover. He turned up his palms. "You already named me. I am a blackmailer and a thief. There's nothing more to tell."

"You are awfully well spoken for a common thief."

"I should hope there's nothing common about me," he said haughtily, drawing a smile from her.

"Then you must be the, er, unacknowledged progeny of some personage?"

"Why, Miss Donne, are you asking whether or not I am a bastard?"

"Excuse me," she mumbled, blushing fiercely, the unexpectedness of it charming him in spite of himself.

"I'm not a bastard. But I'm no longer acknowledged by my father." It was near enough the truth.

"Because of your thieving propensities?"

He stood very still, thinking. He could tell her the truth. It had started out so nobly, so simply. He would anonymously aid the girl to whose life he had brought tragedy. But it was quickly becoming a deeper game he played and he wasn't at all sure what he'd anted or what was at stake. He *should* tell her who he was and let the chips fall where they may.

But then she would leave.

"Just so," he said.

She nodded, her smile an odd mixture of relief and suspicion. A naive liar; an innocent jade. She presented a riveting enigma.

"What about your mother?"

"She's dead." It came out more sharply than he'd intended. He looked up to see Favor's stricken countenance and immediately realized her conjecture.

"No, Favor, she didn't die from heartbreak over her son's criminal propensities. She died well before my *entrée* into the criminal underworld."

"I'm sorry." Her voice was tender with commiseration. "My mother died when I was young, too."

He could not think how to answer her. He remembered well Favor's mother's death.

"What was your mother like?" Favor asked.

"Beautiful. Capricious. A bit vain. Too romantic. Perhaps she was callow. She struggled mightily to believe in fairy tales." He remembered being angry when she asked him and Ash how they'd come by their bruises. She never hesitated to ask but then they'd never hesitated to lie. She never pressed; they never offered more.

"You did not like her very much."

"Like her?" He considered. "I don't know. She was totally absorbed with my father. But when she was with us . . . no one was more entertaining. She was cultured and honest and irreverent." He looked down at the fan in his hand. One could still make out part of the Greek temple painted on one of the sections. "For example, though she loved classical things, she didn't pretend to venerate them. She christened the Greek folly in our garden the Part of None, after the Parthenon, mocking her pretensions."

"You loved her."

"Yes." He set the fan down. "Come, we've work to do and you won't wriggle out of it by such transparent devices."

She grinned. "Since you are so determined to press me into service, O Master Most Severe, where wouldst thou I begin?"

"Did you bring my clothes?" he asked, knowing his tone would dampen her whimsical mood but having no idea how else to alleviate its effect on him.

Either I suppress some of that brilliant vivacity or you pay the consequences, little falcon, he silently abjured her. She'd saved his life and he would not repay her by seducing her no matter how often he flirted with the idea.

"No." She turned away but not before he saw the hurt in her expression. Better a small hurt than a deep wound. "I have no idea where I am to find clothes for you. You're too"—she flung her hand out—"large. Besides, even if I should find some monolithic dandy, I can't very well sneak into his room while he sleeps and pilfer his small clothes."

Monolithic dandy?

"You're a resourceful girl," he returned. "I'm sure you'll think of something. By tomorrow. I'm getting tired of wearing these clothes and I refuse to trick myself out in bygone glory."

"Why not?" she asked. "It seems a commendable notion to me. There are so many clothes here."

"It would amuse you far too much," he answered loftily. "Add to that the fact that you are—or so you tell me—my victim. Victims are not allowed to be amused by their victimizers. 'Tisn't done. I'm certain if there were a rule book for victims and their victimizers, it would be one of the first principles cited."

Her extraordinary eyes widened during this speech and at the end she burst out laughing. *Good God,* he was losing what little mind he possessed. First, he purposefully depressed the girl's spirits and then, not a minute later, unable to bear the downward tilt of her mouth, he wasn't content until he'd returned it to merriment.

"You can help me over here," he said. "The furniture is stacked too high. I cannot reach the top."

"How can I help?" she asked.

"Come here and I'll show you."

She approached him warily, which was amusing seeing how he'd come damn near electing himself to sainthood on the merits of his self-restraint where she was concerned. "Well?"

"I'll lift you up and you take down the smaller items."

"You'll lift me?" she repeated, eyeing him doubtfully.

"Yes. Enough wary glares, Favor. Come here."

She shuffled up to him, tilting her head back and looking squarely in his face, trying to gauge his intention. He glimpsed the edge of that crooked front tooth, a sliver of white in the warm, dark secret of her mouth. At the base of her throat, her pulse fluttered. Her skin there would be warm and satiny.

They were alone.

No matter what he'd told himself, he was no saint, had never aspired to sainthood. She shivered and he felt every muscle in his body tighten instantly in response, a cat watching a fledgling suddenly beat its wings.

If she shivered again he would pounce, as intransigently as that cat lured by that fledgling's helplessness. Dear God. He was a prison-hard-ened knave. What the hell was she doing here with him? He lowered his head, his gaze hooded and alive to opportunity. *Any* opportunity. Let her pulse quicken, let her eyes darken, let her part her lips . . .

It didn't. They didn't. She didn't. She turned, presenting him with her back and said, "I'm ready."

His hands trembled as they circled her waist. The homely dress she'd worn to work in had been a mistake. Not nearly enough separated him from her. No corset stiffened the bodice; no heavy busk acted as armor separating them. Just simple blue worsted wool suffused with her heat.

He felt each breath she took, each rise of her rib cage, the shallow plane of her belly under his fingertips. Only the texture of her skin remained a mystery.

He closed his eyes. A tavern is what he needed . . . and a tavern wench. There used to be a place called The Red Rose a dozen miles east of the north highway. Strong drink and willing wenches, both available for the right price.

"Well?" She sounded breathless.

He lifted her, determinedly pinning his thoughts on unmet ladies with welcoming smiles. He jounced her up onto his shoulder.

"Oh!" She wobbled atop her perch. Her arms flayed out as she sought to keep her balance. He clamped an arm about her legs, and thrust up his free hand. "Take hold of my hand!"

There was a flurry of little adjustments. She grabbed his hand. Her feet beat against his chest and he clasped hold of one delicate ankle and pinned it against his stomach. "Calm down!" he bellowed.

She scrambled instead of calmed.

"Damn it! Do you *want* to fall?" Silk pooled over his wrist as her garter came undone and her stocking fell down her calf and covered his hand.

"Stop wiggling!" He drove his hand up through layers of petticoats until he found her knee and climbed higher, gripping her thigh securely.

She went as still as a heart-struck doe.

Her thighs were smooth and firm, lithe and long-muscled. A young woman who walked more than rode. A satin-skinned siren.

"Has the unhappy Orville shown any further interest?" He had no idea where the words came from. Unplanned. Not even thought before voiced.

"Orville is gone." Her voice sounded faint.

"Good." He heard the gloat of possessiveness, abhorred it, tried again for a neutral tone but it was hard to do when her leg was a smooth, tapering column that begged to be stroked. "I mean, good for him. Mar-ried wasn't he? Waste of time pursuing you, then."

"He left because his face powder could not cover the bruises you gave him."

"Oh."

She shifted and a warm, womanly fragrance rippled forth, escaping from beneath the lace ruffles and the silk stocking sagging about her ankle. Jasmine and heated flesh and earthier, more provocative scents. His grip tightened. Her hand clenched his.

"Favor."

"What?"

He didn't know "what." He only knew their present positions were untenable. He dipped his shoulder, tumbling her from her perch and into his arms, one arm linked under her knees, the other beneath her shoulders. Her hair, dense and matte as a London midnight, escaped its cap and coiled down over her chaste bodice. He caught a handful of it, his knuckles pressed against the soft cushion of her breast.

"Wash it off."

"What?"

"Your hair. It's bright and gleams like molten gold. Wash the black out."

She stared up at him, a shade frightened, a bit anxious and, yes, a little tantalized. "I can't. She . . . I can't."

For a long minute he gazed down at her fresh lovely face, scrubbed clean of powder, her eyes blue not abnormally black. It was too quiet. She would hear the thunder of his heartbeat. He knew because he heard it himself.

Only it wasn't his heartbeat. He lifted his head, listening. It was something else. Something growing closer.

"What is that?" Favor asked.

"The echo you noted," he answered quietly. "Someone's coming down the hall."

He dropped her lightly to her feet and pushed her toward a low cupboard that stood behind where the altar had once been.

"Go through there. It's not a sacristy. It's a corridor that leads to the north wing. You mustn't be found here. Particularly by any of Carr's guests. Believe me, Orville was one of the better sort in this place.

"Hurry, damn it!" he said harshly when she hesitated. "I can't afford to rescue you again. I was lucky Orville's vanity kept him quiet about me."

"But how—"

"I can't fit through there, Favor," he said tersely. "There's other places where I can conceal myself. But they're not big enough for two. Now *go*."

Only after the low, squat door shut behind her did he breathe again. The footsteps were louder now. Nearly to the chapel.

Raine did not bother looking around. He'd lied. There was no other place to hide. He stepped behind the mountain of furniture and waited. A few minutes later he heard the door swing open and then a short series of footsteps, moving slowly.

Whoever it was must not follow Favor through that door. Raine leapt out, fists raised, ready to strike—

A shriveled little woman stood just beyond the light coming through the rosette window.

"Raine!" Gunna crumpled to the floor.

CHAPTER 17

"**G**unna!" Raine sprang to the old lady's side and carefully lifted her in his arms. Weakly, she batted at him. She weighed next to nothing. Her thick, homely clothing gave only the impression of weight.

She still wore a thick mantle draped across her face, leaving only one side of her disfigured countenance exposed. She peered up at him through a sunken eye. She no longer looked as hideous as he remembered, only sadly distorted, like a watercolor portrait left out in the rain.

"Is it really ye, Raine Merrick, and not a ghost?" she whispered. Tears leaked from the corner of her eye and found a deep crevasse to course down.

He pressed a kiss against her cheek. "No ghost, old woman. Just the same brat, back to make your life a misery again."

The gap-toothed mouth turned up at the corner in a weak grin. She closed her eyes and let her head relax against his chest. Contentment flowed from her like resin from spring pines. He gazed down at the wee old woman, both moved and disconcerted. The Gunna he remembered had little time for displays of *"waistie luve."*

As if she'd read his mind, her eyelid snapped open and her tender smile evaporated. She squirmed, struggling to right herself in his arms, swatting and muttering, "Leave me down! I heard ye were in prison. What sort of prison might that be, I'm askin', tha has built ye up like a prize bull?"

Apparently, she hadn't changed much after all.

Raine lowered her to her feet. Immediately, she dashed away any evidence of tears with the back of her elegantly shaped hand. Those gracefully wrought hands had ever been Gunna's only claim to beauty. She set them on her hips now, glaring up at him. "Well? How long have ye been out of that French prison, then?"

"Six months. Near seven."

"And here? How long here without . . . ? How long here?" It struck him that she was hurt, truly, genuinely hurt that he hadn't informed her of his presence. It never occurred to him that she might have fretted over him.

"A few weeks."

She pressed her lips together.

"I'm sorry."

With his heartfelt apology the anger lifted from her expression. "No need to be sorry, Raine. I'm just so . . ." She broke off, embarrassed by such sentiment. She began again. "I'm glad yer here and well and lookin' fit. Yer brother wrote and said he'd gone to pay yer ransom but ye weren't there. I . . . we feared ye'd been killed by the French."

"Ash went to France to ransom me?" Raine echoed. Once more the old woman confounded him. In quick succession, Raine discovered not one but two people who'd cared for him through all those dark years of his imprisonment. The intimacy of such a tie unnerved him.

"Yes." Gunna nodded. "Carr ransomed him near a year ago. Ash set out at once to earn the means to ransom ye. Succeeded, too, much to Carr's chagrin, and won himself a bride in doing so."

"A bride?" Raine asked in amazement. His older brother hardly seemed husband material.

"Aye. Yer father's ward what Ash snatched from whatever plots Carr had devised fer the chit. Ye should have seen yer brother, Raine. Fair besotted with the girl and she with him. And her a Russell lassie, no less." Gunna shook her head, cackling with evident pleasure. "The Russells were some that answered the McClairen call for the Bonny Prince."

"A Jacobite?" Raine asked, amused. "Father must have loved that."

Gunna pulled a grimace. "I'd be surprised if he even remembers the girl's name. That which doesna touch yer da doesn't much exist, to his way of thinkin'. Once Ash married—Well, yer father's not so dull-witted as to think there's ever a chance of him seein' his eldest son agin." She snorted. "At least not in this life."

Raine hesitated. "And Fia?" She'd been such a beautiful child with her black hair and rosy lips. She'd also been his father's little shadow. He waited now to hear to whom Carr had 'sold' her. Which duke, earl, or foreign prince. For clearly that had been Carr's plan.

"Here she be still. For a few months yet. Then it's to London with her. And him, too. Or so he says."

"I thought that King George had forbidden Carr to return to London."

"Aye. Yer da's last wife was the queen's own godchild, and doesn't yer father wish he'd known that before he lost her like the other two. But ye canna hang a peer for murder without proof and who would speak against Carr? So the king banished Carr here," Gunna said. "But now Carr's swearing Fia will make her bow this spring." She shot a glance up at him. "Have ye spoken with her?"

"No. I never imagined she wouldn't have been married by now." Had he seen her? Raine wondered, surprised by his eagerness. He scoured his memory, trying to match a mature face to the youthful one he recalled.

Had one of the women in the ballroom he'd watched from the high overhead been his sister? Would she remember him? Was she even more Carr's creation now than she'd been four years before? Sadness replaced his earlier expectancy. Of course she would be. He shook his head. "I wouldn't know what to say. No one knows I'm here, Gunna. And I'd as soon it remained that way."

"I wouldn't rely too much on that notion, Raine. Carr has been seeing 'things' lately, meaning ghosts and now I'm thinkin' it's ye he's been seein'."

Raine stared at her a minute before breaking out in laughter. "He thinks I'm a ghost? How perfect. He leaves me to rot in prison and then, catching sight of me, expects I'm dead and come back to haunt him?"

His mouth flattened in abrupt and savage bitterness. "He gives himself too much status. Were I dead and doomed to wander this earth for eternity, the last bit of ground I would go near would be the one he occupied —as either man or corpse."

"I don't think he believes it's yer ghost haunting him, Raine." Gunna said quietly. "He thinks it's another."

"What other?"

"His dead wife."

Bitter amusement filled him. "Oh? Which one?"

At this, Gunna tched loudly, her expression aggrieved. "Speak gently of the dead, Raine Merrick. Particularly those poor, cursed brides."

"Forgive me. I have only to be reminded of my paternity and its influence exerts itself. Now, which bride does Carr think cannot stand to be separated from him?"

"Yer mother. That's why I'm here." She shuffled toward an open box, its contents strewn untidily from the top. Her hand moved gently over the contents. "I knew this is where Carr had her things removed and when one of the stable lads claimed to have seen a light in the chapel last night I thought . . ."

"You thought I was Janet? So you came to petition Janet's spirit on Carr's behalf? I hadn't realized you were so devoted to him. I'd always assumed it was Fia who owned your loyalty."

The old woman answered his mockery by swinging around and cuffing his ear. He backed off with a yelp.

"And so she does," she said. "If someone is trying to convince Carr his dead wife is haunting him, it may be not to Miss Fia's best interest."

"You're still her champion," Raine said.

"I've had to be." The old woman hesitated. "Did ye . . . did ye feel it, then, havin' no champion of yer own?"

Raine stared, amazed, and Gunna immediately misread his silence as condemnation.

"Ye were strapping lads when I come to work here," she said defensively. "Both reckless and hotheaded but fer all that yer own creatures entirely. Ye can thank God yer father cared naught fer ye. It let ye become who ye were and not who he would have made ye."

And yet there was a time that Raine would have been glad of that, would have done anything to gain Carr's approval.

"But Fia . . ." Gunna's hands twisted the coarse material of her skirts. "So beautiful and so sad. She was just a wee wraith yer father spoon-fed lies and treachery. Someone had to stand between him and what he would have made of her."

"And that had to be you?"

"Who else?"

"Why?"

The old woman touched her ruined face. "They do say the ugly are powerless to resist the beautiful," she said simply. "But never doubt I cared fer ye and Ash, too. Who was it do ye think that found out the McClairens were plannin' to lynch ye and made sure Carr learned of it?"

Raine returned her unhappy gaze steadily. "Carr hardly came to rescue me, Gunna."

Gunna spat on the stone underfoot. "Of course he wouldna! But he would go after ye quick enough if he thought he could use those pitiful fool McClairens' attack on ye as an excuse to rid himself of the last of their lot. And so he did! Be happy he had that excuse, and forgive the McClairens for not sharing yer joy!" she finished, fierce and vastly upset.

But Carr *hadn't* achieved genocide, Raine thought. Favor and her brother lived. "Carr has much to answer for regarding the McClairens. No wonder he sees ghosts."

"Aye," Gunna returned. "But lately some of Carr's guests has been seeing' things, too. And Carr is actin' odd. Excited. And I coulda sworn I heard a woman's voice as I come down the hall."

"I assure you I was not sharing the chapel with a ghost, female or otherwise." He needed to get Gunna out of here in case Favor should take it into her mind to return. While he did not doubt Gunna's affection, she had made clear where her loyalty lay. If she realized Favor was a Mc-Clairen she might decide that she posed a threat to Fia. After all, all McClairens must hate all Merricks.

"As for Carr's guests, they must have seen me." He smiled charmingly. "I shall strive to be less obvious."

She'd always scented a diversion as keenly as a hound does a hare. She sidled nearer, watching him closely. "Aye. Might be so." She tapped his chest with one long finger. "What are ye doin' here, Raine Merrick? Clearly ye've not come for a family reunion."

"Haven't I?" He took her accusing finger and wrapped it in his fist, and dropped a kiss on its tip. "Perhaps I came just for one more hug from you, Gunna."

"Ye never got hugs from me to begin with so why would ye be thinkin' to get them now?" she said, but her gruffness could not completely mask her pleasure. "Out with it or I'll stay until ye tell me."

He released her finger and she wagged it beneath his chin. "Don't ever think to fool me, Raine Merrick. Yer in a lather to have me gone and gone I'll be soon enough if ye'll tell me why yer searching through yer mother's things."

The decision to tell her took no great deliberation. She would think him as daft as Favor did. Besides Gunna might know where Carr had dumped the rest of Janet's things.

"I'm looking for the McClairen's Trust."

"The what?" More lines added themselves to her already furrowed brow. "What's that be?"

Of course, Gunna must never have heard about the gems. As Favor had remarked, it was only a local legend. And Gunna was not a McClairen. She'd arrived from the north some years after his mother's death, seeking any kind of employment. Carr, seeing how Fia took to her, had hired her immediately. A woman with Gunna's mien worked cheap.

"My mother had a set of jewels, Gunna, which she held in trust for her clansmen."

Gunna shrugged eloquently. "Then Carr's got them now."

"No. He never knew about them. I only know about them because I saw her take them out once."

Gunna looked doubtful.

Raine went on. "There was a necklace and some other pieces. A brooch fashioned in the shape of a lion, embedded with rough stones. It wasn't fine craftsmanship, even my child's eyes could see that. But the gold was as thick as my thumb and the gems were as large as cat's eyes."

"Go on!" Gunna guffawed.

He smiled. "She kept them in a sort of oriental box. Do you remember ever having seen such a thing lying about here or in another room?"

Gunna squinted at the ceiling, rubbing her flattened nose with her thumb. She pondered several moments before shrugging apologetically. "Nay, Raine. I'm sorry. I don't recall ever seein' such a thing. But that don't mean it don't exist. There's so much that lays about in these rooms."

Her words sentenced him to long days of searching through endless piles of cast-offs, litter, and odds-and-ends. Probably many such days.

All in the company of his little "victim."

For whatever reason, he did not find the realization disheartening.

The girl had an aversion to him.

Carr led Favor Donne up toward the picture gallery. Earlier she'd claimed she would not be happy until she'd viewed it and then only under his tutelage.

Her fingers danced above his sleeve on the point of breaking contact. Very odd conduct if she were, indeed, occupied by the spirit of his wife, a wife who'd loved him devotedly, passionately and yes, demonstratively. At least in the earlier years of their marriage.

He was still wondering what to do with her should she prove to be Janet. He couldn't very well marry the chit. What if he did and a *real* accident befell her? He could offer her a position as his mistress, but Janet had, when all was said and done, been a prude about such things. She would not let him touch her until after they'd read their vows. And, too, as he'd already noted, the girl could barely tolerate touching him.

He was not wrong. He'd seduced many women. Yet all evening she'd put herself in his way. How to account for that, except with Pala's explanation, that the girl was directed by Janet's spirit.

He'd had his doubts after the scarf incident but her pursuit of him had been so persistent, having such an element of compulsion, nay, desperation, in it that he'd begun to believe Pala. Besides, the girl did not even know her body housed another tenant.

So he'd acquiesced and here they were, standing before one of Titian's conceits. He'd invested much of his wealth in artwork, jewels, and manuscripts.

"I like the color blue. Particularly peacock blue," Favor said, glancing sideways at him. Dark eyes, he noted, overly dilated and nearly black. Like her hair. Fetching but odd.

"A lovely shade," he allowed.

During the course of their walk here, she'd made several such random comments. She liked shellfish. She found violin music stirring. She announced that she'd read Jonathan Swift and Henry Fielding and clearly expected him to be scandalized. He told her he'd never read either and that he found reading tiresome. Clearly disconcerted, she fell into a lengthy silence from which she roused herself only to make more sporadic, disconnected comments.

The girl could not have so little—or such inane—conversation. Earlier, he'd overhead her talking easily and rather wittily to Tunbridge. Perhaps what he was seeing was Janet's unseen influence and these burbles of erupting nonsense were the result of being possessed.

They stood staring up at Titian's masterpiece some minutes before he grew bored. "Shall we continue?"

He led her by a deplorably murky Flemish painting to something he truly enjoyed, a landscape of near mathematical precision by Poussin, entitled *Dionysus at the City Gates*. The Greek theme appealed to him no less than the analytical purity of the composition. He'd always admired Greek architecture and, to some extent, the Greeks. Not as much as the Romans, of course.

"Lovely," Favor murmured.

"Not only lovely but precise," he instructed. "See these buildings in the background. They are all structures represented in their correct location in Athens."

"Really? I do not read Greek. Nor Latin. I have some French. Less German."

Carr barely heard her. He would have made a fine Greek aristocrat. Or perhaps a Greek philosopher. Or a Greek politician. He would have orated just . . . there.

"See, m'dear? There is the Acropolis and there, just so, the Parthenon."

She replied under her breath. He turned, his gaze sharpening. Her expression was both distant and tender. Her mouth held the promise of a smile yet to be born and her eyes were soft.

"What did you say?" he asked, dipping his head to be certain he heard her correctly. *"What did you say?"*

"Part of None," she murmured, as though recalling something foolish and sweet.

His breath caught; a painful hammering began beating in his chest. He hadn't really believed it. Not really. Not until now.

Janet had returned.

"I bid you good even', Miss Donne."

"Lord Carr." She smiled, entered her room and shut the door behind her. Her eyes squeezed shut as she listened for the sound of his leaving. A full five minutes passed before she finally heard his footsteps retreating down the hall.

With a sob, she slumped against the door; her shoulders hit the panel with a thud. She shoved her knuckles against her mouth, trying to compose herself, failing miserably.

She'd done it. She'd secured Lord Carr's interest. More than secured it. He'd fixated on her. Somewhere in that long, dismal picture gallery he'd become convinced that Janet McClairen's spirit lived within her.

He'd touched her. Stroked her cheek with the back of his hand. God! Her legs began trembling, her joints felt watery. She sank to the floor, upbraiding herself for such childish histrionics.

Of course he touched her! If all went as they'd planned, he'd do much more than touch her. That had been her goal and purpose from the start. For Carr to marry her. It still was.

Tears fell from her eyes. More of them followed and more still, a torrent of tears impossible to check. They coursed down her cheeks and lips, dripping from her chin and jaw, soaking the delicate lace edging her bodice. Treacherous tears, betraying tears, tears impervious to plans and goals and purposes and intentions.

If only, she thought helplessly, Rafe hadn't touched her first.

CHAPTER 18

"Not many of us here yet, are there?" Lady Fia smiled at Favor, a sweet smile that did all the right things to her lovely face and yet managed to make a mockery of its own gentleness.

Favor, standing beside Fia as they awaited the rest of the company, paid the girl little heed. Rafe would wonder where she'd gone. Why she hadn't brought the clothes he'd made her promise to bring him. Perhaps he would curse her and rant against her.

Perhaps he would miss her.

She blinked, amazed by her absurdity. She must force away such thoughts. She'd best find the means to smile before Carr arrived to lead the company to their *déjeuner* alfresco.

The late-October day had been born bright and unseasonably warm. Overnight, the wind had shifted and now meandered up from the south, amiable and unhurried as a maid on a Sunday stroll.

Lady Fia, ever chimerical, had arranged a picnic. Early this morning she'd issued invitations. Even now the more jaded *habitués* of Wanton's Blush slept, their invitations unread. But most of Fia's devoted retinue—having instructed their servants that any *communiqué* from Lady Fia was to be brought immediately to their attention—had sent their acceptance.

Favor was one of the few guests who hadn't been sleeping when the invitation arrived, for the simple expedient that she hadn't slept. She had accepted reluctantly, knowing that by doing so she sentenced herself to the day in Carr's company when she could have been on a treasure hunt with Rafe.

But avoiding Carr only meant delaying what she must do. So now she awaited Carr's arrival, Carr's interest, and ultimately Carr's suit. And her thoughts were as dull and leaden as this fine day was sweet and clear.

"Miss Donne," Lady Fia exclaimed. " 'Struth you look unwell. Perhaps you'd best remain at Wanton's Blush?"

"No."

Lady Fia smiled obliquely. "If you choose to quit our party, I guarantee you won't suffer any lost opportunity for your absence."

"Lady Fia?" Favor queried, finally awakened to the subtle derision in the girl's voice.

"My father, Miss Donne, does not ride."

Favor was immediately alert, shedding her emotional somnambulism as one would a sodden winter cloak. That Lady Fia had noted Favor's attention in her father mattered less than the fact that he would not be among their number today.

"Lord Carr won't be going with us?"

"No," Lady Fia said, studying her. "He seldom rises before noon." She leaned closer, smiling with falsely conspiratorial glee. "There, a bit of useful information for you. Of course, I could give you even better advice, but then, I doubt you'd take it, would you?"

Before Favor could reply, masculine voices hailed them. Fia twirled to return the greeting. Dozens of determined merrymakers surrounded them, sweeping the young women out of the castle's front doors, Favor still bemused by the news of her unexpected reprieve.

An entire day free. Free of Muira's badgering, of Carr's obsessive ardency, and even free of Rafe's troubling magnetism. Her sense of release was nearly palpable. She smiled at Tunbridge, returned another swain's sally, and chatted with the older woman next to her.

They arrived at the stables to find dozens of horses dancing on the end of their leads, tricked into fresh spirits by the springlike weather. The stable master stood among them, gauging the ability of the various riders and matching them with appropriate mounts.

Favor glimpsed Jamie Craigg's gigantic figure lumbering toward her, leading a docile-looking mare. Her spirits sank at this reminder of Muira's far-reaching influence and far-ranging eye. She'd nearly forgotten Jamie's masquerade as Thomas's driver. He looked out of place here on land, the sea seeming to be a more natural element for him. Not for the first time, Favor wondered whether the others whose lives Muira had orchestrated and overturned ever resented her manipulations.

Jamie halted before her, his expression closed. Perhaps, if she asked he wouldn't tell Muira she'd played truant for a day. "Jamie, please—"

"Don't worry none, Miss Donne." Jamie broke in warningly, his gaze fixed over her shoulder. "I put a kinder bit in 'er mouth."

She turned her head. Lord Tunbridge was close behind.

"Of course. Thank you, Jamie. You may tell my aunt . . ."

"Ach, Miss! Yer aunt is bound to be sleepin' until yer return. I'll send a maid to wake her if ye insist but, beggin' me pardon fer me presumption, I'd let the grand lady remain innocent of yer doin's." He gave her a quick, furtive wink. Bless him! He approved. She returned his wink with a gay smile, her spirits fully restored.

She lifted her skirts and waited for Jamie to assist her but before he had taken a step, thin, hard fingers encircled her waist.

"Miss Donne." Tunbridge's breath fanned her ear a second before he smoothly tossed her into the saddle.

She cast a startled glance down into the man's pale, upturned face. "Thank you, Lord Tunbridge."

Tunbridge's thin mouth formed an admiring smile. "May I be so bold as to remark on your rare good looks this day, Miss Donne?"

Perhaps he wasn't so terrible, Favor decided and, remembering his painful infatuation with Lady Fia and that lady's mockery of it, Favor smiled at him. "Thank you, sir."

Without glancing in Jamie's direction, Tunbridge dug a coin from his purse and flipped it in the giant's direction. Mumbling thanks and bobbing his massive head in a fair imitation of humble gratitude, Jamie backed away.

Tunbridge's gaze remained locked on Favor. "You're every bit as lovely as she," she thought she heard Tunbridge mutter beneath his breath, "Damned, if you aren't."

The sound of a boy's voice raised in panic finally severed his regard. "Damn. You'll excuse me, Miss Donne," Tunbridge said. "One of the stable boys is having rather a time with my stallion. Bad-tempered brute. Nasty habit of biting those who cinch his girth. I suppose I best see that he doesn't kill the brat. Put a bit of a pall on the luncheon."

Favor's momentary favor with Tunbridge evaporated. "You're truly a humanitarian, milord."

He smirked and moved away and shortly Favor's pleasure in the day returned. A little while later the others finished mounting and Lady Fia raised her gloved hand.

"Follow me, now!" she called out. "Riders, follow me!"

"Miss Donne rides out with Fia and the rest of her raucous crowd," Carr said, looking down from the tower window as forty riders came milling around the corner of the castle. With an imperious gesture, Fia raised her lace kerchief above her head and whipped it in a circle. As one the group broke, the riders sending the frantic cattle from standstill to full gallop, as though they were beginning a steeplechase and not a jaunt to a picnic site.

"Lud." Carr expelled a gusty sigh. "No one ever rides at a leisurely pace anymore." Carr let the draperies fall back down, giving his attention to Pala. "Will Miss Donne ever recall more of her life as my wife?"

Pala cringed where she stood. She'd better cringe.

It had taken two days to ferret the old crone out. One of his men had finally found her trudging along the cliff path picking her vile weeds and such. How dare she vanish when he'd things he wanted to know?

He tamped down his irritation. "I will assume that you didn't hear me. Now, once more, will Miss Donne ever remember specific incidents as Janet McClairen?"

Pala rubbed the red welt on her cheek. "I don't know."

Carr picked up his riding crop and bounced it in his hand. "Guess." He smiled mildly. "But guess correctly."

The hag flinched. "Please, my lord. I guess . . . no. These things she feels, she . . . *feels*. She doesn't know why."

"Hm." It made a certain sense.

"You not like my guess. I sorry. *I sorry!*" Pala whimpered, ducking her head.

"I'm not." It would make things even more difficult if Janet—Miss Donne—damnation, but this was a coil!—recalled the events of her last day on earth. But then, whose last day on earth had it actually been? Certainly not Miss Donne's and apparently not Janet's. The conundrum fascinated him.

Janet. They could be together, here at Wanton's Blush where it had all begun. He could set things right. If only he could persuade Miss Donne . . .

"In some respects Janet's lack of—what shall we say? presence?—creates a bit of a problem."

Pala flashed him a look of fearful inquiry. Her gray hair hung in filthy ropes on either side of sallow sunken cheeks. "What is that, Lord Carr? What can Pala do? How can she help her most generous Lord Carr?"

She crept closer, the strands of shells and odd bright stones clicking around her throat, her heavy skirts leaving a leaf-strewn trail on the otherwise clean floor. "What is Lord Carr's desire?"

"Well . . ." Carr murmured, examining his nails, "as hard as it is to believe, I have come to the conclusion that Miss Donne dislikes me. I see that you are shocked. I read it in your face. I empathize with your astonishment."

"Y-y-yes, milord!"

" 'Tis, nonetheless, true. Miss Donne has an aversion to my person."

As testament to her incredulity, Pala's head had sprung straight up on the meager stalk of her neck. She met his gaze with her own wide, amazed one. "But how . . . I mean, you tell me she seeks you out. She puts herself in your way! Maybe you only seeing a young girl's shyness and *thinking* it dislike?"

He gave her a dry smile. "I believe I have ample enough experience to be able to distinguish virginal coyness from antipathy."

"But . . . ! I no understand. Why she seek you if she not like you?"

Carr seated himself on the room's only chair, carefully making sure not to rumple the skirts of his new coat. "You, Pala, are but a primitive Gypsy. How could you understand? Still, while explaining a philosophical nicety to such as you may well prove impossible, I have never refused an intellectual challenge. So, attend, Pala, and I shall endeavor to explain."

The old woman nodded eagerly.

"Janet's spirit has survived buried within Miss Donne's body rather like a wharf rat that secretes itself aboard a ship, unsuspected and unwilling to make itself known. Yet from this vantage Janet somehow causes Miss Donne to react to me, again rather like that rat might infect the crew with fleas of the ship upon which he hides. Miss Donne is *infected* with Janet's feelings for me, feelings so deep and intense Miss Donne finds them frightening.

"Thus, Miss Donne desires me—thanks to my former wife—yet has an aversion to me." He held up his hand, forestalling Pala's certain objection. "Hard to believe, isn't it?"

Pala, apparently not conversant with etiquette, merely stared at him dumbly rather than murmuring the expected assent. He sighed forlornly. People were such a disappointment to him.

"If I know my Janet, she is issuing Miss Donne her . . . emotional directives in a most forceful manner." He leaned forward confidingly. "Such passion as Janet had for me might very well overwhelm the delicate sensibilities of a gently raised young girl. How can Miss Donne help but be frightened, directed by what she must consider carnal impulses? Thus, she reacts by stubbornly resisting Janet's directives and forming an aversion to the man who engenders these feelings. *N'est-ce pas?*"

Beneath its coat of grime, Pala's face was utterly blank.

Pearls before swine, Carr thought. Ah well, she was, after all, little more than an animal. But, as many animals, she had her uses. He'd wasted enough time.

"You don't understand, do you? Thankfully, you don't need to understand. All you need do, Pala, is one thing."

"What be that, Lord Carr?" Pala choked out, her voice thick with awe.

Probably still trying to digest that bit about Miss Donne disliking him. 'Struth it was rather incredible.

"You must make me a love potion."

Muira shoved the footstool into the bright midday light coming through the stable door and plopped down on it. She held out her hand in an imperious manner and Jamie placed a mirror in it. She angled her face to better see herself.

"Curse the man!" The pain Carr's blow had caused her was incidental. The mark his crop had left on her face was much harder to bear. It meant a delay in plans and just when things were coursing along so very, very well.

"Damn the man! Damn his black soul to hell!"

"I thought that was yer aim and goal, Muira," Jamie said. "Damning his soul to hell."

Abruptly Muira giggled, an unnerving sound, particularly so hard on the heels of her rage. "Aye, Jamie Craigg. 'Tis. And soon now, soon."

The giant tucked his thumbs into the waistband of his breeches, looming over the small old woman. "Is it, now?" he said. "And here we've all been thinkin' that the plan had more to do with returning to the clan what was stolen from us than yer own personal cravin' for revenge."

Muira shot him a venomous glare. "If I can achieve both, why are you suddenly so reluctant?"

"Because ye haven't told the girl what it is ye plan to do."

Muira's gaze grew flat. She reached beneath her multiple layers of dirty skirts and tore a piece of flounce loose, using it to wipe her face. "She knows."

"Ye told her?"

"I didn't need to tell her. She must know but if she sleeps easier at night by telling herself Carr will live a long life after she weds and leaves him, fine. If it makes it possible for her to do what needs doing, then I'm for it."

Jamie watched her dip the rag into the water bucket and scrub violently at her face. "Yer half mad with what happened that night, Muira Dougal. Ye know that, don't ye?"

She grinned up at him, correctly reading his weary tone as one of capitulation. "And even half mad I'm cannier than most sane, eh?"

He snorted but finally nodded in answer. Immediately the humor left her expression.

"Remember, Jamie Craigg, 'twas me who tended you and the others that survived the demon earl's ride. 'Twas me that found the means to bring back those McClairens that were exported for their 'crimes.' It's me who brought those McClairens to the village on the north coast, that village where you hide your contraband.

"I did it. *Me.* We'll get back the land. A McClairen will live in Wanton's Blush again. And Lord Carr will die. *I swear it.*" Her voice shook with vehemence.

Jamie's brow furrowed as he looked down at the old woman shaking with rage, but he said nothing. For all the years she'd led the clan and held the clan together by force of her will alone, he'd said nothing. Now, just because he looked at Favor McClairen and remembered a time when Highland lassies were courageous and blithe, free-spirited and generous, he had no right to speak. Even if Muira and her plots destroyed her.

"Damnation!" Muira exclaimed, her gaze once more on the mirror, "This mark will never fade by nightfall and no amount of paint will conceal it. The girl will have to plead the headache tonight. Thankfully, tomorrow is the masque and believe me, I shall be wearing one!"

CHAPTER 19

"Innkeep! Another mug of ale," the stranger shouted.

"Me, too," Franny cooed.

The handsome, bruising brute didn't appear to hear her; he kept staring at the foamy waste in the bottom of his mug. She was about to repeat her demand when he raised his head. He stared at her startled-like, as though he'd forgotten she was on his lap. At twelve stone, few men forgot if Franny was on their lap.

It was a testament to the fellow's own big, manly build. Franny wriggled in pleasure. The man held up two fingers. "Her, too, Innkeep."

"Right you are, sir. Be but a minute. Gots to tap another keg, here, and I don't have no help to take care of the place whilst I do it, tha' help be currently helpin' herself to the contents of yer pocket, sir, if yer not careful," the innkeeper returned, shooting Franny a venomous glare.

"I never stole a penny from a gentleman, and well you know, it!" Fran squalled, but her protest was lost on the innkeeper, who was manfully upending another keg. Not that Fran cared a fig for what the innkeeper liked or didn't like. The rough-looking stranger had a look of generosity about him and Fran wasn't one to make a mistake about such a thing. He'd come in an hour before, set on getting drunk if she knew anything about it . . . which she did. Ill-humored, vexed, and needing a release. She'd decided to offer herself as a likely one.

Because, besides being generous-looking, weren't he handsome? Rugged sort of handsome. A bit of wear on him for all that he looked young, but then, she'd a bit of wear on herself, too.

ard. Only time his father even noticed him was when he nearly got
elf hanged for raping a nun."

he stranger's head shot up at that.

ch! Davie, why'd ye want to go dredging up that poor, sordid tale?"
innkeeper called out.

'Cause that's the only sort of tales there are about Raine Merrick!"
ie cackled.

Sounds the very devil," the stranger said.

Well, that's what the McClairen clan thought sure enough—they're
ones that almost snapped his neck," Davie said. " 'Twas a McClairen
the lad was supposed to have raped."

he stranger had returned his attention to his beer.

But wouldn't they have been red in the face if'n they *had* stretched the
?" Davie chuckled.

Why do you say that?" the big man asked dully.

Because it come out later that Merrick didn't rape no one."

What?"

Davie nodded. "Merry McClairen, the girl they caught with him, con-
sed a few years afterward that she and Raine had been lovers. Said she
uldn't live with the lie no longer."

"What did they do to her?"

"Do to her?" Davie looked confused. "Nuthin'. First off, 'cause there
s no one much left to do anything anyway and, second off, because
at are you going to do to a Mother Superior?"

The stranger's sherry-colored eyes had gone wide. "You jest."

"Nope." Franny confirmed Davie's tale. "Mother Perpetua Augusta of
e Sacred Order of—ach! Some sacred order or other. Runs the abbey
out a half day's ride south of here. We keeps discreet up here. No one
entions the abbey, nor Mother Augusta's tame priest."

The stranger smiled, then began to laugh. "Well, if nothing else your
aine Merrick had the devil's own luck."

"Since he was heir to a demon, makes sense, don't it?" Fran said,
ding herself caught up in the story.

"Ah, yes. Carr. The Demon Earl," the tall man said. "I've heard of
m."

"You and everyone else," Davie said smugly. "But *I* knew him. *And*
aine."

Fran nodded wistfully. "Aye. '*Tis* sad. Raine weren't evil, you know.
ust . . . poisoned like."

"I'll tell you about him for the price of a brandy, Mister . . ." Davie
ggested.

"You. Sir!" A voice called from across the sun-dabbed roor
from these parts or just traveling through?"

The stranger's head swung around at the sound of the sl
voice and Fran's mouth twitched with irritation. Damn Davie
way. He rose unsteadily, snagged his beer mug with his free
lumbered over. "Well?" he demanded.

The stranger regarded him evenly. "Why do you ask, frienc

"Because," Davie said, peering down, "you remind me of
knew once. Bosom companion of my misspent youth." He seer
the sound of the phrase, for he repeated it several times. '
youth. Misspent. Youth."

"Do I?" The stranger readjusted Fran on his lap. "Forgive
rising."

"Never!" Fran crowed, thrilled with her witticism. Davie leer
ciatively.

"And who might this lost companion be?" the stranger a
nearly interested enough in the bounty she sought to display.

"Fellow named Raine Merrick. But you're not him, are you
asked.

"Are you so sure?" the stranger asked, and something in his vo
Fran turn her head and look hard at him.

Only took a second to decide he was twitting Davie. He werer
Merrick. She'd known Raine Merrick. Not well, but well enough
a tumble or two with the lad. He'd been a big lad, square and b

This man was taller than Raine and though wide-shoulder
made. His hair was darker and his face more angular than Rair
most of all, she remembered the driving anger in Raine. He humm
it like a piece of metal before a lightning storm. Biting words, c
fist, bitter laugh—that's what she remembered about Raine Merr

Not that this fellow looked like he'd be a stranger to clenched fi
this fellow looked like he owned the devil, whereas Raine Merr
looked like the devil owned him.

Which, seeing how Lord Carr was his father, was probably close
truth.

"—lucky you aren't Raine Merrick. Heard he died in some
crib," Davie was saying.

"Clearly, you grieve for him," the stranger answered with a to
mockery.

"Me? Nah! He weren't really a chum, mind you. I only said that th
you were him. He was just a lad always had a notion to spite his da

Fran, abandoning tender reflections on past lovers, decided it was time to concentrate on the present ones. "Clear off, David Duff!" she exclaimed, "yer not wanted here. The gentleman and I are quite cozy enough without yer company. Besides, who'd want to hear stories about some poor sot of a dead boy?"

"Why, indeed?" the gentleman murmured, smiling down into his empty mug. "Best leave, Davie."

Thwarted, Davie snatched his mug from the table, nursing it to his chest. "Ah, now that I see you, you look nuthin' like him," he said, and with that parting salvo, slunk back to his original companions.

Finally, the innkeeper arrived at their table and thumped two overflowing mugs on the sticky surface. The stranger placed one in her hand. She nudged her thigh between his legs, wriggling deeper onto his lap.

"Ah," she breathed, her eyes lighting with discovery. "There ye are. I was wonderin' when ye'd make yerself known, if ye catch me meaning."

He moved his mouth a few inches from her ear. "I'd sooner make a proper accounting of myself, Franny."

She glanced at the door that led to the only private room the inn boasted. " 'Sblood, I'd like to get to know you better, too . . . but I gots to work."

He tickled her chin. "There's not so many here that you'll be missed for a while."

"A short while?" she asked, tempted.

"If I'm to give a proper account of myself, I demand enough time to do so. I'd hate to rush the process."

She would, too, but she'd always prided herself on her practicality and if this young buck wanted more than a quarter hour of her time, he was going to have to convince her of it. "As sad a thing as it is, 'tis a fact that pleasure don't pay the landlord."

There was nothing overt. Nothing so apparent as a grimace, yet something rueful seeped into his expression. Still, he whispered, "Pleasure might not, but I will."

She promptly shoved herself from his lap and took hold of one of his large hands and tugged him upright. "Well then, come on, love," she said. "Follow me."

A flotilla of fat-bellied white clouds drifted overhead in a slow procession. There would be hours more sun to enjoy before October remembered herself and took her role as winter's vanguard more seriously.

The picnickers from Wanton's Blush took the warmth for granted, being far more interested in earthy diversions. They lounged on wool blankets, masculine heads lolling on female laps, tongues wetting lips, signals flashing amid ribald repartee, assignations covertly arranged.

Raine Merrick stood with his hand on his horse's bridle 'neath the branches of a rowan tree. He was well inured to such behavior, having been raised among its most avid practitioners. He waited a few minutes longer, scanning the party for her.

If she thought to sneak off for a spot of slap-and-tickle with some would-be suitor, she'd best think again. He had no intention of releasing her from their search. His knuckles stretched the black leather of his glove as his hand tightened into a fist. Somehow she'd arrived at the misguided notion that she and he were compatriots of a sort, and that she could follow her own whims, decide when and where she would attend him. She'd soon learn the error of that idea.

He looped his mount's rein over a tree branch, anger building in him and with it his sense of offense at her . . . her faithlessness. And if it occurred to him that he'd originally intended to keep her near him only that he might discover some way in which to repay his debt to her, he did not let that inconsistency trouble him.

As far as he was concerned, she had much to answer for, did Favor McClairen. She infiltrated his thoughts and dreams, disrupted his stratagems, undermined his intentions, and destroyed his desire to bed another woman—damn her to hell! There was no possible way he was going to allow her to indulge herself when he could not.

He'd find her, by God, even if it meant questioning each one of these bejeweled mannequins. He cared little that someone might note he had not been one of their original number. He cared less for the consequences of such a discovery.

He strode toward a small clutch of lounging revelers. A few gentleman watched his approach incuriously. Several of the women noted him with a good deal more interest.

"Where is the wench?" he said in a loud, exasperated voice as he drew near. A dandy, his chin propped in his hand inches from a brunette woman's bosom, raised his brows questioningly.

"We've a veritable buffet of wenches, sir," the dandy said. "Which delectable morsel would you be seeking?"

"Miss Donne."

The dandy *tched* softly. "Too bad, old son. I fear Miss Donne is being . . . sampled even as we speak."

"Really?" Thank God, years of prison had stood him in good stead. He was still smiling. After a manner.

"Coo! Don't 'e look nasty?" A beauty in blue silk breathed, revealing origins that had never included silk. "Don't worry, sir. With your looks you won't 'ave too long a wait afore you find yourself another."

Raine ignored her. "By whom?"

"Tunbridge," another man answered wistfully. "Lucky bastard."

"And where is the happy couple?" Raine asked, less than pleasantly.

The beauty with the dockyard accent pointed. "That way they went, quarter hour at most."

The dandy glanced up at Raine and smiled nastily. "If you run you might just make opening curtain, if you know what I mean. There still might be some good seats left—"

Raine seized a fistful of waistcoat, shirt, and skin. The dandy yelped and thrashed his arms, dangling horizontally three feet above the ground.

The rest grew hushed. The dandy kept yelping. Raine bent over him. "I dislike your manners, sir. Perhaps your friends here"—he cast a harsh smile around the group, daring any interference—"consider your filth wit. I do not. I suggest you remember that."

Raine dropped the dandy. He scuttled away on his bootheels, clutching at his chest. "Who the bloody hell do you think you are?" he ground out, fear and fury matched in his quavering voice.

Raine, already moving in the direction the girl had indicated, did not stop. "No one," he muttered. "No one at all."

CHAPTER 20

Lord Tunbridge intended seduction. An unfortunate intention in Favor's estimation, as nature had not endowed him with those attributes she found necessary for a man to be considered desirable. At least to her.

Warm toffee-brown eyes that crinkled at the corners, *they* were alluring. And glossy dark hair that became ringlets where it touched a strong, broad neck. And a lean, square jaw. And a wry wit. And an impetuous devil-may-care streak. The sort of temperament a man who chased after rumored treasure must own. Now *those* were tempting.

Tunbridge made a guttural sound, drawing Favor's attention. He'd posed beside a lichen-covered outcrop, his hand braced at head level on the rock, one leg bent foot forward, toe angled just so. He leered down at her where he'd seated her, like an actor onstage playing to the front row audience.

"You're a vastly pretty gel, Miss Donne." One of his gingery brown brows rose while the other dipped.

Whatever was she doing here with him? She'd been enjoying her freedom so much that she'd simply floated blithely along with the current and that current happened to have contained Lord Tunbridge.

When his eyebrows' acrobatics failed to entice her, he tried a different tack. "I've always been partial to black-haired chits." He wet his lips. "Bespeaks a fiery temperament, a passionate nature, and an adventuresome—"

Enough of this rubbish, Favor thought.

"My hair isn't black. It's actually quite light," she said blandly. "I dye it."

He dropped his hand and straightened, his expression slackening in surprise. "Oh?"

"I'm sorry to disappoint but I'd hate to have you think I'd . . . led you on. Now, Lady Fia," she added naughtily, "*she* has naturally black hair. I'm sure you noticed. Such a pretty *child*."

"I don't wish to discuss that hell-bred bit of baggage." Tunbridge's nostrils pinched and his eyes narrowed.

The change in demeanor was so startling and so abrupt that Favor was taken aback. She'd assumed Tunbridge nothing more than Lady Fia's pathetic, lovelorn castoff. She saw now a dangerous man, his expression revealing he was well aware of her mockery.

She scrambled to her feet, the huge bell of her skirts hampering her efforts. His thin fingers closed about her upper arm.

"Allow me." He helped her to rise, his thin frame belying the strength in his grip.

She murmured her thanks, and this time *she* was the recipient of the mocking gaze. He did not release her.

"Miss Fia has a powerful parent," Tunbridge said. "It allows her a latitude of behavior that others shouldn't emulate, because they haven't the same guarantee that their taunts will go unanswered."

She'd been a fool and now she needed to retrieve the situation. "You're correct," she apologized. "It was unconscionable of me."

"Unconscionable." He tested the word, disliked it. His grip tightened. "Stupid."

"That, too." She agreed wholeheartedly. Her thoughts raced to find some way out of the danger. "I set a barb without thinking. It's just that this past week I, too, received a set down from one I . . . I am interested in. It rather makes one sharpish."

She'd caught him off guard. His fingers loosened. "You?"

She looked past him, as though pride kept her from meeting his gaze. "Yes. Me."

"But, who?" he asked, clearly surprised. "You haven't shown any favoritism among your followers. In fact, there's even a betting book dedicated to naming the man who first—"

He stopped. Apparently even Tunbridge still owned some decorum, for he obviously regretted revealing what Favor imagined were wagers on who would first bed her. Not that such things mattered. Not if she could use them to her advantage.

"First what?" she prodded sweetly, pleased to have him off balance. "Shall we say, 'breach my defenses?' " She twisted. He let her go.

"Yes," he admitted.

"I wouldn't expect you or your lot to have identified my . . ." Favor let the sentence hang. "He isn't one of your number."

Tunbridge stared at her a second before bursting out laughing. "Don't say he's a groom or a stable boy? Not a footman! Good God, you're not another Lady Orville, are you?"

"No!" she snapped.

Tunbridge's amusement faded. A speculative gleam entered his eyes. "I could make quite a tidy sum if I was to correctly name the fellow who's captured your fancy, Miss Donne."

Of course. Pleasure palace it may well be, but first and foremost, Wanton's Blush was an exalted gaming hell. And Lord Tunbridge one of its deepest players.

"You . . . you rakehell!" Favor breathed in high dudgeon, not in the least displeased with the direction the conversation had taken. She had adroitly sidestepped a potentially ugly confrontation and in doing so set up a perfect opportunity to further pique Carr's interest.

All she had to do now was name Carr her would-be swain. Tunbridge, eager to find favor with Lady Fia's sire, would run to him immediately with the news. What man could resist knowing he was a lady's rumored object of fascination?

"We could, say, split the winnings," Tunbridge suggested slyly.

She gasped. Not because she was shocked but because she couldn't think of anything else to do. She couldn't give up Carr's name quite that easily. Not if she was to be believed. Favor, who was as adept at tale-telling as any minstrel, knew the value of good timing.

Tunbridge sidled closer and she presented him with her back. He touched her lightly on the shoulder, a furtive, conspiratorial touch, nothing of passion in it. She made herself stand still. She felt him bend his head close to hers. His breath tickled her ear.

"Just a first name?"

Now was the time. She'd only to whisper a forlorn "Ronald" to draw Carr to her as surely as iron filings to a magnet. She'd misplayed Carr last night. She'd said the right things, she'd endured his touch, and she'd listened to his every word. But without enthusiasm. He'd known it and it had made him suspicious.

She could easily rectify that error.

Say his name. Tunbridge pressed her shoulder encouragingly.

"Who is he?" he whispered.

She conjured his face, preparing to whisper the answer but instead of Carr's haughty, handsome visage it was Rafe's face that formed behind her closed eyelids.

No, she thought desperately. *Not Rafe. Carr. Say it.*

Her lips parted. She took a breath. "He's—"

Tunbridge's hand was snatched from her shoulder. At the same time she heard him make a sound of angry protest. She spun around. Her heartbeat quickened; happiness raced through her.

Rafe stood before Tunbridge, smiling. It took Favor a second to realize Rafe's smile was far from pleasant.

"Sorry, dear fellow," Rafe drawled. "Didn't want to see the lady's shoulder dampened by your . . . enthusiasm."

The delight she'd experienced on seeing him, a delight she was in no way prepared to examine, faded. He was deliberately provoking Tunbridge. Reality doused her in cold truths. She'd had the matter well in hand. His interference could only cause trouble and the great lout didn't seem to realize that most of that trouble would be his own.

"You insolent cur!" Tunbridge spat.

"At least I don't drool," Rafe answered lightly, but his posture was far from nonchalant. He stood in an attitude of readiness, body angled sideways, weight forward, and arms loose at his sides.

"Who the hell are you?" Tunbridge demanded.

"Just another worshiper at Miss Donne's shrine."

Tunbridge looked as confused as he did angry. Abruptly Favor saw Rafe through Tunbridge's eyes. For Carr's guests, appearance was of paramount importance. Rafe, attired in worn, somewhat shabby but well-cut clothes, clearly hadn't the means for dandification.

"The hell you say! What do you mean by interrupting this lady and myself?" Tunbridge said. "Can you not see we were engaged in a private conversation?"

"Really?" Rafe asked innocently. "I'm *de trop,* am I?"

"Decidedly."

She had to do something and quickly. Rafe mustn't provoke Tunbridge any further. The man was rumored to have skewered five men to their deaths.

"Oh!" she said.

Neither man appeared to hear her breathy gasp of distress.

She redoubled her effort. "Oh! My! *You!*"

At this squawk both men turned. Rafe frowned, apparently displeased she'd interfered with his masculine posturing. She ignored him, keeping

her attention on Tunbridge and saw the moment comprehension seeped
into his expression.

"*Him?*" Tunbridge breathed.

She nodded, eyes wide, not having to reach very deep to produce a
shuddering inhalation. "Him."

"Lucky bastard!" Tunbridge said admiringly, new appreciation in his
expression.

"What the devil are you talking about?" Rafe demanded.

"Please." Favor lifted her head, striving to emulate pride before the fall.
"As you are a gentleman, Lord Tunbridge, I ask you to honor my confidences."

Tunbridge, all eager anticipation, slumped as if she'd pulled a trump
card from nowhere in a game of hazard. "Well . . ."

"Sir!"

"Yes. Fine. Confidence shall be kept. Blast. Damn. Hell."

She didn't believe him for a minute. But she did believe that at this
moment he honestly believed he would keep her secret. He'd at least that
much of honor left. That's all she needed. A little time in which Rafe
might get away. The rash, impetuous . . . *man.*

"Your language, sir, is not fit for this lady's ears," Rafe said.

Favor, who'd heard far worse from Rafe, stared at him, trying to discern
if he'd suddenly decided to make a jest. Clearly not. He was glaring at
Tunbridge, who stood poised to fly to his confederates and learn the
identity of the big, ill-dressed man he'd somehow overlooked these past
weeks. He looked about as trustworthy as a cat near an open bird cage.

"My pardon," Tunbridge muttered hurriedly. "Disrespectful of me. I
am unspeakable. A pig. Forgive me, Miss Donne and Mister . . . Mister? Sorry, sir. I didn't catch your name—"

"You didn't and you won't!" Favor stated emphatically. "Not from
either of us, Lord Tunbridge! Please, sir. Leave us!"

Luckily Raine finally decided it might prove wise to take his cue from
her. He positioned himself between Favor and Tunbridge, his attitude
growing even more threatening. "I believe you heard the lady's request,
Tunbridge. Leave."

Tunbridge looked from one to the other. "Damn!" he burst out. "I
don't know why you won't reveal the fellow's name. Since he's a guest of
Carr's it won't be all that bloody hard to discover and you'll save me a bit
of time."

Favor placed her fingertips over her chest and closed her eyes. "I will
not make my tender heart the object of filthy speculation," she whispered
dramatically.

"What?" Rafe's head snapped around.

"Fine," Tunbridge bit out, and without another word stalked off in the direction from whence they'd come.

They waited in silence until Tunbridge disappeared, before turning to face one another.

"What the hell was that all about?" Rafe asked in bewilderment.

Favor burst out laughing.

She braced her hands on her knees, laughing in that full rich way of hers and there was nothing he could do but smile and then chuckle and then laugh himself. And that was the last thing he'd been expecting to do.

When he'd seen that ass's hand on her he'd reacted instinctively, viscerally, jerking it away from her. He'd expected her to be furious that he'd thwarted her *tête-à-tête*. But when she'd turned he'd seen the welcome in her expression, the surprised second of—God help him—what looked like joy in the smile that sprang full blown to her lips . . . for *him* . . .

And later while he tried to figure out what sort of lies she'd been telling Tunbridge so that he could appropriately play his part, she'd caught his eye and the immediate sense of understanding, the rightness of it, had been like homecoming.

The realization rushed into his thoughts and soul, filling the empty and hollow parts of his life. When he was with Favor, his past did not exist. He felt no anger or bitterness or hatred. He thought of Carr and his mother without choking on the need for redress or recompense. His eye turned out, toward the morrow: not in, toward the past.

And now she made him laugh.

What more could she do to him?

Except make him love her.

"Ah! Me," she finally sniffed, wiping the tears away with the back of her hand. She sighed and smiled at him. "Well, you'd best be off before Tunbridge comes hurrying back bringing witnesses to my deflowering."

"What?"

Favor valiantly withstood another wave of laughter.

"Oh, yes. That's what he was doing whispering in my ear, trying to coax from me the name of the fellow who'd caught my fancy."

She nodded happily, unaware of the havoc she was causing in his heart. "They've a betting book on it, you see. Poor Tunbridge, after discovering he was not destined to be my paramour, decided he might as well make the best of the situation and find out the name of the fellow who was. Being a lady, I, of course, declined to name names and refused to say more than that my beau was not among Tunbridge's circle of friends. Then you arrived. I could not have asked for better timing."

"You jest."

"No!" She grinned broadly, tapping him lightly on the chest with her finger, winsome, naughty, and utterly engaging. "I couldn't make up so rich a tale."

"I'm afraid I have more faith in your skills than you," he said dryly.

"Well, perhaps I could come up with *as* good a tale, but none better," she allowed modestly. "Why *did* you come?"

He wasn't about to tell her he'd come because he'd made the frustrating discovery that he wanted no other woman but her. He glanced about for inspiration.

"Clothes. You were to get me clothes. This afternoon. At one. It's"—he yanked his timepiece from his pocket—"three o'clock."

She drew back and he cursed the distance that separated them even though it was but a mere foot or so.

"You mean you came charging over here because I failed to deliver your clothes at the exact hour you'd decreed? Of all the reckless, self-important, vainglorious masculine— Oh!"

He wasn't attending her words as well as he ought, though something in her tone cautioned him. He was simply too busy enjoying the sight of her, hair tossed by a suddenly capricious breeze, color fresh in her cheeks and lips, eyes as clear as wood violets. "It wasn't that reckless."

"Ah!" Her hands flew up in exasperation.

A thought interrupted the pleasure he took in the picture she made. "Why would that Tunbridge fellow think you had chosen a paramour?"

"Because I told him so."

"You were lying."

Her brow cleared. She smiled sunnily.

Damn. He may as well hand her his heart on a platter and what the bloody good that useless organ would do either of them was, and would forever remain, a mystery. He would do no such thing, for it could only result in more harm to her.

And worse harm for me, an inner voice cautioned. *An irreparably, irredeemably worse harm.*

"Was I?" she asked archly.

He did rise to her bait although it took much effort to stand motionless while she sashayed up to him, tossing her head.

"But of course you were," he said with carefully measured indifference. "If you had found your gull, you'd hardly be out here cavorting with Tunbridge. You'd be close by the poor dupe, setting up a wind what with fluttering all those lashes."

Her impertinent smile wavered, dissolved. "Well, if you think that for one instant I believe you came storming out here simply to demand I produce your purloined wardrobe, you're sadly mistaken."

"Why else would I come here?" he asked coldly. "I thought to teach you that I am not to be discounted at your convenience. Certainly not because my demands interfere with your pleasures."

Her lips pressed tightly together, the full curve of her enticing lower lip disappearing.

"Having achieved my purpose," he went on, "I will now leave you to your . . . diversions. Tomorrow you will bring the clothes."

There. He'd sounded cold and threatening to his own ear. He needed only to leave. Except Favor's lower lip had reappeared and it trembled slightly and the hard brilliance of her eyes was no longer hard, but veiled by a wash of unshed tears, angry tears but tears nonetheless. He couldn't remember when he'd last seen a woman cry. It undid him entirely.

"Why do we always end up fighting?" The words escaping her lips were rife with unhappiness.

He gave up. Reaching out, he captured her easily and spun her about, bending her over his arm.

"Little falcon, don't you honestly know?" he asked. "Why, so *this* won't happen."

And he kissed her.

CHAPTER 21

Rafe's lips moved over hers. His arms were strong and his body an anchor she could cling to and not for an instance did she consider trying to free herself from his embrace. With a sigh, she gave herself up to his kiss, wrapping her arms around his neck and pulling him down.

She closed her eyes, soaking up all of the delicious sensations not only surrounding but filling her. Like a dry sponge thrown in an ocean, her awareness expanded with the influx of perceptions. She cupped his hard jaw, holding his face to hers, alive to each inch of beard-rough skin abrading her palms.

Her pawn. Her blackmailer. Her thief.

His muscular arms, the sinew in the thigh pressed against her hip, the hard chest flattening her own breasts, all of these set her skin tingling with the need to arch closer, rubbing against him like a cat. His scent filled her nostrils, crushed grass and dry pine, astringent soap, mysterious male musk.

And kisses. Kisses such as she'd never known nor dreamed existed: the feathering gentleness of velvety nibbles; the shivery carnality of moist, softly drawing kisses; and, finally, a deep, soul-searing kiss as he angled his mouth sideways over hers and tilted her chin, urging her mouth open. She needed no further encouragement. His tongue stroked the sleek lining of her cheeks, playing with her own tongue: wet, warm, and infinitely wicked.

Abruptly sensation exceeded experience. She'd no words to record the feelings rocketing through her, no terms to even identify them.

Her head fell back and wedged in the lee of his arm. Her eyelids fluttered open, allowing her a glimpse of his rugged face, tense and intent. Then he was kissing her again. But surely kisses alone could not account for the surge of pleasure coursing through her, as sweet and heady as hot mead. Kisses couldn't set a pulse beating high between her thighs, or rouse an aching in the very tips of her breasts.

She wanted to *melt* into him, to feel his body surround hers, to absorb him into herself. She tried. Lord knows, she tried.

She moved her hands around his torso and up his back, clasping the hard, mounded shoulder muscles and pulling herself as close as humanly possible. Her hips burrowed into the niche created by his splayed stance. A sound rumbled from deep in Rafe's chest. He pulled away from her. She voiced an unintelligible but vehement protest, her eyes opening to flash a disbelieving glare at him.

Why would he want to stop? Why, in the name of all the saints, would anyone *ever* want to stop something so wonderful?

He lifted his head and stared down at her. His breath rushed out in pants to fan her hot cheeks and swollen lips.

"Oh, no," he said, sounding amused and winded and angry and tender all at once. "Kisses, yes," he said and rained a dozen lightning-fast busses over her temple, cheeks, and eyelids. Her mouth turned to intercept them but could not. She made a sound of frustration.

"Dear Lord," he whispered, capturing the back of her head in one broad hand and pressing her forehead to his.

"Kisses," he whispered. "Nothing more." He laughed. "I seem to have acquired a taste for punishment. I knew how inadequate kisses would— No! Stay, you!" he commanded as she tipped her chin seeking his lips. "I am no saint and you, lady, are a far greater temptation than this poor mortal flesh has ever endeavored to resist."

She didn't understand the meaning of his words, or why, though his gaze roved like a stalking thing over her countenance, he held himself back. She knew only that a moment earlier she'd been vibrantly whole, and as each moment passed her pleasure dissolved like footprints lapped by an incoming tide.

She'd had too little happiness of late. She'd forgotten its flavor. She worked her hands up to his face, bracketing the tense jaw between her hands and polishing his lips with hers.

"Kiss me," she whispered. He stared down at her, the shadows of his lashes making mysteries of his warm brown eyes. She could read nothing there. The very world seemed to hold its breath. She brushed her fingertip across the silky sable fringe of his lashes. "Kiss me."

His head moved slowly down—

" 'Sblood! Tunbridge was right!" A woman's voice broke Favor's hushed anticipation.

Instantly, Rafe straightened, carrying her to his side and behind him, shielding her from curiosity seekers.

"Pray excuse us." His voice was vitriolic and cold, like burning ice. "I hadn't realized we were being offered as voyeuristic entertainment," he said, "or I should have endeavored a more licentious tableau."

Silently, Favor cursed the intruders, far more furious at their interruption than embarrassed by it. She raised her chin to a haughty angle and stepped from behind Rafe's broad back.

"Lady Fia." She acknowledged the slender girl and brace of snickering men on either side of her. "Were you seeking me?"

But Fia didn't appear to hear Favor. Her gaze was trained on Rafe, as blank and fixed as a sleepwalker's.

"Fia?" Rafe echoed, scowling.

One of the swains—a handsome blond man whose name Favor could not recall but whose fetid breath she did—stepped forward. His lip curled in derision. "The Lady Fia Merrick. Lord Carr's daughter. You do know Lord Carr, don't you, fellow? For either he's your host"—he turned to Fia, doubtless so he could witness the appreciation his next sally was sure to bring—"or your employer."

The other swain, a green lad who'd the previous night confessed to Favor his fervent desire "to be baptized in the ways of sin," took his blond friend's cue.

He shot a quick, guilty glance in Favor's direction before averting his eyes and addressing her. "Miss Donne, never say your taste for rural pleasures is what's kept you from sampling a more cosmopolitan fare. I didn't believe Tunbridge when he claimed it so, but"—he hid his mouth behind his hand—"I can scarce doubt my own eyes."

"You must have gone to some trouble to locate me, Lady Fia." Favor tried once more to divert attention from Rafe. He'd been mad to walk into the center of one of Carr's parties. If she didn't think quickly, he'd be found out. "And in quite a hurry to do so. Lord Tunbridge left not ten minutes ago. Was there something imperative that you needed to see me about? Or were you eager to see *us*?" The innuendo was sharp and unflattering yet Fia barely glanced in her direction.

The men, either too dull-witted to catch the inference or simply uncaring, were watching Rafe, who had gone mute—strange behavior from a man who hadn't lacked for words a few minutes before. Favor studied him. But though at first glance one might have supposed that he, too, had fallen under Fia's siren spell, there was nothing of desire in his gaze. It was searching and somehow sad.

"*Is* this brute one of your employees, Lady Fia?" the youth asked. Favor held her breath, willing Rafe not to take umbrage.

Fia answered without removing her gaze from Rafe. "No."

"You know him, then?" the blond man said.

"I don't know," Fia said reflectively. "There's something familiar about him." She stepped forward.

"Here now," she said imperiously, "do you know me, sir?"

Rafe hesitated. The sorrow intensified in his eyes. He shook his head. "No. I do not know you."

A shadow passed over Fia's countenance, making her beauty suddenly tragic. Then it was gone and one high-curving brow rose haughtily.

"I thought not. Nor do I know you." She turned away but checked her step and turned her head. "Ah. I have it. I know where I've seen this fellow. Do you know my father?"

An unpleasant smile curved Rafe's wide lips. "Oh, yes. Him I know."

Fia nodded, clearly satisfied. "There you are. He is one of my father's special guests and that is why we have not seen him. That, and his having apparently been"—her gaze passed to Favor—"preoccupied with other companions. Tell me, Miss Donne, does my father know you are dallying with his . . . guest? He won't like it."

Favor's heart beat thickly. Silently she prayed Fia would not reveal her interest in Carr to Rafe. Not yet. She needed time. Time to . . .

"He doesn't like sharing," Fia went on. "Never got the knack of it." Her three-point smile lit her smooth, youthful countenance and she motioned for her swains. They came like puppies to a milk bowl and she linked her arms to each, one on either side.

"Come, gentlemen. Despite Miss Donne's conviction that we were sneaking through the woods hoping to surprise her and this fellow in an indiscretion, I still desire to find the stag's antlers Mrs. Petrie claimed to have seen. Oh, yes. I heard your query, Miss Donne, and no, I did not come to *see* you."

She did not look back as she allowed her sniggering male companions to draw her away. In minutes they were lost to sight in the rocky, tree studded landscape.

Favor, flooded with relief that Rafe had escaped more dangerous notice, sank to the grassy floor.

"Why did she warn you about Carr?" Rafe asked, standing above her. "What did she mean?"

Her recent relief died. She should tell him the truth: that she was here to become affianced to Lord Carr. She kept her head averted, steeling herself to say the words. And why shouldn't she tell him? He already knew half of it: He'd accepted that she was seeking to make a brilliant match, to refill her clan's coffers with a rich husband's money. Why not Carr?

Carr's face rose in her mind's eye. Other girls had wed men with far more years than Carr. It wasn't age alone that stayed her tongue. It was the knowledge that she knowingly sought to take as her mate a man so evil.

But Rafe wouldn't know that. Rafe hadn't stood beneath Carr's lathered steed and stared up at him while he decided one's fate with less thought than he'd give to drowning a kitten. Rafe hadn't witnessed Carr's satisfaction as he'd ridden off with his devil's brood, leaving her alone in a blood-stained night rail among the dead and dying.

Rafe wouldn't know she maneuvered to become a monster's bride.

"Favor?"

How sweet her name sounded coming from him. But he couldn't match her Christian name with her surname. He didn't know it. Just as she didn't know his. And it didn't matter.

But it did. They'd followed their inclinations on instinct and emotion. Their relationship was a castle built on quicksand, doomed to disappear, swallowed by harsh realities and grim truth, surnames and pasts, obligations and penalties.

But she could not see it fall apart yet. Not yet. She could cling to whatever she had of happiness, stretch it out a few more hours or days or . . .

"I think she was talking about you, Rafe."

He'd squatted down on his heels beside her, his brow worried. "What?"

"When she said Carr didn't like sharing. I think she mistook you for one of the gamblers and I believe she meant Carr would not like sharing you with me. I might divert your attention from the tables."

"I see." He'd accepted her lie, too concerned about her to give it much heed. "Are you all right? Did those men offend you? I can—"

"No!" She reached up, grabbing hold of his forearm. The muscle tightened beneath her grip. Sensual awareness ambushed her anew. She drew back her hand. "No. You can't do anything. You have to keep hidden or you'll be found out."

"No one will find me out."

"They almost did! You're safe now only because of Fia Merrick's certainty that no one could breach her father's castle."

That wholly engaging lopsided smile once more graced his bold features, making boyish what was normally so unremittingly male and mature. "Thank you for caring."

She made an exasperated face. "It's not as though I want to care."

His smile spread into a grin. "I'm sure of that."

He knelt down beside her on one knee and raised a hand to touch her cheek. She scooted backward on her seat. She could resist him if he didn't touch her. But why would she want to res—

Ah, no! she thought, *that way lies disaster!*

No similar cautionary thought seemed to occur to Rafe. He'd eased forward, prowling toward her. The smile still teased the corners of his mouth, a lazy smile now and quite, quite predatory. As were the dark eyes and intent gaze belying that charming, casual smile. He looked like the proverbial wolf come to court the lamb.

She gulped, scooted back again, slipped and landed flat on her back. Before she could scramble up he was over her, arms braced on either side of her shoulders, blotting out the sky with his breadth.

He reached down and grinned as she flinched, but his hand moved harmlessly past the quivering agitation of her mouth and chest and tangled in her hair.

Her pulse galloped. The memory of his kisses was so fresh she could still feel his lips.

"Why would you conceal its true color?" The smile slowly vanished from his face. "Ah, yes. The would-be suitors like a dark lass."

He released the strand of black dyed hair and in one easy movement rose to his feet. He extended his hand down to her. She wriggled up onto her elbows, gazing blankly at his hand. Disappointment quickly replaced her trepidation. So, there was to be no dalliance, then?

"Let me help you up," he said mildly, as though he'd never held her, caressed her, molded her body to his and his lips to hers.

"No, thank you," she said, aware she sounded disgruntled.

As if he knew the reason for her glum expression he grinned. "Here, little falcon. I may not be one of Carr's well-heeled *roués* but at least my character is not so poor that I would ply my slight amorous skills here for any chance passerby to view. Neither, do I think, would you want that."

"Of course not!" she huffed, dusting off nonexistent pieces of grass, avoiding his amused eyes. Damn the man's arrogance!

"I don't know what momentary aberration clouded my judgment, but you may be well assured there shan't be a second such lapse," she said.

She clambered to her feet, ignoring his offer of assistance and turned a quelling eye on him. She acknowledged with gratification his bow in deference to her terse statement.

And missed the smile his deferential pose concealed.

CHAPTER 22

Favor meandered toward her suite, peeling back her riding gloves as she went. She'd been away from Rafe only an hour and already she missed him. Not that she'd ever allow him to know that. And truly it had been insanity to let him kiss her.

Let him?

An impish smile appeared on her face, born of the knowledge that he was attracted to her far beyond what he was willing to admit. And if she suffered from similar pride—or fear—well, she didn't really care.

She'd just arrived at her chambers when the door swung open. Muira seized her wrist and yanked her inside, slamming the door behind her. Startled, Favor jerked away from her, only then realizing that Muira wore none of the makeup that created Pala or Mrs. Douglas. Instead a livid red welt crossed one weathered cheek.

"What happened?" Favor asked in concern.

"What *hasn't* happened?" Muira snapped in reply. "While you've been licking icing from your fingers beneath some tree, 'Pala' had an audience with Carr."

"Did he do that?"

"Do what?" Muira asked irritably, and then, seeing the direction of Favor's shocked gaze, she touched her cheek. She made a dismissive sound. "This is nothing. We have far graver matters to consider."

"I don't understand."

"Of course not, you stupid girl," Muira said. "I'll tell you what you've done. Because you were too delicate, too sensitive to endure Carr's attentions, he's decided that he needs a *love* potion to make you more receptive."

"What!"

"Yes. A love potion. Which I will provide him. And later, when he hands you a drink, my girl, you will take it and drink it and within an hour act like his Cheapside doxy."

"I will not," Favor breathed, repelled.

"Don't worry," Muira sneered. "You'll have at least one day to practice puckering your lips. Carr made sure of that by marking me with this." She touched her cheek. "No paint will cover it and you can't appear unchaperoned. I'll send word that you have the headache. Tomorrow you'll be ready to play Carr's cooing lovebird."

Every fiber of her body rebelled at the notion. "No," she said. "I will not do it."

"By God, you will!" Muira's hand darted out with the speed of a striking snake, slapping Favor hard across the face.

Instinctively self-protective, Favor grabbed hold of Muira's arms above the elbow, stopping a second blow. Stunned, Muira stared at Favor's hands. Her mouth fell open.

Instinct might have incited Favor's action, anger caused her hands to tighten.

"Listen, old woman," she said in a low, hard voice. "Long ago, you assured me that simply showing interest in Carr would be enough. I've been able to carry my role this far only because I did *not* have to pretend I was smitten.

"I would *never* be able to carry off such a farce and not all your slaps or threats can make it so. I can barely tolerate his breath on my cheek! If you force me to try, you, and only you, will be responsible for the failure of your plan. Do you understand me?" She shook Muira, rage and pain and regret overwhelming her.

"Now," she grated out. "I shall not drink any vile brew and pretend that that bastard fills me with lust. Do we understand each other?"

Muira, eyes wide and unblinking, nodded. "But what shall we do? He trusts Pala to make him a potion. She dare not show up without one. And it must work or he will never again trust her."

Favor released Muira's arm and stood back, as disgusted with her violence toward the elderly woman as with Muira herself. She wondered if Muira was even aware that more and more often lately she spoke of Pala as if the character were a real woman.

"Make your potion," she said. "Deliver it to Carr. He'll have to combine it with drink or food he intends to give me. I shall find excuses not to eat or drink anything he offers me. At the same time, I'll make clear that the only time he will be alone with Janet is after he marries me."

"You think this will work?" Muira said, her shock at Favor's ferocity fading. She eyed the girl with hidden acrimony. *She* was the one who'd held the clan together for the last bleak decade, not this little uppity bitch. It was *her* plan that would return the McClairens to power and prestige, not this . . . *child*'s. She, Muira Dougal, was the dark heart of the clan. And now this barely weaned little slut challenged her.

"Yes," Favor said, unaware of the dark path of Muira's thoughts.

Muira, her gaze never leaving Favor's hard, determined countenance, nodded her compliance. And made plans of her own.

". . . and if what yer da says is true, ye'll be in London by Christmas," Gunna prattled on, she who was not given to chatter. Fia continued watching Gunna's reflection in the mirror hanging above the dressing table. The twisted old woman brushed through Fia's hair, turning the curly mass into a rippling, shimmering veil of black. "I'm thinking ye'll like London. What do ye think?"

"How can I fail to like it? It's not Wanton's Blush," Fia replied.

"Aye," Gunna said. "That's for certain and right ye are to be putting this wretched place behind ye. It's no but a mausoleum yer father's guests use like a brothel."

"What lovely imagery," Fia said, softly ironic. "You've such a gift for words, Gunna."

Gunna cackled. "Well, I have no love of the great gloomy place but"— her eye fixed on Fia—"I thought ye'd a bit of care fer it."

"I'd an interest," Fia corrected. "I should have liked to have known the castle when it was called Maiden's Blush. As a matter of curiosity."

Gunna did not reply, concentrating on a snarl. Moments passed. The setting sun filled the bedchamber with amber light. Outside, the bare limbs of the oak trees tapped lightly on the windows, like a lover come begging.

"You know he's here, don't you?" Fia said.

Gunna's hand checked. "Who be that?"

"Raine," Fia replied, and turned in her chair to search Gunna's face. The ravaged countenance gave little away. It never had. "You knew he was here, didn't you?"

"Aye," Gunna admitted.

Fia nodded as she turned back around, facing the mirror. She'd thought so. And that Gunna, whom she'd always trusted, had kept this from her caused only a small prick of anguish. She was used to being disillusioned. "When did you find out?"

"Yesterday. He's been here some weeks and me never knowing, nor anyone else neither."

"How enterprising of him. Not even Father?"

"No. I dinna tell ye because he did not want ye to know and I wouldna have ye hurt by his seeming indifference, though I do believe it's not indifference as much as mistrust." She caught Fia's eye. "He doesna know ye, Fia," she said flatly. "And what he remembers is that ye were yer father's shadow."

"He's quite right on both counts," Fia replied calmly. "He has no reason to show interest in me or to trust me."

"Do not act callous for my poor benefit, Fia Merrick. 'Tis a waste of a good performance. I know ye better than that."

"Do you?" Fia whispered suddenly. Her voice was that of a lost little girl unable to hide her wistful hope that deep within she really was decent and honorable and . . . good, when she knew how unlikely that to be. She bowed her head, ashamed of such emotions.

Gunna's hand hovered briefly above Fia's bowed head, hesitated and was retracted. She cleared her throat. "How did ye find out about Raine?"

Relieved that Gunna would not pursue other topics, Fia answered. "He was on the picnic this afternoon. Attending Miss Donne."

"Miss Donne?"

"Thomas Donne's sister."

"Aye. I remember ye remarking ye were surprised by yer father's interest in her. Ye thought it odd as he hadn't paid much attention to her until the last week or so."

"Yes. Apparently not only my father but my brother is interested in Miss Donne. The Donnes hold some sort of fatal magnetism for us Merricks." She regretted the words as soon as she'd said them. Even Gunna did not know exactly how much Thomas Donne had hurt her. She would just as soon not hint that the injury she'd sustained still bled.

She could still hear Thomas's voice, carrying above the gales blowing up from the sea to the garden where he'd led Rhiannon Russell for privacy. It had carried, too, over the garden wall where she'd knelt, listening:

"This isn't simply a rather nasty family. It's evil."

"Carr killed his first wife."

"Merrick skewered a man's hand just for cheating."

"His brother raped a nun."

"They are all as bad as their sire."

And finally, the mortal thrust,

"Fia is nothing but Carr's whore, groomed to fetch the largest marriage settlement possible."

Her entire body jerked in physical repudiation of the memory. She closed her eyes, hating that it still had such power, hating more that she, who'd spent her life building walls, was so vulnerable in this one last area. Once she'd loved Thomas Donne. But now, as with all love betrayed, she hated him with surpassing fervor.

If only she could stir within herself some animosity for his sister, she might find she liked the taste of revenge. But she couldn't.

She glanced at Gunna. The old woman stood motionless, the half of her face revealed by her mantilla taut with concentration. "What is it, Gunna?"

"What was Raine doing at yer picnic?"

Fia lifted her shoulders. "I don't know. He pretended not to know me and I returned the favor. Why is he here, Gunna? What is going on?"

"He's looking fer some treasure he says his mother had keep of. He came to find it without yer father's knowledge and to take it away."

Fia smiled, slightly bemused, a trifle sad. How in keeping with what she remembered of her brawny middle brother. Impetuous. Bold. Doomed.

"Ye say ye found Raine and this girl together?" Gunna asked.

"Like a dovetailed joint," Fia replied flatly, "fitted at the lips. Quite protective of her, he was. Nearly snapped my head off when we came upon them. And she . . . well, she was obviously intent on distracting me and my companions from asking too closely about him."

"I *thought* someone had been there with him," Gunna murmured.

"What?"

"I found him in the old chapel. Or he found me, is more like. Sprung at me, arms raised to strike and his face hard with violence. It makes sense now. *She'd* been with him and he'd been protecting her.

"And later, as we spoke his eyes kept moving about the room, touching on bits of trash and turning tender. He was thinking of her." She passed her slender hand over her face. "Oh, Raine!"

"Why do you say that?" Fia asked, perplexed. "So, Raine has found himself a light-skirts. What of it? You can't be surprised? Not what with Raine's reputation. Even I have heard tales about him, tales old by the time he was sixteen."

"Ach!" Gunna shook her head, setting the mantilla swinging. "Ye never knew him at all if ye think that. He was ever the reckless one, set on racing the devil to damnation, but only because no one ever bade him stay. No one ever cared enough to stop him.

"He knew plenty about tupping, I'll grant ye that, but naught about

love, either the giving or the receiving of it. But I always ken that once
he'd learned to love, he'd do it as he did everything. Wholeheartedly,
recklessly, without a thought to consequence or the risks to his heart."

"You think he *loves* Miss Donne?" Fia asked, taken aback.

"I don't know," Gunna answered flatly. "I do know he deserves to be
loved. He's waited for it long enough."

Fia laughed, made nervous by the pity and confusion Gunna's revelation awakened in her heart. "And Miss Donne? Have you any thoughts on
her emotional state?"

"Don't use that tone on me, Fia. Save it for yer sophisticated friends,"
Gunna reprimanded her sharply and Fia's eyes fell. "I know nothing of
this girl; perhaps she's no better than she should be, but Raine . . . yer
father's taken so much from him already. He mustn't take her, too."

Lord Carr uncorked the crude bottle a footman said had been delivered
by a raggedy-looking tinker a few hours earlier. He waved it under his
nose, his nostrils quivering.

Not too vile a brew: a hint of almond, a soupçon of orange blossoms.
But then, Carr reminded himself, it was a love potion. What would it smell
like, brimstone?

He lit the candles on his desk before working a key into the lock on one
set of drawers. It was dusk and he'd need to hurry to finish his prepara-
tions.

He opened a drawer and removed a short tray. Several small vials
clinked together as he set it on his desktop. He removed an empty one
and fitted it with a small funnel, humming as he filled it with the potion.
By midnight, Miss Donne—and Janet—would follow him anywhere.

Not that he couldn't have brought the girl round entirely with his own
charms. But when so expeditious a solution was at hand, why exert oneself
needlessly?

Having filled the vial, he sealed and pocketed it before returning the
tray to its original location. He locked the drawer. He had to remember to
take the tray with him when he vacated Wanton's Blush. Its contents
might prove useful in London.

He chanced to catch sight of his reflection in the mirror and frowned.
This would never do. One simply couldn't commence a seduction in a
plain white periwig. He would see that the increasingly—and thankfully—
close-mouthed Rankle prepared a lavender powder for his new bagwig for
this evening.

But first. . . . He moved to the wall and yanked on a silk bell pull. A
footman arrived in a few minutes.

"Go to the conservatory and have the gardener cut several of whatever bloom is most exotic. Deliver them immediately to Miss Favor Donne with my regards and tell her I look forward to her company this evening."

"Ah. Er. Yes," the tall, strapping, and exceedingly ornamental young man said. "Ah. Sir?"

Unfortunately the best-looking of this sort were invariably the most dull-witted.

"What?" Carr snapped irritably. He'd much to do before this evening's *soirée* began.

"Miss Donne ain't going to be coming down to dine this evening, sir. Her old auntie sent her regrets, saying as how the young lady had the headache and how the old lady would sit by her."

"Damnation!" Carr thundered. "Get out of here!" The footman began to bolt. "No. Wait. Go get the bloody flowers and deliver them to her anyway. With my regrets that she's feeling vaporish."

The footman ducked his head and backed out of the room. Carr slammed the door after him and commenced pacing. *Headache?* He'd been all set for the next part of his plan and now she had a *headache?* Of all the gall.

Clearly, Janet had done this to the chit simply to taunt him. Or maybe the chit had done this to Janet, simply to thwart her. It was hard enough understanding the primitive workings of one female mind but to have to deal with two conjointly! A lesser man would fail in so tortuous a task.

CHAPTER 23

"The momentary aberration" Favor had promised would not return the day before had, apparently, returned. Not only did it cloud Favor's mind, it had eclipsed her reason as well. Raine wasn't even certain how it was they'd started kissing. And he didn't care.

Then thought receded and pleasure took precedence as Favor's soft lips found the base of his neck. He groaned as she nibbled her way up the side of his throat to the angle of his chin, his small measure of self-restraint fast being depleted.

When she'd appeared in the room he'd been searching, her mouth sulky and succulent and the purloined men's garb draped over her arm, he'd promised himself he would treat her as the convent-bred lady she was, not the girl her presence in this Scottish Sodom declared her. It quickly became a task far more arduous than he'd imagined.

Favor sighed, her fingers exploring beneath his shirt with shattering eagerness. Her eyes were closed and her head had fallen against his shoulders, inviting more kisses. Genteel, sweet kisses, nectar when he was fast growing thirsty for a more potent brew. But he would be good. He would hold back. He would keep control of the hunger rumbling through his body like distant thunder. Not only because he was no longer a willful, irresponsible boy, not only because her upbringing cautioned any wooer to use restraint to bring this little falcon to hand, but because, just as Favor had never been wooed, he had never courted.

It was a rich, complicated dance and one not without its own subtle, piquant rewards. All of his early sexual experiences with women had ended in bed. All of it, the petting and licking and kissing, had been accomplished too hastily and most often frantically, an obligatory prelude to mating.

This was . . . exquisite.

Delectable. Ambrosial. Honeyed kisses, pulpy sweet, open-mouthed exchanges, wet and yearning and deep. Caresses like satin. Smooth, deep polishing strokes. Skimming feathering touches. He'd never known such delicious torment.

She nestled trustingly in his embrace, unskilled yet wise in a way no woman in his past had ever been wise—with a deep understanding of unselfishness, of pleasure gained through pleasure given. She was a treasure.

"Treasure," he murmured against her forehead.

Her eyes opened. "Yes." She sighed. "You're right. We should get back to it."

"I . . . I didn't mean—" He stopped. What was he going to do, admit he'd been speaking about her? Unwise. Not with everything so bloody complicated and daily growing more so.

She didn't appear to note his stumbling near-confession. Her arms slid languidly away from his throat. She smiled regretfully. Regretfully, he released her.

"I have to leave. Tonight is Carr's masque." Her cheeks colored and he knew she was remembering his comments on masques and their attendees.

"You don't have to go," he said.

Her gaze was fixed on the opposite wall. She'd pinned a faux smile to her countenance. He hated it.

"You should leave Wanton's Blush," he said, unable to keep his frustration from sounding like anger. "Pack up your aunt and go back to your brother's home.

"If you must find a rich husband, go to London when your brother returns. I assure you, this isn't the only society that would welcome you. There are better hunting grounds, Favor. You don't have to be *here*."

She turned her head toward him. She looked weary, in some unfathomable manner depleted, as though all her reserves had suddenly found an end.

"There you're wrong. I need to . . . marry soon."

"Why? Can't your family fend for themselves for an additional few months?" he asked angrily. "Are they such poor specimens that they would sacrifice you to provide them an easier life for a few weeks more?"

Her blue eyes quickened with anger. Better lightning than emptiness. "You don't know anything about it!"

"Then tell me!"

"Ach!" She backed away, driven off by his words. But he wouldn't retreat. He couldn't.

"Tell me."

She crossed her arms under her breasts and glared at him. "Men! You think you have a monopoly on honor. That only males need the catharsis of discharging a debt. But you're wrong."

"Why would you need catharsis?" he asked, holding his breath, afraid she'd tell him, terrified she wouldn't. He wanted her trust. He didn't deserve it. He hadn't even told her who he was. "Why?"

"I did something. Years ago." She hesitated. He searched her face and saw a young woman, little more than a girl, torn by indecision, wanting desperately to share the most intimate details of her life with a man she knew next to nothing about. Desperate because there was no one else to tell.

How alone she must be to have come to such a pass. How achingly alone.

"My actions cost my . . . it cost people their lives," she said finally.

"Did you know they would pay such a price?"

"No!"

"Then if unintentional, you cannot be blamed."

"Ignorance is no excuse." She recited the words in such a way that he knew she'd heard them many, many times.

He started toward her but she held up her hand, denying him, stopping him. "Explain."

"I . . . I was a child," she mumbled, eyes averted. "My . . . people were seeing that a criminal was brought to justice."

"A criminal?"

"A rapist."

Odd he should flinch now, upon hearing that label on her lips, when years ago he'd not only refused to flinch but had endured blow after blow without giving satisfaction.

She misunderstood his recoil and nodded. "They brought him to where we lived to see justice meted out by my father. But he was gone and my mother, who was a lady of standing, bade me stop them."

"Why?"

"Because she feared that if they hanged this rapist, my brothers would be killed in retaliation."

"I see."

"I did what she asked. I stopped them"—her arms tightened about her —"just long enough for *his* family to arrive with armed men. They killed most all of those people. Slaughtered them. Cut them down like wheat before the scythe. I found out later that my brother was already dead."

Her eyes were dazed, her expression ravaged, stunned anew by the memory. He had to draw her back from that terrible inner vista he knew so well himself. "Bedamned, Favor! What else could you have done?"

Her brow puckered, looking for an answer to a riddle posed years before and never answered. "I should have let them kill the boy. If I hadn't stopped them they could have hanged him and been gone by the time the soldiers arrived. And even if they hadn't been gone, at least justice would have been served. A rapist would have died."

"You did what your mother asked," he said soberly. "It wasn't your fault."

He had the distinct impression that he'd failed her, that she'd been waiting hungrily for an answer she'd yet to hear.

"I know," she said, as though he were being purposefully obtuse. "But 'fault' isn't part of this. Nor blame. This is about what I can live with, what I need to do."

"And marrying a wealthy maggot is the only way you can live with yourself?" he asked, frustration spawning sarcasm.

"Aye." Her voice was distant.

"Why not don a hair shirt?" Raine asked bitterly. "I'm sure I can find a flail somewhere about to help aid you in your pleasure. This is Wanton's Blush after all."

"Don't," she said, not angry, not pricked, simply resigned. " 'Tis you who are being unreasonable, not I. I'm not the first woman who chooses a husband for what he can bring her family. Indeed, I have it better than most, for I do this of my own free will." She appealed to him helplessly. "Would you rather I disobeyed the dictates of my conscience just to please my selfish heart?"

Joy was a piercing blade, killing him with never-to-be's. He couldn't say a word. He could only stand, drinking in the implication of her words.

"Rafe." She smiled, shy and forlorn. He held out his hand. She pretended not to see it and turned and walked away. He closed his eyes.

"Raine," he whispered back in so low a voice she could not hear him. He knew now why poets spoke of a heart breaking for something spilled in his chest, something hot and hurtful. He opened his eyes. Her slender back was to him. The slope of her shoulders was burdened, her steps heavy.

She stopped, looking around the room, trying to find an excuse to stay, knowing she should go. "You." She cleared her voice, tried again. "You said you were looking for an oriental box." Her tone tried hopelessly for its former brightness.

He answered in kind, searching for a place hidden from the demands and machinations of the world outside, the place they'd found in these empty rooms, searching for a fabled treasure and finding another even greater, one they'd never sought and knew they could never keep.

"Yes," he said dully. "An oriental box."

"Dark? About two feet across?" Irrepressible interest flickered to life in her expression.

"Yes," he muttered. "A tea chest."

Her eyelids were stained mauve with fatigue. Her skin looked ethereal, clean of the white face powder she usually wore, fragile and all too mortal.

"Does it look like that?" She pointed.

He glanced in the direction she indicated. This room was less crammed than the others: a pair of water-stained sideboards; a moldy rolled-up carpet; a leather-clad traveling trunk; and, against the wall, a huge bookcase, one door missing, the shelves dark and empty. Atop this monstrosity sat several boxes that, because of the bookcase's height, had hitherto gone unnoticed. Only now, looking up from across the room, could one see them.

One was intricately carved. Foreign in appearance. Black.

"Yes," Raine said, his heart beginning to race. Inside that box could be the answer to the dream he forced himself to forget upon waking each day. But now, with the box within reach, that dream emerged from the nether world he'd relegated it to and became dazzling potential.

With McClairen's Trust *he* would be wealthy. *He* would be a prize to any woman who would marry for money.

Immediately, he slaughtered the ridiculous notion. She was a McClairen. She held him accountable for her clan's massacre. Not ten minutes earlier she'd been regretting his having lived.

He grabbed hold of one of the mahogany sideboards and leaned into it, grunting as he shoved the mammoth piece across the floor toward the bookcase. He could not ask Favor for her hand but at least with McClairen's Trust in his possession he could make sure she didn't have to marry some bleeding idiot like Tunbridge. He could give her the bloody jewels.

He gave the sideboard a final heave, bringing it within a few feet of the bookcase, and jumped atop it. He peered at the dark box. It *was* his mother's tea chest. He recalled the rippling inlaid back of the dragon that danced across the lid. He pulled it into his hands and jumped down.

An intricate bronze clasp swung listlessly from the back hinge. One tiny set of drawers was completely missing. But the top, the portion that had opened to reveal the jewels, was still seamlessly closed.

"Do you really think it holds the treasure?" Favor asked. Raine could not read either her tone or her odd, unhappy expression.

"I don't know. Let's find out." He seized a heavy candlestick holder and brought it smashing down on the tea chest's lid. The fragile, delicately carved wood splintered and flew apart.

Together Raine and Favor stared down at the shattered chest. For a full minute they stood. Slowly, Raine reached down and lifted a large, covered tray from the ruined box. He pulled it open, revealing a faded velvet lining and nothing else. Favor knelt beside the splintered pieces, lifting and discarding splintered boards, peering into the few interior trays that survived the demolition. Raine nudged the last of the pieces with his foot, turning them over. There was no place a ring could hide let alone a complete parure of heavy gold and gems.

"I'm . . . I'm sorry," he heard Favor whisper.

Desolation swept through him. He'd nothing left now. Not pipe dreams. Not honorable intentions.

He stared in bemusement. He should leave. The chances of his finding McClairin's Trust among the dozens of rooms crammed with hiding places was infinitesimal—assuming it still existed. But that wasn't the real reason he wanted to flee. How could he stay while she sought some other bastard for her spouse?

"I guess we'll just have to continue looking," he heard Favor say in a small, rough voice.

He looked up, read her face, and understood. As far as Favor was concerned, she'd found that place where they could be together, separated from debts and duty. And she found the excuse she needed to stay with him: searching for the Trust.

She wasn't smiling but guilty happiness illumined her face like sunlight.

He didn't stand a chance.

"Yes," he agreed softly.

CHAPTER 24

Tunbridge burst through Carr's library door. "Carr! Great news! At last!"

Carr, in the process of searching through a pile of promissory notes, deeds, wills, letters, and the occasional confession, looked up sharply. "Pray shut the door, Tunbridge," he said, and began stacking the papers.

He'd been looking for a particularly damning love letter but that could wait. It was more important that he must not seem overly concerned with the sheets on his desk. He mustn't let Tunbridge know that he was seeing the source upon which hung Carr's future power and prestige.

"Now," Carr said, snipping off a length of twine and tying the papers into two separate bundles, "What is this wondrous news?"

"The king is dead! George is dead!" Tunbridge said. He braced his hands flat on the desk and leaned over it. "Do you hear me, Carr? George II died October 25. His grandson is now king."

"Grandson?" Carr repeated. After all these years finally . . .

"Yes." Tunbridge nodded vigorously. "And as all Hanovers hate their successors, George hated his grandson and the grandson returned the sentiment. This new king is young, Carr, malleable and eager."

"He will rescind his grandfather's edict concerning me?" Carr asked, careful not to reveal his anxiety.

"He wouldn't even *know* about it."

Carr surged forward, thrusting his face close to Tunbridge's smirking visage. "Be careful, sir. I will not be disappointed in this."

"I am certain of it!" Tunbridge avowed. "George spent so many of his last years abroad he barely knew the boy. The young king will have scant time for his grandfather's personal enmities, I assure you."

"Where did you hear this news?"

"From Lord Edgar, not an hour ago. I was leaving the castle as he arrived. He'd come directly from St. James's Palace itself."

"Where is he now?"

"In his chambers, asleep I should imagine. He's exhausted. Rode straight through."

Slowly, Carr straightened. "I see."

Tunbridge took a deep breath and pushed himself upright from the desk. "I have served you well these many years, Carr."

"Ay? Oh. Yes," Carr acknowledged distractedly.

No more George. How very ironic. He'd intended to return to London this winter regardless of the old king's banishment of him. He'd finally accrued enough "influences"—his fingertips caressed the stack of papers to his right—to defy the edict that had exiled him to Scotland.

Now, with that sentence finally reprieved he could . . . by God! He could marry again!

"Your Grace?"

Tunbridge broke through his thoughts. He was inclined to feel magnanimous toward the bearer of such wonderful news. "Yes?"

"You'll want to alert your staff."

"Good idea, Tunbridge. I shall set them to packing forthwith. I don't suppose I can expect to leave before week's end?"

"Sir?" Tunbridge blinked.

"Well, you don't think I'd leave my treasures behind here? The place can burn for all I care but not before I divest it of its valuables." Carr pulled his stack of correspondence toward him. "I'll want all the silver and jewelry to come directly with me. The paintings and statuary should follow in wagons at the same time—art makes a fine investment and that's as good a piece of financial advice as ever you're likely to get."

"Ah, yes, sir. Thank you."

"Come, come, Tunbridge. Why do you look so confused?"

"I was speaking of alerting the staff to the matter of tonight's masque."

"What of the masque?" He would need to see about those tapestries, too. Hideous gloomy things but he'd been told they were worth a pretty penny.

"The king has died. The castle must go into mourning."

Mourning, when all he wanted to do was celebrate? Nonsense. Besides, with George's death things between him and Janet had suddenly, drastically, changed. The thought brought with it a smile.

He was rushing his fences. First he needed to summon Janet to him and in order to do that he needed to see Favor Donne. Alone. It had been a task he'd yet to achieve; it would prove impossible if she followed what would become an exodus heading back to London for the king's funeral.

"You say Edgar has retired to his chambers. Did he come with any others?"

"No."

"Did he speak to anyone else?"

"No," Tunbridge said thoughtfully. "The Highgates arrived with a large party as we spoke but poor Edgar was so exhausted he barely nodded before seeking his bed."

"Then the Highgates know nothing of the king's death."

"That's correct."

Carr's glance fell to the drawer that held his special elixirs. "Tunbridge, you will leave for London on the morrow. In the meantime keep to your room. That way no one can accuse you of keeping the sovereign's death secret, nor me of hearing and then disregarding it."

"You are risking a great deal," Tunbridge said. "There are those who would call knowingly holding a revelry during a period of national mourning sedition. What if Edgar tells someone?"

"Edgar," Carr said smoothly, "will not be waking anytime soon. His trip, which you already noted left him depleted, has turned into something more dire." He tapped his chin thoughtfully.

"But what of his servants?"

"I shall send them away. What with Edgar's undiagnosed malady, I cannot risk the health of my guests by exposing them to possible contaminants."

"They may already have told other servants."

Carr sighed. He was fast tiring of Tunbridge's fretfulness. Most unmanly. He'd been considering giving Tunbridge back the deed to his family manse. Now he saw that the fellow didn't deserve such a gift.

"Let them," Carr said. "There have been rumors of George's death half a dozen times in as many years. Who is going to blame me for not listening to servants' gossip?"

"You have, as always, accounted for every contingency," Tunbridge said admiringly.

"Yes," Carr said, "I have."

"And soon you will reign once more in London, powerful, respected, feared, courted—"

"Yes, yes, yes. Out with it, Tunbridge before your tongue rots the leather of my new boots."

The thin, pale man grew paler. Bloodless white outlined the flesh about his narrow lips.

"Well?"

"You've achieved your goal without having to threaten, blackmail, or coerce another man."

"Yes," Carr said, wondering a little at the dissatisfaction that suddenly crept over him. "So?"

"You don't need me anymore."

"I never did need you, Tunbridge. I found you convenient." Carr smiled. "I still do."

The heat was stultifying and the racket ear-splitting. The spectacle of three hundred people vying to be the brightest, the gaudiest, and the most outrageous hurt the eye and robbed breath from the lungs. Carr had declared this to be Wanton's Blush's Last Masque and since rumors had spread that Carr intended to quit Wanton's Blush for London, his guests were rabidly determined to make the ball memorable.

Encased in bizarre costumes, burdened by towering headdresses and extravagant wigs, they strutted about with a formality belied by the open leer that was their universal expression, made prim by clothes stiff with gems, brilliants, and paste. Like grotesque hedgehogs in bejeweled armor, they circled the rooms in a stately waddle, undressing each other with their eyes.

And, truth be told, they'd not much undressing to do. Skirts dragged the floor under the weight of pearl and crystal and heavy gold trim. Coats crunched as gemstones grated against each other with the slightest movement. But other parts of their anatomy were bare—both men's and women's—displaying only salved and scented flesh. A great deal of flesh.

There was no risk. For who could tell who hid beneath Prospero's black silk domino, or the feathered mask of the Swan Queen? And if the answer to that was "many," few would admit it. For anonymity was the *raison d'être* of a masque. Tonight no one would know with whom they flirted and danced and dallied.

Except Carr. He knew every one of his guests' identities. Later he would make certain they all knew it. At the moment, however, he cared little who groped whom. Only one woman concerned him. His little Scot.

He'd spotted her a few minutes earlier. He was still amazed by her audacity even though Miss Donne was one of the few women who had not contrived to bare at least one breast.

She'd found another way to excite the most jaded of interest.

She wore an *arisaid,* the traditional plaid scarf of the Highland Scotswoman, prohibited since 1747 in an act of Parliament. Or rather *they'd* dressed themselves in plaid. This could only be Janet's unbiddable spirit at work.

The long rectangular piece of rough silk plaid veiled her black hair and hung over the lose sacque gown she wore. Not a particularly modish dress, being in vogue some twenty years earlier, but attractive on her.

Favor was speaking to her doughy and doughty old aunt, a pudding in unstructured puce draperies with a serpent perched atop her cap and a semitransparent veil pinned over her mouth. 'Sblood, the woman was portraying Cleopatra.

Carr hailed a footman carrying a tray of punch-filled cups. It was time to address the problem posed by his dead—yet still amazingly obstinate—wife. He withdrew the vial containing Pala's elixir and emptied it into a cup and then, careful not to spill any, wove his way through the crowd.

"Mrs. Douglas," he greeted the old lady when he'd reached them. He inclined his head toward Favor. "Miss Donne."

She'd seen him coming. The mask she wore over her eyes did not conceal the way her full lower lip tightened with aversion. Before daylight, he swore, he would chew on that provocative lip and she would sigh with pleasure for it.

"Lord Carr!" The aunt giggled into her plump, glove-clad hand. "Such an extravagant *soirée*! I've never seen the like."

"Nor hope to again," Favor said sweetly, and then, in answer to her chaperone's gasp, "How could I? How could anything compare to . . . this?" She waved toward a satyr chasing Lucrezia Borgia. "I would never dare to imagine I could experience another like it."

Carr smiled. "You might experience its like and more, Miss Donne, if you continue to honor me with your presence."

"But that's most unlikely, isn't it?" the aunt interjected mournfully. "However much my dear niece might desire it otherwise."

"Why is that, Mrs. Douglas?"

"You'll be going to London soon, or so 'tis rumored, and we, perforce, will retire to Thomas's manor. We couldn't possibly venture to London without Thomas and heaven alone knows how long the dear boy will be gone. It may be months or years before he's back."

"I see." He stared into Favor's shadowed eyes. "Perhaps I can yet find some way to enjoy Miss Donne's company."

He heard the aunt's sharp inhalation, a response he'd hoped to draw from Favor. The girl must know he was implying marriage. And even if she had currently found his person distressing, shouldn't Janet be supplanting the girl's reaction with her own rapturous response to the hinted promise?

Instead Favor had frozen. Frowning, Carr sought an answer. Happily, one was not long in coming. She simply didn't dare believe that she'd understood him correctly. She was stunned by the honor he bestowed on her.

Given that, he would forgive her lack of enthusiasm.

"Miss Donne, I don't believe I've mentioned how delightful you look. I saw you across the room and remarked it immediately. But that"—he motioned toward the heathenish *arisaid*—"looks rather warm. So I've brought you a punch to cool you."

He held out the cup of punch.

"Thank you," Favor answered, and began reaching for the cup but suddenly changed her mind and withdrew her hand. Her smile became shy. She backed up a step, leaving him standing there with cup still extended.

"A minute, sir, before I accept your kind offer. Tell me"—she placed her hand on her hips, striking a winsome pose—"can you tell who I am?"

Damn the chit. He just wanted her to take the damn cup of punch and drain it down.

"No," he said as pleasantly as possible. "I can't. Here." He thrust the cup at her. She ignored it.

"Oh, *do* guess!" she pleaded, unexpectedly playful.

Her aunt, her gaze fixed on her niece, nodded slowly. "She's a child still," she said, "and will have her games as all children must. Pray indulge her, Lord Carr."

"I don't know," he exclaimed in exasperation. She was, indeed, frolicsome and girlish. He'd always found both qualities tiresome. "Queen Boadicea?"

"No . . ." She waggled her finger playfully.

"Enough," he snapped. "Who are you, then?"

"Janet McClairen. Your dead wife."

The cup fell from his hand and hit the floor; any sound it might have made swallowed by the surrounding din.

"What did you say?" He stepped toward her, crushing the cup beneath his foot. *"How came you by the idea to dress as my wife?"*

She shrank back, eyeing him fearfully.

"I found th-this in a box at the bottom of the—the chest in my b-bedchamber!"

"Impossible!" He'd had all of Janet's belongings removed and stored in the farthest reaches of the castle. Nothing of hers remained in these inhabited wings. Unless Janet herself . . .

"*Why* did you dress as my first wife?"

"I found the *arisaid*. Someone had told me the story of the first ball held at Wanton's Blush"—her lip trembled—"and how your wife didn't come down and your guests went searching for her. I heard how they first found her scarf and then spied her but before they could get to her body, it was swept out to sea. I'd heard, too, how devoted you were and I thought—" She hesitated. "It just seemed right that for this last masque she should be here, too."

The aunt's gaze flickered nervously between them. "She didn't mean any harm. It's my fault if she's offended you. I should have asked her who she was impersonating."

"No," Carr replied. "I know she meant no harm. I was taken aback because I had been thinking of wives and marriage and how very alone I am." He reached out and secured one of Favor's hands. It lay limply in his own. "Then to suddenly hear my wife's name on Miss Donne's lips . . . ! It seemed more than happenstance, indeed, a sign."

"Ah!" The aunt clasped her hands at her ample bosom in an attitude of rapture.

Favor wet her lips. "I cannot begin to fathom your meaning, sir," she whispered.

"Really? I can," Fia pronounced. Carr looked around to find his daughter standing at his elbow. She was dressed all in silver and white satin, even to the slight mask over her eyes. Long, soft feathers plaited in her hair nodded in the soft currents of air. More feathers covered her shoulders and the long, tight sleeves of her dress. She'd dressed as the Swan Princess.

"I have years of experience in interpreting everything Carr says. Should I translate, Miss Donne?" Fia asked.

"Ah, Fia my dear," Carr acknowledged her coldly. "Forgive my daughter, ladies. One would think she was fresh from the nursery with such manners. I'm afraid I've overindulged her. She continually makes the unwarranted assumption that she is welcomed everywhere."

Instead of being cut to the quick as he'd intended, Fia laughed. He should have known his sarcasm would be lost on her.

"Don't fret, Carr. I shall take myself off before you"—she glanced at Favor—"end up on your knees." Before he could respond, she drifted away.

"Whatever could she mean?" the aunt chirped.

"I am sure I couldn't fathom," Favor said forcefully. Her skin had turned very pale.

"Soon you will not have to fathom anything. I will reveal all." He gazed tenderly down at her, cursing himself for dropping the love potion. Ah, well. The night was young. He'd simply refill the vial and return. Or he could try . . .

"Mrs. Douglas"—he smiled respectfully at the old woman—"though I am a man in the prime of my life and one of both experience and sophistication, I find myself in the odd position of having to beg your leave to be private with your niece."

"Oh?" The aunt blinked myopically. "Oh. Oh no, sir! Thomas would never forgive me were I to countenance such goings-on. My niece is a well-brought-up young girl, sir, not some light-skirts!"

So, the fluffy little lap pisser dared lift her lips and reveal her ancient teeth at him, eh? "Of course. How thoughtless of me."

"Thoughtless, indeed, sir. And one gets only one chance to be careless with so lovely a lady."

Carr turned irritably toward the male voice, prepared to spear the interloper with a quelling glare. He found himself staring into the broad tanned throat of a . . . well, damned if he knew what the Goliath-sized creature was supposed to be. A jinn, perhaps.

The newcomer wore a long coat in an oriental style, made of bronzy satin figured with geometric patterns. Over one broad shoulder hung a plum-colored cape. A huge turban wound above a face stained dark as a Moor's.

Jinn or Turk, Carr thought, eyeing the scimitar suspended from the man's waist. He looked up and met the rogue's interested gaze. He was unfamiliar. "You must have come with Highgate this afternoon, sir."

The tall man inclined his head.

"I don't have your name."

"You may call me Mahomet."

"May I?" Carr stretched his lips into a host's smile. "How gracious of you."

'Struth! Whose idiot idea had this bloody masque been anyway? Everywhere he met impertinence. He'd had enough of it. He'd find out this bastard's name tomorrow, if it still interested him. Right now he needed to refill that vial.

The Turk shouldered his way past Carr to Favor's side. She stared up at him with wide-eyed trepidation. "If I might have the pleasure of this lovely Scottish lassie's company I can promise nothing more unacceptable than a dance." Though he spoke to Mrs. Douglas his eyes never left Favor's pale face. "Miss?"

"Ach," demurred the auntie, clucking fearsomely. "I don't know you, sir and—"

"Ah!" The tall Turk swung his head around, displaying a very large, very white set of teeth. "But I came with Highgate, one of Lord Carr's special friends! Surely that's voucher enough?"

He'd caught the old bitch off guard and she knew it, Carr thought. His eyes narrowed appreciatively on this unexpected rival. Mrs. Douglas didn't dare refuse him now lest she insult her host.

"Miss Donne?" The Turk held out his hand.

Slowly, mutely, Favor nodded and laid her hand within his great, strong-looking paw. His fingers closed tightly on hers.

And she clenched his in turn.

"Ah! Allah blesses me!" The tall Turk laughed in triumph and took her arm, sweeping her into the crowd as he led her to the ballroom. Immediately, Mrs. Douglas mumbled an apology and hied off in pursuit, leaving Carr alone.

Yes. He would still be interested in the man's name come the morrow. He felt certain of it.

CHAPTER 25

"**Y**ou must be mad!" Favor gasped as Rafe swung her in a dizzying circle. "Do you know who that was?"

"Who? The fellow in the lilac wig?" Rafe caught Favor's hand and laid it on his forearm. He kept his own hand over hers, his fingertips lightly stroking her wrists, sending shivers of pleasure coursing up her arm as they commenced the sedate promenade the dance prescribed.

"Favor?" His sherry-brown eyes warmed with knowledge.

"Hm?" Favor murmured, distracted by his caresses.

"Is that the fellow you meant?"

"Hm . . . ? Yes. Yes! That, my boy, was Lord Carr."

He drew back in mock horror. "Say not so! The Demon Earl himself? But where is his tail? His horns?"

"Who could see horns under all that hideous purple hair?" Favor muttered, winning Rafe's laughter. She eyed him severely. "Aye. We'll see how amused you are when Carr has you hauled out and whipped until your back is nothing but shredded flesh."

He grinned. "Would you care?"

She felt herself blush and looked away. "No."

"You would."

She heard the tender smile in his voice and could not deny him. "Yes."

His hand pressed hers and she listed toward him, pulled by a need to be nearer, much nearer than this too public place allowed. A sense of urgency underscored that desire.

Carr was going to offer for her. Possibly tonight, but if not, soon. He'd all but declared himself already. Wherever he'd gone, soon he'd come back and expect her to fawn over him. As would Muira.

She couldn't be here when he returned. She glanced at Rafe. A lightness of expression had gentled his aggressive profile. Her declaration had pleased him because, she suddenly understood, he cared for her. She sensed it in the deepest part of her, knew the truth of it just as surely as she knew . . .

"I love you."

His head whipped around. He pulled up short in the middle of the dance floor, arrested in midstride. He gripped her arms, turning her to face him. He stared down at her, his brows snapped together in concentration as he searched her face.

Around them the other couples, thrown out of their patterned dance, milled and hesitated and finally split and flowed on either side of them, leaving them an island in a river of streaming satin.

"What?"

"I love you, Rafe. You knew that though, didn't you?" she said simply.

"No," he said faintly. "No. I didn't."

He looked up as though searching the heavens for inspiration. She tugged lightly on his arm; they'd already attracted far too much attention. Like a sleepwalker, Rafe moved back into the dance steps, his rhythm wanting, his steps mechanical and graceless.

On the far side of the room Favor glimpsed Muira's furious mien, her glare lethal enough to kill at any closer range. If Favor had her way, that's as near as Muira would come to her for the rest of the night.

She looked up at Rafe. He still appeared bemused. She supposed she ought to feel like a slattern for being so forward. She didn't. She'd no time to be less. She had one night. This night.

There would be no happy ending for her and Rafe. He was a thief and an escaped prisoner, without family, future, or even, she suspected in spite of his denial, a surname. Not that he need envy those.

She had a family . . . a clan to which she owed a debt that only one act could repay. She'd a surname . . . which kept her chained to her past as inescapably as Rafe's manacles had once chained him to the prison walls. And she had a future . . . as Lady Carr.

She owed her clan that. But she did not owe Carr anything. Including the privilege of breaking her maidenhead. That gift she would insist on giving in love, not sacrifice. To Rafe.

"Let's leave here," she whispered.

"What?" Dear, reckless, baffled Rafe.

"I want to be alone with you. But if my aunt makes it across the ballroom—a task she's presently engaged upon—I guarantee she'll keep me by her side the rest of the night." Rafe looked in the direction she indicated. Muira had waded into the thick ring of spectators lining the dance floor. Her step was determined, her mouth grim. "Not only will we be unable to share another dance but we won't trade another unchaperoned phrase."

It was threat enough. Without another word, Rafe took hold her arm, pulling her after him as he strode toward the opposite side of the room.

Muira elbowed her way through the last of the posing and primping fools that stood between her and the dance floor. She was sweating profusely under the layers of stuffing and wadding that formed "Mrs. Douglas's" matronly figure. Dark rings circled her armpits and she could feel the paste, made of sweat and powder, trickling down the side of her face.

Damn the girl to bloody hell! Now she'd need to go and repair her makeup before the welt on her cheek was laid bare. And where was the little bitch anyway? A moment ago she'd been panting up at that big, dark-skinned man as if she'd seen Robert the Bruce himself. And him looking down at her like a starving man at a feast . . .

She scanned the dance floor. It only took a few minutes to discern that they were no longer on it. Furiously, Muira began stalking the perimeter of the room but the crush was growing by the minute and soon she could see nothing.

She'd no choice but to give up. No one knew Wanton's Blush better than she, but the castle was huge and the places they might have gone too numerous to count. Besides, Carr would reappear soon. She couldn't take the chance of Favor's being with Carr unchaperoned. She didn't trust the chit not to make a bloody hash of it.

No. She would just have to wait, bide her time and bite her tongue. If Carr asked after Favor, she'd make excuses he would swallow. She'd spent too many years half-starved and half-frozen, plotting and planning and begging and stealing her way to this place, to this point in time. All for the sake of her clan. For the McClairens.

And tomorrow she would make sure Favor McClairen understood just what that meant.

"You don't even know me," Raine said. He clasped her shoulders lightly, pushing her back against the tapestry-covered wall. They were in one of the castle's solars, a chamber attached to what had once been the private quarters of Lizabet McClairen, the first lady of Maiden's Blush.

Favor touched his face. "I know you."

He shook his head in patent disbelief. She was young and he'd be-friended her in a place populated by predators. Of course she thought she loved him.

"I am"—*dying with hope I know to be hopeless*—"honored by your words."

The gentle comedown he'd hoped to give her did not have the desired effect. She smiled tenderly.

"I should hope so. I don't give my heart readily." One fingertip swept along his lower lip. "Lud, you have a beautiful mouth."

"Stop that!" He sounded panicked, which he was. "You're mistaken. You must be. How can you give a thief and blackmailer, a man you mistrust—and with ample cause, I do admit—your love?"

"Had I any choice perhaps I would heed your sage advice," she mur-mured, "but my heart, graceless thing, did not ask my opinion. It loved without first seeking my counsel."

"You speak too sweetly and wake a craving for more such words." *Such sweet words that I would give anything to believe.*

He dared not move. Her hand brushed down his chin and traced his jaw, trailing a lightning strike of sensation. She covered the pulse beating at the base of his throat with her palm.

"Think you so? 'Tis you who make me a poetess then. And I thank Him who gave me so canny a tongue. But I must return the compliment yet complain, for, in truth, sir, your tongue has its own sweet tricks that I do crave to learn." Her other hand had moved up, unbuttoning the ancient Persian coat and pulling loose the strings tying his shirt.

"How can I get you to divulge your secrets? I would recite you more poetry but, sir," she whispered, "longing takes my breath away."

He groaned. His eyes shut. Her hand burrowed under his shirt, stroking his naked chest.

It was all too much.

With a growl, he wrapped his arms about her waist. He lifted her slight form, imprisoning her between the wall and his body. His mouth slanted over hers, his tongue thrust between her lips, seeking and finding the sweet, warm interior and—blessed bounty!—her own eager tongue.

She denied him nothing, either by word or act. He swept her loose frock from her shoulder, baring one of her breasts to his greedy eyes. He cupped the firm pale globe gently. She whimpered with pleasure, pushing the tightening nipple against his palm.

Hungry, desperate and half-dazed with the unexpected heat of her response, he lowered his mouth and swirled his tongue against the silky brown aureole. Her hands came to life on his shoulders, biting deep into his muscles as her gasp set the ripe flesh to jiggling against his tongue. He suckled greedily, sweeping a hand under her buttock and lifting her higher against the wool-softened wall. The rich, crisp cloth of her skirt crumpled in his fists. Gossamer lace drifted over his arms. A creamy smooth thigh slid beneath his hand.

"Yes," she whispered rapturously, her eyelids fluttering half shut. "Please. Yes."

"Yes," he echoed, his lips sliding to the outer arc of her breast. He would drown in her physical response.

"Oh! Please. Don't stop," she pleaded when he sought a less urgent pace and he, both supplicant and sovereign, gladly complied.

He rucked her skirt up about her waist, inhaling sharply when he felt the warmth of her mons press tight against him, separated from her nakedness only by his breeches' thin material. Instinctively, he thrust against her.

Her mouth parted, revealing the erotic unevenness of her front teeth. He rolled his hips and her thighs fell apart.

"Make love to me," she said.

Love. Dear God. Yes, he wanted to make love to her, to love her, to give her some of the physical pleasure he knew this act could bring and in doing so find for himself that deeper . . . *something* he suddenly had cause to believe existed.

He had to think but he couldn't, not with her dampness seeping through his breeches and her gaze sultry and inviting. He tore his mouth from hers. She made a sound of protest. Lightly, he clasped her chin, turning her face away and resting his forehead on the wall beside her head. She took his free hand and lifted it to her mouth.

"I want you." A siren call. She didn't know what she asked.

Once, a decade earlier, she'd saved his life. He wouldn't ever again be the cause of her anguish or her guilt. He couldn't bed her and risk ruining her future. While he put no great store in virginity, most men did. And Favor, if what she'd told him had been true, had nothing else to offer a groom but the presumed paternity of her child. She herself had once told him it was the only thing of value she owned.

Bloody, bloody son of a bitch! If only he'd found the bleeding jewels. If only her name wasn't McClairen. If only she would tell him to stop . . .

But she didn't. She nipped the tender pads at the base of each finger before sucking on his thumb's knuckle. "You have the most beautiful hands. I want to know what artistry they might work on my flesh."

Good intentions faded. His clasp on her chin became a caress. "You don't want this. It isn't going to lead to some blessed union, Favor," he rasped out. "I have nothing. Nothing at all to offer you."

"You have your name," she suggested in a whisper as fearful as it was hesitant.

God, yes. His name. "I assure you, my name would be no recommendation to you."

She came back with a reply at once. "I don't care."

"I do! Damn it, don't you think I want to feel you under me, around me?" he ground out. "I want to drink your cries, I want to make you scream with pleasure. I want to take you. Now. Here."

"Yes!" One of her long thighs climbed up his leg and hooked over his hip. She rocked her pelvis against him. Desire careened through him, splintering his resolve.

"You can't. We can't." His breath had grown thick in his chest; his body burgeoned with need.

She tipped her upper body away from his and yanked his shirt open. Her expression was heated with desire, fixed with determination. She started at his throat and worked down his chest, her fingers flowing over his pectorals, her nails raking through the soft hair, past the thickened V of fur low at his waist, beneath the waistband of his breeches. He held his breath.

Her hand closed about his cock. He jerked at the contact, impaled by want, torn by conflicting desires. A rumbling growl issued from deep in his throat.

"You're a virgin," he panted, his eyes hot and accusing. It was an act of masochism holding himself still like this, fighting to retain his self-control.

Her hand tightened into a silky fist and slid down over his throbbing shaft. Sweat shimmered on his forehead and above his upper lip. His body trembled. She leaned back, still holding him, and whispered, "No, I'm not."

Her words shredded what was left of his resistance.

It ought to make no difference. He still had nothing to give her, no future, no name, no recompense for a childhood destroyed. But if he had nothing to give her, at least he couldn't hurt her by taking her virginity away.

"Please," she said, her hips rocking against him in a thought-destroying rhythm. She released him, pulling his head down to hers, her mouth open and seeking, the flavor of desperation on her tongue and in the tightness with which her arms wrapped around him.

He made no further attempts at chivalry. He reached between them and wrenched the cloth away from his straining manhood. Then he found her opening and pushed his finger into the sleek cleft, found her ready, wet and heated.

He moved his finger inside of her, testing, stimulating. Her interior muscles clamped tight about him, a little sob—pleasure? pain?—fanned his ear as she nestled her face against his throat. He withdrew his finger and found the nubbin hidden between the plump folds of her sex. He flicked it gingerly, eliciting from her a breathy series of gasps.

He prayed for strength and plucked again, in short, rhythmic pulls. She keened, trying to mount higher on him, her shoes falling to the floor with a dull thud, as her feet climbed the backs of his calves.

"Little falcon," he urged. "Let me pleasure you. Let me show you."

Her hips surged forward to comply in a rough, bucking rhythm. She moved in gorgeous abandonment, her head thrown back, her hair streaming past her hips, her arms taut with strain.

He licked the salty moisture from the base of her throat. His own arousal was near a fever pitch now, contained only by his need to see her climax, to be fully aware of each second of her crisis and to revel in the knowledge that he'd brought her there.

"Please!" she sobbed.

"Yes." His hand worked deftly between her legs, his gaze growing hot and fiercely possessive.

He'd not long to wait. Her thighs clamped about his hips, her toes flexed with exertion. She arched, her spine curving over his arm, her skirts piled about her waist, her breasts bare in the soft shadows.

"Oh, please. I can't . . . I can't . . ."

"Yes. Yes. And yes," he murmured, stroking the damp hair from her face as he drove her toward fulfillment.

Her gaze found his, focused. "Rafe!"

Rafe, not Raine. He refused to think. He would not think. He would just feel.

And then her fierce pants dissolved into a high cry of effort that broke into the sweetest sound he'd ever heard.

He positioned himself and pushed into her heated core. Her shallow pants of repletion became a single sob. She was tight. Some beast within purred with the evidence of her relative innocence. He pushed harder. Her arms tightened convulsively about his throat.

"Mine," he intoned, surging slowly forward.

She moved, not in unison with him, but as though to avoid the deeper coupling he sought. He hesitated.

"Yes," she whispered.

He set his hands beneath her thighs, spreading her legs wider and with one long thrust came up against a barrier. Her maidenhead. He clenched his teeth in a feral snarl, near violent with frustration, desire building to a near explosive pitch in his loins. He trembled. He swore.

"You're a bloody virgin! Aren't you?"

She was crying.

"Aren't you?"

"Yes!"

He jerked his swollen member out of her, heedless of his roughness until he heard her gasp of pain. He looked down. Her brilliant eyes were filled with despair. Tears streamed down her face. With a groan he wrapped his hand about the back of her head and dragged her into his arms.

She'd only wanted to gift him with her maidenhead. He could not rail against her for that. But rail he could against all else.

He threw back his head and cursed the heavens and his fate with every foul and blasphemous word he knew. He would have howled in fury but for fear of scaring her even more. So he simply stood, cursing in dark and vehement tones while stroking her head with exquisite tenderness.

CHAPTER 26

Muira flung herself down from the carriage and reached back, grabbing hold of Favor's arm and jerking her out. Favor stumbled and fell to her knees in the mud, staining the bright scarlet skirts of her antique Highland gown.

"Where are we?" she asked, blinking into the bright morning sun, dazed with anguish and lack of sleep. She'd returned to her room last night to find Muira waiting in the hall. Wordlessly, Muira had seized her arm and dragged her down the corridor, ignoring Favor's stammered demands for an explanation as well as the speculative gazes that followed them out the back door to the stable yard where Jamie had awaited them atop Thomas's carriage.

Favor had resisted then, but Muira had backhanded her across the face, stunning her with the brutal strength of her blow. She'd shoved Favor into the carriage and followed her in, yanking the door shut and slamming her hand against the ceiling, calling out for Jamie to whip up the horses.

They'd driven most of the night. Muira had settled in the corner and stabbed Favor with a malevolent glare. Favor had been bitterly unsurprised by how quickly she'd gone from Rafe's passionate embrace and heated words to this cold, silent carriage on a nameless road.

"Where are we?" Favor repeated now.

"You don't know?" Muira seized hold of Favor's hair and yanked her head up, half hauling her to her feet. "Look around!"

"Muira, careful. She's but a girl . . ." Jamie objected from atop the carriage.

Muira swung round, bruising Favor's upper arm. *"Girl,* is she?" she hissed. "Well, this *girl* has jeopardized everything we've worked and sacrificed for, all so she can rut with some pretty English hound!"

An expression of shocked betrayal flashed over Jamie's rough features at Muira's accusation. "Not quite the little novitiate you'd imagined, is she, Jamie me boy?"

Jamie turned his head, fixing his gaze on the horizon.

"It wasn't like that," Favor whispered.

"Wasn't like what?" Muira turned on her. "Wasn't he any good then, lassie? Didn't he spread your legs wide and make you scream with it?"

Favor bit hard on the inner flesh of her cheeks. She wouldn't weep. Not in front of this woman. No matter how much she wanted to—and God knew she wanted to break down and cry.

When she'd agreed to Muira's plan she hadn't known what she would be giving up. Now she did. Now she knew just what and just whom she was losing. And that knowledge threatened to swallow her whole.

"Well?" Muira demanded brightly. "Didna scream, eh?" She pointed behind Favor. *"They* did."

She said it so matter-of-factly, so conversationally, that for a moment Favor did not grasp her meaning.

With a sense of inevitability, she looked around. Backed by a swollen leaden sky, a tower's rough shell stood wearily in the misting rain. The roof was gone, the western wall tumbled, exposing the rooms on the second story. Within, black rotted beams leaned against bare interior walls. It was the room where Favor's mother had birthed her stillborn brother and then, dying in the process, given Favor her fateful charge. The rain's soft susurration could not conceal her mother's weak voice.

"They're killing my sons!" She'd grasped Favor's hand, but her clasp was weak and her skin hot and dry. *"You* must *stop them, Favor. There's no one else."*

"How?"

"I don't know!" her mother's voice had risen frantically. *"But you must. If they kill Carr's son, the king will never have mercy on mine. They'll be gutted and hanged by month's end and not all your father's pleading will stop it. Go, Favor. Stop them!"*

And she had.

"Do you know where you are now?" Muira's voice had lost its savagery, becoming nearly gentle. She released Favor's arm and moved about the muddy ground with a dazed look of wonder, like a Muslim in Mecca.

"There is where Cam McClairen died," she said, pointing. "That great rock there, that split his head as he fell from a soldier's blow."

She turned, her skirts belling out as lightly as a girl on a dance floor. "And here is where my Bobbie was killed. He was my youngest, ever falling over his own feet."

She smiled at Favor in bizarre camaraderie, as though they were two women chatting about their family's foibles. "He took a lead ball in his brain." She pursed her lip and nodded. "Quick at least, not like his father, whose gut was split open and took three days to die."

Favor's stomach rose, sickened by the light voice reciting the horrendous memories she shared: screaming men, horses impaled, blood licked by torchlight, and the pure snow glistening on the mountainside far away.

Muira returned and wrapped her arm about Favor's waist. Pulling lightly, she began walking her toward the tower's arched gate. "Did you see who fell and who didn't? Who gave as good as he got? I would have stayed and fought, but as soon as we saw the redcoats the men shoved us down into the moat to hide."

She cocked her head. "I didn't see much. But you . . . you were right in the thick of it the whole time, clinging to that Merrick boy like a limpet. I always wanted to know if my men acquitted themselves well. Did they?"

"I couldn't say," Favor whispered, images of horrors piling up in her mind's eye.

Muira nodded understandingly. "Aye. It was dark and over so quick and you didn't know any of those men now, did you?"

She stopped just short of the gate. Favor began to tremble. Muira didn't appear to notice; she was scowling. "Jamie? Was it Russell who was cut down here? 'Faith, I be growing old for I canna remember whether it was Russell or Gavin Fraser. 'Twas Russell, was it not?"

"Aye," Jamie called back. "Russell."

Muira brightened, sighing with pleasure. "I dinna forget then," she said, and tugged Favor back into motion. "Jamie was here, too, did you know? Being so big, they made him hold the cattle. But when the redcoats came down the horses panicked and bolted and just plain ran over Jamie Craigg. He came to his senses a few days later. In my house."

Her knees felt liquid and weak. The mud sucked at her shoes as she stumbled forth. The mist soaked her uncovered head, condensed on her frozen flesh, and leaked down her cheeks.

"I have it all in here," Muira confided, touching her free hand to her temple. "Each moment. Each cry. Like acid it burned its way into my brain so that everything I see, I see overlaid with the images from that night. Like a shadow play on my every thought . . ." Her voice trailed off.

The shivering in Favor's body had become shaking. She could hear her teeth clattering against each other. They stopped at the gate.

"Right here is where you stood." She gave Favor a little shove and then backed up. "I stood . . . yes. Right there. Imagine that, Favor. For a few minutes nine years ago I was within reach of you . . . and him. And after, when they'd taken him away and left you standing here, barefoot and cold, your night rail soaked with blood, I could have taken my wounded and gone, leaving you here."

The smile twisted, became ugly. "I would have, too, if I'd known you would betray us twice."

She *was* going to be sick. Her head spun and her knees knocked together. She didn't want to be here. She'd never wanted to come back here. All that was here was terror, terror and a boy's filthy, blood-slick torso, the shouts of men, the stench of gunpowder, and . . . and the gentle, pitying brush of a rapist's lips against the top of her head—the only bit of comfort in that night, given by her enemy and yet one she'd gladly accepted, one she'd never forgive herself for accepting.

She wrapped her arms around her waist and hugged tightly, afraid that if she let go she would burst into a million fragments and be lost in a black, all-consuming abyss.

"You see it again now, don't you, Favor?" Muira asked gently. "You'd forgotten, hadn't you? Aye, I thought it was so. I didn't think anyone who remembered could fail us."

Numbly she nodded.

"Seventeen men and boys of clan McClairen died that night. Those that didn't die, I patched together. Two died later. That's what saving that rapist did, Favor."

"Muira!" Jamie suddenly called out, his voice worried.

The gentleness bled from Muira's eyes. "Quiet you, Jamie! She saved the life of a rapist and nineteen died because of it."

Muira turned back to Favor, her expression fierce and commanding.

"The nine men that lived have worked as hard as I for restitution. They're smugglers and thieves, hard laborers and servants now, struggling to earn enough not only for the families of them that died, but also for you. So that *you* could become Lady Carr and return the land and the castle to us.

"That's where the money for your convent and your clothes and your jewels came from, Favor. That's who you've betrayed."

"No!" Favor cried weakly. How could she have forgotten? How could she have for a minute risked what they'd worked so hard to achieve?

"Are you ready to be Carr's bride?"

Numbly, Favor nodded.

Raine prowled through the shrouded empty rooms and dark echoing corridors, an animal set loose in a graveyard. Favor had not come to him yesterday, nor had she come today. Last night, he'd waited high above the ballroom for her to appear, suffused with a feeling such as he'd never known. His heart thumped thickly in his chest; his breath lodged in his throat.

He was, he realized, afraid. Afraid she'd regretted it. All of it. Her words, her passion . . . her love. But then she'd entered at Carr's side, clinging to his arm like an invalid. Her face was white, her gait unsteady.

A new fear swelled, eclipsing the other. Was she ill? The thought tormented him until finally, late last night, he'd gone to her room. She wasn't there and a word with a scurrying maid informed him that she slept in her chaperone's room.

All day he'd watched, trying to catch sight of her. At noon he'd seen her being hustled from the orangery by her aunt. Again her gait had been unsteady.

Now it was late afternoon. If he did not speak to her and discover if she was, indeed, unwell and if so, with what and to what extent, he would go mad. He *was* going mad. And he'd never been one to wait.

Without another thought, he strode to the room where he slept and snatched his coat from the table where he'd thrown it. He shrugged into it, heading down the empty hallway to the tower door. From there he followed the spiraling staircase to the main floor and opened the door leading to the north wing.

Few people were about in the great salon. A cluster of aged *roués* played hazard at a green baize-covered table while a single footman kept watch on the decanter sitting on the floor beside them. A woman attended by a phalanx of gentlemen stood at the great leaded window looking out over the terrace below. She turned and caught sight of him.

It was his sister, Fia. He wished that he'd known her better as a child. But Carr had always kept the little princess far away from her brothers and when they had seen her, she'd seldom spoken, only watched them with the same considering expression she now wore. Or had that expression been wistfulness?

A little frown turned her lips; she glanced outside and then came toward him. The men at her side began to follow, but she bade them stay. Raine watched her approach.

"Ah, Mister . . . ?" She waited. He regarded her evenly. "Mr. Mystery." She smiled. "But not Miss Donne's Mr. Mystery anymore, eh?"

"I do not take your meaning," he replied. "Do you know where Miss Donne is?"

"Oh, yes. I do, indeed," she said, snapping open the pearl-handled fan that hung from her wrist. "But first, aren't you curious about why I say you are no longer Miss Donne's . . . well, anything, I should imagine."

"Not particularly. I dislike word games."

"Oh, yes. I recall." At his startled look her dimples deepened. "From our previous encounter. The thing is, sir, I *do* like games. They hone one's intellect."

"Miss Fia, I am sure your gamesmanship is unsurpassed. Now, please—"

"You aren't Miss Donne's anything anymore because," Fia cut in, leaning close and raising her fan to conceal what she was about to say, "she's somebody else's something now. Somebody who would dislike very much finding out that she'd had a somebody before him." Her smile was buttery soft and innocent.

He stared at her, frozen. "Who?"

"That's the amazing part. If I hadn't heard him all but propose myself, I wouldn't have believed it!"

"Who?" he demanded.

"Why, my father." Abruptly her voice went flat. "Lord Carr."

No. She couldn't. He couldn't. No.

The word rolled through his mind, his thoughts, his heart. His entire being hummed denial. *No. No. No.*

"Fascinating creature, Miss Donne," Fia continued. "Why right this minute she's keeping company with a quart of gin, either celebrating her imminent engagement . . . or consoling herself."

"Where is she?"

"She's down below, on the terrace—" He'd left so there was no reason to give further direction. The brittle smile faded from Fia's face. "—brother."

"You can pack a trunk of my clothes for London tonight, Gunna. I shall be leaving on the morrow."

Gunna paused in helping Fia off with her day gown. "I didn't ken that yer father's plans had come so quick to profit," she said in amazement. "Still and all, how can he leave so sudden? There's so much to do."

"Carr knows nothing about my leaving," Fia said uninterestedly. "I shall be staying with Lady and Lord Wente. They have been kind enough to extend to me an open-ended invitation to be their guest."

She untied the ribbons around her waist. Her hoops collapsed to the floor. Gracefully, she stepped out of them. "Of course," she said, "Lord Wente's well-documented indebtedness to Tunbridge has, I fear, more to do with their gracious invitation than my own, ineluctable charm. Be that as it may, I intend to take them up on the offer. At least until I can secure my own establishment. Then I'll send for you, Gunna."

The chill left her expression and a degree of human warmth softened the hard brilliance of her eyes. "I promise, it won't be long."

"I don't understand," Gunna said, untying Fia's corset with trembling fingers. "Yer own establishment? Yer a girl, Fia, not a woman."

"Oh, Gunna," Fia said, "I've never been a 'girl' and well you know it."

"But it isn't done! Ye can't have yer own establishment. Carr will insist ye live with him. He'd never allow anything different. I . . ." She hesitated, her half-exposed face lined with worry. "I don't even know if he'll allow me to come to London."

The glimpse of vulnerability disappeared from Fia's face, leaving it coolly serene. "I will handle Carr, Gunna. I will handle everything: the house, the funds, and your arrival."

Gunna had no choice but to believe her. Fia had never made an idle promise in her life. "But why? Why now? Why not wait?"

Once more a shadow of the young girl that might have been crept into Fia's expression, looking out through the smooth, artificial, and ravishing visage with infinite sadness. "Because I am tired unto death of tragedies and I don't wish to stay and witness the one unfolding now."

CHAPTER 27

Favor tucked the heavy wool blanket around her legs and gazed with sullen satisfaction at the storm swelling above the castle turrets. She did not think she could quite endure a bright, clear day.

Morosely she motioned a servant to her side and indicated the empty glass on the wrought-iron table before her. He filled it from the bottle standing beside it again, bowed, and left. Favor lifted the glass in both hands and took a long draught before returning it unsteadily to its place.

The courtyard, which had been set up for a late-afternoon repast when the day had promised better, held only a few people. Indeed, it seemed to Favor that the castle was quickly emptying of its population. Everywhere, people were in the process of leaving this place. Godspeed to them.

Those left sat in little groups at tables, warming their palms on china cups filled with tea or coffee while Favor attempted to warm a deeper chill with a more potent distillation. She sat alone, her table somewhat removed from the others, the expression on her face dissuading any approach.

That's the way she wanted it. Getting drunk, Favor had decided, was a solitary occupation. She swept the glass up once more, tipped its contents into her mouth and grimaced as she swallowed.

"Does it help?"

Favor closed her eyes, despair sweeping over her. Of course he would come. Why should he stay away? Why would she think for a moment that common sense would have any influence at all over him and that he might realize the risk of discovery he ran?

"Go away," she muttered, refusing to look at him.

"I asked you if it helped." His voice was low and quite savage, as enraged as he'd sounded when he'd discovered her virginity two days before. But then he'd held her as though she were the most precious thing he'd ever known. He'd made love to her. She must cling to that sole benefit in this vile stew. Longings struggled to rise from deep in the cold, dark place she'd buried them.

She kept her eyes tightly shut, trying not to cry. Her nails dug fiercely into her palms. She would focus on that pain—but how, when this other one so utterly eclipsed it? She must just send him away. She'd not shed tears for Muira, she wouldn't shed them now.

He was waiting. She braced herself. She was a good liar. The best the convent of Sacré Coeur had ever known. She opened her eyes. He loomed above her table, his clenched fists planted on either side of her on the tabletop. His feet were spread wide as though bracing himself for a fight.

"Help with what?" she asked, furtively cataloguing each beloved feature—the amber color of his eyes, the texture of his beard-rough jaw, the breadth and height of him—hungrily hoarding each impression so that she would have his image for all time.

She did not worry about remembering his touch. The tensile strength in his fingers, the warmth of his mouth, his kiss, his whispered words, these were part of her now. She would no sooner forget them than she would forget how to breathe.

For a long moment they stared at each.

"Is it true?" he finally asked.

She'd begun shivering. She hadn't shivered since Muira had brought her back from the tower even though she was cold, so cold she doubted she'd ever be warm again.

"Is what true?" she asked feebly, dull-witted with gin. Ah, yes. Gin. The promised void. She snagged the glass and brought it to her lips. He seized her wrist and slammed it down on the table. The liquid leapt from the glass, spilling over the linen table covering.

She tried to pull free. Around them the low murmur of conversation died. Interested faces turned in their direction.

"Stop!" she whispered hoarsely. "The footman will be on you in a minute if you continue like this!"

His smile was feral and dark. "Let him."

"No, I beg you," she said. "You'll only be found out. Leave. *Please.*"

"Not before you tell me whether it's true," he ground out between clenched teeth. "Are you going to marry Carr?"

"What does it matter who I wed?" she asked in a low, taut voice. "You knew I was trolling for a trophy. What grander trophy than Carr? Who wealthier?"

"You little fool," he said, his eyes blazing. "You don't know what you're doing. You can't."

"Why are you suddenly so loathe to see me marry?" she asked bitterly, unable to contain her words. "Remember? You have nothing to offer in substitute. Not even a name. Or should I just acquiesce to your demands, give you *carte blanche* and become your mistress?"

He leaned forward. She could see his braced arms tremble with barely contained emotion. "If I don't already have a place in hell, that would surely win it," he said in a low, intense voice, "but by God, if that is what you want . . . if that would keep you from him . . . my hand is yours, Madame."

Hand, not heart.

"My path is set," she said vacantly. "I've other masters to serve besides myself."

His bronze skin dulled. He straightened, towering over her. "Carr will destroy you."

She shook her head. "I can manage Carr. You see, I have been *bred* to manage Carr."

"You fool," he said again with quiet venom. "You don't know what you're dealing with. If you won't have me, have some other knave. I swear to God, I could gladly give you to another if by doing so I kept you from him."

"I won't have another."

"Vanity or suicide, which one?" His eyes condemned her, his knuckles were white where he gripped the edge of the table.

"Neither. My family."

"Oh, Favor," he said, suddenly appealing to her. "Refuse them. You'll be doing them a benefit by setting them free from their expectations of you. Let them find their own fate and not rely on you to find it for them."

She stared at the sodden linen, soaked with the spilled oblivion she'd been courting to no avail all afternoon. The wind had picked up, driving most of the others in the courtyard inside though a few remained seated at a distance. One of them would tell Carr. Rafe would be exposed.

She rose unsteadily to her feet, separated from him by a table and a decade of obligation. "I have a debt I need to repay."

"A curse on your damned debt!" he grated out.

Too late. Already damned. She made a last appeal to him, trying to make him understand. "How could I live with myself if I asked less of myself than you would ask of yourself?"

He slammed his fist down on the table once more. His face was flushed, his teeth bared. "I don't give a bloody damn about your moral conscience. This is *Carr*. A man who's known to have killed three wives already. Is it your desire to be the fourth?"

"I will die—"

"Bloody right."

"—long after we marry. I will outlive him. I'm far younger than he—"

He surged across the table, grabbing her hand and dragging her halfway across it. She did not resist, even when he thrust his face within inches of hers. "You are a little girl," he said tightly. "A foolish little girl raised on stupid romantic notions about sacrificing yourself for a lofty and noble purpose. But you won't just sacrifice your youth, your beauty, your bravery and— Damn you! You'll sacrifice your *life*, Favor!

"You'll *die* at Carr's convenience and the only thing lofty about it will be the heights from which he'll pitch you like he did m—his first bride."

His words scared her, undermined her resolve, and she couldn't let that happen. She closed her eyes, forcing herself to return to that tower, to see her clansmen's broken bodies and hear their dying screams.

She'd been raised with this one purpose. And she would fulfill it but, the Blessed Virgin help her, she could no longer stand to see the bitter condemnation in Rafe's expression or hear the contempt in his voice. He'd been a lover. He deserved the truth.

"My name is Favor McClairen," she said dully. "The Earl of Carr robbed my family of this island, this castle. He stole not only our wealth but our heritage."

He was watching her, not only unimpressed but unsurprised. "Why must you be the one to regain it?"

"Because," she said, "ten years ago I was responsible for the massacre of those who could have fought for it."

"No." He shook his head.

"Carr's son had raped a novitiate and they brought him to—but you'd know, wouldn't you?" she asked. "If Ash Merrick told you about something as paltry as the Trust, he surely recited to you that fascinating bit of his family history. I see I'm right." Her smile felt like a grimace. "Well, Rafe, *I* was the girl who saved Raine Merrick's life. I delayed his hanging long enough for Carr to ride down on my clan with a hundred redcoats."

His face was hard, intractable. "You can't repay the dead with your life."

"I'm repaying the living," she said tiredly. "I'll marry Carr and I'll leave him. I'll return to France. He wouldn't dare follow me there. I'll wait for him to die and then—"

"And then what?" Rafe sneered.

"Then McClairen's Isle will belong to the McClairens once more. In Scotland a widow inherits her husband's property."

He shook his head, his eyes bleak, and shook his head again. "You cannot be so naive," he whispered. "Whoever put you to this cannot be so naive. 'Wait for Carr to die?' "

"It's what I'll do," she said. "It's what will happen."

He kept shaking his head, his lips curled back to reveal the edge of his teeth, a pulse pounding in his temple. "No," he said. "No. I'll stop it."

"No. You can't. You're too late." Her gaze fell before his, her voice dropped to a harsh whisper. "Carr proposed this morning. I accepted."

He went absolutely still. She closed her eyes, unable to stand the condemnation in his expression. His contempt washed over her like a physical thing. Not that she could blame him. It was why she was here with this bottle of gin when she did not drink spirits. It was why she'd drunk Carr's gift—a carafe of Madeira doubtless laced with Muira's "love potion"—throughout luncheon. It was why she would stay here, drinking, after he left. She opened her eyes. He was still there.

"I will ask you this and, damn you, you'd better answer," he said in a hard voice, "Did you declare yourselves? Were witnesses there?"

She understood then. He thought Carr had tricked her into the old Scottish custom of declaration and that they'd already wed.

"Did you?" he shouted, rattling the heavy iron furniture like a piece of tin.

"What difference does it make?" she said.

"I'll ask once more 'ere I throttle you, Madame—and be warned, I have never so desired to do a person harm as I do you at this moment."

"I assure you, I hurt every bit as much as you could want," she replied softly. He jerked forward and caught himself short as though held by invisible chains.

"Did you declare?"

"No," she said tiredly. "No. I would have and so, too, would Carr but Muira—Mrs. Douglas—insisted on finding a priest. She said the McClairens would not accept the marriage as real unless it had been sanctioned by the Church."

She lifted tragic eyes to him. "Is that not funny? Do you not see the joke? They want this marriage blessed when it is from its conception cursed."

A sound of anguish and fury rose in Rafe's throat, frightening the hollow humor from her.

"You can't stop it, Rafe," she whispered. "A priest rides for Wanton's Blush even as we speak."

His fury erupted in a roar of pain. He seized the table and pitched it over, hurling it across the terrace. Without another glance at her, he strode from the windswept courtyard.

Gunna was waiting for Raine when he reached the room he'd been using for sleep. "They say the king is dead!" she greeted him.

Raine didn't reply. He moved past her and began a hurried hunt through a pile of discarded clothing.

"Everyone is leaving Wanton's Blush. Everyone!" Gunna went on. "Fia is already gone. The house is in an uproar: servants scurrying everywhere, packing trunks; the grooms and stable boys working round the clock to hitch the proper horses to the proper carriage."

He found his greatcoat and swung it over his shoulder, stopped in the middle of the room, and looked about for the small leather purse containing all the wealth he owned, a dozen gold guineas.

"And Carr prowls the castle like an aged badger, snarling and gloating, and while all his guests leave he keeps servants in the tower looking for the arrival of a carriage!"

"Aye," Raine swept the debris from a table. His purse wasn't there. "He's sent for a priest."

"Why?" Gunna asked, her confusion mirrored in her ravaged face.

"To marry him and Miss Donne."

He heard the sharp whistle of her indrawn breath. "Aye. A new stepmama for Fia and myself. Aren't we lucky?" He spied the purse on the windowsill. He snagged it, tossing it in the air with a predacious smile.

"Oh, Raine. I am sorry," Gunna said softly.

"Don't be. You'd be wasting your pity. She'll not wed Carr. I swear it."

"But, Raine, how can you stop them?"

He shoved the purse into his belt and wheeled around, grasping her by the shoulders. "I'll be gone for a while, a couple of days at the most. If you ever had any affection for me, I need you to do something for me now, Gunna. And never fail."

She studied his face, saw something there that caused her breath to catch in her scarred old lungs. "Of course, Raine. But where are you going?"

His expression turned hard. "There's an old debt I have to collect."

CHAPTER 28

"Wake up!"

Favor rolled onto her side, swatting at the hands pulling her. She blinked owlishly into the dark. It was still night. Her mouth was cottony and rancid, her eyes crusted with the residual salt from countless tears. And she was still half-drunk.

Not that it helped.

She remembered each eternal moment since yesterday when Rafe had left. She must not think of Rafe. He was gone. "Go 'way," she mumbled.

"Nay!" Muira grabbed her arm and hauled her upright. The sound of a flint strike preceded the flash of a flame as Muira lit a candle. "The priest is here. You're to be wed in an hour's time."

Favor came wide awake, snatching herself out of the old woman's grip and scooting to the far side of the bed, yards of rumpled and stained pink satin heaped about her. She stared at them uncomprehendingly until she recognized the skirts of last night's gown. She hadn't taken it off before falling into her bed last night and no maid had disrobed her.

"No," she mumbled, tucking her knees to her chest. "Carr is too sick. He's been abed since yesterday. So sick he hasn't even come to see his guests off."

"He must have gotten better," Muira said, seizing Favor's ankle and dragging her across the bed. "He sent word a few minutes ago. He's found a priest but the man won't stay long, fearing the antipapists at Wanton's Blush. You must get up!"

"I am cursed then," Favor said, and as Muira began to drag her farther she reached down and pried her fingers from her ankle. "I'll come. I said I would marry him and I will, now let me be."

"Stupid girl! You can't appear like that! Look at you. I've ordered a bath brought up." She pointed at a tub standing in the center of the room. "You'll use it and clean yourself!"

Favor's lip curled back. "If you think to deck me out like some virgin sacrifice, you'll get no satisfaction, I promise you. I'd sooner go to him dressed in black."

The old woman's mouth flattened with impatience. "Ach! Fine, then. Carr isn't marrying you anyway, he's marrying Janet."

She stood back, waiting while Favor pulled herself to the edge of the bed and stood. Her head swam and she closed her eyes against the ache in her temple. When she opened them she caught sight of herself in a dark mirror on the far wall.

She was ghastly white, her eyes sunk deep and ringed with shadows. Her hair fell in thick black ropes about her face and shoulders, lending her a feral appearance. She glared at her image with satisfaction. A worthy bride for a murderer. With a sharp movement, she gestured Muira ahead of her.

Muttering, Muira led her down empty black halls and long-echoing corridors. Already Wanton's Blush wore an air of abandonment, her denizens having fled in a steady stream over the last few days.

"They're in here, waiting," Muira whispered. "I'll look over the marriage certificate. You bob your head when the priest bids you do so and then, finally, it will be done." She opened the door and waited for Favor to enter and followed her in.

The room was small and dark and of indeterminate usage. The few lit candles did little to chase the shadows from the corners. At least it is not a chapel, Favor thought. A priest, sitting on a hardback chair near the doorway, rose as they entered, his gaze darting anxiously. A small man stood beside the priest, his expression closed. Probably a witness.

Favor looked about. No one else was in the room. Certainly not Carr. Relief flooded through her. Perhaps he was, indeed, too sick to leave his room. Perhaps he'd overestimated his strength. Perhaps he wouldn't come. Hope uncoiled in Favor's heart.

"Where's His Lordship?" Muira asked, her honeyed 'Mrs. Douglas' tones so unlike her real voice that for a second Favor did not realize who'd spoken.

"His Lordship is too ill to leave his bed." The small man beside the priest stepped forward.

"Ah!" An involuntary cry, small and quickly smothered, rose from Muira.

"But," he said, "His Lordship is most anxious, indeed, *most* anxious to wed Miss Donne, and as the priest"—his gaze flickered derisively at the silent man—"is afraid to leave his sanctuary for long, Lord Carr insists we do not delay."

"I don't understand," Muira snapped, in her confusion over this unforeseen turn of events forgetting her harmless mien.

"If it pleases you, he would like to go through with the ceremony by proxy," the small man continued. "I will stand for him. My name is Rankle. I am His Lordship's valet."

"His *valet*? This is most irregular," Muira exclaimed. "Some would say ridiculous. Why I doubt such a marriage is legal or"—she looked at the priest—"even valid."

"I can assure you as to its validity, Madame," the priest said quietly, "and as far as the world is concerned, you know that a simple declaration before witnesses is all that Scottish law requires to marry."

"I want to see the certificate," Muira said, holding out her hand.

Wordlessly, Rankle gave it to her. She tilted the paper into the candlelight while Favor held her breath, praying she would find some irregularity, a few more days in which—if God would but show mercy—Rafe's face would begin to fade from memory.

Muira raised her face, a gloating smirk on her lips. Favor's hope died.

"It's legal and it's clear as day. Aye!" Muira said. She grasped Favor's elbow and propelled her forward. "Say your piece, priest, and make sure to heed her answer well."

She could not say what held her upright, Muira's grasp or her own will. With Muira's triumph her last bit of hope died. The room faded to a dim stage, the others became caricatures mumbling unintelligible lines in a play in which she had no interest. She stared at the candles' haloes, heard the priest's voice drone above the dull throbbing in her temples. Her limbs seemed liquid, her thoughts disjointed. She answered in a faint voice when prodded, nodding in continual agreement while deep inside she chanted his name like an incantation against the devil: *Rafe. Rafe. Rafe.*

And then it was done. Rankle wished her well and plopped a purse into the priest's outstretched hand. Muira, eyes ablaze with triumph, folded the certificate and stuffed it into her bodice.

"I must go at once and show this to those left of the clan."

"Don't leave," Favor whispered, and knew she had finally reached the end of her strength, for she was asking for Muira's aid. She should have known she wouldn't receive any.

Muira grasped her chin between her thumb and forefinger and shook it with horrible playfulness. "Don't be ridiculous. The village where the last McClairens live is less than a five-hour drive. There's no reason for you to become all over vaporish, m'girl." She leaned close, whispering in Favor's ear, "Carr is too ill to perform his husbandly duties." She smiled thinly. "If you're very lucky, he'll die and never will."

Favor stared at the old woman as she swept from the room. The priest followed her, his face taut with worry.

"Lady Carr." Rankle bowed and he, too, left.

She was alone.

She stood until her gaze slowly focused on a dark, oily lock snaking across her bodice. She lifted the tress as one would a dead thing. It filled her with revulsion.

She'd dyed her hair black to ensnare Carr. She'd achieved that goal. Now she wanted only to rid herself of the noxious stain. Rafe had hated it.

She must clean it off now. She *had* to get it off.

She returned to her room and undressed, dropping the foul garments about her feet and peeling stays, chemise, and petticoats from her body. Then, naked, she scooped water from the hipbath Muira had ordered into a smaller basin. She dunked her head.

She began slowly, using the bar of harsh soap Muira had used to clean off her own makeup. With numb fingers, she worked the soap deep into her hair. But as the water grew dark, so grew her eagerness to be rid of the dye. Harder and faster she scrubbed, digging her fingers into the sodden mass, working up a thick lather of gray foam.

Desire became obsession. She dumped the dirty water on the floor and stood in the spreading pool, refilling the basin with clear water. Again and again she washed and rinsed her hair, until finally the lather remained white and the water held no tint of color. Only then did she fall exhausted and trembling to her knees, wrapping her arms around her middle and rocking back and forth. Because though she'd removed the blight from her hair, she still felt unclean.

Warmth flowed over her. Slowly, Favor opened her eyes. A hazy glow filled her room. Dawn had finally come.

"Favor, beloved, wake up."

She turned her head, certain she was dreaming. She was not.

Rafe stood over her, the gentle sunlight revealing each harsh and beloved feature. No anger remained in his expression, all the rage was gone; he knew he'd lost. They'd lost.

"Your hair," he murmured, tenderness filling his voice. He reached down and fingered a tress. " 'Tis as bright as I recall. Brighter."

"You're too late," she whispered.

"Aye," he answered sadly. "Years too late 'twould seem."

Reality sliced through the languor binding her. She struggled to rise, heedless of her nakedness beneath the bedsheets. "You must go! If you're found—"

"Gently, sweet falcon." He grasped her shoulders, sitting down on the bed beside her and pushing her against the pillows. "There's no cause for alarm. Your dragon *doyenne* is gone, the servants are otherwise occupied, and Carr is sick in his den."

Relief flowed through her and hard on its heels, gratitude. She'd never expected to see him again, yet here he was, filled with such poignance, such loss. She turned her head and kissed the back of his hand where it still lightly cupped her shoulder.

Without hesitation he wrapped his long fingers around the back of her head and brought her mouth to his. Surprise briefly touched her; he'd taken this kiss, not courted it, and he was a man not given to taking. But then his lips moved over hers and she couldn't think beyond the moment. 'Twas her beloved who embraced her, kissed her, caressed her. 'Twas Rafe.

With a sob, she wrapped her arms about his throat, deepening the kiss. His hands moved up and tilted her face, gently urging her mouth to open. She complied and his tongue plundered deep within, finding hers and mating with it. Her head spun, her body burned bright as the sun outside and was just as ignorant of morality.

"You're mine, Favor," he whispered against her mouth.

Her body was ignorant, but she was not. "I'm married, Rafe."

"I know." His tone was serrated with anguish. He pulled back and stared into her eyes, ferocity flickering to life in the amber depths of his own. "It doesn't matter. You are mine, Favor. You always will be no matter what name you take or where you flee. I love you."

Yes, she thought hopelessly. *Yes*. His words speared her with their essential truth. She could not deny them any more than she could deny her own heart. But she could not acknowledge them either.

Rafe's she might be, and he her own love, but still she *did* have another name and she *would* soon flee to France. . . .

But not now. Not yet. She'd been granted a few hours' reprieve, a few hours to make enough memories to last a lifetime. Her embrace tightened.

It was enough of an answer. He eased her onto her back, following her down. His body had been her anchor before, a rock she'd clung to as he'd held her upright, buffeted by a tempest of sensations as he'd pleasured her. Now she learned the weight and breadth of him covering her and gloried in it.

His fingers skated lightly over her collarbone and found the pulse at the base of her throat. He measured the rapid beat with his lips, trailing lower, just above the line of the blanket. She arched upward, wanting more, wanting what he'd given her just a few nights before, wanting what she thought she would never know again. He brushed the linen away, exposing her breasts to his hungry gaze.

He inhaled sharply. "Let me take my shirt off, Favor. Let me feel your skin naked against mine. Please."

She nodded. She could do nothing else; her voice was lost. He stripped his shirt off over his head, the movement feline and graceful, the muscles cloaking his laddered ribs sliding smoothly beneath velvety skin. His chest and belly were as hard and muscular as her caresses had described them, his arms long and powerful-looking, capped by thick dense muscle.

Dark hair covered his chest and thickened into a dark line that traveled beneath the waist of his breeches. Her gaze traveled lower. She caught her breath. His breeches were tight, too small and old, and the faded cloth hugged the big bulge of his sex closely, clearly revealing his arousal.

Her eyes fluttered shut remembering the feel of him pressed inside her. It had ached. Now that ache had returned but this time it seemed only the instrument that had then caused the ache could now ease it.

"Favor?"

She opened her eyes, swallowed hard. He was watching her intently, his expression taut.

"Is it . . . can I . . ." He trailed off and speared a hand through his hair, further rumpling the glossy sable locks. "Favor, I would not frighten you. I swear—"

She reached for him. He dropped to one knee, sliding his arms beneath her and lifting her clear off the linens, crushing her to his naked flesh. He inhaled sharply. "Dear God, you feel good."

She twisted in his embrace, dragging her nipples across his chest. The sensation was carnal, the sweet abrasion causing the peaks of her breasts to throb. She rubbed them again in the soft hair on his chest, assuaging the ache.

He clenched his teeth, his eyes narrowing with pleasure. She threaded her fingers through his hair and pulled his head close, drinking in the scent of him, the crisp, silky texture of the loose curls between her fingers.

"You are beautiful, too beautiful, and I want you too much," he whispered, and she realized that he worried he would hurt her.

She didn't. He'd shown her the most exquisite care, given her profound pleasure, and taught her passion. She'd taken all he'd had to give and offered nothing in return. Except her love, and that she gave in abundance. Now she wanted to please him, to show him her love in the most intimate way possible.

She gripped his upper arms, reveling in the feel of his muscles bunching beneath the clear, smooth skin. She pushed. He was heavy. She would never have been able to dislodge him by her strength alone and yet he shifted at once, his gaze quiet and askance, allowing her whatever she would have of him. Or not have.

She pushed again, harder, and he acquiesced to the unspoken command by rolling on his back, catching her to keep her from falling on top of him. But that's where she wanted to be. She snuggled down, lying fully on him, her breasts flattened against his chest, her hair a shimmering curtain flowing on either side of his rib cage.

She lowered her head and kissed his flat belly. It jerked into taut delineation. His hands, barely clasping her shoulders, tightened painfully. She opened her mouth and flicked the heated skin with the tip of her tongue.

"Favor!" The choked word came out a warning.

Her longing preempted his caution. She curled her fingers beneath the waist of his breeches, tugging the cloth down over his narrow hips. His sex sprang free. Touch alone had not prepared her for the sight of him, big, swollen, and rigid. She raised her eyes in apprehension and found Rafe watching her, his smile rueful. Instantly, her fears disappeared.

"I swear I won't hurt you," he said hoarsely, trying to pull her up.

She would have none of it. She twisted out of his grip and scooted farther down. Lightly, she clasped him between her palms. His hips bucked slightly in response.

She lowered her head, placing a fleeting kiss on the thick tip. He made a throaty sound, half anguish, half pleasure. It was all the impetus she needed. She opened her lips over his sex and took him into her mouth. He pulsed, silky and smooth against her tongue—

His hands swooped down to bracket her face. "No, Favor. You don't—" Whatever else he'd been about to say was lost in a shuddering groan.

Carnal satisfaction flooded her. This strong, broad man, this huge male, trembled with the pleasure she gave him. She reveled in the power. Her ability to inspire his desire was intoxicating.

She glazed the head of his sex with her tongue. His fists twisted in her hair, his knuckles shivering against her temples in his efforts to control the building lust she drew forth with each long, sultry pull of her mouth. She did not want his restraint; she wanted his passion. She tasted the salty essence, drawing him deeper—

With a low, guttural roar, he grabbed her upper arms and hauled her up and over him, holding her upper body suspended above him. His biceps trembled, veins roping thickly under the tanned skin.

"My turn." He lifted his head to her breast and opened his mouth wide over her nipple, sucking the velvety peak deep into his mouth.

She gasped, her hips undulated instinctively against his thick staff. Liquid warmth seeped from between her legs.

He released her nipple and clamped his big hands on either hip, repositioning her higher on his body. She bowed backward, her hands seeking purchase and finding it on his own hips, her swinging curtain of hair lightly teasing his thighs.

He pressed his mouth to the soft flesh of her inner thigh and nibbled higher, closer to the jointure— Her eyes flew open. He'd covered her mound with his mouth, and was sucking softly.

Dear God! His tongue swept deep within the folds, grazing the nubbin buried within, robbing her of cohesive thought. Lightning raced along her nerves, spun behind the black shield of her eyelids, taunting her with the promise of more.

She moaned, no longer able to tell what he did or how. Her whole body was caught in a vortex of driving need, the pitch to the crescendo building within her with painful intensity . . .

The crisis broke. Her cry rose to a soundless keen as the climax engulfed her, narrowing all sensation down to one essential point. She tensed, impaled on the very apex of pleasure, rocking slightly until the feel of his tongue, flickering lightly over her sex, became too acute. She shivered, drew back. Gently he shifted and lowered her to the mattress, covering her with his body.

He came into her on a long, smooth thrust, breaking through the thin barrier of her maidenhead without hesitation. The pain was sharp and brief, supplanted by a quickening need. He stopped deep within her.

Her eyes fluttered open. He was watching her, his breathing harsh, his bronze skin dusky. He reached down and lifted first one then the other of her hands, and set them on his shoulders.

"Hold on to me, Favor. Please. Cling to me. Want me. For the love of God, hold on to me this one time." And then he moved.

The pace he set was hard and brutal, his thrusts deep. He stretched and filled her, yet still she wanted, needed. Her recalcitrant hands strayed from his shoulders and swept down the muscular straining back to his taut buttocks. She dug her fingers into the hard round muscle, wrapped her thighs about his hips and tilted her pelvis in ancient welcome, greedily absorbing the agressiveness of his possession.

Just this one time. Just once to last the rest of her life.

Climax after climax seized her and carried her like a scrap on a tidal wave, peaking and crashing, wild and tumultuous and exquisite. Suddenly Rafe tensed. He rose like Vulcan, hard and burnished beneath the sheen of sweat, masterful and potent. He braced himself on his arms, and with a deep cry, pushed deep within her. He held himself still, his body shuddering with his release.

When it was over he sank down on her, heavy with repletion. He slid his arms beneath her, cradling her tenderly.

She started to rise.

"Stay, Favor," he said softly. "Rest with me. It isn't only sex I would have but its sweet aftermath, too. Stay."

"I can't. He'll send a servant. We'll be found."

She tried once again to free herself but her attempt was a pitiful parody. His sadness bound her to him. She allowed him to draw her back down to his side and wrap his long arms around her. She laid her head on his chest and listened to the low, deep beat of his heart. And there, against all chance, she fell asleep.

"Raine! Rouse yerself! Carr is up!" Gunna stood in the bedchamber doorway, the light from the hall making a black silhouette of her misshapen figure.

Raine surged upright, carrying Favor with him. Instinctively, he shielded her.

"Rafe?" He heard her voice, soft and groggy, yet a sliver of fear sliced through it.

"It's all right, Favor." He mouthed the words knowing them for a lie. It was not all right. How could it be? She would hate him and he would have to live with that hatred the rest of his life.

"But who is that? What does she say?"

"Raine," Gunna repeated. "There's no time for this. He's up and he's looking for her. 'Tis only a matter of time before he comes here."

"Why does she call you Raine?" Favor whispered. "Why. . . . Dear God."

He closed his eyes. He'd hoped . . . for what? Another hour before he was destroyed?

"Because that is my name. Raine. Raine Merrick."

CHAPTER 29

Raine felt her scuttle away from him, dragging the bed linen with her. He turned. She was staring at him with wide, uncomprehending eyes, her golden hair streaming about her bare shoulders.

"No." She shook her head. "It cannot be."

"Yes. I'm . . . I'm so damn sorry."

"Sorry? Dear God, that's how you knew about the Trust and the castle and all about Carr and what he . . . why?" The last word was a heart-wrenching whisper. "Why?"

"I didn't want Carr to know I was here. Then I found you and later I discovered who you were. I owed you my life, Favor. I thought that if you knew my name you wouldn't allow me to help you—"

"Help me?" she echoed, lifting the pitiful sheet as though that could somehow hide her from him. "And making me an adulteress is how you *helped* me? By cuckolding your father?"

She scooted off the far side of the bed, backing away from him. Her eyes revealed her horror.

"Raine!" Gunna shut the door and hobbled forward.

"You said you'd kept him sick with some drug!" Raine said desperately, keeping his gaze on Favor who trembled before him. "That he'd be abed. You're probably misinformed. He's probably still sick."

"Nay!" Gunna said. "I saw him myself. He must not have drunk the drugged water this morning. If Carr finds ye in here with her he'll kill ye!"

A sob broke from Favor, dispelling all other considerations. "What sort of hellish family is this? Did you see bedding me after my marriage to him as a chance to pay him back for the years you spent in prison?"

"No, Favor, I swear it's not so." He stretched out his hand; only on seeing her expression did he realize he was still naked. With a snarl he rose, snatching up his breeches and pulling them on. Gunna grabbed his forearm. "Raine!"

Angrily he shook her off and went to Favor. She backed away from him, panic suffusing her lovely features. "No. No. Oh God, how could you?"

He'd no choice but to tell her now, with Gunna hovering. "You're not an adulteress, Favor."

"What?" Favor whispered.

"You married *me* last night, Favor. Not Carr."

"No," she breathed. "Impossible."

" 'Tis true. Gunna kept Carr drugged while I rode to an abbey south of here. The Abbess there owed me a good deed. She sent her priest here."

"But the valet . . ." She was trembling, her skin blanched white as cream. He longed to enfold her in his arms, took a step forward, and saw her gaze dart wildly about, seeking escape. He had to keep talking, trying to explain.

"Rankle stood proxy for me, knowing that while he played the part of Carr's stand-in he was in truth acting for me."

"Why?"

"You've seen how Carr treats his servants. Rankle was only too happy to repay him in kind."

"But the certificate! Muira said it was all in order!"

"Muira believed what she wanted to see. The certificate named R. Merrick as your husband. It gave no peer's title."

"R. Merrick. Raine Merrick." She swayed slightly.

"I couldn't let you marry him, Favor. He would have killed you. This plan, this godforsaken plan of yours, could never have worked."

"*You* stopped it from working. You stopped me from repaying my obligation," she said, a new horror in her voice. "You ruined it all. Why . . . Oh God." Her head shot up and she gazed at him out of terrible, wounded eyes. "You even made love to me this morning to ensure the marriage couldn't be annulled. Didn't you?"

He could not deny the charge. In truth he had entered her room with just such a motive. But that motive hadn't survived the passion that had ignited as soon as he'd seen her. Then his only consideration had been to make love to her, to find in a life rife with pain and regret and sorrow one short interlude for love. But she was right, that hadn't been his plan when he'd gone to her. She read the guilt on his face and flinched.

"Not in the end," he whispered hoarsely. "Not—"

"Go!" she panted desperately. "Get out of here! Leave me! Go!"

"Favor, please, I beg you—"

"Go! Haven't you done enough? Stolen my heart, my honor, and my pride and—go!" She crumpled to the floor, sobbing. Her slender back, so vulnerable and pale, shook with a tempest of tears.

"Heed her," Gunna insisted, yanking on his arm. "Ye'll do no good here, Raine, and ye'll surely do her no good dead!"

"Won't I?" Raine asked numbly, staring at the slight figure at his feet, afraid to touch her, unable to leave.

"Think!" Gunna ground out. "Carr will kill ye and take yer place, Raine. No one knows yet about the marriage. Rankle can be silenced and Carr's Christian name still begins with an 'R'."

She was right. He couldn't die. He had to leave.

"Favor . . ."

She huddled closer, refusing to look at him. With an oath, he swung away and strode from the room.

She heard him leaving with the old hunched woman in the veil. For a long moment she lay where she'd fallen, huddled among the tangled bedsheets still scented with their lovemaking.

Raine Merrick: Rapist. Her enemy's son. Her betrayer. Her husband. And soon Carr would come . . . and he would want to know . . . and Muira was gone . . . and she was alone, far more alone than she'd ever been before because even last night she'd had Raf—Raine. She jerked upright, the thought a physical pain.

She had to get out of there. Leave. But where? All her life she'd been shunted from place to place. The small town of her birth, these fatal shores, the French convent. She had no home. She'd only had her goal and that had been rendered unattainable. She only knew she couldn't stay here.

She rose and dressed with trembling haste. Quickly she donned a cloak, then she opened the door to the hallway and peeked outside. No one moved. She crept down the corridor, past the main staircase to the servants' stairwell, and descended on clattering heels. Downstairs she hastened through the kitchens and larders, the curtseys and bobs of startled servants following her progress.

She burst through the back door and raced across the small open courtyard for the stables. There she stole inside. A surprised groom harnessing a team of matched grays stumbled to a halt and tugged his forelock submissively.

"Where is Jamie Craigg?" she asked him.

"He be—"

"Right here, Miss Donne." The giant emerged from a stall, wiping his huge paws on a leather apron.

"Where's Muira?"

Jamie darted a warning glance at the groomsman. What matter? It was all over now.

"*Mrs. Douglas* drove herself out early this morning," he said. "She said she was going to visit relatives up north and would be back by dinner. Beggin' yer pardon, Miss, but ye don't look so well. Are ye all right?" His craggy face was riddled with concern.

"Yes," she whispered. "Except I have a desire . . . that is I *need* to go away." She prayed he would not ask her where, for she did not have any idea. She only knew she had to leave and Jamie was her only hope.

"Now, Miss?"

"Oh yes, please, Jamie."

Again he darted an anxious look at the groom, who stood watching with undisguised interest.

"Please."

"Of course, Miss. Right away, Miss. I'll just hitch the carriage and we'll be off." He turned away, his gaze passing scathingly over the eavesdropping groom. "Ye can tell me where once we're on our way."

In the end there was no place to go except her brother's manor twenty miles inland.

"What has happened? I returned to the castle to find Carr beside himself and the two of you missing." Favor heard Muira's voice rise stridently from the small entry hall below. She heard Jamie's low rumble in reply.

She rose from her chair. She would not hide up here from Muira. Muira no longer mattered. Nothing mattered.

"What did Carr say?" Jamie asked.

"I didn't speak to Carr, you great oaf! I couldn't very well show up without his doting bride, now could I? Nor tell him she'd fled like a rabbit from a hound. I come straight here to fetch her back and that's exactly what I'll do."

"The girl is sick, Muira," Jamie muttered. "As white as new snow and eyes as bleak and deep as a new dug grave."

"I don't care. Where is the silly bitch? I'll teach her to—"

"I'm here, Muira."

The old woman swung around and looked up at where Favor stood on the landing. "Get your cloak on!" she spat. "Your husband's waiting for you."

"No. He's not."

"Stupid girl, he's not had you yet. He can still have the marriage annulled. Now get down here!"

Favor laughed, a hopeless choked sound. In response, Muira stormed up the steps, grabbed her arm in a viselike grip and wrenched her forward.

"No." Favor shook her head frantically. "No! Listen to me, Muira! Listen!" Her shout had the desired effect. Muira dropped her arm.

"I didn't marry Carr. I married his son, Raine!"

Muira turned to Jamie. His forehead rippled with a fierce frown of confusion. "And you said *I* was daft," she muttered grimly. "Well, mad or no, she'll lay beneath Carr this day."

"I will not. I've already lain with his son. My husband."

The supreme confidence in Muira's expression faltered. "She's mad."

Favor looked past her to Jamie. " 'Twas Raine Merrick who we finagled from that French prison. He came to Wanton's Blush without Carr's knowledge, seeking McClairen's Trust. He found me instead. But he didn't tell me who he was, I swear it."

"Oh, lassie," Jamie breathed.

"Ignore her," Muira said flatly, but something skittered behind her opaque eyes. "She's just looking for some way out. And she'll not find it."

"You foolish old woman! 'Twas Raine who danced with me at the masque. 'Twas Raine whom I stayed with that night. 'Twas Raine's name on that certificate."

She could see Muira's throat working convulsively. "No."

"Look at it!" Favor said, and the old woman withdrew the folded sheet from her bodice with trembling fingers. "It says 'R' Merrick, 'R' for Raine not Ronald. If it were Carr I'd married, the paper would read 'Merrick, Earl of Carr.' Look! What date does it give for my groom's birth?"

Her answer was a howl of rage that rose from the depths of Muira's belly. Fearfully, Favor backed away. Muira crumpled the certificate into her fist and tore at the rumpled wad, tearing it to pieces with hands whose bones showed white. When she was done she hurled the pieces to the hall below and swung around.

"NO! I won't let this happen. All the years, the planning, the sacrifices and scratching to make . . . No! McClairen's Isle will be the McClairens' once more!"

Jamie, his face still and wary, moved cautiously up the steep flight of stairs. "It's over, Muira," he said.

"No, it's not," she panted, her gaze wild and staring. "It's not over.

There has to be a way . . ." She swung on Favor. "You vile thing. You wretched curse on our clan!"

Her words beat at Favor, each word a blow. "For what did you sell out your honor and your debt?" Muira demanded.

"I didn't know. God help me, 'tis true I love . . . loved him but I swear I didn't know who he was. I didn't know 'twas Raine Merrick I married. I swear I thought I'd wed Carr! I only learned of his duplicity this morning after he . . ."

"Tupped you," Muira finished in tones so ugly Favor closed her eyes. "Who else knows of your filthy betrayal?"

Favor flinched before the raw hatred in Muira's voice. "No one. Only the priest and the valet and Raine."

"*Raine,*" she sneered. "Could you not have waited to lay with him? A few months and I would have made you a widow."

She laughed at Favor's bewildered expression, a dark and hideous sound. "Oh, so innocent! Did you not ken that was part of the plan, dearie? Did you honestly believe I'd trust God to take Carr's life before yours? God is not to be trusted. I planned to kill Carr within the week.

Murder? She should have known. She should have realized. But she hadn't. Yet another thing she was guilty of, but at least in marrying Raine she had been spared a part in murder. "I would never have agreed to let you kill Carr," she whispered. "No matter how evil he is."

"Of course not," Muira sneered. "You haven't the guts. You've too much blood of your whey-faced mother in you and not enough McClairen. You sold us out to squirm beneath a rapist, to grow a belly full of Merrick demon. May the fires of hell consume you!"

"Leave off, Muira!" Jamie said, his voice cold with warning. "Merrick never raped that nun and well you know it. Merry confessed her guilt and absolved him."

"What?" Favor asked. "All these years you had me think I'd traded my people's lives for a rapist."

"What matter?" Muira sneered. "He's demon spawn and I'll see him to his rightful home in hell. There's time yet to make this work. The valet and priest can be dealt with later. And once I find—"

"No!" Immediately Favor grasped the black permutations of Muira's mad thoughts. "No, you—"

Muira swung, all her rage invested in the blow that caught Favor across the temple and sent her tumbling down the stairs. The world was gone before she reached the bottom.

CHAPTER 30

"Where's Muira?" Favor asked faintly. Her head throbbed and a burning pain drove through her back to her shoulder blades. Blackness skirted about her consciousness, beckoning her toward oblivion.

"She's gone too far," she heard Jamie mutter. "No piece of land is worth the price of yer soul."

The darkness swallowed her. When it released her again she grew slowly aware that someone held her, pressing a cool, moist cloth against her forehead. "Raine," she whispered.

"I'm sorry, Favor McClairen," Jamie said. "I'm sorry fer all we done to ye. The boy was no rapist. Ye saved us from the sin of murdering an innocent lad. And that's all ye did. Carr would have found another way to rid us from his land. Ye were just convenient."

"Please," she said trying to turn. She had to stop Muira. Raine. Dear God, why hadn't she stayed with him? Listened? The swirling darkness beckoned her once more; she fought against it, concentrating on Jamie's soft litany.

"Ye were convenient for Muira, too. Fer us. I'll not deny it. We shouldn't have used ye so. It's just that we owed Muira. Please, try and understand.

"We were scattered after the massacre. She found us. She gave us a goal, a purpose, something besides scrabbling from one day to the next without pride or future or past. But she got lost somewhere. I knew it and I didna stop her and that's somethin' I'll have to live with fer the rest of me days."

The blackness receded enough for her to struggle upright in Jamie's great arms. She didn't care about his guilt. She'd had a bellyful of guilt. She only wanted Raine. "Where is she?"

"I dunno. Back to the castle I'd guess. She whipped those horses something fierce." He shook his great shaggy head sadly. "Best rest, Miss Favor. It's all over now."

"No. It's not." She pulled away from him, wincing as she rose. A sea of darkness lapped at her vision. She fought and won the battle against drowning in it. "I have to get to Raine, Jamie. You have to take me to Wanton's Blush."

"Now, Miss Favor. What good will that do?" Jamie said mournfully.

She reached out her hand and braced it on the newel post at the bottom of the stairs. She could not lose him to Muira's mad obsession. Nor to anything else.

"Didn't you hear her, Jamie? And you, who know her so well, didn't you realize what she plans?"

He reached up to steady her by the elbow. She shook off his hand. "What's that, Miss Favor?"

"She plans to kill all three—the valet, priest, and Raine—and by doing so clear the way for my marriage to Carr."

Jamie stared at her, his muteness testifying to his agreement. "But ye'll never agree to it. She must know that."

"It doesn't matter. She's mad!" Favor said, seizing Jamie's hand and tugging. "Now drive me to Wanton's Blush, Jamie Craigg. Drive like the devil himself is chasing you."

Wanton's Blush stood preternaturally dark in the deepening dusk. Few lights brightened the narrow embrasures of her central façade; and her two ells, completely dark, seemed to fold in toward the gloomy courtyard like the wings of some huge, sentient night bird. Jamie drew the lathered horses up before the enormous front doors. Favor jumped from the carriage before the poor beasts had stopped.

"Miss Favor!" Jamie called. "I'll wait without for ye!"

She didn't reply. She wrenched one massive door open, darting past the flummoxed footman and up the central stairs, heading for the abandoned east rooms.

At the top she turned and flew down the corridor to a small passageway leading to the sea-facing rooms. Raine's lair was near the north tower. If he was here that was the place she'd most likely find him. *If* he was, indeed, still here. The thought that he'd left eased a small part of Favor's panic.

Still, Muira would be hunting—a mad, obsessed woman thwarted in her designs—and as knowledgeable about Wanton's Blush as Muira was, she would soon figure out Raine's whereabouts.

Favor slowed her pace, adjusting her eyes to the gloom. Near the center of the hallway she saw a sliver of light from under a door. It was the chapel where most of Janet McClairen's things had been abandoned.

The thought invoked an image of Raine looking at the detritus that had once been his mother's treasured items. She hadn't understood his pensive mood when she'd come upon him there. He'd accepted her intrusion with relief. Raine, too, had dealt with his share of ghosts.

She opened the door and stepped inside, looking about. An ornate silver candelabra stood on the floor, the lights from a dozen tapers glinting from its polished surface. Otherwise, the room looked empty. She frowned, moved forward, and heard the door bang shut behind her.

She swung around. Ronald Merrick, Earl of Carr, stood behind her. He was dressed like a prince, gleaming from head to foot. At his side he wore a sword in a jewel-encrusted scabbard, on his head a snowy bagwig secured with a diamond clasp. The deep cuffs and buttons of his coat shimmered with crystals and metallic threads. Even the buckles of his shoes glittered.

"You've done something to your hair," he said mildly. "Begad, I rather like it. Pretty."

She didn't know what to say, how to respond. His eyes were odd though his face was composed.

"I knew you'd come, Janet. You always liked your pretty things, though"—he cast a sad look around—"they're not very pretty anymore."

"I'm not Janet, sir."

"Of course you're not. You're Favor Donne, or should I say McClairen? Did you think I didn't know? Of course I knew. Although, I will admit, I only recently found out. Rankle told me, just before he succumbed. Chicken bone, I believe."

Dear God, he'd killed that little valet.

"Don't worry, m'dear, though I will probably have to have a little talk with your brother when . . . *if* he returns. But that has naught to do with you and me. I don't care if you are a McClairen. It doesn't matter who you are because . . ."—he moved toward her—". . . because I also know that you carry the spirit of my dear Janet."

She released her breath slowly, holding very still as he picked up a strand of her hair and coiled it nonchalantly around his finger. "Really quite lovely. I declare myself utterly taken with the hue."

Her smile was tremulous.

"It really is too bad you have to die."

She jerked back, unprepared for the sudden death sentence and he smiled, clucking softly as one would to a frightened mare. "There now, Janet. You are somewhere in there listening, aren't you, Janet? Because everything I have to say would, I'm afraid, simply be wasted on Miss Donne."

He was going to kill her anyway. It made no sense. "Why?" she pleaded in a hoarse little voice.

"Because I can't have you hounding me through London. You're a Scottish nobody, both in this body and in your last. You aren't"—he twirled his hand, searching for the right words—"rich enough, or well-connected enough, or *special* enough to be my wife. And Janet, you were ever too proud to be anything less.

"Perhaps Miss Donne, too, suffers from this elevated sense of herself because I certainly gave her—you?—every chance to become my mistress, but she—you?—tiresomely insisted on matrimony."

"I'm not Janet," she protested weakly, uncertain whether she should reveal Muira's plot, fearful that doing so would incite him to a murderous rage.

"Of course not." He patted her cheek as one would a child, his gaze slowly warming as he studied her features. "Do you know, Janet, I actually considered for a moment acquiescing to your wishes? I'd almost decided to marry you with—of course—the caveat that I could rid myself of you when I found it expedient to do so.

"But then old farmer George died and the ban on my matrimonial aspirations lifted. There are countless heiresses in London, m'dear. Countless rich, *well-connected* heiresses. You, I'm afraid, never stood a chance."

"Why did you propose to me, then?" she asked. "Why did you send for the priest?"

"I didn't. I simply told your aunt I did." He *tched* softly. "I thought if I proposed, the old hag that guards you would finally allow us a moment alone. So I proposed. In fact, I believe dear Fia even overheard me. Then I told your aunt I'd sent for the priest. I even had a few servants look for a carriage.

"It would have worked, too. I would have insisted we spend an hour or so alone. But then I took sick. I can't begin to describe to you my frustration," he said confidingly. "Happily all has come to rights, however, for here we are."

Her eyes darted about the room, looking for a likely weapon, finding nothing. "I'll just come back," she whispered desperately. "As many times as you kill me, I'll come back."

"Ho-ho!" he chuckled, bussing her under the chin. "I knew I could draw you out. Threats now, Janet? I would have thought you'd learned the error of that particular behavior on those cliffs." He opened his palm in the direction of the windows and she saw that in spite of his jocular tone, she had, indeed, enraged him.

His pupils were pinpoints of black in his dazzling blue eyes. A tiny tic twitched at the corner of his mouth. "Do your damnedest, Janet. Come back as many times as you like, I'll simply kill you again."

She'd made a grave error. She backed up until she banged into a wall of boxes and crates. She edged along the mass, hands behind her, groping for some weapon. Carr advanced.

"But you know something, Janet? I've been reading about haunts and ghoulies and such. It's fascinating. You ghosts seem a peculiarly hearth-loving mob. Unless you find a human vessel to house you, and that little endeavor took you how long this time? A dozen years?"

He was only a few feet away and she'd worked her way into a corner with nothing to show for it. "The point I'm trying to make, Janet"—he spoke through his teeth now, the soft, urbane tones coming from the choleric face frightening her far more than his words—"is that I don't think you—or your clan—*can* leave here. Let's find out, shall we?"

He seized her around the throat. She flailed frantically in his grip but her heavy skirts smothered her struggles. She clawed at his wrists, tearing violently but his fingers dug deep.

"You would kill your own son's wife?" she choked out.

He laughed, entertained by what he clearly imagined was a paltry diversionary tactic, his grip loosening just enough for her to gulp another lungful of air.

"I swear 'tis true!" she gasped, working at his implacable hold on her throat. "I am married to your son Raine."

"Raine?" He chuckled, his handsome face made even handsomer by his amusement. But his clasp on her throat did not tighten. Instead, it loosened slightly. He didn't seem to care how deeply she scored his arms and hands with her nails. Like a cat with a mouse, he was playing with her, curious to see what she would say next.

"Yes. He's here. And he'll kill you if you hurt me," she said, and as she spoke she realized it was the truth. She did not for one minute doubt Raine would avenge her with all the formidable power he possessed. Because he loved her.

Stunned at learning his identity, bewildered and uncomprehending, she'd ascribed to him fantastic and horrendous motives. Now she saw that everything he'd done he'd done to protect her. Including marrying her. If only she'd listened to her heart.

Carr had tired of his play. His hands were tightening incrementally, torturously, slowly squeezing the life from her. Light-spattered darkness careened about the perimeter of her vision. Her limbs felt weightless. Her lungs burned.

"So Raine will kill me if I hurt you?" he said, chuckling as he studied her face.

"Yes, I will."

She had to be imagining Raine's voice. But Carr's body had gone as still as a hound on point, his head snapping up. His hands dropped from her throat and she crumpled to the ground, gasping for breath as he wheeled to face his son.

Raine strode from the shadowed doorway. In his hand he held a primed pistol, pointed at Carr. His shirt was open, his long hair in disarray, his boots splattered with mud. Compared to Carr's exquisite figure he looked coarse, rough, and incredibly beautiful. Gabriel come to challenge Lucifer.

"Well, blast me if it isn't my large middle child," Carr murmured, his eyes hooded. "And tell me, is the rest true, also? Are you wed to her?" He flung his hand down toward Favor. She skittered back. He did not notice.

"Yes," Raine said. His gaze was watchful, his jaw tense with barely contained fury.

"Rather incestuous, or did you not know she also carries your mother's soul?"

Raine snickered. "You've grown foolish, old man. We duped you, made you believe my mother had returned in order to keep you occupied while I searched the castle for McClairen's Trust."

We? Dear God, he must have heard her talking and deduced Muira's plan. Now he was drawing Carr's attention away from her. Carr stared, fury born of shock simmering in his expression. His lips twitched, his eyes flickered. A palsy began in his right hand.

"No," Carr said. "I don't believe it." He jerked his head around, impaled Favor with a killing glare. "You're Janet. You knew about the Part of No—" His voice trailed off, his gaze flew back, returned to Raine. "You told her what to say."

Raine grinned, a one-sided smile. Janet's smile. The same smile Muira had made her practice so many hours. Why had she never seen it?

The light of fanaticism faded from Carr's eyes, replaced by cold, killing enmity. He would hate above all things being made a fool of and Raine knew it. He deliberately goaded him.

"I should like to kill you," Carr said.

"Please, do try," Raine returned seriously, uncocking the pistol and tossing it away. It skittered across the room and lodged against a chest twenty feet away from where Favor cowered.

With a roar, Carr drew his sword and charged. Raine grabbed a crate lid, flinging it up in front of his face just as Carr's sword slammed into it, biting deep into the wood. Raine wrenched back, hurling away the lid and the sword buried in it and, for that moment, exposed his torso.

Favor saw the short, lethal blade flash from beneath the cuff of Carr's coat and slip into his hand.

"He's got a dagger!" Her warning came too late. Raine twisted as Carr lunged forward, the knife plunging inches into Raine's ribs. He gasped, staggering back, but Carr, well versed in the foulest forms of fighting, followed him. He released the blade, leaving it impaled in Raine's body and battered at his son's face.

He was going to kill Raine.

Favor scrambled along the wall to where the pistol lay. She lifted it as Raine jerked the dagger from his side. Slick with blood, it fell to the ground. Favor pulled back the hammer, pointed the pistol with shaking hands, and pulled the trigger.

Nothing happened.

Sobbing, she banged the cursed instrument against the floor. An explosion ripped through the air, echoing in the chamber as the pistol fired, catching Carr by surprise. He turned his head toward the sound. It was all the advantage Raine needed.

His fist met Carr's jaw with a sickening crunching sound. His other fist drove deep into Carr's gut, felling him to his knees. He clasped his hands together and raised them overhead, swinging them in a telling blow on the back of Carr's neck. Carr fell flat on his face.

"Get up!" Raine demanded, standing over his fallen sire. Blood soaked the right side of his shirt and oozed from a gash over his cheek.

"I said, get up!" He reached down and grabbed the back of Carr's coat with one hand. Beads and crystals popped, skittering about the floor. He hauled Carr half up with one hand, with the other striking him backhanded across the face. Again and again he beat Carr, his lips peeled back in a feral grimace, his breath a harsh rasp punctuated by the sound of his fists meeting Carr's face.

Dear God, thought Favor. Carr had killed the mother. Now the son would kill the father. Merrick blood running true. No! She knew Raine.

No matter how evil Carr was, Raine could never endure committing the sin of patricide.

"Raine!" she cried, struggling upright and stumbling across the room. "No!"

He looked up, his face savage, and she flung her arms around his neck, pressing herself to him. "No, Raine! For my love, please, I beg you stop!"

A heartbeat. Another. She felt Carr fall to her feet and then Raine seized her in a tight embrace, his arms trembling.

"He's nothing to us. Nothing," she whispered fervently. "Let him go, Raine."

"He killed my mother! He's killed and wounded and . . . Dear God, Favor, he's a plague that needs to be wiped out!"

"But not by you. Not by me. Look at him, Raine. He'll not be going anywhere. Jamie's outside now. We'll give him to Jamie and let the Mc-Clairen decide his fate."

"No!" Raine shook his head violently. "You don't know him! He'll get away!"

"No, he won't," Favor said, pleading. Her hand moved down Raine's body, grew sticky with blood. He was wounded. Bleeding copiously. Carr wasn't worth debating while Raine bled to death. "Let it go. As you asked me, so I beg you. I love you. Be *mine*."

"I've nothing to give you," he said harshly. "Nothing but the assurance that this . . . creature will never be able to harm you again. Let me give you that, Favor," he pleaded in a hoarse voice. "Let me do that, at least, for you."

Her hands crept up and cupped his wounded face in tender palms. "You've already given me more than I dreamed the world contained," she returned, her voice aching with love. "All I want is within your ability to give. Your heart."

" 'Tis already yours."

"Then don't take it away from me. Let him live."

He did not hesitate this time; his capitulation came with his kiss, tender, yearning, and reverent. He lifted her in his arms and buried his face against her throat.

"No," she protested. "Your side."

" 'Tis no great matter," he murmured.

Below, Carr stirred. Favor turned in Raine's embrace as Carr fumbled to hands and knees, his handsome face battered beyond recognition, his clothes torn and stained with blood.

"You haven't any more guts now than you did as a child," he muttered, his voice thick and muddled. "You haven't inherited anything from me, not guts, not brains, not looks. Nothing of value. Nothing! You never found the Trust, did you?"

"No. I found something infinitely more precious."

At that Carr's face snapped up, a questioning greedy gleam lit his swelling eyes. "What?" he demanded on a choked cough. "What did you find?"

"You'll never know," Raine answered, turning toward Favor. Gently he set her on her feet. Carr's gaze followed Raine's. "I'll kill you if you say a word to her," Raine promised. "If you so much—"

A figure from a child's night terror burst from the portal behind the nave, brandishing a pair of torches. Her face was livid, her mouth a gaping hole, her eyes pinpoints of madness.

"Traitorous bitch!" Muira shrieked. "You've destroyed it all, all my work and planning but you'll not reap the rewards of your treachery! If the McClairens cannot have Maiden's Blush, no one can!"

And she flung the torch into the tinderbox of rotting detritus that was all that was left of Janet McClairen.

CHAPTER 31

The flames leapt from rotting wood to paper boxes, traveling at breakneck haste. Cloth and books, *papier-mâché* and curtains, linens and leather fed its rapacious hunger. It danced in brilliant waves, bubbled and flowed, enveloping in an instant anything in its path.

A sudden move caught Favor's attention. As she watched, Carr rose and stumbled through the door into the outer hall. "No!" Muira screamed, seeing her quarry escape.

Raine grabbed Favor's arm, yanking her toward the door but her feet caught in her voluminous skirts. She would have fallen had not Raine caught her up in his arms and dashed toward the hall. But the delay cost them dearly.

Muira was quicker.

She darted across the room, waving her second torch in the air, shedding a cloud of living embers in her wake. She halted in the doorway beside the huge ancient armoire teetering under the weight of half-packed crates and boxes. Madly, she feinted at them with her torch, using it like an épée.

Raine reached out to seize her and caught instead the burning end of the torch. With a hiss of pain, he jerked his hand back. Favor darted forward to deal with the madwoman but Raine caught her around the waist and yanked her back just as Muira swung the flaming brand, missing Favor's face by inches. He pushed Favor behind him, scanning the narrowing tunnel of darkness behind the madwoman. Already, Favor could feel the heat from the growing inferno at her back.

"Let her go!" Raine demanded hoarsely.

"Nay! Nay!" Muira shrieked, dancing from side to side. "You'll next have yer pleasure of her in hell, Raine Merrick!" Her expression grew sly; her gaze darted to the side. She touched her torch to the wardrobe's rotting contents, setting it ablaze.

"No!" Raine shouted. Before he could act she grabbed the door of the wobbling armoire and pulled. She jumped back into the open hallway just as it crashed to the floor, choking the entrance with its flaming contents.

In the black corridor, they could see her dart down the hall, touching her torch to anything in her path. And then she stumbled. The torch fell against her skirts, catching fire to them. She shrieked not with pain but with horrific laughter. She spun her way down the hall, a burning effigy, and in seconds was lost to view.

"God have mercy," Favor whispered.

"Hurry!" Raine shouted.

Favor looked behind them. The exit by the altar was unreachable. A wall of liquid flames undulated over the wall behind them, searing the back of her neck and shoulders. They'd only one chance. She hurled herself at the mound of burning crates, grabbing hold of any unlit portion and jerking it away from the doorway. Raine was already working feverishly, hurling crates and trunks away heedless of burning his hands and arms.

Frantically and silently they worked, side by side. Smoke, a churning black miasma, rose toward the high ceiling, already billowing as it sought another egress. In minutes it would envelop them. Already her lungs burned with the noxious fumes and her eyes streamed.

Outside in the hall, the fire had taken hold. It skittered along the floorboards, tasted the walls with hungry licks. It bloomed in orange brilliance at rotted wooden door frames and raced toward the main part of the castle.

Raine seized the edge of the toppled wardrobe and with one enormous grunt shoved it away from the door. Favor darted through the small opening he'd made, reaching back and grasping Raine's wrist.

"Go!" he shouted, trying to pull free. " 'Tis too small. Go! I'll be right behind you!"

She let go, but she didn't leave. She hurled her small body against the mammoth piece of furniture and pushed with all her strength.

"GO!" he shouted.

"Not"—she gritted her teeth—"without"—she closed her eyes and offered a prayer—"you!" She rammed her shoulder against the monolithic piece.

"Damn you, Favor McClairen!" she heard Raine roar, and then the wardrobe slithered a few blessed inches. He swung himself up and over the armoire, through an opening just wide enough to allow him through, turned, seized her hand, and pulled her to him.

Down the blazing hallway they ran, the snapping and crackling of the flames following them like manic laughter. They burst through the tower doorway into complete blackness, clattering and half-falling down the narrow spiraling steps to the main floor. Muira had done her job well; Wanton's Blush was an inferno.

The castle was burning, set ablaze by a madwoman. Carr crept step by painful step along the hall, heading for his library.

His eyes were swollen nearly shut. A red haze obscured vision that kept fading and then resolving itself. His nose was broken and his head echoed with dull noise. Pain lanced his side with each breath he took. He ignored the pain just as he ignored the deeper agony of being duped by his son—with the aid of that little Scottish heathen.

He'd no time for that now. Already the air in the stairwell behind him shimmered with heat, the vanguard of the blaze that followed.

The few guests left emerged wild-eyed from the rooms where they'd been carousing, befuddled and stupid as lemmings on a cliff. Wild-eyed and uncertain, they stood frozen, mouthing inanities and pleas for help. Carr ignored them. A few of his footmen screamed for water. Fools! No water could save Wanton's Blush now.

He made it to the door of his library, and with swollen hands fumbled for the key in his pocket and fit it in the lock. A roar like hell's hound boomed above him. Suddenly the ceiling a few yards behind him collapsed. Fire rose like Atlas unchained and surged from the burning timbers, pounced upward, gorging itself on rich tapestries and gilt-framed masterpieces.

Carr ground his teeth in impotent fury and pushed the library door open. He'd little time. Less than little. He lumbered across the room toward the ornately carved mantel and, gritting his teeth in agony, fit his fingernails beneath a tile and pried it up. He shoved his hand down into the revealed compartment and fished until his hand closed on a packet. He removed it, stuffing the bundle beneath his shirt.

He looked at the door leading to the hall. Tendrils of smoke crept beneath it in gentle exploration, insidiously delicate. He turned and hobbled quickly to his adjoining bedchamber, bent on retrieving at least the gold he kept in the trunk beneath Janet's portrait. The thought of Janet brought a snarl to his lips, twisting the cut lips painfully. He reached for the handle and thrust the door open.

The sight that met his gaze sent him reeling backward, gasping and clutching at his chest.

Janet stood beneath her portrait.

She was silhouetted by the fire he insisted always be kept burning in the hearth of his private chambers, posed in profile, her hands folded at her waist. Her chin was tilted up at an angle as though she were studying the picture; a small smile curved her soft lips.

"No!" he whispered.

"Leave here, Ronald." Her voice seemed to come from within his own head, echoing and dim, soft and implacable. She did not turn to face him. Her figure wavered slightly. "Leave here *now*."

She'd come to save him.

Ronald Merrick, Earl of Carr, obeyed the haunt's advice.

"It's barred from outside!" Favor shouted, clawing at Raine's arm as he banged his shoulders again and again into the small door at the foot of the tower stairway. It was pitch black; only a sullen sliver of light beneath the door gave any illumination. "We have to go back up—"

"No! We'll die up there!"

He'd been working to open the door for ten minutes, though it felt like hours. The stone tower had as yet stood proof against the blaze's fury but soon the fire would find entry and they would be burned alive at the tower's base.

"Favor," he said urgently, "I need something with which to pry the hinges off. See what you can do, I'll keep battering at this."

Nodding, Favor scrambled back up the stairs, her hands feeling about for anything to use as a pry bar, her feet sliding over the width of the steps for anything that might be lying there. Halfway to the second story she almost impaled herself on a sharp edge protruding from the wall. She groped until she caught hold of a curved piece of metal. It was an old iron banister some worthy McClairen had fitted along the steep staircase and promptly left to erode. Double blessings on his head.

Favor wrapped her fingers around the cold metal and twisted. The railing moved and she heard plaster pieces falling. She leaned back against the central core of the spiral staircase, braced her foot against the wall and heaved back with all her might. With a distinct snap, a heavy section of metal came loose in her hands.

Panting and triumphant, she clambered down to Raine. Patting her way down his arm, she found his hand and slapped the three-foot section of metal in his palm.

"Now, please, get us out of here," she said.

"Yes, Milady." His tone told her he was smiling. She heard him feeling for the hinge, the scrape of metal against metal as he fit the end beneath the hinge, and then a grunt as he shoved.

The metal snapped.

For a second neither spoke.

"We're going to die here, aren't we?" she asked quietly.

In answer she heard his shoulder strike the door with a loud *boom,* the sound reverberating through the small enclosure.

"Please, Raine," she said. "If we have to die here, I don't want to die without feeling your arms around me once more."

Boom!

"I love you, Raine. I want you to know that."

"God!" His roar was part fury, part supplication.

"Please—"

Strong arms caught her up in a fervent embrace. Lips salty with blood and sweat touched hers in a kiss so tender that tears sprang to her eyes.

"I love you, Favor McClairen Merrick. I would have done everything in my power to make you happy. I swear I would."

"Where would we have gone?" she asked, an unnatural calm overtaking her. How could she feel so content in such a hell? A benefit of loving, she imagined.

"America?" he said, sounding as if he, too, struggled to reconcile himself to this fate but fared far worse than she. "Perhaps . . . India. Yes. I think India."

"It's warm there, is it not?" she asked wistfully. "I never realized how much I like to be warm until I'd returned here."

"I promise, you would have never been cold again," he swore in a rough voice.

"I should have dressed in silk saris and lain beneath white canopies and fed you pomegranates."

"No, sweet one," he replied in a hushed voice. "I would have fed *you* pomegranates and kissed the juice from your lips."

"Then I should have been the first woman on earth to have grown fat on pomegranates," she said, smiling softly.

He did not reply and she felt a shiver pass through him, heard the hiss of a breath drawn in pain. She hurried on, determined to take him away from this black place and, for a brief moment, to the brilliant future they would never know.

She touched his mouth, trying to soothe him. "And how many children would we have had?"

"Dozens." His voice was hushed. "All with shining hair and fierce dark brows and . . . Oh, God, I cannot do this. *I will not do this!"* He pounded his fist against the door.

Silently, it swung open.

She stared as Raine grabbed her hand and pulled her out after him. They were in the front hall, leading to the main staircase. Part of the ceiling had fallen in midway. Flames shot from the hole above and curtained one wall in a sheet of rippling fire.

A footman carrying an empty sack ran far ahead of them and disappeared into the dining room. A scullery maid emerged shrieking from a doorway, beating at the fire climbing up her skirts but refusing to drop the silver tray she carried. She wheeled back into the room from whence she came and was lost to sight.

They stopped. They needed only to make it past the blazing mound of plaster and wood that the ceiling had dumped in the corridor. The heat was intense, scorching their cheeks and singeing their hair. They were so close; they'd need only to turn the corner to be at the front door. But the pile was deep and the flames engulfing it were high.

Abruptly, Raine spun her around. He clutched handfuls of her satin gown and with a mighty jerk, tore the heavy skirts off her. He scooped her up, tossing her over his shoulder and with a muttered oath, ran straight over the pile of burning debris. On the far side he dropped her, slapping his smoldering boots before motioning her ahead. She took hold of his hand. A few more yards. They turned the corner leading to the front entrance.

There, impossibly, set on the floor directly in front of the door to the outside, stood a life-sized portrait of Janet McClairen. Some hand must have set it there, barring that portal. Yet who? It was afire, the painted canvas curling at the corners, little yellow flames lapping from the edges in toward the painted visage, burning away the beautiful one-sided smile, the haughty nose, and the gorgeous too-knowing eyes. As they watched, thunderstruck, Janet's face disappeared exposing the backing and secured to it a large leather satchel. Then the backing, too, caught fire and the pocket dropped from where it had once been lodged.

"Raine . . . ?"

He knelt and quickly retrieved the heavy leather bundle, untying the thong and lifting the flap. A fierce Celtic lion the size of a man's hand glared up at him with marble-sized ruby cabochon eyes.

"McClairen's Trust," Raine murmured.

"Do you think that . . . that someone put it here just for you to find?" she asked. The flames behind them were growing nearer.

Someone had. Raine gazed at the empty picture frame, a scowl hardening his features and then, just as the fire had burned away Janet's lovely visage, the frown disappeared from his face replaced by tenderness and warmth and fierce certainty. He retied the bundle and thrust it inside his shirt.

"Raine?" Favor asked again.

"Aye," he said. "I do. My mother, Favor. She gave it to us as a wedding present and that belief I will carry to my grave."

He held out his hand. She took it.

Together they walked out of the burning castle and down the granite steps and past the huddled, whimpering queues of guests and servants.

And they did not look back.